40p

GW00500749

Suffolk Co

2006

6

6

7

7

# THREE CASES FOR CHIEF INSPECTOR WEXFORD

# Also by Ruth Rendell

# Ruth Rendell

## THREE CASES FOR CHIEF INSPECTOR WEXFORD

KISSING THE GUNNER'S DAUGHTER
SIMISOLA
ROAD RAGE

HUTCHINSON
London

First published in the United Kingdom in 2002 by Hutchinson

1 3 5 7 9 10 8 6 4 2

Copyright © Kingsmarkham Enterprises 2002

Ruth Rendell has asserted her right under the Copyright, Designs and Patents Act, 1988 to be identified as the author of this work

*Kissing the Gunner's Daughter* was first published by Hutchinson in 1991 © Kingsmarkham Enterprises 1991
*Simisola* was first published by Hutchinson in 1994 © Kingsmarkham Enterprises 1994
*Road Rage* was first published by Hutchinson in 1997 © Kingsmarkham Enterprises 1997

The Author and publisher thank Faber & Faber for kind permission to quote from Philip Larkin's 'Going, Going' from his collection, *High Windows*

Hutchinson
The Random House Group Limited
20 Vauxhall Bridge Road, London SW1V 2SA

Random House Australia (Pty) Limited
20 Alfred Street, Milsons Point
Sydney, New South Wales 2061, Australia

Random House New Zealand Limited
18 Poland Road, Glenfield, Auckland 10, New Zealand

Random House (Pty) Limited
Endulini, 5a Jubilee Road, Parktown 2193, South Africa

The Random House Group Limited Reg. No. 954009

www.randomhouse.co.uk

A CIP record for this book is available from the British Library

Papers used by Random House are natural, recyclable products made from wood grown in sustainable forests. The manufacturing processes conform to the environmental regulations of the country of origin.

Typeset by Deltatype Ltd, Birkenhead, Merseyside
Printed and bound in Great Britain by Clays Ltd, St Ives plc

ISBN 0 09 179442 0 (Hardback)
ISBN 0 09 179447 1 (Trade Paperback)

# Contents

# KISSING THE GUNNER'S DAUGHTER

In memory of Eleanor Sullivan
1928–1991
a great friend

# 1

The thirteenth of May is the unluckiest day of the year. Things will be infinitely worse if it happens to fall on a Friday. That year, however, it was a Monday and quite bad enough, though Martin was scornful of superstition and would have engaged in any important enterprise on 13 May or gone up in a plane without a qualm.

In the morning he found a gun in the case his son took to school. They called it a satchel in his day but it was a briefcase now. The gun was among a jumble of textbooks, dog-eared exercise books, crumpled paper and a pair of football socks, and for a single frightening moment Martin thought it was real. For about fifteen seconds he thought Kevin was actually in possession of the largest revolver he had ever seen, though of a type quite beyond his ability to identify.

Recognising it as a replica didn't stop him confiscating it.

'You can say goodbye to this weapon and that's a promise,' he said to his son.

The discovery was made in Martin's car just before nine on the morning of Monday 13 May on the way to Kingsmarkham Comprehensive. Kevin's briefcase, insecurely fastened, had fallen off the back seat and some of its contents had come out on to the floor. Kevin watched ruefully and in silence as the replica gun found its way into the pocket of his father's raincoat. At the school gates he left the car with a muttered goodbye and did not look back.

This was the first link in a chain of events which was to lead to five deaths. If Martin had found the gun before he did and Kevin left the house, none of it would have happened. Unless you believe in pre-destination and fate. Unless you believe our days are numbered. If

3

you can imagine it, if you can perceive them numbered in reverse, from death to birth, Martin had reached Day One.

Monday 13 May.

It was also his day off, this Day One of his life, Detective Sergeant Martin of Kingsmarkham CID. He had come out early, not only to take his son to school – that was incidental, a by-product of leaving the house at ten to nine – but to have a new pair of windscreen wipers fitted to his car. It was a fine morning, the sun shining from a clear sky, and the forecast was good, but still he wouldn't risk taking his wife to Eastbourne for the day with wipers that failed to function.

The people at the garage behaved in typical fashion. Martin had made this arrangement by phone two days before but that did not prevent the receptionist reacting as if she had never heard of him, or the only available mechanic shaking his head and saying it was just possible, it could be done, but Les had been called out unexpectedly in an emergency and Martin had better let them phone him. At last Martin got a promise of sorts out of him that the job would be done by ten thirty.

He walked back along Queen Street. Most of the shops were not yet open. The people he passed were commuters on their way to the British Rail station. Martin could feel the gun in his pocket, its weight and its shape, the heaviness of it weighing him down on the right side. It was a big heavy gun with a four-inch barrel. If the British police were eventually armed, this was how it would feel. Every day, all day. Martin thought this might have its drawbacks as well as its advantages, but anyway he couldn't imagine such a measure getting through Parliament.

He wondered whether he should tell his wife about the gun, he seriously wondered if he should tell Chief Inspector Wexford. What does a boy of thirteen want with a replica of what was probably a Los Angeles policeman's weapon? He was too old for a toy gun, certainly, but what could be the purpose of a replica except to threaten, to make others believe it was real? And could this be for anything but criminal intent?

There was nothing Martin could do about it at present. Tonight, of course, whatever else he decided on, he must have a serious talk with Kevin. He turned into the High Street, from where he could see the blue and gold clock on the tower of St Peter's Church. It was coming up to half past nine. He was heading for the bank, intending

4

to draw out enough to cover the garage charges as well as pay for petrol, lunch for two, incidental expenses in Eastbourne, and have a bit left over for the next couple of days. Martin distrusted credit cards and though he possessed one, seldom used it.

His attitude was the same in respect of the cash-point dispenser. The bank was still closed, its solid oak front door firmly shut, but there was the automatic bank, installed in the granite façade for his convenience. The card was in his wallet and he went so far as to get it out and look at it. Somewhere he had written down the vital number. He tried to recall it – fifty-fifty-three? Fifty-three-O-five? He heard the bolts shifted, the hammers in the lock fall. The front door swung inwards to reveal the inner door of glass. The huddle of bank customers who had been waiting when he arrived went in before him.

Martin made his way to one of the counters which were provided with a blotter and a ballpoint chained to a false ink-well. He took out his chequebook. His credit card would not be needed here to back the cheque, for everyone knew him, this was where he had his account; he had already caught the eye of one of the cashiers and said good morning.

Few, however, knew his Christian name. Everyone called him Martin and always had. Even his wife called him Martin. Wexford must know what he was called, and the accounts department must, and whoever attended to such things in this bank. When he was married he had uttered it and his wife had repeated it. Quite a lot of people thought Martin was his first name. The truth of it was a secret he kept locked within himself so far as he could, and now as he made out the cheque he signed it as always, 'C. Martin'.

Two cashiers dispensed cash or received deposits behind their glass screens: Sharon Fraser and Ram Gopal, each with name tag on the glass and overhead light to flash to indicate they were free. A queue had formed in the area newly designated for waiting in with chrome uprights and turquoise-blue ropes.

'As if we were cattle in a market,' said the woman in front of him indignantly.

'Well, it's fairer,' said Martin, who was deeply committed to justice and order. 'It makes sure no one goes out of turn.'

It was then, just after he had spoken, that he was aware of disturbance. There is something very calm in the atmosphere of a bank interior. Money is serious, money is quiet. Frivolity, amusement, swift movement, haste, can have no place in this seat of custom, of pecuniary exchange. So the slightest change of mood is felt at once. A raised voice is remarked on, a pin dropped becomes a clatter. Any minor disturbance makes waiting customers start. Martin felt a draught as the glass door was opened too suddenly, he sensed the falling of a shadow as the front door, which was never shut in the daytime, which remained permanently fastened back during opening hours, was carefully and almost silently closed.

He turned round.

Everything happened very fast after that. The man who had closed the door, who had bolted the door, said sharply, 'All get back against the wall. Quickly, please.'

Martin noticed his accent, which was unmistakably Birmingham. He would have called it Brum. When the man spoke, someone screamed. There is always someone who screams.

The man, who had the gun in his hand, said in his flat nasal tones, 'Nothing will happen to you if you do as you're told.'

His companion, a boy really, who also had a gun, advanced up the passage of turquoise rope and chrome uprights, towards the two cashiers. There was a cashier behind a window to the left of him and another behind a window to the right of him, Sharon Fraser and Ram Gopal. Martin got back against the left-hand wall with all the others from the queue; they were all on that side, covered by the man's gun.

He was pretty sure the gun in the boy's gloved hand was a toy. Not a replica like the one in his own pocket, but a toy. The boy looked very young, seventeen or eighteen, but Martin knew that, although not himself old, he was old enough not to be able to tell if someone was eighteen or twenty-four.

Martin made himself memorise every detail of the boy's appearance, not knowing, not dreaming then, that any memorising he might succeed in doing would be in vain. He noted the man's appearance with similar care. The boy had a curious rash on his face, or spots perhaps. Martin had never seen anything like them before. The man was dark with tattooed hands. He had no gloves on.

The gun in the man's hand might not be real either. It was impossible to tell. Watching the boy, he thought of his own son, not so many years younger. Had Kevin contemplated something of this sort? Martin felt the replica in his pocket, met the eyes of the man

6

fixed on him. He removed his hand and brought it up to clasp the other.

The boy had said something to the woman cashier, to Sharon Fraser, but Martin hadn't caught what it was. They must have some alarm system in the bank. He confessed to himself that he didn't know what kind. A button that responded to foot pressure? Was an alarm going off even now in the police station?

It did not occur to him to commit to memory any details of the appearance of his companions, those people cowering with him against the wall. In the event it would have made no difference if he had. All he could have said of them was that none of them was old, though all but one were adults. The exception was the baby in a sling on its mother's chest. They were shadows to him, a nameless, faceless public.

Inside him was rising an urge to do something, take some action. He felt an enormous indignation. It was what he always felt in the face of crime or attempted crime. How dare they? Who did they think they were? By what imagined right did they come in here to take what was not their own? It was the same feeling that he had when he heard or saw that one country had invaded another. How dare they commit this outrage?

The woman cashier was handing over money. Martin didn't think Ram Gopal had set off an alarm. He was staring, petrified with terror or merely inscrutably calm. He was watching Sharon Fraser pressing those keys on the cash dispenser at her side which would tumble out banknotes already packed into fifties and hundreds. The steady eyes watched pack after pack pushed under the glass barrier, through the metal valley, into the greedy gloved hand.

The boy took the money in his left hand, scooping it up, shovelling it into a canvas bag strapped round his hips. He kept the gun, the toy gun, trained on Sharon Fraser. The man was covering the rest of them, including Ram Gopal. It was easy from where he stood. The bank interior was small and they were all huddled together. Martin was aware of the sound of a woman crying, quiet sobs, soft whimpers.

His indignation threatened to spill over. But not yet, not quite yet. It came to him that if the police had been authorised to bear arms he might now be so used to them that he would be able to tell a real gun from a false. The boy had moved to stand in front of Ram Gopal. Sharon Fraser, a young plump girl whose family Martin slightly

7

knew, whose mother had been at school with his wife, sat with her hands in fists and her long red nails digging into the palms. Ram Gopal had begun passing packs of notes under the glass barrier. It was nearly over. In a moment it would all be over and he, Martin, would have done nothing.

He watched the dark stocky man retreat towards the doors. It made very little difference, they were still all covered by his gun. Martin slid his hand down to his pocket and felt there Kevin's huge weapon.

The man saw but did nothing. He had to get that door open, the bolts drawn, for them to make a getaway.

Martin had known at once that Kevin's gun wasn't real. By the same process of recognition and reasoning, if not from experience, he knew this boy's gun wasn't real either. The clock on the wall above the cashiers, behind the boy's head, pointed to nine forty-two. How swiftly it had all happened! Only half an hour earlier he had been in that garage. Only forty minutes ago he had found the replica in the satchel and confiscated it.

He put his hand into his pocket, snatched Kevin's gun and shouted, 'Drop your guns!'

The man had turned for a split second to unbolt the door. He backed against it, holding the gun in both hands like a gangster in a film. The boy took the last pack of notes, swept it into his canvas bag.

Martin said it again. 'Drop your guns!'

The boy turned his head slowly and looked at him. A woman made a strangled whimpering sound. The feeble little gun in the boy's hand seemed to tremble. Martin heard the front door crash back against the wall. He didn't hear the man go, the man with the real gun, but he knew he had gone. A gust of wind blew through the bank. The glass door slammed. The boy stood staring at Martin with strange impenetrable, perhaps drugged, eyes, holding his gun as if he might at any moment let it fall, as if he were carrying out a test to see how loosely he could suspend it from a finger before it dropped.

Someone came into the bank. The glass door swung inwards. Martin shouted, 'Get back! Call the police! Now! There's been a robbery.'

He took a step forwards, towards the boy. It was going to be easy, it *was* easy, the real danger was gone. His gun was trained on the boy

8

and the boy was trembling. Martin thought, I will have done it, I alone, my God!

The boy pressed the trigger and shot him through the heart.

Martin fell. He did not double up, but sank to the floor as his knees buckled under him. Blood came from his mouth. He made no sound beyond a little cough. His body crumpled, as in some slow-motion film, his hands grasped at the air, but with weak graceful movements, and gradually he collapsed into utter stillness, his eyes cast up to stare unseeing at the bank's vaulted ceiling.

For a moment there had been silence, then the people burst into noise, into screams and shouts. They crowded round the dying man. Brian Prince, the bank manager, came out from the office behind and members of his staff came with him. Ram Gopal was already on the phone. The baby began to utter desperate heartrending cries as its mother screamed and gibbered and flung her arms round the sling and the small body. Sharon Fraser, who had known Martin, came out into the bank and knelt beside him, weeping and twisting her hands, crying out for justice, for retribution.

'Oh God, oh God, what have they done to him? What's happened to him? Help me, someone, don't let him die . . .'

But by then Martin was dead.

# 2

Martin's Christian name appeared in the newspapers. It was spoken aloud that evening on the BBC's early-evening news and again at nine o'clock. Detective Sergeant Caleb Martin, aged thirty-nine, married and the father of one son.

'It's a funny thing,' said Inspector Burden, 'you won't credit it, but I never knew he was called that. Always thought he was John or Bill or something. We always called him Martin like a first name. I wonder why he had a go? What got into him?'

'Courage,' said Wexford. 'Poor devil.'

'Foolhardiness.' Burden said it ruefully, not unkindly.

'I suppose courage never has much to do with intelligence, does it? Not much to do with reasoning or logic. He didn't give the pale cast of thought a chance to work.'

He had been one of them, one of their own. Besides, to a policeman there is something peculiarly horrible in the murder of a policeman. It is as if the culpability is doubled and the worst of all crimes compounded because the policeman's life, ideally, is dedicated to the prevention of such acts.

Chief Inspector Wexford did not expend more effort in seeking Martin's killer than he would have in the hunt for any other murderer, but he felt more than usually emotionally involved. He hadn't even particularly liked Martin, had been irritated by his earnest, humourless endeavours. 'Plodding' is an adjective, pejorative and scornful, often applied to policemen, and it was the first which came to mind in Martin's case. 'The Plod' is even a slang term for the police force. But all this was forgotten now Martin was dead.

'I've often thought,' Wexford said to Burden, 'what a poor piece of psychology that was on Shakespeare's part when he said that the evil

10

men do lives after them, the good is oft interred with their bones. Not that poor Martin was evil, but you know what I mean. It's the good things about people that we remember, not the bad. I remember how punctilious he was and how thorough and – well, dogged. I feel quite sentimental about him when I'm not bloody angry. But God, I'm so bloody angry I can hardly see out of my eyes when I think of that kid with the spots shooting him in cold blood.'

They had begun with the most careful in-depth interviewing of Brian Prince, the manager, and Sharon Fraser and Ram Gopal, the cashiers. The customers who had been in the bank – that is, those customers who had come forward or whom they had been able to find – were seen next. No one was able to say exactly how many people had been in the bank at the time.

'Poor old Martin would have been able to tell us,' Burden said. 'I'm sure of that. He knew, but he's dead, and if he wasn't none of it would matter.'

Brian Prince had seen nothing. The first he knew of it was when he heard the boy fire the shot that killed Martin. Ram Gopal, a member of Kingsmarkham's very small Indian immigrant population, of the Brahmin caste from the Punjab, gave Wexford the best and fullest description of both men. With descriptions like that, Wexford said afterwards, it would be a crime not to catch them.

'I watched them very carefully. I sat quite still, conserving my energy, and I concentrated on every detail of their appearance. I knew, you know, that there was nothing I could do but that I could do, and I did it.'

Michelle Weaver, on her way at the time to work in the travel agency two doors away, described the boy as between twenty-two and twenty-five, fair, not very tall, with bad acne. The mother of the baby, Mrs Wendy Gould, also said the boy was fair but a tall man, at least six feet. Sharon Fraser thought he was tall and fair but she had particularly noticed his eyes which were a bright pale blue. All three of the men said the boy was short or of medium height, thin, perhaps twenty-two or twenty-three. Wendy Gould said he looked ill. The remaining woman, Mrs Barbara Watkin, said the boy was dark and short with dark eyes. All agreed he had a spotty face but Barbara Watkin was doubtful about the cause being acne. More like a lot of small birthmarks, she said.

The boy's companion was described invariably as much older than he, ten years older or, according to Mrs Watkin, twenty years older.

11

He was dark, some said swarthy, and with hairy hands. Only Michelle Weaver said he had a mole on his left cheek. Sharon Fraser thought he was very tall but one of the men described him as 'tiny' and another as 'no taller than a teenager'.

Ram Gopal's confidence and concentration inspired belief in Wexford. He described the boy as about five feet eight, very thin, blue-eyed, fair-haired and with acnaceous spots. The boy wore blue denim jeans, a dark T-shirt or sweater and a black leather jacket. He had gloves on, a point no other witness thought to mention.

The man wore no gloves. His hands were covered in dark hairs. The hair on his head was dark, nearly black, but receding severely, giving the effect of a superlatively high forehead. He was at least thirty-five and dressed similarly to the boy except that his jeans were of some dark colour, dark grey or dark brown, and he wore some sort of brown pullover.

The boy had only spoken once, to tell Sharon Fraser to hand over the money. Sharon Fraser was unable to describe his voice. Ram Gopal gave his opinion that the accent was not cockney but not an educated voice either, probably from south London. Could it be the local accent, 'Londonised' as it was by the spread of the capital and by television? Ram Gopal admitted that it could be. He was unsure about English accents, which Wexford discovered by putting him to the test and finding he defined a Devon accent as Yorkshire.

So how many people were in the bank? Ram Gopal said fifteen including the staff and Sharon Fraser said sixteen. Brian Prince didn't know. Of the customers, one said twelve and another said eighteen.

It was clear that, however many or however few there had been in the bank, not all had come forward in response to police appeals. During the time between the raiders' departure and the arrival of the police, perhaps as many as five people had quietly left the bank while the rest concerned themselves with Martin.

As soon as they saw their opportunity, they made their escape. Who could blame them, especially if they had seen nothing relevant? Who wants to be drawn into a police investigation if they have nothing to contribute? Even if they do have something to contribute, but something small and trivial which other more observant eye-witnesses can supply?

For peace of mind and a quiet life, how much simpler to slip away and continue to work or the shops or home. Kingsmarkham Police faced the fact that four or five people had kept mum, knew something or nothing but kept silent and hidden. All the police knew was that not one of these people, four or five or perhaps only three, were known by sight to the bank staff. So far as they could remember. Neither Brian Prince, nor Ram Gopal, nor Sharon Fraser could remember a face they recognised in that queue in the roped-off area. Apart from, that is, those regular customers who had all remained inside the bank after Martin's death.

Martin himself had of course been known to them, and Michelle Weaver and Wendy Gould among others. Sharon Fraser could say only this: she had an impression that the missing bank customers were all men.

The most sensational piece of evidence given by any of the witnesses was that of Michelle Weaver. She said she had seen the boy with acne drop his gun just before he escaped from the bank. He had thrown it on to the floor and run away.

At first, Burden hardly believed she expected him to take this statement seriously. It seemed bizarre. The act which Mrs Weaver described he had read of somewhere, or been taught, or gleaned from some lecture. It was a classic Mafia technique. He even said to her that they must have read the same book.

Michelle Weaver insisted. She had seen the gun skid across the floor. The others had crowded round Martin but she had been the last in the line of people the gunman had directed to stand against the wall, so therefore the furthest from Martin who had been at the head of it.

Caleb Martin had dropped the gun with which he made his brave attempt. His son Kevin later identified it as his personal property, taken from him by his father in the car that morning. It was a toy, a crude copy, with several design inaccuracies, of a Smith and Wesson Model 10 Military and Police Revolver with four-inch barrel.

Several witnesses had seen Martin's gun fall. A building contractor called Peter Kemp had been standing next to him and he said Martin dropped the gun at the moment the bullet struck him.

'Could it have been Detective Sergeant Martin's gun that you saw, Mrs Weaver?'

'Pardon?'

'Detective Sergeant Martin dropped the gun he was holding. It skidded across the floor among people's feet. Could you be mistaken? Could it have been that gun which you saw?'

13

'I saw the boy throw it down.'

'You said you saw it skid across the floor. Martin's gun skidded across the floor. There were two guns skidding across the floor?'

'I don't know. I only saw one.'

'You saw it in the boy's hand and then you saw it skid across the floor. Did you actually see it leave the boy's hand?'

She was no longer sure. She thought she had seen it. Certainly she had seen it in the boy's hand and then seen a gun on the floor, skating across the shiny marble among the people's feet. An idea came that silenced her for a moment. She looked hard at Burden.

'I wouldn't go into court and swear I saw it,' she said.

In the months that followed, the hunt for the men who had carried out the Kingsmarkham bank robbery became nationwide. Gradually, all the stolen banknotes turned up. One of the men bought a car for cash before the numbers of the missing notes were circulated, and paid out six thousand pounds to an unsuspecting second-hand car dealer. This was the older, darker man. The car dealer furnished a detailed description of him and gave, of course, his name. Or the name the man had given him – George Brown. After that, Kingsmarkham Police referred to him as George Brown.

Of the remaining money, just under two thousand pounds came to light wrapped in newspapers in a town waste-disposal dump. The missing six thousand was never found. It had probably been spent in dribs and drabs. There was not much risk in doing that. As Wexford said, if you give the girl on the check-out two tenners for your groceries she doesn't do a spot-check on the numbers. All you need to do is be prudent and not go there again.

Just before Christmas Wexford went north to interview a man on remand in prison in Lancashire. It was the usual thing. If he co-operated and offered helpful information, things might go rather better for him at his trial. As it was, he was likely to go down for seven years.

His name was James Walley and he told Wexford he had done a job with George Brown, a man whose real name was George Brown. It was one of his past offences he intended to ask to be taken into consideration. Wexford saw the real George Brown at his home in Warrington. He was quite an elderly man, though probably younger than he looked, and he walked with a limp, the result of falling off a scaffold some years before when attempting to break into a block of flats.

14

After that, Kingsmarkham Police started talking of their wanted man as o.k.a. (otherwise known as) George Brown. Of the boy with acne there was never any sign, not a whisper. In the underworld he was unknown, he might have died for all that was heard of him.

O.k.a. George Brown surfaced again in January. He was George Thomas Lee, arrested in the course of a robbery in Leeds. This time it was Burden who went up to see him in the remand prison. He was a small, squinting man with cropped carroty hair. The tale he spun Burden was of a spotty boy he had met in a pub in Bradford who had boasted of killing a policeman somewhere in the south. He named one pub, then forgot it and named another, but he knew the boy's full name and address. Already sure that the motive behind all this was revenge for some petty offence, Burden found the boy. He was tall and dark, an unemployed lab technician with a record as spotless as his face. The boy had no memory of meeting o.k.a. George Brown in any pub, but he did remember calling the police when he found an intruder in the last place he worked at.

Martin had been killed by a shot from a Colt Magnum .357 or .38 revolver. It was impossible to tell which, because although the cartridge was a .38, the .357 takes both .357 and .38 cartridges. Sometimes Wexford worried about that gun and once he dreamed he was in the bank watching two revolvers skating round the marble floor while the bank customers stared like spectators at some arena event. Magnums on Ice.

He went to talk to Michelle Weaver himself. She was very obliging, always willing to talk, showing no signs of impatience. But five months had gone by and the memory of what she had seen that morning when Caleb Martin died was necessarily growing dim.

'I can't have seen him throw it down, can I? I mean, I must have imagined that. If he'd thrown it down it would have been there and it wasn't, only the one the policeman dropped.'

'There was certainly only one gun when the police arrived.' Wexford talked to her conversationally, as if they were equals in knowledge and sharers of inside information. She warmed to this, she grew confident and eager. 'All that we found was the toy gun DS Martin took away from his son that morning. Not a copy, not a replica, a child's toy.'

'And was that really a toy I saw?' She marvelled at it. 'They make them look so real.'

Another conversational interview, this time with Barbara Watkin,

15

revealed not much more than her obstinacy. She was tenacious about her description of the boy's appearance.

'I know acne when I see it. My eldest son had terrible acne. That wasn't what the boy had. I told you, it was more like birthmarks.'

'The scars of acne, perhaps?'

'It wasn't anything like that. You have to picture those strawberry marks people have, only these were the purple kind, and all blotched, dozens of them.'

Wexford asked Dr Crocker, and Crocker said no one had birthmarks of that description, so that was the end of that.

There was not much more to say, nothing left to ask. It was the end of February when he talked to Michelle Weaver and the beginning of March when Sharon Fraser came up with something she had remembered about one of the missing men among the bank customers. He had been holding a bunch of banknotes in his hand and they were green notes. There had been no green English banknotes since the pound note had been replaced by a coin several years before. She could remember nothing else about this man – did it help?

Wexford couldn't say it did, much. But you don't discourage that kind of public-spiritedness.

Nothing much else happened until the 999 call came on 11 March.

# 3

'They're all dead.' The voice was a woman's and young, very young. She said it again. 'They're all dead,' and then, 'I'm going to bleed to death!'

The operator who had taken the call, though not new to the job, said afterwards she turned cold at those words. She had already uttered the formula of asking if the caller wanted police, the fire service or an ambulance.

'Where are you?' she said.

'Help me. I'm going to bleed to death.'

'Tell me where you are, the address . . . '

The voice started giving a phone number.

'The address, please . . . '

'Tancred House, Cheriton. Help me, please help me . . . Make them come quickly . . . '

The time was eight twenty-two.

The forest covers an area of something like sixty square miles. Much of it is coniferous, man-made woods of Scots pine and larch, Norway spruce and occasionally a towering Douglas fir. But to the south of this plantation a vestige of the ancient forest of Cheriton remains, one of seven which existed in the County of Sussex in the Middle Ages, the others being Arundel, St Leonard's, Worth, Ashdown, Waterdown and Dallington. Arundel excepted, they once all formed part of a single great forest of three-and-a-half-thousand square miles which, according to the Anglo-Saxon Chronicle, stretched from Kent to Hampshire. Deer roamed it and in the depths, wild swine.

The small area of this which remains is woodland of oak, ash, horse chestnut and sweet chestnut, birch and the wayfarer's tree,

17

which clothes the southern slopes and borders of a private estate. Here, where all was parkland until the early thirties, green turf on which grew Douglas firs, cedars and the rarer Wellingtonia, an occasional half-acre of mature woodland, a new forest was planted by the new owner. The roads up to the house, one of them no more than a narrow track, wind through the woods, in places between steep banks, in others through groves of rhododendron, past trees in the prime of life and here and there overshadowed by an ancient giant.

Sometimes fallow deer can be seen among the trees. Red squirrels have been sighted. The blackcock is a rarity, the Dartford warbler common, and hen harriers are winter visitors. In late spring, when the rhododendrons come out, the long vistas are rosy pink under a green mist of unfolding beech leaves. The nightingale sings. Earlier, in March, the woods are dark, yet glowing with the coming life, and underfoot the ground is a rich ginger-gold from beech mast. The beech trunks shine as if their bark were laced with silver. But at night there is darkness and silence, a deep quiet fills the woods, a forbidding hush.

The land is not fenced but there are gates in the boundary hedge. All are of red cedar and five-barred. Most give access only to paths, impassable except on foot, but the main gate closes off the woods from the road that turns northwards from the B2428, linking Kingsmarkham with Cambery Ashes. There is a sign, a plain board attached to a post and bearing the words, TANCRED HOUSE. PRIVATE ROAD. PLEASE CLOSE THE GATE, which stands to the left of it. The gate is required to be kept closed, though no key, code or device is needed to open it.

On that Tuesday evening, eight fifty-one on 11 March, the gate was shut. Detective Sergeant Vine got out of the first car and opened it, though he was senior to most of the officers in the two cars. He had come to Kingsmarkham to replace Martin. There were three vehicles in the convoy, the last being the ambulance. Vine let them all through and then he closed the gate once more. It was not possible to drive very fast but once they were inside, on this private land, Pemberton went as fast as he could.

Later they were to learn, using it daily, that this road was always known as the main drive.

It was dark, sunset two hours past. The last streetlamp was a hundred yards down the B 2428 before the gate. They relied on their headlights alone, lights which showed up the mist that drifted through the woods as streamers of greenish fog. If eyes looked out of the forest the lights did not show them up. The tree trunks were colonnades of grey pillars, swathed in scarves of mist. In the depths between was impenetrable dark.

No one spoke. The last person to speak had been Barry Vine when he said he would get out and open the gate. Detective Inspector Burden said nothing. He was thinking about what they would find at Tancred House and telling himself not to anticipate, for speculation was useless. Pemberton had nothing to say and would not have considered it his place to initiate a conversation.

In the van behind were the driver, Gerry Hinde, a scene-of-crimes officer called Archbold with a photographer called Milsom, and a woman officer, Detective Constable Karen Malahyde. The paramedics in the ambulance were a woman and a man, and the woman was driving. A decision had been taken at an early stage to display no blue lamps and sound no sirens.

The convoy made no sound but for that produced by the engines of the three vehicles. It wound through the avenues of trees where the banks were high and where the road passed across sandy plateaux. Why the road should wind like this was a mystery, for the hillside was shallow and there were no features to avoid except perhaps the isolated giant trees, invisible in the dark.

The whim of a forest planter, thought Burden. He tried to remember if he had seen these woods in their younger days but he did not know the region well. Naturally, he knew who owned them now, everyone in Kingsmarkham knew that. He wondered if the message left for Wexford had reached him yet, if the Chief Inspector was even now on his way, in a car a mile or two behind them.

Vine was staring out of the window, pressing his nose against the glass, as if there was something to be seen out there besides darkness and mist and the verges ahead, yellowish and shining and wet-looking in the headlights. No eyes looked out from the depths, no twin points of green or gold, and there was no movement of bird or animal. Even the sky was not to be discerned here. The tree trunks stood separated like columns but their top branches seemed to form an unbroken ceiling.

Burden had heard there were cottages on the estate, houses to accommodate whatever staff Davina Flory kept. These would be near Tancred House, no more than five minutes' walk away, but they passed no gates, no paths leading into the woods, saw no distant lights, dim or bright, on either side. This was fifty miles from London but it might have been northern Canada, it might have been Siberia. The woods seemed endless, rank upon rank of trees, some of them forty feet in height, others half-grown but tall enough. As each bend was turned and you knew that round this corner must be an opening, must be a break, a sight of the house must at last be granted, there were only more trees, another platoon in this army of trees, still, silent, waiting.

He leaned forward and said to Pemberton, his voice sounding loud in the silence, 'How far have we come from the gate?'

Pemberton checked. 'Two miles and three-tenths, sir.'

'It's a hell of a way, isn't it?'

'Three miles according to the map,' said Vine. He had a whitish squash mark on his nose where it had pressed against the window.

'It seems to be taking hours,' Burden was grumbling like this, peering out at the endless groves, the infinite reaches of cathedral-like columns, when the house came into view, rearing suddenly into sight with an effect of shock.

The woods parted, as if a curtain was drawn aside, and there it was, brilliantly lit as for some stage-set, bathed in a flood of artificial moonlight, greenish and cold. It was strangely dramatic. The house gleamed, shimmered in a bay of light, thown into relief against a misty dark well. The façade itself was punctured with lights, but orange-coloured, the squares and rectangles of lighted windows.

Burden had not expected light, but dark desolation. This scene before him was like the opening shot of a film about characters in a fairy story living in a remote palace, a film about the Sleeping Beauty. There should have been music, a soft but sinister melody, with horns and drums. The silence made you feel an essential was missing, something had gone disastrously wrong. The sound was lost without fusing the lights. He saw the woods close in again as the road wound into another loop. Impatience seized him. He wanted to get out and run to the house, break in there to find the worst, what the worst was, and he kept his seat petulantly.

That first glimpse had been a brief foretaste, a trailer. This time the woods fell away for good, the headlights showed the road crossing a grassy plain on which a few great trees stood. The occupants of the cars felt very exposed as they began to cross this plain, as if they were the outriders of an invading force with an ambush ahead of them.

20

The house on the other side of it was now illuminated with absolute clarity, a fine country manor that looked Georgian but for its pitched roof and candlestick chimneys. It looked very large and grand and also menacing.

A low wall divided its immediate surroundings from the rest of the estate. This ran at right angles to the road they were on, bisecting the treeless open land. A left-hand turn branched off just before the gap in the wall. It was possible to go straight on, or turn left on this road which looked as if it would take you to the side and back of the house. The wall itself concealed the floodlights.

'Go straight ahead,' said Burden.

They passed through the gap, between stone posts with ogee tops. Here the flagstones began, a vast space paved in Portland stone. The stone was golden-grey, pleasingly uneven, too close-set for even moss to spring between. Plumb in the centre of this courtyard was a large circular pool, coped in stone, and standing in the midst of it, on a stone island laden with flowers and broad-leaved plants in varied marbles, green and pinkish and bronze-grey, a group of statuary, a man, a tree, a girl in grey marble, that might or might not have been a fountain. If it was, it was not at present playing. The water lay stagnant, unruffled.

Shaped like an E without the central crosspiece, or like a rectangle missing one long side, the house stood unadorned beyong this great plain of stone. Not a creeper softened its smooth plasterwork or shrub grew nearby to compromise its bands of rusticated stone. The arc lamps on this side of the wall showed up every fine line and every tiny pit on its surface.

The lights were on everywhere, in the two side wings, in the central range and the gallery above. They glowed behind drawn curtains, pink or orange or green according to the colours of the curtains, and they shone too out of uncurtained panes. Light from the arc lamps competed with these softer glowing colours but was not able entirely to quell them. Everything was quite motionless, windless, giving the impression that not only the air but time itself had been stilled.

Though, as Burden asked himself afterwards, what was there that could have moved? If a gale-force wind had been glowing there was nothing here for it to move. Even the trees were behind them now, and thousands more beyond the house, lost in that cavern of darkness.

The convoy drove up to the front door, passing to the left of the pool and the statuary. Burden and Vine threw open their doors and Vine made it first to the front door. This was approached by two wide, shallow stone steps. If there had ever been a porch it was gone now, and all that remained on either side of the door were a couple of unfluted recessed columns. The front door itself was gleaming white, shining in this light as if the paint on it was still wet. The bell was the kind you pull, a sugarstick rod of wrought iron. Vine pulled it. The sound it made when he tugged at the spiral rod must have clanged through the house, for it was clearly audible to the paramedics, getting out of their ambulance twenty yards away.

He pulled at the bell a third time and then he banged the brass knocker. The door furniture gleamed like gold in the bright light. Remembering the voice on the phone, the woman who had cried for help, they listened for a sound. There was nothing. Not a whimper, not a whisper. Silence. Burden banged the knocker and flapped the letter-box. Nobody thought of a back door, of what numerous rear doors there might be. No one considered that one might be open.

'We're going to have to break in,' Burden said.

Where? Four broad windows flanked the front door, two on each side of it. Inside could be seen a kind of outer hall, an orangery with bay trees and lilies in tubs on the mottled white marble floor. The lily leaves glistened under the light from two chandeliers. What was beyond, behind an arch, could not be seen. It looked warm and still in there, it looked civilised, a well-appointed gentle place, the home of rich people fond of luxury. In the orangery, against the wall, was a mahogany and gilt console table with a chair placed negligently beside it, a spindly chair with a red velvet seat. From a Chinese jar on the table spilled out the long tendrils of a trailing plant.

Burden turned away from the front door and began to walk across the stone-flagged plain of this vast courtyard. The light was like moonlight much magnified, as if the moon had doubled or reflected itself in some celestial mirror. Afterwards, he said to Wexford that the light made it worse. Darkness would have been natural, he could have handled darkness more comfortably.

He approached the west wing where the window at the end, a shallow bow, had its base only a foot above the ground. The lights were on inside, reduced, from where he was, to a soft green glow. The curtains were drawn, their pale lining towards the glass, but he guessed that on the other side they must be of green velvet. Later he

22

was to wonder what instinct had led him to this window, to reject those nearer and come to this one.

A premonition had come to him that this was it. In there was what there was to see, to find. He tried to look through the knife-blade sliver of bright light that was the gap between the edges of those curtains. He could see nothing but a dazzlement. The others were behind him, silent but close behind him. To Pemberton he said, 'Break the window.'

Pemberton, cool and calm, prepared for this, broke the glass in one of the largish rectangular panes with a car spanner. He broke one of the flat panes in the centre of the window, put his hand through the space, lifted the curtain aside, unlocked the lower sash and raised it. Ducking under the bar, Burden went in first, then Vine. Heavy thick material enveloped them and they pushed it away from their faces, drawing the curtain back with a swish, its rings making a gentle clicking sound along the pole.

They stood a few feet into the room, on thick carpet, and saw what they had come to see. From Vine came a strong indrawing of breath. No one else made a sound. Pemberton came through the window and Karen Malahyde with him. Burden stepped aside to allow them space, aside but not for the moment forward. He did not exclaim. He looked. Fifteen seconds passed while he looked. His eyes met Vine's blank stare, he even turned his head and noted, as if on another plane somewhere, that the curtains were indeed of green velvet. Then he looked again at the dining table.

It was a large table, some nine feet long, laid with a cloth and with glass and silver; there was food on it, and the tablecloth was red. It looked as if it was meant to be red, the material scarlet damask, except that the area nearest the window was white. The tide of red had not reached so far.

Across the deepest scarlet part someone lay slumped forward, a woman who had been sitting or standing at the table. Opposite, flung back in a chair, another woman's body was slung, the head hanging and the long dark hair streaming, her dress as red as that tablecloth, as if it had been worn to match.

These two women had been sitting facing one another across the precise middle of the table. From the plates and the place settings, it was apparent someone else had sat at the head and someone else at the foot, but no one was there now, dead or alive. Just the two bodies and the scarlet spread between them.

There was no question but that the two women were dead. The elder, she whose blood had dyed the cloth red, had a bullet wound in the side of her head. You could see that without touching her, and no one touched her. Half her head and the side of her face were destroyed.

The other had been shot in the neck. Her face, curiously undamaged, was as white as wax. Her eyes were wide open, fixed on the ceiling where a sprinkling of dark spots might have been blood-stains. Blood had splashed the dark-green papered walls, the green and gold lampshades in which the bulbs remained alight, had stained the dark-green carpet in black blotches. A drop of blood had struck a picture on the wall, trickled down the pale thick oil-paint and dried there.

On the table were three plates with food on them. On two of them the food remained there, cold and congealing, but recognisably food. The third was drenched with blood, as if sauce had been poured liberally over it, as if a bottle of sauce had been emptied on to it for some horror meal.

There was doubtless a fourth plate. The woman whose body had fallen forward, whose blood had fountained and seeped everywhere, had plunged her mutilated head into it, her dark hair, grey-streaked, had been loosened from a knot on her nape and spread out among dining litter, a saltcellar, an overturned glass, a crumpled napkin. Another napkin, soaked in blood, lay on the carpet.

A trolley with food on it was drawn up close to where the younger woman was, she whose hair streamed over the back of her chair. Her blood had splashed the white cloths on it and the white dishes, and sprayed across a basket of bread. The drops of blood sprinkled the slices of French bread in speckles like currants. There was some sort of pudding in a large glass dish but Burden, who had looked at everything without his gorge rising, could not look at what the blood had done to that.

It was a long time, an age, since he had felt actual physical nausea at such sights. On the other hand, had he ever before seen such a sight as this? He felt a blankness, a sensation of being stricken dumb, of all words being useless. And although the house was warm, of sudden bitter cold. He took the fingers of his left hand in the fingers of his right and felt their iciness.

He imagined the noise there must have been, the huge noise of a gun barrel emptying itself – a shotgun, a rifle, something more

24

powerful? The noise roaring through the silence, the peace, the warmth. And those people sitting there, talking, halfway through their meal, disturbed in this terrible untimely way . . . But there had been *four* people. One on either side and one at the head and one at the foot. He turned and exchanged another blank glance with Barry Vine. Each was aware that the look he gave the other was of despair, of sickness. They were dazed by what they saw.

Burden found himself moving stiffly. It was as if he had lead weights on his feet and hands. The dining-room door was open and he passed slowly through it into the house, a constriction in his throat. Afterwards, several hours later, he reminded himself that then, during those minutes, he had forgotten about the woman who had phoned. The sight of the dead had made him forget the living, the possibly still living . . .

He found himself not in the orangery but in a majestic hall, a large room, whose ceiling, lanterned high up in the centre of the roof of the house, was also lit by a number of lamps, but less brightly. There were lamps with silver bases and lamps with glass and ceramic bases, their shades in colours of apricot and a deep ivory. The floor was of polished wood, scattered with rugs that Burden perceived as Oriental, rugs patterned in lilac and red and brown and gold. A staircase ascended out of this hall, branching into two at first-floor level where the double set of stairs mounted out of a gallery, balustered with ionic columns. At the foot of the staircase, spread-eagled across the lowest treads, lay the body of a man.

He too had been shot. In the chest. The stair carpet was red and his shed blood showed like dark wine-stains. Burden breathed in and, finding that he had put up his hand to cover his mouth, resolutely brought it down again. He looked round him with a slow deliberate gaze and then he saw a movement in the far corner.

The jangling crashing sound that came suddenly had the effect of unlocking his voice. This time he did exclaim.

'My God!' His voice struggled out as if someone held a hand across his throat.

It was a telephone which had fallen on to the floor, had been pulled to the floor by some sudden involuntary movement which jerked its lead. Something was crawling towards him out of the darkest part, where there was no lamp. It made a moaning sound. The phone lead was caught round it and the phone dragged behind,

25

bouncing and sliding on polished oak. It bounced and jiggled like a toy on a string pulled by a child.

She was not a child, though she revealed herself as not much more, a young girl who crept towards him on all fours and collapsed at his feet, making the bewildered gibbering moans of a wounded animal. There was blood all over her, matting her long hair, sodden in her clothes, streaking her bare arms. She lifted her face and it was blotched with blood, as if she had dabbled in it and finger-painted the skin.

He could see, to his horror, blood welling out of a wound in her upper chest on the left side. He fell on his knees in front of her.

She spoke. It came in a clotted whisper. 'Help me, help me . . .'

# 4

Within two minutes the ambulance was off, on its way to the infirmary at Stowerton. This time its lamp was on, and its siren, blaring its two-tone shriek through the dark woods, the still groves.

It was going so fast that the driver had to brake for dear life and pull over sharply to avoid Wexford's car which entered the main gateway from the B2428 at five minutes past nine.

The message had reached him where he was dining with his wife, his daughter and her friend. This was at a new Italian restaurant in Kingsmarkham called La Primavera. They were halfway through their main course when his phone started bleeping and saved him in a peculiarly drastic way, as he thought afterwards, from doing something he might be sorry for. With a quick word to Dora and a rather perfunctory goodbye to the others, he left the restaurant immediately, abandoning his veal Marsala uneaten.

Three times he had tried calling Tancred House and each time got the engaged signal. As the car, driven by Donaldson, negotiated the first bend in the narrow woodland road, he tried again and this time it rang and Burden answered.

'The receiver was off. It fell on the floor. There are three people dead here, shot dead. You must have passed the ambulance with the girl in it.'

'How bad is she?'

'I don't know. She was conscious, but she's pretty bad.'

'Did you talk to her?'

Burden said, 'Of course. I had to. There were two of them got into the house but she only saw one. She said it was eight when it happened, or just after, a minute or two after eight. She couldn't talk any more.'

27

Wexford put the phone back in his pocket. The clock on the car's dashboard told him it was twelve minutes past nine. When the message came he had been not so much in a bad temper as disturbed and increasingly unhappy. Already, sitting at that table in La Primavera, he had begun struggling with these feelings of antipathy, of positive revulsion. And then as he checked, for the third or fourth time, the sharp comment which rose to his lips, controlling himself for Sheila's sake, his phone had rung. Now he pushed aside the memory of a painful meeting. There would be no time for dwelling on it; everything must now give place to the killing at Tancred House.

The illuminated house showed through the trees, was swallowed in darkness, reappeared as Donaldson drove up the drive and across a wide empty plain. He hesitated at the gap in the low wall, then accelerated and went ahead, swinging on to the forecourt. A statue that probably represented the pursuit of Daphne by Apollo was reflected in the dark waters of a shallow pool. Donaldson drove to the left of it and in among the cars.

The front door stood open. He saw that someone had broken one of the panes in a bow window on the left-hand or west wing of the house. Inside the front door, from an orangery full of lilies, a pillared screen at each end of it in what he thought was called the Adam style, an arch opened on to the big hall where there was blood on the floor and the rugs. Blood made a map of islands on the pale oak. As Barry Vine came out to him, he saw the man's body at the foot of the staircase.

Wexford approached the body and looked at it. It was a man of about sixty, tall, slim, with a handsome face, the features finely cut and of the kind usually called sensitive. His face was now waxen and yellowish. The mouth hung open. The blue eyes were open and staring. Blood had dyed scarlet his white shirt and stained blacker his dark jacket. He had been formally dressed in a suit and tie, had been shot twice from the front at close range, in the chest and in the head. His head was a mess of blood, a brownish stickiness matting the thick white hair.

'Do you know who this is?'

Vine shook his head. 'Should I, sir? Presumably the guy who owned the place.'

'It's Harvey Copeland, former MP for the Southern Boroughs and

28

husband of Davina Flory. Of course you haven't been here long, but you'll have heard of Davina Flory?'

'Yes, sir. Of course.'

You could never tell with Vine, whether he had or not. That deadpan face, that unruffled manner, stolid calm.

He went into the dining room, preparing himself, but just the same what he saw made him catch his breath. No one, ever, becomes entirely hardened. He would never reach a stage of looking at such scenes with indifference.

Burden was in the room with the photographer. Archbold as Scene-of-Crimes officer was measuring, making notes, and two technicians had arrived from forensics. Archbold stood up when Wexford came in and Wexford motioned to him to carry on.

When he had allowed his gaze to rest for a few moments on the bodies of the two women, he said to Burden, 'The girl, tell me everything she said.'

'That there were two of them. It was about eight. They came in a car.'

'How else would you get up here?'

'There were sounds from upstairs. The man who's dead on the stairs went to investigate.'

Wexford walked round the table and stood beside the dead woman whose head and streaming hair hung over the back of her chair. From there he was able to get a different view of the woman opposite. He looked at the remains of a face, laid left cheek downwards in a blood-filled dinner plate, on the red cloth.

'That's Davina Flory.'

'I guessed it must be,' Burden said quietly. 'And no doubt the man on the stairs is her husband.'

Wexford nodded. He felt something unusual for him, a kind of awe. 'Who's this? Wasn't there a daughter?'

The other woman might have been about forty-five. Her eyes and hair were dark. Her skin, white and drained in death, had probably been very pale in life. She was thin, dressed in gypsyish clothes, trailing patterned cottons with beads and chains. The colours had been predominantly red, but not so red as they now were.

'It would have made a hell of a din, all this.'

'Someone may have heard,' Wexford said. 'There must be other people on the estate. Someone looked after Davina Flory and her

29

husband and daughter. I'm sure I've heard there's a housekeeper and maybe a gardener live in houses up here, tied cottages on the estate.'

'I've seen to that. Karen and Gerry have gone out to try and locate them. You'll have noticed we didn't pass a house on the way in.'

Wexford moved round the table, hesitated, came closer than he had hitherto been to the body of Davina Flory. Her copious dark hair, threaded with white, escaping from a loose knot on the back of her head, lay spread in blood-dabbled tendrils. The shoulder of her dress, a red silk which clung closely to her thin shape, bore a huge blackish stain. Her hands lay on the blood-dyed tablecloth in the position of someone at a seance. They were the kind of preternaturally long thin hands such as are seldom seen except on oriental women. Age had done little to damage them, or else death had already shrunk the veins. The hands were unadorned but for a plain gold wedding ring on the left one. The other had half-closed in death as the fingers contracted to clutch a handful of bloody damask.

His sense of awe increasing, Wexford had stepped back to take in more fully this scene of horror and destruction, when the door crashed open and in walked the pathologist. Some moments before Wexford had heard a car draw up outside but had assumed it was only the return of Gerry Hinde and Karen Malahyde. It had in fact brought Dr Basil Sumner-Quist, a man who was anathema to Wexford. He would have much preferred Sir Hilary Tremlett.

'Dear, oh dear,' said Sumner-Quist, 'how are the mighty fallen!'

Bad taste, no, worse than that, outrageous, revolting lack of any taste at all, characterised the pathologist. He had once referred to a garrotting as 'a tasty little titbit'.

'I suppose that's her?' He prodded at the blood-stained red silk back. The prohibition on touching dead bodies applied to all but himself. 'We think so,' Wexford said, keeping the note of disapproval in his tone to a minimum. He had no doubt shown enough disapproval for one night. 'This is most probably Davina Flory, the man on the stairs is her husband Harvey Copeland and we guess that's her daughter. I don't know what she's called.'

'You finished?' Sumner-Quist said to Archbold.

'I can come back, sir.'

The photographer took one last shot and followed Archbold and the forensics men from the room. Sumner-Quist did not delay. He lifted up the head by grasping the mass of grey-threaded dark hair. The pathologist's body hid the ruined half of this face and a noble profile was revealed, majestically high forehead, straight nose, a wide curved mouth, the whole scored with a thousand fine lines and deeper indentations.

'Cradle-snatching when she picked him, wasn't she? She must have been at least fifteen years older.'

Wexford dipped his head.

'I've just been reading her book, Part One of the autobiography. A life packed with incident, you might say. Part Two must remain for ever unwritten. Still, there are too many books in the world, in my humble opinion.' Sumner-Quist let out his shrill braying laugh. 'I've heard it said that all women when they get old turn into goats or monkeys. She was a monkey, I'd say, wouldn't you? Not a sagging muscle to be seen.'

Wexford walked out of the room. He was aware that Burden was following him but he didn't look round. The anger which had been brewing in the restaurant, fermenting now from another cause, threatened to explode.

He said in a cold dull voice, 'When I kill him, at least it'll be old Tremlett doing the post-mortem.'

'Jenny's a great admirer of her books,' said Burden, 'the anthropology ones or whatever you call it. Well, I suppose they're political too. A remarkable woman, she was. I gave Jenny the autobiography for her birthday last week.'

Karen Malahyde came into the hall. She said, 'I wasn't certain what to do, sir. I knew you'd want to talk to the Harrisons and Gabbitas before it got too late, so I told them the bare facts. It seems to have come as a complete shock.'

'You did quite right,' said Wexford.

'I said it was likely you'd be along within the half-hour, sir. The houses, they're a pair, semi-detached, are about two minutes away down the lane that runs from the back garden.'

'Show me.'

She led him to the side of the west wing, past the broken bow window, and pointed to where the road skirted the garden and disappeared into the dark.

'Two minutes in a car or two minutes on foot?'

'I'd say ten minutes on foot, but I'll tell Donaldson where they are, shall I?'

'You can tell me, I'll walk.'

*

Donaldson was to follow with Barry Vine. Wexford set out along the lane that was separated from the garden by a high hedge. On the other side of it the forest encroached. There was very little mist here and the moon had risen. Out of the reach of the arc lamps, the moonlight washed the path ahead with a greenish phosphorescence on which conifers laid smooth or feathery black shadows. Also black against the clear shining sky were the silhouettes of marvellous trees, specimen trees planted decades before, and even by night discernible as fantastic or strange by their immense height or curious leaf formations or contorted branches. The shadows they cast were like letters in Hebrew on an old stained parchment.

He thought of death and of contrast. He thought of the ugliest of all things happening in this most beautiful place. Of 'right perfection wrongfully disgraced'. The memory of that blood splashing the room and the table like spilt paint made him shudder.

Here, so near by, was another world. The path had a magical quality. The wood was an enchanted place, not real, a backdrop perhaps to *The Magic Flute* or a setting for a fairy tale, an illustration, not living landscape. It was totally silent. Underfoot he trod on pine needles and his shoes made no sound. On and on, as the path wound, opened new moonlit vistas of leafless larches, araucarias with monkey puzzle branches like anchored reptiles, cypresses pointing spires into the sky, Scots pines whose crowns were concertinas, macrocarpas dense as tapestries, junipers slender and frondy, firs with last year's cones knobbing their tufted boughs. Moonlight, gaining strength, flooded the pinetum, glimmered through its alleys, was here and there excluded by a dense barrier of needled branches or trunks like twisted hanks of rope.

Nature, which should have risen up and howled, sent a gale roaring through these woods, driven the wild things to protest, the branches of trees to toss and lament, was quiet and sweet and placid. The stillness was almost unnatural. Not a twig moved. Wexford rounded a bend in the path, saw it peter out, the woods thin before him and a clearing emerge. A narrower path opened out of it, penetrating a screen of the more common sort of conifers.

The lights of houses showed gleaming at the end of the path.

Barry Vine and Karen Malahyde had been upstairs to the first and second floors to check that there were no more bodies. Curious to know what might be up there, Burden was nevertheless chary of

32

passing Harvey Copeland until Archbold had logged the body's position, it had been photographed from all angles and the pathologist had given it his preliminary examination. To pass it he would have had to step over the dead man's outflung right arm and hand. Vine and Karen had done so, but an inhibition, squeamishness and a sense of what was fitting, stopped Burden. He made his way instead across the hall and looked into what turned out to be the drawing room.

Beautifully furnished, exquisitely tidy, a museum of pretty things and *objects d'art*. Somehow, he would not have imagined Davina Flory living like this, but in a more slapdash or Bohemian fashion. He would have pictured her, robed or trousered, seated with like-minded spirits at some ancient and battered refectory table in a big warm untidy place, drinking wine and talking long into the night. A kind of banqueting hall it was that his imagination had conjured up. Davina Flory inhabited it, dressed like a matriarch in a Greek tragedy. He smiled to himself shamefacedly, looked again at the festooned windows, portraits in gilded frames, the jardinière of kalanchoe and ferns, the spindle-legged eighteenth-century furniture, and closed the door on it.

At the back of this east wing and behind the hall were two rooms that seemed to be his and her studies, another that opened into a large glazed room full of plants. One or more of the dead had been an enthusiastic gardener. The place was sweet-scented from bulb plants in bloom, narcissi and hyacinths, and with that damp green feel, humid and mild, peculiar to conservatories.

He found a library behind the dining room. All these rooms were as orderly, as sleek and tended as the first one he had looked into. They might have been in some National Trust mansion where certain rooms are open to the public. In the library all the books were contained behind screen doors of trellis-work, dark-red wood, fine gleaming glass. A single book only lay open on a lectern. From where he stood Burden could see that the print was old and he guessed at long S's. A passage led away to kitchen regions.

The kitchen was big but in no way cavernous. It had been newly fitted in the pseudo-farm dairy style, but he thought the cabinet doors were oak not pine. Here was the refectory table he had been imagining, glowingly polished and with fruit on a polished wooden platter in the centre of it.

A cough behind him make him look round. Archbold had come in with Chepstow, the fingerprint man.

'Excuse me, sir. Prints.'

Burden held up his right hand to show the glove on it. Chepstow nodded, got to work on the door handle on the kitchen side. The house was too grand to have that kitchen exit known as the 'back door'. Burden gingerly approached the open doors, one which led to a laundry room with washing machine, dryer and ironing things, the other to a kind of lobby with shelves, cupboards and a rack where coats hung. Yet another room had to be passed through before an exit to the outside was reached.

He looked round as Archbold came through. Archbold gave a half-nod. The door had bolts but they were not secured. A key was in the lock. Burden wouldn't touch the doorknob, glove or no glove.

'You're thinking they came in this way?'

'It's a possibility, isn't it, sir? How else? All the other outside doors are locked.'

'Unless they were admitted. Unless they came to the front door and someone opened it and invited them in.'

Chepstow came through and did his test on the doorknob, the fingerplate, the jamb. A cotton glove on his right hand, he carefully turned the knob. It gave and the door came open. Outside was cool greenish darkness with a remote wash of moonlight. Burden could make out a high hedge, enclosing a paved court.

'Someone left the door unlocked. The housekeeper when she went home, maybe. Maybe she always left it unlocked and they only locked it before they went to bed.'

'Could be,' said Burden.

'Terrible thing to have to lock yourselves in when you're in an isolated place like this.'

'They evidently didn't,' Burden said, irritated.

He made his way through the laundry room which led, by a doorway where the door stood open, into a kind of back hall lined with cupboards. An enclosed staircase, much narrower than the principal one, mounted between walls. These then were the 'back stairs', a feature of big old houses Burden had often heard of but seldom if ever seen. He went up, found himself in a passage with open doors on both sides.

The bedrooms seemed innumerable. If you lived in a house this size you might lose count of how many bedrooms you had. He

34

turned lights on and then off as he proceeded. The passage turned to the left and he knew he must be in the west wing, above the dining room. The only door here was closed. He opened it, pressed the switch his fingers felt on the left-hand wall.

Light flooded on to the sort of disorder he had imagined Davina Flory living in. It took him an instant only to realise that this was where the gunman or gunmen had been. The disturbance had been caused by them. What was it Karen Malahyde had said?

'They took her bedroom apart, looking for something.'

The bed had not been stripped but the covers thrown back and the pillows tossed aside. The drawers in the two bedside tables were pulled out and so were two of those in the dressing table. One of the wardrobe doors was open and a shoe from inside lay on the carpet. The lid of the ottoman at the foot of the bed had been raised and a length of silken fabric, a rose and gold floral pattern, trailed over the side of it.

It was odd, this feeling Burden had. His image of the kind of life he had expected Davina Flory to lead, the kind of person he would have thought she was, kept returning to him. This was how he would have envisaged her bedroom, beautifully appointed, cleaned and tidied daily, but subjected by its owner to a continuous untidying process. Not through wanton disregard of a servant's labours but because she simply did not know or notice, was indifferent to the neatness of her surroundings. It had not been so. An intruder had done this.

Why then did he find something incongruous about it? The jewel box, a red leather case, empty and upturned on the carpet, expressed the truth plainly enough.

Burden shook his head ruefully, for he would not have expected Davina Flory to have possessed jewels or a case to put them in.

Five people in the Harrisons' small front room turned it into a crowded place. John Gabbitas, the woodsman, had been fetched from next door. There were not enough chairs and an extra had to be brought from upstairs. Brenda Harrison had insisted on making tea, which no one had seemed to want, but of which, Wexford thought now, they all needed the relief and comfort.

She was cool about it. She had had, of course, some half-hour in which to adjust to the shock before he got there. Nevertheless, he found her briskness disconcerting. It might have been some minor disaster befalling her employers that Vine and Malahyde had told her about, a bit of the roof blowing off, for instance, or water through a ceiling. She bustled about with the teacups and a tin of biscuits while her husband sat stunned, his head occasionally moving from side to side as if in disbelief, his eyes staring.

Before running outside to boil a kettle and lay a tray – she seemed a hyperactive restless woman – she had confirmed his own identification. The dead man on the stairs was Harvey Copeland, the elder of the dead women at the table Davina Flory. The other woman she identified as certainly Davina Flory's daughter Naomi. In spite of the exalted status, in anyone's estimation, of her employers, it appeared that they were all on Christian-name terms here, Davina and Harvey and Naomi and Brenda. She even had to think for a moment before recalling Naomi's surname. Oh, yes, Jones, she was Mrs Jones, but the girl called herself Flory.

'The girl?'

'Daisy was Naomi's daughter and Davina's granddaughter. Her name was Davina too, she was sort of Davina Flory the younger, if you see what I mean, but they called her Daisy.'

'Not "was",' said Wexford. 'She's not dead.'

She lifted her shoulders a little. Her tone seemed to him indignant, perhaps only because she had been proved wrong. 'Oh. I thought the policewoman said they all were.'

It was after this that she made the tea.

He could already tell that of the three she was to be his principal informant. Her apparent callousness, an indifference that was almost repulsive, was of no particular account. Because of it, she might make the best witness. In any case, John Gabbitas, a man in his twenties, though living in one of the Tancred Wood houses and managing the woodland, worked for himself as well, as a woodsman and tree expert, and said he had only returned an hour before from a job on the other side of the county. Ken Harrison had scarcely uttered a word since Wexford and Vine arrived.

'When did you last see them?' Wexford asked.

She answered quickly. She was not the kind of woman to take thoughts. 'Seven thirty. I always did, regular as clockwork. Unless she had a dinner party. When it was just them, the four of them, I'd cook whatever it was and dish it up and put in on the heated trolley and wheel it into the dining room. Naomi always served it, or so I presume. I was never there to see. Davina liked to be at the table by seven forty-five sharp, same every night when she was home. It was always the same.'

'And it was the same tonight?'

'It was always the same. I wheeled the trolley in at seven thirty. It was soup and sole and apricots with yoghurt. I put my head round the sare door, they were all there . . .'

'Round the what?'

'The sare. That's the name they had for it. The conservatory. I said I was off and I went out the back way like I always do.'

'Did you lock the back door?'

'No, of course I didn't. I never do that. Besides, Bib was still there.'

'Bib?'

'She helps out. Comes up on her bike. She's got a morning job some mornings so she mostly comes here in the afternoons. I left her here, finishing off the freezer, and she said she'd be off in five minutes.' A thought suddenly struck her. Her colour changed – for the first time. 'The cat,' she said, 'is the cat all right? Oh, they didn't kill the cat!'

'Not so far as I know,' Wexford said. 'Well, no, certainly not.'

Before he could add, as he had begun to, suppressing a tone of irony, 'Only the people', she exclaimed, 'Thank God for that!'

Wexford gave her a moment. 'Around eight, did you hear anything? A car? Shots?'

He knew the shots would not have been heard from here. Not shots fired inside the house. She shook her head.

'A car wouldn't go past here. The road ends here. There's only the main road in and the by-road.'

'The by-road?'

She answered him impatiently. She was one of those people who expect everyone to know, as well as they themselves do, the workings and rules and geography of their little private world. 'It's the one comes up from Pomfret Monachorum, isn't it?'

Gabbitas said, 'That's the way I came home.'

'What time was that?'

'Twenty past eight, half past. I didn't see anyone, if that's what you're asking. I didn't meet a car or pass one or anything like that.'

Wexford thought that came out rather too pat. Then Ken Harrison spoke. The words came slowly, as if he had suffered an injury to his throat and was still learning how to project his voice. 'We didn't hear a thing. There wasn't a sound.' He added, wonderingly – and

37

incomprehensibly – 'There never was.' He explained. 'You can never hear anything at the house from here.'

The others seemed long to have registered and accepted what had happened. Mrs Harrison had adjusted to it almost at once. Her world had altered but she would contend with it. Her husband reacted as if the news had just that moment been broken to him, 'All dead? Did you say they were all dead?'

It sounded to Wexford like something out of *Macbeth,* though he wasn't sure it was. A lot of tonight was like something out of *Macbeth.*

'The young girl, Miss Flory, Daisy, she's alive.'

But, he thought, is she? Is she still alive? Then Harrison shocked him. He thought that was impossible but Harrison did it.

'Funny they didn't finish her off, wasn't it?'

Barry Vine coughed.

'Have another cup of tea, will you?' said Brenda Harrison.

'No, thank you. It's getting late and we'll be off. You'll want to get to bed.'

'You've finished with us, then, have you?'

Perhaps it was a favourite word with him. Ken Harrison was looking with a kind of glazed wistfulness at Wexford.

'Finished? No, by no means. We shall want to talk to you all again. Perhaps you'll let me have Bib's address. What's her other name?'

No one seemed to know. They had the address but no surname. She was just Bib.

'Thanks for the tea,' said Vine.

Wexford went back to the house by car. Sumner-Quist had gone. Archbold and Milsom were working away upstairs. Burden said to him, 'I forgot to mention it but I had road blocks put on all the roads out of here when the message came through.'

'What, before you knew what it was about?'

'Well, I knew it was in the nature of a – a massacre. She said, "They're all dead," when she made her 999 call. You think I over-reacted, do you?'

'No,' said Wexford slowly, 'no, not at all. I think you were right, insofar as it's possible to block all roads. I mean, there must be dozens of ways out.'

'Not really. What they call the by-road goes to Pomfret Monachorum and Cheriton. The main drive goes directly to the B2428 into town and there happened to be a squad car on that about half a mile along. In the other direction the road goes to Cambery Ashes, as you know. It was a piece of luck for us, or it looked that way. The pair in the squad car knew about it within three minutes of her call. But they didn't go that way, they must have gone by the by-road, and then there wasn't much of a chance. No description, no index number or approximation to it, no idea what to look for. We haven't now. I couldn't have asked her anything more, could I, Reg? I reckoned she was dying.'

'Of course you couldn't. Of course not.'

'I hope to God she doesn't die.'

'So do I,' said Wexford. 'She's only seventeen.'

'Well, naturally one hopes for her sake she'll live, but I was thinking of what she can tell us. Pretty well everything, don't you think?'

Wexford just looked at him.

# 5

The girl could tell them everything. Davina Jones called Daisy Flory could tell them when the men came and how they came, what they looked like, even perhaps what they wanted and took. She had seen them and perhaps spoken to them. She might have seen their car. Wexford thought it likely she was intelligent and hoped she was observant. He hoped very much she would live.

Entering his own house at midnight, he thought of phoning the hospital to check on her. What good would it do, his knowing whether she lived or died?

If they told him she was dead he wouldn't sleep, because she had been young and with all of her life before her. And for Burden's reason too, he had better be honest. Because if she was dead the case would be all that much harder. But if they told him she was all right, she was doing well, he would be too hyped up at the prospect of talking to her to sleep.

Anyway, they wouldn't tell him that, but either that she was dead or 'holding her own' or 'comfortable'. In any case WPC Rosemary Mountjoy was with her, would sit outside the ward door till morning and be relieved at eight by WPC Anne Lennox.

He went quietly upstairs to see if Dora was still awake. The light from the open door fell, not on her face, but in a wide band across the arm that lay outside the covers, the sleeve of her nightdress, the rather small neat hand with round pink fingernails. Deep sleep held her and her breathing was steady and slow. She could sleep easily then, in spite of what had happened earlier that evening, in spite of Sheila and the fourth member of their party he was already calling 'that wretched man'. He felt unreasonably exasperated by her. Retreating he pulled the door to behind him, went down again and in

40

the living room hunted through the paper rack for the *Independent on Sunday* of two days before.

The review section was still there, pushed between the *Radio Times* and some freebie magazine. It was the Win Carver interview he was looking for and the big portrait photograph he remembered as a double-page spread. Page eleven. He sat down in an armchair, found the page. The face was before him, the face he had seen an hour before in death when Sumner-Quist had lifted it from the table by a handful of hair like an executioner holding aloft a severed head.

The text began as a single column on the left-hand side. Wexford looked at the picture. The portrait was of a kind a woman would only tolerate seeing of herself if she had succeeded overwhelmingly in fields distant from the triumph of youth and beauty. These were not lines on the face but the deep scoring of time and the pleating of old age. From a bird's nest of wrinkles the nose stood out beak-like and the lips curved in a half-smile that was both ironic and kindly. The eyes were still young, dark, burning irises and clear unveined whites in the tangle of gathered folds.

The caption read: Davina Flory, the first volume of whose autobiography *The Youngest Wren of Nine* is published by St Giles Press at £16.00. He turned the page and there she was when young: a little girl in a velvet dress with lace collar, ten years later a grown-up girl with a swan neck, mysterious smile, shingled hair and one of those dresses with no waist and a belt round the hips.

The print swam before his eyes. Wexford gave a huge yawn. He was too tired to read the piece tonight and leaving the paper open on the table, he went back upstairs. The evening past seemed immensely long, a corridor of events with at the opening of the tunnel, distant but very much there, Sheila and that wretched man.

While the reader had recourse to a magazine, the non-reader went to a book for help.

Burden let himself into his house to the sound of his son yelling. By the time he was upstairs the noise had stopped and Mark was being comforted in his mother's arms. Burden could hear her telling him, in that rather didactic confident way of hers which was immediately reassuring, that diplodocus the two-ridged reptile had not walked the earth for two million years and in any case had never been known to inhabit toy cupboards.

By the time she came into their bedroom Burden was in bed, sitting up with her birthday copy of *The Youngest Wren of Nine* resting against his knees.

She kissed him, went into a detailed description of Mark's dream, which for a little while distracted him from the biographical note he had been reading on the back flap of the book jacket. In that moment he decided to say nothing to her of what had happened. Not till the morning. She had deeply admired the dead woman, followed her travels and collected her works. Their pillow talk of the previous night had been about this book, Davina Flory's childhood and the early influences which helped to form the character of this distinguished anthropologist and 'geo-sociologist'.

'You can't have my book till I've finished it,' she said sleepily, turning over and burying her head in the pillows. 'Anyway, can't we have the light out?'

'Two minutes. Just to let me unwind. Good-night, love.'

Unlike many writers past a certain age, Davina Flory had had no reservations about her birth date appearing in print. She had been seventy-eight, born in Oxford, the youngest of the nine children of a professor of Greek. Educated at Lady Margaret Hall, with later a Ph.D. from London, she had married in 1935 a fellow undergraduate at Oxford, Desmond Cathcart Flory. Together they had set about the redemption of the gardens of his home, Tancred House, Kingsmarkham, and had begun the planting of the famous woods.

Burden read the rest, put the light out, lay looking into the dark, thinking of what he had read. Desmond Flory had been killed in France in 1944, eight months before his daughter Naomi was born. Two years later Davina Flory began her travels in Europe and the Middle East, re-marrying in 1951. He had forgotten the rest of it, the new husband's name, the titles of all the works.

None of this would matter. That Davina Flory had been who she was would turn out to be no more important than if she had been what Burden called 'an ordinary person'. It was possible that the men who had killed her had no idea of her identity. A good many of the kind of people Burden came across in his work were, in any case, unable to read. To the gunman or gunmen at Tancred House she had been only a woman who possessed jewellery and lived in an isolated place. She and her husband and daughter and granddaughter were vulnerable and unprotected and that was enough for them.

The first thing Wexford saw when he woke up was the phone.

Usually the first thing he saw was the little black Marks and Spencer alarm clock, the arch-shaped clock that was either braying away or about to go off. He couldn't remember the phone number of Stowerton Royal Infirmary. WPC Mountjoy would have phoned if anything had happened.

In the post, on the doormat, was a card from Sheila. It had been posted in Venice four days before, while she was there with that man. The picture was of a gloomy baroque interior, a pulpit and drapery over it, marble probably but cunningly contrived to look like cloth. Sheila had written, 'We have just been to see the Gesuiti, which is Gus's favourite joke-church in all the world and not to be confused, he says, with the Gesuati. Stone Wilton is a bit cold on the feet and it is freezing here. Much love, S.'

He would make her as pretentious as himself. Wexford wondered what on earth the card meant. What was a joke-church, and come to that what was Stone Wilton? It sounded like a village in the Cotswolds.

The *Independent on Sunday* review section in his pocket, he drove himself to work. The removal of furnishings and equipment had already begun for the setting up of an incident room at Tancred House. The investigation would be conducted from there. DC Hinde told him as he came in that a Kingsmarkham systems manufacturer on the industrial estate was offering them, free of charge as a gesture of good will, computers, word processors with laser printers, printer ancillaries, workstations, software and faxes.

'The managing director's chairman of the local Tories,' Hinde said. 'Chap called Pagett, Graham Pagett. He's been on the blower. He says this is his way of implementing the Government's policy that fighting crime is up to the private individual.'

Wexford grunted.

'We can do with that kind of support, sir.'

'Yes, it's very good of him,' Wexford said absently. He wouldn't go up there yet but waste no time, take Barry Vine with him and find the woman called Bib.

It had to be straightforward, this business. It had to be murder for robbery or murder in the course of robbery. Two villains in a stolen car after Davina Flory's jewellery. Maybe they'd been reading the *Independent on Sunday*, except that this newspaper hadn't mentioned jewellery other than Win Carver's comment that Davina wore a wedding ring, and they'd be more likely anyway to read the *People*.

If they could read. Two villains certainly, but not strangers to the place. One who knew all about it, one who didn't, his mate, his pal, met perhaps in prison . . .

Someone connected with those servants, the Harrisons? With this Bib? She lived at Pomfret Monachorum, which probably meant she had gone home by the by-road. Wexford fancied the by-road as an exit for the gunman and his companion. That was their most likely way out, especially as one of them must have known the place. He could almost hear one saying to the other that this was the way to avoid the Plod coming in.

The forest separated Pomfret Monachorum from Tancred and Kingsmarkham and almost from the rest of the world. Behind it the road ran to Cheriton and to Pomfret. The ruined walls of an abbey still stood, the church was pretty outside, wrecked inside by Henry VIII and later Cromwell, and the rest of the place consisted of the vicarage, a cluster of cottages and a small council estate. Out on the Pomfret road was a row of three shingle-and-slate cottages.

It was in one of these that Bib lived, though neither Wexford nor Vine knew which one. All the Harrisons and Gabbitas knew was that it was in the row called Edith Cottages.

A plaque bearing this name and the date 1882 was embedded in the shingles above the upper windows of the middle one. All the cottages needed painting, none looked prosperous. Each one had a television aerial on its roof and the one on the left a dish sticking out from the side of a bedroom window. A bicycle leant up against the wall by the front door of the cottage on the right and a Ford Transit van was parked half on the grass verge outside its gate. A wheelie-bin stood in the garden of the middle cottage, on a piece of concrete with a manhole cover in it. There were daffodils in bloom in this garden but no flowers in either of the others, and the one with the bicycle was overgrown with weeds.

Because Brenda Harrison had told him Bib rode a bicycle, Wexford decided to try the house on the right. A young man came to the door. He was rather tall but very slight, dressed in blue jeans and an American college sweatshirt so worn and washed and faded that only the U of University and a capital S and T were discernible on the greyish background. His was a girlish face, the face of a pretty tomboy. The youths who played heroines in sixteenth-century drama must have looked like him.

He said, 'Hi', but in a dazed way and rather slowly. Seeming considerably taken aback, he looked past Wexford at the car outside, then back warily at his face.

'Kingsmarkham CID. We're looking for someone called Bib. Does she live here?'

He was studying Wexford's warrant card with great interest. Or even anxiety. A lazy grin transformed his face, suddenly making him appear more masculine. He shook back the long lock of black hair that fell over his forehead.

'Bib? No. No, she doesn't. Next door. The one in the middle.' He hesitated, said, 'Is this about the Davina Flory killings?'

'How do you know about that?'

'Breakfast TV,' he said, and added, as if Wexford was likely to be interested, 'We studied one of her books at college. I minored in English Literature.'

'I see. Well, thank you very much, sir.' Kingsmarkham Police called everyone 'sir' or 'madam' or by their name and style until they were actually charged. It was for politeness's sake and one of Wexford's rules. 'We won't trouble you any further,' he said.

If the young American had the look of a girl cross-dressing, Bib might have been a man, so few concessions had she or nature made to her gender. Her age was equally an enigma. She might have been thirty-five or fifty-five. Her dark hair was cropped short, her face was reddish and shiny as if scrubbed with soap, her fingernails square cut. In one ear lobe she wore a small gold ring.

When Vine had explained what they had come for, she nodded and said, 'I saw it on telly. Couldn't believe it.' Her voice was gruff, flat, curiously expressionless.

'May we come in?'

In her estimation the question was no mere formality. She seemed to be considering it from several possible angles before giving a slow nod.

Her bicycle she kept in the hall, resting against a wall papered in sweet peas faded to beige. The living room was furnished like the abode of a very old lady and it had that sort of smell, a combination of camphor and carefully preserved not very clean clothes, closed windows and boiled sweets. Wexford expected to encounter an ancient mother in an armchair but the room was empty.

'For a start, could we have your full name, please,' Vine said.

If she had been in court on a murder charge brought there

peremptorily and without counsel to defend her, Bib could not have behaved with greater caution. Every word must be weighed. She brought out her name with slow reluctance and a hesitation before each word.

'Er, Beryl – er Agnes – er, Mew.'

'Beryl Agnes Mew. I believe you work on a part-time basis at Tancred House and were there yesterday afternoon, Miss Mew?'

'Mrs. Missus.' She looked from Vine to Wexford and said it again, very deliberately. 'Mrs Mew.'

'I'm sorry. You were there yesterday afternoon?'

'Yes.'

'Doing what?'

It might be shock that affected her like this. Or a general distrust and suspicion of humanity. She seemed stunned by Vine's question and looked at him stonily before lifting her heavy shoulders in a shrug.

'What do you do there, Mrs Mew?'

Again she considered. She was still but her eyes moved rather more than most people's. Now they moved quite wildly.

She said, incomprehensibly to Vine, 'They call it the rough.'

'You do the rough work, Mrs Mew,' Wexford said. 'Yes, I see. Scrubbing floors, washing paint and so on?' He got a ponderous nod. 'You were cleaning the freezer, I think.'

'The freezers. They've got three.' Her head swayed slowly from side to side. 'I saw it on telly. Couldn't believe it. They was all right yesterday.'

As if, Wexford thought, the inhabitants of Tancred House had succumbed to a visitation of plague. He said, 'What time did you leave for home?'

If the imparting of her own name had caused such inner searching, a question such as this might be expected to give rise to whole minutes of pondering, but Bib answered fairly quickly. 'They'd started on their meal.'

'Mr and Mrs Copeland and Mrs Jones and Miss Jones had gone into the dining room, do you mean?'

'I heard them talking and the door shut. I put me bits back in the freezer and switched it on. My hands was froze, so I put them under the hot tap for a bit.' The effort of saying so much silenced her for a moment. She seemed to be recouping unseen forces. 'I got me coat

46

and then I went to fetch me bike as was in that bit round the back with hedges like round.'

Wexford wondered if she ever talked to the man next door, the American, and if she talked like this, would he understand a word? 'Did you lock the back door after you?'

'Me? No. It's not my job to lock doors.'

'So this would have been – what? Ten to eight?'

A long hesitation. 'I reckon.'

'How did you get home?' said Vine.

'On my bike.' She was made indignant by his stupidity. He should have known. Everyone knew.

'Which route did you take, Mrs Mew? Which road?'

'The by-road.'

'I want you to think very carefully before you answer.' But she always did. That was why this was taking so long. 'Did you see a car on your way home? Did you meet one or did one overtake you? On the by-road.' More explanation was doubtless called for. 'A car or a van or a – a vehicle like the one next door.'

For a moment Wexford feared he had made her think her American neighbour might be involved in this crime. She got up and looked out of the window in the direction of the Ford Transit. Her expression was confused and she bit her lip.

At last she said, 'That one?'

'No, no. Any one. Any vehicle at all. Did you meet any vehicle on your way home last evening?'

She thought. She nodded, shook her head, finally said, 'No.'

'You're sure of that?'

'Yes.'

'How long does it take to get home?'

'It's downhill going home.'

'Yes. So how long did it take you last evening?'

'About twenty minutes.'

'And you met no one? Not even John Gabbitas in the Land-Rover.'

The first flash of any sort of animation showed. It came in her restless eyes. 'Does he say I did?'

'No, no. It's unlikely you would have if you were home here by, say, eight fifteen. Thank you very much, Mrs Mew. Would you like to show us the road you take from here to the by-road?'

A long pause and then, 'I don't mind.'

47

The road where the cottages were fell steeply down the side of the little river valley. Bib Mew pointed their way down this road and gave some vague instructions, her eyes straying to the Ford Transit. Wexford thought he must have ineradicably planted in her mind the notion that she should have met this van last night. As they drove off down the hill, she could be seen leaning over the gate, following their progress with those darting eyes.

At the foot of the hill the stream was not bridged but forded. A wooden footbridge spanned it for the use of foot passengers and cyclists. Vine drove through the water which was perhaps six inches deep and flowing very fast over flat brown stones. On the other side they came to what he insisted on calling a T-junction, though the extreme rusticity of the place, steep hedge banks, overhanging trees, deep meadows with cattle glimpsed beyond, made this a misnomer. Bib's instructions, if such they could be called, were to turn left here and then take the first right. This was the Pomfret Monachorum way in to the by-road.

There came a sudden sight of forest. The hedge trees parted and there it was, a dark, bluish canopy hanging high above them. Half a mile up the road it appeared again, was quickly all round them, as the deep tunnel of lane running between high banks plunged into the start of the by-road where a sign said: TANCRED HOUSE ONLY. TWO MILES. NO THROUGH-ROAD.

Wexford said, 'When we think it's only one mile I'm going to get out and walk the rest of the way.'

'Right. They'd have had to know the place if they came this way, sir.'

'They knew it. Or one of them did.'

He left the car at an auspicious moment, when he saw the sun come out. The woods would not begin to grow green for another month. There was not even a green haze to mist the trees which flanked this sandy path. All was bright brown, a sparkling vigorous colour that gilded the branches and turned the leaf buds to a glowing shade of copper. It was cold and dry. Late on the previous night, when the sky had cleared, a frost had come. The frost was gone now, not a silver streak of it remaining, but a chill hung in the clear still air. Above the dense or feathery treetops, through spaces in the groves, the sky was a light delicate blue, so pale as to be almost white.

The Win Carver interview told him about these woods, when they

48

had been planted, which parts dated from the thirties and which were older but augmented with planting from that time. Ancient oaks, and here and there a horse chestnut with looped boughs and glutinous leaf buds, towered above ranks of smaller neater trees, vase-shaped as if by a natural process of topiary. Wexford thought they might be hornbeams. Then he noticed a metal label secured to the trunk of one of them. Yes, common hornbeam, *Carpinus betulus*. The taller graceful specimens a little way along the path were the mountain ash, he read, *Sorbus aucuparia*. Identifying trees when bare of leaves must be a test for the expert.

The groves gave place to a plantation of Norway maples (*Acer platanoides*) with trunks like crocodile skin. No conifers were here, not a single pine or fir to provide a dark green shape among the shining leafless branches. This was the finest part of the deciduous woodland, man-made but a copy of nature, pristinely ordered but with nature's own neatness. Fallen logs had been left when they fell and were overgrown with bright fungus, frills and ruffs and knobbed stalks in yellow or bronze. Dead trees still stood, their rotting trunks weathered to silver, a habitation for owls or a feeding ground for woodpeckers.

Wexford walked on, expecting each twist in the narrow road to bring him out to face the east wing of the house. But every new curve only afforded another vista of standing trees and fallen trees, saplings and underbrush. A squirrel, blue and silvery brown, snaked up the trunk of an oak, sprang from twig to twig, took a flying leap to the branch of a nearby beech. The road made a final ellipse, broadened and cleared and there was the house before him, dream-like in the veils of mist.

The east wing rose majestically. From here the terrace could be seen and the gardens at the rear. Instead of the daffodils, which filled the public gardens in Kingsmarkham and the council flower-beds, tiny scillas sparkling like blue jewels clustered under the trees. But the gardens of Tancred House had not yet wakened from their winter sleep. Herbaceous borders, rosebeds, paths, hedges, pleached walks, lawns, all still had the look of having been trimmed and manicured, coiffed and in some cases packaged, and put away for hibernation. High hedges of yew and cypress made walls to conceal all outbuildings from sight of the house, dark screens cunningly planted for a privileged privacy.

He stood looking for a moment or two, then made his way to

where he could see the parked police vehicles. The incident room had been set up in what was apparently a stable block, though a stables that no horse had lived in for half a century. It was too smart for that and there were blinds at the windows. A blue-faced gilt-handed clock under a central pediment told him the time was twenty to eleven.

His car was parked on the flagstones, so were Burden's and two vans. Inside the stable block a technician was setting up the computers and Karen Malahyde was arranging a dais, lectern, microphone and half-circle of chairs for his press conference. They had scheduled it for eleven.

Wexford sat down behind the desk provided for him. He was rather touched by the care Karen had taken – he was sure it must be Karen's work. There were three new ballpoint pens, a brass paperknife he couldn't imagine he would ever use, two phones, as if he hadn't got his Vodaphone, a computer and printer he had no idea how to work, and in a blue and brown glazed pot a cactus. The cactus, large, spherical, grey, covered in fur, was more like an animal than a plant, a *cuddly* animal, except that when he poked it a sharp thorn went into his finger.

Wexford shook his finger, cursing mildly. He could see he was honoured. These things seemingly went by rank and though there was another cactus on the desk evidently designated Burden's, it had nowhere near the dimension of his, nor was it so hirsute. All Barry Vine got was an African violet, not even in bloom.

WPC Lennox had phoned in soon after she took over hospital duty. There was nothing to report. All was well. What did that mean? What was it to him if the girl lived or died? Young girls were dying all over the world, from starvation, in wars and insurrections, from cruel practices and clinical neglect. Why should this one matter?

He punched out Anne Lennox's number on his phone.

'She seems fine, sir.'

He must have misheard. 'She *what*?'

'She seems fine – well, heaps better. Would you like to talk to Dr Leigh, sir?'

There was silence at the other end. That is, there was no voice. He could hear hospital noise, footsteps and metallic sounds and swishing sounds. A woman came on.

'I believe that's Kingsmarkham Police?'

'Chief Inspector Wexford.'

'Dr Leigh. How can I help you?'

The voice sounded lugubrious to him. He detected in it the gravity which these people were perhaps taught to assume for some while after a tragedy had taken place. Such a death would affect the whole hospital. He simply gave the name, knowing that would be enough without enquiry.

'Miss Flory. Daisy Flory.'

Suddenly all the gloom was gone. Perhaps he had imagined it. 'Daisy? Yes, she's fine, she's doing very well.'

'What? What did you say?'

'I said she's doing well, she's fine.'

'She's *fine*? We are talking about the same person? The young woman who was brought in last night with gunshot wounds?'

'Her condition is quite satisfactory, Chief Inspector. She will be coming out of intensive care sometime today. I expect you'll want to see her, won't you? There's no reason why you shouldn't talk to her this afternoon. For a short while only, of course. We'll say ten minutes.'

'Would four o'clock be a good time?'

'Four p.m., yes. Ask to see me first, will you? It's Dr Leigh.'

The press came early. Wexford supposed he should really call them the 'media' as, approaching the dais, he saw from the window a television van arriving with a camera crew.

51

# 6

'Estate' sounded like a hundred semi-detached houses crowded into a few acres. 'Grounds' expressed land only, not the buildings on it. Burden, unusually fanciful for him, thought 'demesne' might be the only word. This was the demesne of Tancred, a little world, or more realistically a hamlet: the great house, its stables, coachhouses, outbuildings, dwellings for servants past and present. Its gardens, lawns, hedges, pinetum, plantations and woods.

All of it – perhaps not the woods themselves – would have to be searched. They needed to know what they were dealing with, what this place was. The stables where the centre had been set up was only a small part of it. From where he stood, on the terrace which ran the length of the back of the house, scarcely anything of these outbuildings could be seen. Cunning hedge-planting, the careful provision of trees to hide the humble or the utilitarian, concealed everything from view but the top of a slate roof, the point of a weather vane. After all, it was winter still. The leaves of summertime would shield these gardens, this view, in serried screens of green.

As it was, the long formal lawn stretched away between herbaceous borders, broke into a rose garden, a clockface of beds, opened again to dip over a ha-ha into the meadow beyond. Perhaps. It was a possibility, though too far away to see from here. Things had been so arranged as to have the gardens blend gently into the vista beyond, the parklands with its occasional giant tree, the bluish lip of woods. All the woods looked blue in the soft, misty late-winter light. Except the pinetum to the west with its mingled colours of yellow and smoky black, marble green and reptile green, slate and pearl and a bright copper.

Even in daylight, even from here, the pair of houses where the

Harrisons and Gabbitas lived were invisible. Burden walked down the stone steps and along the path and through a gate in the hedge to the stables and coachhouses area where the search had begun. He came upon a row of cottages, dilapidated and shabby but not derelict, that had once no doubt housed some of the many servants the Victorians needed to maintain outdoor comfort and order.

The front door of one of them stood open. Two constables from the uniformed branch were inside, opening cupboards, investigating a hole of a scullery. Burden thought about housing and how there were never supposed to be enough houses, and he thought about all the homeless people, even on the streets of Kingsmarkham these days. His wife who had a social conscience had taught him to think this way. He never would have done before he married her. As it was, he could see that a surplus of accommodation at Tancred, at the hundreds and hundreds of houses like this there must be all over England, solved no problems. Not really. He couldn't see how you could make the Florys and Copelands of this world give up their unused servants' cottage to the bag lady who slept in St Peter's porch, even if the bag lady would want it, so he stopped this line of thought and walked once more round the back of the house to the kitchen regions where he was due to meet Brenda Harrison for a tour.

Archbold and Milsom were examining the flagged areas here, looking no doubt for tyre marks. They had been working on the broad space at the front when he first arrived that morning. It had been a dry spring, the last heavy rain weeks ago. A car could come up here and leave no trace of its passage behind.

In the still waters of the pool, when he bent over to look, he had seen a pair of large goldfish, white with scarlet heads, swimming serenely in slow circles.

White and scarlet ... The blood was still there, though the tablecloth, along with a host of other items, had gone off in bags to the forensics laboratory at Myringham. Later on in the night the room had been filled with sealed plastic bags containing lamps and ornaments, cushions and table napkins, plates and cutlery.

With no qualms about what she might see in the hall, for sheets covered the foot of the stairs and the corner where the phone was, he had been steering Brenda clear of the dining room, when she side-stepped and opened the door. She was such a quick mover, it was a risk taking his eyes off her for an instant.

She was a small thin woman with the skinny figure of a young girl. Her trousers scarcely showed the outline of buttock and thigh. But her face was as deeply lined as if by knife cuts, her lips sucked in by a constant nervous pursing. Dry reddish hair was already thin enough to make it likely Mrs Harrison would need a wig in ten years' time. She was never still. All night long she probably fidgeted in her fretful sleep.

Outside the bow window, gaping in, stood her husband. The night before they had sealed up the broken pane but not drawn the curtains. Brenda gave him a swift look, then surveyed the room, swivelling her head. Her eyes rested briefly on the worst spattered area of wall, for a longer time on a patch of carpet beside the chair where Naomi Jones had been sitting. Archbold had scraped off a bloodstained section of the pile here and it had gone to the lab with the other items and the four cartridges which had been recovered. Burden thought she was going to comment, to make some remark on the lines of police destroying a good carpet which cleaning would have restored to pristine condition, but she said nothing.

It was Ken Harrison who made – or mouthed, for inside the room it was nearly inaudible – the expected censure. Burden opened the window.

'I didn't quite catch that, Mr Harrison.'

'I said that was eight-ounce glass, that was.'

'No doubt it can be replaced.'

'At a cost.'

Burden shrugged.

'And the back door wasn't even locked!' exclaimed Harrison in the tone a respectable householder uses to refer to an act of vandalism.

Brenda, left to herself to examine this room for the first time, had turned very pale. That frozen look, that increasing pallor, might be the prelude to a faint. Her glazed eyes met his.

'Come along, Mrs Harrison, there's no point in remaining here. Are you all right?'

'I'm not going to pass out, if that's what you mean.'

But there had been a danger of it, he was sure of that, for she sat down on a chair in the hall and hung her head forward, trembling. Burden could smell blood. He was hoping she wouldn't know what the stench was, a mixture of fishiness and iron filings, when she jumped up, said she was quite all right and should they go upstairs?

She bounded quite jauntily over the sheet that covered the steps where Harvey Copeland had lain.

Upstairs, she showed him the top floor, a place of attics that were perhaps never used. On the first floor were the rooms he had already seen, those of Daisy and Naomi Jones. Three-quarters of the way along the passage to the west wing, she opened a door and announced that this was where Copeland had slept.

Burden was surprised. He had assumed that Davina Flory and her husband shared a bedroom. Though he didn't say this, Brenda followed this thought. She gave him a look in which prudery was curiously mixed with lubriciousness.

'She was sixteen years older than him, you know. She was a very old woman. Of course you wouldn't have said that of her, if you know what I mean, she sort of didn't seem to have much to do with age. She was just herself.'

Burden knew what she meant. Her sensitivity was unexpected. He gave the room a quick glance. No one had been in there, nothing was disturbed. Copeland had slept in a single bed. The furniture was dark mahogany but in spite of its warm rich colour, the room had an austere look with plain cream curtains, a cream carpet and the only pictures prints of old county maps.

The state of Davina Flory's bedroom seemed to upset Brenda more than the dining room had. At least it stimulated her to an outburst of feeling.

'What a mess! Look at the bed! Look at all that stuff out of the drawers!'

She ran about, picking things up. Burden made no attempt to stop her. Photographs would provide a permanent record of how the room had been.

'I want you to tell me what's missing, Mrs Harrison.'

'Look at her jewel box!'

'Can you remember what things she had?'

Brenda, as agile as a teenager and as thin, sat on the floor, reaching out all round her for scattered objects; a brooch, a pair of eyebrow tweezers, a suitcase key, an empty perfume bottle.

'That brooch, for instance, why would they leave that?'

Her short laugh was like a snort. 'It wasn't worth anything. I gave it her.'

'You did?'

'For a Christmas present. We all gave each other presents, so I had

55

to get something. What d'you give the woman who has everything? She used to wear it, maybe she liked it, but it was only worth three quid.'

'What's missing, Mrs Harrison?'

'She didn't have much, you know. I say "the woman who has everything" but there are things you can afford you don't always want, aren't there? I mean fur, even if you could afford it. Well, it's cruel, isn't it? She could have had diamonds galore but it wasn't her style.' She had got up and was rummaging through drawers. 'I'd say the lot was gone, what there was. She had some good pearls. There was rings her first husband gave her; she never wore them, but they were here. Her gold bracelet's gone. One of the rings had enormous diamonds in it, God knows what it was worth. You'd have thought she'd have kept it in the bank, wouldn't you? She told me she thought of giving it to Daisy when she was eighteen.'

'When would that be?'

'Soon. Next week or the week after.'

'Only "thought of"?'

'I'm telling you what she said and that's what she said.'

'Do you think you could make me a list of the jewellery you think is missing, Mrs Harrison?'

She nodded, slammed the drawer shut. 'Fancy, this time yesterday I was in here doing the room – I always did the bedrooms on a Tuesday – and she came in, Davina that is, and was talking ever so happily about going off to France with Harvey to do some programme on French TV, some very important book programme for her new book. Of course she spoke French like a native.'

'What do you think happened here last night?'

She was walking ahead of him down the back stairs. 'Me? How should I know?'

'You must have had ideas. You know the house and you knew the people. I'd be interested to know what you think.'

At the foot of the stairs they met a large cat of a colour known to Burden as 'Air Force blue', which had come out of the opposite door and was crossing the back hall. When it saw them it stopped in its tracks, opened its eyes very wide, laid back its ears and began to swell until its dense fluffy smoky fur stood on end. Its attitude was of a brave animal menaced by hunters or some dangerous predator.

'Don't be silly, Queenie,' said Brenda fondly. 'Don't be such a silly old girl. You know he won't hurt you while I'm here.' Burden felt a little affronted. 'There's some chicken livers for you on the back step.'

The cat turned tail and fled the way it had come. Brenda Harrison followed it through a door Burden had not entered on the previous evening, and along a passage which opened into the morning room. The sun-filled conservatory was as warm as summer. He had been in here briefly the night before. It looked different by day and he saw that this was the glazed building, of classical shape and curved roof, which protruded into the centre of the terrace where he had stood surveying the lawns and the distant woods.

The scent of hyacinths was stronger, sweet and cloying. Sunlight had opened the narcissi to show their orange corollas. In here it was humid and warm and perfumed, the way you thought a rain forest might be, the air damply tangible.

'She wouldn't let me have a pet,' Brenda Harrison said suddenly.

'I'm sorry?'

'Davina. Like I say, there was no side to her, all of us was equal – I mean, that's what she *said* – but I wasn't allowed to have a pet. I'd have liked a dog. Have a hamster, Brenda, she said, or a budgie. But I never liked the idea of that. It's cruel keeping birds in cages, don't you reckon?'

'I shouldn't fancy one myself,' said Burden.

'God knows what'll become of us now, me and Ken. We've got no other home. The way property prices are we don't have a chance – well, it's a joke, isn't it? Davina said this was our home for ever but when all's said and done it's a tied cottage, isn't it?' She bent down and picked up a dead leaf from the floor. Her expression became coy, a little wistful. 'It's not easy starting afresh. I know I don't look my age, everyone says so, but when all's said and done we're not getting any younger, either of us.'

'You were going to tell me what you think happened here last night.'

She sighed. 'What do I think happened? Well, what does happen in these awful cases, I mean it's not the first, is it? They got in and went upstairs, they'd heard about the pearls and maybe the rings. There's always bits in the papers about Davina. I mean, anyone'd know there was money here. Harvey heard them, went to go upstairs after them and they came down and shot him. Then they had to shoot the others to stop them talking – I mean, telling people what they looked like.'

'It's a possibility.'

57

'What else?' she said, as if there was no room for doubt. Then, briskly, astonishing him: 'I'll be able to have a dog now. Whatever becomes of us no one can stop me having a dog now, can they?'

Burden returned to the hall and contemplated the staircase. The more he thought of it the less he could match up the mechanics with the evidence.

Jewellery was missing. It might be very valuable jewellery, worth as much as a hundred thousand pounds, but kill three people for it and intend to kill a fourth? Burden shrugged. He knew that men and women have been murdered for fifty pence, for the price of a drink.

The memory of his television appearance rankling a little, Wexford was still able to congratulate himself on the discretion he had maintained in the matter of Daisy Flory. Television was no longer a mysterious and frightening medium. He was getting used to it. This was his third or fourth appearance in front of the camera and if he was not blasé, he was at least assured.

One question only had ruffled him. It had seemed to have little or nothing to do with the Tancred House murders. Were they any more likely to find the men responsible for this than those guilty of the bank shooting? He had replied that he was certain both crimes would be solved and Sergeant Martin's killer caught as the Tancred House killers would be. A small smile appeared on the face of his interrogator, which he tried to ignore, keeping calm.

The question had not been asked by the 'stringer' for the national papers, nor by either of the national paper representatives who were there, but by a reporter from the *Kingsmarkham Courier*. This was a very young man, dark-haired, rather handsome, cocky-looking. His was a public-school voice without trace of London accent or the local burr.

'It's getting on for a year since the bank killing, Chief Inspector.'

'Ten months,' said Wexford.

'Isn't it a fact that statistics show the longer time goes by, the less likely . . .'

Wexford pointed to another questioner with her hand up and the *Courier* reporter's words were drowned by her enquiry. How was the young Miss Flory? Davina or Daisy, didn't they call her?

Wexford meant to be discreet about that at this stage. He replied that she was in intensive care – possibly, at this hour, still true – that she was stable but seriously ill. She had lost a lot of blood. No one

58

had told him this but it was bound to be true. The girl stringer asked him if she was on the 'danger list' and Wexford had been able to tell her that no hospital kept such a list and so far as he knew never had.

He would go alone to see her. He wanted no one accompanying him at this first questioning. DC Gerry Hinde, in his element, was feeding into his computer masses of collated information from which, he had mysteriously announced, he would produce a database to be distributed to every system in the stable block. Sandwiches had been brought in, fetched from the Cheriton High Road supermarket. Opening his own package with the paperknife, understanding how useful it would after all prove to be, Wexford wondered what the world had done before the arrival of the wedge-shaped plastic sandwich-container. Worthy to be ranked in the scale of blessed inventions, he thought with a glance of distaste at Gerry Hinde, at least on a level with facsimile machines.

Just as he was leaving, Brenda Harrison arrived with a list of Davina Flory's missing jewellery. He only had time to give it a quick scan before passing it on to Hinde. That was a real snip for the database that would give him something to mouse through his systems.

To his annoyance, the *Courier* reporter was waiting for him as he came out of the stables. He was sitting on a low wall, swinging his legs. Wexford made it a rule never to talk 'cases' to the press except at the arranged conferences. This man must have been hanging about for an hour, on the chance he must emerge sooner or later.

'No. Nothing more to say today.'

'That's very unfair. You ought to give priority to us. Support your local sheriff.'

'That means you supporting *me*,' Wexford said, amused in spite of himself, 'not me feeding facts to you. What's your name?'

'Jason Sherwin Coram Sebright.'

'A bit of a mouthful, isn't it? Too long for a by-line.'

'I've not decided what to call myself for professional purposes yet. I only started at the *Courier* last week. The point is I've got a distinct advantage over the rest of them. I know Daisy, you see. She's at my school, or where I *was*. I know her very well.'

All this was delivered with a confident brashness that was uncommon, even these days. Jason Sebright seemed entirely at ease.

'If you're going to see her I hope you'll take me with you,' he said. 'I'm hoping for an exclusive interview.'

'Then your hopes are doomed to be dashed, Mr Sebright.'

He shepherded Sebright out, waited there watching until he had got into his own car. Donaldson drove him down the main drive, the way they had come on the previous night. Sebright's tiny Fiat followed close behind. A quarter of a mile on, in an area where there were many fallen trees, they passed Gabbitas operating something Wexford thought might be a planking machine. The hurricane of three years before had done damage here. Wexford noticed cleared areas where there had been recent planting, the two-feet-high saplings tied to posts and sheathed in animal guards. Here too seasoning sheds had been built to protect the planked wood and under tarpaulins were stacked boards of oak and sycamore and ash.

They came to the main gate and Donaldson got out to open it. Hanging from the left-hand gatepost was a bouquet of flowers. Wexford wound down the window to get a better look. This was no ordinary florist's confection but a flower-filled basket with one side deeply curved over to afford the maximum display. Golden freesias, sky-blue scillas and waxen-white stephanotis spilled over the gilded lip of the basket. Attached to the handle was a card.

'What does it say?'

Donaldson stumbled over the words, cleared his throat and began again. '"Now, boast thee, death, in thy possession lies, A lass unparallel'd."'

He left the gate open for Jason Sebright, who, Wexford saw, had also got out to read the words on the card. Donaldson turned on to the B 2428 for Cambery Ashes and Stowerton. They were there in ten minutes.

Dr Leigh, a tired-looking woman in her mid-twenties, met Wexford in the corridor outside MacAllister Ward.

'I can understand it's urgent to talk to her, but could you keep it down to ten minutes today? I mean, as far as I'm concerned and if it's all right with her, you can come back tomorrow, but just at first I think it should be limited to ten minutes. That will be enough to get the essentials, won't it?'

'If you say so,' said Wexford.

'She has lost a lot of blood,' she said, confirming what he had told the press. 'But the bullet didn't break the collarbone. More important, it didn't touch the lung. A bit of a miracle, that. It's not so

60

much that she's physically ill as that she's very distressed. She's still very very distressed.'

'I'm not surprised.'

'Would you come into the office a moment?'

Wexford followed her into a small room which had 'Charge Nurse' on the door. It was empty and full of smoke. Why did hospital staff, who must hear more than most people of the evils and dangers of cigarettes, smoke more than anyone else? It was a mystery that often intrigued him. Dr Leigh clicked her tongue and opened the window.

'A bullet was extracted from Daisy's upper chest. Her shoulder-blade prevented it from exiting. Do you want it?'

'Certainly we do. She was only shot once?'

'Only once. In the upper chest on the left side.'

'Yes.' He wrapped the lead cylinder in his handkerchief and put it in his pocket. The fact that it had been in the girl's body brought him a slight unexpected flutter of nausea.

'You can go in now. She's in a side room; we're keeping her on her own because she's a very unhappy girl. She doesn't need company at the moment.'

Dr Leigh took him into MacAllister Ward. The corridor walls of the single rooms were panelled in frosted glass and each door had an insertion of clear glass. Outside the room with '2' printed on the glass Anne Lennox sat on an uncomfortable-looking stool, reading a Danielle Steel paperback. She jumped up when Wexford appeared.

'Do you need me, sir?'

'No, thanks, Anne. You stay where you are.'

A nurse came out of the room and held the door open. Dr Leigh said she would be waiting for him when he had finished and repeated her injunction about a time limit. Wexford went in and the door was closed behind him.

# 7

She was sitting up in a high white bed, propped by a mass of pillows.
Her left arm was in a sling and her left shoulder thickly bandaged. It
was so warm in the ward that instead of an enveloping hospital
gown, she wore a little white sleeveless shift that exposed her right
shoulder and upper arm. An intravenous line was attached to her
bare right arm.

The photograph from the *Independent on Sunday* came to mind.
This was Davina Flory all over again, this was Davina Flory as *she*
had been at seventeen.

Instead of shingled hair, Daisy wore hers long. It was copious
straight hair of a very fine, very dark brown, which fell down to and
half-covered the wounded shoulder and the bare, whole shoulder.
Her forehead was high like her grandmother's, her eyes large and
deep-set, not brown but a bright clear hazel with a black ring round
the pupils. The skin was white for such a dark woman and the rather
thin lips very pale. A prettier nose than her grandmother's eagle's
beak tilted a little at the tip. Wexford recalled Davina Flory's dead
hands, narrow and long-fingered, and saw that Daisy's were the
same but with the skin still soft and childish. She wore no rings. On
the pale pink lobes of her ears the pierce-marks showed as tiny pink
wounds.

When she saw him she did not speak but began to cry. The tears
rolled silently down her face.

He pulled out a handful of tissues from the box on her bedside
cabinet and handed them to her. She wiped her face, then dropped
her head, screwing up her eyes. Her body heaved with suppressed
sobs.

'I'm sorry,' he said. 'I'm very sorry.'

She nodded, clutching the damp tissues in her left hand. It was something he hadn't given much thought to, that she had lost her mother in the violence of the previous night. She had lost a grandmother too, who might have been as much beloved, and a man who had been like a grandfather since she was five years old.

'Miss Flory . . . '

Her voice came out muffled as she held the tissues up against her face. 'Call me Daisy.' He could tell she was making an effort as she swallowed hard and lifted her head. 'Call me Daisy, please. I can't be doing with "Miss Flory", I'm called Jones really anyway. Oh, I must stop crying!'

Wexford waited a moment or two, though mindful of how few moments he had. He saw she was trying to expel pictures from her mind, to wipe them away, expunge the videotape, come to the here and now. She drew a long breath.

He waited a while but he couldn't afford to wait too long. A minute only for her to breathe steadily in, smooth the tears away with her fingers. 'Daisy,' he began, 'you know who I am, don't you? I'm a policeman, Chief Inspector Wexford.'

She was nodding quickly.

'They're only allowing me ten minutes with you today but I'm going to come back tomorrow if you'll let me. I want you to answer one or two questions now and I'll try not to make them painful questions. Will that be all right?'

A slow nod and another gasp.

'We have to go back to last night. I'm not going to ask you exactly what happened, not yet, just when you first heard them in the house and where.'

The hesitation was so long he couldn't help looking down at his watch.

'If you could just tell me what time you heard them and where it was . . . '

She spoke suddenly and in a rush. 'They were upstairs. We were eating our dinner, we'd got to the main course. My mother heard them first. She said, "What's that? It sounds like someone upstairs."'

'Yes. What next?'

'Davina, my grandmother, said it was the cat.'

'The *cat*?'

'She's a big cat called Queenie, a Blue Persian. Sometimes, in the

63

evenings, she sort of rampages about the house. It's amazing what a racket she can make.'

Daisy Flory smiled. It was a wonderful wide smile, a young girl's smile, and she held it steady for a moment before it trembled on her lips. Wexford would have liked to take her hand but of course he couldn't do that.

'Did you hear a car?'

She shook her head. 'I didn't hear anything but the noise upstairs. A bumping noise and footsteps. Harvey, that's my grandmother's husband, he went out of the room. We heard the shot and then another. It was a terrible noise, it was really terrible. My mother screamed. We all jumped up. No, I jumped up and my mother did and I – I sort of started to go out and my mother shouted, "No, don't," and then he came in. He came into the room.'

'*He*? There was only one?'

'I only saw one. I heard the other one, I didn't see him.'

The recollection of it silenced her again. He saw the tears come back into her eyes. She rubbed her eyes with her right hand.

'I only saw one,' she said in a choked voice. 'He had a gun, he came in.'

'Take it easy,' Wexford said. 'I have to ask you. It'll soon be over. Think of it like that, it's something that must be. All right?'

'All right. He came in . . . ' Her voice went dead, automatic machine tones. 'Davina was still sitting there. She never got up, she just sat there but with her head turned towards the door. He shot her in the head, I think. He shot my mother. I don't know what I did. It was so terrible, it was like nothing you could imagine, madness, horror, it wasn't real, only it was – oh, I don't know . . . I tried to get on to the floor. I heard the other one getting a car started outside. The one in there, the one with the gun, he shot me and I don't know, I don't remember . . . '

'Daisy, you're doing very well. Very well indeed. I don't suppose you can remember what happened after you were shot. But can you remember what he looked like? Can you describe him?'

She shook her head, put her right hand up to her face. He had the impression it wasn't that she couldn't describe the man with the gun but was unable for the present to bring herself to do so. She murmured, 'I didn't hear him speak, he didn't speak.' Though he hadn't asked, she whispered, 'It was just after eight when we heard them and ten past when they went. Ten minutes, that was all . . . '

64

The door opened and a nurse came in. 'Your ten minutes is up. I'm afraid that's all for today.'

Wexford got up. Even if they had not been interrupted he would hardly have ventured to go on. The girl's ability to answer him was almost exhausted.

In a voice just above a whisper, she said, 'I don't mind you coming back tomorrow. I know I have to talk about it. I'll talk some more tomorrow.'

She took her eyes from his and stared hard at the window, slowly lifting her shoulders, the one that was wounded and the one that was whole, and brought her right hand up to cover her mouth.

The piece in the *Independent on Sunday* was imbued with a kind of clever bitchiness. Wherever it was possible to be snide, Win Carver was snide. No opportunity for a sneer was neglected. Yet it was a good essay. Such was human nature, Wexford confessed to himself, that it was *better* for its ironic and slightly malicious tone than a blander article would have been.

A journalist on the *Kingsmarkham Courier* would have adopted a sycophantic style when describing Davina Flory's reafforestation, her dendrology studies, her gardening and her collecting of rare specimen trees. Ms Carver treated the whole subject as if were slightly funny and an instance of mild hypocrisy. 'Planting' a wood, she implied, was a not quite accurate way of referring to an exercise others did for you while all you forked out was the money. Gardening might be a very pleasant way of passing the time if you were only obliged to do it when at a loose end and on fine days. Strong young men did the digging.

Davina Flory, she went on to say in much the same vein, had been a stupendously successful and acclaimed woman, but she hadn't exactly had to struggle, had she? Going to Oxford had been an obvious step, given her intelligence and with her father a professor and there being no shortage of money. A great landscape gardener she might be, but the acreage and the wherewithal fell into her lap when she married Desmond Flory. Being widowed in the last stages of the war had been sad but surely mitigated by inheriting on her first husband's death an enormous country house and a huge fortune.

She was a little scathing too about the short-lived second marriage. However, when she came to the travels and the books, the uniqueness of Davina Flory's penetration of eastern Europe and her political and sociological investigations of it, this at the most difficult and dangerous of times, Win Carver had nothing but praise to offer. She wrote of the 'anthropological' books to which these travels had given rise. She harked back with a charming adulatory nostalgia to her own student days some twenty years before, and to her reading of Davina Flory's only two novels, *The Hosts of Midian* and *A Private Man in Athens*. Her appreciation she compared to Keats's feeling for Chapman's Homer, she even said she had been silenced 'upon a peak in Darien'.

Finally, but not briefly, she came to the first volume of the autobiography: *The Youngest Wren of Nine*. Wexford, who had supposed this title a quotation from *Twelfth Night,* was pleased to have his guess confirmed. A résumé of Davina Flory's childhood and youth, as described in these memoirs, came next, a passing reference to her meeting with Harvey Copeland, and Ms Carver ended with a few words – a very few – about Miss Flory's daughter Naomi Jones who had a part-share in a Kingsmarkham craft gallery, and Miss Flory's granddaughter and namesake.

In the last lines of the article Win Carver speculated as to the chances of a DBE in a future honours' list and judged them pretty high. A year or two only must pass, she implied, before Miss Flory became Dame Davina. Mostly (wrote Ms Carver) 'they wait till you've passed you eightieth birthday so that you won't live too long.'

Davina Flory's life had not been sufficiently protracted. Death had come unnaturally to her and with the maximum violence. Wexford, who was still in the incident room, laid the newspapers aside and studied the print-out Gerry Hinde had produced for him of the missing items of jewellery. There were not many, but what there were sounded valuable. Then he walked across the courtyard to the house.

The hall had been cleaned. It reeked of the kind of disinfectant that smells like a combination of lysol and lime juice. Brenda Harrison was rearranging ornaments which had been put back in the wrong places. Her prematurely lined face wore an expression of intense concentration, the cause no doubt of the lines. On the staircase, three stairs up, where the carpet, perhaps ineradicably stained, was covered in a sheet of canvas, sat the Blue Persian called Queenie.

'You'll be glad to hear Daisy is making a good recovery,' Wexford said.

66

She already knew. 'One of the policemen told me,' she said without enthusiasm.

'How long had you and your husband worked here, Mrs Harrison?'

'Getting on for ten years.'

He was surprised. Ten years is a long time. He would have expected more emotional involvement with the family after so long an association, more *feeling*.

'Mr and Mrs Copeland were good employers then?'

She shrugged. She was dusting a red and blue Crown Derby owl and she replaced it on the polished surface before she spoke. Then she said in a thoughtful way, as if considerable cogitation had been going on before she came up with it, 'There was no side to them.' She hesitated, then added proudly, 'Not with us at any rate.'

The cat got up, stretched itself and walked slowly in Wexford's direction. It stopped in front of him, bristled up, glowered and quite suddenly fled up the stairs. After a moment or two the noises began. Sounds like a miniature horse galloping along the passage, bumps, crashes, reverberations.

Brenda Harrison switched a light on, then another. 'Queenie always carries on like that about this time,' she said.

'Does she do any damage?'

A small smile moved her features, spread her cheeks an inch or so. It told him she was one of those who find their amusement in the antics of animals. Their sense of humour is confined almost exclusively to tea-partying chimpanzees, anthropomorphic dogs, kittens in bonnets. They are the sort that keep circuses going.

'You could go up in half an hour,' she said, 'and you wouldn't know she'd been there.'

'And it's always at this time?' He looked at his watch: ten to six.

'Give or take a bit, yes.' She gave him a sidelong glance, grinning a very little. 'She's as bright as a button but she can't tell the time, can she?'

'I want to ask you just one more thing, Mrs Harrison. Have you seen any strangers about in the past days or even weeks? Unfamiliar people? Anyone you wouldn't expect to see near the house or on the estate?'

She thought. She shook her head. 'You want to ask Johnny. Johnny Gabbitas, that is. He gets about the woods, he's always outside.'

67

'How long has he been here?'

Her answer slightly surprised him. 'Maybe a year. Not more. Wait a minute, I reckon it'll be a year in May.'

'If you think of anything, anything odd or unusual that may have happened, you'll be sure to tell us, won't you?'

By now it was growing dark. As he walked round the side of the west wing, the lights in the lee of the wall came on, controlled by a time switch. He paused and looked back towards the woods and the road which led out of them. Last night the two men must have come that way or else along the by-road; there was no other possible route.

Why had none of the four people in the house heard a car? Perhaps they had. Three of them were no longer alive to tell him. Daisy had not, that was all he could know or would know. But if one of them had heard a car he or she had not remarked on it in Daisy's hearing. Of course he would hear much more from Daisy tomorrow.

The two men in the car would have seen the lighted house ahead of them. By eight the wall lights had been on for two hours and lights indoors for much longer. The road ran up to the courtyard, passed between the stone-pillared opening in the wall. But suppose the car had not come up to the house but turned to the left *before* the wall was reached. Turned left and right on to the road where he now was, the road that led past the west wing, twenty yards from it, curved past the kitchen regions and the back door, skirted the garden and its high hedge, and penetrated the pinetum, which led to the Harrisons' house and that of John Gabbitas.

Taking this route would presuppose knowledge of Tancred House and its grounds. It might presuppose knowledge that the back door was not locked during the evenings. If the car in which they came was driven that way and parked near the kitchen door, it was possible, even likely, that no one in the dining room would have heard it.

But Daisy had heard the man she had not seen start a car she had not seen after the man she *had* seen had shot her and her family.

Probably he had left the house by the back door and brought the car round to the front. He had escaped when he heard noises overhead. The man who shot Daisy also heard noises overhead, which was why he had not fired another shot, the shot that would have killed her. The noises were, of course, made by the cat Queenie, but the two men were not to know that. Very likely, neither of them

68

had been to the top floor, but they knew there *was* a top floor. They knew someone else might be up there.

This was an entirely satisfying explanation in all respects but one. Wexford was standing by the side of the road, looking behind him, pondering on this single exception, when car lights came up out of the wood on the main road. They turned off to the left just before the wall was reached and in the light from the house Wexford saw that it was Gabbitas's Land-Rover.

Gabbitas stopped when he saw who it was. He wound down the window. 'Were you looking for me?'

'I'd like a word, Mr Gabbitas. Can you spare me half an hour?'

For answer, Gabbitas leaned across and opened the passenger door. Wexford hauled himself in. 'Would you come over to the stables, please?'

'It's a bit late for that, isn't it?'

'Late for what, Mr Gabbitas? Pursuing a murder enquiry? There are three people dead here and one seriously injured. But on second thoughts I think your house might be the better venue.'

'Oh, very well. If you insist.'

This little exchange had served to inform Wexford of things he had not noticed at their first meeting. From his accent and his manner, the woodsman showed himself a considerable cut above the Harrisons. He was also extremely good-looking. He was the type of a Cold Comfort Farm hero. He had the looks of an actor some casting director might pick to play the male lead in a Hardy or Lawrence adaptation. Byronic but rustic too. His hair was black, his eyes very dark. The hands on the wheel were brown with black hairs on the backs of them and on the long fingers. The half-grin he had given Wexford when asked to drive down the by-road had shown a set of very white, even teeth. He was a swashbuckler and of the type that is supposed more than any other to be attractive to women.

Wexford climbed into the passenger seat. 'What time was it you told me you came home last night?'

'Eight twenty, eight twenty-five, that's the nearest I can make it. I didn't think I'd have any reason to be precise about the time.' There was an edge of impatience to his tone. 'I know I was back in my house when my clock struck the half-hour.'

'Do you know Mrs Bib Mew who works at the house?'

Gabbitas seemed amused. 'I know who you mean. I didn't know she was called that.'

69

'Mrs Mew left here on her bicycle at ten to eight last night and reached home in Pomfret Monachorum at about ten past. If you reached home at twenty past it's likely you might have met her on your way. She too used the by-road.'

'I didn't meet her,' Gabbitas said shortly. 'I've told you, I met no one, I passed no one.'

They had driven through the pinetum and reached the cottage where he lived. Gabbitas's manner, when ushering Wexford in, had become slightly more gracious. Wexford asked him where he had been on the previous day.

'Coppicing a wood near Midhurst. Why?'

It was a bachelor's house, tidy, functional, a little shabby. The living room into which he took Wexford was dominated by objects which turned it into an office, a desk with laptop computer, grey metal filing cabinet, stacks of box files. Bookcases full of encyclopaedias half filled a wall. Gabbitas cleared a chair for him by lifting off its seat an armful of folders and exercise books.

Wexford persisted. 'And you came home along the by-road?'

'I told you.'

'Mr Gabbitas,' said Wexford rather crossly, 'you must have seen enough television, if you know it from no other source, to understand that a policeman's purpose in asking you the same thing twice is, frankly, to catch you out.'

'Sorry,' said Gabbitas. 'OK, I do know that. It's just that a – well, a law-abiding person, doesn't much like to have it thought he's done anything to be caught out about. I suppose I expect to be believed.'

'Yes, I daresay. That's rather idealistic in the world we live in. I wonder if you've been thinking about this business much today. While you've been in your woodland solitude near Midhurst, for instance? It would be natural to give it some thought.'

Gabbitas said shortly, 'I've been thinking of it, yes. Who could help thinking of it?'

'About the car these people who perpetrated this – this massacre, arrived in, for instance. Where was it parked while they were in the house? Where was it when you came home? Not making its escape by the by-road or you would have passed it. Daisy Flory made her 999 call at twenty-two minutes past eight, within a few minutes of their leaving. She made it as fast as she could crawl because she was afraid she might bleed to death.' Wexford watched the man's face while he said this. It remained impassive but the lips tightened a little.

70

'So the car can't have gone by the by-road or you would have seen it.'

'Obviously it went by the main road.'

'There happens to have been a squad car on the B2428 at this time and it was alerted to block the road and note all vehicles from eight twenty-five. According to the officers in that car no vehicle of any kind passed until eight forty-eight when our own convoy with the ambulance came. A roadblock was also set up on the B2428 in the Cambery Ashes direction. Perhaps our block was put on too late. There's something you can perhaps tell me: is there any other way out?'

'Through the woods, d'you mean? A jeep could perhaps get out if the driver knew the woods. If he knew them like the back of his hand.' Gabbitas sounded extremely dubious. 'I'm not sure I could do it.'

'But you haven't been here all that long, have you?'

As if he thought explanation rather than an answer required, Gabbitas said, 'I teach one day a week at Sewingbury Agricultural College. I take private work. I'm a tree surgeon among other things.'

'When did you first come here?'

'Last May.' Gabbitas put his hand up to his mouth, rubbed his lips. 'How is Daisy?'

'She's well,' Wexford said. 'She's going to be very well – physically. Her psychological state, that's another thing. Who lived here before you came?'

'Some people called Griffin.' Gabbitas spelt it. 'A couple and their son.'

'Was their work confined to the estate or did they have outside jobs like you?'

'The son was grown-up. He had a job, I don't know what. In Pomfret or Kingsmarkham, I should think. Griffin, I think his first name was Gerry or maybe Terry, yes, Terry, he managed the woodland. She was just his wife. I think she sometimes worked up at the house.'

'Why did they leave? It wasn't just a job to leave, it was a house too.'

'He was getting on. Not sixty-five but getting on. I think the work got too much for him, he took early retirement. They had a house to go to, a place they'd bought. That's just about all I know about the

Griffins. I met them just the once, when I got this job and I was shown the house.'

'The Harrisons will know more, I imagine.'

For the first time, Gabbitas really smiled. His face was attractive and friendly when he smiled and his teeth were spectacular. 'They weren't on speaking terms.'

'What, the Harrisons and the Griffins?'

'Brenda Harrison told me they hadn't spoken since Griffin insulted her months before. I don't know what he said or did, that's all she told me.'

'Was that the real reason for their leaving?'

'I wouldn't know.'

'Do you know where this house they moved to is? Did they leave an address?'

'Not with me. I think they said Myringham way. Not all that far. I have a distinct memory of Myringham. Would you like a coffee? Or tea or something?'

Wexford refused. He also refused Gabbitas's offer of a lift back to where his car was parked outside the incident room.

'It's dark. You'd better take a torch.' He called after Wexford, 'That was her place, Daisy's. Those stables, they were her private sort of sanctuary. Her grandmother had them done up for her.' He had a kind of genius for minor bombshells, small revelations. 'She spent hours in there on her own. Doing her own thing, whatever that was.'

They had taken her sanctuary over without asking permission. Or, if permission had been asked and obtained, it was not from the stables' owner. Wexford walked along the winding path through the pinetum, aided by the torch Gabbitas had lent him. It occurred to him as the now dark bulk, the unlit rear, of Tancred House came into sight, that all this now probably belonged to Daisy Flory. Unless there were other heirs, but if there were, newspaper articles and obituaries had made no mention of them.

She had come into all this narrowly. If the bullet had been an inch lower, death would have robbed her of her inheritance. Wexford wondered why he was so sure that her inheritance would be a liability to her, that when she knew of what some would call her good fortune, she would recoil from it.

Hinde had checked the items listed by Brenda Harrison with Davina Flory's insurance company. A string of jet beads, a rope of pearls that, whatever Brenda might insist, were probably not real, a couple of silver rings, a silver bracelet, a silver and onyx brooch, she had not bothered to insure.

On both lists were a gold bracelet valued at three thousand five hundred pounds, a ruby ring with diamond shoulders valued at five thousand pounds, another set with pearls and sapphires at two thousand, and a ring described as a diamond cluster, a formidable piece of jewellery this, valued at nineteen thousand pounds.

The whole seemed to be worth rather more than thirty thousand. They had taken the less valuable pieces as well, of course, not knowing. Perhaps they had been even more ignorant and had supposed their loot worth far more than it was.

Wexford poked at the grey furry cactus with his forefinger. Its colour and texture reminded him of Queenie the cat. No doubt she too had thorns concealed by silky fluff. He locked the door and went to his car.

# 8

Five cartridges had been used in the Tancred murders.

The cartridges, according to the ballistics expert who had examined them, had come from a Colt Magnum .38 revolver. The barrel of every pistol is scored inside by distinct lines and grooves which in turn leave their mark on the bullet as it leaves the gun. The interior of each barrel contains unique marks, as individual as a fingerprint. The marks on the .38 cartridges found at Tancred House – all had passed through the bodies of Davina Flory, Naomi Jones and Harvey Copeland – matched and could therefore be concluded to have come from the same gun.

Wexford said, 'At least we know that only one gun was used. We know it was a Colt Magnum .38. The man Daisy saw did all the shooting. They didn't share it out, he did all the shooting himself. Is that odd?'

'They only had one gun,' said Burden. 'Or only one real gun. Do you know, I read somewhere the other day about a town in the United States where a serial killer was on the loose, that all the students on the university campus were permitted to go out and buy guns for their own protection. Kids of nineteen and twenty they must have been. Think of that. Handguns are still hard to come by in this country, thank God.'

'We said that when poor Martin was shot, remember?'

'That was a Colt .38 or .357 too.'

'I'd noticed,' Wexford said sharply. 'But the cartridges used in the two cases, Martin's killing and this one, don't match anyway.'

'Unfortunately. If they did we'd really be getting somewhere. One cartridge used and five left to go? Michelle Weaver's story wouldn't look quite so fantastic.'

74

'Has it occurred to you it was odd using a handgun at *all*?'

'Occurred to me? It struck me at once. Most of them use a sawn-off shotgun.'

'Yes. The great British answer to Dan Wesson. I'll tell you something else that's odd, Mike. Let's say there were six cartridges in the cylinder, it was full to capacity. Four people were in the house but the gunman didn't fire four times, he fired five times. Harvey Copeland was the first to be shot, yet, knowing he had only six cartridges he *fired twice at Copeland*. Why? Perhaps he didn't know there were three more people in the dining room, perhaps he panicked. He goes into the dining room and shoots Davina Flory, then Naomi Jones, one cartridge each, then Daisy. One cartridge remains in the cylinder but he doesn't shoot Daisy twice to "finish her off", as Ken Harrison might put it. Why doesn't he?'

'Hearing the cat upstairs surprised him. He heard the noise and ran?'

'Yes. Maybe. Or there weren't six cartridges in the cylinder, there were only five. One had already been used before he came to Tancred.'

'Not on poor old Martin, though,' Burden said briskly. 'Anything come in from Sumner-Quist yet?'

Wexford shook his head. 'I suppose we must expect delays. I've put Barry on to checking where John Gabbitas was on Tuesday, what time he left and so on. And then I'd like you to take him with you and find some people called Griffin, a Terry Griffin and his wife living in the Myringham area. They were Gabbitas's predecessors on the Tancred estate. We're looking for someone who knew this place and the people who lived here. Possibly for someone with a grudge against them.'

'A former employee then?'

'Perhaps. One who knew all about them and what they possessed, their habits and so on. One who's an unknown quantity.'

After Burden had gone, Wexford sat looking at the scene-of-crime photographs. Stills from a snuff movie, he thought, the kind of pictures no one but himself would ever see, the results of *real* violence, *real* crime. Those great dark splashes and stains were *real* blood. Was he privileged to see them, or unfortunate? Would the day ever come when newspapers displayed such photographs? It might. After all, it was not so long ago that no publication ever showed a picture of the dead.

He made the mental adjustment that shifted him from being a sensitive man with a man's feelings to a briskly functioning machine, an analysing eye, a printer-out of question marks. In this avatar, he looked at the photographs. Tragic, appalling, monstrous as the scene in the dining room might be, there was nothing incongruous about it. This was how the women would have fallen if one of them had been sitting at the table facing the door, the other, opposite her, standing up and staring past her. The blood on the floor in the empty corner near the foot of the table was Daisy's blood.

He saw what he had seen that night. The bloody napkin on the floor and the blood-dappled napkin in Davina Flory's hand, clutched by her dying, contracting fingers. Her face lying dipped in a plate of blood, and the dreadful ruined head. Naomi lay back in her chair as if in a swoon, her long hair trailed over the barred back of it and dipping nearly to touch the floor. Spangles of blood on the lampshades, the walls, black blotches on the carpet, dark spray spots on the bread in the basket, and the tablecloth dark where the blood had seeped in a dense smooth tide.

For the second time in this case – and he was later to experience it again and again – he had a perception of a prevailing order destroyed, of beauty outraged, of chaos come again. With no evidence for believing it, he thought he detected in this perpetrator a gleeful passion for destruction. But there was nothing incongruous in these photographs. Given the dreadful events, it was what he would expect. On the other hand, the pictures of Harvey Copeland, showing him spreadeagled on his back at the foot of the staircase, his feet towards the front hall and door, presented a problem. One perhaps which Daisy's testimony would solve.

If the men had come downstairs and met him coming up to look for them, why had he, when the gunman shot him, not fallen *backwards* down those stairs?

Four was the hour he had in mind, it was at four that he had been to see her yesterday, though today he had named no definite time. The traffic was light and he reached the hospital rather early. It was ten to four when he stepped out of the lift and walked along the corridor towards MacAllister Ward.

This time there was no Dr Leigh waiting to meet him. He had called Anne Lennox off her watch. There seemed to be no one about. Perhaps the staff were all having a quick breather (or choker) in the charge nurse's room. He came quietly to Daisy's room. Through the frosted-glass panels he could see she had someone with her, a man in a chair on the left side of the bed.

A visitor. At least it wasn't Jason Sebright.

The pane of glass in the door clarified this man's image for him. He was young, about twenty-six, biggish and thickset, and such was his appearance that Wexford could immediately place him, or make a good guess at doing so. Daisy's visitor belonged to the upper middle class, had been to a distinguished public school but probably not to a university, was 'something in the city' where he worked all his days with a computer and a phone. For this job he would be – as Ken Harrison might have said – finished before he was thirty, so he was coining in the maximum before that date. The clothes he wore were suitable for a man twice his age; navy blazer, dark-grey flannels, a white shirt and old school tie. The one concession he made to vague ideas of fashion and suitability was the wearing of his hair rather longer than that shirt and blazer required. It was fair curly hair and from the way it was combed and the way it curled round his ear lobes Wexford guessed he was vain about it.

As for Daisy, she sat up in bed, her eyes on her visitor, her expression inscrutable. She was not smiling, nor did she look particularly sad. It was impossible for him to tell if she had begun to recover from the shock she had received. The young man had brought flowers, a dozen red roses in bud, and these lay on the bedcover between him and her. Her right hand, the good hand, rested on their stems and on the pink and gold patterned paper in which they were wrapped.

Wexford waited for a few seconds, then tapped on the door, opened it and walked in.

The young man turned round, bestowing on Wexford precisely the stare he had expected. At certain schools, he had often thought, they teach them to look at you like that, with confidence, contempt, a degree of indignation, just as they teach them to talk with a plum in their mouths.

Daisy didn't smile. She managed to be polite and cordial without smiling, a rare feat. 'Oh, hello,' she said. 'Hi.' Her voice today was subdued but measured, the edge of hysteria gone. 'Nicholas, this is Inspector – no, *Chief* Inspector Wexford. Mr Wexford, this is Nicholas Virson, a friend of my family.'

She said it calmly, without a flicker of hesitation, though she had no family left.

The two men nodded to each other. Wexford said, 'Good afternoon.' Virson only gave a second nod. In his idea of a hierarchy, his great Chain of Being, policemen had their low place.

'I hope you're feeling better.'

Daisy looked down. 'I'm OK.'

'Do you feel well enough for us to have a talk? To go into things rather more deeply?'

'I must,' she said. She stretched her neck, lifted her chin. 'You said it all yesterday when you said we had to, we didn't have a choice.'

He saw her close her fingers round the paper that wrapped the roses, saw her clutch the stems tightly, and had the strange notion she was doing it to make her hand bleed. But perhaps they were thornless.

'You'll have to go, Nicholas.' Men with this Christian name are almost always called by one of its diminutives, Nick or Nicky, but she called him Nicholas. 'It was sweet of you to come. I adore the flowers,' she said, squeezing their stems without looking at them.

Wexford had known Virson would say it or something like it, it was only a matter of time. 'I say, I hope you aren't going to put Daisy through any sort of interrogation. I mean, at the end of the day what can she in fact tell you? What can she remember? She's a very confused lady, aren't you, lovey?'

'I'm not confused.' She spoke in a calm low monotone, giving each word equal weight. 'I'm not at all confused.'

'Now she tells me.' Virson managed a hearty laugh. He got up, stood there, suddenly seeming not quite sure of himself. Over his shoulder he threw at Wexford, 'She may manage a description of the villain she did see, but she never even caught a glimpse of the vehicle.'

Now why had he said that? Was it simply that he needed something to say to fill up the time while he considered attempting a kiss? Daisy lifted her face to him, something Wexford hadn't expected, and Virson, bending down quickly, put his lips to her cheek. The kiss stimulated him to use an endearment.

'Is there anything I can do for you, darling?'

'There is one thing,' she said. 'On your way out could you find a vase and put these flowers in it?'

This, evidently, was not at all what Virson had meant. He had no option but to agree.

'You'll find one in a place they call the sluice. I don't know where it is, down to the left somewhere. The poor nurses are always so busy.'

Virson went off, carrying out the roses he had carried in.

Today Daisy had a hospital gown on that fastened with tapes down the back. It covered and enclosed her left arm with the bandages and the sling. The IV line was still there. She followed his eyes.

'It's easier for putting drugs into you. That's why they keep it there. It's coming off today. I'm not *ill* any more.'

'And you're not confused?' He was quoting her.

'Not in the least.' She spoke for a moment like someone much older. 'I have been thinking about it,' she said. 'People tell me not to think of it but I have to. What else is there? I knew I'd have to tell you everything as best I could so I've been thinking about it to get things straight. Didn't some writer say violent death wonderfully concentrates the mind?'

He was surprised but he didn't show it. 'Samuel Johnson, but it was knowing one was going to be hanged on the morrow.'

She smiled a little, a very little, narrowly. 'You're not much like my idea of a policeman.'

'I daresay you haven't met many.' He thought suddenly, she looks like Sheila. She looks like my own daughter. Oh, she was dark and Sheila was fair but it wasn't those things, whatever people said, that made one person look like another. It was similarity of feature, facial shape. It made him a bit cross when they said Sheila was like him because they had the same hair. Or had, before his went grey and half of it fell out. Sheila was *beautiful*. Daisy was beautiful and her features were like Sheila's. She was looking at him with a sadness close to despair. 'You said you'd been thinking about it, Daisy. Tell me what you thought.'

She nodded, her expression unchanging. She reached for the glass of something on the bedside cabinet – lemon squash, barley water – and drank a little. 'I'll tell you what happened, everything I remember. That's what you want, isn't it?'

'Yes. Yes, please.'

'You must interrupt me if something isn't clear. You'll do that, won't you?'

Her tone, suddenly, was that of someone used to telling servants, and not only servants, what she wanted, and having them obey. She

79

was habituated, he thought, to telling one to come and he cometh, another to go and he goeth and a third, do this and he doeth it. Wexford suppressed a smile. 'Of course.'

'It's hard to know how far back to begin. Davina used to say that when she was writing a book. How far back to begin? You could start at what you thought was the beginning and then you'd realise it began long, long before that. But here, in this case – shall I start with the afternoon?'

He nodded.

'I'd been to school. I'm a day student at Crelands. As a matter of fact, I'd love to have boarded but Davina wouldn't let me.' She seemed to recollect something, perhaps only that her grandmother was dead. *De mortuis* . . . 'Well, it would have been silly really. Crelands is only the other side of Myfleet, as I expect you know.'

He knew. This was also the alma mater of Sebright, apparently. A minor public school, it nevertheless belonged in the Headmasters' Conference, as Eton and Harrow did. The fees were similar to theirs. Exclusively a boys' school from its founding by Albert the Good in 1856, it had opened its doors to girls some seven or eight years ago.

'Afternoon school stops at four. I got home at four thirty.'

'Someone fetched you by car?'

She gave him a glance, genuinely puzzled. 'I drove myself.'

The great British car revolution had not passed him by, but he could still recall very clearly the days when a three- or four-car family was something he thought of as an American anomaly, when a great many women couldn't drive, when few people possessed a car until they were married. His own mother would have stared in astonishment, suspected mockery, if asked if she could drive. His mild surprise wasn't lost on Daisy.

'Davina gave me my car for my birthday when I was seventeen. I passed my test next day. It was a great relief, I can tell you, not having to depend on one of them or be driven by Ken. Well, as I was saying, I got home by four thirty and went to my place. You've probably seen my place. That's what I call it. It used to be stables. I garage my car there and there's this room that's mine, that's private.'

'Daisy, I've a confession to make. We're using your place as an incident room. It seemed the most convenient. We do have to be there. Someone should have asked you and I'm very sorry we overlooked it.'

'You mean there are lots of policemen and computers and desks and a – a blackboard?' She must have seen something like it on television. 'You're sort of investigating the case from there?'

'I'm afraid so.'

'Oh, don't be afraid. I don't mind. Why should I mind? Be my guest. I don't mind anything any more.' She looked away, wrinkled up her face a little, said in the same cool tone, 'Why would I care about a little thing like that when I've nothing to live for?'

'Daisy . . . ' he began.

'No, don't say it, please. Don't say I'm young and I've all my life before me and this will pass. Don't tell me time is a great healer and this time next year I'll have put it all in the past. Don't.'

Someone had been saying those things to her. A doctor? Some psychologist on the hospital staff? Nicholas Virson?

'All right. I won't. Tell me what happened after you got home.'

She waited a little, drew in her breath. 'I've got my own phone, I expect you've noticed. I expect you're using it. Brenda phoned to ask if I'd like tea and then she brought it. Tea and biscuits. I was reading, I get a lot of prep. A levels for me in May – or it was to have been.'

He didn't comment.

'I'm no intellectual. Davina thought I was because I'm – well, quite bright. She couldn't bear to think I might take after my mother. Sorry, you won't want to hear about that. It doesn't matter any more, anyway.

'Davina expected us to change for dinner. Not dress exactly but change. My – my mother came home in her car. She works in a crafts gallery – well, she's a partner in a crafts gallery – with a woman called Joanne Garland. The gallery's called Garlands. I expect you think that's yucky but it's the woman's name so I suppose it's OK. She came home in her car. I think Davina and Harvey were home all afternoon but I don't know. Brenda would know.

'I went to my room and put a dress on. Davina used to say jeans were a uniform and should be used as such, for work. The others were all in the *serre* having drinks.'

'In the what?'

'The *serre*. It's French for "greenhouse", it's what we always called it. It sounds better than "conservatory", don't you think?'

Wexford thought it sounded pretentious but he said nothing.

'We always had drinks in there or in the drawing room. Just sherry, you know, or orange juice or fizzy water. I always had fizzy water and so did my mother. Davina was talking about going to

Glyndebourne; she is – was – a member or a friend or whatever and she always went three times a year. Everything like that she went to, Aldeburgh, the Edinburgh Festival, Salzburg. Anyway, her tickets had come. She was asking Harvey about what she should order for dinner. You have to order your dinner months in advance if you don't want to picnic. We never did picnic; it would be so awful if it rained.

'They were still talking about that when Brenda put her head round the door and said dinner was in the dining room and she was off. I started talking to Davina about going to France in a fortnight's time, she was going to Paris to be in some television book programme and she wanted me to go with her and Harvey. It would have been Easter holidays for me but I didn't much want to go and I was telling her I didn't and – but you won't want to hear all this.'

Daisy put her hand up to her lips. She was looking at him, looking through him. He said, 'It is very hard to realise, I know that, even though you were there, even though you saw. It will take you time to accept what has happened.'

'No,' she said remotely, 'it's not hard to accept. I'm not in any doubt. When I woke up this morning I didn't even have a moment before I remembered. You know –' she shrugged at him '– how there's always that moment, and then everything comes back. It's not like that. Everything's there all the time. It'll always be there. What Nicholas said, about me being confused, that's absolutely not so. OK, never mind, I'll go on, I'm digressing too much.

'My mother usually served dinner. Brenda left it all there for us on the trolley. We didn't have wine except at the weekends. There was a bottle of Badoit and a jug of apple juice. We had – let me see – soup, it was potato and leek, sort of vichyssoise, but it was hot. We had that and bread, of course, and then my mother cleared away the plates and served the main course. It was fish, sole something or other. Is it called sole *bonne femme* when it's in a sauce with creamed potatoes round?'

'I don't know,' Wexford said, amused in spite of everything. 'It doesn't matter. I get the picture.'

'Well, it was that with carrots and French beans. She'd served us all and sat down and we'd started eating. My mother hadn't even started. She said, "What's that? It sounds like someone upstairs."'

'And you hadn't heard a car? No one had heard a car?'

'They'd have said. You see, we were expecting a car. Well, not

82

then, not till a quarter past eight, only she's always early. She's one of those people who are as bad as the unpunctual ones, always at least five minutes early.'

'Who is? Who are you talking about, Daisy?'

'Joanne Garland. She was coming to see Mum. It was Tuesday, and Joanne and Mum always did the gallery books on a Tuesday. Joanne couldn't do them on her own, she's hopeless at arithmetic even with a calculator. She always brought the books and she and Mum worked on them, the VAT and all that.'

'All right. I see. Go on, will you?'

'Mum said she heard a noise upstairs and Davina said it must be the cat. Then there was quite a lot of noise, more than Queenie usually makes. It was like something crashing on to the floor. I've thought about it since and I've thought maybe it was a drawer being pulled out of Davina's dressing table. Harvey got up and said he'd go and look.

'We just went on eating. We weren't worried – not then. I remember my mother looked at the clock and said something about how she wished Joanne would make it half an hour later on Tuesdays because she had to eat her meal too fast. Then we heard the shot and then another, a second one. It made this terrible noise.

'We jumped up. My mother and I, Davina went on sitting where she was. My mother sort of cried out, screamed. Davina didn't say anything or move – well, her hands sort of closed round her napkin. She clutched her napkin. Mum stood staring at the door and I pushed my chair away and started going to the door or I think I did, I meant to – maybe I was just standing there. Mum said, "No, no" or "No, don't" or something. I stopped, I was just standing there, I was sort of frozen to the spot. Davina turned her head towards the door. And then he came in.

'Harvey had left the door half-open – well, a little bit open. The man kicked it open and came in. I've tried to remember if anyone screamed but I can't remember, I don't know. We must have. He – he shot Davina in the head. He held the gun in both hands, like they do. I mean like they do on telly. Then he shot Mum.

'I haven't a clear memory of what happened next. I've tried hard to remember but something blocks it off, I expect it's normal when you've had a thing like that happen, but I wish I could remember.

'I've a sort of idea I got on to the floor. I crouched on the floor. I know I heard a car start up. That one, the other one, had been upstairs, I think, he was the one we heard. The one who shot me, he was downstairs all the time, and when he shot us the other one got out fast and started the car. That's just what I think.'

'The one who shot you, can you describe him?'

He was holding his breath, expecting her to say, fearing she would say, that she couldn't remember, that this too had been absorbed and destroyed by shock. Her face had been contorted, almost distorted, with the effort of concentration, the recollection of almost intolerably painful events. It seemed to clear as if a little rest had come to her. Alleviation soothed her, like a sigh of relief.

'I can describe him. I can do that. I've *willed* myself to that. What I could see of him. He was – well, not too tall but thickset, heavily built, very fair. I mean his hair was fair. I couldn't see his face, he had a mask over his face.'

'A mask? D'you mean a hood? A stocking over his head?'

'I don't know. I just *don't know*. I've been trying to remember because I knew you'd ask but I don't know. I could see his hair. I know he had fair hair, shortish, and thick, quite thick fair hair. But I wouldn't have been able to see his hair if he'd had a hood over it, would I? D'you know what's the impression I keep getting?'

He shook his head.

'That it was a mask like the sort people wear in smog, in pollution, whatever you call it. Or even one of those masks the woodsmen wear when they're using a chain saw. I could see his hair and his chin. I could see his ears – but they were just ordinary ears, not big or sticking out or anything. And his chin was ordinary – well, it might have had a cleft in it, a sort of shallow cleft.'

'Daisy, you've done very well. You've done supremely well to take all this in before he shot you.'

At those words she shut her eyes and screwed up her face. The shooting, the attack on herself, he saw was still too much for her to discuss. He understood the terror it must evoke, that she too could so easily have died there in that death room.

A nurse put her head round the door.

'I'm all right,' Daisy said. 'I'm not tired, I'm not overdoing it. Really.'

The head retreated. Daisy took another drink from the bedside glass. 'We're going to have a picture made of him, based on what you've been able to tell me,' Wexford said. 'And when you're better and out of here, I'm going to ask you if you will say this all over again in the form of a statement. Also, with your permission, a tape will be made of it. I know it will be hard for you but don't say no now, think about it.'

'I don't have to think,' she said. 'I'll make a statement, of course I will.'

'In the meantime, I should like to come back and talk to you again tomorrow. But first, I'd like you to tell me one more thing. Did Joanne Garland in fact come?'

She seemed to be pondering. She was very still. 'I don't know,' she said at last. 'I mean, I didn't hear her ring the bell or anything. But all sorts of things might have happened after – after he shot me, and I didn't hear them. I was bleeding, I was thinking of getting to the phone, I was concentrating on crawling to the phone and getting you, the police, an ambulance, before I bled to death, I really thought I'd bleed to death.'

'Yes,' he said, 'yes.'

'She could have come after they, the men, after they left. I don't know, it's no use asking me, I just don't know.' She hesitated, said very quietly, 'Mr Wexford?'

'Yes?'

For a moment she said nothing. She hung her head and the copious dark-brown hair fell forward, covering face and neck and shoulders with its veil. Her right hand went up, that slim white long-fingered hand, and raked her hair, took a handful of it and threw it back. She looked up and looked at him, the expression taut, intense, her upper lip curled back in pain or incredulity.

'What's going to become of me?' she asked him. 'Where will I go? What will I do? I've lost everything, everything's gone, everything that matters.'

Now was not the time to remind her she would be rich, that not everything had gone. That which for many makes life worthwhile remained to her in abundance. He had never been a man to believe blindly in the adage which told him that money doesn't bring happiness. But he remained silent.

'I should have died. It would have been better for me if I'd died. I was terrified of dying. I thought I was dying when the blood was pumping out of me and I was terrified – oh, I was so frightened. The funny thing was, it didn't hurt. It hurts more now than it did then. You'd think something going into your flesh would hurt so terribly but there wasn't any pain. But it would have been best if I'd died, I know that now.'

He said, 'I know I risk your thinking of me as one of those who hand out the old placebos. But you won't continue to feel like this. It *will* pass.'

She stared at him, said rather imperiously, 'I shall see you tomorrow then.'

'Yes.'

She held out her hand to him and he shook it. The fingers were cold and very dry.

# 9

Wexford went home early. His feeling was that this might be the last time he got home by six for a long while.

Dora was in the hall, replacing the phone receiver, as he let himself in. She said, 'That was Sheila. If you'd been a second sooner you could have talked to her.'

A sardonic retort rose to his lips and he suppressed it. There was no reason for being unpleasant to his wife. None of it was her fault. Indeed, at that dinner on Tuesday, she had done her best to make things easier, to dull the edge of spitefulness and soften sarcasm.

'They *are* coming,' Dora said, her tone neutral.

'Who's coming where?'

'Sheila and – and Gus. For the weekend. You know Sheila said they might on Tuesday.'

'A lot of things have happened since Tuesday.'

At any rate, he probably wouldn't be home much during the weekend. But tomorrow was the weekend, tomorrow was Friday, and they would arrive in the evening. He poured himself a beer, an Adnam's which a local wine shop had begun to stock, and a dry sherry for Dora. She laid her hand on his arm, moved it to enclose the back of his hand. It reminded him of Daisy's icy touch. But Dora's was warm.

He burst out, 'I've got to have that miscreant here for a whole weekend!'

'Reg, don't. Don't *begin* like that. We've only met him twice.'

'The first time she brought him here,' said Wexford, 'he stood in this room in front of my books and he took them out one by one. He looked at them in turn with a little contemptuous smile on his face. He took out the Trollope and looked at it like that. He took out the

87

short stories of M. R. James and shook his head. I can see him now, standing there with James in his hand and shaking his head slowly, very slowly from side to side. I expected him to turn his thumbs down. I expected him to do what the Chief Vestal did when the gladiator had the net-man at his mercy in the arena. Kill. That's the verdict of the supreme judge, kill.'

'He has a right to his opinion.'

'He hasn't a right to despise mine and show he despises it. Besides, Dora, that's not the only thing and you know it isn't. Have you ever met a man with a more arrogant manner? Have you ever – well, as a friend in your own family circle or that you know well – have you ever come across anyone who so plainly made you feel he despised you? You and me. Everything he said was designed to show his loftiness, his cleverness, his wit. What does she see in him? *What does she see in him?* He's small and skinny, he's ugly, he's myopic, he can't see further than the end of his twitching nose . . . '

'You know something, darling? Women *like* small men. They find them attractive. I know big tall ones like you don't believe it, but it's true.'

'Burke said . . . '

'I know what Burke said. You've told me before. A man's handsomeness resides entirely in his height, or something like that. Burke wasn't a woman. Anyway, I expect Sheila values him for his mind. He's a very clever man, you know, Reg. Perhaps he's a genius.'

'God help us if you're going to call everyone who was short-listed for the Booker prize a genius.'

'I think we should make allowances for a young man's pride in his own achievements. Augustine Casey is only thirty and he's already seen as one of this country's foremost novelists. Or so I read in the papers. His books get half-page reviews in the book section of *The Times*. His first novel won the Somerset Maugham Award.'

'Success should make people humble, modest and kind, as the donor of that prize said somewhere.'

'It seldom does. Try to be indulgent towards him, Reg. Try to listen with – with an older man's wisdom when he airs his opinions.'

'And you can say that after what he said to you about the pearls? You're a magnanimous woman, Dora.' Wexford gave a sort of groan. 'If only she doesn't really care for him. If only she can come to see what I see.' He drank his beer, made a face as if the taste were after all not congenial to him. 'You don't think –' he turned to his wife, appalled '– you don't think she'd *marry* him, do you?'

'I think she might live with him, enter into – what shall I call it? – a long-term relationship with him. I do think that, Reg, really. You have to face it. She's told me – oh, Reg, don't look like that. I have to tell you.'

'Tell me what?'

'She says she's in love with him and that she doesn't think she's ever been in love before.'

'Oh, God.'

'For her to tell me that, she never tells me things – well, it has to be significant.'

Wexford answered her melodramatically. He knew it was melodramatic before the words were out but he couldn't stop it. The histrionics brought him a tiny consolation.

'He'll take my daughter from me. If he and she are together that's the end of Sheila and me. She will cease to be my daughter. It's true. I can see it. What's the use of pretending otherwise, what is ever the use of pretending?'

He had blocked off that Tuesday evening's dinner. Or the events at Tancred House and their consequences had blocked them off for him, but now he opened his mind to them, the second beer he poured opened his mind, and he saw that man entering the little provincial restaurant, eyeing his surroundings, whispering something to Sheila. She had asked how her father, their host, would like them to sit at the table they were shown to, but Augustine Casey, before Wexford had a chance to speak, had chosen his seat. It was the chair backing a corner of the room.

'I shall sit here where I can see the circus,' he had said with a small private smile, a smile that was for himself alone, excluding even Sheila.

Wexford had understood him to mean he wanted to watch the behaviour of the other diners. It was perhaps a novelist's prerogative, though scarcely that of such an extreme post-post-modernist as Casey was. He had already written at least one work of fiction without characters. Wexford had still been trying to talk to him then, to get him to talk about something, even if the subject was himself. Back at the house he had spoken, had delivered some obscure opinions on poetry in eastern Europe, every phrase he used consciously clever, but once in the restaurant he became silent, as if

89

with boredom. He confined his speech to answering briefly requests that had to be made.

One of the things about him which had angered Wexford was his refusal ever to use an ordinary phrase or to indulge in the usage of good manners. When 'How do you do?' was said to him, he replied that he was not at all well but it was useless to enquire because he seldom was. Asked what he would drink he requested an unusual kind of Welsh mineral water which came in dark-blue bottles. This unavailable, he drank brandy.

His first course he left after one mouthful. Halfway through the meal he broke his silence to talk about pearls. The view from where he sat had afforded him a sight of no fewer than eight women wearing pearls round their necks or in their ears. After using the word once he didn't repeat it but referred to 'concretions' or 'chitinous formations'. He quoted Pliny the Elder who spoke of pearls as 'the most sovereign commodity in the whole world', he quoted Indian Vedic literature and described Etruscan jewellery, he delivered a thousand words or so on the pearls of Oman and Qatar that come from waters one hundred and twenty feet deep. Sheila hung upon his words. What was the use of deceiving himself? She listened, gazing at Casey, with adoration.

Casey was eloquent on the subject of Hope's baroque pearl that weighed eleven ounces and on *La Reine des Perles* which was among the crown jewels of France stolen in 1792. Then he talked of the superstitions associated with 'concretions', and with his eyes on the modest string round Dora's neck, spoke of the folly of older women who used to believe, and no doubt still did, that such necklaces would restore their lost youth.

Wexford had made up his mind then to speak, to rebuke, but his phone had started bleeping and he had left without a word. Or without a word of admonition. Naturally, he had said goodbye. Sheila kissed him and Casey said, as if it were some received rubric of farewell, 'We shall meet again.'

Anger had fulminated, he had been boiling with rage, up through the dark, the cold woods.

Enormous tragedy neutralised it. But the Tancred tragedy was not his, and this was, or might well be. The pictures kept on coming, the imagined future scenarios, *their* home. He thought of how it would be when he phoned her and that man answered. What message of arcane wit would that man have recorded on his and Sheila's

90

answering machine? How would it be when, on some necessary trip to London, Sheila's father dropped in on Sheila as he so dearly loved to do, and that man was there?

His mind was filled with it and when he went to bed he expected a dream of Casey to be its natural consequence. But the nightmare which came, towards dawn, was of the massacre at Tancred. He was in that room, at that table, with Daisy and Naomi Jones and Davina Flory, Copeland having gone to investigate the noises upstairs. He could hear no noises, he was examining the scarlet tablecloth, asking Davina Flory why it was such a bright colour, why it was red. And she, laughing, told him he was mistaken, perhaps he was colour-blind, many men were. The cloth was white, as white as driven snow.

She didn't mind using a hackneyed expression like that one? he had asked her. No, no, she said and she smiled, she touched his hand with her hand, clichés like that were often the best way to describe something. You could be too clever.

The shot came and the gunman walked into the room. Wexford slipped out, he escaped unseen, the window with its panes of curved eight-ounce glass melted to allow his passage, so that he was in time to see the getaway car slide on to the courtyard, driven by the other man. The other man was Ken Harrison.

At the stables in the morning – he had stopped calling it an incident room, it was the stables – they showed him the composite picture made from Daisy's description. It would appear in television news programmes that evening, on all networks.

She had been able to tell him so little! The pictured face was blander and blanker than any real face ever can be. Those features she had been able to describe, the artist seemed to have accentuated, perhaps unconsciously. After all, these were all he had to work on. So the man who looked out of the paper at Wexford had blank wide-apart eyes and a straight nose, and lips neither full nor thin, but a strong chin with a cleft dividing it, large dramatic ears and a copious thatch of pale hair.

He gave Sumner-Quist's post-mortem reports a summary exam-ination, then had himself driven down to Kingsmarkham to put in an appearance at the inquest. As he expected, it was opened, the pathologist's evidence heard, and the proceedings adjourned. Wexford walked across the High Street, down York Street and into the Kingsbrook Centre, to find Garlands, the craft gallery.

Although a notice inside the glass door informed prospective shoppers that the gallery would be open five days a week from 10 a.m. until 5.30 p.m., on Wednesdays from 10 a.m. until 1 p.m. and closed on Sundays, it was shut. The windows on either side of this door contained a familiar assortment of pottery, dried flower arrangements, basketwork, marble photograph frames, shell pictures, ceramic cottages, silver jewellery, inlaid wooden boxes, glass baubles, carved, woven, moulded, knitted, blown-glass and sewn miniature animals, as well as a great quantity of household linen with birds and fish and flowers and trees printed on it.

But no lights were on to illuminate this plethora of uselessness. A dimness, becoming a darkness in the depths of the gallery, just allowed Wexford to make out larger items hanging from fake antique beams, gowns perhaps, shawls and robes, and a cash desk set up between a pyramid of what seemed like grotesque felt animals, the reverse of cuddlesome, and a display case showing behind dim glass, terracotta masks and porcelain wall-vases.

It was Friday and Garlands was closed. The possibility that Mrs Garland had closed her gallery for the remainder of the week out of respect for the memory of Naomi Jones, her partner, who had died so dreadfully, did not escape him. Or she might have failed to open because she was simply too upset. The degree of her friendship with Daisy's mother was still unknown. But the purpose of Wexford's call had been to enquire about the visit she might or might not have paid to Tancred House on the Tuesday evening.

If she had been there why had she not come to tell them? The publicity, the coverage, had been enormous. Everyone with the least knowledge of events, everyone with the smallest connection with Tancred House, had been appealed to. If she had not been there why had she not told them why not?

Where did she live? Daisy had not said, but it was a simple matter to find out. Not over the gallery, at any rate. The three floors of the centre were entirely devoted to the establishments of retailers, boutiques, hairdressers, a vast supermarket, a DIY place, two fast-food restaurants, a garden centre and a gym. He could call in to the incident room and have the address within minutes, but the main Kingsmarkham Post Office was only on the other side of the road. Wexford went in and, avoiding the queue for stamps, pensions and allowances, which coiled serpentinely around a roped-off winding lane, asked to see the electoral register. It was what he would have done long ago, before the advent of all this technology. Sometimes, defiantly, he liked doing these old-fashioned things.

The voters' list was arranged by street, not surname. It was a task for a subordinate but he was there now, he had begun. Anyway, he wanted to know, he very much wanted to know, and as soon as possible, why Joanne Garland had closed her shop, and presumably closed it for three days.

He found her at last, and only a couple of streets from where he lived himself. Joanne Garland's house was in Broom Vale, a somewhat more spacious building and a rather superior location to his own. She lived alone. The register told him that. Of course, it wouldn't have told him if she had anyone under eighteen living with her, but this was unlikely. Wexford went back to the court where his car was. Parking in the town was not something to be engaged in lightly these days. He could just imagine the piece in the *Kingsmarkham Courier,* some bright young reporter – perhaps Jason Sebright himself? – spotting that it was Chief Inspector Wexford's car on the double yellow line, trapped in the jaws of the wheel clamp.

There was no one at home. Next door, on both sides, there was no one at home either.

When he was young, you usually found a woman at home. Things had changed. For some reason, this reminded him of Sheila, and he sternly chased away the thought. He had a look at the house, which he had never bothered to study before, though he had passed it hundreds of times. It was quite ordinary, detached, set in its garden, well kept, newly painted, probably four-bedroomed, two-bathroomed, with a television dish sticking out by an upstairs window. An almond tree was coming into bloom in the front garden.

He considered for a moment, then walked round the back. The house looked closed up. But at this time of the year, early spring, it *would* look closed up, windows wouldn't be open. He looked through the kitchen window. Inside it was tidy, though there were dishes on the draining board, washed and stacked against each other to dry.

Back to the front of the house and a squint through the keyhole in the garage door. There was a car inside but he couldn't make out what kind. A glance through the tiny window to the right of the door showed him newspapers on the floor and a couple of letters. Perhaps only this morning's papers? But no, he could see one *Daily Mail* masthead against the edge of the mat and another half-hidden by a brown envelope. Wexford twisted his head, striving to make out the name of the third paper of which he could only see a corner and a section of a picture. The photograph was a full-length shot of the Princess of Wales.

Returning to Tancred House, he had the car stop at a newsagent. As he had expected, the Princess of Wales's photograph was on today's *Mail*. Therefore, three newspapers had arrived for Joanne Garland since she had last been in the house. Therefore she had not been there *since Tuesday evening*.

Barry Vine said in his slow laid-back way, 'Gabbitas may have been in that wood on Tuesday afternoon, sir, and he may not. Witnesses are what you might call thin on the ground out where he was. Or says he was. The wood's on land belonging to a man who owns five hundred acres. He calls it organic farming what he does on some of it, cattle just roaming around, if you know what I mean. He's planted some new woodland and he's got some of that set-aside the Government pays you not to grow things on.

'The point is, the wood where Gabbitas says he was is miles from anywhere. You go down this lane for two miles, it's like the end of the world, not a roof to be seen, not even a barn. Well, I've lived in the country all my life but I wouldn't have believed there was anything like that in the Home Counties.

'They call it coppicing, what he was doing. It'd be pruning if it was roses, not trees. He's done some, that's for sure, and you can see he's been there – we checked the track marks with his Land-Rover. But your guess is as good as mine, sir, if he was there on Tuesday.'

Wexford nodded. 'Barry, I want you to get down to Kingsmarkham and find a Mrs Garland, Joanne Garland. Failing finding *her* – I don't think you'll find her – see if you can discover where she's gone, in fact her movements since Tuesday afternoon. Take someone with you, take Karen. She lives in Broom Vale, at number fifteen, and she's got one of those kitschy shops in the Centre. See if her car's gone, talk to the neighbours.'

'Sir?'

Wexford put up his eyebrows.

'What's a kitschy shop?' Vine placed the stress on the first word, as in fish shop. 'I'm sure I ought to know but it's slipped my mind.'

Somehow, this reminded Wexford of distant days and his grandfather, who managed an ironmonger's in Stowerton, telling a lazy boy assistant to go out and buy a pound of elbow grease and the boy obediently going. But Vine was neither lazy nor stupid, Vine – *de mortuis* notwithstanding – was cuts above poor Martin. Instead of telling this tale to Vine, he explained the word he had used.

Wexford found Burden eating lunch at his desk. This was behind screens in the corner where Daisy's furniture, bookcases, chairs, floor cushions, were carefully covered up in dust sheets. Burden was eating pizza and coleslaw, not among Wexford's favourite foods, either apart or associated, but he asked where it came from just the same.

'Our caterers' van. It's outside and will be every day from twelve thirty till two. Didn't you fix it?'

'It's the first I've heard of it,' said Wexford.

'Get Karen to go out and fetch you something. That's quite a selection they've got.'

Wexford said Karen Malahyde had gone down to Kingsmarkham with Barry Vine but he'd ask Davidson to get his lunch. Davidson knew what he liked. He sat down opposite Burden with a mud-coloured coffee from the machine.

'How about these Griffins then?'

'The son's unemployed, living on the dole – well, no, Income Support, he's been unemployed too long for the dole. He lives at home with his parents. He's called Andrew or Andy. The parents are Terry and Margaret, late middle-age to elderly.'

'Like me,' said Wexford. 'What telling phrases you do use, Mike.'

Burden ignored him. 'They're retired people with not enough to do, they struck me as being at a loose end. And they're raving paranoiacs as well. Everything's wrong and everyone's against them. When we got there they were waiting for Telecom to fix their phone, that's who they thought we were, and they both gave us a blast before we got a chance to explain. Then as soon as the name Tancred was mentioned, they started whingeing on about the best years of their lives they gave up to the place and the iniquities of Davina Flory as an employer, you can imagine. The funny thing was that although they must have known, I mean it was clear that they knew, all about what happened on Tuesday night – there was even yesterday's paper lying there with all the photos – they never said a word about it till we did. I mean, not even a comment on how terrible it was. Just an exchanged glance when I said I believed they'd worked there, Griffin said rather grimly that they'd worked there all right, they'd never forget it, and then they were off, the pair of them, until we had to – well, stem the tide.'

Wexford quoted, '"An event has happened on which it is difficult to speak and impossible to be silent."' He got a suspicious look in return. 'Did the Telecom man come?'

'Yes, he did at last. I was going spare, what with her toddling to the front door every five minutes to look up and down the road for him. By the way, Andy Griffin wasn't there, he came in later. His mother said he was out jogging.'

They were interrupted by Davidson, coming round the screens with a waxed paper carrier containing tandoori chicken, pilaf rice and mango chutney for Wexford.

'I wish I'd had that,' said Burden.

'Too late now. No swaps, I hate pizza. Did you find out what they quarrelled about with the Harrisons?'

Burden looked surprised. 'I didn't ask.'

'No, but if they're so paranoid they might have volunteered the information.'

'They didn't mention the Harrisons. Maybe that's significant. Margaret Griffin went on about the immaculate state she'd left the cottage in and how the one time they met Gabbitas he'd had tar on his boots and it came off on their carpet. He'd soon turn the place into a tip, she could tell that.

'Andy Griffin came in. I suppose he might have been jogging. He's overweight, not to say fat. He was wearing a tracksuit but not everyone who wears them goes on tracks. He looks as if he couldn't run for a bus that was going at five miles an hour. He's shortish and fair but there's no way you could stretch Daisy Flory's description to fit him.'

'She wouldn't have to describe him. She'd know him,' said Wexford. 'She'd know him even behind a mask.'

'True. He was out on Tuesday night, he says with mates, and his parents confirm he went out at around six. I'm checking it out with the mates. They're supposed to have gone the round of pubs in Myringham and for a Chinese in a place called the Panda Cottage.'

'Those names! Sounds like a haunt for gay endangered species. He's on the *dole*?'

'Like I say, one of those benefits. They're always changing the names. There's something funny about him, Reg, though I can't tell you what. I know that's not helpful but what I'm really saying is, we have to keep our eye on Andrew Griffin. His parents give the impression of disliking everyone and they've got a lot of resentment built up for some reason – or no reason – against Harvey Copeland and Davina Flory, but Andy, he hates them. His whole manner and voice change when he talks about them. He even said he was glad they were dead – "scum" and "shit" are the words he uses about them.'

'Prince Charming.'

'We'll know a bit more when we find out if he really was out round the pubs and this Panda Cottage on Tuesday.'

Wexford glanced at his watch. 'Time for me to get off over to the Infirmary. D'you feel like coming? You could put a few Griffin queries to Daisy yourself.'

The moment the words were out of his mouth he regretted them. Daisy was accustomed to him by now, she would almost certainly not want another policeman arriving with him and arriving unannounced. But he need not have worried. Burden had no intention of coming. Burden had an appointment for another interview with Brenda Harrison.

'She'll keep,' he said of Daisy. 'She'll feel easier about talking when she's out of there. By the way, where's she going when she *is* out of there?'

'I don't know,' Wexford said slowly. 'I really don't know. It hadn't occurred to me.'

'Well, she can't go home, can she? If it's her home, I suppose it is. She can't go straight back where it happened. Maybe one day but hardly now.'

'I'll be back,' said Wexford, as he went, 'in time to see what the television networks do for us. I'll be back in time for the ITN news at five forty.'

Once again, at the hospital, he did not declare himself but entered unobtrusively, almost secretly. No Dr Leigh was about and no nurses. He knocked on the door of Daisy's room, unable to see much through the frosted glass, the shape of the bed only, enough to tell him no visitor sat at the bedside.

No one said to come in. Of course, he was rather earlier than he had been on previous occasions. Alone, unescorted, he did not like to open the door. He knocked again, now certain, without evidence for his certainty, that the room was empty. They must have a day room and she might be in it. He turned away and came face to face with a man in a short white jacket. The charge nurse?

'I'm looking for Miss Flory.'

'Daisy went home today.'

'She went *home*?'

'Are you Chief Inspector Wexford? She left a message that she'd phone you. Her friends came for her. I can give you the name, I've got it somewhere.'

Daisy had gone to Nicholas Virson and his mother in Myfleet. That, then, was the answer to Burden's question. She had gone home to her friends, perhaps her closest friends. He wondered why she hadn't told him of this on the previous day, but perhaps she hadn't known. No doubt, they had been in touch with her, had invited her and she had agreed in order to escape. Almost every patient longs to escape from hospital.

'We'll be keeping an eye on her,' the charge nurse said. 'She has an appointment here for an examination on Monday.'

Back at the stables, he watched television, one news broadcast after another. The artist's impression of what the Tancred gunman looked like came on to the screen. Seeing it like that, enlarged, somehow more convincing than a drawing on paper could be, Wexford knew who it reminded him of.

Nicholas Virson.

The face on the screen was exactly as he remembered Virson's face at Daisy's bedside. Coincidence, chance and something fortuitous on the artist's part? Or some unconscious displacement on Daisy's? Did that make the picture, which had now vanished from the screen to be succeeded by some pop star's wedding, worthless? The mask the gunman had worn had served its purpose if the result of wearing it had been to make himself look like the witness's boyfriend!

Wexford sat in front of the television, unseeing. It was getting on for half past six, the time Sheila and Augustine Casey might be expected to arrive. He felt no compulsion to go home.

He went back to his own desk where a dozen messages awaited him. The top one told him what he already knew, that Daisy Flory could be found care of Mrs Joyce Virson at The Thatched House, Castle Lane, Myfleet. It also gave him something he didn't know, a phone number. Wexford took his own phone out of his pocket and punched the digits.

A woman's voice answered, superior, sweeping, imperious. 'Hello?'

Wexford said who he was and that he would like to talk to Miss Flory on the following day, in the afternoon at about four.

'But it's Saturday!'

He agreed. There was no denying it.

'Well, I suppose so. If you must. Can you find this cottage? How do you intend to get here? The bus service isn't at all reliable ...'

He said he would be there at four and pressed the cut-off button. There was much to be said for this new phone. The door opened, a strong draught of cold evening air swept in and Barry Vine appeared.

'Where have you sprung from?' Wexford said rather sourly.

'It sounds ridiculous, but she's disappeared. Mrs Garland. Joanne Garland. She's missing.'

'What d'you mean, missing? You mean she's not there? That's hardly the same thing.'

'She's missing. She told no one she was going away, she left no messages or instructions for anyone. No one knows where she's gone. She hasn't been seen since Tuesday evening.'

# 10

The old people were watching television. Their last meal of the day was over, it had been served at five, and this was evening for them, with bedtime scheduled for eight thirty not too far off.

Armchairs and wheelchairs were arranged in a semicircle in front of the set. The elderly viewers were confronted by a brutish face, the Identikit-picture maker's idea of the Tancred gunman. It was the kind of face that once, long ago, was defined by the phrase 'a blond beast'. And this was the expression one of them used to describe him, uttering it in a loud stage whisper to the man next to her:

'Look at him, a real blond beast!'

She seemed one of the livelier inmates of the Caenbrook Retirement Home and Burden felt relief when it was to her chair that the thin worried-looking girl who had received them ushered him and Sergeant Vine. She looked round, smiled, surprise rapidly giving place to a very real delight when she understood that the visitors, whoever they might be, were for her.

'Edie, there's someone to see you. They're policemen.'

The smile remained. It widened.

'Hey, Edie,' said the old man she had whispered to, 'what have you been up to then?'

'Me? Chance'd be a fine thing.'

'Mrs Chowney, my name is Inspector Burden and this is Detective Sergeant Vine. I wonder if we could have a word with you. We're anxious to find the whereabouts of your daughter.'

'Which one? I've got six.'

As Burden told Wexford later, that almost stunned him. It certainly silenced him, if briefly. Edie Chowney compounded matters by announcing proudly – to an audience, who had evidently heard it many times before – that she also had five sons. All alive, all doing well for themselves, all in this country. It struck Burden then as dreadful, as something which in many other societies would be incomprehensible, that out of those eleven children none had taken their mother to live in their home, under their wing. Indeed, to avoid this, they had preferred to raise the money, among them all most likely, which would keep her in this doubtless expensive end-of-the-road for the discarded old.

As they went along the corridor to Mrs Chowney's room, a plan put forward by the thin warden, which drew forth more ribaldry from the old man, Burden reflected that one of those ten siblings of Joanne Garland might have been a better source for the information he was seeking. But there he was wrong, for Edie Chowney, walking to her room without asistance, ushering them in and complaining to the warden that the heating was less than adequate, showed herself as much in command of her mind and her speech as someone thirty years younger.

She looked to be in her late seventies, a small sprightly woman, thin but broad and rather bandy. It was a strong body that had borne many children. Her wispy hair was dyed dark-brown. Only her hands, tree-root-like and with knobbed knuckles, revealed it must have been arthritis that betrayed her and committed her to Caenbrook.

The room had its basic furnishings and it had Edie Chowney's own things. Mostly framed photographs. They crowded on to the window sill and the table tops, the bedside cabinet and the little bookcase, these pictured people with their own posterity, their spouses, their dogs, their homes in the background, all of them aged between forty and fifty-five. One was very likely Joanne Garland but there was no knowing which.

'I've got twenty-one grandchildren,' said Mrs Chowney when she saw him looking. 'I've got four great-grandchildren and with any luck, if Maureen's eldest gets on with it, I'll have a great-great-grand-child one of these fine days. What d'you want to know about Joanne?'

'Where she's gone, Mrs Chowney,' said Barry Vine. 'We'd like the address of where she is. Her neighbours don't know.'

'Joanne never had kids. Married twice but no kids. Women aren't barren in our family so I reckon it was from choice. Didn't have much choice in my day but times change. Joanne'd be too selfish, wouldn't put up with their noise and the mess. You get a lot of mess one way and another with kids. I should know, I've had eleven. Mind you, she was the eldest of the girls, so she *knew*.'

'She's gone away, Mrs Chowney. Can you tell us where?'

'Her first husband was a hard worker but he never made good. She divorced him, I didn't like that, I said, you're the first person in our family ever to go through the divorce court, Joanne. Pam got divorced later and so did Trev but at the time Joanne was the first. Anyway, she met this wealthy man. Do you know what he used to say? He used to say, I'm only a poor millionaire, Edie. Oh, they lived it up, I can tell you, spend, spend, spend, but it all came to grief like the first time round. He had to pay up – ooh, she made him pay through the nose. That's how she's got that house and started that business she's got and bought that big car and all. It's her keeps me in here, you know. It costs as much to be in here as a posh hotel in London, which is a mystery when you look round you. But she pays, the others couldn't run to it.'

Burden had to stem the tide. Edie Chowney had only paused to draw breath. He had heard of lonely people's verbosity when at last in company but this (as he told himself) was ridiculous.

'Mrs Chowney . . .'

She said, more sharply, 'All right. I've done. I know I talk too much. It's not my age, it's my nature, I've always been a chatterbox, my husband used to go on at me. What was it you wanted to know about Joanne?'

'Where is she?'

'At home, of course, or at business. Where else would she be?'

'When did you last see her, Mrs Chowney?'

She did a curious thing. It was as if she were reminding herself about which particular child they were enquiring. She viewed the photograph collection by the bed, paused for calculation, then selected a coloured one in a silver frame and looked at it, nodding.

'It would have been Tuesday evening. That's right, Tuesday, because it was the day the chiropodist comes and she always comes on a Tuesday. Joanne came in while we were having our teas. Five-ish. Maybe a quarter past five. I said, you're early, what about the shop? and she said, gallery, Mother, you always say that, the gallery's OK, Naomi's there till half past. You know who she meant by Naomi? Naomi's one of them that got murdered – no, massacred like they say on the telly, massacred at Tancred House. Wasn't that a terrible thing? I suppose you've heard about it – well, you would, being policemen.'

'While your daughter was with you, did she say anything about going to Tancred House that evening?'

Mrs Chowney handed Burden the photograph. 'She always went up there on Tuesday evening Her and that poor Naomi, the one that was massacred, they did the shop accounts. That's her, that's Joanne, it was taken five years back but she hasn't changed much.'

The woman looked overdressed in a bright pink suit with gilt buttons. A great deal of gold costume jewellery huddled round her neck and swung from her ears. She was tall with a good figure. Her blonde hair was rather rigidly and elaborately dressed and she seemed heavily made-up, though this was hard to tell.

'She didn't tell you she was going away on holiday?'

'She wasn't,' Edie Chowney said sharply 'She wasn't going anywhere. She'd have told me. What makes you think she's gone away?'

That was something Burden hardly liked to answer. 'When would you expect her to visit you again?'

Bitterness entered her voice. 'Three weeks. A good three weeks. It wouldn't be sooner. Joanne never comes more than once every three weeks and sometimes it's a month. She pays up and she thinks she's done her duty. Comes once in three weeks and stops ten minutes and thinks she's the good daughter.'

'And your other children?' It was Vine who asked. Burden had resolved not to.

'Pam comes. I mean, she only lives two streets away, so coming every day wouldn't kill her. Not that she does come every day. Pauline's in Bristol, so you can't expect it, and Trev's on one of them oil rigs. Doug's in Telford, wherever that may be. Shirley's got four kids and that's her excuse, though God knows they're all in their teens. John drops in when it suits him, which isn't often, and the rest of them crop up around Christmas. Oh, they all turn up together at Christmas, a whole troop of them. What's the use of that to me? I said that to them last Christmas, what's the good of you all coming at once? Seven of them on Christmas Eve in one go, Trev and Doug and Janet and Audrey and . . . '

'Mrs Chowney,' said Burden, 'can you give me the addresses of . . . ' he hesitated, hardly knowing how to put it '. . . one or two of your children who live nearest? Who live around here and might know where your daughter Joanne has gone?'

*

103

It was eight before Wexford finally left for home. When the car reached the main gates and Donaldson got out to open them, he noticed something tied to each gatepost. It was too dark under the crowding trees to make out more than shapeless bundles.

He switched on the headlamp beam, left the car and went to look. More bouquets, more tributes to the dead. Two this time, one on each gatepost. They were simple bouquets but exquisitely arranged, one a Victorian posy of violets and primroses, the other a sheaf of snow-white narcissi and dark green ivy. Wexford read on one card: *In grief for the great tragedy of 11 March*. The other said: *These violent deaths have violent ends and in their triumph die*. He returned to the car and Donaldson drove out through the gateway. The message on the first bunch of flowers left on the gatepost had seemed innocuous, a rather apt quotation from *Antony and Cleopatra* – well, apt if you had extravagantly admired Davina Flory. This later one had a faintly sinister ring. It too was probably Shakespeare but he couldn't place it.

He had more important things to think about. Phone calls to John Chowney and Pamela Burns née Chowney had elicited only that they had no idea where their sister was and had not known she was going away. No neighbour had been told she would be absent. Her newsagent had not been alerted. Joanne Garland was not in the habit of taking a milk delivery. The manager of the card shop next door to Garlands in the Kingsbrook Centre had expected her to arrive and open the gallery on Thursday morning, one day's grace having been allowed out of respect to Naomi Jones.

John Chowney named two women he called close friends of his sister. Neither was able to tell Burden anything of her whereabouts. Each was surprised to hear of her absence. She had not been seen since five forty on Tuesday evening when she left the Caenbrook Retirement Home and the warden on duty saw her get into her car she had parked on the forecourt. Joanne Garland had disappeared.

In different circumstances, the police would hardly have noticed it. A woman who goes away for a few days without telling her friends or relatives is not a missing woman. That arrangement to call at Tancred House at quarter past eight on Tuesday evening altered things. If Wexford was sure of anything it was that she had been there, she had kept her promise. Was her disappearance due to what she had seen at Tancred House or to what she had done?

He let himself into his house and immediately heard laughter from

104

the dining room, Sheila's laughter. Her coat was hanging up in the hall, it must be hers – who else would wear synthetic snow-leopard a petrol-blue fake fox collar?

In the dining room they had had their soup and moved on to the main course. Roast chicken, not sole *bonne femme*. Why had he thought of that? It was an altogether different house, the whole of it would have got lost in Tancred House, they were very different people. He apologised to Dora for his lateness, kissed her, kissed Sheila and held out his hand to Augustine Casey for Casey to ignore it.

'Gus has been telling us about Davina Flory, Pop,' Sheila said.

'You knew her?'

'My publishers,' said Casey, 'don't belong among those whose policy is to pretend to one author that they have no others on their list.'

Wexford hadn't known he and the dead woman shared a publisher. He said nothing but went back to the hall and took his hat and coat off. He washed his hands, telling himself to be tolerant, to be magnanimous, to make allowances, be kind. When he was back in there and sitting down Sheila made Casey repeat everything he had said so far about Davina Flory's books, much of it unedifying as far as Wexford was concerned, and repeat too an unbelievable story that Davina Flory's editor had sent the manuscript of her autobiography to Casey for his opinion before they made her an offer for it.

'I'm not usually thick,' said Casey, 'I'm not, am I, love?'

Wexford, wondering what was coming, winced at that 'love'. Sheila's response when appealed to nearly made him cringe, it was so adoring and at the same time so appalled that anyone, even the man himself, might deprecatingly suggest he was less than a genius.

'I'm not usually thick,' Casey repeated, presumably expecting a further chorus of incredulous denial, 'but I really had no idea that all that happened down here and that you . . .' he turned small pale eyes on Wexford '. . . I mean, Sheila's father, were in – what's the term, there must *be* a term – oh, yes, in *charge* of the case. I know nothing about these things, less than nothing, but Scotland Yard still exists, doesn't it? I mean, isn't there something called a Murder Squad? Why you?'

'Tell me your impressions of Davina Flory,' Wexford said equably, swallowing a rage that filled his mouth with hot sourness and put up red screens before his eyes. 'I'd be interested to hear from someone who had met her professionally.'

'*Professionally*? I'm not an anthropologist. I'm not an explorer. I met her at a publisher's party. And, no, thank you very much, I don't think I will tell you my *impressions*, I don't think that would be at all wise. I shall keep mum. It would only remind me of the time I was done for reckless driving and the funny little cop who chased me on his motorbike read back everything I said to him in court, the whole of it ineluctably distorted by the filtering process of semi-literacy.'

'Have some wine, darling,' said Dora smoothly. 'You'll like it, Sheila brought it specially.'

'You haven't put them in the same room, have you?'

'Reg, that's the kind of remark I should be making, not you. You're supposed to be the liberal one. Of course I've put them in the same room. I'm not running a Victorian workhouse.'

Wexford had to smile in spite of himself. 'That's typical unreason, isn't it? I don't mind my daughter sleeping under my roof with a man I like but I hate the whole idea when it's a shit like him.'

'I've never heard you use that word before!'

'There has to be a first time for everything. Me throwing someone out of my house, for instance.'

'But you won't.'

'No, I'm sure I won't.'

Next morning Sheila said she and Gus would like to take her parents to dinner at the Cheriton Forest Hotel that evening. It had recently changed hands and had a new reputation for wonderful food at high prices. She had booked a table for four. Augustine Casey remarked that it would be amusing to see that sort of thing at first hand. He had a friend who wrote about places like that for a Sunday paper, in fact about manaifestations of nineties' taste. The series was called *More Money Than Sense*, a title which was his, Casey's, brainchild. He would be interested not only in the food and the ambience, but in the kind of people who patronised it.

Unable to resist, Wexford said, 'I thought you said last night you weren't an anthropologist.'

Casey gave one of his mysterious smiles. 'What do *you* put on your passport? Police officer, I suppose. I've always kept *student*. It's ten years since I left my university but I still have *student* in my passport and I suppose I always shall.'

Wexford was going out. He was meeting Burden for a drink in the Olive and Dove. A rule, made to be broken, was that they never did this on a Saturday. He had to get out of the house for short spells, though he knew it was wrong of him. Sheila caught him up in the hall.

'Dear Pop, is everything all right? Are you OK?'

'I'm fine. This Flory case is a bit of a strain. What are you going to do with yourselves today?'

'Gus and I thought we'd go to Brighton. He's got friends there. We'll be back in heaps of time for dinner. You will be able to make it for dinner, won't you?'

He nodded. 'I'll do my best.'

She looked a little crestfallen. 'Gus is marvellous, isn't he? I've never known anyone like him.' Her face brightened. It was such a lovely face, as perfect as Garbo's, as sweet as Marilyn Monroe's, as transcendentally beautiful as Hedy Lamarr's. In his eyes, at least. He thought so. Where did the genes dredge up from to create that? She said, 'He's so clever. Half the time I can't keep up with him. The latest thing is he's going to be the writer-in-residence at a university in Nevada. They're building up a library of his manuscripts there, it's called the Augustine Casey Archive, they really appreciate him.'

Wexford had scarcely heard the end of this. He was stuck – and blissfully – in the middle of her remarks.

'He's going to live in *Nevada*?'

'Yes – well, for a year. It's a place called Heights.'

'In the *United States*?'

'He intends to write his next novel while he's there,' said Sheila. 'It will be his masterwork.'

Wexford gave her a kiss. She threw her arms around his neck. Walking down the street, he could have burst into song. All was well, all was better than well, they were going to Brighton for the day and *Augustine Casey was going to America for a year*, the man was practically emigrating. Oh, why hadn't she told him last evening and given him a good night's sleep? It was useless worrying about that now. He was glad he had decided to go to the Olive on foot, he could have a real drink now and celebrate.

Burden was there already. He said he had come from Broom Vale where, on a warrant sworn out two hours before, they were searching Joanne Garland's house. Her car was in the garage, a dark-grey BMW. She kept no pets to be fed or walked. There were no houseplants to be watered, no flowers left dying in vases. The television set had been unplugged, but some people did this every

107

night before they went to bed. It looked as if she had left the house of her own free will.

A desk diary, with engagements meticulously entered, told Burden only that Joanne Garland had been to a drinks party on the previous Saturday, to lunch on Sunday with her sister Pamela. Her visit to her mother was marked in for Tuesday 11 March – and that was that. The following spaces remained blank. Her handwriting was small, neat and very upright, and she had managed to squeeze quite a lot of information into the inch by three inches allowed for each entry.

'We've come across this sort of thing before,' Wexford said, 'someone apparently disappearing and it turns out they've been on holiday. But in neither of those cases had the missing persons a host of relatives and friends, people, mark you, who in the past had been quite used to being told whenever the missing person was going away. The facts are that Joanne was going to Tancred House at a quarter past eight on Tuesday evening. She was an over-punctual person, we're told by Daisy Flory, in other words too early for appointments as a general rule, so we may take it she got to the house soon after eight.'

'If she went there. What are you going to have?'

Wexford wasn't going to say anything to him about celebrations. 'I was thinking of Scotch, but I'd better think again. The usual half of bitter.'

When he came back with the drinks, Burden said, 'We've no reason to believe she went there.'

'Only the fact that she always did on a Tuesday,' Wexford retorted. 'Only the fact that she was expected. If she hadn't been going, wouldn't she have phoned? There was no phone call received at Tancred House that evening.'

'But look, Reg, what are we saying? It doesn't add up. These are ordinary villains, aren't they? Trigger-happy villains after jewellery? One of them a stranger, the other possibly with special knowledge of the house and its occupants. That presumably is why only the blond beast, as Mrs Chowney calls him, let himself be seen by the three he killed and the one he attempted to kill. The other, the familiar face, kept out of the way.

'But they're typical villains, they're not the sort who carry off a possible witness and dispose of her elsewhere, are they? You see what

108

I mean about it not adding up. If she came to the door why not shoot her too?'

'Because the chamber of the Magnum was empty,' Wexford said quickly.

'All right. If it was. There are other means of killing. He'd killed three people and wouldn't jib at killing a fourth. But, no, he and his pal carry her off. Not as some sort of hostage, not for information she may have, just to get rid of her elsewhere. Why? It doesn't add up.'

'OK. You've said that three times, you've made your point. If they killed her at Tancred House, what became of her car? They drove it home and put it neatly in her garage?'

'I suppose she could be involved. She could be the other one. We only assume it was a man. But, Reg, is it even worth considering? Joanne Garland is a woman in her fifties, a prosperous, successful businesswoman – because, God knows how or why, that gallery is successful, it does work. She's well enough off to be independent of it, anyway. Her car's a last year's BMW, she's got a wardrobe of clothes I know nothing about but Karen says are top designers, Valentino and Krizia and Donna Karan. Have you ever heard of them?'

Wexford nodded. 'I do read the papers.'

'She's got every kind of equipment there you can think of. One of the rooms is a gym full of exercising gear. She's obviously rich. What would she want with the sort of money some fence would give her for Davina Flory's rings?'

'Mike, I've thought of something. Is there an answering machine? What's her phone number? There may be a message on it.'

'I don't know the number,' Burden said. 'Can you get Enquiries on that thing of yours?'

'Sure.' Wexford asked for the number and was quickly given it. At their table in a dim corner of the Olive's lounge, he dialled Joanne Garland's number. It rang three times, then clicked softly and a voice that was not at all what they expected came on. Not a strong self-assertive voice, not confident and strident, but soft, even diffident:

'This is Joanne Garland. I am not available to speak to you now but if you would like to leave a message I will get back to you as soon as I can. Please speak after the tone.'

The routine statement of identity and availability recommended in most answering-machine literature.

'We'll check on what messages have been left, if any. I'm going to try it again and hope this time they realise and pick up the phone themselves. Is Gerry up there?'

'DC Hinde,' said Burden, keeping a straight face, 'is busy working, but elsewhere. He has constructed what he calls a tremendous database of all the crime committed in this area in the past twelve months and he's mousing away in it – I've probably got the terminology all wrong – looking for coincidences. Karen's up there and Archbold and Davidson. You'd think one of them would have the sense to answer.'

Wexford dialled the number again. It rang three times and the message began to repeat itself. Next time, Karen Malahyde picked up the receiver after the second ring.

'About time too,' said Wexford. 'You know who this is? Yes? Good. Play back the messages, would you? If you're not familiar with the working of these things, you should look for a button marked PLAY. Do it once only, note what's on it and take the tape out. It's probably the kind that will only play the same thing back twice. All right? Call me back on my personal number.' He said to Burden, 'I don't think she's involved in Tuesday night's murders, of course not, but I do think she saw them. Mike, I'm wondering if instead of searching her house we should be looking for her body up at Tancred.'

'It's not in the vicinity of the house. It's not in the outbuildings. You know we've searched.'

'We haven't searched the woods.'

Burden gave a sort of groan. 'D'you want the other half?'

'I'll get them.'

Wexford went up to the bar, holding the empty glasses. Sheila and Augustine Casey would be on their way to Brighton now. With satisfaction – because it would soon come to an end, soon only be heard under the shadow of the Sierra Nevada – he imagined the conversation in the car, the monologue rather, as Casey gave vent to streams of wit and brilliance, esoterica, malicious anecdotes and self-aggrandising tales, while Sheila listened enraptured.

Burden looked up. 'They might take her away with them because she saw them or was a witness to the murders. But take her where and kill her how? And how did her car get back into her garage?'

Wexford's phone bleeped. 'Karen?'

'I've taken the tape out like you said, sir. What would you like me to do with it?'

'Have it copied, phone me and play the copy to me, then bring it to me. At my home. The tape and the copy. What were the messages?'

'There are three. The first one's from a woman calling herself Pam and I think that's Joanne's sister. I've written it down. It says to phone her about Sunday, whatever that means. The second's a man, it sounds like a sales rep. He's called Steve, no surname. He says he tried the shop but got no answer so he thought he'd phone her at home. It's about the Easter decorations, he says, and would she call him at home. The third's from Naomi Jones.'

'Yes?'

'This is it verbatim, sir: "Jo, this is Naomi. I wish it was you sometimes and not always that machine. Can you make it eight thirty tonight and not earlier? Mother hates having dinner interrupted. Sorry about that but you understand. See you." '

Lunch at home, just the two of them.

'He's going to be writer-in-residence in the Wild West,' said Wexford.

'You oughtn't to rejoice when it's making her so unhappy.'

'Is it? I don't see any signs of unhappiness. More likely the scales are falling from her eyes and she sees what a good miss he'll be.'

What Dora might have said in reply to these remarks was lost in the ringing of the phone. Karen said, 'Here it is, sir. You asked me to play it.'

Like the murmur of a ghost, the dead woman's voice spoke to him. ' . . . Mother hates having dinner interrupted. Sorry about that but you understand. See you.'

He shivered. Mother had had her dinner interrupted. An hour or so after that message was left her life had been interrupted for ever. He saw the red cloth again, the seeping stain, the head lying on the table, the head flung back to hang over the back of a chair. He saw Harvey Copeland spreadeagled on the staircase and Daisy crawling past the bodies of her dead, crawling to the phone to save her own life.

'You needn't bring it, thanks, Karen. It'll keep.'

At half past three he set off for Myfleet and the house where Daisy Flory had found her refuge.

# 11

The first thing that came into his mind was that she was in the attitude of her dead grandmother. Daisy had not heard him come in, she had heard nothing, and she was slumped across the table with one arm stretched out and her head beside it. So had Davina Flory fallen across a table when the gun found its aim.

Daisy was abandoned to her grief, her body shaking though she made no sound. Wexford stood looking at her. He had been told where she was by Nicholas Virson's mother but Mrs Virson had not accompanied him to the door. He closed it behind him and took a few steps into what Joyce Virson had called 'the little den'. What names these people had for parts of their houses others would have designated 'greenhouse' or 'sitting room'!

It was a thatched house, as its name indicated, something of a rarity in the neighbourhood. A kind of self-deprecatory snobbery might cause its owners to call it a cottage but in fact it was a sizeable house, of picturesquely uneven construction and pargeted patterns on the walls. The windows were large or medium-sized or very small, and several peeped out under eyelid gables close up to the roof. The roof was a formidable reed construction, ornately done and with a woven design round where the ribbed and pargeted chimney pots protruded. A garage, of the kind estate agents call 'integral', was also roofed by this dense layer of thatch.

Their popularity on calendars had made thatched houses faintly absurd, the butt of a certain kind of wit. But if you cleared your mind of chocolate-box images, this house could be made to appear what it was, a beautiful English antiquity, its garden pretty with wind-blown spring flowers, its lawns the brilliant green result of a damp climate.

Inside, a certain shabbiness, an air of make-do-and-mend, made

112

him doubt his own original assessment of Nicholas Virson's city successes. The little den where Daisy hung slumped over the table had a worn carpet and stretch-nylon covers on the chairs. A weary houseplant on the window sill had artificial flowers stuck into the soil around it to perk it up.

She made a little sound, a whimper, an acknowledgement perhaps of his presence.

'Daisy,' he said.

The shoulder that was not bandaged moved a little. Otherwise she gave no sign of having heard him.

'Daisy, please stop crying.'

She lifted her head slowly. This time there was no apology, no explanation. Her face was like a child's, puffy with tears. He sat down in the chair opposite her. It was a small table between them, such as might be used in a room of this kind for writing, for playing cards, for a supper for two. She looked at him in despair.

'Would you like me to come back tomorrow? I have to talk to you but it need not be now.'

Crying had made her hoarse. In a voice he hardly recognised she said, 'It may as well be now as any other time.'

'How is your shoulder?'

'Oh, all right. It doesn't hurt, it's just sore.' She said something then which, if it had come from someone older or someone *else,* he would have found ridiculous. 'The pain is in my heart.'

It was as if she heard her own words, digested them and understood how they sounded, for she burst into a peal of unnatural laughter. 'How stupid I sound! But it's true – why does saying what's true sound false?'

'Perhaps,' he said gently, 'because it isn't quite real. You've read it somewhere. People don't really have pains in their hearts unless they're having a heart attack and then I believe it's usually in the arm.'

'I wish I was old. I wish I was as old as you and wise.'

This couldn't be treated seriously. 'Will you be staying here for a while, Daisy?' he asked her.

'I don't know. I suppose so. I'm here now, it's as good a place as any. I made them let me out of the hospital. Oh, it was bad in there. It was bad being alone and worse being with strangers.' She shrugged. 'The Virsons are very kind. I'd like to be alone but I'm afraid of being alone too – do you know what I mean?'

113

'I think so. It's best for you to be with your friends, with people who'll leave you alone when you want to be on your own.'

'Yes.'

'Would you feel like answering some questions about Mrs Garland?'

'Joanne?'

This, at any rate, was not what she had expected. She wiped her eyes with her fingers, blinked at him.

He had made up his mind not to tell her of their fears. She could know that Joanne Garland had gone away to some unknown destination but not that she was a 'missing person', not that they were already assuming her dead. Censoring what he said, he explained how she couldn't be found.

'I don't know her very well,' Daisy said. 'Davina didn't like her much. She didn't think she was good enough for us.'

Recalling some of what Brenda Harrison had said, Wexford was surprised and his astonishment must have shown on his face, for Daisy said, 'Oh, I don't mean in a snobby way. It was nothing to do with class with Davina. I mean –' she lowered her voice '– she didn't much care for –' she cocked her thumb towards the door '– them either. She hadn't any time for people she said were dull or ordinary. People had to have character, vitality, something individual. You see, she didn't know any ordinary people – well, except the people who worked for her – and she didn't want me to either. She used to say she wanted me to be surrounded by the best. She'd given up on Mum, but she didn't like Joanne just the same, she'd never liked her. I remember one phrase she used, she said Joanne dragged Mum down into a "quagmire of the commonplace".'

'But your mother took no notice?' Wexford had observed that Daisy could now talk of her mother and grandmother without a break in her voice, without a lapse into despair. Her grief was stemmed while she talked of the past. 'She didn't care?'

'You have to understand that poor Mum was really one of those ordinary people Davina didn't like. I don't know why she was, something to do with genes I suspect.' Daisy's voice was strengthening as she talked, the hoarseness conquered by the interest she could still take in this subject. She could be distracted from her sorrow for these people by talking of them. 'She was just as if she was the daughter of ordinary people, not someone like Davina. But the strange thing was that Harvey was a bit like that too. Davina used to

114

talk a lot about her other husbands, number one and number two, saying how amusing and interesting they were, but I did wonder. Harvey never had much to say, he was a very quiet man. No, not so much quiet as passive. Easy-going, he called it. He did what Davina told him.' Wexford thought he saw a spark burn in her eyes. 'Or he tried to. He was dull, I think I've always known that.'

'Your mother went on being friends with Joanne Garland in spite of your grandmother's disapproval?'

'Oh, Mum had had Davina disapproving of her and sort of laughing at her all her life. She knew there was nothing she could do that would be right, so she'd got to do what she liked. She'd even stopped rising when Davina poked fun at her. Working in that shop suited her. You probably don't know this – why should you? – but Mum tried to be a painter for years and years. When I was little I can remember her painting and Davina coming into this studio they'd made for her and – well, criticising. I remember one thing she said, I didn't know what it meant at the time. She said, "Well, Naomi, I don't know what school you belong to but I think we could call you a Pre-Raphaelite Cubist."

'Davina wanted me to be all the things Mum wasn't. Maybe she wanted me to be all the things *she* wasn't too. But you don't want to hear about that. Mum loved that gallery and earning her own money and being – well, what she called "my own woman".'

For the time being Daisy's tears were in abeyance. Talking did her good. He doubted whether she was right when she said the best thing for her was to be alone. 'How long had they worked together?'

'Mum and Joanne? About four years. But they'd been friends for ever, since before I was born. Joanne had a shop in Queen Street, and that was where Mum first started with her, then she got that place for the gallery when the Centre was built. Did you say she'd gone away? She didn't mean to go away. I remember Mum saying – well, on *the* day, that's how I think of it, as *the* day – Mum said she'd wanted to take Friday off for something but Joanne wouldn't let her because they'd got the VAT inspector coming in and she'd have to go through the books with him, I mean Joanne would. It took hours and hours and Mum would have to see to clients – they didn't call them customers.'

'Your mother phoned her and left a message on her answering machine not to come before eight thirty.'

115

Daisy said indifferently, 'I expect she did. She often did but it never seemed to make much difference.'

'Joanne didn't phone during the evening?'

'No one phoned. Joanne wouldn't phone to say she'd come later. I don't think she *could* have come later even if she'd tried. Those extra-punctual people can't, they can't help themselves.'

He watched her. A little colour had come into her face. She was perspicacious, she was interested in people, their compulsions, how they behaved. He wondered what they talked about, she and these Virsons, when they were alone together, at meals, in the evening. What had she in common with them? As if she read his mind, she said, 'Joyce – Mrs Virson – is arranging about the funeral. Some undertakers came today. She'll speak to you, I expect. I mean, we can have a funeral, can we?'

'Yes, yes. Of course.'

'I didn't know. I thought it might be different for murdered people. I hadn't thought anything about it till Joyce said. It gave us something to talk about. It's not easy talking when there's only one thing in your life to talk about and that's the one you have to avoid.'

'It's fortunate you can talk about it with me.'

'Yes.'

She tried to smile. 'You see, there aren't any family left. Harvey hadn't any relations, except a brother who died four years ago. Davina was "the youngest wren of nine" and nearly all the rest are dead. Someone has to organise things and I wouldn't know how on my own. But I'll say what I want the service to be and I'll go to the funeral, I will do that.'

'No one would expect you to.'

'I think you may be wrong there,' she said thoughtfully, and then, 'Have you found anyone yet? I mean, have you got any clues to who it was that – did it?'

'I want to ask you if you are quite sure of the description you gave me of the man you saw.'

Indignation made her frown, her dark eyebrows push together. 'What makes you ask? Of course I'm sure. I'll tell you it again, if you like.'

'No, that won't be necessary, Daisy. I'm going to leave you now but I'm afraid this isn't likely to be the last time I'll want to talk to you.'

She turned away from him, twisting her body like a child turning

116

its back out of shyness. 'I wish,' she said, 'I wish there was someone, just one person, I could pour out my heart to. I'm so alone. Oh, if I could only open my heart to someone . . .'

The temptation to say, 'Open it to me' was resisted. He knew better than that. She had called him old and implied he was wise. He said, perhaps too lightly, 'You're talking of hearts a lot today, Daisy.'

'Because,' she faced him, 'he tried to kill me in my heart. He aimed at my heart, didn't he?'

'You mustn't think of that. You need someone to help you not to,' he said. 'It's not for me to advise you, I'm not competent to do that, but do you think you need some counselling? Would you consider it?'

'I don't need that!' She uttered it scornfully, an adamant denial. He was reminded of a psychotherapist he had once met in the course of an enquiry who had told him that saying you don't need counselling is one sure way of estimating that you do. 'I need someone to – to *love me,* and there's no one.'

'Goodbye.' He held out his hand to her. There was Virson to love her. Wexford was sure he did and would. The idea was rather dispiriting. She took his hand and her grip was strong, like a powerful man's. He felt in it the strength of her need, her cry for help. 'Goodbye for the time being.'

'I'm sorry to be such a bore,' she said quietly.

Joyce Virson was not exactly hovering in the passage, though he guessed she had been. She emerged from what was probably a drawing room, into which he wasn't invited. She was a big tall woman, perhaps sixty or rather less. The remarkable thing about her was that she seemed altogether on a larger scale than most women, taller, wider, with a bigger face, bigger nose and mouth, a mass of thick curly grey hair, man's hands, surely size nine feet. A shrill, affected upper-class voice went with all this.

'I simply wanted to ask you, I'm sorry but rather a delicate question – may we go ahead with the – well, the funeral?'

'Certainly. There's no difficulty about that.'

'Oh, good. These things must be, mustn't they? In the midst of life we are in death. Poor little Daisy has some wild ideas but she can't do anything, of course, and one wouldn't expect it. I have actually been in touch with Mrs Harrison, that housekeeper person at Tancred House, on this very subject. It seemed tactful to include her in, don't you think? I thought of next Wednesday or Thursday.'

117

Wexford said that seemed a sensible course to take. He wondered what Daisy's position would be. Would she need a guardian until she was eighteen? When would she be eighteen? Mrs Virson shut the front door rather sharply on him, as befitted one who in her estimation would once, in better days, have been expected to come and go by a tradesman's entrance. As he walked to his car, an MG, old but stylish, swept in through the open gateway and Nicholas Virson got out of it.

He said, 'Good evening,' which made Wexford look at his watch in alarm, but it was only twenty to six. Nicholas let himself into the house without a backward glance.

Augustine Casey came downstairs in a dinner jacket.

If he had had any fears about the way Sheila's friend might dress himself for dinner at the Cheriton Forest, Wexford would have guessed at jeans and a sweatshirt. Not that he would much have minded. That would have been Casey's business, to have put on the proffered tie the hotel produced or to have refused and the lot of them gone home. Wexford wouldn't have cared either way. But the dinner jacket seemed to invite comment, if only for a comparison with his own not very smart grey suit. He could think of nothing to say beyond offering Casey a drink.

Sheila appeared in a peacock-blue miniskirt and peacock-blue and emerald sequinned top. Wexford didn't much like the way Casey eyed her up and down while she told *him* how marvellous he looked.

The disquieting thing was that everything went very well for half the evening – the first half. Casey talked. Wexford was learning that things usually went well while Casey talked, while, that is, he talked about a subject chosen by himself, pausing to allow intelligent and appropriate questions from his audience. Sheila, Wexford noticed, was an adept at these questions, seeming to know the precise points at which to interject them. She had tried to tell them about a new part that had been offered her, a wonderful opportunity for her, the name part in Strindberg's *Miss Julie,* but Casey had little patience with that.

In the lounge, he talked about post-modernism. Sheila said, humbly resigned to no more interest being taken in her career, 'Could you give us some examples, please, Gus,' and Casey gave a large number of examples. They went into one of the several dining rooms the hotel now boasted. It was full and not one of the men sitting at

118

tables was in a dinner jacket. Casey, who had already drunk two large brandies, ordered another and immediately went to the men's room.

Sheila had always appeared to her father as an intelligent young woman. He hated having to revise this opinion but what else could he do when she said things like this?

'Gus is so brilliant, it makes me wonder what on earth he sees in someone like me. I feel really inferior while I'm with him.'

'What a bloody awful basis for a relationship,' he said, at which Dora kicked him under the cloth and Sheila looked hurt.

Casey came back laughing, something Wexford hadn't seen him often doing. A guest had taken him for a waiter, had asked for two dry martinis, and Casey had said in an Italian accent that they were coming up, sir. This made Sheila laugh inordinately. Casey drank his brandy, made a big show of ordering some special wine. He was extremely jovial and began to talk of Davina Flory.

All talk of 'keeping mum' and 'funny little cops' was apparently forgotten. Casey had met Davina on several occasions, the first time at a launch party for someone else's book, then when she came into his publisher's offices and they encountered each other in the 'atrium', a word for 'hall' which occasioned a disquisition on Casey's part on fashionable words and otiose importations from dead languages. Wexford's interruption was received as well-timed.

'You didn't know I was published by the St Giles Press? I'm not, you're perfectly right. But we're all under the same umbrella now – or sunshade might be the more appropriate word. Carlyon, St Giles Press, Sheridan and Quick, we're all Carlyon Quick now.'

Wexford thought of his friend and Burden's brother-in-law, Amyas Ireland, an editor at Carlyon-Brent. He was still there, as far as he knew. The takeover hadn't squeezed him out. Would there be any point in phoning Amyas for information on Davina Flory?

For Casey's own reminiscences seemed not to amount to much. His third meeting with Davina had been at a party given by Carlyon Quick at their new premises in Battersea – or the 'boondocks', as Casey called it. Her husband had been with her, a rather too sweet and gracious old 'honey' who had once been the Member for a constituency in which Casey's parents lived. A friend of Casey's had been taught by him some fifteen years before at the LSE. Casey called him a 'cardboard charmer'. Some of this charm had been exercised on the hordes of publicity girls and secretaries who were always at such parties, while poor Davina had to talk to boring editors-in-chief and marketing directors. Not that she had taken any sort of back seat, but had thrown her opinions about in her nineteen-twenties Oxford voice, boring everyone with east European politics and details of some trip she and one of her husbands had made to Mecca in the fifties. Wexford smiled inwardly at this example of projection.

He, Casey, had personally liked none of her books, with the possible exception of *The Hosts of Midian* (this novel Win Carver had described as the least successful or well-received by the critics) and his own definition of her was as the undiscerning reader's Rebecca West. What on earth made her think she could write novels? She was too bossy and didactic. She had no imagination. He was pretty sure she was the only person at that party who hadn't read his own Booker short-listed novel, or at any rate couldn't be bothered to pretend to have done so.

Casey laughed self-deprecatingly at this last remark of his. He tasted the wine. It was then that things began to go wrong. He tasted the wine, winced and used his second wine-glass as a spittoon for receiving the offending mouthful. Then he gave both glasses to the waiter.

'This plonk is disgusting. Take it away and bring me another bottle.'

Talking about it afterwards with Dora, Wexford said that it was odd nothing like this had happened on the previous Tuesday at La Primavera. Casey wasn't the host there, Dora said. And, after all, if you tasted wine and it was really unpalatable, where were you supposed to spit it out? On the cloth? She was always making excuses for Casey, though she was finding it difficult this time. She hadn't, for instance, much to say in Casey's defence when, after their starters had been sent back, with three waiters and the restaurant manager grouped round the table, he told the head waiter he had about as much idea of *nouvelle cuisine* as a school dinner-lady with PMT.

Wexford and Dora were not the hosts but the restaurant was in their neighbourhood, they were in a sense responsible for it. Wexford felt too that Casey was not sincere in what he was doing, it was all for effect, or even what in his youth the old people called 'devilment'. The meal proceeded in miserable silence, broken by Casey, after he had pushed aside his main course, saying very loudly that he for one wouldn't let the bastards get him down. He returned to the subject of

120

Davina Flory and began making scurrilous remarks about her sexual history.

Among them was the suggestion that Davina had still been a virgin eight years after her first wedding. Desmond, he said in a loud raucous voice, had never been able 'to get it up', or not with her and who could wonder at it? Naomi, of course, had not been his child. Casey said he wouldn't hazard a guess at who her father might have been and then proceeded to hazard several. He had spotted an elderly man at a distant table, a man who was not, though he strongly resembled him, a distinguished scientist and Master of an Oxford college. Casey began speculating as to the possibilities of this man's *doppelgänger* being Davina Flory's first lover.

Wexford stood up and said he was leaving. He asked Dora to come with him and said the others could do as they pleased. Sheila said, 'Please, Pop,' and Casey asked what in Christ's name was the matter. To his chagrin, Sheila succeeded in persuading Wexford to stay. He wished very much he had stuck to his guns when the time came to pay the bill. Casey refused to pay it.

A frightful scene ensued. Casey had consumed a great deal of brandy and though not drunk had become reckless. He shouted and abused the restaurant staff. Wexford had resolved that come what might, even if the *police* should be sent for, he would not pay that bill. In the end Sheila paid it. Stony-faced, Wexford sat by and let her. He said to Dora afterwards that there must have been times in his life when he felt more miserable but he couldn't remember them.

That night he had no sleep.

The missing pane of glass in the dining-room window was patched over with a sheet of plywood. It served its purpose of keeping out the cold.

'I've taken it upon myself to send away for some eight-ounce glass,' Ken Harrison said gloomily to Burden. 'Don't know how long they'll take coming up with that. Months, I shouldn't be surprised. These criminals, the villains who do this sort of thing, they don't think of the trouble they cause to the little folk like you and me.'

Burden didn't much like being numbered among the 'little folk', it made him feel (as he remarked to Wexford) like an elf, but he said nothing. They strolled towards the gardens at the rear, towards the pinetum. It was a fine sunny morning, cold and crisp, frost still silvering the grass and the box hedges. In the woods, among the dark leafless trees, the blackthorn was coming into flower, a white scattering on the network of dark twigs like sprinkled snow. Harrison had pruned the roses during the weekend, hard, nearly to the ground.

'We may be finished here for all I know,' he said, 'but you have to carry on, don't you? You have to carry on normal, that's what life's about.'

'How about these Griffins, Mr Harrison? What can you tell me about them?'

'I'll tell you one thing. Terry Griffin helped himself to a young cedar out of here for a Christmas tree. Couple of years back, it was. I came on him digging it up. No one'll miss that, he said. I took it upon myself to tell Harvey – Mr Copeland, that is.'

'Was that the cause of your falling out with the Griffins, then?'

Harrison gave him a sidelong look, truculent and suspicious. 'They never knew it was me told on them. Harvey said he'd discovered it himself, he made a point of not involving me.'

They passed among the trees into the pinetum, where the sun penetrated only in streaks and bars of light between the low coniferous branches. It was cold. Underfoot the ground was dry and rather slippery, a carpet of pine needles.

Burden picked up a curiously shaped cone, as glossy-brown and pineapple-shaped as if it had been carved from wood by a master hand. He said, 'D'you know if John Gabbitas is at home or if he's off in the woods somewhere?'

'He goes out by eight but he's down there about a quarter of a mile ahead, felling a dead larch. Can't you hear the saw?'

The whine of it, coming then, was the first Burden had heard. From the trees ahead came the harsh cry of a jay. 'Then what was it you and the Griffins did quarrel about, Mr Harrison?'

'That's private,' Harrison said gruffly. 'A private matter between Brenda and me. She'd be finished if that got out, so I'm saying no more.'

'In a murder case,' Burden said with the deceptive smooth mildness he had learned from Wexford, 'as I have already told your wife, there is no such thing as privacy for those involved in the enquiry.'

'We're not involved in any enquiry!'

'I'm afraid you are. I'd like you to think about this matter, Mr Harrison, and decide whether you'd like to tell us about it, or your wife would, or the two of you together. Whether you'd like to tell me

122

or DS Vine and whether it's to be here or at the police station, because you're going to tell us and there'll be no two ways about it. See you later.'

He walked off along the path through the pinetum, leaving Harrison standing and staring after him. Harrison called out something but Burden didn't hear what it was and he didn't look back. He rolled the fir cone between the palms of his hands like someone with a worry egg, and he found the feeling good. When he saw the Land-Rover ahead and Gabbitas operating the chain saw, he put the fir cone into his pocket.

John Gabbitas was dressed in the protective clothing, blade-repellent trousers, gloves and boots, mask and goggles, which sensible younger woodsmen put on before using a chain saw. After the hurricane of 1987 surgical wards of the local hospitals, Burden recalled, had been populated by amateur tree-fellers with self-amputations of feet and hands. Daisy's description of the gunman, now on tape, returned to him. She had described the mask he wore as 'like a woodsman's'. When he saw Burden, Gabbitas switched off the saw and came over. He lowered his visor and pushed up the mask and goggles.

'We're still interested in anyone you might have seen when you were coming home last Tuesday.'

'I've told you I didn't see anyone.'

Burden sat down on a log, patted the smooth dry area of bark beside him. Gabbitas came reluctantly to sit there. He listened, his expression mildly indignant, while Burden told him of Joanne Garland's visit.

'I didn't see her, I don't know her. I mean, I didn't pass any car or see any car. Why don't you ask *her*?'

'We can't find her. She's missing.' He said, though it was unusual for him to announce moves to possible suspects, 'In fact, we start searching these woods today.' He looked hard at Gabbitas. 'For her body.'

'I came home at twenty past eight,' Gabbitas said doggedly. 'I can't prove it because I was alone, I didn't see anyone. I came along the Pomfret Monachorum road and I didn't pass a car or meet a car. There were no cars outside Tancred House and no car at the side of it or outside the kitchens. I *know* that, I'm telling you the truth.'

Burden thought, I find it hard to believe that coming at that time you didn't see both cars. That you saw neither, I find impossible to

123

believe. You're lying and your only motive for lying must be a very serious one indeed. But Joanne Garland's car was in her garage. Had she come in some other vehicle and if so, where was it? Could she have come in a taxi?

'What did you do before you came here?'

The question seemed to surprise Gabbitas.

'Why do you ask?'

'It's the kind of question,' Burden said patiently, 'that does get asked in a murder enquiry. For instance, how did you come to get this job?'

Gabbitas back-tracked. Having considered for a long silent moment, he reverted to Burden's first query. 'I've got a degree in forestry. I told you I do a bit of teaching. The hurricane, as they call it, the storm of 1987, that got me started really. As a result of that there was more work than all the woodsmen in the county could handle. I even made a bit of money, for a change. I was working near Midhurst.' He looked up, slyly, it seemed to Burden. 'At that place, as a matter of fact, where I was the evening this business happened.'

'Where you were coppicing and no one saw you.'

Gabbitas made an impatient gesture. He used his hands a lot to express his feelings. 'I told you, mine is a lonely job. You haven't got people keeping an eye on you all the time. Last winter, I mean the winter before last, the major part of the work there was coming to an end and I saw this job advertised.'

'What, in a magazine? In the local rag?'

'In *The Times*,' said Gabbitas, with a little smile. 'Davina Flory interviewed me herself. She gave me a copy of her tree book but I can't say I actually read it.' He moved his hands again. 'It was the house which attracted me.'

He said it quickly, for all the world, thought Burden, as if to forestall being asked if the attraction had been the girl.

'And now if you'll excuse me, I'd like to get this tree down before it falls down and does a lot of unnecessary damage.'

Burden made his way back through the woods and the pinetum, this time crossing the garden and making for the wide gravelled area beyond which the stables were. Wexford's car was there, two police vans and DS Vine's Vauxhall as well as his own car. He went inside.

Wexford he found in an uncharacteristic attitude, confronting and gazing at a computer screen. Gerry Hinde's computer screen. The Chief Inspector looked up and Burden was shocked by his face, by

124

that grey look, those surely new ageing lines, something like misery in his eyes. It was as if Wexford were, for a brief moment, out of control of his face, but then he seemed to make some inner adjustment and his expression returned to normal, or nearly so. Hinde sat at the computer keyboard, having summoned on to the screen a long, and to Burden impenetrable, list.

Wexford, recalling Daisy Flory's sentiments, would have liked someone in whom he could freely confide. Dora was in this matter unsympathetic. He would dearly have liked someone he could talk to of Sheila's avowal that he, her father, was prejudiced against Augustine Casey and determined to hate him. That she was so in love with Casey as to be able to say, strange as it might sound, as to be discovering what that meant for the first time. That if it came to a choice – and this was the worst thing – she would 'cleave' (her curious biblical word) to Casey and turn her back on her parents.

All this, expressed tête-à-tête while out on an unhappy walk, Casey being in bed recovering from the brandy, had cut him to the heart. As Daisy might put it. If there was any comfort to be found it was in the knowledge that Sheila had the offer of a role she couldn't forgo and Casey was off to Nevada.

His wretchedness showed in his face, he knew that, and he did his best to wipe it away. Burden saw the effort he made.

'They've started searching the woods, Reg.'

Wexford moved away. 'It's a big area. Can we rope in some of the locals to help?'

'It's only missing kids they're interested in. They won't turn out for adult corpses for love or money.'

'And we're offering neither,' said Wexford.

# 12

'He's away,' Margaret Griffin said.

'Away where?'

'He's a grown-up man, isn't he? I don't ask him where he's going and when he's coming home, all that. He may live at home but he's a grown man, he can do as he likes.'

At mid-morning the Griffins had been drinking coffee and watching television. No coffee was offered to Burden and Barry Vine. Barry said to Burden afterwards that Terry and Margaret Griffin looked much older than they were, elderly already, set into a routine, which was apparent if not explicit, of television-watching, shopping, small regular meals, togetherness in solitude and early bedtimes. They answered Burden's questions with resigned truculence that threatened, at any moment, to yield to paranoia.

'Does Andy often go away?'

She was a small round white-haired woman with bulging blue eyes. 'He's nothing to keep him here, has he? I mean, he's not going to get work, is he? Not with another two hundred laid off at Myringham Electrics last week.'

'Is he an electrician?'

'Turn his hand to anything, will Andy,' said Terry Griffin, 'if he gets the chance. He's not one of your unskilled workers, you know. He's been PA to a very important businessman, has Andy.'

'An American gentleman. He placed implicit trust in Andy. Used to go backwards and forwards abroad and he left everything in Andy's hands.'

'Andy had the run of his house, had his keys, let to drive his car, the lot.'

Taking this with more than a grain of salt, Burden said, 'Does he go away looking for work, then?'

'I told you, I don't know and I don't ask.'

Barry said, 'I think you should know, Mr Griffin, that though you told us Andy went out at six last Tuesday, according to the friends he said he was with, no one saw him that evening. He didn't do the round of the pubs with them and he didn't meet them in the Chinese restaurant.'

'What friends he said he was with? He never told us no friends he was with. He went to other pubs, didn't he?'

'That remains to be seen, Mr Griffin,' said Burden. 'Andy must know the Tancred estate very well. Spent his childhood there, did he?'

'I don't know about "estate",' said Mrs Griffin. '"Estate's" a lot of houses, isn't it? There's only the two houses there and that great place where *they* live. Lived, I should say.'

Demesne, Burden thought. How would it be if he had said that instead? A lifetime of police work had taught him never to explain if he could avoid it. 'The woods, the grounds, Andy knows them well?'

'Of course he does. He was a little kid of four when we first went there and that girl, that granddaughter, was a baby. Now you'd think it'd have been normal for them to play together, wouldn't you? Andy would have liked that, he used to say, "Why can't I have a little sister, Mum?" and I had to say, "God isn't going to send us any more babies, lovely", but let her play with him? Oh, no, he wasn't good enough, not for little Miss Precious. There was only the two children there and they wasn't allowed to play together.'

'And him calling himself a Labour MP,' said Terry Griffin. He gave a low hoot of laughter. 'No wonder they kicked him out at the last election.'

'So Andy never went in the house?'

'I wouldn't say that.' Margaret Griffin was suddenly huffy. 'I wouldn't say that at all. Why d'you say that? He'd come with me sometimes when I went to help out. They had a housekeeper woman living next door on her own before those Harrisons came but she couldn't do the lot, not when they had company. Andy'd come with me then, go all over the house with me, whatever they said. Mind you, I don't reckon he ever did after he was – well, ten, like.'

This was her first mention of Ken and Brenda Harrison, the first

127

indication either of them had given of the existence of their erstwhile neighbours.

'When he goes away, Mrs Griffin,' Barry put in, 'how long is he usually away for?'

'Might be a couple of days, might be a week.'

'I understand you weren't on speaking terms with Mr and Mrs Harrison at the time you left . . .'

Burden was cut short by the crowing Margaret Griffin made. More than anything else it was like the wordless utterance of a heckler at a meeting. Or, as Karen said afterwards, a child's jeer at a playmate proved wrong, a reiterated, 'Aah, aah, aah!'

'I knew it! You said, didn't you, Terry, you said they'd get on to that. It'll come out now, you said, for all Mr Harvey *Labour* Copeland's promises. They'll get hold of that to smear poor Andy after all this time.'

In his wisdom, Burden didn't betray by the movement of a muscle or the flicker of an eyelid that he hadn't the faintest idea what she meant. He maintained a rather stern omniscient gaze as they told him.

The valuation of Davina Flory's jewellery joined the rest of Gerry Hinde's data on the computer.

Barry Vine discussed it with Wexford. 'A lot of villains would consider thirty thousand pounds worth killing three people for, sir.'

'Knowing they'd get maybe half that for it in the sort of markets they use. Well, yes, maybe. We've got no other motive.'

'Revenge is a motive. Some real or imaginary injury perpetrated by Davina or Harvey Copeland. Daisy Flory had a motive. So far as we know, she inherits and no one else does. She's the only one left. I know it's a bit far-fetched, sir, but if we're talking motives . . .'

'She shot her whole family and wounded herself? Or an accomplice did? Like her lover Andy Griffin?'

'All right. I know.'

'I don't think the place interests her much, Barry. She hasn't realised yet what sort of money and property she's come into.'

Vine turned from his computer screen. 'I've been talking to Brenda Harrison, sir. She says she and the Griffins quarrelled because she didn't like Mrs Griffin hanging washing out in the garden on a Sunday.'

'You believe that?'

'I think it shows Brenda's got more imagination than I gave her credit for.'

Wexford laughed, then became instantly serious. 'We can be sure of one thing, Barry. This crime was committed by someone who didn't know this place and these people at all and by someone else who knew both very well indeed.'

'One in the know and one to take instruction from him?'

'I couldn't put it better myself,' said Wexford.

He was pleased with Burden's sergeant. You must not say, even to yourself, when someone had died a heroic death, or any death at all, that his replacement was a positive improvement or that tragedy was a blessing in disguise. But the feeling was there, or just the inescapable relief that Martin's successor was so promising.

Barry Vine was a strong muscular man of medium height. If he had held himself less well he might have been called short. Not exactly secretly but certainly privately, he went in for weight lifting. He had reddish hair, short and thick, the kind that recedes but never goes bald, and a small moustache that had grown dark, not red. Some people always look the same and are instantly recognisable. Their faces can be conjured up by memory and screened on the inner eye. Barry's was not like that. There was something protean about him, so that in certain lights and at certain angles you would have called him a sharp-featured man with a hard jawline, while at others his nose and mouth looked almost feminine. But his eyes never varied. They were rather small, a fleckless, very dark blue, that fixed friend and suspect alike with an unvarying steady gaze.

Wexford, whom his wife called a liberal, tried to be tolerant and forbearing, and often succeeded (or so he believed) in being merely irascible. Until his second marriage it had never occurred to Burden – or he had not listened when these things had been pointed out to him – that there might be any wisdom or virtue in holding views other than those of an inflexible conservative. He would have found nothing to dispute in the notion of the police force as the Tory Party with helmet and truncheon.

Barry Vine thought little about politics. He was the essential Englishman, more English in a curious way than either of his superiors. He voted for the party which had done most for him and his immediate circle in the recent past. It mattered very little whether they called themselves right or left wing. 'Most for him' meant, in his book, most in the area of finance, saving him money, reducing taxes and prices, and making life more comfortable.

While Burden believed that the world would be a better place if others behaved more like he did, and Wexford that things would improve if people learned to think, Vine made no incursions into even such primitive metaphysics. For him there existed a large (but not large enough) population of decent law-abiding people who worked and owned houses and raised families in varying degrees of prosperity, and a swarm of others, instantly recognisable by him even if they had, as yet, committed no offence. The interesting thing was that this was not a matter of class, as it might be in Burden's case. He could spot, he said, a potential villain even if this person had a title, a Porsche and several million in the bank; an accent like an art history don at Cambridge or the intonation of the man who digs up the roads. Vine was no snob and often started off with a bias towards the road-digger. His villain-spotting rested on quite other pointers, something intuitive perhaps, though Vine called it common sense.

Therefore, when he found himself in the Myringham pub called the Slug and Lettuce, having discovered that this was where Andy Griffin's friends congregated most evenings, his antennae were quickly at work assessing the criminal potential of the four men for whom he had bought halves of Abbot.

Two of them were unemployed. That hadn't inhibited their regular attendance at the Slug and Lettuce, which Wexford would have excused on the grounds that human beings need circuses as well as bread, which Burden would have called fecklessness but which Vine set down as characteristic of men on the lookout for lucrative ways to break the law. One of the others was an electrician, grumbling about a fall-off in work caused by recession, the fourth a messenger for an overnight delivery company who described himself as a 'mobile courier'.

A phrase particularly offensive to Vine's ears was that so often heard in court, uttered by defendants or even witnesses: 'I might have been.' What did it mean? Nothing. Less than nothing. Anybody, after all, might have been almost anywhere or done almost anything.

So when the unemployed man called Tony Smith said that Andy Griffin 'might have been' in the Slug and Lettuce on the night of 11 March, Vine ignored him. The others had already told him, days ago, that they hadn't seen him that evening. Kevin Lewis, Roy Walker and Leslie Sedlar were adamant that Andy hadn't been with them, nor

130

afterwards at the Panda Cottage. They were less positive about his present whereabouts.

Tony Smith said he 'might have been in the old Slug' on Sunday evening. The others couldn't say. That was one evening on which they gave the pub a miss.

'He goes up north,' Leslie Sedlar offered.

'Is that what he tells you, or do you know it?'

This was a distinction hard for any of them to make. Tony Smith insisted that he knew it.

'He goes up north with the lorry. He goes up regular, don't he?'

'He hasn't got a job any more,' said Vine. 'He hasn't had a job for a year.'

'When he had his driving job he went up regular.'

'How about now?'

He said he went up north, so he did. They believed him. The fact was they weren't much interested in where Andy went. Why should they be? Vine asked Kevin Lewis, whom he had assessed as the most sensible and probably the most law-abiding, where he thought Andy was now.

'Off on his bike,' Lewis said.

'Where, then? Manchester? Liverpool?'

They barely seemed to know where those places were. To Kevin Lewis, Liverpool dredged up recollections of his 'old man' talking about something popular in his youth called the Mersey Sound.

'He goes up north then. Suppose I said he doesn't, he hangs about down here?'

Roy Walker shook his head. 'He don't. Not Andy. Andy'd be in the old Slug.'

Vine knew when he was beaten. 'Where does his money come from?'

'He gets the dole, I reckon,' said Lewis.

'And that's it? That's all?' Keep it simple. No use asking about 'supplementary sources of income'. 'He's no other money coming in?'

It was Tony Smith who answered. 'He might have.'

They were silenced. They had no more to offer. An enormous strain had been put on their imaginations and the result was to exhaust them. More Abbot might have helped – 'might have'! – but Vine felt the game wasn't worth the candle.

\*

Mrs Virson's voice was loud, expansive, the product of an expensive girls' boarding school attended some forty-five years before. She opened the front door of The Thatched House to him and welcomed him in with a kind of high graciousness. The floral printed dress she wore upholstered her like a voluminous chair cover. Her hair had been done that day. The scrolls and undulations looked as fixed as if they had been carved. It was unlikely that all this was for him, but something had happened to change her attitude to him since his previous visit – Daisy's own insistence on her willingness to see and talk to him?

'Daisy's asleep, Mr Wexford. She's still very deeply shocked, you know, and I insist on her having plenty of rest.'

He nodded, having no comment to make.

'She'll be awake in time for her tea. These young things have a very healthy appetite, I've noticed, however much they may have been through. Shall we go in here and wait for her? I expect there are things you want to chat to me about, aren't there?'

He was not the man to neglect such an opportunity. If Joyce Virson had something to say to him, which was what 'chat' must mean, he would listen and hope for the best. But when they were in Mrs Virson's drawing room, sitting in faded chintz-covered chairs and facing each other across an arts-and-crafts coffee table, she seemed to have no inclination to begin a conversation. She was not embarrassed or awkward or even diffident. She was simply thoughtful and perhaps doubted where to begin. He was very wary of helping her. In his position any help would look like interrogation.

She said suddenly, 'Of course what happened up there at Tancred House was a terrible thing. After I heard about it I didn't sleep for two whole nights. It was simply the most appalling thing I've ever heard in the whole course of my life.'

He waited for the 'but'. People who began like that, with an admission of their appreciation of tragedy or extreme misfortune, usually went on to qualify it. Initial empathy was to be an excuse for subsequent abuse.

There was no 'but'. She surprised him by her directness. 'My son wants Daisy to be engaged to him.'

'Really?'

'Mrs Copeland didn't like the idea. I suppose I should call her Davina Flory or Miss Flory or something, but old habits die hard, don't they? I'm sorry, I suppose I'm old-fashioned, but a married

132

woman will always be "Mrs" and her husband's name to me.' She waited for Wexford to say something and when he said nothing, continued, 'No, she didn't care for the idea. Of course I don't mean she had anything against Nicholas. It was just some silly notion – I'm sorry but I thought it silly – about Daisy having her life to lead before she settled down. I could have said to her that when she was Daisy's age girls got married just as young as they could.'

'Did you?'

'Did I what?'

'You said you could have said this to her. Did you in fact say it?'

A pucker of wariness crossed Mrs Virson's face. It passed. She smiled. 'It was hardly my business to interfere.'

'What did Daisy's mother think?'

'Oh, really, it wouldn't have mattered what Naomi thought. Naomi didn't have opinions. You see, Mrs Copeland was much more like a mother than a grandmother to Daisy. *She* made all the decisions for her. I mean, where she went to school and all that. Oh, she had very big ideas for Daisy, or Davina as she insisted on calling her, most confusing. She had her whole future mapped out, university first, Oxford *naturally,* and then poor little Daisy was to have a year travelling. Not anywhere a young girl would want to go to, I mean not Bermuda or the south of France or anywhere nice, but places in Europe with art galleries and history, Rome and Florence and those sort of places. And then she was to go on doing something at another university, if you please, another degree or whatever they call them. I'm sorry, but I don't see the purpose of all this education for a pretty young girl. Mrs Copeland's idea was for her to bury herself at some university, she wanted her to be a – what's the name I want?'

'An academic?'

'Yes, that's right. Poor little Daisy was to have got there by the time she was twenty-five and then she was supposed to write her first book. I'm sorry, but it just seems ridiculous to me.'

'What about Daisy herself. How did she feel?'

'What does a girl of that age know? She knows nothing about life, does she? Oh, if you go on talking about Oxford and make it sound a glamorous place and then you keep saying how wonderful Italy is and seeing this picture and that statue, and how much more you can appreciate things if you've been educated in this way and that – well,

133

naturally, it has some effect on you. You're so impressionable at that age, you're just a baby.'

'Marrying,' said Wexford, 'would of course put a stop to all that.'

'Mrs Copeland may have been married three times but I don't think she was too keen on marriage just the same.' She leant towards him confidingly, lowering her voice and looking briefly over her shoulder as if someone else was in a far corner of the room. 'I don't know this, I mean I don't actually know it, it's pure guesswork but I think it's pretty sound – I'm positive Mrs Copeland wouldn't have turned a hair if Nicholas and Daisy had wanted to live together without marriage. She was obsessed with sex, you know. At her age! She'd probably have welcomed a relationship, she was all for Daisy having experience.'

'What sort of experience?' he asked curiously.

'Oh, you mustn't take me up on every little thing I say, Mr Wexford. I mean, she used to say she wanted her to *live*. She'd really *lived,* she used to say, and I suppose she had with all those husbands and all that travelling. But marriage, no, she wasn't at all happy about that idea.'

'Would you like your son to marry Daisy?'

'Oh, *yes,* I would. She's such a sweet girl. And clever, of course, and good-looking. I'm sorry, but I shouldn't like my son to marry a plain girl. I don't expect you think that's very nice but it does seem such a waste, a handsome man with a plain wife.' Joyce Virson preened herself a very little. There was no other word for that slight elongating of her neck, for the way she ran a thick finger along her jawline. 'We're a good-looking family on both sides.' The smile she gave Wexford was arch, was nearly flirtatious. 'Of course the poor little thing's madly in love with him. You've only got to see the way she follows him with her eyes. She adores him.'

Wexford thought she was going to preface her next remarks with her usual expression of sorrow for an opinion she very obviously did not in the least regret, but she only elaborated on Daisy's qualifications for a union with a member of the Virson family. Daisy was so fond of *her,* had such nice manners, was so even-tempered and good-humoured.

'And so rich,' said Wexford.

Mrs Virson actually jumped. She started as violently as someone in the early stages of a seizure. Her voice rose twenty or thirty decibels.

'That has nothing whatsoever to do with it. When you look at the size of this house and the standing we have in the community, you can hardly imagine there's any shortage of money, surely. My son has a very good income, he's quite able to support a wife in the . . . '

He thought she was going to add something about the style to which Daisy was accustomed, but she checked herself and glowered at him. Sick of her hypocrisy and affectations, he had decided the time had come for a sharp thrust below the belt. It had gone home better than he had hoped for. He smiled to himself.

'You're not worried she may be too young?' he said. Now the smile was extended to her as well, wide and disarming. 'You called her a baby just now.

Joyce Virson was saved from answering by the entry of Daisy into the room. He had heard her footsteps on the hall floor as he spoke the word 'baby'. She gave him a wan smile. Her arm was still bandaged but less bulkily and the sling was lighter. This, he realised, was the first time he had seen her standing up, moving about. She was thinner than he had expected, her shape more fragile.

'What am I too young for?' she said. 'I'm eighteen today, it's my birthday.'

Mrs Virson shrieked. 'Daisy, you terrible girl, why didn't you tell us? I hadn't the least idea, you didn't say a word.'

She attempted an astonished laugh but Wexford could tell she was very displeased. She was chagrined. Daisy's revelation gave the lie to her claims of an intimate knowledge of the young woman staying in her house.

'I suppose you just dropped a hint to Nicholas, so that he could plan a surprise.'

'As far as I know, he doesn't know either. He won't remember. I have no one in the world now to remember my birthday.' She looked at Wexford, said lightly, stagily, 'Goodness, how sad!'

'Many happy returns of the day.' He used the old-fashioned formula.

'Ah, you're tactful, you're careful. You couldn't say "Happy birthday", could you? Not to me. It would be frightful, it would be an insult. Will you remember my birthday next year, d'you think? Will you say to yourself on the eve of it, it's Daisy's birthday tomorrow? You may be the only one who will.'

'What nonsense, dear. Nicholas will certainly remember. It'll be your job to keep him up to that. I'm sorry, but men need a hint, you know, not to say a little twist of the arm.' Joyce Virson's expression

135

was ferociously arch. Daisy allowed her eyes to meet Wexford's for a short moment and looked away. Not looking at him, she said, 'Shall we go in the other room, then?'

'Oh, why not stay here, dear? It's nice and warm in here and I won't listen to what you're saying. I'll be too wrapped up in my book. I won't hear a word.'

Determined not to speak to Daisy in Mrs Virson's presence, before making this point he waited to hear what Daisy would say. She looked so far away, so remotely sorrowful, that he expected an apathetic acquiescence, but instead she spoke firmly.

'No, it's better it should be private. We won't turn you out of your room, Joyce.'

He followed her to the 'little den', the room where they had been on Saturday. There she remarked, 'She means well.' He marvelled at how young she could be – and how old. 'Yes, I'm eighteen today. After the funeral I think I'll go home. Quite soon after. I can do what I like now I'm eighteen, can't I? Absolutely what I like?'

'As far as any of us can, yes. Apart from breaking the law with impunity, you can do as you please.'

She sighed heavily. 'I don't want to break the law. I don't know what I want to do but I think I'd be better at home.'

Warningly, he said, 'Perhaps you don't quite realise how you'll feel confronting your home again. After what happened there. It will bring that night back to you very painfully.'

'That night is always with me,' she said. 'It can't be there more strongly than it is every time I close my eyes. That's when I see the picture of it, you see. When I close my eyes. I see that table – before and after. I wonder if I'll ever be able to bear sitting at a dining table again? She gives me my meals on a tray here. I asked for that.' She was silent, smiled suddenly and looked at him. He saw a strange glow in her dark eyes. 'We always talk about me. Tell me about you. Where do you live? Are you married? Have you got children? Have you got people who remember your birthday?'

He told her where he lived, that he was married, had two daughters, three grandchildren. Yes, they remembered his birthday, more or less.

'I wish I had a father.'

Why had he neglected to ask about this? 'But surely you have? You see him sometimes?'

'I've never seen him. Or not that I remember. Mum and he were

136

divorced when I was a baby. He lives in London but he's never shown any sign of wanting to see me. I don't mean I wish I had him, I wish I had *a* father.'

'Yes, I expect your – er, your grandmother's husband filled the place of a father in your life.'

It was unmistakable, the incredulity in the look she gave him. She made a sound in the back of her throat, somewhere between a snort and a cough. 'Has Joanne turned up?'

'No, Daisy. We're worried about her.'

'Oh, nothing will have happened to her. What could have?'

Her serene innocence only served to exacerbate his concern. 'When she came to see your mother on Tuesdays,' he said, 'did she always come by car?'

'Of course.' She looked surprised. 'Oh, you mean, did she walk? It would be a good five miles. Anyway, Joanne never walked anywhere. I don't know why she lived here, she hated country things, everything to do with the country. I suppose it was on account of her old mum. I'll tell you what, she did sometimes come by taxi. It wasn't that her car had broken down. She liked a drink, did Joanne, and then she'd be scared to drive.'

'What can you tell me about some people called Griffin?'

'They used to work for us.'

'The son, Andy, have you seen him since they left?'

She gave him a curious look. It was as if she marvelled that he had hit on something so unexpected or secret. 'I did once. How funny you should ask. It was in the woods. I was walking in the woods and I saw him. You probably don't know our woods at all but it was near the by-road, that little road that goes off to the east, it was near where the walnuts are. He may have seen me, I don't know, I should have said something to him, asked him what he was doing, but I didn't, I don't know why. It *frightened* me, seeing him like that. I didn't tell anyone. He was trespassing, Davina would have hated that, but I didn't tell her.'

'When was this?'

'Oh, last autumn sometime. October, I should think.'

'How would he have got here?'

'He used to have a motorbike. I expect he still has.'

'His father says he had a job with an American businessman. I had a hunch – that's all it was – they might have got in touch through your family.'

She thought. 'Davina would never have recommended him. I suppose it could be Preston Littlebury. But if Andy worked for him it would only have been – well . . .'

'As a driver perhaps?'

'Not even that. Maybe to clean his car.'

'All right. It's probably not important. One last question. Could the other man, the man you didn't see, leave the house and start the car – could that have been Andy Griffin? Think before you answer. Take it as a possibility and then think if there was anything, anything at all, that might have identified him with Andy Griffin.'

She was silent. She seemed neither shocked nor incredulous. It was plain she was obeying his instruction and thinking it over. At last she said, 'It *could* have been. Can I say there was nothing to make me certain it wasn't? That's all I can say.'

He left her then, telling her he would be at the funeral on Thursday morning.

'I'll tell you my idea of what happened, if you like,' Burden said. They were in his house, his son Mark in pyjamas on his lap, Jenny having gone to her evening class in advanced German. 'I'll get you another beer and then I'll tell you. No, you can get the beer so I don't have to shift him.'

Wexford came back with two cans and two steins.

'Those tankards, you see they're identical. There's a third one on the shelf. It's quite an interesting illustration in economics. The one you've got – let me have a closer look – yes, the one you've got Jean and I bought on our honeymoon in Innsbruck for five shillings. Before decimal coinage, you see, well before. The one I've got, it's actually a fraction smaller, I bought ten years ago when we took the kids there. Same difference and it cost four quid. The one on the shelf's a good deal smaller and in my opinion not such a good piece of work. Jenny and I bought it in Kitzbühel while we were on holiday last summer. Ten pounds fifty. What does that tell you?'

'The cost of living's gone up. I didn't need three beer mugs to tell me that. Could we have your Tancred scenario instead of these disquisitions on comparative ceramics?'

Burden grinned. He said to his son rather sententiously, 'No, you can't have Daddy's beer, Mark, just as Daddy can't have your Ribena.'

138

'Poor old Daddy. I bet that's a real sacrifice. What happened on Tuesday evening, then?'

'The gunman in the bank, the one with the acne, I shall call him X.'

'That's really original, Mike.'

Burden ignored the interruption. 'The other man was Andy Griffin. Andy was the man with the knowledge, X had the gun.'

'Gun,' said Mark.

Burden put him on the floor. The little boy picked up a plastic whistle from the heap of toys, pointed it at Wexford, said, 'Bang, bang.'

'Oh, dear, Jenny doesn't like him to have guns. He hasn't in fact got a gun.'

'He has now.'

'D'you think it would be all right for him to watch half an hour's television before I put him to bed?'

'For God's sake, Mike, you've more children than I have, you should know.' When Burden still looked dubious, he said impatiently, 'So long as it's not more bloody than what you're going to tell me, and it's unlikely to be.'

Burden switched the set on. 'X and Andy set off for Tancred House in X's jeep.'

'In *what*?'

'It has to be a vehicle that can handle rough ground.'

'Where did they meet, these two, X and Andy?'

'In a pub. Maybe in the Slug and Lettuce. Andy tells X about Davina's jewellery and they make their plan. Andy knows Brenda Harrison's habits. He knows that she announces dinner every evening at seven thirty and goes home, leaving the back door unlocked.'

Wexford nodded. 'A good point in favour of Griffin's involvement.'

Looking pleased, Burden went on, 'They drive up by the main road through the gates from the B2428, but take the left-hand branch just before the wall and the courtyard are reached. Brenda has gone home, Davina Flory, Harvey Copeland, Naomi Jones and Daisy Flory are all in that conservatory place. So no one hears a vehicle arrive or sees its lights, as Andy has calculated they won't. The time is twenty-five to eight.'

139

'Cutting it fine. Suppose Brenda had been five minutes late leaving or the others five minutes early going into the dining room?'

'They weren't,' said Burden simply. He proceeded, 'X and Andy enter the house by the back way and go up the back stairs.'

'They can't have done. Bib Mew was there.'

'You can get to the back stairs without passing through the main kitchen. That's where she was, working on the freezer. In Davina's room they search for and find her jewellery and they also search the other women's bedrooms.'

'They would need to in order to take twenty-five minutes over it. Incidentally, why leave the other women's bedrooms tidy but Davina's in a mess if they searched them all?'

'I'm coming to that. They went *back* to Davina's room because Andy believed there was some more valuable piece they had missed. It was while they were flinging the stuff about in there that they were heard by the people downstairs and Harvey Copeland went to investigate. They must have assumed he was coming up the front stairs, so they went down the back . . .'

'And out of the back door with their loot to make their getaway with no harm done beyond the loss to Davina of some heavily insured jewellery she didn't much care for anyway.'

'We know it wasn't like that,' Burden said very seriously. 'They came through the house into the hall. I don't know why. Perhaps they had some reason to fear the return of Brenda or they believed Harvey was upstairs, intending to walk the length of the gallery and go down the back stairs. Whatever it was, they came into the hall and encountered Harvey, who was halfway up the stairs. He turned and saw them, immediately recognising Andy Griffin. He took a couple of steps down, shouted some threat at Andy or called to the women to phone the police . . .'

'Daisy didn't hear him if he did.'

'She's forgotten. She's admitted herself she can't recall details of what happened. She says on that tape we made, "I've tried hard to remember but something blocks it off." Harvey threatened Andy, and X shot him. He fell backwards across the bottom stairs. Andy was now obviously terrified, *more* terrified, of being recognised. He heard a woman scream from the dining room. While X kicked open the dining-room door, Andy ran to the front door and out.

'X shot the two women, he shot Daisy. From upstairs he heard someone racketing about. It was the cat but he didn't know that.

140

Daisy was on the floor, he thought she was dead, he followed Andy out of the front door where the jeep had been brought round for him. Andy had fetched the jeep from where it was parked at the back . . . '

'It won't work, Mike. This was the time Bib Mew was leaving. She was leaving on her bike from the back of the house. Daisy heard a car start up, not "brought round".'

'It's a small point. Would she swear to that, Reg? Her mother and grandmother had been shot before her eyes, she was shot, she's on the floor wounded and bleeding – just imagine the noise that Magnum would have made, for one thing – and she can differentiate between a car starting up and one being driven?'

Turning his eyes from a nature programme on lions killing and disembowelling wildebeests, Mark said happily, 'Wounded and bleeding.' He nodded and pointed the whistle at his father.

'Oh God, I must get him to bed. Just let me finish this, Mark. While Andy is round the back fetching the jeep and X is making mayhem in the dining room, Joanne Garland arrives *in a taxi*. Once again she is afraid to drive because she has had a drink or two . . . '

'Where? Who with?'

'That remains to be seen. That remains to be discovered. She paid the driver and he left. Her intention was to phone for another taxi when she was through with her book-keeping with Naomi. The time is ten past eight. She isn't supposed to be there until eight thirty but we know she was one of these over-punctual people, always early.

'The front door is open. She steps inside, perhaps she calls out. She sees Harvey's body spreadeagled across the stairs, perhaps she hears the last shot. Does she turn and run? Perhaps. Andy has appeared by now with the jeep. He jumps out and seizes her. X comes out, kills Joanne, *with the sixth and last cartridge in the chamber,* and they put her body in the back.

'Fearing they might meet someone on the road, Gabbitas, us, some visitor, they take off *through* the wood, using paths negotiable by a jeep but not by your average saloon car.' Burden picked up his son, switched off the television. The little boy was still grasping his whistle. 'Subject to a few minor amendments, I suggest that's the only way it could have happened.'

Wexford said, 'What did the Harrisons and the Griffins quarrel about?'

Indignation had briefly contorted Burden's face. Was that all? Was that the only reception his analysis was going to get? He shrugged. 'Andy tried to rape her.'

'*What?*'

'That's what she says. The Griffins say *she* made advances to him. Apparently, he tried a sort of blackmail on those grounds and Brenda told Davina Flory. Hence, if we were to be kept out of it, the Griffins had to go.'

'We'd better have him in, Mike.'

'We will,' said Burden, and he carried his son away to bed, Mark firing the whistle over his shoulder and shouting, 'Wounded and bleeding, wounded and bleeding', all the way upstairs.

# 13

Had they no friends but the Virsons and Joanne Garland, this family who were wealthy and distinguished, whose nucleus was a famous writer and an economist and former MP? Where were Daisy's school friends? Their local acquaintances?

These questions had interested Wexford from the first. But the nature of the crime was such as to preclude hitherto law-abiding members of the public from being involved, and his usual investigation in a murder case of everyone known to the victims had not been carried out. It had simply occurred to him, while talking to Daisy, and to a lesser extent to the Harrisons and Gabbitas, that there seemed to be a dearth of Flory family friends.

The funeral showed him how right he had been – and how wrong. In spite of the fame of one of the dead and the distinction, by association with her, of the others, he had supposed those who mourned Davina Flory and her family would wait to attend the memorial service. Daisy, as well as Joyce Virson, had said a service would be held. St James's, Piccadilly, had been suggested, in two months' time. The service in Kingsmarkham parish church would surely have a small congregation, a few people only proceeding to the distant cemetery. As it turned out, they were queuing up.

Jason Sebright from the *Kingsmarkham Courier* was taking names at the church gates when he arrived. Wexford quickly perceived that the queue was the press and he pushed past them producing his warrant card. St Peter's was very large, one of those English churches that would be called cathedrals anywhere else, with an enormous nave, ten side chapels and a chancel as big as a village church. It was nearly full.

Only the front pews on the right-hand side awaited occupants, and

143

a few scattered seats among the congregation. Wexford made his way to one of these, a vacant space next to the aisle on the left. The last time he was there had been to give Sheila away when she married Andrew Thorverton, the last time he had sat like this, in the body of the church, was to hear her banns called. A marriage come to grief, a love affair or two, and now Augustine Casey . . . He pushed it out of mind and eyed the congregation. A voluntary was playing, Bach probably.

The first person he recognised was someone he had met at a book launch, taken there by Amyas Ireland. The book, he recalled, had been a family saga with a policeman in every generation since Victorian times, its author's editor this man three rows in front of him. All the others in the pew looked like publishers to him, though he couldn't have said how. He identified (again without much to go on) a plump yellow-haired woman in a large black hat as Davina Flory's agent.

A preponderance of elderly women, some of them scholarly-looking, in groups or sitting alone, led him to believe these were old cronies of Davina, perhaps from as far back as Oxford days. From photographs he had seen in the newspapers, he recognised a distinguished woman novelist now in her seventies. Wasn't that the Minister for the Arts in the pew next to her? His name escaped Wexford for the moment, but that was who it was. A man with a red rose in his buttonhole – in questionable taste? – he had seen on television on the Opposition benches. An old parliamentary friend of Harvey Copeland's? Joyce Virson had secured herself a place very near the front. Of her son there was no sign. And there wasn't a young girl in sight.

Just as he was wondering who would take the empty seat next to him, Jason Sebright hurried in to sit in it.

'Hordes of glitterati here,' he said happily, barely able to conceal his enjoyment of the occasion. 'I'm going to do a piece called "The Friends of a Great Woman". Even if I get nine refusals out of ten I should get at least four exclusive interviews.'

'I'd rather have my job than yours,' said Wexford.

'I've learned my technique from US TV. I'm half American, I spend my vacations there visiting with my mom.' This he said in a horrible parody of a midwest accent. 'We've a lot to learn in this country. At the *Courier* they're dead scared all the time of treading on people's toes, everyone's got to be handled with gloves on and what I . . . '

144

'Sshh, will you? It's going to start.'

The music had stopped. A hush fell. There was no whispering. It was as if the congregation had even ceased to breathe. Sebright shrugged and put one finger up to his lips. The silence was of a kind that only ever prevails in a church, oppressive, cold, but for some transcendent. Everyone was waiting, expectant and gradually enclosed by awe.

The first chords from the organ broke the silence with a heavy and terrible multiplication of decibels. Wexford could hardly believe his ears. Not the *Dead March in Saul,* no one ever had the *Dead March in Saul* any more. But that was what it was. Dum-dum-de-boom-dum-de-dum-de-dum-dum-boom, he murmured under his breath. The three coffins were borne up the aisle with ineffable slowness in time to that wonderful and dreadful music. The men who supported them on their shoulders moved in the steps of a stately pavane. Someone with a sense of the dramatic had arranged for that, someone young and intense and steeped in tragedy.

Daisy.

She followed the three coffins and she was alone. Or, rather, Wexford thought she was alone until he saw Nicholas Virson, who must have escorted her in, searching for an empty seat. She was in deepest mourning, or perhaps only in the clothes every girl her age had in abundance in her wardrobe, funereal garments habitually worn to discos and parties. Daisy's dress was a narrow black tube, reaching to her black-booted ankles. Vague black draperies covered her, among them something that could almost be discerned as a coat of roughly coat shape. Her face was paper-white, her mouth painted crimson, and she stared ahead of her, moving at last alone into that empty front pew.

'I am the resurrection and the life, saith the Lord . . . '

Her sense of the dramatic – and of the fitting? – had prompted her also to make sure the Prayer Book of 1662 was used. Was he attributing too much to her and was that Mrs Virson's work or even the parson's good taste? She was a remarkable girl. He was aware of a sense of warning, of alarm, whose source he couldn't trace.

'Lord, let me know mine end and the number of my days, that I may be certified how long I have to live . . . '

The wind had not been noticeable in the town. Perhaps, on the other hand, it had only got up in the past half-hour. Wexford remembered some sort of gale warning in the forecast of the night before. The wind had a knife edge feel to it as it whistled across this place of burial that a few years ago had been a meadow on a hillside.

Why burial and not cremation? More of Daisy's dramatic ideas, perhaps, or else a wish expressed in wills. There was to be no will-reading after this, the solicitor had told him, no anything after this, none of that gathering together for sherry and cake. 'In the circumstances,' said the solicitor, 'it would be wholly inappropriate.'

No flowers. Daisy, it appeared, had asked for donations instead to a number of causes, none of them likely to meet with a sympathetic response from many of these people, charities for Bangladesh, a fund to counter famine in Ethiopia, the Labour Party and the Cats' Protection League.

A single grave had been prepared for the married couple. The one beside it was for Naomi Jones. Each was lined with sheets of artificial turf of a sicklier green than the grass. The coffins went down and one of those aged scholars stepped forward to cast a handful of earth upon the last of Davina Flory.

'Come, ye blessed children of my Father, receive the kingdom prepared for you from the beginning of the world . . . '

It was over, the drama past. The most significant thing now for all was the biting of the wind. Collars were turned up, arms hugged shivering bodies inside inadequate clothes. Undeterred, Jason Sebright was going from person to person, boldly putting his request. Instead of the notebook of former times, he had a receiver and recording device. Wexford wasn't altogether surprised to see how many people responded favourably. Some of them very likely thought they were going out live on radio.

He had not spoken to Daisy. He watched one mourner after another approach her and saw her lips move in monosyllabic response. One old woman pressed a kiss on her white cheek.

'Oh, my dear, and poor Davina wasn't even a believer, was she?'

Another said, 'That lovely service, it does send shivers down one's spine.'

An elderly man, speaking in what Wexford called an Ivy League voice, embraced her and, and with an impulsive gesture, apparently an expression of sudden emotion, pressed her face into his neck. When she lifted her head Wexford saw her lips had left a crimson imprint on his white collar. He was a tall man, paper-thin, with a small grey moustache and a bow tie. Preston Littlebury, the erstwhile employer of Andy Griffin?

'You have my deepest sympathy, my dear, you know that.'

Wexford saw that he had been wrong about the young girls. One at any rate had braved the grimness of the day and the bad weather, a thin pale teenager in black trousers and a raincoat. The elderly woman with her was saying, 'I'm Ishbel Macsamphire, my dear. Last year in Edinburgh? Remember? With poor Davina. And then I met you with your young man. This is my granddaughter . . . '

Daisy behaved beautifully to all of them. Her sadness gave her an enormous dignity. She managed the difficult feat he had seen her achieve before, of responding with courtesy yet without a smile. One by one they moved away from her and for a moment she was alone. She stood, surveying the people as they moved towards their cars, as if searching for someone, her eyes wide, her lips a little parted. It was as if she was looking for a mourner whose presence she expected but who had not come, who had failed her. The wind snatched the long black scarf she wore and pulled it out in a fluttering streamer. She shivered, hunched herself for a moment before coming up to Wexford.

'That's over. Thank goodness. I thought I might burst out crying, or faint, but I didn't, did I?'

'Not you. Were you looking for someone who hasn't come?'

'Oh, no. Whatever gave you that idea?'

Nicholas Virson was approaching them. In spite of her denial, it must have been he she was looking for, her 'young man', for she gave a little dip of the head as if bowing to some necessity, as if resigned. She took his arm and let him lead her to his car. His mother was already seated inside it, peering through the steamy glass.

Wexford thought, as he had occasionally thought of Sheila years ago, and thought of her with accurate foresight, what an actress she would make! Well, Sheila had made an actress, but Daisy wasn't acting, Daisy was sincere. She was simply one of those people who cannot help extracting drama from their personal tragedies. Hadn't Graham Greene said somewhere that every novelist has a splinter of ice in his heart? Perhaps she would follow in her grandmother's footsteps here too.

Grandmother's footsteps. He smiled to himself as he thought of the game children played, tiptoeing up close, seeing how near they

147

could get, before the one in front with her back to them turned round, and they fled screaming . . .

'We found two sets of keys inside, sir,' said Karen. 'We found her chequebook, but no cash or credit cards.'

The house was lavishly furnished, the kitchen luxuriously appointed. In the bathroom, which was *'en suite'* with Mrs Garland's bedroom, was a bidet and a power shower, a hair dryer attached to the wall.

'As in the best hotels,' Karen said with a giggle.

'Yes, but I thought they only did that to stop the guests stealing them. This is a private house.'

Karen looked doubtful. 'Well, you couldn't lose it this way, could you? You wouldn't wonder where you'd left it last time you washed your hair.'

To Wexford it looked more as if Joanne Garland had spent money for the sake of spending it. She had hardly known what to spend her income on. An electric trouser press? Why not? Even though the clothes cupboard revealed only a single pair of trousers. A phone extension in the bathroom? No more running dripping into the bedroom, wrapped in a towel. The 'gym' contained an exercise bicycle, a rowing machine, a contraption that looked to Wexford like nothing so much as pictures he had seen of the Iron Maiden of Nuremberg, and something that might have been a treadmill.

'They used to make poor devils in workhouses stomp up and down on those,' Wexford said. 'She has it for *fun*.'

'Well, for her fitness, sir.'

'And all this, is this for her fitness?'

They were back in the bedroom where he confronted the most comprehensive collection of cosmetics and beauty products he had ever seen outside a department store. These items were not in the drawers of a dressing table or on a shelf, but contained in a large cabinet, there exclusively to accommodate them.

'There's another lot in the bathroom,' said Karen.

'This looks more like something you'd stick up your nose,' said Wexford, holding up a brown bottle with a gold top and dropper. He unscrewed the top from a jar and sniffed the contents, a thick sweet-scented yellow cream. 'You could eat this one. They don't work, do they?'

'I suppose it gives the poor old things hope,' said Karen with all

148

the arrogant indifference of twenty-three. 'You believe what you read, don't you think, sir? You believe what you read on labels. Most people do.'

'I suppose so.'

What struck him most was how tidy the place was. As if its owner was going away and had known well in advance she was going. But no one goes away without telling anyone. A woman with such a large family as Joanne Garland doesn't go away without a word to her mother, to her brothers and sisters. His mind went back to that evening and Burden's scenario. It hadn't been a satisfactory scenario but it had its points.

'How are we getting on with checking out all the cab companies in the district?'

'There are a lot of them, sir, but we're getting through them.'

He tried to think of possible reasons for a wealthy, single, middle-aged woman suddenly taking off on a trip in March without telling her family, her neighbours or her business partner. Some lover from the past who had turned up and swept her off her feet? Unlikely in the case of a hard-headed businesswoman of fifty-four. A summons from the other side of the world that someone close to her was dying? In that case, she would have told her family.

'Was her passport in the house, Karen?'

'No, sir. But she may not have had one. We could ask her sisters if she ever went abroad.'

'We could. We will.'

Back at the stables of Tancred House, a call was put through to him. It was no one he knew or had even heard of: the deputy-governor of Royal Oak Prison outside Crewe in Cheshire. Of course he knew all about Royal Oak, the famous high-security, Category B prison that was run as a therapeutic community and still, years after such theories ceased to be fashionable, held to the principle that criminals can be 'cured' by therapy. Though with just the same rate of recidivism as any other British jail, it at least appeared not to make its inmates worse.

The deputy-governor said he had a prisoner who wanted to see Wexford, who had asked for him by name. The prisoner was serving a long sentence for attempted murder and robbery with violence and at present he was in the prison hospital.

'He thinks he's going to die.'

'Is he?'

149

'I don't know. He's called Hocking, James. Known as Jem Hocking.'

'I've never heard of him.'

'He's heard of you. Kingsmarkham, isn't it? He knows Kingsmarkham. Didn't you have a police officer shot down dead there getting on for a year ago?'

'Oh, yes,' said Wexford. 'Yes, we did.'

O.k.a. George Brown. Was Jem Hocking the man who had bought a car in the name of George Brown?

Mrs Griffin told them Andy hadn't come back yet. 'But we had a phone call, didn't we, Terry? He rung up last night from up north. Where did he say he was, Terry? Manchester, was it?'

'He rung up from Manchester,' Terry Griffin said. 'He didn't want us to worry, he wanted us to know he was all right.'

'Were you worried?'

'It's not a matter of whether we was worried or not. It's a matter of Andy thinking we might be worried. We thought it was very considerate. It's not every son that'd ring up his mum and dad to tell them he was all right when he'd only been away two days. You do worry when he's on that bike. A bike wouldn't be my choice but what's a young boy to do with the price cars are? It was very considerate and thoughtful ringing us up.'

'Typical of Andy,' said his mother complacently. 'He was always a very considerate boy.'

'Did he say when he was coming back?'

'I wouldn't ask. I wouldn't expect him to tell us his every movement.'

'And you don't know his address in Manchester?'

Again Mrs Griffin had been too sensitive and the relationship too finely tuned for him to risk disturbing it by bald enquiries of that nature.

The woman called Bib admitted Wexford to the house. She wore a red tracksuit with an apron over it. When Wexford said that Mrs Harrison was expecting him she gave a sort of grunt and nodded but said not a word. She walked ahead of him with a rollicking gait like someone who has been too long on board ship.

Brenda Harrison was in the conservatory. It was very warm, faintly damp and sweet-smelling. The scent came from a pair of lemon trees in tubs of blue and white faïence. They were simultaneously in flower and fruit, the flowers white and waxy. She had been busy with watering can, houseplant food and tissues for putting a gloss on leaves.

'Though who it's all for I'm sure I don't know.'

The blue and white printed blinds were drawn up in ruffles high up in the glass roof. Queenie, the Persian, sat on one of the sills, her hyacinth eyes fixed on a bird on a branch. The bird was singing in the rain and its cadences made the cat's teeth chatter.

Brenda got up off her knees, wiped her hands on her overall and subsided into a wicker chair.

'I'd just like to hear their version, those Griffins. I'd really like to hear what they told you.'

Here Wexford refused to oblige her. He said nothing.

'Of course I'd made up my mind I wasn't going to say a word. Not to you lot, I mean. It wasn't fair on Ken. Well, that's the way I saw it. Not nice for Ken, I thought. And when you think about it, what's that Andy Griffin taking a fancy to me for some reason and trying all that funny business, what's that got to do with criminals shooting Davina and Harvey and Naomi? Well, nothing, has it?'

'Tell me about it, will you, Mrs Harrison?'

'I suppose I must. It's very distasteful. I know I look a lot younger than I am – well, people are always telling me – so maybe I shouldn't have been surprised when that Andy got fresh.'

It was an expression Wexford hadn't heard for years. He marvelled at Mrs Harrison's vanity, the delusion that made this shrivelled lined woman imagine she looked younger than her fifty-odd years. And what was there, after all, to be so pleased and proud about, in looking younger than one was? It had always perplexed him. As if there was some particular virtue attached to looking forty-five when one was fifty. And what anyway did fifty look like?

She was staring at him, seeking the words in which to reveal it or perhaps obfuscate it. 'He touched me. I nearly jumped out of my skin.' As if anticipating the question, she placed her hand against her left breast, looking away. 'It was in my own house. He'd come in the kitchen, I was having a cup of tea, so of course I gave him one. Not that I liked him, don't think that.

'He's evil. Oh, yes, I'm not exaggerating. He's not just peculiar, he's evil. You've only got to look at his eyes. He was just a little kid when we first came here, but he wasn't like other kids, he wasn't

151

normal. His mother, she wanted him allowed to play with Daisy – well, you can just see that happening, can't you? Even Naomi said no, not just Davina. He used to have these screaming tantrums, you'd hear him through the walls, it'd go on for hours. They couldn't do a thing with him.

'He can't have been a day over fourteen when I caught him here peering at me through the bathroom window. I'd got all my clothes on, thank God, but he didn't know that when he started looking, did he? That was the point, to catch me with no clothes on.'

'The *bathroom*?' Wexford said. 'What did he do, climb a tree?'

'The bathrooms are downstairs in these houses. Don't ask me why. They were built that way with the bathrooms downstairs. He only had to come through from theirs through the hedge and hang about outside. It wasn't long after that his mother told me a lady in Pomfret had complained about him for the same thing. Called him a Peeping Tom. Of course *she* said it was a wicked lie and the woman had got it in for her poor Andy, but I knew what I knew.'

'What happened in the kitchen?'

'When he touched me, d'you mean? Well, I don't want to go into details and I won't. When it was done, after he'd gone, I thought to myself, it's only because he's madly attracted to you and he can't help himself. But he could help himself when he came back next day, asking for money, couldn't he?'

Queenie gave a tap with her paw on the glass. The bird flew away. The rain suddenly came down heavily, the water lashing against the panes. The cat got down and stalked towards the door. Instead of getting up to assist her, which Wexford would have expected from such a committed animal lover, Brenda sat intently watching. It soon became clear what she was waiting for. Queenie stood up on her hind legs, took hold of the door handle with her right paw and pulled it down. The door came open and she passed through, tail erect.

'You can't tell me they're not more intelligent than any human being,' said Brenda Harrison fondly.

'I'd like to hear about this attempted rape, Mrs Harrison.'

She didn't care for the word. A deep blush coloured her worn face. 'I'm sure I don't know why you're so keen on all these details.' Having implied that Wexford's interest in the matter was of a prurient kind, she looked down, twisting her neck, and began kneading a corner of her overall. 'He touched me, like I said. I said, don't. He said, why not? Don't you like me? It's not a matter of like

152

or dislike, I said, I'm a married woman. Then he got hold of me by the shoulders and he pushed me back against the sink and started rubbing up against me. Well, you said you wanted details. It doesn't give me any pleasure talking about it.

'I struggled but he was a lot stronger than me, it stands to reason he was. I said to let me go or I'd go straight in and tell his father. He said, had I got anything on under my skirt, and he tried pulling at my skirt. I kicked at him then. There was a knife laying on the draining board, only a little knife I use for doing the veg, but I grabbed hold of it and I said I'd stick it in him if he didn't let go. Well, he let go then and called me a name. He called me an aitch, oh, ar, ee, and said it was my fault for wearing my skirts tight.'

'Did you tell his father? Did you tell anyone?'

'I thought if I kept quiet it'd all blow over. Ken's a very jealous man, I suppose it's only natural. I mean, I've known him make a scene over a fellow just looking at me on a bus. Anyway, next day that Andy came back. He knocked on the front door and I was expecting the man to service the tumble-dryer, so naturally I opened it. He pushed his way in. I said, this is it, this time you've gone too far, Andy Griffin, I'm telling your dad *and* Mr Copeland.

'He didn't touch me. He just laughed. He said I was to give him five pounds down or he'd tell Ken I'd asked him to – well, to go with me. He'd tell his mum and dad and he'd tell Ken. And folks'd believe him, he said, on account of me being older than him. "So much older" was what he said, if you must know.'

'Did you give him any money?'

'Not me. D'you think I'm daft? I wasn't born yesterday.' The irony of this last remark was entirely lost on Brenda Harrison, who went on serenely, 'I said, publish and be damned! I'd read that in a book and I'd always remembered it, don't know why. Publish and be damned, I said, go on, do your worst. He wanted five pounds down and five pounds a week till further notice. That's what he said, "till further notice".

'The minute Ken came in I told him everything. He said, come along, my girl, we're going next door to have it out with those Griffins. That'll finish them with Davina, he said. I know it's unpleasant for you, he said, but it'll soon be over and you'll feel better for knowing you did the right thing. So next door we went and I told them everything. In a quiet way, not getting excited, I just quietly told them what he'd done and about the Peeping Tom too. Of

153

course Mrs Griffin went hysterical, shouting her precious Andy wouldn't do that, him so clean and pure and not knowing what a girl was for and all that. Ken said, I'm going to Mr and Mrs Copeland – we never called them by their Christian names to those Gnffins, of course, that wouldn't have been suitable – I'm going to Mr and Mrs Copeland, he said, and he did and me with him.

'Well, the upshot of it was Davina said Andy'd have to go. They could stay but he'd have to go. The alternative – that's what she said, the alternative – was calling the police and she didn't want to do that if she could help it. Mrs Griffin wouldn't have that, she wouldn't be separated from her Andy, so they said they'd all go, Mr Griffin'd take early retirement, though what she meant by "early" I don't know. He looks knocking seventy to me.

'Of course we had to put up with them next door for weeks and weeks after that, months. Mind you, Andy had a job then, some labouring job for an American friend of Harvey's he put him on to out of the goodness of his heart, so we never saw much of *him*. I'd said to Ken, come what may, I'd said, I shan't speak a work to any of them. I'll look through them if we happen to meet outside, and that's what I did, and in the end they went like they were bound to, and Johnny Gabbitas came.'

Wexford remained silent for a moment or two. He watched the rain. Drifts of crocuses made purple stains across the green grass. The forsythia was out, brilliant yellow like sunshine on this dull wet day.

He said to Brenda Harrison, 'When did you last see Mrs Garland?'

She looked surprised at this apparent change of subject. Wexford suspected that now the matter had been brought out into the open she was not at all averse to talking of her husband's jealousy and her own irresistible attractions. She answered him rather peevishly.

'Not for months, years. I know she came up here most Tuesday nights but I never saw her. I'd always gone home.'

'Mrs Jones told you she came?'

'I don't know as she ever mentioned it,' Brenda said indifferently. 'Why should she?'

'Then . . . ?'

'How did I know? Oh, I see what you mean. She used Ken's brother's cars, didn't she?' Wexford's obvious bewilderment fetched an explanation from her. 'Between you and I, she liked a drink, did Joanne Garland. And sometimes two or three. Well, you can understand it, can't you? After a day in that shop. Beats me how they

154

ever sold a thing. It really beats me how those places keep going. Anyway, sometimes when she'd had one too many, I mean when she reckoned she was over the limit, she wouldn't drive her car, she'd give Ken's brother a ring for one of his. Well, to bring her up here for one thing and take her wherever else she might fancy going. She's rolling in money, of course, never thought twice about ringing up for a car.'

'Your brother-in-law runs a taxi service?'

Mrs Harrison put on a look of refinement, rarefied, slightly sour. 'I wouldn't put it that way. He doesn't advertise, he has a private clientele, a few special selected clients.' She became alarmed. 'It's all above board, you needn't look like that. I'll tell you his name, we've nothing to hide, I'll give you all the details you want, I'm sure you're welcome.'

Occasionally in the past, when he had published a book he thought might interest his friend, Amyas Ireland had made a present of a copy to Wexford. It was always a pleasure, on arriving home in the evening, to find the parcel addressed to him, the padded bag with the publisher's name and logo on its label. But since the takeover of Carlyon-Brent he had received nothing, so it was a surprise to see a larger than usual parcel waiting for him. This time the logo was the St Giles Press's lion with fritillary in its mouth but inside, tucked among the books, was a letter on the familiar headed paper and an explanation from Amyas.

In the particular circumstances, he had thought Wexford might be interested in three of Davina Flory's books, which they were currently re-issuing in a new format: *The Holy City, The Other Side of the Wall* and *The Hosts of Midian*. If Reg would like a copy of the first – and now, sadly, to be the only – volume of the autobiography, he had only to ask. He was sorry he hadn't been in touch before. Reg would be aware they had been taken over, but perhaps not of the subsequent shake-up and Amyas's fear for the fate of his own imprint. It had been an anxious time. However, all now seemed well, Carlyon Quick, as they were now to be known, had a wonderful autumn list in view. They were most specially delighted to have secured the rights in Augustine Casey's new novel, *The Lash*.

This was almost enough to spoil Wexford's pleasure in the Davina Flory books. The phone rang as he was glancing desultorily through the first of them. It was Sheila. Thursday was her evening for

155

phoning. He listened to Dora speaking to her, indulging himself in a favourite pastime of trying to guess what she was saying from his wife's astonished, delighted or merely interested replies.

Dora's words fell into none of those categories this evening. He heard her expression of disappointment, 'Oh, dear,' and a more intense regret, 'Is that a good idea? Are you sure you know what you're doing?' He had a feeling as of his heart growing heavy, a tension in his chest. He half got up from the table, sat down again, listened.

Dora said in the cold stiff tone he hated when it was directed at himself, 'You'll want to talk to your father, I suppose.'

He took the receiver. Before she spoke he found himself thinking, she has the most beautiful voice I ever heard from a woman's mouth.

The beautiful voice said, 'Mother's cross with me. I expect you will be. I've turned down that part.'

A glorious lightness, a splendid relief. Was that *all* it was? 'In *Miss Julie*? I expect you know what you're doing.'

'God knows if I do or not. The thing is I'm going to Nevada with Gus. I turned it down to go to Nevada with Gus.'

# 14

At Kingsmarkham station, illuminated digital letters announced that an experimental queueing system was in operation. In other words, instead of waiting comfortably, two or three to each ticket window, you lined up between ropes. It was as bad as Euston. In the concourse, up near the platform from which the Manchester train would depart, was a sign instructing travellers: 'Form queue here.'

Nothing about the train, nothing welcoming, nothing to say when it would leave, only the assumption made that there would be a queue. It was worse than wartime. Wexford could remember wartime – just – and then, while they might take queueing for granted, they at least put no official stamp on it.

Perhaps he should have let Donaldson drive him. He hadn't done so because of a weary dread of the motorways and their congestion. Trains were fast these days, trains didn't get into jams with other trains, and on weekdays at any rate railway tracks weren't being constantly excavated and mended as roads were. Unless there was snow or a hurricane, trains *ran*. He had bought himself a paper at Kingsmarkham and read it on the journey to Victoria. He could always buy another here, anything to keep his mind off Sheila and what had happened last night. On the other hand, *The Times* hadn't stopped him thinking about it, so why should the *Independent*?

The queue wound quite elegantly round the broad concourse. No one protested, just joined the tail of it, uncomplaining. It had formed a near-circle, as if these travellers were about to join hands and start singing 'Auld Lang Syne'. Then the barrier opened and everyone was let in, not exactly surging, but pushing a bit, impatient to reach the train.

A nice, newish, smart, modern train. Wexford had a reserved seat.

157

He found it, sat down, looked at the front page of his paper and thought about Sheila, heard Sheila's voice. The ring of it, in his head, made him flinch.

'You'd made up your mind to hate him before you'd even met him!'

How she could rail! Like Petruchio's Shrew, a role of which she had oddly not made a success.

'Don't be ridiculous, Sheila. I've never made up my mind to hate anyone before I've met them.'

'There's always a first time. Oh, I know why. You were jealous, you knew you had real cause. You knew none of the others meant a thing to me not even Andrew. I was in love for the first time in my life and you saw the red light, you saw the danger, you were determined to hate anyone I loved. And why? Because you were afraid I'd love him better than you.'

They had often quarrelled before. They were the kind of people who rowed hotly, lost their tempers, made up and forgot the cause of it within minutes. This time it was different.

'We're not talking about love,' he had said. 'We're talking about common sense and reasonable behaviour. You'd throw up maybe the best part you've ever had to tag along to the middle of nowhere just to be with that . . .'

'Don't say it! Don't abuse him!'

'I couldn't abuse him. What would be abuse to a miscreant like him? To that drunken foul-mouthed clown? The biggest insults I could find would flatter him.'

'My God, whatever I've inherited from you, I'm glad it isn't your tongue. Listen to me, Father . . .'

He gave a whoop of laughter. 'Father? Since when have you called me Father?'

'Right, I'll call you nothing. Listen to me, will you? I love him with all my heart. I'll never leave him!'

'You're not on stage at the Olivier now,' said Wexford very nastily. He heard her draw in her breath. 'And if you go on like this I frankly doubt if you ever will be again.'

'I wonder,' she said distantly – oh, she had inherited much from him! – 'I wonder if it's ever occurred to you to think about how unusual it is for a daughter to be as close to her parents as I've been to you and Mother, how I phone you a couple of times a week, how I'm always coming down to see you. Have you ever wondered why?'

158

'No. I know why. It's because we've always been nice and sweet and loving to you, because we've spoiled you to hell and let you stomp all over us, and now that I've summoned up the nerve to confront you and tell you a few home truths about you and that ugly little pseud . . . '

He never finished the sentence. What he was going to cite as the consequence of his 'nerve' he never reached, and now he had forgotten what it was. Before he could get another word out she had slammed down the receiver.

He knew he shouldn't have spoken to her like that. His mother, long ago, had used a regretful phrase which was perhaps current in her youth: 'Come back all I said!' If only it were possible to call back all one had said! By saying those words of his mother's, to cancel out abuse and sarcasm, to make five minutes disappear. But it wasn't possible, and none knew better than he that no word uttered could ever be lost, only, one day, like everything else that ever happened in human existence, it might be forgotten.

His phone was in his pocket. The train, as usual these days, was full of people using phones, mostly men making business calls. It had been a novelty not long ago, now it was commonplace. He could phone her, she might be at home. She might put the receiver down when she heard his voice. Wexford, who didn't usually care for the opinion of others, very much disliked the idea of his fellow passengers witnessing the effect this would have on him.

A trolley came round with coffee and those ubiquitous sandwiches, the kind he liked in three-dimensional plastic boxes. In this world are two kinds of people – among the fed, that is – those who when worried eat for comfort and those whose appetite is killed by anxiety. Wexford belonged in the first category. He had had breakfast and presumably he would have lunch, but he bought a bacon and egg sandwich just the same. Eating it appreciatively, he found himself hoping that what he encountered at Royal Oak would to some extent drive Sheila from his mind.

At Crewe he got a taxi. The taxi driver knew all about the prison, where it was and what sort of institution it was. Wexford wondered who were the fares he habitually drove up there. Visitors perhaps, sweethearts and wives. There had been a move here a year or two ago to allow 'conjugal visits in private' but this had been smartly vetoed. Sex was evidently rated highly among amenities not to be countenanced.

159

The prison turned out to be well out in the country, in, according to the driver, the valley of the River Wheelock. Royal Oak, he told Wexford in a practised guide-like way, came from an ancient tree, long since disappeared, in which King Charles had hidden from his enemies. Which King Charles he didn't say and Wexford wondered how many such trees proliferated in England, as many as there were beds slept in by Elizabeth I, no doubt. There was certainly one in Cheriton Forest, a favourite picnic spot. Charles must have spent years of his life climbing them.

Huge, sprawling, hideous. Surely what must be the highest and longest wall in the Midlands. No trees here. So barren, indeed, was the plain on which the cluster of crimson brick buildings stood, as to make the name absurd. 'Her Majesty's Prison: Royal Oak'. He had arrived.

Would the taxi come back for him? Wexford was presented with the hire company's card. He could phone. The taxi disappeared rather quickly as if, unless a speedy escape was made, there might be problems about getting away at all.

One of the governors, a man called David Cairns, gave him a cup of coffee in a rather nice room with carpet on the floor and framed posters on the walls. The rest of the place looked like all such places, but smelt better. While Wexford drank his coffee Cairns said he supposed he knew all about Royal Oak and its survival in spite of official distrust and Home Office dislike. Wexford said he thought so, but Cairns proceeded to describe the system just the same. He was obviously proud of the place, an idealist with shining eyes.

Paradoxically, it was the most violent and recalcitrant prisoners who were referred to Royal Oak. Of course, they also had to want to come. So many wanted to come that there was currently a waiting list of over a hundred. Staff and inmates were on Christian-name terms. Group therapy and mutual counselling were the order of the day. Prisoners mixed, for, uniquely, there was no Rule 43 segregation here and no hierarchy of murderers and violent criminals at the top and sex offenders at the bottom.

All inmates came to Royal Oak on referral, usually the recommendation of a prison Senior Medical Officer. Which reminded him, their own Senior Medical Officer, Sam Rosenberg, would like to see him before he went to meet Jem Hocking. As he'd said, it was all first names here. None of your 'Sir' this and 'Dr' that.

A member of staff conducted Wexford to the hospital, which was

160

just another wing. They passed men walking about freely – freely up to a point – dressed in tracksuits or pants and sweatshirts. He couldn't resist a glance through an interior window where a group therapy session was in progress. The men sat round in a circle. They were opening their hearts and baring their souls, the member of staff said, learning how to bring to the surface all their inner confusions. Wexford thought they looked as hangdog and wretched as most incarcerated people.

A smell just like Stowerton Infirmary hung about the hospital; lime juice, lysol and sweat. All hospitals smell the same, except private ones which smell of money. Dr Rosenberg was in his room which was like the charge nurse's room at Stowerton. Only the cigarette smoke was absent. It commanded a view of the empty green plain and a line of electricity pylons.

Lunch had just arrived. There was enough for two, unexciting piles of brown slime on pillows of boiled rice, chicken curry probably. 'Individual' fruit pies to follow and a carton of non-dairy creamer. But Wexford was eating for comfort and he accepted at once Sam Rosenberg's invitation to join him while they talked about Jem Hocking.

The medical officer was a short thickset man of forty with a round childlike face and a thatch of prematurely grey hair. His clothes were like those of the prisoners, a tracksuit and trainers.

'What d'you think?' he said, waving a hand towards door and ceiling. 'This place, I mean. Bit different from the "System", eh?'

Wexford understood the 'System' to refer to the rest of the prison service and agreed it was.

'Of course it doesn't seem to work. If by "work" we mean stopping them doing it again. On the other hand, that's rather hard to tell because most of them hardly get the chance to do anything much again. They're lifers.' Sam Rosenberg wiped up the remains of his curry with a hunk of bread. He seemed to be enjoying his lunch. 'Jem Hocking asked to come here. He was convicted in September, was sent to the Scrubs or it may have been Wandsworth, and set about tearing the place apart. He was referred here just before Christmas and he got into what we do here, roughly an on-going "talking it through", like a – well, a duck to water.'

'What did he do?'

'What was his conviction for? He went to this house where the owner was supposed to keep her shop takings over the weekend, found five hundred pounds or so in a handbag and half-beat to death the woman who lived there. She was seventy-two. He used a seven-pound hammer.'

'No gun involved?'

'No gun, so far as I know. Have one of these pies, will you? They're raspberry and redcurrant, not bad. We have the non-dairy creamer because I'm a bit of a cholesterol freak. I mean, I'm scared of it, I believe in battling against it. Jem's ill at the moment. He thinks he's dying but he's not. Not this time.'

Wexford raised an eyebrow. 'Not a cholesterol problem, I'm sure.'

'Well, no. As a matter of fact, I've never tested his cholesterol.' Rosenberg hesitated. 'A lot of the Bill – sorry, didn't mean to be insulting – a lot of the police still have gay prejudice. I mean, you'll hear coppers make these jokes about queens and queers and then they'll mince about. Are you one of those? No, I can see you're not. But you may still think homosexuals are all hairdressers and ballet dancers. Not *real men*. Ever read any Genet?'

'A bit. It was a long time ago.' Wexford tried to remember titles and recalled one. '*Our Lady of the Flowers.*'

'*Querelle of Brest* was what I had in mind. Genet, more than anyone, makes you understand gay men can be as tough and as ruthless as the heterosexual sort. Tougher, more ruthless. They can be killers and thieves and brutal criminals as well as dress designers.'

'Are you saying Jem Hocking is one of those?'

'Jem doesn't know about closets, being in them or coming out of them, but one of the reasons he wanted to come here was to talk openly to other men about his homosexuality. Talk about it day after day, unchecked, in groups. The world he lived in is perhaps the most prejudiced of all worlds. And then he got ill.'

'You mean he's got AIDS, don't you?'

Sam Rosenberg gave him a narrow look. 'You see, you *do* associate it with the gay community. I tell you, it'll be as common among heterosexuals in a year or two. It is not a gay disease. Right?'

'But Jem Hocking has it?'

'Jem Hocking is HIV Pos. He's had a very bad go of flu. We've had a flu epidemic at Royal Oak and he just happened to get it worse than the others, badly enough to come in here for a week. With luck, he'll be back in the community by the end of the week. But he insists he's had AIDS-related pneumonia and he thinks I'm jibbing at telling him the truth. Hence, he believes he's dying and he wants to see you.'

162

'Why does he?'

'That I don't know. I haven't asked and if I asked he wouldn't tell me. He wants to tell you. Coffee?'

He was a man of the doctor's age but dark and swarthy, a week's growth of beard on cheeks and chin. Aware of modern hospital trends, Wexford had expected him to be up, dressing-gowned, seated in a chair, but Jem Hocking was in bed. He looked far more ill than Daisy ever had. The hands which rested on the red blanket were dark blue with tattoos.

'How are you?' Wexford said.

Hocking made no immediate reply. He put one blue-configured finger up to his mouth and rubbed it. Then he said, 'Not good.'

'Are you going to tell me when you were in Kingsmarkham? Is that what it's about?'

'Last May. That's making bells ring for you, isn't it? Only I reckon they've rung already.'

Wexford nodded. 'Some of them have.'

'I'm dying. Did you know that?'

'Not according to the medical officer.'

Derision altered Jem Hocking's face. He sneered. 'They don't tell you the truth. Not even in here. Nobody ever tells the truth, not here, not anywhere. They can't, it's not possible to. You'd have to go into too much detail, you'd have to search your soul. You'd insult everyone and every word'd show you up for the bastard you are. Have you ever thought of that?'

'Yes,' said Wexford.

Whatever Hocking had expected it wasn't a bald affirmative. He paused, said, 'Most of the time you'd just say, "I hate your guts, I hate your guts" over and over. That'd be what the truth is. And, "I want to die but I'm fucking scared of dying."' He drew a breath. 'I know I'm dying. I'll get another bout of what I've had but a bit worse and then a third and that one'll carry me off. It might be quicker than that. It was a fucking sight quicker for Dane.'

'Who's Dane?'

'I reckoned on telling you before I died. Might as well. What can I lose? I've lost everything except my life and that's on the way out.' Hocking's face narrowed and his eyes seemed to draw closer together. He suddenly looked one of the nastiest customers Wexford had ever come across. 'D'you want to know something? It's the last

163

pleasure I've got left, talking to people about me dying. It embarrasses them, see, and I enjoy that, them not knowing what to say.'

'It doesn't embarrass me.'

'Well, fucking Bill, what can you expect?'

A nurse came in, a man in jeans and a short white coat. In Wexford's youth he would have been called a 'male nurse'. That was what they said then: 'male nurse' and 'lady doctor'. There was nothing particularly sexist about it, but it shed a lot of bright illumination on people's expectations of the sexes.

The nurse heard Hocking's last words and said not to be rude, Jem, there was no call for that, mud-slinging didn't help, and it was time for his antibiotics.

'Fucking useless,' said Hocking. 'Pneumonia's a virus, right? You're all fuckwitted in here.'

Wexford waited patiently while Hocking took his pills under feeble protest. He really looked very ill. You could believe this was death's threshold. He waited till the nurse had gone, hung his head, contemplated the designs on his blue hands.

'Who's Dane? you said. I'll tell you. Dane was my mate. Dane Bishop. Dane Gavin David Bishop, if you want the lot. He was only twenty-four.' 'I loved him' hung unspoken in the air. Wexford could see it in Hocking's face, 'I loved him', but he wasn't a sentimentalist, especially about killers, especially about the kind who hammer old women. So what? Does loving someone redeem a man? Does loving someone make you good? 'We did the Kingsmarkham job together. But you knew that. You knew that before you came or you wouldn't have come.'

'More or less,' said Wexford.

'Dane wanted money to buy this drug. It's American but you can get it here. Initials it goes by, doesn't matter.'

'AZT.'

'No, as a matter of fact, clever cop. DDI it's called, stands for Di-deoxy-innosine. Not available on the fucking NHS, needless to say.'

Don't give me your excuses, Wexford said to himself. You ought to know better. He thought of Sergeant Martin, foolish and foolhardy but quite bright by turns, a good man, an earnest, well-intentioned good man, the salt of the earth.

'This Dane Bishop, he's dead, is he?'

Jem Hocking just looked at him. It was a look full of hatred and pain. Wexford thought the hatred was due to the fact that the man couldn't embarrass him. Perhaps the sole purpose of the exercise, this 'confession', was to cause an embarrassment in which Hocking had hoped to revel.

'Died of AIDS, I guess,' he said, 'and not long after.'

'Dead before we could get the drug. It took him fast at the end. We saw that description you put out, spots on his face, all that. That wasn't fucking acne, that was Kaposi's Sarcoma.'

Wexford said, 'He used a gun. Where did he get

An indifferent shrug from Hocking. 'Are you asking me? You know as well as I do, it's easy to get a shooter if you want one. He never said. He just had it. A Magnum, it was.' The sly sidelong look came back. 'He chucked it away, threw it down, getting out of the bank.'

'Ah,' said Wexford almost silently, almost to himself.

'Scared to be found with it. He was ill then, it makes you weak, weak like an old man. He was only twenty-four but he was weak as water. That's why he shot that fuckwit, too weak to keep up the pressure. I got us away, I wasn't even in there when he shot him.'

'You were concerned with him. You knew he had a gun.'

'Am I denying it?'

'You bought a car in the name of George Brown?'

Hocking nodded. 'We bought a vehicle, we bought a lot of things with cash, we reckoned we could sell the vehicle again on account of we never dared keep any of the notes. I wrapped them in newspaper and stuffed them in a dump. We sold the vehicle – not a bad way of handling things, was it?'

'It's called laundering money,' Wexford said coldly. 'Or it is when done on a grander scale.'

'He died before he got the drug.'

'You told me before.'

Jem Hocking heaved himself up in bed. 'You're a frozen bastard, you are. If it was anywhere else in the system I was doing bird they wouldn't have left you alone with me.'

Wexford got up. 'What could you do, Jem? I'm three times your size. I'm not embarrassed and I'm not impressed.'

'Just fucking helpless,' said Hocking. 'The world's helpless against a dying man.'

'I wouldn't say that. There's nothing in the law to say a dying man can't be charged with murder and robbery.'

165

'You wouldn't!'

'I certainly will,' said Wexford, leaving.

The train took him back to Euston in pouring rain. It was raining all the way down from Victoria to Kingsmarkham. As soon as he got in he tried to phone Sheila and got her Lady Macbeth voice, the one that said, 'Give me the daggers', asking callers to leave a message.

# 15

It was a job Barry Vine might have done, or even Karen Malahyde, but he did it himself. His rank seemed to frighten Fred Harrison, a nervous man who looked an older and shorter version of his brother. Wexford asked him when he had last driven Joanne Garland to Tancred House and, looking through his book, he named a date four Tuesdays before.

'I wouldn't have touched her with a bargepole if I'd known it was going to lead to trouble,' Fred Harrison said.

In spite of himself and his wretched feelings, Wexford was amused. 'I doubt if it's going to lead to trouble for you, Mr Harrison. Did you see Mrs Garland or hear from her on Tuesday 11 March?'

'Nothing, not a dicky-bird since whenever it was, what I said, 26 February.'

'And on that evening, what happened? She phoned you and asked you to drive her to Tancred House at – what? Eight? Eight fifteen?'

'I'd not have taken her anywhere if I'd known it was going to lead to trouble. You've got to believe that. She rung up like she always did around seven, said she had to be at Tancred by half eight. I said like I always did I'd pick her up a few minutes after eight, be ample time, but she said, no, she didn't want to be late, and to come at ten to. Well, I fetched up at Tancred eight ten, eight fifteen. Going the shortest way, I'd be bound to, but she never listened, she was scared stiff of being late. That always happened. Sometimes I'd wait for her, she'd ask me to wait she'd be an hour, and I'd take the opportunity to pop in and see my brother.'

Wexford was uninterested in this. He persisted. 'You're sure she didn't phone you on 11 March?'

167

'Believe me, I'd make a clean breast of it. Trouble's the last thing I want.'

'Do you think she ever used another taxi service?'

'Why would she? She's nothing to complain about with me. Time and time again she's said, I don't know what I'd do without you, Fred, to come to my rescue. And then she'd say I was the only one round here she'd trust to drive her.'

There seemed no more to be got out of the nervous Fred Harrison. Wexford left him to return to Tancred. He was driving himself and he took the Pomfret Monachorum road. This was only the second time he had been this way. After yesterday's rain it was a fine mild day and the woods were full of life, the quiet, stirring, fresh life of early spring. The road wound as it ascended the shallow wooded hill to Tancred. It was too soon for the trees to show leaf except for the hawthorns which were already misted all over with green. Blossom hung on the wild plums like white spotted veils.

He drove slowly. As soon as his mind emptied of Fred Harrison and his anxieties, Sheila came in to fill it. He could almost have groaned aloud. Every angry word that had been uttered during that hideous interchange was fresh in his memory, was persistently repeating itself.

' . . . you were determined to hate anyone I loved. And why? Because you were afraid I'd love him better than you.'

Driving on through the wood where aconites grew in yellow rings like patches of bright sunlight, he opened the car window to feel the sweet air against his face, the equinoctial air of the first, or maybe the second, day of spring. Last night, with the rain lashing against the windows, he had tried to ring her, and Dora had tried. He wanted to apologise to her and ask her forgiveness. But the phone rang and rang unanswered and when he tried again, despairing, at nine and again at nine thirty, her answering-machine voice came on. Not one of her characteristic messages: 'If that's someone offering me the female lead in the Scottish play or wanting to take me to dinner at Le Caprice . . . ' 'Darling' – the actress's universal *darling* that would serve for him or Casey or the woman who cleaned – 'Darling, Sheila's had to go out . . . ' It was neither of those but, 'Sheila Wexford. I'm out. Leave a message and there's a chance I'll get back to you.' He hadn't left a message but at last had gone to bed, sick at heart.

He thought, I've lost her. It had nothing much to do with her going six thousand miles away. Casey would have taken her from him in the same way if they had both decided to buy a house and settle down in Pomfret Monachorum. He had lost her and things would never be the same for them again.

The lane made its last wind, coming to the straight and the level ground. On either side stretched acres of young trees, planted perhaps twenty years before, their slender branches that reached for the light a bright russet colour, the hawthorn and blackthorn amongst them bouquets of misty green and snow white. The ground between, strewn with dry brown leaves, was dappled with spots of sunlight.

In the distance he saw a movement. Someone was walking towards him, along the lane, a long way head, someone young, a young girl. More and more was revealed as he approached and she approached. It was Daisy. Unlikely as it was that she should be here, in this place, at this time, it was undoubtedly Daisy.

She stopped when she saw the car. Of course, from that distance, she could have no idea who the driver was. She wore jeans and a Barbour jacket, the left sleeve empty, a bright red scarf wound twice round her neck. He knew the precise moment when she recognised him by the way her eyes widened. She remained unsmiling.

He stopped and wound down the window. She didn't wait for the question.

'I've come home. I knew they'd try to stop me so I waited till Nicholas had gone off to work and then I said, I'm going home now, Joyce, thank you for having me, and that was it. She said I couldn't, not on my own. You know how she talks, "I'm sorry, dear, but you can't do that. What about your luggage? Who'll look after you?" I said I'd already phoned for a cab and I'd look after myself.'

The thought came to Wexford that she had never in fact done much of that and, as in the past, Brenda Harrison would be looking after her. But she only had the kind of illusions all the young have. 'And now you're taking a walk round your domain?'

'I've been out long enough. I'm going back. I soon get tired.' The bleak look was back in her face, her sorrowful eyes. 'Will you give me a lift?'

He reached across and opened the passenger door. 'Now I'm eighteen,' she said, though not enthusiastically, 'I can do as I like. How d'you do up this seat belt? My sling and all this padding get in the way.'

169

'You needn't put it on if you don't want to. Not on private land.'

'Really? I never knew that. You've got yours on.'

'Force of habit. Daisy, are you planning to stay here on your own? To *live* here?'

'It's mine.' Her voice was as grim as it could get. It became bitter. 'It's all mine. Why shouldn't I live in what's mine?'

He didn't answer. There was no point in telling her things she already knew, that she was young and a woman and defenceless, and things she might not have realised, that it might very well be in someone's interest to finish off the job he had begun two weeks before. If he took that seriously he would have to put a day and night guard on Tancred, not alarm Daisy with his fears.

Instead, he reverted to a subject they had discussed when he last saw her at the Virsons. 'I don't suppose you've heard from your father?'

'My *father*?'

'He *is* your father, Daisy. He must know about all this. There's no one living in this country could have missed it on television and in the papers. And unless I'm much mistaken, it'll revive today with the funeral all over the dailies. I think you should expect him to get in touch.'

'If he was going to, wouldn't he have already?'

'He wouldn't have known where you were. For all we know, he's been ringing up Tancred House every day.'

Suddenly he wondered if it was this man she had looked for in vain at the funeral. That shadowy father no one talked of but who must exist. He parked the car beside the pool. Daisy got out and stared into the water. Perhaps because the sun was shining, several fish had come close to the surface, white, or colourless rather, with scarlet heads. She lifted her face to the statuary, the girl metamorphosed into a tree, a sheath of bark enclosing her limbs, the man closing upon her with uplifted yearning face, with arms outstretched.

'Daphne and Apollo,' she said. 'It's a copy of the Bernini. Supposed to be a good one. I wouldn't know, I don't really care about things like that.' She made a face. 'Davina loved it. She *would*. I suppose the god was going to rape Daphne, don't you think? I mean, they have nice words for it, make it sound romantic, but that's what he was going to do.'

Saying nothing, Wexford wondered what event in her own past prompted this sudden savagery.

170

'He wasn't going to *court* her, was he? Take her out to dinner and buy her an engagement ring? What fools people are!' She changed tack as she turned from the pool with a little toss of her head. 'When I was younger I used to ask Mum about my father. You know how kids are, they want to know all that. She had this way, had my mother, if there was something she didn't like talking about she'd tell me to ask Davina. It was always, "Ask your grandmother, she'll tell you." So I asked Davina and she said – you won't believe this but it's what she said – "Your mother was a soccer groupie, darling, and she used to go and watch him playing football. That's how they met." And then she said, "Not to put too fine a point on it, he was among the low life." She liked those expressions, sort of trendy slang, or what she thought was trendy slang, "soccer groupie" and "low life". "Forget him, darling," she said. "Imagine you were born by parthenogenesis like the algae," and then she explained to me what parthenogenesis was. Typical of her, that was, to turn everything into a lesson. But it didn't exactly make me feel much love or respect for my father.'

'Do you know where he lives?'

'Somewhere in north London. He's married again. Come into the house, if you want, and we could find where he lives.'

The front door and the inner door were not locked. Wexford followed her in. The closing of the door behind them made the chandeliers tremble and ring. The lilies in the orangery had an artificial smell, like the perfumery department of a big store. Here in the hall she had crawled to the telephone, leaving a trail of blood across this shiny floor, had crawled past the body of Harvey Copeland, spreadeagled across those stairs. He saw her glance at the stairs where a great area of carpet had been cut away to show the bare wood beneath. She went to the door at the back which led into Davina Flory's study.

He had not previously entered it. Every wall was lined with books. Its single window gave on to the terrace, of which the *serre* formed one wall. He had expected this, but not the fine terrestrial globe of dark-green glass on the table, nor the bonsai garden in a terracotta trough under the window, nor the absence of word processor, typewriter, electronic equipment of any kind. On the desk, beside a leather writing case, lay a gold Mont Blanc fountain pen. In a jar, made perhaps of malachite, were ballpoints, pencils and a bone-handled paperknife.

'She wrote everything by hand,' Daisy said. 'She couldn't type, never wanted to learn.' She was searching a top drawer of the desk. 'Here. This is it. She called it her "unfriendly" address book. She kept it for people she didn't like or it didn't – well, benefit her to know.'

There were an uncomfortably large number of names in the book. Wexford turned to the J's. The only Jones had the initials G.G. and an address in London N5. No phone number.

'I don't quite understand this, Daisy. Why would your grand-mother have your father's address and not your mother? Or did your mother have it too? And why "G.G."? Why not his first name? After all, he'd been her son-in-law.'

'You really don't understand.' She managed a fleeting smile. 'Davina liked keeping tabs on people. She'd want to know where he was and what he was doing, even if she'd never see him again as long as she lived.' At this she bit her lip but continued, 'She was very manipulative, you know. Very organising. She'd know exactly where he was, no matter how often he'd moved. You can be sure that's the right address you've got. I expect she thought he'd turn up sometime and – well, ask for money. She used to say that most people out of her past turned up sooner or later, she called it "coming out of the woodwork". As for Mum, I doubt if Mum even kept an address book.'

'Daisy, I'm trying to find a kind and tactful way of asking this and I'm not sure if there is one. About your mother.' He hesitated. 'Your mother's friends . . .'

'You mean, did she have boyfriends? Lovers?'

Once again, he was astonished at her intuitiveness. He nodded. 'She can't have seemed young to you but she was only forty-five. Besides, I don't think age is of much importance in this area, in spite of what people say. People have friends of the opposite sex, friends in the romantic sense, at any age.'

'Like Davina would have had.' Daisy grinned suddenly. 'If Harvey had dropped off his perch.' She realised what she had said, the awfulness of it. Her hand went up to cover her mouth and she gasped. 'Oh, God! Forget I said that. I didn't say it. Why do we say these things?'

Instead of answering, for he couldn't answer ('Come back all I said'), he reminded her gently that she had been telling him about her mother.

She sighed. 'I never knew her go out with anyone. I never heard her mention a man. I just don't think she was interested. Davina used to tell her to get herself a man, that would "take her out of herself", and even Harvey had a go. I remember Harvey bringing some chap home, some political bloke, and Davina saying wouldn't he do for Mum? I mean, they didn't think I understood what they meant but I did.

'When we were all up in Edinburgh last year – you know we went up for the Festival, Davina was doing something at the Book Festival – Mum got flu, she spent the whole two weeks in bed, and Davina moaned about what a shame it was because she'd met this son of a friend of hers who would just have done for Mum. That's what she said to Harvey, that he'd just have done for Mum.

'Mum was all right as she was. She liked her life, she liked pottering about in that gallery and watching the telly and not having any responsibilities, doing her bit of painting and making her own clothes and all that. She couldn't be bothered with *men.*' A look of extreme despair suddenly descended upon Daisy's face. It fell into a disconsolate childlike grief. She leant forward across the table where the green glass globe was and pressed her fist up against her forehead. She pushed her fingers through her hair. He expected a sudden outburst of anger against life and the way things were, a cry of protest at what had happened to her simple, innocent, contented mother, but instead she lifted her head and said quite coolly, 'Joanne's the same, so far as I know. Joanne spends thousands on clothes and having her face done and her hair and massage and whatever, but it's not for a man. I don't know what it's for. Herself, maybe. Davina was always on about love and men, she called it having a full life, she thought she was so *modern,* her word, but actually women don't care about that any more, do they? They're just as pleased to be seen about with women friends. You don't have to have a man to be a real woman, not any more.'

It was as if she were justifying something in her own life, making it seem right. He said, 'Mrs Virson says your grandmother wanted you to be like her, to do all the same things.'

'But without her mistakes, yes. I told you she was manipulative. I wasn't asked if I wanted to go to university and travel and write books and – and have sex with a lot of different people.' Daisy looked away from him. 'It was just taken for granted I would. I don't as a matter of fact. I don't even want to go to Oxford and – and,

173

well, if I don't even do my A levels I *can't*. I want to be *me,* not someone else's creation.'

So time had begun doing its stuff, he thought. It was working. And then what she said next made him revise.

'Insofar as I want to do anything. So far as I give a toss what happens.'

He made no comment. 'There's one thing you might want to do. Would you like to come and see how we've turned your sanctum into a police station?'

'Not now. I'd like to be alone now. Just me and Queenie. She was so pleased to see me, she jumped on to my shoulder from the banisters the way she used to, purring like a lion roaring. I'm going to go all over the house and just look at it, get reacquainted with it. It's changed for me, you see. It's the same but it's quite different too. I shan't go into the dining room. I've already asked Ken to seal up the door. Just for a while. He's going to seal it up so that I can't open it if I – if I forget.'

It is rare to see people shiver. Wexford, watching her, did not see this galvanic movement of the body, only the outward signs of the inner shudder, the draining of colour from her face, a goose-pimpling on her neck. He considered explaining to her what he had in mind for her protection but thought better of it. Decidedly more sensible would be to present her with a *fait accompli.*

She had closed her eyes. When she opened them he saw she had made an effort not to cry. The lids were swollen. He thought that after he had gone she would allow herself a transport of grief, but as he was leaving the telephone rang.

She hesitated, lifted the receiver, and he heard her say, 'Oh, Joyce. It's nice of you to phone but I'm quite all right. I'll be fine . . .'

Karen Malahyde would spend the night at Tancred House with Daisy, Anne Lennox the following night, Rosemary Mountjoy the next one, and so on. He thought of mounting a further guard from the stables, two men on duty throughout the twenty-four hours, but his heart quailed at the idea of the Deputy Chief Constable's response to that. They were short-handed, anyway, they usually were. The girl had no business to be there on her own, she had friends to stay with, he could hear Freeborn saying it; it wasn't for them to spend public money for the protection of a young woman who had chosen to return to this great lonely place on a whim.

But Karen and Anne and Rosemary were only too pleased. None of them had ever slept under a roof that covered more than a three-bedroomed semi or a block of flats. His decision to let Karen tell Daisy was formed on the spur of the moment. He was protecting her but this was to protect himself. Whenever it was avoidable, he must not see her. Briefly, he thought he understood the meaning of that sense of warning and alarm he had experienced in St Peter's.

It horrified him. For a whole ten minutes, sitting at his desk in the stables, staring at the Persian cat cactus, but unseeing, unseeing, he believed he was in love with her. He saw it as some terminal disease Dr Crocker might have enlightened him about, some fearful blight, he saw it as Jem Hocking saw the fate that would surely overtake him.

Of course there had been instances in the past. He had been married to Dora for more than thirty years, so of course there had been instances. That young Dutch girl, pretty Nancy Lake, others apart from his work. But he loved Dora, his was a happy marriage. And this was so ridiculous, he and this *child*. But how the whole day lit up for him when he saw her, when he saw her sad face! How happy he was when she talked to him, when they sat together talking! How beautiful she was, and clever, and good!

He put it to the test, the only test. He tried to imagine making love to her, her nakedness and wanting to make love to her, and the whole concept was grotesque. It wasn't that he *wanted* her, it wasn't that at all. A positive revulsion from that made him flinch. He couldn't have contemplated touching her with the tip of his finger, not even in some secret fantasy. No, he knew what it was he felt. Instead of groaning, which he had felt like doing ten minutes before, he let out a sudden guffaw, a bellow of laughter.

Barry Vine, previously glued to a report he was reading, turned round to stare. Wexford cut off the laughter and made his face grim. He thought Vine was going to say something, ask some fool question as poor Martin might have done, but he constantly underestimated DS Vine. The man was back to his clipboard and Wexford revelling now in the realisation of what it was that had happened. Not sex, not being 'in love', thank God. His mind had merely replaced the lost Sheila with Daisy. He had lost a daughter and found one. What a strange thing was the human psyche!

Thinking about it, he saw that this was exactly what had happened. He saw her as a daughter, for he was a man who needed

175

daughters. Guilt touched him that he had not instead turned to that other, to Sylvia, his elder girl. Why go a-whoring after strange goddesses when he had his own near at hand? Because the feelings and the needs blow where they list, he thought, without regard for what is fitting and what is appropriate. But he made up his mind to see Sylvia soon, perhaps to take her a present. She was moving house, moving to some old rectory in the countryside. He would go and ask her about her move, how he could help. And meanwhile that resolve to see less of Daisy might stand, lest the less dangerous love become as consuming as that other fearful sort.

He sighed and this time Barry Vine didn't turn round. The London phone directories had been brought here when they moved in and Wexford went to look in the book that used to be pink, E-K, and on whose cover pink still predominated in the picture. Of course there were hundreds of Joneses, but not too many G.G. Joneses. Daisy had been right when she said Davina would have the correct address for her father. Here it was: Jones, G.G., 11 Nineveh Road, N5, and a phone number on the 832 exchange. On the 071 area code, no doubt, it was inner London. But Wexford didn't pick up the phone. He sat wondering what those initials stood for, and wondering too why such an absolute breach had been established between Jones and his daughter.

He thought about inheritance too and the variously different outcomes there might have been if, say, Davina had been the one not to die, or Naomi had been. And what, if any, significance was there in the fact that neither Naomi nor her friend Joanne Garland had been interested in men, had apparently preferred each other's company?

A report in front of him expressed the opinion of a small-arms expert. His mind relieved, he read it again and more carefully. The first time, when he feared he was in the grip of the most overwhelming of obsessions, he hadn't taken it in. The expert was saying that though the cartridges used in the Martin killing appeared different from those used at Tancred House, they might not in fact be. It was possible, if you knew what you were doing, to tamper with the barrel of a pistol, to *engrave* on the inside of it lines which would be themselves imprinted on a cartridge passing through it. In his view this might well have been done in the present case . . .

He said, 'Barry, it was true what Michelle Weaver said. Bishop threw down the gun. It skidded across the floor of the bank. Strange as it seems, there *were* two guns careering around that floor after Martin was shot.'

Vine came over, sat on the edge of his desk.

'Hocking told me Bishop threw the gun down, the Colt Magnum. It was a Colt Magnum .357 or .38, no way of telling. Someone in the bank picked that gun up. One of the people who didn't hang around till we came. One of the men. Sharon Fraser had the impression the ones that went were all men.'

'You only pick up a gun with malice aforethought,' said Vine.

'Yes. But perhaps no particular malice. A mere generalised bias towards law-breaking.'

'In case it might come in useful one day, sir?'

'Something like that. The way my old dad used to pick up every nail he saw lying in the gutter. In case it came in handy.'

His phone was bleeping. Dora or the police station. Anyone who wanted them in connection with the Tancred murders would presumably know to call on the freephone number that had daily appeared on television screens. It was Burden, who had not come up to the stables that day.

He said, 'Reg, a call's just come through. Not a 999. A man with an American accent. Phoning on behalf of Bib Mew. She lives next door to him, hasn't got a phone, says she's found a body in the woods.'

'I know who you mean. I've spoken to him.'

'She found a body,' said Burden, 'hanging from a tree.'

# 16

She let them in but said nothing. To Wexford she gave the same sort of blank hopeless stare she might have bestowed on a bailiff come to make an inventory of her goods. That typified her attitude from the beginning. She was stunned, despairing, unable to struggle against these waters which had closed over her head.

Oddly enough, she looked more masculine than ever in corduroy trousers, check shirt and V-necked pullover, the earring missing today. 'I could find it in my heart to disgrace my man's apparel and cry like a woman,' thought Wexford. But Bib Mew wasn't crying and wasn't that a fallacy anyway, that women wept and men did not?

'Tell us what happened, Mrs Mew,' Burden was saying.

She had led them into the stuffy little parlour that lacked for romantic authenticity only a shawled old woman in an armchair. There, without a word to them, she subsided on to the old horsehair sofa. Her eyes never left Wexford's face. He thought, I should have brought a WPC with me, for here is something I haven't understood till now. Bib Mew is not simply eccentric, slow, stupid if the term isn't too harsh. She's backward, mentally handicapped. He felt a rush of pity. For such people shocks were worse, they penetrated and somehow overturned their innocence.

Burden had repeated his question. Wexford said, 'Mrs Mew, I think you should have a hot drink. Can we get that for you?'

Oh, for Karen or Anne! But his offer had unlocked Bib's voice. 'He gave me that. Him next door.'

It was no good expecting what Burden expected. This woman wasn't going to be able to give them any sort of factual account of what she had found. 'You were in the woods,' Wexford began. He looked at the time. 'On your way to work?'

The nod she gave was more than frightened. It was the terrified movement of a creature cornered. Burden left the room silently, in search, Wexford guessed, of the kitchen. Now for the hard part, the bit that might set her off screaming.

'You saw something, *someone*? You saw something hanging from a tree?'

Again a nod. She had begun to wring her hands, a series of rapid dry washing movements. Speech from her surprised him. She said, very warily, 'A dead person.'

Oh God, he thought, unless it's in her mind, and I don't think it's in her poor mind, this is Joanne Garland. 'Man or woman, Mrs Mew?'

She repeated what she had said. 'A dead person,' and then, 'hanging up.'

'Yes. Could you see it from the by-road?'

A fierce shake of the head and then Burden came in with tea in a mug printed with the faces of the Duke and Duchess of York. A spoon stuck out of it and Wexford guessed Burden had put enough sugar in to make the spoon stand up.

'I phoned in,' he said. 'Got Anne to come up here.' He added, 'And Barry.'

Bib Mew held the mug close to her chest and closed her hands round it. Incongruously Wexford recalled someone telling him how the people of Kashmir carry pots of hot coals under their clothes to warm them. If they hadn't been there he thought Bib would have put the mug up under her sweater. She seemed to take comfort from the tea as a heater rather than a drink.

'Went in the trees,' she said. 'I had to go.'

It took Wexford a moment or two to understand what she meant. In court they still called it 'for a natural purpose'. Burden seemed baffled. She could only have been ten minutes from her own house but of course it was possible, even then, one could be 'caught short', that she might be troubled in that way. Or be in awe of using the bathrooms at Tancred House?

'You left your bike,' he said gently, 'and went in among the trees and then you saw it?'

She began to tremble.

He had to persist. 'You didn't go on to Tancred, you came back?'

'Scared, scared, scared. I was scared.' She pointed a finger at the wall. 'I told him.'

'Yes,' Burden said. 'Could you – could you tell us *where*?'

She didn't scream. The sound she made was a kind of gibbering and her body shook. The tea rocked in the cup and splashed over the side. Wexford took it gently from her. He said in the calmest, most soothing voice he could achieve, 'It doesn't matter. Don't worry about it. You've told Mr Hogarth?' She looked uncomprehending. He fancied her teeth had begun to chatter. 'The man next door?'

A nod. Her hands went back to the mug of tea, clasped it. Wexford heard the car, nodded to Burden to let them in. Barry Vine and Anne Lennox had taken precisely eleven minutes to get there.

Leaving them with her, Wexford went next door. The young American's bicycle rested against the wall. There was no bell or knocker, so he flapped the letter-box lid up and down. The man inside took a long time coming and when he did he looked far from pleased to see Wexford. No doubt he resented this involvement.

'Oh, hi,' he said rather coldly, and then, with resignation, 'We've met before. Come on in.'

It was a pleasant voice. Educated, Wexford supposed, though not up to the immaculate Ivy League standard of Mr Littlebury's. The boy showed him into a grubby sitting room, just what he would have expected someone of his age – twenty-three or four – to be living in on his own. There were a lot of books in bookcases made by resting planks on stacks of bricks, a smartish television set, a broken-down old green settee, a gateleg table weighed down with books, papers, typewriter, indefinable metal instruments of the clamp and wrench type, plates, cups and a half-empty glass of something red. Newspapers occupied the only other thing provided for sitting on, a Windsor wheelback chair. The young American swept them off and on to the floor, removing from the wheelback, where they were hanging, a dirty white T-shirt and a pair of muddy socks.

'Can I have your full name?'

'I guess.' But he didn't give it. 'Do I get to know what for? I mean, I'm not involved in all this.'

'Routine, sir. Nothing for you to worry yourself about. Now I'd like your full name.'

'OK, if that's the way you want it. Jonathan Steel Hogarth.' His manner changed and he became expansive. 'They call me Thanny. Well, I call me Thanny, so everyone else does now. You can't all be

180

Jon, can you? I figured if a girl named Patricia can be Tricia, I can be Thanny.'

'You're an American citizen?'

'Yeah. Should I be calling my consul?'

Wexford smiled. 'I doubt if that will be necessary. Have you been here long?'

'I've been in Europe since last summer. Since the end of May. I guess I'm doing what they call the Grand Tour. I've lived *here* maybe a month. I'm a student. Well, I've been a student and hopefully I'm going to be one again. At USM in the fall. So I found this place – what would you call it? A cabin? No, a cottage – and settled in and the next thing there's this massacre on the property up there and the lady next door finds some poor guy hanging off of a tree.'

'A guy? It was a man?'

'Funny that, I don't know. I sort of presumed it was.'

He gave Wexford a rueful grin. It was a delicate face, not so much handsome as sensitive, the features fine as a girl's, large dark-blue eyes with thick long lashes, a short straight nose, roseleaf skin – and the heavy stubble of a dark man who hasn't shaved for two days. The contrast was strangely arresting. 'You want me to tell you what happened? I guess it was lucky I was here. I'd just got back from USM . . . '

Wexford interrupted him. 'You said that before, USM. What's USM?'

Hogarth looked at him as if he must be simple-minded and Wexford quickly saw why. 'I'll be going to school there, right? University of the South, Myringham, USM. What do *you* call it? They do this postgrad creative writing course and I've applied. I only minored in English Literature at college, Military History was my major, so I figured I needed more training if I'm going to write novels. I'd filled out the application and been over with it.' He grinned. 'It's not that I don't have confidence in the British mails, I wanted to take a look at the campus. Well, like I said, I'd delivered my application and got back here – when? I guess around two, ten after two. There came this hammering on my door and the rest I guess you know.'

'Not quite, Mr Hogarth.'

Thanny Hogarth put up his delicate dark eyebrows. He had recovered perfect command of himself, a remarkable command in one so young. 'She can't tell you herself?'

181

'No,' Wexford said thoughtfully. 'No, it appears she can't. What exactly *did* she tell you?' The idea had come to him, not too far-fetched, that Bib had been seeing ghosts, phantasms or bogies, that perhaps she had done this before. There was no body, or what hung from that tree was a sheet of plastic, a windblown sack. The English countryside, after wind and rain, was sometimes festooned with rags of grainy greyish polythene . . . 'What did she say to you? Precisely?'

'Her exact words? It's hard to recall. She said there was a body, hanging . . . She told me *where* and then she started sort of laughing and crying.' An idea struck him, it seemed with pleasure. He suddenly wanted to help. 'I could show you. I guess I could find where she said and show you.'

The wind had dropped and it was very silent and still in the woods. There was a little muted birdsong, but songbirds rarely live in forests and a more usual sound was the shriek of a jay and the woodpecker's distant drilling. They left the car at the point where the by-road twisted to the south. It was an old part of Tancred woods with old standing trees and many fallen.

Gabbitas or his predecessor had done some logging in here but had left a few tree trunks lying, overgrown now with brambles, as habitats for wildlife. So much light penetrated that whole areas of the forest floor were bright with spring grass, but deeper in, where the trunks crowded together, a dense leafmould lay underfoot, crisp on the surface with brown oak leaves.

Here it was that Bib Mew had come, according to Thanny Hogarth. He showed them where he calculated she had abandoned her bicycle. Modest, inhibited Bib must have gone a long way in among the trees before she was satisfied she had found privacy. So long a way, in fact, that Wexford's earlier notion returned to him: that they would find nothing – or nothing but a rag of plastic wrap flapping from a branch.

The silence they all maintained, the grim speechlessness, would seem folly, a pointless over-reacting, when the hanging object, the fluttering rag, the empty sack, was found. He was thinking along these lines, beginning to think as if it were all over, Bib's bogey seen for what it was, the whole thing to be dismissed with an exasperated exclamation – when he saw it. They all saw it.

There were holly trees, a wall of them. They screened a clearing, and in the clearing, from one of the lower branches of a great tree, an ash or perhaps a lime, it hung by the neck. A bundle, tied up at the neck, but no rag or sack. It had weight, the weight of flesh and bones, to suspend it with a heavy ponderousness. This had once been human.

The policemen made no sound. Thanny Hogarth said, 'Wow!'

It was sunny in the clearing. The sun lit the hanging body with a gentle golden gleam. Rather than swinging like a pendulum, it rotated to the extent perhaps of a quarter circle as a metal weight might on the end of a plumb line. This was a beautiful place, a sylvan dell with budding branches around and the tiny yellow and white star flowers of spring underfoot. The body in this setting was obscene. An earlier thought returned to Wexford, that the man or men who did this took pleasure in destruction, delighted in spoliation.

Having stopped briefly to stare, they approached the pendant thing. The policemen went close up, but Thanny Hogarth hung back. His face was unchanged but he hung back and lowered his eyes. It wasn't in fact the exciting discovery he had envisaged, jaunty and eager back at the cottage, Wexford thought. At least, he wasn't going to throw up.

They were a yard from it now. A trousered body, tracksuited, once fat, the neck stretched horribly by the noose, and Wexford saw that he had been wrong, so wrong.

'That's Andy Griffin,' Burden said.

'It's not possible. His parents had a phone call from him on Wednesday night. He was up in the north of England somewhere and he phoned his parents Wednesday evening.'

Sumner-Quist seemed unimpressed. 'This man has been dead at least since Tuesday afternoon and very likely longer.'

For further information they would await his report. Burden was indignant. You cannot directly reproach bereaved parents for telling you lies about their dead son. However much he longed to have it out with them, he would have to desist. Freeborn was very keen on his officers maintaining what he called 'civilised and sensitive' relations with the public.

In any case, Burden could make an intelligent guess at what had happened. Terry and Margaret Griffin wanted to postpone any questioning of Andy as long as possible. If they could maintain a fiction that he was far away – and how much of a fiction, after all, was it? – if they could, when he turned up, persuade him to go to ground again, by the time his reappearance was inevitable the case might be concluded and the whole thing blown over.

'Where was he those three days, Reg? This "up north" stuff is just a blind, isn't it? Where was he between Sunday morning and Tuesday afternoon? Staying with someone?'

'Better get Barry back to his favourite hostelry, the Slug and Lettuce, and see what Andy's mates have to suggest.' Wexford pondered. 'It's a horrible way to kill someone,' he said, 'but there are no "nice" ways. Murder is horrible. If we can talk about it dispassionately, hanging has a lot of advantages for the perpetrator. No blood, for a start. It's cheap. It's certain. Provided you can immobilise your victim, it's easy.'

'How was Andy immobilised?'

'We'll find out when we hear something final from Sumner-Quist. Could be whoever it was did it administered a Mickey Finn first, but that would have its own problems. Andy was the second man? The man Daisy didn't see?'

'Oh, I think so, don't you?'

Wexford made no answer. 'Hogarth was distinctly put out when I came to his door. That may be natural enough, not wanting to get involved. He perked up when he appointed himself our guide, though. Probably just likes being the centre of attention. He looks about seventeen, though he's very likely twenty-three. They go to university for four years in the United States. He says he came here at the end of last May, so that would be after he'd graduated, they do that in May over there, and he'd have been twenty-two. Making the Grand Tour, he called it. Got a well-off father, I'd guess.'

'Have we checked up on him?'

'I thought it wise,' Wexford said rather austerely. He told Burden of a call he had made privately to an old friend, the Vice-Chancellor of Myringham University, and of Dr Perkins's equally private scanning of the enrolment applications computer.

'I wonder what Andy was up to?'

'You and me both,' said Wexford.

He went to see Sylvia. He was too busy to take time to see her, and that was all the more reason. On the way he did something he had never done for her before, bought her flowers. In the florist's he found himself wishing for one of the gorgeous confections sent to dead Davina, a cushion or a heart of blossoms, a basket of lilies.

184

There was nothing of that sort here and he had to settle for golden freesias and pheasant's eye narcissus. The scent of them, stronger than any perfume in a glass flagon, filled his car overpoweringly.

She was strangely touched. He thought for a moment she was going to cry. Instead she smiled and buried her face in the yellow trumpets and white petals.

'They're beautiful. Thank you, Dad.'

Did she know of the quarrel? Had Dora told her?

'How are you going to feel about leaving this house?' It was a nice one, just off prestigious Ploughman's Lane. He knew why she kept moving, why she and Neil hankered after repeated change, and it added nothing to the sum of his happiness. 'No regrets?'

'Wait till you see the Rectory.'

He omitted to tell her he had driven past, back and forth, with her mother. He didn't tell her how appalled they had been by the size of it and its state of dilapidation. She made him tea and he ate her fruit cake, though he didn't want it and it wasn't good for him.

'You and Mother absolutely mustn't fail to come to our house-warming.'

'Why should we fail?'

'Now he asks me! You're famous for never going to parties.'

'This will be the exception that proves the rule.'


Three days had passed since he had seen Daisy. His only contact with her was to assure himself that the watch on her at Tancred House was maintained. To this end he spoke to her on the phone. She was indignant but not angry.

'Rosemary wanted to answer the phone! I can't be doing with that. I told her I wasn't afraid of heavy breathers. Anyway, there haven't been any. I can't really be doing with Karen at all, or with Anne. I mean, they're very nice, but why can't I be here on my own?'

'You know why, Daisy.'

'I just don't believe one of them's going to come back and finish me off.'

'Nor do I, but I like being on the safe side.'

He had tried several times to ring up her father but there was no answer from G.G. Jones in Nineveh Road, wherever – Highbury? Holloway? That evening, having read Davina Flory's novel, *The Hosts of Midian*, the one Casey liked, he began her first book about Eastern Europe and found that he didn't much like Davina. She was a high-toned snob, both social and intellectual; she was bossy, she thought herself superior to most people; she was unkind to her daughter and feudal to her servants. Although avowedly left-wing, she referred not to a 'working' but to a 'lower' class. Her books revealed her as that always suspect creature, the rich socialist.

A mixture of elitism and Marxism imbued these pages. Down-to-earth humanity was conspicuously absent, as was humour, except in a single area. She appeared to be one of those people who relish the idea of unbridled sex for all, find the very notion of sex lubriciously, lip-lickingly delightful and the only provoker of fun, as readily available to the old (the intelligent and attractive old) as to the young. But in the case of the young indispensable, to be indulged in with fabulous frequency, as necessary as food and as positively nourishing.

As a result of his request in the matter of the enrolment computer, he and Dora were invited to the Perkinses' for drinks. The Vice-Chancellor of Myringham University surprised him by confessing a one-time close acquaintance with Harvey Copeland. Harvey, years before, had been a visiting professor of business studies at an American university during the time he, Stephen Perkins, had taught a history class there while working for his Ph.D. According to Dr Perkins, Harvey was at that time, in the sixties, a startlingly handsome man and what he called a 'wow on campus'. There was a minor scandal over a pregnant third-year student and a rather bigger one over his affair with the wife of a head of department.

'Pregnancy wasn't a commonplace among undergraduates then, especially not in the midwest. He didn't have to leave, nothing like that. He stayed his full two years, but a good many sighs of relief were heaved when he took his departure.'

'What was he like, apart from that?'

'Pleasant, ordinary, rather dull. He just looked amazing. They say a man can't tell that about another man but there was no escaping poor Harvey's looks. I'll tell you who he looked like. Paul Newman. But he was a bit of a bore. We went over there to dinner once, didn't we, Rosie? To Tancred, I mean. Harvey was just the same as he was twenty-five years ago, a terrible bore. Still looked like Paul Newman. I mean, the way Paul Newman looks *now*.'

'He was gorgeous, poor Harvey,' said Rosie Perkins.

'And Davina?'

'D'you remember a few years back that graffiti the kids used to

186

write up, "Rambo Rules", "Pistols Rule", that stuff? Well that was Davina. You could have said "Davina Rules". If she was there, she presided. Not so much the life and soul of the party as the boss. In a reasonably subtle way, of course.'

'Why did she marry him?'

'Love. Sex.'

'She used to talk about him in a very embarrassing way. Oh, I shouldn't tell him this, should I, darling?'

'How should I know when I don't know what it is?'

'Well, she was always saying very confidingly, you know, what a wonderful lover he was. She'd look sort of roguish and put her head on one side – it really was embarrassing – one would be alone with her, I mean, there wouldn't be any men there, and she'd just say rather winsomely how he was a marvellous lover. I can't imagine saying such a thing to anyone about my husband.'

'Thank you very much, Rosie,' Perkins laughed. 'She did in fact say it in my hearing once.'

'But she was in her mid sixties when she married him.'

'Has age to do with love?' said the Vice-Chancellor loftily in what sounded to Wexford like a quotation, though he couldn't place it. 'Mind you, she didn't pay him any other compliments. Let's say his intellect didn't stand very high in her regard. But she liked to surround herself with ciphers. People like that do. They acquire them, as in the case of Harvey, or create them, as in the case of that daughter of hers, and then they spend the rest of their lives railing at them for not being witty and scintillating.'

'Did Davina do that?'

'I don't know. I'm guessing. Poor woman's dead and in a hideous way.'

The four of them at the table, two ciphers, as Perkins called them, two sparklers, and then the gunmen entered the house and it was over, the railing and the wit, the dullness and the love, the past and the hope. He often thought of it, he thought about the *mise-en-scène* more than he ever had in any murder case before. The red and white tablecloth, red and white like those fishes in the pool, was a recurring image no one would believe a seasoned policeman like himself could keep seeing. As he read Davina's account of her travels in Saxony and Thuringia, he thought of that tablecloth, dyed with her blood.

'It's a horrible way to kill someone,' he had said to Burden of Andy Griffin's hanging. 'Murder is horrible.' But had it been a clever murder? Or a murder that was mystifying only through a concatenation of unforeseeable circumstances? Were they to believe that the gunman had been clever enough to engrave grooves in the barrel of a .38 or a .357? Some chum of Andy Griffin's had been clever enough for that?

Rosemary Mountjoy stayed at Tancred House with Daisy on Monday night, Karen Malahyde on Tuesday and Anne Lennox on Wednesday. Dr Sumner-Quist furnished Wexford with a full report of the port-mortem on Thursday and a national tabloid daily carried a story on its front page enquiring why the police had made no progress at all in the hunt for those responsible for the Tancred House massacre. The Deputy Chief Constable had Wexford up to his house, wanting to know how he had come to let Andy Griffin die. Or that was what it amounted to, couched differently.

The inquest on Andy Griffin was opened and adjourned. Wexford studied a detailed analysis from the forensic lab on the state of Andy's clothes. Particles of sand, loam, chalk and fibrous leafmould were found in the seams of his tracksuit pants and top and the pockets of his jacket. A very small amount of jute fibre as used in the manufacture of ropes adhered to the neck of his tracksuit top.

Sumner-Quist had found no traces of any sedative or narcotic substance in the stomach or intestines. A blow had been struck to the side of the head prior to death. It was Sumner-Quist's opinion that this blow had been struck by a heavy instrument, probably a metal instrument, wrapped in cloth. The blow was not severe but would have been enough to stun Griffin, to lay him out cold for a few minutes. For long enough.

Wexford didn't shudder. He only felt like shuddering. It was an awful picture that this conjured up, somehow not of this modern world as he knew it, but of a long past time, arcane, brutish and crudely rustic. He could see the unsuspecting man, the fat, stupid and foolishly confident man perhaps believing he had a henchman in his power, and the other creeping behind him with his prearranged weapon, his padded weapon. The blow to the head, quick and expert. Then, no time to waste, the prepared noose, the rope slung over the great limb of an ash tree . . .

Where had the rope come from? Gone were the days of small private ironmongers, ownership passed down in a family from generation to generation. Now you bought rope at a DIY emporium or in the hardware section of some vast general supermarket. It made things harder, for a shop assistant remembers serving an individual customer who asks for specific items far better than does the girl or boy on the check-out. They look at the price rather than the nature of an object as it is lifted from the trolley, they may even pass it unseeing under the scrutiny of an electronic eye, and they may not look at the customer at all.

He had managed to get to bed early. Dora had a cold and was sleeping in the spare room. This had nothing, or not much, to do with the heated words they had had earlier over Sheila. Several times on the phone Dora had spoken to Sheila, but always in the daytime when her father was at work. She was bitter against him, Dora told Wexford, but willing to 'talk it through'. The terminology made Wexford snort. That sort of jargon was all very well at Royal Oak, quite another thing from the lips of his daughter.

Dora's idea was that Sheila should come down for another weekend. Of course, Casey would have to come too, they were a couple now, one of those unmarried couples, who do everything together and put their names side by side on Christmas cards. Casey would come with her as naturally as Neil would with Sylvia. Over his dead body, said Wexford.

So Dora had sniffed and taken her cold into the spare room. With her went the pile of literature Sheila had sent – addressed pointedly to her mother – on the little town of Heights in Nevada where the university campus was. This included a prospectus of Heights University with details of the courses it offered and photographs of its amenities. A city guide presented panoramic views of the scenery in which it was set and pages and pages of advertisements from local traders to offset, no doubt, the cost of this glossy production. Wexford had given them both a miserable glance before handing these productions back to Dora without comment.

He sat up in bed with a fresh pile of books Amyas Ireland had sent. He read all the writing on the cover of the top one, which Ireland had told him was called 'jacket copy'. He read enough of the introduction to understand that *Lovely As A Tree* was going to be about Davina Flory's efforts with her first husband to replant the ancient woods of Tancred, before the onset of sleep dropped his eyelids and shook him with a violent galvanic start. He put out the light.

His phone was bleeping. He reached for it and knocked the tree book on to the floor.

Karen said, 'Sir, this is DC Malahyde at Tancred House. I've phoned in.' This was the term they all used for contacting the police station to summon help. 'They're on their way. But I thought you'd want to know. There's someone outside, a man, I think. We heard him and then we – well, Daisy, she *saw* him.'

'I'm on my way too,' said Wexford.

# 17

It was one of those rare nights when the moon shines nearly bright enough to read by. Up in the woods Wexford's car lights quenched the moonlight but once he emerged on to the open land and came into the courtyard, everything showed as clear as day in the still white radiance. No breath of wind stirred the trees. To the west of the great pile of the house and behind it showed the tops of the pines and firs and cedars in the pinetum, serrated, spired, pinnacled, fronded, black silhouettes against the gleaming pearl-grey sky. A single greenish star shone very brightly. The moon was a white sphere, alabaster-like and glowing, so that you could understand the ancients believing a light burned inside it.

The arc lamps under the wall were out, had perhaps gone out on a time clock. It was twenty to one. Two police cars were parked on the flagstones, one of them Barry Vine's Vauxhall. Wexford pulled his car alongside Barry's. In the dark water of the pool the moon was reflected, a white globe. The front door was open, the inner glass door was closed but not locked. Karen opened it to him as he approached. She told him, before he could get a word out, that four men from the uniformed branch were searching the woods nearest to the house. Vine was upstairs.

He nodded, went past her into the drawing room. Daisy was walking up and down, clenching and unclenching her hands. He thought for an instant that she was going to throw herself into his arms. But she only came close to him, about a yard from him, bringing her fists up to her face and holding them to her mouth as if she meant to gnaw her knuckles. Her eyes were enormous. He understood at once that she had been frightened almost unendurably, was near hysteria with terror.

'Daisy,' he said gently, and then, 'Won't you sit down? Come and sit down. Nothing is going to happen. You're quite safe.'

She shook her head. Karen went to her, hazarded a touch on her arm, and when that was repulsed, took her arm and led her to a chair. Instead of sitting down, Daisy turned fully to face Karen. Her wound must be nearly healed by now, only a slight padding on the shoulder showed through her sweater.

She said, 'Hold me. Please hold me for a minute.'

Karen put her arms round her and held her tight. Wexford noticed that Karen was one of those rare people who can hug another without patting shoulderblades. She held on to Daisy like a mother with a child that has been endangered newly restored to her, then she released her gently and propelled her into the chair, *placed* her in the chair.

'She's been like this ever since she saw him, haven't you, Daisy?' Nurse-like, Karen went on, 'I don't know how many times I've cuddled you, it doesn't seem to do much good. Would you like another cup of tea?'

'I didn't want the first cup!' Wexford had never before heard Daisy sound like this, her voice all over the place, jagged, like the run-up to a scream. 'Why do I have to have tea? I'd like something to stun me, I'd like something to make me go to sleep for ever!'

'Make us all a cup of tea, would you, Karen?' He disliked making this request of women officers, it smacked too much of the old days, but he told himself he would have asked for tea to be made if it had been Archbold standing there or Davidson. 'For you and me and Sergeant Vine and whoever else is about. And would you bring Daisy a small brandy? I think you'll find it in the cabinet in the –' Not for anyone was he going to call it the *serre* '– the greenhouse.'

Daisy's eyes darted this way and that, to the windows, to the door. When the door swung slowly and silently inwards she drew in her breath in a long tremulous gasp, but it was only the cat, the big dignified blue cat, walking majestically in. The cat gave Wexford one of those stares of contempt that only a spoilt pet can achieve, went up to Daisy and leapt lightly into her lap.

'Oh Queenie, oh Queenie!' Daisy hung forward, burying her face in the dense blue fur.

'Tell me what happened, Daisy.'

She went on nuzzling the cat, murmuring feverishly. Queenie's purr was a deep heavy throb.

'Come on,' Wexford said more roughly. 'Get a grip on yourself.' He talked to Sheila like that when she tried his patience, *had* talked to her like that.

Daisy lifted her head. She swallowed. He saw the delicate movement of the thorax between the curtains of shining dark hair.

'You must tell me what happened.'

'It was *so* awful.' Still the ragged voice, hoarse, shrill, broken. 'It was *terrible*.'

Karen came in with the brandy in a wine-glass. She held it to Daisy's lips like medicine. Daisy took a sip and choked.

'Let her drink it herself,' said Wexford. 'She's not ill. She's not a child or a geriatric, for God's sake. She's just had a fright.'

That shook her. Her eyes flashed. She took the glass from Karen as Barry Vine came in with four cups of tea on a tray, and threw the brandy down her throat in a bold defiant gesture. A violent choking ensued. Karen banged her on the back and the tears came into Daisy's eyes, overflowed and streamed down her face.

Having watched this performance inscrutably for a few seconds, Vine said, 'Good morning, sir.'

'I suppose it is morning, Barry. Yes, well, it must be. Now Daisy, dry your eyes. You're better now. You're all right now.'

She rubbed at her face with the tissue Karen handed her. She stared at him rather mutinously but it was in her old voice that she spoke.

'I've never had brandy before.'

It rang a bell. Years and years before, he remembered Sheila uttering those same words and the young ass that was with her saying, 'Another virginity gone, alas!' It made him sigh. 'OK, where were you both, you and Karen? In bed?'

'It was only just after eleven thirty, sir!'

He had forgotten that to these young things eleven thirty was mid-evening. 'I asked Daisy,' he said sharply.

'I was in here, watching the telly. I don't know where Karen was, in the kitchen or somewhere, making herself a drink. We were going to go to bed when the programme finished. I heard someone outside but I thought it was Karen . . .'

'What do you mean, you heard someone?'

'Footsteps out in the front. The outside lights had just gone off. They're set to go off at half past eleven. The footsteps came right up to the house, to the windows there, and I got up to look. The moon was very bright, you didn't need lights. I saw him, I saw him out

193

there in the moonlight as near as you are to me now.' She paused, breathing quickly. 'And I just started screaming, I screamed and screamed, till Karen came.'

'I'd already heard him, sir. I heard him before Daisy did, I think, footsteps outside the kitchen door and then going round the back of the house, along the terrace. I ran through the house and into the – the conservatory, and I heard him again but I never saw him. That was when I phoned in. I phoned in before I heard Daisy screaming. I came in here and found Daisy at the window screaming and hammering on the glass and then I – I phoned you.'

Wexford turned to Daisy again. She had grown calm, the brandy apparently having had that stunning effect she craved. 'What exactly did you see, Daisy?'

'He had a thing over his head, like a sort of woolly helmet with eyeholes. He looked like those pictures you see of terrorists. The thing he was wearing, I don't know, maybe a tracksuit, dark, could have been black or dark blue.'

'Was it the same man as the gunman who killed your family and tried to kill you here on 11 March?'

Even as he uttered it he thought what a terrible question it was to have to put to an eighteen-year-old, a sheltered girl, a gentle frightened girl. Of course she couldn't answer him. The man had been masked. She returned his look with one of despair.

'I don't know, I don't know. How can I tell? It might have been. I couldn't tell anything about him, he might have been young or not so young, he wasn't *old*. He looked big and strong. He seemed – he seemed to know this place, though I don't know how I knew that, it's just that he seemed to know what he was doing and where he was going. Oh, what will become of me, what will happen to me!'

Wexford was saved from trying to find an answer by the entry into the room of the Harrisons. Though Ken Harrison was fully dressed, his wife was in the kind of garment Wexford had heard, long ago, called a 'housecoat', red velvet with whitish swansdown round the neck, the front open from the waist to show blue spotted pyjama legs. In time-honoured fashion, she was carrying a poker.

'What's going on?' said Harrison. 'There's men everywhere. The place is bristling with cops. I said to Brenda, you know what this could be? This could be those villains come back to finish Daisy off.'

'So we put some things on and came straight here. I wasn't

194

walking, I made Ken get the car out. You're not safe here, I wouldn't count on being safe even *inside* a car.'

'Mind you, we should have *been* here. I said it from the first, when we first heard there was going to be some policewoman stopping in the house. Why didn't they just get us? You don't want some bit of a girl, policewoman or no policewoman so-called. Johnny and us, we should have been called in, God knows there's bedrooms enough, but oh no, nobody suggested it, so I never said a word. If Johnny and us had been here and the word had gone round we was here, d'you reckon any of this would have happened? D'you reckon that gunman would have had the nerve to come back here with ideas of finishing her off? Not a . . . '

Daisy cut him short. Wexford was astonished by what she did. She jumped up and said with cold clarity, 'I'm giving you notice' You must be on some sort of notice and I don't know what it is, but a month's if possible. I want you out of here and the sooner the better. If I had my way, you'd be out tomorrow.'

She was her grandmother's granddaughter all right. She stood with her head thrown back, confronting them contemptuously. And then, quickly, her voice broke and slurred. The brandy had done its work and now it was doing work of a different kind.

'Haven't you any feelings? Haven't you any care for me? Talking about finishing me off? I hate you! I hate you both! I want you out of my house, off my land, I'm going to take your cottage away from you . . . '

Her cry disintegrated into a wail, a hysterical sobbing. The Harrisons stood dumbfounded, Brenda's mouth actually hanging open. Karen went up to Daisy and Wexford thought for a moment she was going to administer one of those slaps that are supposed to be the best remedy for hysteria. But instead she took Daisy in her arms and, with one hand on the dark head, brought it to rest against her own shoulder.

'Come, Daisy, I'm going to take you up to bed now. You'll be quite quite safe now.'

Would she? Wexford wished he could have provided such a confident reassurance. Vine's eyes met his and the sedate sergeant performed the action most nearly possible to him of casting up the gaze. He moved his eyeballs a few millimetres to the north.

Ken Harrison said excitedly, 'She's overwrought, she's in a state, she didn't mean that. She didn't mean that, did she?'

'Of course she didn't mean it, Ken, we're all a family here, we're part of the family. Of course she didn't mean it – did she?'

'I think you'd better go home, Mrs Harrison,' said Wexford. 'Both of you should go home.' He rejected saying that things would seem different in the morning, though they undoubtedly would. 'Get on home and get some sleep.'

'Where's Johnny?' said Brenda. 'That's what I'd like to know. If we could hear those men, and they were making enough racket to wake the dead, why didn't Johnny hear them? Why's he laying low? That's what I'd like to know.' She went on with venom, 'Can't even be bothered to come up here and see what's going on. If you ask me, if someone's going to get the push it should be him, lazy devil. What's he got to lay low about?'

'He slept through it.' Wexford couldn't resist adding, 'He's young.'

Karen Malahyde, twenty-three years old, far from fitting Ken Harrison's image of a 'policewoman', that now derogatory and disused term, was a black belt who taught a judo class. Wexford knew that if she had encountered the Tancred intruder on the previous night and that man had either been unarmed or slow on the draw, she would have been capable of rendering him harmless very rapidly. Once she had described how she went alone everywhere fearlessly at night, having proved herself by throwing a mugger the width of a street.

But was she an adequate bodyguard for Daisy on her own? Were Anne or Rosemary adequate? He must persuade Daisy to leave the house. Not exactly to go into hiding but certainly to go some distance and hole up with friends. Still, he confessed to himself and later to Burden that this was a development he hadn't expected. He had supplied a 'minder' for Daisy but only to be on the safe side. That one of those men, the gunman necessarily if the other, the unseen, had been Andy Griffin, should in fact come back to 'get her' was the stuff of dreams, of fiction, of wild imaginings. *It did not happen.*

'It did,' said Burden. 'She's not safe here and she ought to go. I don't see how it's going to make much difference if we move the Harrisons and Gabbitas into the house. There were four people in the house that first time, remember? That didn't deter him.'

The white tablecloth with the glass on it and the silver. The food on the heated trolley. The curtains cosily drawn against the March

196

night. The first course finished, the soup, Naomi Jones serving the fish, the sole *bonne femme,* and when everyone has a plate, as everyone begins to eat, the sounds from overhead, the noises Davina Flory says are made by the cat Queenie on the rampage.

But Harvey Copeland goes to look, handsome Harvey who looked like Paul Newman and had been a 'wow on campus', that his elderly wife had married for love and sex. Silence outside, no car, no footsteps, only a distant commotion overhead.

Harvey has gone upstairs and come down again or has never reached upstairs, but turned at the foot as the gunman comes out of the passage . . .

How long had all this taken? Thirty seconds? Two minutes? And in those two minutes what was going on in the dining room? They were calmly eating their fish in Harvey's absence? Or simply waiting for him, talking about the cat, the way the cat ran up the back stairs and down the front every night. Then the shot and Naomi getting to her feet, Daisy getting to her feet, starting for the door. Davina remained where she was, seated at the table. Why? Why would she do that? Fear? Simple fear holding her fast to the spot?

The door flies open and the gunman enters and the shots are fired and the tablecloth is no longer white but scarlet, dyed by a dense stain that was to spread across nearly the whole of it . . .

'I'll talk to her in a minute,' Wexford said. 'Of course I can't force her to leave if she doesn't want to. Come with me, will you? We'll both have a go.'

'She may be very anxious to go by now. Morning makes all the difference.'

Yes, but it doesn't make that kind of difference, thought Wexford. The light of day makes you less afraid, not more. Sunshine and the morning make you dismiss last night's terrors as exaggerated. Light is practical and dark is occult.

They went outside, crossed the yard and came slowly round the side of the house, the west wing. He had not used those words to himself metaphorically. The sun shone with a hard strong light where the moon had shed a pale glow. The sky was a deep blue without cloud. It might have been June, for the air felt mild as if the chill had been lifted for an assured stretch of months.

'He came round the back here, then,' Burden said. 'What was he trying to do, find a way in? An open window downstairs? It wasn't a cold night.'

'There were no open windows downstairs. All the doors were locked. Unlike that previous time.'

'It was a bit funny, wasn't it, pattering round the house so that two people inside could plainly hear you? With all the windows closed, they could still hear? You disguise yourself in a hood but you don't mind making a hell of a racket while you're looking for a way in.'

Wexford said thoughtfully, 'I wonder if the truth is he didn't mind if he was heard or seen? If he believed Daisy was alone and he meant to kill her, so what if she did see him?'

'In that case, why wear a mask?'

'True.'

An unfamiliar car was parked a few yards from the front door. That door opened as they approached the car and Joyce Virson came out with Daisy behind her. Mrs Virson was in a fur coat, the kind of garment neither favoured nor fashionable, that the Oxfam shop baulked at and the church sales couldn't sell, unmistakably made from the pelts of many foxes.

Never had Wexford seen Daisy so punkish. There was something defiant about her gear, the black tights and lace-up boots, black sweatshirt with something white printed on it, the scuffed black leather motorbike jacket. Her face was a mask of misery but her hair, heavily gelled, stuck out in spikes all over her head like a forest of burnt tree stumps. She seemed to be making a statement – perhaps only that this was Daisy *contra mundum*.

She looked at him, she looked at Burden, in silence. It took Joyce Virson a moment or two to recall who this was. A big toothy smile transfigured her as she came up to Wexford with both hands outstretched.

'Oh, Mr Wexford, how are you? I'm so pleased to see you. You're just the man to persuade this child to come back with me. I mean, she can't stay here on her own, can she? I was so utterly horrified when I heard what happened here last night, I came straight over. She should never have been allowed to leave us.'

Wexford wondered how she had heard. Not through Daisy, he was sure.

'I'm sorry, but I don't understand the way things are allowed to be these days. When I was eighteen I wouldn't have been permitted to stay anywhere on my own, let alone in a great lonely house like this one. You can't tell me things have changed for the better. I'm sorry, but as far as I'm concerned the old days were the best.'

198

Stony-faced, Daisy watched her through half this speech, then turned aside to fix her eyes on the cat which, perhaps seldom permitted to escape from the front of the house, was sitting on the stone coping of the pool, watching the white and red fish. The fish swam in concentric circles and the cat watched.

'Do say something to her, Mr Wexford. Persuade her. Use your authority. You can't tell me there's no way of bringing pressure to bear on a *child*.' Mrs Virson was rapidly forgetting that persuasion necessarily must include elements of niceness and perhaps flattery if it is to succeed. Her voice rose. 'It's so stupid and downright foolhardy! What does she think she's playing at?'

The cat dipped a paw into the pool, found an element different from what it expected and shook water drops from its pads. Daisy bent down and lifted it up in her arms. She said, 'Goodbye, Joyce,' and with an edge of irony, not lost on Wexford, 'Thank you so much for coming.' She stalked into the house with her fluffy armful, but left the door open.

Burden followed her in. With no idea what to say, Wexford muttered something about having it all in hand, the police had it under control. Joyce Virson gave him a scathing glare, as well she might.

'I'm sorry, but that's just not good enough. I'm going to have to see what my son says about that.'

From her it sounded like a threat. He watched her making heavy weather of turning the little car round and positioning it without – just without – scraping its nearside wing on the gateway post as she drove off. Daisy was in the hall with Burden, sitting in a high-backed, velvet-cushioned chair with Queenie on her lap.

'Why do I care so much if he does kill me?' she was saying. 'I don't understand myself. After all, I want to die. I've nothing to live for. Why did I scream and make all that fuss last night? I should have walked out there and gone up to him and said, Kill me, go on, kill me. Finish me off, like that horrible Ken says.'

Wexford shrugged. He said with some taciturnity, 'Don't mind me, will you? If you get done in I'll have to resign.'

She didn't smile but made a sort of grimace. 'Talking of resigning, what d'you think? It was that Brenda phoned her, Joyce, I mean. She phoned her up first thing this morning and told her I'd given them the sack and to *make* me keep them on. How about that? As if I was

199

a child or a psychiatric case. That's how Joyce knew about last night. There's no way I'd have told her, interfering old bat.'

'You must have other friends, Daisy. Isn't there someone else you could stay with for a little while? For a couple of weeks?'

'You'll have caught him in two weeks?'

'It's more than probable,' Burden said stoutly.

'It makes no difference to me, anyway. I'm staying here. Karen or Anne can come if they like. Well, it's if *you* like, I suppose. But it's a waste of time, they needn't bother. I shan't be afraid any more. *I want him to kill me*. That'll be the best way out, to die.'

She hung her head forward and buried her face in the cat's fur.

Tracing Andy Griffin's movements from the time he left his parents' house proved impossible. His usual drinking companions from the Slug and Lettuce knew nothing of any other address he might have, though Tony Smith spoke of a girlfriend 'up north'. That empty expression always came up in conversation concerning Andy. Now there was a girlfriend in that vague region, that never-never land.

'Kylie, she was called,' said Tony.

'I reckon he made her up,' Leslie Sedlar said with a sly grin. 'He got her off the telly.'

Until losing his job just over a year before, Andy had been a long-distance lorry driver for a company of brewers. His usual route had taken him from Myringham to various London outlets and to Carlisle and Whitehaven.

The brewers had few good words to say of Andy. They had in the past two or three years been enlightened as to the reality of sexual harassment. Andy spent little time in the office but on the few occasions he had been there he had made offensive remarks to a woman marketing executive and had once taken hold of her secretary from behind in an arm lock round her neck. Status did little to deter Andy Griffin, it was apparently enough that his quarry should be female.

The girlfriend seemed a myth. There was no evidence of her and the Griffins denied her existence. Terry Griffin gave reluctant permission for a search of Andy's bedroom in Myringham. He and his wife were stunned by the death of their son and both looked as if they'd aged by ten years. They sought the remedy of television as others in their situation might look to sedatives or alcohol. Colours and movement, faces and violent action, flowed across the screen to provide a solace that needed only to be *there,* not to be absorbed or even comprehended.

The whitewashing of her son's reputation was now Margaret Griffin's only aim. It might have been said that this was the last best thing she could do for him. Accordingly, still watching the flowing images, she denied all knowledge of any girl. There had never been a girl in Andy's life. Taking hold of her husband's hand and gripping it tightly, she repeated this last phrase. She managed, in the way she repudiated Burden's suggestion, to make a girlfriend sound like a venereal disease, in a mother's eyes as disgraceful, as irresponsibly acquired and as potentially damaging.

'And you last saw him on Sunday morning, Mr Griffin?'

'Early morning. Andy was always up with the lark. About eight, it was. He made me a cup of tea.' The man was dead and he had been a thug, a sexual menace, idle and stupid, but his father would continue pathetically to do for him this splendid public relations job. Even *post mortem* his mother would advertise the purity of his conduct and his father eulogise over his punctual habits, his thoughtfulness and his altruism. 'He said he was off up north,' Terry Griffin said.

Burden sighed, and suppressed his sigh.

'On that bike,' said the dead man's mother. 'I always hated that bike and I was right. Look what's happened.'

From some curious emotional need, she was beginning the metamorphosis of her son's murder into death in a road accident.

'He said he'd give us a ring. He always said that, we didn't have to ask.'

'We never had to ask,' his wife said wearily.

Burden put in gently, 'But he didn't in fact phone, did he?'

'No, he never did. And that worried me, knowing he was on that bike.'

Margaret Griffin held on to her husband's hand, drawing it into her lap. Burden went down the passage to the bedroom where Davidson and Rosemary Mountjoy were searching. The stack of pornography an exploration of Andy's clothes cupboard had revealed didn't surprise him. Andy would have known that his mother's discretion where he was concerned would have kept herself and her vacuum cleaner honourably away from the inside of that cupboard.

Andy Griffin had not been a correspondent, nor had he been attracted by the printed word. The magazines relied on photographs solely for effect and the briefest of crudely titillating captions. His girlfriend, if she had existed, had never written to him and if she had given him a photograph of herself he had not kept it.

The only discovery they made of real interest was in a paper bag in the bottom drawer of a chest of drawers. This was ninety-six American dollar bills in various denominations, tens, fives and singles.

The Griffins insisted they knew nothing about this money. Margaret Griffin looked at the notes as if they were phenomenal, currency from some remote culture perhaps, a find from an archaeological dig. She turned them over, peering, her grief temporarily forgotten.

It was Terry who put the question she perhaps thought asking would make her look foolish. 'Is it money? Could you use it to buy things?'

'You could in the United States,' Burden said. He corrected himself. 'You could use it almost anywhere, I daresay. Here in this country and in Europe. Shops would take it. Anyway, you could take it to a bank and change it into sterling.' He put it more simply. 'Into – well, pounds.'

'Why didn't Andy spend it then?'

Burden balked at the idea of asking them about the rope but he had to ask. In the event, to his relief, neither of them seemed to make the awful connection. They knew the means by which their son had died but the word 'rope' did not immediately conjure for them the notion of hanging. No, they possessed no rope and they were sure Andy had not. Terry Griffin harked back to the money, the haul of dollars. Once the idea of it was planted in his mind, it seemed to take precedence over everything.

'Those notes you said could be changed into pounds, they belonged to Andy?'

'They were in his room.'

'Then they'll be ours, won't they? It'll be like compensation.'

'Oh, Terry,' said his wife.

He ignored her. 'How much d'you reckon they're worth?'

'Forty to fifty pounds.'

Terry Griffin considered. 'When can we have them?' he said.

# 18

He answered the phone himself.

'Gunner Jones.'

Or that was what Burden thought he said. He might have said 'Gun*nar* Jones'. Gunnar was a Swedish name but such as might possibly be held by an Englishman if, say, his mother had been a Swede. Burden had been at school with someone called Lars who had seemed as English as himself, so why not Gunnar? Or else he *had* said 'Gunner' and it was a nickname he'd got through having been in the Royal Artillery.

'I'd like to come and see you, Mr Jones. Would later on today be convenient? Say six?'

'You can come when you like. I'll be here.'

He didn't ask why or mention Tancred or his daughter. It was slightly disconcerting. Burden didn't want a wasted journey.

'You *are* Miss Davina Jones's father?'

'So her mother told me. We have to believe the ladies in these matters, don't we?'

Burden wasn't getting himself involved with that one. He said he'd see G.G. Jones at six. 'Gunner' – on an impulse he looked it up in the dictionary from which Wexford was never parted for long and found it could also be another name for a gunsmith. A *gunsmith*?

Wexford's phone call was to Edinburgh.

Macsamphire was such an odd name, though unmistakably Scots, that he had counted on the single one in the Edinburgh telephone directory being Davina Flory's friend, and he was right.

'Kingsmarkham *Police*? What help can I possibly be to you?'

'Mrs Macsamphire, I believe Miss Flory and Mr Copeland with

203

Mrs Jones and Daisy all stayed with you last August when they came up for the Edinburgh Festival?'

'Oh, no, whatever can have given you that idea? Davina very much disliked staying in private houses. They all stayed in a hotel, and then when Naomi was taken ill, she had a really severe flu, I suggested she be moved here. So dreadful being ill in an hotel, don't you think, even a grand one like the Caledonian? But Naomi wouldn't, afraid of giving it to me, I expect. Davina and Harvey were in and out, of course, and we all went to a good many of the shows together. I don't think I saw poor Naomi at all.'

'Miss Flory was taking part in the Book Fair herself, I believe?'

'That's so. She gave a talk on the difficulties which arise in the writing of autobiography and she also took part in a writer's panel. The subject was something about the practicalities of writers being versatile – that is, writing fiction as well as travel and essays and so on. I attended the lecture and the panel and both were really most interesting . . .'

Wexford managed to cut her short. 'Daisy was with you as well?'

Her laugh was musical and rather girlish. 'Oh, I don't think Daisy was much interested in all that. As a matter of fact, she'd promised her grandmother she'd come to the lecture but I don't believe she turned up. She's such a sweet unaffected girl, though, you'd forgive her anything.'

This was the kind of thing Wexford wanted to hear from her – or he could persuade himself he wanted to hear it.

'Of course, she had this young man of hers there with her. I only saw him once and that was on their last day, the Saturday. I waved to them across the street.'

'Nicholas Virson,' said Wexford.

'That's right. Davina did mentioned the name Nicholas.'

'He was at the funeral.'

'Oh, was he? I was rather upset at the funeral. I don't remember. Was that all you wanted to ask me?'

'I haven't begun to ask you what I really want, Mrs Macsamphire. It's to do me a favour.' Was it? Or to exact from him a great sacrifice? 'Daisy should be away from here for various reasons I needn't go into. I want to ask if you'd invite her to stay with you. Just for a week –' He hesitated '– or two. Would you ask her?'

'Oh, but she wouldn't come!'

'Why not? I'm sure she likes you. I'm sure she would like to be with someone she could talk to about her grandmother. Edinburgh is a beautiful and interesting city. Now, what's the weather like?'

Again that pretty giggle. 'I'm afraid it's *pouring*. But of course I'll ask Daisy; I'd love to have her, it's just that I never thought of asking her myself.'

The drawbacks of the system sometimes seemed to outweigh the points in favour of setting up an incident room on site. Among the advantages were that you could see with your own eyes who came calling. Not a Virson vehicle this morning, drawn up between the pond and the front door, not one of the Tancred cars, but a small Fiat Wexford couldn't immediately place. He had seen it before but whose was it?

This time he was to be granted no timely opening of the door and egress of the visitor. There was nothing of course to stop him pulling the sugarstick bellpull, gaining admittance and making a third at whatever tête-à-tête was in progress. He disliked the idea. He mustn't take over her life, rob her of all privacy, her right to be solitary and free.

Queenie, the Persian, sat on the coping of the pool, looking into the mirror-like surface of the water. A lifted paw briefly distracted its attention. The cat contemplated the underside of fat grey pads, as if deciding on the paw's fitness as a fishing implement, then tucked both paws under its chest, folded itself into the sphinx position and resumed its staring at the water and the circling fish.

Wexford walked back past the stables, round the house and on to the terrace. He had a vague feeling of trespassing, but she knew they were there, she wanted them there. While he was here she was protected, she was safe. He looked up at the back of the house and saw for the first time that the Georgianisation had not reached so far. This was much the way it had been in the seventeeth century, the half-timbering exposed, the top windows mullioned.

Had Davina built the conservatory? Before Listed Building consent was needed? He thought he disapproved, without knowing enough about architecture to have a firm opinion. Daisy was in there. He caught sight of her get up from where she had been sitting. Her back was to him and he quickly left the terrace before she had seen him. Her companion was invisible.

It was chance that allowed Wexford an encounter with him an

hour later. He was coming out in his own car and he told Donaldson to wait when he saw someone getting into the Fiat.

'Mr Sebright.'

Jason gave him a broad smile. 'Did you read my piece on the mourners? The sub cut it to bits and changed the title. They called it "A Farewell to Greatness". What I don't like about local journalism is the way you have to be nice about everybody. You can't be *acerbic*. For instance, the *Courier* has a gossip column but there's never a snide line in it. I mean, the sort of thing you want is speculation about who's screwing the Mayoress and how the Chief Constable wangled his holiday in Tobago. But that's anathema on a local paper.'

'Don't worry,' said Wexford. 'I doubt if you'll be there long.'

'That sounds a bit double-edged. I've had an amazing interview with Daisy. "The Masked Intruder".'

'She told you about that?'

'Everything. The works.' He gave Wexford a sidelong look, a little smile twitching. 'I couldn't help thinking, anyone could do that, couldn't they? Come up here in a mask and frighten the ladies?'

'Appeals to you, does it?'

'Only as a story,' said Jason. 'Well, I'll be off home.'

'And where's home?'

'Cheriton. I'll tell you a story. I only read it the other day, I think it's wonderful. Lord Halifax said to John Wilkes, "Upon my word, sir, I do not know if you will first perish on the gallows or of the pox," and Wilkes said back, quick as a flash, "That depends, my lord, on whether I first embrace your Lordship's principles or your Lordship's mistress."'

'Yes, I've heard it before. Is it apt?'

'It sort of reminds me of *me*,' said Jason Sebright. He waved to Wexford, got into his car and drove off rather too fast down the by-road.

Gunther, or Gunnar, appears in the saga of the Nibelungen. Gunnar is the Norse form, Gunther the German or Burgundian. Gunther resolved to ride through the flames which encircled Brünnhilde's castle and thus win her for his wife. He failed and it was Siegfried who succeeded in Gunther's shape, remaining with Brünnhilde for three nights, lying beside her but with a sword between. Wagner had composed operas about it.

This account was given Burden by his wife before he set off for London. Burden sometimes thought his wife knew everything – well, everything *of that sort*. Far from resenting this, it met with his unqualified admiration and it was very useful. She was better than Wexford's dictionary and, he told her, much nicer-looking.

'How did they do that, d'you think? The sword, I mean. It wouldn't have been much of a hindrance if they laid it down flat. You could just have pulled the sheet up and over it and you'd hardly have known it was there.'

'I think,' said Jenny gravely, 'they must have laid it sharp side upwards, the hilt resting on the bedhead, if you can imagine. Only I expect they only wrote about it, never actually did it.'

Barry Vine drove. He was one of those who enjoyed driving, whose wives are never allowed to drive, who will drive distances of enormous and terrible lengths and still appear to enjoy themselves. Barry had once told Burden how he had driven all the way home from the West of Ireland single-handed and without a break except for the bit on the ferry to Fishguard. This time he only had to drive fifty miles.

'You know that expression, sir, "kissing the gunner's daughter"?'

'No, I don't.' Burden was beginning to feel an ignoramus. Was DS Vine about to tell him the further adventures of all these Wagnerian people, who seemed to find their way from Norse sagas into German operas and back?

'It's a phrase that means something completely different, only I can't remember what.'

'Does it come in an opera?'

'Not so far as I know,' said Barry.

Daisy's father's house was near Arsenal football ground, a small grey-brick Victorian house in a street of terraces. There was no restriction on parking and Vine could leave the car by the kerb in Nineveh Road.

'Be light this time tomorrow,' Barry said, feeling for the latch on the gate. 'Clocks go on tonight.'

'They go on, do they? I can never remember when they go on and when they go back.'

'Spring forward, fall back,' said Barry.

Burden, tiring of always being the one at the receiving end of instruction, was about to protest that you might as well say, fall forward, spring back, when a brilliant flood of light from the front door suddenly washed over them and made them blink.

A man came out on to the step. He held out his hand to each of them as if they were invited guests or even old friends.

'You found your way all right then?'

It was one of those remarks which must have received a prefatory affirmative in order to be made at all, but people go on making them. G.G. Jones even made another.

'Put your car somewhere, have you?'

His tone was jolly. He was a younger man than Burden had expected, or he looked younger. Inside, with the light on him rather than behind him, he was revealed as not much more than forty. Burden had also expected a resemblance to Daisy but there was none, or none that an early cursory study showed.

Jones was fair, his face ruddy. The look of youth was partly due to that face being round and babyish, snub-nosed, wide at the cheekbones. Daisy was no more like him than she was like Naomi. She was her grandmother's child.

He was also overweight, too much overweight for his big frame to carry it well. The beginnings of a formidable belly swelled out his sweater in a barrel shape. He seemed perfectly at ease, with nothing to hide, and the impression of their being invited, even honoured guests, was enhanced by his producing a bottle of whisky, three cans of beer and three tumblers.

Both policemen refused. They had been shown into a living room that was comfortable enough but lacked what Burden would have called 'a woman's touch'. He was aware that this was (mysteriously to him, since he could only see it as flattering women) a sexist theory. His wife would have told him off for holding it. But secretly he adhered to it, it was *fact*. Here, for example, was a comfortable, decently furnished room with pictures on the walls and a calendar hanging up, a clock on the mantelpiece over the Victorian fireplace, even a rubber plant struggling to survive in a dim corner. But there was nothing of care or taste, nothing of interest in what a place looked like, no symmetry, no arrangement, no home-making. No woman lived in this house.

He was aware that he had been silent too long, even though Jones had filled the interval with fetching the diet coke he had pressed Barry into accepting and with pouring his own beer. Burden cleared his throat.

'D'you mind telling us your name, Mr Jones? What do the initials stand for?'

'My first name's George but I'm always called Gunner.'

'E,r or a,r?'

'I'm sorry?'

'Gunner or Gunn*ar*?'

'Gunner. On account of I used to play for Arsenal. Didn't you know?'

No, they didn't know. Barry's lips twitched. He took a swig of his diet coke. So Jones had once, maybe twenty years ago, played for Arsenal, the Gunners, and Naomi the 'soccer groupie' had hero-worshipped from the stand . . .

'George Godwin Jones, that's my full name.' Gunner Jones's face wore a pleased look. 'I've been married since Naomi,' he said unexpectedly, 'but that one wasn't a roaring success either. She packed her bags five years ago and I'm not thinking of taking the plunge again. Not when it's like the song says and you can have it all and not get hooked.'

'What do you do for a living, Mr Jones?' Barry asked.

'Sell sports equipment. I've got a shop in the Holloway Road, and don't talk to me about recessions. As far as I'm concerned, business is booming, never better.' He wiped the broad, self-satisfied smile from his face as if with some swift inner switch. 'That was a bad business at Tancred,' he said, his voice dropping an octave. 'That's what you're here about, yes? Or, let's say you wouldn't be here if it hadn't happened?'

'I don't believe you've had much contact with your daughter?'

'I haven't had any, my friend. I haven't had sight nor sound of her for a good seventeen years. How old is she now? Eighteen? I haven't seen her since she was six months old. And the answer to your next question is, no, not a lot. No, I don't care. It doesn't worry me one way or the other. Men may get to like their kids when they're older, fair enough, but babies? Don't mean a thing, do they? I washed my hands of the lot of them and I've never had a moment's regret.'

It was startling how fast his bonhomie could become belligerence. His voice rose and fell as the subject matter changed, a crescendo when he spoke of things personal to himself, a low purr when paying lip service to society's requirements.

Barry Vine said, 'You didn't think of getting in touch when you heard your daughter had been injured?'

209

'No, sport, I didn't.' Only a momentary hesitation preceded Gunner Jones's opening of a second can. 'No, I didn't think about it and I didn't do it. Get in touch, I mean. Since you ask, I was away when it happened. I went fishing, a not unusual pastime with me, in fact it's what I'd call my hobby if anyone was interested in knowing what my hobby is. It was the West Country this time, I was staying in a cottage on the River Dart, nice little place I often go to for a few days at this time of the year.' He spoke with a self-confident aggressiveness. Or perhaps this amount of pugnacity was never really confident? 'I'm there to get away from it all, so the last thing I do is watch the news on TV. The first I knew of it was on the fifteenth when I got back.' His tone altered a little. 'Mind you, I'm not saying I wouldn't have felt a pang if the kid'd gone the same way as the rest of them, but you'd feel like that about any kid, doesn't have to be your own.

'I don't mind telling you something else. Maybe you think I'm incriminating myself but I'm saying it just the same. Naomi was nothing, *nothing*. I'm telling you, *there wasn't anything there*. There was quite a pretty face and what you might call an affectionate nature. A hand-holder and a cuddler. Only the cuddling strictly stopped at bedtime. As for empty-headed, well, I'm not educated and I don't reckon I've read more than say six books in all my life, but I was a bloody genius compared to that one. I was the personality of the year . . .'

'Mr Jones . . .'

'Yes, sport, you can have your say in a minute. Don't cut me short in my own house. I haven't said what I started to say yet. Naomi was nothing and I never had the pleasure of Mr Copeland MP's acquaintance, but I'll tell you something, I'll tell you what I'm working up to, any bloke who'd take on Davina Flory, *any* bloke, he'd have to be a soldier, a fighting soldier, gentlemen. He'd have to be brave as a lion and strong as a horse and with a skin as thick as a bleeding hippo. Because that lady was some queen-sized bitch and she *never got tired*. You couldn't tire her, she only needed about four hours' sleep and then she was raring to go – or raring to attack, I should say.

'I had to live there. Well, they called it "staying there while we found somewhere", but it was plain Davina'd never let go, especially after the baby came along.' He barked at Burden, 'D'you know what a Goth is?'

Something like Gunnar and those Nibelungen, Burden thought. 'You tell me.'

'I looked it up.' Gunner Jones had evidently, long ago, learnt the definition by heart. '"One who behaves like a barbarian, a rude, uncivilised or ignorant person." That's what she used to call me, "the Goth" or just "Goth". She'd use it like a Christian name. I mean, I had those initials, didn't I? G. G. She wasn't common, oh dear, no, or she'd have called me Horse. "What's Goth going to sack and pillage today?" she'd say, and "Have you been battering at the gates of the city again, Goth?"

'She set out to break up the marriage, she once actually told me how she saw me, as someone who'd give Naomi a child, and once that was done my usefulness was over. Just an animal at stud, that's me. A champion Goth. I had the face to complain once, said I was sick of living there, we wanted a place of our own, and all she said was, "Why not go off and find somewhere, Goth? You can come back in twenty years and tell us how you've got on."

'So I went but I never came back. I used to read the ads in the papers for her books, the things they said, "Wise and witty, compassion combined with a statesmanlike grasp, humanity and a deep empathy for the humble and the oppressed . . ." Christ, but that made me laugh. I wanted to write to that paper and say, you don't know her, you've got it all wrong. Well. I've got that off my chest and maybe I've given you some idea of why wild horses wouldn't have driven me to make contact with Davina Flory's daughter and Davina Flory's grandchild.'

Burden felt slightly winded by it all. It was as if a juggernaut of hatred and bitter resentment had rolled through the little room, leaving him and Barry Vine to recover gradually from the flattening they had had. Gunner Jones had the look of a man who has been through a catharsis, liberated and pleased with himself.

'Have another of those diet cokes?'

Vine shook his head.

'Time for a chaser.' Jones poured himself a generous two fingers of whisky into the third glass. He was writing something down on the back of an envelope he had taken from behind the mantelpiece clock. 'There you are. The address of the place I was in on the Dart and the name of the people at the pub next door, the Rainbow Trout.' He had suddenly grown enormously good-humoured. 'They'll give me an alibi. You check up all you want, be my guest.

211

'I don't mind freely admitting something, gentlemen. I would gladly have killed Davina Flory if I'd thought I could do it and get away with it. But that's when you come to the crunch, isn't it? Getting away with it? And I'm speaking of eighteen years ago. Time heals all, or so they say, and I'm not the crazy young madcap, I'm not the Goth I was in the days when I thought once or twice I'd wring Davina's neck and to hell with the fifteen years inside.'

You could have fooled me, thought Burden, but he said nothing. He wondered if Gunner Jones was the stupid man Davina Flory had believed him to be, or very, very clever. He wondered if he was acting or all this was real, and he couldn't tell. What would Daisy have made of this man if she had ever met him?

'As a matter of fact, I may be called Gunner but I can't handle a gun. Never so much as fired an airgun. I ask myself if I could even find my way to that place, that Tancred House, these days and I don't know, I honestly don't know. I reckon there'll have been some trees grown up and others fallen down. There were some folk there – Davina called them the "help", I reckon she thought that a fraction more democratic than "servants" – lived in a cottage, name of Triffid, Griffith, something of that sort. They had a kid, some kind of retard, poor little sod. What became of them? The place'll go to my daughter, I suppose. Lucky little lass, eh? I don't reckon she'll have been crying her eyes out, whatever she may say. Does she look like me?'

'Not a bit,' said Burden, though by this time he had seen Daisy in the turn of Gunner Jones's head, a certain lift to the corner of his mouth, the slant of his eyes.

'So much the better for her, eh, my friend? Don't think I can't tell what's going on behind that blank look of yours. If you've done, seeing it's Saturday night, I'll bid you a fond farewell and be off to my local watering-hole.' He opened the front door and ushered them out. 'If you're thinking of lying low for a bit, keeping an eye on me, I'll be leaving my vehicle where it's parked right outside there and taking what the old folks call shanks's pony.' As if they were traffic police. 'I'd hate to give you the satisfaction of finding me over the limit, as by now I surely am.'

'D'you want me to drive?' said Burden when they were in the car, knowing his offer would be refused.

'No, thanks, sir, I enjoy driving.'

Vine started the ignition.

212

'Is there a map-reader's light in this car, Barry?'

'Under the dashboard shelf. It pulls out on a flexible what-d'you-call-it.'

It was impossible to turn here. Barry took the car a hundred yards down the street, swung round in the entrance to a side street and returned the way they had come. The place was too much of an unknown, a mystery, for him to attempt the experiment of getting back to the crossroads by a sortie round the block.

Gunner Jones went across a pedestrian crossing in front of them. There was no one else on foot and they were the only car. Jones put up his hand in an imperious gesture to halt them but he didn't look into the car or give any other sign that he knew who the driver and passenger were.

'A strange man,' Barry said.

'This is a very odd thing, Barry.' Burden had the map-reader's light trained on the envelope Gunner Jones had given him and on which he had written the address. But it was the other side, the previously used side with the stamp, that he was looking at. 'I noticed it when he first took it off the mantelpiece. It's addressed to him, here at Nineveh Road, to Mr G.G. Jones, nothing peculiar about that. But the handwriting, it's a very distinctive handwriting, I last saw it in a desk diary, I'd know it anywhere. It's Joanne Garland's writing.'

# 19

It was broad daylight now at six. Nothing could have made it feel more like spring, the late sunsets, the lengthening evenings. Less pleasing, according to the Deputy Chief Constable, Sir James Freeborn, was the length of time Wexford's team had been quartered at Tancred House without results. And the bills they were running up! The cost! A day and night guard on Miss Davina Jones? What was it going to cost? The girl shouldn't be there. He had never heard of such a thing, an eighteen-year-old imperiously insisting on staying alone in that barrack of a place.

Wexford came out from the stables just before six. The sun was still shining and the evening air untouched by chill. He heard a sound ahead that might have been made by heavy rain, but rain couldn't be falling out of that unclouded sky. As soon as he came to the front of the house he saw that the fountain was playing.

Until now he had scarcely know it *was* a fountain. The water spouted from a pipe that came up somewhere between Apollo's legs and the tree trunk. It cascaded through slanting sunbeams to make rainbows. In the little waves the fish cavorted. The fountain in full play transformed the place so that the house no longer looked austere, nor the courtyard bare, nor the pool stagnant. The sometimes oppressive silence had given place to a delicate musical splashing.

He tugged at the sugarstick bellpull. Whose car was that on the drive behind him? A sports car, an uncomfortable-looking, by no means new MG. Daisy came to let him in. Her appearance had undergone another alteration and she was feminine again. In black, of course, but clinging, flattering black with a skirt and not trousers,

214

shoes and not boots, the back of her hair hanging loose, the sides looped up, like an Edwardian girl's.

And there was something else different about her. He was unable at first to say what this was. But it was in all of her, her step, her demeanour, the lift of her head, her eyes. A light shone out of her. You meaner beauties of the night, That poorly satisfy our eyes . . . What are you when the moon cloth rise?

'You answered the door,' he said reproachfully, 'when you didn't know who it was. Or did you see me from the window?'

'No, we're in the *serre*. I turned on the fountain.'

'Yes.'

'Isn't it lovely? Look at the rainbows it makes. With the water washing down you can't see that nasty leer on Apollo's face. You can believe he loves her, you can see he only wants to kiss her . . . Oh, please don't look like that. I knew it would be all right, I sensed it. I sensed it was someone nice.'

With less faith in her intuition than she had herself, he followed her through the hall, wondering who the other half of 'we' was. The entrance to the dining room was still sealed up, door taped to architrave. She walked ahead of him with springy step, a different girl, a changed girl.

'You remember Nicholas,' she said to him, pausing on the threshold of the conservatory, and to the man inside, 'This is Chief Inspector Wexford, Nicholas, that you met in the hospital.'

Nicholas Virson was sitting in one of the deep wicker armchairs and he didn't get up. Why should he? He didn't extend a hand, but nodded, said, 'Ah, good evening,' like a man twice his age.

Wexford looked about him. He looked at the prettinesses of the place, the green plants, an early azalea in flower in a tub, the lemon trees in their blue and white china, a pink cyclamen, burdened with blossoms in a bowl on the glass table. At Daisy, who was back in the seat she must have vacated a moment before, close to Virson's chair. Their two drinks, gin or vodka or plain spring-water, were side by side, no more that two inches apart, beside the cyclamen flowers. He knew quite suddenly what had caused the change in her, brought pink into her cheeks and removed the pain from her anxious eyes. If it hadn't been impossible in these circumstances, after what had happened and she had gone through, he would have said she was happy.

'Can I offer you a drink?' she said.

215

'Better not. If that's mineral water I'll accept and have a glass.'
'Let me do it.'

Virson spoke as if the request Wexford had made implied some gargantuan task, for the water to be fetched from a well, for instance, or brought up a dangerous ladder out of the cellar. Daisy must be saved from an exertion Wexford had no right to ask of her. A reproachful glance accompanied his handing over of the half-full glass.

'Thank you. Daisy, I've come to ask you if you won't reconsider your decision to stay here.'

'How funny. So has Nicholas. I mean, come here to ask me that.' She turned on the young man a smile of great candlepower. She took his hand and held it. 'Nicholas is so good to me. Well, you all are. Everyone's so kind. But Nicholas would do anything for me, wouldn't you, Nicholas?'

It was a strange thing to say. Was she serious? Surely the irony was in his imagination?

Virson seemed a little taken aback, as well he might be. An uncertain smile trembled on his mouth. 'Anything in my power, darling,' he said. He seemed reluctant to have more to do with Wexford than he could help, but now he forgot prejudices and what was perhaps snobbism and said almost impulsively, 'I want Daisy to come back to Myfleet with me. She should never have left us. But she's so absurdly stubborn – can't you do something to make her see she's in danger here? I worry about her night and day, I don't mind telling you. I can't sleep. I'd stay here myself only I suppose it wouldn't be quite the thing.'

That made Daisy laugh. Wexford didn't think he had ever heard her laugh before. Nor did he believe he had ever heard a young man make such a remark, not even in the old days when he was young himself and people still found something improper in unmarried persons of opposite sexes sleeping under the same roof.

'It wouldn't be at all the thing for you, Nicholas,' she said. 'All your things are at home. And it takes yonks to get to the station from here, you've no idea till you try it.' She spoke fondly, she still held his hand. Momentarily, her face blazed with happiness when she looked at him. 'Besides, you're not a policeman.' She spoke teasingly. 'Do you think you could defend me?'

'I'm a bloody good shot,' said Virson like an old colonel.

Wexford said drily, 'I don't think we want any more guns here, Mr Virson.'

That made Daisy shiver. Her face went dull, like a shadow crossing the sun. 'An old friend of my grandmother's rang up at the weekend and asked me to go and stay with her in Edinburgh. Ishbel Macsamphire. You remember my pointing her out to you, Nicholas? She said she'd invite her granddaughter as well and that was supposed to be an attraction! I shuddered. Of course I said no. Maybe later in the year, but not now.'

'I'm sorry to hear that,' Wexford said, 'very sorry.'

'She's not the only one. Preston Littlebury invited me to his house in Forby. "Stay as long as you like, my dear. Be my guest." I don't think he knows "be my guest" is a sort of joke thing to say. Two girls from school have asked me. I'm really popular, I suppose I'm a kind of celebrity.'

'You've turned all these people down?'

'Mr Wexford, I'm going to stay on here in my own house. I know I'm going to be safe. Don't you see that if I ran away now I might never come back?'

'We shall catch these men,' he said stoutly. 'It's only a matter of time.'

'An extremely long time.' Virson drank his water or whatever it was in slow sips. 'It's getting on for a month.'

'Just three weeks, Mr Virson. Another idea that occurred to me, Daisy, was that when you go back to school whenever it is the Crelands term starts – two or three weeks' time – you might think of boarding for your final term.'

She answered him as if she saw the suggestion as extremely odd, almost improper. The gap of temperament and taste he had always sensed between her and Virson quickly closed. They suddenly became highly compatible young people with the same values and reared in an identical culture. 'Oh, I'm not going back to school! Why would I ever do that? After everything that's happened? A levels aren't something I'm likely to need in my future life.'

'Haven't you got a university place consequent on how well you do in your A levels?'

Virson gave Wexford a look implying that it was impertinent of him to believe anything of the sort. 'University places,' said Daisy, 'don't have to be taken up.' She spoke strangely. 'I only tried for it to please Davina and now – now there's no pleasing her any more.'

217

'Daisy has left school,' said Virson. 'All that's over.'

Wexford was suddenly sure some revelation was to be offered or announcement made. *Daisy has just promised to be my wife* – or something old-fashioned and pompous but nevertheless a bombshell. No revelatory statement was made. Virson sipped his water. He said, 'I think I'll stay on a while, darling, if you'll let me. Could you give me a spot of dinner or shall we go out?'

'Oh, the place is groaning with food,' she said lightly. 'It always is. Brenda was cooking all morning, she doesn't know what to do with herself now – now there's only me.'

'You're feeling better,' was all Wexford said to her as she saw him to the door.

'I'm getting over it, yes.' But she looked as if things had gone further than that. He had the impression that from time to time she tried to revert to her old misery, for form's sake, for decency. But to be miserable was no longer natural. Naturally, she was happy. Yet she said, as if feelings of guilt had caught up with her. 'In a way I'll never get over it, I'll never forget.'

'Not for a while, anyway.'

'It would be worse somewhere else.'

'I wish you'd reconsider. Both about going away from here and about university. Of course, university – that's no business of mine.'

She did something astonishing. They were on the doorstep, the door was open and he was about to leave. She flung her arms around his neck and kissed him. The kisses landed, warm and firm, on both his cheeks. He felt against the length of him a body seething with delight, with joy.

Firmly, he disengaged himself. 'Please me,' he said as he had sometimes said to his daughters, long ago and usually to no avail, 'please me by doing what I ask.'

The water continued to splash steadily into the pool and the fish leapt in the little waves.

'Are we saying,' said Burden, 'that the vehicle they used left, and perhaps arrived, through the woods themselves? It was a jeep or a Land-Rover or something built for use on rough ground and the driver knew those woods like the back of his hand.'

'Andy Griffin certainly knew them,' said Wexford, 'and his father does, perhaps better than anyone else. Gabbitas knows them and so, to a lesser extent, does Ken Harrison. No doubt the three dead people knew them and, for all we know, Joanne Garland may have done, members of her family may do.'

'Gunner Jones says he doesn't think he could find his way through them now. Why say that to me if he wasn't pretty confident he *could*? I didn't ask him. It was simply a piece of gratuitous information. And we're talking about someone *driving* through the woods, not running through on foot, which provided you followed your nose or a compass would be bound to bring you out on a road sooner or later. This guy would have to be prepared to drive a cumbersome four-wheel-drive vehicle through woods in the dark and the only lights he'd dare to have on would be sidelights and maybe not even those.'

The other one walked in front of him with a lantern,' Wexford said drily, 'like in the early days of motoring.'

'Well, perhaps he did. I find it all hard to picture, Reg, but what alternative is there? There's no way they wouldn't have passed Bib Mew or Gabbitas wouldn't have met them if they were on the Pomfret Monachorum road – unless Gabbitas was one of them, unless he was the other one.'

'How d'you like the idea of a motorbike? Suppose they made their way through the woods in the dark on Andy Griffin's motorbike?'

'Wouldn't Daisy distinguish between the sound of a motorbike starting up and the sound of a car? I can't somehow see Gabbitas riding pillion on Andy's bike. Gabbitas, I don't need to remind you, has no alibi for the afternoon and early evening of 11 March.'

'You know, Mike, something rather strange has happened to alibis in recent years. It's getting progressively more difficult to establish hard-and-fast ones. That works against villains, of course, but it also works for them. It's got something to do with people leading more isolated lives. There are more people than ever before but individual lives are more lonely.'

The glazed look appeared on Burden's face which often settled there when Wexford began to talk what he categorised as 'philosophy'. Wexford was becoming ultra-sensitive to this change of expression and, since he had nothing more to say of value in the present case, he cut short his remarks and bade Burden good-night. But his thoughts on alibis remained with him as he drove home, how suspects were able to call on less and less corroboration in support of their claims.

Men, in times of recession and high unemployment, went to the pub less frequently than they had used. Cinemas were empty as television lured away their audiences. The Kingsmarkham cinema had closed five years before and been converted into a DIY emporium. More people lived singly than ever before. Fewer grown-up children lived at home. In the evenings and by night the streets of Kingsmarkham, of Stowerton, of Pomfret, were empty, not a car parked, not a pedestrian, only freight traffic rolling through, each truck with a lone driver. At home, in single rooms, or tiny flats, a lone man or lone woman sat watching television.

This accounted, in some measure, for the problems in establishing the certain whereabouts of almost all these people on that date in March. Who was there to support the claims of John Gabbitas and Gunner Jones, or come to that, Bib Mew? Who could corroborate where Ken Harrison had been, or John Chowney or Terry Griffin, but in the case of two of them their wives, whose testimony was useless? They had all been at home, or on their way home, alone or with their wives.

To say that Gunner Jones had disappeared would be putting it too strongly. A call to the sports equipment shop in the Holloway Road ascertained that Gunner had gone on a few days' holiday, he hadn't said where, he often went away. Wexford would hardly help seeing the coincidence here, if coincidence it was. Joanne Garland kept a shop and had gone away. Gunner Jones, who knew her, who corresponded with her, kept a shop and 'often went away'. Another thing, which Wexford was prepared to admit might be seen as way-out, had struck him. Gunner Jones sold sports equipment, Joanne Garland had converted a room in her house to a gym and filled it with sports equipment.

Were they together and if so, why?

The proprietors of the Rainbow Trout Inn at Pluxam on the Dart were most willing to tell DS Vine everything they knew about Mr G.G. Jones. He was a regular customer when in the neighbourhood. They let a few rooms to visitors and he had once stayed there, but only once. Since then he had always rented the cottage next door. It was not exactly next door, in Vine's eyes, but a good fifty yards down the lane which led to the river bank.

The eleventh of March? The licensee of the Rainbow Trout knew exactly what Vine was talking about and needed no explanation. His eyes sparkled with the excitement of it. Mr Jones had certainly been there from the tenth to the fifteenth. He knew because Mr Jones never paid for his drinks till he left and there was a record of his expenditure for those days. To Vine it seemed an incredibly large sum for one man. As to the eleventh, the licensee couldn't say, he had no record of Mr Jones coming in that evening, he didn't write the dates on his 'slate'.

Since then he hadn't seen Gunner Jones and hadn't expected to. There was no one in the cottage at present. The landlord told Vine he had no further bookings for Gunner Jones in the current year. He had rented the cottage four times and had always been alone. That is, he had never moved into it with someone else. The landlord had once seen him having a drink in the Rainbow Trout with a woman. Just a woman. No, he couldn't describe her beyond saying she hadn't impressed him as being too young for Gunner or, come to that, too old. The probability was that Gunner Jones was at present off fishing in some other part of the country.

But what had been contained in the envelope on the mantelpiece in Nineveh Road? A love letter? Or the outline of some kind of plan? And why had Gunner Jones kept the envelope when he had evidently discarded the letter? Why, above all, had he written those addresses on it and handed it so insouciantly to Burden.

Wexford ate his dinner and talked to Dora about going away for the weekend. She could go if she liked. He saw no prospect of his getting away. She was reading something in a magazine and when he asked her what interested her so deeply, she said it was a profile of Augustine Casey.

Wexford made the sound the Victorians wrote as, 'Pshaw!'

'If you've finished with *The Hosts of Midian*, Reg, can I read it?'

He handed her the novel, opened *Lovely As A Tree* which he still hadn't got very far with. Without looking up, his head bent, he said, 'Do you speak to her?'

'Oh, for God's sake, Reg, if you mean Sheila why can't you say so? I speak to her the same as always only you aren't here to snatch the receiver from me.'

'When is she going to Nevada?'

'In about three weeks' time.'


Preston Littlebury had a small Georgian village house in the middle of Forby. Forby has been called the fifth prettiest village in England, which he explained as his reason for having a weekend house there.

If the so-called prettiest village in England was as near to London he would have lived there, but it happened to be in Wiltshire.

It was not strictly a weekend house, of course, or he wouldn't have been there on a Thursday. He smiled as he made these pedantic remarks and held his hands together up under the chin, the wrists apart and the fingertips touching. His smile was small and tight and patronising in a twinkling way. Apparently, he lived alone. The rooms in his house reminded Barry Vine of the partitioned-off areas in an antiques emporium. Everything looked like a beautifully preserved, well-tended antique, not the least silver-haired Mr Littlebury in his silver-grey suit, his pink Custom Shop shirt and his rose and silver spotted bow tie. He was older than he looked at first, as is also true of some antiques. Barry thought he might be well into his seventies. When he spoke he sounded like the late Henry Fonda playing a professor.

His circumlocutory style of speaking left Vine very little the wiser as to what he did for a living than when he began describing his occupation. He was an American, born in Philadelphia, and had been living in Cincinnati, Ohio, while Harvey Copeland had been teaching at a university there. That was how they came to meet. Preston Littlebury was also acquainted with the Vice-Chancellor of the University of the South. He had been some sort of academic himself, had worked at the Victoria and Albert Museum, had a reputation as an art expert and had once written a column about antiques for a national newspaper. It seemed that he now bought and sold antique silver and porcelain.

This much Vine managed to sort out from Littlebury's obscurities and digressions. All the while he talked he was nodding like a Chinese mandarin.

'I travel rather a lot, back and forth, you know. I pass a considerable amount of time in eastern Europe, a fecund marketplace since the cessation of the Cold War. Let me tell you of rather an amusing thing that happened as I was crossing the frontier between Bulgaria and Yugoslavia . . .'

An anecdote on the perennial theme of bureaucratic bumbling threatened. Vine had endured three already and hastily cut him short.

'About Andy Griffin, sir. You employed him at one time? We're anxious to know his whereabouts during the days before he was killed.'

Like most raconteurs, Littlebury was not happy to be interrupted.

222

'Yes, well, I was coming to that. I haven't set eyes on the man for nearly a year. You're aware of that?'

Vine nodded, though he wasn't. If he demurred he might get to hear the further adventures of Preston Littlebury in the Balkans during that year. 'You did employ him?'

'In a manner of speaking.' Littlebury spoke very carefully, weighing each word. 'It depends on what you mean by "employ". If you mean, did I have him on what I believe in common parlance is called a "payroll", the answer must be an emphatic no. There was, for instance, no question of making National Insurance contributions on his behalf or applying myself to certain Income Tax adjustments. If, on the other hand, you refer to *casual labour*, to a role as *odd-job man*, I must tell you that you are right. For a short time Andrew Griffin was in receipt of what I will call an elementary emolument from me.'

Littlebury put the tips of his fingers together and twinkled at Vine over the top of them. 'He performed such menial tasks as washing my car and sweeping my yard.' The use of this word was the first hint he had given of his Philadelphian origins. 'He took my little dog – now, alas, passed on to the rabbit warren in the sky – for walks. Once, I recall, he changed a wheel when I had a flat – a puncture, I should say to you, Sergeant.'

'Did you ever pay him in dollars?'

If anyone had told Vine that this man, this epitome of refinement and pedantry, or as he himself would doubtless put it, of civilisation, would use the old lag's favourite phrase, he wouldn't have believed it. But that was what Preston Littlebury did.

'I might have done.'

It was uttered in as shifty a way as Vine had ever heard. Now, he thought, the man would probably start using those other giveaways: 'To be perfectly honest with you' was one of them; 'To tell you the absolute truth' another. Littlebury would doubtless have no occasion to use the defendant's biggest whopper: 'I swear on the lives of my wife and children I'm innocent.' He appeared, anyway, to have neither wife nor children and his dog was dead.

'Did you, sir, or didn't you? Or can't you remember?'

'It was a long time ago.'

What was he afraid of? Not much, Vine thought. No more than the Inland Revenue catching up with his back-pocket transactions.

Very likely he dealt in dollars. Countries in eastern Europe liked them better than sterling, far better than their own currencies.

'We found a certain number of dollar notes . . .' He corrected himself '. . . er, bills, in Griffin's possession.'

'It's a universal currency, Sergeant.'

'Yes. So you may have paid him occasionally in dollars, sir, but you can't remember?'

'I may have done. Once or twice.'

No longer tempted to illustrate every rejoinder with an amusing tale, Littlebury seemed suddenly ill at ease. He was bereft of words. He no longer twinkled and his hands fidgeted in his lap.

Vine was inspired and said quickly, 'Do you have a bank account in Kingsmarkham, sir?'

'No, I do not.' It was snapped out. Vine remembered that he lived in London, this was only a weekend or occasional retreat. No doubt, though, he sometimes stayed on over Mondays and needed cash . . . 'Have you anything else you want to ask me? I was under the impression this enquiry was concerned with Andrew Griffin, not my personal pecuniary arrangements.'

'The last days of his life, Mr Littlebury. Frankly, we don't know where he spent them.' Vine told him the relevant dates. 'A Sunday morning till a Tuesday afternoon.'

'He didn't spend them with me. I was in Leipzig.'

Greater Manchester Police confirmed the death of Dane Bishop. The death certificate gave the cause as heart failure and the contributory cause as pneumonia. He had been twenty-four years old and living at an address in Oldham. The reason for his failing to come to Wexford's notice before had been his lack of a record. There was only one offence recorded against him and that had taken place some three months after the death of Caleb Martin: shop-breaking in Manchester.

'I'm going to have that Jem Hocking charged with murder,' Wexford said.

'He's already in jail,' Burden half-objected.

'Not my idea of jail. Not real jail.'

'That doesn't sound like you,' said Burden.

224

# 20

'If Miss Jones had died, Miss Davina Jones, that is,' said Wilson Barrowby, the solicitor, 'there is no question but that her father, Mr George Godwin Jones, would have inherited the estate, would indeed have inherited everything.

'No other heirs exist. Miss Flory was the youngest of her family.' He gave a rueful smile. 'Indeed, we know she was the "youngest wren of nine", and was in fact five years younger than her youngest sibling and no less than *twenty* years younger than her eldest sister.

'There were no first cousins. Professor Flory and his wife were both only children. They were not a prolific family. Professor Flory might well have expected to have eighteen or twenty grandchildren. In fact, he had six, one of those being Naomi Jones. Only one of Miss Flory's siblings had more than one child and of those two the elder died in infancy. Among Miss Flory's four surviving nieces and nephews ten years ago, three were not much younger than she herself and the fourth was only two years younger than she. That niece, Mrs Louise Merritt, died in the South of France in February.'

'And their children?' Wexford asked. 'The great-nieces and nephews.'

'Great-nieces and nephews don't inherit under an intestacy or, if a will exists as in this case, unless they are specifically named in that will. There are only four, the children of Mrs Merritt, both living in France, and the son and daughter of an elder nephew and niece. But as I've told you, there was no question of their inheriting. Under the terms of the will, as I believe you already know, everything was left to Miss Davina Jones with the proviso that Mr Copeland have a life interest in Tancred House and be allowed to live there for life, and the same in the case of Mrs Naomi Jones, who was to be allowed to live there until her own death. I believe you also know that in addition to the house and grounds and the extremely valuable furniture and the jewellery, alas lost, a fortune of just under a million pounds had accumulated, not I'm afraid a vast sum in these days. There are also the royalties from Miss Flory's books, what I believe is called a "backlist", amounting to some fifteen thousand pounds per annum.'

It seemed big enough to Wexford. It justified his description to Joyce Virson of Daisy as 'rich'. He was paying this belated visit to Davina Flory's solicitors because it was only now that he had come fully to believe that the Tancred murders were in a sense an 'inside job'. Gradually, he had come to see that robbery, at least actual on-the-spot robbery of jewels, had little to do with these deaths. The motive was closer to home. It lay somewhere in this web of relationships, yet where? Was there somewhere somehow a relative who had slipped through Barrowby's net?

'If a blood relation of Davina Flory wouldn't have inherited,' he said, 'I mean a great-niece or nephew, I don't quite see why George Jones would have done. By all accounts, Miss Flory hated Jones and he hated her and he's not named in the will.'

'You could say it had nothing to do with Miss Flory,' said Barrowby, 'and everything to do with Miss Jones. I'm sure you know how the order of deaths is presumed to be when several people who are related to each other are killed. We assume that the youngest survives longest.'

'Yes, I know that.'

'Therefore, in this case, though it hasn't come to that, the assumption would be that Davina Flory died first, then her husband, then Mrs Jones. In fact, we know that it wasn't so from the testimony of Miss Jones. We know that Mr Copeland died first. But let us say that the perpetrator was successful and Miss Jones had died. Then assumptions of this kind would have had to be made, since there would be no surviving witness to help us. We would assume, in the absence of precise medical evidence of the time of death, in this case obviously not forthcoming, that Davina Flory died first, her granddaughter immediately inheriting under the will with the proviso that Mr Copeland and Mrs Jones have a life interest in the house.

'Then, in order of age, we suppose Mr Copeland to die, then Mrs Jones, thus by death forfeiting their life interest. The property, in those few crucial moments, perhaps seconds only, is Miss Davina

Jones's alone in its entirety. Therefore, if and when she should die, her natural heirs would inherit under an intestacy, regardless of whether they were of Miss Flory's blood or anyone else's. Davina Jones's *only natural heir*, after her mother's death, is her father George Godwin Jones.

'If she had died, as she might well have done, the entire property would have passed to Mr Jones. I cannot see that there would be any dispute about it. Who would contest such a thing?'

'He's never seen her since she was a baby,' Wexford said. 'He hasn't seen or spoken to her for over seventeen years.'

'No matter. He is her father. That is, he most probably is her father and certainly he is in the law. He was married to her mother at the time of her birth and his paternity has never been disputed. He is her natural heir as much as, in the event of his death, if he died without making testamentary disposition, she would be his.'

The engagement would be announced any day, Wexford had begun to believe. *Nicholas, only son of Mrs Joyce Virson and the late whatever-it-was Virson, and Davina, only daughter of George Godwin Jones and the late Mrs Naomi Jones* . . . Virson's car was outside Tancred House even earlier the next day, soon after three. He must be taking time off work, perhaps, with acute opportunism, part of his annual holiday. But Wexford really had no doubt that neither opportunism nor luck was needed. Daisy had been persuaded, Daisy would be Mrs Virson.

He found himself very much disliking the idea. Not only was Virson a pompous ass with absurd notions of his own importance and status, but Daisy was too young. Daisy was only just eighteen. His own daughter Sylvia had been married at that age, rather against his and Dora's wishes at the time, but she had gone ahead in spite of them and the wedding had taken place. She and Neil were still together but, Wexford sometimes suspected, only for the children's sake. It was an uneasy marriage, full of tensions and incompatibilities. Of course Daisy had turned to Nicholas Virson to console her in her grief. And he had consoled her. The change in her had been remarkable, she was as nearly happy as anyone in her situation could be. The only explanation for that happiness had been a declaration of love on Virson's part and of acceptance on hers.

He was one of the few young people she appeared to know, apart from those schoolfellows who may have invited her to stay but were

227

certainly conspicuous by their absence from Tancred House. Well, there was Jason Sebright, if you could count him. Her family had approved of Nicholas Virson. At any rate, they had permitted him to accompany them to Edinburgh last year as Daisy's acknowledged escort. It might have been true that Davina Flory would have smiled more graciously on a plan for the two of them to live together rather than marry, but that was itself approval. He was a good-looking man, of suitable age, with a satisfactory job, who would make a good, dull, and very likely faithful husband. But for Daisy, at eighteen?

It seemed to him a great waste. The kind of life Davina Flory had mapped out for her, though perhaps imperiously conceived, was surely the life that would just have suited her with its potential for adventure, for study, for meeting people, for travel. Instead, she would marry, bring her husband to live at Tancred and, Wexford had little doubt, after a few years divorce him when it was growing too late for the education and the self-discovery.

He was reflecting on all this as he had himself driven from the solicitors to the Caenbrook Retirement Home. He had not yet met Mrs Chowney, though he had spent an unproductive half-hour with her daughter Shirley. Mrs Shirley Rodgers was the mother of four teenagers, her excuse for seldom visiting her mother. She seldom visited her sister Joanne either and seemed to know very little about her life. At *her* age? was her immediate rejoinder when Wexford asked her if her sister had men friends. But he hadn't been able to forget the wardrobe of clothes, the cosmetic aids to beauty and the gym full of fitness equipment.

Edith Chowney was in her own room but not alone there. A woman on the staff, receptionist or nurse, took him up to the room and knocked on the door. It was opened a crack by a woman who might have been Shirley Rodgers's twin. She admitted him, he was expected, and Mrs Chowney in a bright red wool dress, red ribbed tights covering her bandy legs and pink bedsocks on her feet, was all smiles.

'Are you the head one?' she said.

He thought he might reasonably say he was. 'That's right, Mrs Chowney.'

'They've sent the head one this time,' she said to the woman she then proceeded to introduce as her daughter Pamela, the good

228

daughter who came most often, though she didn't say this. 'My daughter Pam. Mrs Pamela Burns.'

'I'm glad you're here, Mrs Burns,' he said with some diplomacy, 'because I think you too may be able to help us. It's now more than three weeks since Mrs Garland went away. Have either of you heard from her?'

'She's not gone away. I told the others – didn't they tell you? She's not gone away, she wouldn't go away and not say a word to me. She's never done such a thing.'

Wexford baulked at telling this old woman they were by now seriously worried not simply for Mrs Garland's whereabouts but for her life. He was expecting any day another one of those calls that announced a gruesome discovery. At the same time he wondered if Mrs Chowney might not take it all in her stride. What a life hers must have been! The eleven children and all the consequent worries and stresses and even tragedies. Unwelcome marriages, even less acceptable divorces, partings, deaths. And yet he hesitated.

'Wouldn't you have expected her to have been in to see you by now, Mrs Chowney?'

'What I expect,' she retorted sharply, 'and what they do are two different things altogether. She's been gone three weeks before without showing her face in here. Pam's the only one you can rely on. The only one in the whole lot of them isn't for self, self, self morning, noon and night.'

Pamela Burns looked a little smug. A small modest smile appeared on her lips. Mrs Chowney said shrewdly, 'This is about that Naomi, isn't it? It's got something to do with what happened up there. Joanne was worried about her. She used to talk to me about it, when she wasn't talking about herself.'

'Worried in what way, Mrs Chowney?'

'Said she had no life, ought to find a man. Said her life was empty. Empty, I thought to myself, and her living in that house, never known money worries, playing at selling china animals, never had to fend for herself. That's not an empty life, I said, that's a sheltered life. Still, she's gone and it's all water under the bridge.'

'Your daughter had a man in her own life, did she?'

'Joanne,' said Mrs Chowney. He remembered too late that with so many it was necessary to specify. 'My daughter Joanne. She's had two, you know, two husbands.' She spoke as if some kind of rationing scheme existed in this area of life and her daughter had

229

already used up the best part of her allocation. 'There might be someone, she wouldn't tell me, not if he wasn't loaded. What she'd do is show me the things he'd given her and there was nothing of that, was there, Pam?'

'I don't know, Mother. I wasn't told and I wouldn't ask.'

Wexford came to the question that was the point of his visit. He trembled on the brink of it. So much depended on a guilty or defensive or indignant response.

'Did she know Naomi's ex-husband, Mr George Godwin Jones?'

They both looked at him as if such sublime ignorance was only to be pitied. Pamela Burns even leant a little towards him as if to encourage him to repeat what he had said, as if she had not, could not, have heard aright.

'Gunner?' said Mrs Chowney at last.

'Well, yes. Mr Gunner Jones. Did she know him?'

'Of course she knew him,' said Pamela Burns. 'Of course she did.' She made a gesture of locking her forefingers. 'They were like that, thick as thick, her and Brian and Naomi and Gunner, weren't they? Used to do everything together.'

'Joanne had just got married for the second time,' put in Mrs Chowney, 'oh, it'll be getting on for twenty years ago.'

They were still incredulous that all this might not be widely known. It was as if he had to be indignantly reminded of the facts, not be told them for the first time.

'It was through Brian Joanne got to know Naomi. He was a pal of Gunner's. I remember her saying what a coincidence it was Gunner marrying a girl from round here and I thought, not just a girl from round here, come on, a girl from that background! Still, Joanne had got a leg-up in the world. Brian used to say he was just a poor millionaire, but that was him trying to be funny.'

'They were that close,' said Mrs Chowney, 'I said to Pam, I wonder Gunner and Naomi don't take those two on their honeymoon with them.'

'And the closeness persisted after the two divorces?'

'Pardon?'

'I mean, did these four people continue to know each other after their marriages ended? Of course I know Mrs Garland and Mrs Jones remained friends.'

'Brian went to Australia, didn't he?' Mrs Chowney asked the question in the tone she might have used to ask Wexford if the sun had risen in the east that morning. 'They couldn't be hob-nobbing with him even if they'd wanted to. Anyway, Gunner and Naomi'd split up long before. That marriage was doomed from the start.'

'Joanne took Naomi's part,' said Pamela Burns eagerly. 'Well, you would, wouldn't you? A close friend like that. She lined herself up with Naomi. She and Brian were together then and even Brian took against Gunner.' She added sententiously, 'You don't give up on a marriage just because you can't get on with your wife's mother, especially when you've got a baby. That baby was only six months old.'

The caterer's van, as was its daily habit, was drawn up on the courtyard between Tancred House and the stables. It was fragrant with curry and the scent of Mexican spices.

'Freebee would have a word to say about that too, if he did but know about it,' said Wexford to Burden.

'We have to eat.'

'Yes, and it's a cut above the station canteen or any of our cheaper haunts in town.' Wexford was eating chicken pilaf and Burden an individual ham and mushroom quiche.

'Funny to think of that girl, only a few yards away from us really, being waited on by a servant, her meals cooked for her, just as a matter of course.'

'It's a way of life, Mike, and one we don't happen to be used to. I doubt if it contributes much to personal happiness or detracts from it. When does that shop of his expect Gunner Jones back?'

'Not till Monday. But that doesn't mean he won't be home sooner. Unless he skipped off, left the country. I wouldn't put it past him.'

'Gone to join her, d'you reckon?'

'I don't know. I was certain she was dead, but now I just don't know. I'd like to be able to make another of what you call my scenarios for those two but when I try it it doesn't work. Gunner Jones has the best motive of anyone for these killings – provided Daisy had died, and no doubt whoever shot her thought she would die. In that case, he would have inherited everything. But where does Garland come in? Was she his girlfriend, going to share the loot with him? Or was she an innocent visitor who interrupted him – and who else? We've established no connection at all between Jones and Andy Griffin beyond Gunner's seeing him a couple of times as a kid. Then there's the vehicle they came in. Not Joanne Garland's car. The forensic boys have been over that with a toothcomb. Not the BMW. There's not a sign to indicate anyone but Joanne herself had been in it for months.'

'And where does Andy come in?

Bib Mew had returned to work at Tancred House and there Wexford and Vine had each had a further go at talking to her. Mention of the body hanging from the tree, however carefully couched in soothing language, resulted in more trembling fits and once a kind of attack which manifested itself in a series of short sharp screams.

'She won't go past where it was,' Brenda Harrison volunteered with ghoulish relish. 'She goes all that long way round. All the way down to Pomfret and along the main road and up to Cheriton. Takes her hours and it's no joke when it's raining. Daisy –' here a loud sniff '– says to Ken to fetch her in the car, it's the least we can do, she says. Let her fetch her herself if she's so keen, I said. We're under notice, I said, I don't see why we should put ourselves out. I hope you're still baking our own bread, Brenda, she says, and I've got someone for dinner tonight, Brenda, and we're getting pushed out into the street. Davina would turn in her grave if she knew.'

The next time Wexford tried to see her Bib hid in the room off the kitchen where the freezer was and locked herself in.

'I don't know what you've done to scare her,' Brenda said. 'She's a bit simple, you know. You did know that?' She tapped her head with two fingers. A silent mouthing offered: 'Damage to her brain in the birth.'

There were a good many things Wexford would have liked to know. If Bib had seen anyone near the hanging tree. If she had seen anyone at all in the woods that afternoon. Thanny Hogarth was his only link with what might have happened; Thanny Hogarth must be her interpreter.

'Accordingly,' Wexford said, finishing his pilaf, 'I've got him coming up here this afternoon to make a statement. On what happened when Bib arrived at his door and told him about finding Andy Griffin's body. But I don't think it's going to supply any shattering revelations.'

Thanny Hogarth arrived on his bicycle. Wexford saw him from the window. He came across the courtyard towards the stables, no hands, pedalling away, his arms folded, his face rapt as he listened to the Walkman clamped to his head.

The headset was draped round his neck when he sauntered in. Karen Malahyde intercepted him and brought him over to Wexford. Thanny's hair was tied back today, apparently with a shoelace, in that style which Wexford loathed on a man, while recognising his dislike as prejudice. He was unshaven to exactly the same degree as he had been last time they met, that is with two or three days' growth of beard. Was it always so? Wexford allowed himself to wonder how he managed it. Did he trim it to that level with scissors? In a pair of Western boots, chestnut brown, stitched and studded, and with a red scarf knotted round his neck, he looked like a handsome young pirate.

'Before we begin, Mr Hogarth,' Wexford said, 'I'd like you to satisfy my curiosity on one point. If your creative writing course doesn't start until the autumn, why are you here six months early?'

'Summer school. It's a preliminary course for students taking the MA.'

'I see.'

He would check that with Dr Perkins but he had no doubt he would find all above-board. Karen had a shorthand notebook and took down Thanny Hogarth's statement. It was also recorded on tape.

'For what it's worth,' he said cheerfully, and Wexford was inclined to agree with him. What was it worth, this brief account of a few blurted-out terrified words?

'She said, "A dead person. Hanging up. Hanging up off of a tree." I guess I didn't believe her. I said "Come on," or something like. Maybe I said, "Wait a minute," I said to tell me again. I'd just made coffee and I made her have some, though I guess she didn't care for it. Too strong. She spilt it all down her, she was kind of shaking.

'I said, "How about you take me and show me?" but that was the wrong thing to say. It started her off again. "OK, then," I said, "you have to call the police, right?" It was then she said she hadn't a phone. Isn't that incredible? I said to use mine but she wouldn't. I mean, naturally I see she wouldn't want to do that, so I said OK, I'll do it, and I guess I did.'

'She said nothing about seeing anyone else in the woods? Then or on a previous occasion near where the body was?'

'Nothing. You have to understand she didn't talk much, not actual *talk*. She made a whole lot of noises, but real speech, no.'

In addition to the other means of recording this statement,

Wexford had been noting down some of it when his ballpoint ceased to work. The tip of it began making grooves instead of marks on the page. He looked up, reached for another pen out of the jar beside the furry cactus and saw that Daisy had come into the stables and was standing just inside the door, looking rather wistfully about her.

She saw him a fraction after he saw her and immediately came over, smiling and holding out her hands. This might have been a social visit, long-promised, that she was paying. That it was, to all intents and purposes, a police station, that these were police officers conducting a murder enquiry, had not in the least deterred her. She was unaware of the implications and innocent of the knowledge which would have inhibited others.

'You asked me to come the other day, and I said no, I was tired or I wanted to be alone or something, and ever since I've thought how rude that was. So I thought, today I'll go and see the place and here I am!'

Karen was looking scandalised and Barry Vine not much less so. The open-plan arrangement of the stables had its disadvantages.

Wexford said, 'I'll be delighted to give you a conducted tour in ten minutes' time. Meanwhile, Sergeant Vine will show you our computer system and how it works.'

She was looking at Thanny Hogarth, just a glance she gave him before taking her eyes away, but it was a glance full of curiosity and speculation. Barry Vine said to come this way, please, and he'd explain the computer phone-link with the police station. Wexford had the impression she didn't want to go but that she recognised she hadn't much choice.

'Who was that?' said Thanny.

'Davina, called Daisy, Jones, who lives at the house.'

'You mean the girl who was shot?'

'Yes. I'd like you to read this statement, please, and if you find everything satisfactory, to sign it.'

Halfway through his reading, Thanny lifted his eyes from the sheet to have another look at Daisy, who was being instructed by Vine in the formatting of software. A line came into Wexford's head: 'What lady's that which cloth enrich the hand of yonder knight?' Romeo and Juliet . . . well, why not?

'Thank you very much. I shan't need to trouble you any longer.'

Thanny seemed not at all anxious to go. He asked if he too could be shown the computer system. It was interesting to him because he was considering replacing his typewriter. Wexford, who wouldn't have got where he was if unable to deal with this kind of thing, said no, sorry, they were far too busy.

With a shrug, Thanny ambled off towards the door. There he lingered for a moment as if deep in thought. There he might have stood until Daisy herself had taken her leave, had not DC Pemberton opened the door for him and firmly ushered him out.

'Who was that?' said Daisy.

'An American student called Jonathan Hogarth.'

'What a nice name. I do like names with *th* sounds in them.' For a moment, a disconcerting moment, she sounded exactly like her grandmother. Or as Wexford guessed her grandmother must have sounded. 'Where does he live?'

'In a cottage at Pomfret Monachorum. He's here to do a creative writing MA at the University of the South.'

Wexford thought she looked wistful. If you like the look and the sound of him, he felt like saying, go to university and you'll meet plenty like him. He felt like saying it but he didn't. He wasn't her father, however paternal he might feel, and Gunner Jones was. Gunner Jones couldn't have cared less whether she went to Oxford or she went on the streets.

'I don't suppose I'll ever use this place again,' she said. 'Well, not as my own special private place. I won't need to. It would be a funny thing to do now I've got the whole house. But I shall always have happy memories of it.' She spoke like someone of seventy, grandma again, looking back to a distant youth. 'It was really nice, getting home from school and having here to come to. And I could bring my friends, you know, and no one would disturb us. Yet I'm sure I didn't appreciate it as I should have done when I had it.' She looked out of the window. 'Did that boy come on a bike? I saw a bike leaning up against the wall.'

'Yes, he did. It's not all that far.'

'Not if you know the way through the woods, though I suppose he wouldn't. And, anyway, not on a bike.'

After she had gone back to the house, Wexford permitted himself a small fantasy. Suppose they were really attracted to each other, those two. Thanny might ring her up, they might meet and then – who could tell? Not a marriage or a serious relationship, he wouldn't want that for Daisy at her age. But to put Nicholas Virson's nose out

235

of joint, to change Daisy's repudiation of Oxford to enthusiastic acceptance, how desirable all that seemed.

Gunner Jones returned home rather earlier than expected. He had been in York, staying with friends. Burden, on the phone, asked him for the name and address of the friends and he refused to give these details. In the meantime, he had learned from the Metropolitan Police that, far from being unable to handle a gun, Jones was a member of the North London Gun Club and had been issued with firearms certificates for a rifle and a handgun, in respect of both of which he was subject to periodic inspections by the police.

The handgun was not a Colt but a Smith and Wesson Model 31. Nevertheless, all this led Burden to ask him, in no uncertain terms, to come to Kingsmarkham police station. At first Jones again refused but something in Burden's tone must have made it clear to him that he had little choice.

To the police station, not to Tancred House. Wexford would talk to him in the austerity of an interview room, not up here with his daughter only a stone's throw away. He hardly knew how he came to the decision to drive home by the Pomfret Monachorum road. It was much further, a very long way round. The beauty of the sunset perhaps or, more practically, to avoid, by driving eastwards, heading straight for that flaming red ball whose light blinded as it penetrated the woodland in dazzling shafts. Or simply to see how spring had begun to veil the young trees with green.

After half a mile he saw them. Not the Land-Rover. That was either hidden among the trees or not in use today. And John Gabbitas was not dressed in his protective clothing, there was no chain saw or other tools to be seen. He was in jeans and a Barbour jacket and Daisy too wore jeans with a heavy sweater. They stood on the edge of a recent plantation of young trees, a long way away, glimpsed only because there happened to be an aisle here, a swathe cut through. They were talking, they were close together and they did not hear his car.

The sun gilded them with red-gold so that they looked like painted figures brushed into a landscape. Their shadows were dark and stretched out on the reddened grass. He saw her lay her hand on Gabbitas's arm and her shadow copy the gesture, and then he drove on.

# 21

A woodsman uses rope. Burden remembered 'surgery' being performed on a tree in a neighbour's garden. It was during his first marriage, when his children were young. They had all watched from an upstairs window. The tree surgeon had roped himself to one of the great limbs of the willow before beginning the work of sawing off a dead branch.

Whether or not John Gabbitas would be working on a Saturday he didn't know but he made a point of getting to the cottage early just in case. It was only a minute or two past eight thirty. A repeated ringing of the doorbell failed to rouse him. Gabbitas either wasn't yet up or had already gone out.

Burden walked round the back and looked at the various outbuildings, a woodshed and a machinery shed and a structure for keeping wood dry while it seasoned. All had been searched at the beginning of the case. But when they searched, what had they been looking for?

Gabbitas appeared as Burden returned to the front of the house. He seemed not to have come along the path through the pinetum but from among the trees themselves, from that area of woodland that lay to the south of the gardens. Instead of working boots, he was wearing trainers and instead of protective clothing or even his Barbour, jeans and a sweater. If there was a shirt under it this was not apparent.

'May I know where you've been, Mr Gabbitas?'

'A walk,' Gabbitas said. It was short and sharp. He looked affronted.

'A fine morning for a walk,' Burden said mildly. 'I want to ask you about rope. Do you use rope in your business?'

'Sometimes.' Gabbitas looked suspicious, he looked as if he was going to ask why, but he must have thought better of it – or remembered how Andy Griffin had died. 'I haven't used any lately but I've always got it to hand.' As Burden had expected, he was in the habit of roping himself to a tree if the work he had to do was above a certain height or otherwise dangerous.

'It'll be in the machinery shed,' he said. 'I know exactly where. I could put my hand on it in the dark.'

But he couldn't. Not in the dark or broad daylight. The rope had gone.

Wexford, who had wondered where those features of Daisy's appearance came from that were not direct hand-downs from Davina Flory, saw them uncannily present in the man before him. But no, not perhaps uncannily. Gunner Jones was her father, a fact manifest to all except those who saw likenesses only in physical size and in colour of hair and eye. He had her – or, rather Daisy had *his* – way of looking sideways with a tilt to eye and mouth, the curve of the nostrils, the short upper lip, the straight eyebrows that described a curve only at the temples.

His weight obscured other, possible, resemblances. He was a big heavy man with a truculent look. When he was brought to the interview room where Wexford was, he behaved as if on a social visit or even fact-finding mission. Eyeing the window (which gave on to a back yard and repository for wheelie-bins), he remarked breezily that the old place had changed out of all conscience since he was last here.

There was an insolent defiance in the way he spoke, Wexford thought. He ignored the hand that was extended to him with a false cordiality, and pretended to be studying a folder of papers on the table between them.

'Sit down, please, Mr Jones.'

It was a cut above the usual interview room, that is the walls were not whitewashed roughcast, the window had a blind and no metal grille, the floor was not concrete but tiled and the chairs in which the two men sat had padded backs and seats. But there was nothing to raise it to 'office' standard and over by the door sat a uniformed policeman, PC Waterman, trying to look insouciant and as if sitting in the corner of a bleak chamber in the police station was the way he preferred to spend his Saturday mornings.

Wexford added a note to the notes in front of him, read what he had written, looked up and began to speak about Joanne Garland. He fancied Jones was surprised, perhaps even disconcerted. This was not what he had expected.

'We were friends once, yes,' he said. 'She was married to my pal Brian. We used to go about a bit together, the two couples, I mean. Me and Naomi, Brian and her. As a matter of fact, I was working for Brian while I lived here, I had a job with his company as a sales rep. I did my leg in, as you may know, and the world of sport was closed to me at the tender age of twenty-three. Hard cheese, wouldn't you reckon?'

Treating the question as rhetorical, Wexford said, 'When did you last see Mrs Garland?'

Jones's laughter was a honking sound. 'See her? I haven't seen her for whatever it is, seventeen, eighteen years? When me and Naomi split up she took Naomi's side, which I daresay you could call being loyal. Brian took her side too and that was the end of my job. What you'd call that, my friend, I don't know but I'd call it treachery. Nothing was bad enough for those two to say about me – and what had I done? Not a lot, to be honest with you. Had I beaten her up? Did I go with other women? Did I drink? No way, there was none of that. All I'd done was get driven round the bend by that old bitch till I couldn't stand another bloody day of it.'

'You haven't seen Mrs Garland since then?'

'I told you. I haven't seen her and I haven't spoken to her. Why would I? What was Joanne to me? I never fancied her, for a start. As you may by now have gathered, bossy meddling women don't exactly turn me on, besides her being a good ten years older than me. I haven't seen Joanne and I haven't been near this place from that day to this.'

'You may not have seen or spoken to her but you've communicated,' Wexford said. 'You recently had a letter from her.'

'Did she tell you that?'

He should have known better than to ask. Wexford wouldn't have described his blustering manner and quick protests as good acting. But perhaps they were not acting at all.

'Joanne Garland is missing, Mr Jones. Her whereabouts are unknown.'

His expression was the extreme of incredulity, the look of a character in a horror comic confronted by disaster.

'Oh, come *on*.'

'She's been missing since the night of the murders at Tancred House.'

Gunner Jones pushed out his lips. He lifted his shoulders in a massive shrug. He no longer looked surprised. He looked guilty, though Wexford knew this meant nothing. It was merely the air of a person who is not habitually honest and straightforward. His eyes fixed themselves on Wexford's but the gaze soon faltered and fell.

'I was in Devon,' he said. 'Maybe you haven't heard that. I was fishing at a place called Pluxam on the Dart.'

'We've found nobody to support your story that you were there during March the eleventh and twelfth. I'd like you to come up with the name of someone who might corroborate that. You told us you had never handled a gun, yet you're a member of the North London Gun Club and hold firearms certificates in respect of two weapons.'

'It was a joke,' said Gunner Jones. 'I mean, come on, surely you can see that? It's funny, isn't it, being called Gunner and never had a gun in my hand?'

'I think I must have a different sort of sense of humour from yours, Mr Jones. Tell me about the letter you had from Mrs Garland.'

'Which one?' said Gunner Jones. He went on as if he hadn't asked the question. 'It doesn't matter because they were both about the same thing. She wrote me three years ago – it was when I got divorced from my second wife – and said Naomi and me should get back together. I don't know how she knew about the divorce, someone must have told her, we still knew some of the same people. She wrote to say now I was "free", her word, there was nothing to stop me and Naomi "remaking our marriage". I'll tell you something, I reckon these days folk only write letters when they're scared to talk on the phone. She knew what I'd say to her if she phoned me.'

'Did you reply?'

'No, sport, I didn't. I consigned her letter to the bin.' A look of ineffable shiftiness took command of Jones's face. It was pantomimic. It was also, probably, unconscious. He had no idea how sly he looked when he lied. 'I had another one like it around a month ago, maybe a bit more. That went the same way as the first.'

Wexford began questioning him about his fishing holiday and his prowess with guns. He took Gunner Jones over the same ground as when he had first asked him about the letter, and got similar evasive answers. For a long time Jones refused to say where he had been

240

staying in York but he yielded at last and admitted sulkily that he had a girlfriend there. He provided a name and an address.

'However, I shan't be taking the plunge again.'

'Until today you haven't been to Kingsmarkham for getting on for eighteen years?'

'That's right.'

'Not on Monday, 13 May of last year, for instance?'

'Not on that day, *for instance*, or any other instance.'

It was the middle of the afternoon and two hours since a sandwich lunch had been provided from the canteen, when Wexford asked Jones to make a statement and reluctantly and inwardly decided he must let him go. He had no hard evidence on which to hold him. Jones was already talking about 'getting a lawyer down here', which seemed to tell Wexford that he knew more about crime from American television imports than from actual experience, but again he could be acting.

'Now I'm here I might think about taking a cab up to meet my daughter. How about that?'

Wexford said neutrally that this, of course, would be up to him. The idea was not pleasant but he had no doubt Daisy would be perfectly safe. The place was swarming with police officers, the stables still fully staffed. In advance of his own arrival, he put through a call to Vine, alerting him to Jones's intention.

In the event, Gunner Jones, who had come by train, returned to London at once by the same means, putting up no resistance to the offer of police transport to Kingsmarkham British Rail Station Wexford found himself uncertain as to whether Jones was really quite clever or deeply stupid. He concluded that he was one of those people to whom lies are as reasonable an option as the truth. What is chosen is that which makes life easier.

It was growing late and it was Saturday but he had himself driven back to Tancred just the same. Another floral offering had been hung on the right-hand post of the main gate. He wondered who might be the donor of these flowers, this time a heart composed of dark-red rosebuds, if it was a series of people or always the same person, and he got out of the car to look while Donaldson opened the gate. But on the card was written only the message, 'Good night, sweet lady', and there was no name or signature.

Halfway up the woodland road a fox ran across in front of them but far enough away for Donaldson not to have to brake. It

241

disappeared into the thick greening underbrush. On the banks, among the grass and new April growth, primroses were opening. The car window was open and Wexford could smell the fresh mild air, scented with spring. He was thinking of Daisy, as the fear of her father's surprise visit had led him to do. But thinking of her – he realised with careful self-analysis – with no excessive anxiety, no passionate fear, no absolute love, to speak truly.

He felt slightly shaken. He had no great desire to see Daisy, no need to be with her, place her in that daughter's position, be her father and have that role acknowledged by her. His eyes were opened. Perhaps by the fact that he had not been horrified or angered by Gunner Jones's declared intention of coming up here. He had been no more than annoyed and on his guard. For he was fond of Daisy but he did not love her.

It was self-revelation that the experience brought him. He had been taught the difference, the huge division, between love and being fond of someone. Daisy had been there when, for the first time in her life, Sheila defected. No doubt any amicable pretty young woman who was nice to him would have served the purpose.

He had been given his allotment of love, for wife, children and grandchildren, and that was it, there would be no more. He wanted no more. What he felt for Daisy was a tender regard and a hope that all would go well with her.

This final reflection was forming itself in his mind when he caught sight, from the car window, of a running figure in the distance among the trees. The day was fair and shafts of sunlight penetrated the woods everywhere in slanting misty rays, in places almost opaque. These hindered his view rather than helping him to see whose the figure might be. It ran, apparently joyously and with abandon, through the clear spaces and into the dense bars of light, then between them again. Impossible to tell whether the flying figure was a man or a woman, young or middle-aged. Wexford could only be confident that the runner was not old. It disappeared in the vague direction of the hanging tree.

When the phone rang Gerry Hinde was talking to Burden, asking him if he had seen the flowers on the gate. You never saw flowers like that in a flower shop. When you wanted to buy some for your wife, for instance, you got them all bunched together, not looking very attractive, and she had to arrange them. His wife said that she didn't really like people bringing her flowers because the first thing she had to do, whatever else she might be doing, was put them in water. And that might take ages when the chances were she was cooking a meal or getting one of the kids to bed.

'It would be a useful thing to know. I mean, where whoever he is got those flowers from. Done like that.'

Burden didn't like to say they would very likely be beyond DC Hinde's means. He picked up the phone.

The puritan ethic still played an important role among the forces that ruled his thinking. It told him not to use a car if you could walk the distance, and that phoning the people next door was almost a sin. Therefore, when Gabbitas said he was at home in his cottage, Burden was on the point of asking sharply why he couldn't have come over if he had something to say. A note of gravity and perhaps of shock in the woodsman's voice stopped him.

'Could you come here, please? Could you come and bring someone with you?'

Burden didn't say what he might have, that Gabbitas had seemed far from keen on his company that morning. 'Give me some idea of what this is about, would you?'

'I'd rather wait until you're here. It's nothing to do with the rope.' The voice wavered a little. It said awkwardly, 'I haven't found a body or anything.'

'For God's sake,' said Burden to himself as he put the receiver back.

He emerged on to the courtyard and walked round the front of the house. Nicholas Virson's car was parked on the flagstones. The sunshine was still very bright but the sun by now quite low in the sky. Its oblique rays turned the car approaching along the main road out of the woods to a dazzling globe of white fire. Burden was unable to look at it, so that it had drawn up not far from him and Wexford was getting out before he saw who this was.

'I'll come with you.'

'He said to bring someone with me. I thought it a bit of a nerve.'

They took the narrow road through the pinetum. On either side the placid sunshine of early evening showed the varying colours of the conifers, smooth spires, serrated cones, Christmas tree spruces and sweeping cedars, green, blue, silver, gold and almost black. The sunlight stood in pillars and hung in bands between the symmetrical shapes. There was a strong aromatic, tarry scent.

243

Underfoot it was dry and rather slippery, for brown needles covered the road surface as well as the interstices of the wood. The sky was a great blue-white dazzlement above them. How lucky they were to live here, Wexford thought, those Harrisons and John Gabbitas, and how much they must fear the loss of it. Uneasily, he remembered his homeward journey of the previous evening and the woodsman and Daisy standing side by side in the sunlit aisle. A girl might lay her hand on a man's arm and look up into his face in that confiding way and it all meant nothing. They had been a long way distant from him. Daisy was a 'toucher', she tended to touch you as she talked, to lay a finger on your wrist, pass her hand lightly across your arm in a gesture near a caress . . .

John Gabbitas was out in his front garden, waiting for them, his right hand beating time with a frenzied impatience as if he found this delay intolerable.

Once again Wexford was struck by his looks, a spectacular handsomeness which, if it had belonged to a woman, would have led you to call it a waste, buried in such a place. The same sort of comment simply never applied to a man. He was reminded suddenly of Dr Perkins's remarks about Harvey Copeland and his appearance, and then Gabbitas was ushering them into the little house, into the living room and pointing with the same quivering finger that had beat time, at something which lay on a woven-raffia-topped stool in the middle of the room.

'What is this, Mr Gabbitas?' Burden asked him. 'What's going on?'

'I found it. I found *that*.'

'Where? Where it is now?'

'In a drawer. In the chest of drawers.'

It was a large handgun, a revolver, of a dark leaden colour, the metal of the barrel of a slighty paler and browner shade. They looked at it, in a moment of silence.

Wexford said, 'You took it out and put it there?'

Gabbitas nodded.

'You know, of course, that you shouldn't have touched it?'

'OK, I know now. It was a shock. I opened the drawer, I keep paper and envelopes in there, and it was the first thing I saw. It was lying on top of a packet of paper for printing out. I know I shouldn't have touched it, but it was instinctive.'

'May we sit down, Mr Gabbitas?'

244

Gabbitas cast up his eyes, then nodded furiously. These were the gestures of a man wondering at the triviality of the request at such a time. 'It's the gun they were all killed with, isn't it?'

'It may be,' said Burden. 'It may not. That remains to be established.'

'I phoned you as soon as I found it.'

'As soon as you'd removed it from where you found it, yes. That would have been at five fifty. When was the last time you looked in that drawer, prior to five fifty?'

'Yesterday,' Gabbitas said after a small hesitation. 'Yesterday evening. About nine. I was going to write a letter. To my parents in Norfolk.'

'And the gun wasn't there then?'

'Of course it wasn't!' Gabbitas's voice was suddenly ragged with exasperation. 'I'd have got in touch with you then if it had been. There was nothing in the drawer but what's always in it, paper, notepaper, envelopes, cards, that sort of thing. The point is the gun wasn't there. Can't you understand? I've never seen it before.'

'All right, Mr Gabbitas. I should try to keep calm if I were you. Did you in fact write to your parents?'

Gabbitas said impatiently, 'I posted the letter in Pomfret this morning. I spent the day felling a dead sycamore in the centre of Pomfret and I had two kids doing community service to help me. We finished at four thirty and I was back here by five.'

'And fifty minutes later you opened the drawer because you meant to write another letter? You seem to be an enthusiastic correspondent.'

It was with a scarcely restrained fury that Gabbitas turned on Burden. 'Look, I didn't have to tell you about this. I could have chucked it out with the rubbish and no one the wiser. It's nothing to do with me, I simply found it, I found it in that drawer *where someone else must have put it*. I opened the drawer, if you must know, for a piece of paper on which to write an invoice for the job I did today. To the borough council's environment department. That's the way I work. I have to. I can't hang about for weeks and weeks. I need the money.'

'All right, Mr Gabbitas,' Wexford said. 'But it was unfortunate you handled this weapon. I suppose it was with bare hands? Yes. I'm going to put through a call to DC Archbold to come over here and take care of it. It'll be wiser for no other unauthorised person to touch it.'

Gabbitas was sitting down, leaning forward, his elbows resting on the arms of the chair, his expression truculent and peevish. It was the look of someone who has been baulked of his desire to have authority thank him for his services. Wexford considered that there were two possible views to take. One was that Gabbitas was guilty, perhaps only of possessing this gun, but guilty of that and now afraid to hang on to it. The other was that he simply did not realise the gravity of the matter or understand what this meant, if the revolver on the stool was indeed the murder weapon.

He made his call, said to Gabbitas, 'You were out all day?'

'I told you. And I can give you the names of dozens of witnesses to prove it.'

'It's a pity you can't give us the name of one to corroborate where you were on 11 March.' Wexford sighed. 'All right. I suppose there are no signs of a break-in? Who else has a key to this house?'

'Nobody, so far as I know.' Gabbitas hesitated, and quickly emended what he had said. 'I mean, the lock wasn't changed when I moved in. The Griffins might still have a key. It's not my house, it doesn't belong to me. I suppose Miss Flory or Mr Copeland had a key.' More and more names seemed to come to mind. 'The Harrisons had a key between the Griffins going and me coming. I don't know what happened to it. I never go out and leave the house unlocked, I'm careful about that.'

'You might as well not bother, Mr Gabbitas,' said Burden drily. 'It doesn't seem to make much difference.'

You lost a rope and found a gun, Wexford reflected when he was alone with Gabbitas. Aloud he said, 'I suppose much the same applies to the keys to the machinery shed. A lot of people have keys?'

'There's no lock on the door.'

'That settles that, then. You came here last May, Mr Gabbitas?'

'At the beginning of May, yes.'

'No doubt you have a bank account?'

Gabbitas told him where, told him without hesitation.

'And when you came here you immediately transferred your account to the Kingsmarkham branch? Yes. Was this before or after the murder of the police officer? Can you remember that? If it was before or after DS Martin was murdered in that bank branch?'

246

'It was before.'

Wexford fancied Gabbitas sounded uneasy, but he was used to his imagination telling him things like that. 'The gun you found just now was almost certainly the weapon used in that murder.' He watched Gabbitas's face, saw nothing there but a kind of blank receptiveness. 'Of the public who were in the bank that morning, 13 May, not all came forward to make statements to the police. Some left before the police came. One took that gun with him.'

'I know nothing about any of this. I wasn't in the bank that day.'

'But you had already come to Tancred?'

'I came on May the fourth,' Gabbitas said sullenly.

Wexford paused, then said in a conversational way, 'Do you like Miss Davina Jones, Mr Gabbitas? Daisy Jones?'

The change of subject caught Gabbitas off guard. He burst out, 'What's that got to do with it?'

'You're young and apparently unattached. She's young too and good-looking. She's very charming. As a result of what has happened she's in possession of a considerable property.'

'She's just someone I work for. All right, she's attractive, any man would find her attractive. But she's just someone I work for, so far as I'm concerned. And may not be working for much longer.'

'You're leaving this job?'

'It's not a matter of leaving the job. I'm not employed here, remember? I did tell you. I'm self-employed. Is there anything else you want to know? I'll tell you one thing. Next time I find a gun I won't tell the police, I'll chuck it in the river.'

'I wouldn't do that if I were you, Mr Gabbitas,' Wexford said mildly.

In the *Sunday Times* review section was an article by a distinguished literary critic on material he had collected for a biography of Davina Flory. Most of this was correspondence. Wexford glanced at it, then began to read with mounting interest.

Many of the letters had been in the possession of the niece in Mentone, now dead. They were from Davina to her sister, the niece's mother, and indicated that Davina's first marriage, to Desmond Cathcart Flory, had never been consummated. Long passages were quoted, instances of unhappiness and bitter disappointment, all written in Davina's unmistakable style that alternated between the plain and the baroque. The author of the article speculated, basing

247

his argument on evidence in later letters, as to who might have been Naomi Flory's father.

This accounted for something Wexford had wondered about. Though Desmond and Davina had married in 1935, Davina's only child had not been born until ten years later. He called to mind, painfully, that horrible scene at the Cheriton Forest Hotel when Casey had loudly averred that Davina had still been a virgin for eight years after her marriage. With a sigh, he finished the piece and turned over to the double-page spread on the newspaper's Literary Banquet held at Grosvenor House on the previous Monday. Wexford looked at it only in the hope of seeing a photograph of Amyas Ireland, who had been at the banquet the previous year and might be again.

The first face he saw, that leapt at him from a page of photographs, was Augustine Casey's. Casey was sitting at a table with four other people. At any rate, there were four other people in the picture. Wexford wondered if he had spat in his wineglass, and then he read the caption.

*From left to right: Dan Kavanagh, Penelope Casey, Augustine Casey, Frances Hegarty, Jane Somers.*

All were smiling pleasantly except Casey, whose face wore a sardonic smirk. The women were in formal evening gowns.

Wexford looked at the picture and reread the caption, looked at the other pictures on the two pages, returned to the first one. He sensed Dora's silent presence at his left shoulder. She was waiting for him to ask but he hesitated, not knowing how to frame what he wanted to say. The question came carefully.

'Who is the woman in the shiny dress?'

'Penelope Casey.'

'Yes, I know. I can see that. What is she to him?'

'She's his wife, Reg. It looks as if he's gone back to his wife or she's come back to him.'

'You knew this?'

'No, darling, I didn't know. I didn't know he had a wife until the day before yesterday. Sheila didn't phone this week so I phoned her. She sounded very upset, but all she told me was that Gus's wife had come back to their flat and he'd gone back there "to talk it through".'

That expression again . . . He put his hand up to his eyes, perhaps to hide the picture from sight. 'How unhappy she must be,' he said, and then, 'Oh, the poor child . . .'

248

# 22

'I can't tell you if this is the same weapon as was used in the bank killing last May,' the expert witness said to Wexford. 'It certainly is the weapon that was used at Tancred House on 11 March.'

'Then why can't you say if it was the same gun?'

'It probably is. Evidence in favour of that theory is that the chamber accommodates six cartridges – it's a classic 'six-gun' – and one of these was used at the bank killing, while five were used at Tancred House. Very likely the remaining five in the chamber. In a society where handguns appear constantly as murder weapons one would hardly care to hazard that. But I think it's an intelligent guess here.'

'But you still can't be sure it's the same gun?'

'As I've said, I can't be sure.'

'Why not?'

'The barrel's been changed,' the expert said laconically. 'It's not such an amazing task to undertake, you know. The Dan Wesson line of revolvers, for instance, with their variety of barrel lengths, are all capable of being changed at home by any amateur. The Colt Magnum might be more difficult. Whoever embarked on that would have to have the tools. Well, he must have had because this is definitely not the barrel this gun started life with.'

'Would a gunsmith have them?'

'Depends on what kind of gunsmith, I should say. Most specialise in shotguns.'

'And that's what makes the marks on the five cartridges fired at Tancred House different from the one that killed Martin? A change of barrel?'

'Right. That's why I can only say this and that is probable, not that it definitely happened. This is Kingsmarkham, after all, not the Bronx. There aren't going to be unlimited caches of firearms about. It's the numbers really that point to it, the one for that poor fellow who was one of you, and the five for Tancred. And the calibre, of course. And his intent to deceive. How about that? He wasn't changing gun barrels for fun, it wasn't his hobby.'

He was angry. The relief he might have felt that Sheila had been divided from that man, that she would no longer go to Nevada, was subsumed in anger. For Casey she had turned down *Miss Julie*, for Casey she had changed her life and, it seemed to him, her very personality. And Casey had gone back to his wife.

Wexford hadn't spoken to her. Only the answering machine replied when he dialled her number and there were no more cheerful messages, only the clipped name and request for a message to be left. He left a message, asking her to phone. Then, when she didn't, he left another, one that said he was sorry – for her, for what had happened, and for all the things he had said.

He called into the bank on the way to work. It was the branch where Martin had been killed, not his bank, but the nearest to the route Donaldson took and it had its own small car park at the back. Wexford had his Transcend card that enabled him to draw cash at all banks and all branches in the United Kingdom. The name made him grind his teeth at the misuse of words, but it was a useful card.

Sharon Fraser was still there. Ram Gopal had obtained a transfer to another branch. The second cashier this morning was a very young and pretty Eurasian woman. Wexford, who had resolved not to do this, could not keep his eyes from turning to the place where Martin had stood and had died. There should be some mark, some lasting memorial. He half-expected to see Martin's blood still there, some vestige of it, while castigating himself for such nonsensical ideas.

Four people were in the queue ahead of him. He thought of Dane Bishop, ill and frightened, perhaps not even of sound mind by that time, shooting Martin from about this spot, running out and throwing down his gun as he went. The frightened people, the screams, those men who had not remained but had quietly slipped away. One of them, standing perhaps where he was standing now, had, according to Sharon Fraser, been holding a bunch of green banknotes in his hand.

250

Wexford looked round to see the length of the queue behind him and saw Jason Sebright. Sebright was trying to write a cheque where he stood instead of using one of the bank's tables and chained-up ballpoint. The woman in front of him turned round and Wexford heard him say, 'Do you mind if I rest my chequebook on your back, madam?'

This aroused uneasy giggles. Sharon Fraser's light came on and Wexford went up to her with his Transcend card. He recognised the look in her eyes. It was apprehensive, unwelcoming, the look of someone who would rather attend to anybody except you because, by your profession and your searching questions, you endanger her privacy and her peace and perhaps her very existence.

When Martin died people had come into the bank and laid flowers on the spot where he fell, donors as anonymous as whoever had brought these bouquets to hang on the Tancred gates. The latest offerings were dead. Night frosts had blackened them until they looked like a nest made by some untidy bird. Wexford told Pemberton to remove them and throw them on Ken Harrison's rubbish heap. No doubt they would soon be replaced by others. Perhaps it was because his mind was dwelling abnormally on love and pain and the perils of love that he had begun speculating who the donor of these flowers might be. A fan? A silent – and rich – admirer? Or more than that? The sight of the withered roses made him think of those early letters of Davina's and her loveless years until Desmond Flory went away to war.

As he approached the house, he saw a workman at the west-wing window, replacing the pane of eight-ounce glass. It was a dull still day, the kind of weather the meteorologists had taken to calling 'quiet'. The mist that hung in the air showed itself only in the distance where the horizon was blurred and the woods turned to a smoky blue.

Wexford looked through the dining-room window. The door to the hall was open. The seals had been taken off and the room opened up. On the ceiling and walls the blood splash marks still showed but the carpet was gone.

'We'll be making a start in there tomorrow, governor,' the workman said.

So Daisy was beginning to come to terms with her loss, with the horror of that room. Restoration had begun. He walked across the flagstones, past the front of the house, towards the east wing and the

251

stables behind. Then he saw something he hadn't noticed when he first arrived. Thanny Hogarth's bicycle was leaning up against the wall to the left of the front door. A fast worker, Wexford thought, and he felt better, he felt more cheerful. He even felt like speculating as to what might happen when Nicholas Virson arrived – or was Daisy too good a manager in these matters to let that happen?

'I think Andy Griffin spent those two nights here,' Burden said to him as he walked into the stables.

'*What?*'

'In one of the outbuildings. We searched them, of course, when we did the general search of the house after it happened, but we never went near them again.'

'Which outbuilding are you talking about, Mike?'

He followed Burden along the sandy path behind the high hedge. A short row or terrace of cottages, not dilapidated but not well-maintained either, stood parallel to this hedge, the roadway a sandy track. You might be quartered here for a month, as they had been, without ever knowing the cottages were there.

'Karen came out here last night,' Burden said. 'She was doing her rounds. Daisy said she heard something. There was no one in fact about but Karen came this way and looked through that window.'

'She shone a torch, d'you mean?'

'I suppose so. There's no electricity to these cottages, no running water, no amenities at all. According to Brenda Harrison they've not had anyone living in them for fifty years – well, since before the war. Karen saw something which made her go back this morning.'

'What d'you mean "saw something"? You're not in court, Mike. This is me, remember?'

Burden made an impatient gesture. 'Yes, sure. Sorry. Rags, a blanket, remains of food. We'll go in. It's still there.'

The cottage door opened on a latch. The most powerful of a variety of smells that greeted them was the ammoniac one of stale urine. There was a floor of bricks on which a makeshift bed had been contrived from a pile of dirty cushions, two old coats, unidentifiable rags, a good, thick and fairly clean blanket. Two empty Coke cans stood in the grate in front of the fireplace. An iron fire-basket contained grey ash and on top of the ash, thrown there perhaps after the cinders had cooled, was a wad of greasy screwed-up paper that had wrapped fish and chips. The smell of this was marginally more unpleasant than that of the urine.

252

'You think Andy slept here?'

'We can try the Coke cans for prints,' Burden said. 'He could have been here. He would have known about it. And if he was here on those two nights, 17 and 18 March, no one else was.'

'OK. How did he get here?'

Burden beckoned him through the unsavoury room. He had to duck his head, the lintels were so low. Beyond the hole of a scullery and the back door, bolted top and bottom but not locked, was a wired-in plot of overgrown garden and a small walled area that might have been a coal-hole or a pig sty. Inside, half-covered by a waterproof sheet, was a motorbike.

'No one would have heard him come,' Wexford said. 'The Harrisons and Gabbitas were too far away. Daisy hadn't come back home. She didn't come until several days later. He had the place to himself. But, Mike, why did he *want* the place to himself?'

They strolled along the path that bordered the wood. In the distance, to the south of the by-road, the whine of Gabbitas's chain saw could be heard. Wexford's thoughts reverted to the gun, to the extraordinary thing that had been done to the gun. Would Gabbitas have had the means and the knowledge to change the barrel on a revolver? Would he have the tools? On the other hand, would anyone else?

'Why would Andy Griffin want to sleep up here, Mike?' he said.

'I don't know. I'm starting to wonder if this place had some sort of particular fascination for him.'

'He wasn't our second man, was he? He wasn't the one Daisy heard but didn't see?'

'I don't see him in that role. That would have been too big for him. Beyond his class. Blackmail was his line, small petty blackmail.'

Wexford nodded. 'That's why he was killed. I think he started in a small way and it was all for cash. We know that from his Post Office Savings account. He may have operated from here quite a bit while he and his parents still lived here. I don't suppose he began on Brenda Harrison. He may well have tried it successfully on other women. All he had to do was pick an older woman and threaten to tell her husband or her friends or some relative that she'd made advances to him. Sometimes it would work and sometimes it wouldn't.'

'Do you think he tried something on the women here? Davina

herself, say, or Naomi? I can still hear the venom in his voice when he talked to me about them. The choice language he used.'

'Would he dare? Perhaps. It's something we're never likely to know. Who was he blackmailing when he left home that Sunday and camped here? The gunman or the one Daisy didn't see?'

'Maybe.'

'And why did he have to be here to do that?'

'This sounds more like one of your theories than mine, Reg. But as I've said I think he was fascinated by this place. It was his *home*. He may have bitterly resented being turned away from it last year. We may well discover that he spent far more time up here and in the woods and just spying out the land than anyone's dreamed of. All those times he was away from home and no one knew where, I reckon he was up here. Who knew this place and these woods? He did. Who could have driven through them and not got bogged down or hit a tree? He could.'

'But we've said we don't see him as our second man,' said Wexford.

'OK, forget his ability to drive through the wood, forget any involvement in the murders. Suppose he was camping in here on 11 March? Let's say he intended to stay here for a couple of nights for purposes we as yet know nothing of. He left home on the motorbike at six and brought his stuff up here. He was in the cottage when the two men arrived at eight – or maybe he wasn't in the cottage but outside, prowling about or whatever he did. He saw the gunmen and one of them he recognised. How about that?'

'Not bad,' said Wexford. 'Who would he recognise? Gabbitas, certainly. Even under a woodsman's mask. Would he recognise Gunner Jones?'

The bicycle was still there. The workman was still there, putting the finishing touches to his mended window. A thin persistent drizzle began to fall, the first rain for a long time. The water washed down the stables windows and made it dark inside. Gerry Hinde had an angled lamp on above the computer on which he was building a new database: every subject or suspect they had interviewed with his or her alibis and corroborative witnesses.

Wexford had begun to wonder if there was any point their remaining so close to the scene of the murders. It was four weeks tomorrow since what the newspapers called 'the Tancred Massacre' and the Assistant Chief Constable had made an appointment for an interview with him. Wexford was to go to his house. It would seem like a social engagement, a glass of sherry featuring somewhere in the proceedings, but the purpose of it all was, he was sure, to complain to him about the lack of progress made and the cost of it all. The suggestion would be made, or more likely the order given, that they move back to Kingsmarkham, to the police station. He would again be asked how he could continue to justify the night guard on Daisy. But how could he justify to himself the removal of that guard?

He phoned home to ask Dora if there had been any sign from Sheila, got a worried negative and walked outside into the rain. The place had a dismal look in wet weather. It was curious how the rain and the greyness changed the presence of Tancred House, so that it seemed like a building in one of those rather sinister Victorian engravings, austere, even dour, its windows dull eyes and its walls discoloured with water stains.

The woods had lost their blueness and grown pebble-grey under a scummy sky. Bib Mew came out from round the back, wheeling her bicycle. She dressed like a man, walked like a man, you would unhesitatingly put her down as male from here or nearer. Passing Wexford, she pretended not to see him, twisting her head round awkwardly and looking skywards, studying the phenomenon of rain.

He reminded himself of her handicap. Yet she lived alone. What must her life be? What had it been? She had been married once. He found that grotesque. She mounted her bike in man's fashion, swinging one leg over, pushed hard on the pedals, swung off along the main drive. It was apparent that she was still avoiding the by-road and the proximity of the hanging tree, and this brought him a little inner shiver.

Next morning the builders arrived. Their van was on the flagstones by the fountain before Wexford got there. Not that they called themselves builders, but 'Interior Creators' from Brighton. He went carefully through his case notes, filling by now a large file. Gerry Hinde had them all on a small disc, smaller than the old single record, but useless to Wexford. He saw the case slipping through his fingers now that so much time had elapsed.

Those irreconcilables remained. Where was Joanne Garland? Was she alive or dead? What connection had she with the murders? How did the gunmen get away from Tancred? Who put the gun in Gabbitas's house? Or was this some ploy of Gabbitas's own?

255

Wexford read Daisy's statement again. He played over Daisy's statement on tape. He knew he would have to talk to her again, for here the irreconcilables were most obvious. She must try to explain to him how it was possible for Harvey Copeland to have climbed those stairs yet be shot as if he were still at the foot of them and facing the front door; account for the long time – a long time measured in seconds – between his leaving the dining room and being shot.

Could she also account for something he knew Freeborn would laugh to scorn if he heard the matter raised? If the cat Queenie normally, indeed, it seemed, invariably, galloped about the upper floors at six in the evening, *always* at six, why had Davina Flory thought the noise upstairs was Queenie when she heard it at eight? And why had the gunman been frightened off by sounds from upstairs, which were in fact made by nothing more threatening than a cat?

There was another question he had to ask, though he was almost sure time would have blotted out her accurate memory of this just as trauma had begun to do so immediately after the event.

The car on the flagstones, as far away from 'Interior Creators of Brighton' as could possibly be managed without parking on the lawn, was one he thought he recognised as Joyce Virson's. He was probably right in thinking Daisy would welcome a respite from Mrs Virson, perhaps an excuse for getting rid of her altogether. He rang the bell and Brenda came.

A sheet had been hung up over the dining-room door. From behind came muffled sounds, not bangs, not scraping noises, but soft liquid floppings and sluicings. Accompanying these was the builders' invariable *sine qua non*, but turned low, the mindless dribble of pop music. You couldn't hear it in the morning room nor in the *serre* where they were sitting, not two but three people: Daisy, Joyce Virson and her son.

Nicholas Virson took time off whenever he felt like it, Wexford thought, saying an austere good-morning. Whatever he did, was business so bad in this recession time that it mattered very little whether he went in or not?

They had been talking when Brenda brought him in and he fancied their talk had been heated. Daisy was looking determined, a little flushed. Mrs Virson's expression was more than usually peevish and Nicholas seemed put out, baulked in some endeavour. Were they here for lunch? Wexford hadn't previously noticed that it was past noon.

Daisy got up when he came in, hugging close to her the cat which had been lying in her lap. Its fur was almost the same shade as the blue denim she wore, a bomber jacket, tight jeans. The jacket was embroidered and between the coloured stitching were a multiplicity of gilt and silver studs. A black and blue checked T-shirt was under the jacket and the belt in the jeans' waistband was of metal, woven silver and gold with bosses of pearly and clear glass. Inescapable was the feeling that this was a statement she was making. These people were to be shown the real Daisy, what she wanted to be, a free spirit, even an outrageous spirit, dressing as she pleased and doing as she liked.

The contrast between what she wore and Joyce Virson's clothes – even allowing for the great age difference – was so marked as to be ludicrous. It was a mother-in-law's uniform, burgundy wool dress with matching jacket, round her neck a silver rhomboid on a thong, trendy in the sixties, her only rings her large diamond engagement ring and her wedding band. Daisy had an enormous ring on her left hand, a two-inch-long turtle in silver, its shell studded with coloured stones, that looked as if it was creeping down her hand from first finger-joint to knuckles.

Having an objection to the word 'intrude', Wexford apologised for disturbing them. He had no intention of leaving and agreeing to come back later, and he indicated that he was sure Daisy wouldn't expect this. It was Mrs Virson who answered for her.

'Now you're here, Mr Wexford, perhaps you'll come in on our side. I know how you feel about Daisy being here alone. Well, she's not alone, you put girls in here to protect her, though what they could do in an emergency, I'm sorry but I really can't imagine. And, frankly, as a ratepayer, I rather resent our money being spent on that sort of thing.'

Nicholas said unexpectedly, 'We don't pay rates any more, Mother, we pay poll tax.'

'It's all the same thing. It all goes the same way. We came here this morning to ask Daisy to come back and stay with us. Oh, it's not the first time as you know as well as I do. But we thought it worth another try, particularly as circumstances have changed as regards – well, Nicholas and Daisy.'

Wexford watched a terrible blush suffuse Nicholas Virson's face. It

257

wasn't a blush of pleasure or gratification but, to judge by the wince which accompanied it, of intense embarrassment. He was nearly sure circumstances hadn't changed except in Joyce's Virson's mind.

'It's obviously absurd for her to be here,' Mrs Virson reflected, and her remaining words came out in a rush. 'As if she was *grown up*. As if she was able to make her own decisions.'

'Well, I am,' Daisy said calmly. 'I am grown-up. I *do* make decisions.' She seemed quite untroubled by all this. She looked faintly bored.

Nicholas made an effort. His face was still pink. Wexford suddenly remembered the description of the masked gunman Daisy had given him, the fair hair, the cleft chin, the big ears. It was almost as if it was this man she had been thinking of when she described him. And why would she do that? Why would she do it even unconsciously?

'We thought,' Nicholas said, 'that Daisy might come over to dinner with us and – and stay the night and sort of see how she felt. We were planning to give her her own sitting room, a sort of suite, you know. She wouldn't actually have to live with us, if you see what I mean. She could be absolutely her own woman, if that's what she wants.'

Daisy laughed. Whether it was at the whole idea or Nicholas's use of the fashionable absurdity Wexford couldn't tell. He had thought her eyes troubled and the disturbance, the anxiety in them remained, but she laughed and her laughter was full of merriment.

'I've already told you, I'm going out to dinner tonight. I don't expect to be back until quite late and my friend will certainly bring me home.'

'Oh, Daisy . . .' The man couldn't help himself. His misery broke through the pompous manner. 'Oh, Daisy, you might at least tell me who you're going to dinner with. Is it someone we know? If it's a friend can't you bring her with you to us?'

Daisy said, 'Davina used to say that if a woman talks about her friend, or her cousin even, or "someone" she works with or "someone" she knows, people will always assume it's another woman. Always. She said it's because deep down they don't really want women to have relationships with the opposite sex.'

'I haven't the faintest idea what you're talking about,' Nicholas said and Wexford could see he hadn't. He really hadn't.

'Well, I'm sorry,' said Joyce Virson, 'but all this is beyond me. I should have thought a girl who had an understanding with a young

258

man would want to spend time with him.' Her temper was going and with it her self-control. It was always a tremulously balanced function. 'The truth is that when freedom and a lot of money come to people too soon it goes to their heads. It's power, you see, they become power-mad. It's the greatest pleasure in life some women have, exercising power over some poor man whose only crime is he happens to be fond of them. I'm sorry, but I hate that sort of thing.' She grew wilder, her voice tipping over the edge of control. 'If that's women's lib or whatever they call it, women's something, horrible nonsense, you can keep it and much good may it do you. It won't find you a good husband, that I do know.'

'Mother,' said Nicholas, with a flash of strength. He spoke to Daisy. 'We're on our way to lunch with . . .' he named some local friends '. . . and we hoped you'd come too. We do have to go very soon.'

'I can't come, can I? Mr Wexford's here to talk to me. It's important. I have to help the police. You haven't forgotten what happened here four weeks ago, have you? Or have you?'

'Of course I haven't. How could I? Mother didn't mean all that, Daisy.' Joyce Virson had turned her head away and was holding a handkerchief up to her face while apparently staring with great concentration at the newly-opened tulips in the terrace tubs. 'She's set her heart on your coming and so – well, so had I. We really thought we could win you over. May we come back later, on our way home from this lunch? Can we just drop in again and try to explain to you just what we had in mind?'

'Of course. Friends can call on each other when they want, can't they? You're my friend, Nicholas, surely you know that?'

'Thank you, Daisy.'

'I hope you'll always be my friend.'

They might not have been there, Wexford and Joyce Virson. For a moment the two were alone, enclosed in whatever their relationship was, had been, whatever secrets of emotion or events they shared. Nicholas got up and Daisy gave him a kiss on the cheek. Then she did a curious thing. She strode to the door of the *serre* and flung it open. Bib was revealed on the other side of it, taking a step backwards, clutching a duster.

Daisy said nothing. She closed the door and turned to Wexford. 'She's always listening outside doors. It's a passion with her, a sort of

259

addiction. I always know she's there, I can hear her start breathing very fast. Strange, isn't it? What can she get out of it?'

She returned to the theme of Bib and eavesdropping as soon as the Virsons had gone. 'I can't sack her. How would I manage with no one?' She sounded suddenly like someone twice her age, an embattled housewife. 'Brenda's told me they're going. I said I only sacked them in a rage, I didn't mean it, but they're going just the same. You know his brother runs that hire-car business? Ken's going in with him, they plan to expand and they can have the other flat over Fred's office. John Gabbitas has been trying to buy a house in Sewingbury since last August and he's just heard his mortgage has come through. He'll still look after the woods, I suppose, but he won't live here.' She gave a kind of dry giggle. 'I'll be left with Bib. D'you think she'll murder me?'

'You've no reason to think . . . ?' he began seriously.

'None at all. She just looks like a bloke and never speaks and listens at doors. She's feeble-minded too. As a murderer she makes a really good cleaner. Sorry, that wasn't funny. Oh God, I sound like that awful Joyce! You don't think I ought to go there, do you? She persecutes me.'

'You wouldn't do what I thought anyway, would you?' She shook her head. 'Then I shan't waste my breath. There are one or two things, as you rightly guessed, I'd like to talk to you about.'

'Yes, of course. But there's something I have to tell you first. I was going to before, but they kept on and on.' She smiled rather ruefully. 'Joanne Garland phoned.'

'*What*?'

'Don't look so amazed. She didn't *know*. She didn't know any of it had happened. She came back last night and went down to the gallery this morning and saw it all shut up, so she phoned me.'

He realised Daisy might not be aware of their fears for Joanne Garland, might not know anything beyond the fact that she had gone away somewhere. Why should she?

'She thought she was phoning Mum. Wasn't that awful? I had to tell her. That was the worst part, telling her what had happened. She didn't believe me, not at first. She thought it was a ghastly joke. This was only – well, half an hour ago. It was just before the Virsons came.'

260

# 23

She was in tears.

It was because she was crying on the phone, incoherent with tears and gasps, that he had relented and, instead of asking her to come to the police station, had said he would go to her. In the house in Broom Vale he sat in one armchair and Barry Vine in another while Joanne Garland, incapacitated by the first question he had asked her, sobbed into the sofa arm.

The first thing Wexford noticed when she admitted them to the house was that her face was bruised. They were old marks, healing now, but the vestiges were there, greenish, yellowish, bruises around the mouth and nose, darker abrasions, plum-coloured at the eyes and the hairline. Her tears couldn't disguise them, nor were they the aftermath of tears.

Where had she been? Wexford asked her that before they sat down and the question drew more tears. She gasped out, 'America, California,' and threw herself down on the sofa in floods of weeping.

'Mrs Garland,' he said after a while, 'try to get a grip on yourself. I'll get you a drink of water.'

She sat bolt upright, her bruised face streaming. 'I don't want *water*.' She said to Vine, 'You could get me a whisky. In that cupboard. Glasses in there. Have yourselves one.' A heavy choking sob cut the end of the last word. From a large red leather handbag on the floor she pulled a handful of coloured tissues and rubbed at her face. 'I'm sorry. I *will* stop. When I've had a drink. My God, the shock.'

Barry showed her the soda bottle he had found. She shook her head fiercely and took a swig of the neat whisky. She seemed to have forgotten all about the offer she had made them, which in any case would have been refused. The whisky was evidently welcome. The effect it had on her was quite different from that on someone who seldom drinks spirits. It was not so much as if she had been in need of a drink – that is, an alcoholic drink – as thirsty. Some special kind of thirst seemed quenched by what she drank and relief spread through her.

The tissues came out again and once more she wiped her face, but carefully this time. Wexford thought she looked remarkably young for fifty-four, or if not exactly young, remarkably smooth-faced. She might have been a tired and rather battered thirty-five. Her hands, though, were those of a much older woman, webs of stringy tendons, wormed with veins. She wore a jersey suit of goose-turd green and a great deal of costume jewellery. Her hair was a bright pale gold, her figure shapely if not quite slim, her legs excellent. In anyone's eyes she was an attractive woman.

Breathing deeply now, sipping the whisky, she took a powder compact and lipstick out of the bag and restored her face. Wexford could see the gaze arrested by the worst of the bruises, one under her left eye. She touched it with a fingertip before applying powder in an attempt at concealment.

'We have a lot of things we'd like to ask you, Mrs Garland.'

'Yes. I suppose.' She hesitated. 'I didn't know, you know, I didn't have a clue. They don't have foreign news – well, it's foreign to them – in American papers. Not unless it's a war or something. There wasn't anything about this. The first I knew was when I phoned that girl, Naomi's girl.' Her lip trembled when she spoke the name. She swallowed. 'Poor thing, I suppose I should be sorry for *her*, I should have told her I was sorry, but it threw me, it just flattened me. I could hardly speak.'

Vine said, 'You told no one you were going away. You didn't say a word to your mother or your sisters.'

'Naomi knew.'

'Maybe.' Wexford didn't say what he felt, that they would never know the truth of that, since Naomi was dead. The last thing he wanted was a fresh gush of tears. 'Would you mind telling us when you went and why?'

She said, like children do, 'Do I have to?'

'Yes, I'm afraid you do. Eventually. Perhaps you'd like to think about your answer. I have to tell you, Mrs Garland, that your vanishing into thin air like this has caused us considerable trouble.'

'Could you get me some more Scotch, please.' She held the empty glass up to Vine. 'Yes, all right, you needn't look like that, I do like a drink but I'm not an alcoholic. I specially like a drink in times of stress. Is there anything wrong with that?'

'I'm not in the business of answering your enquiries, Mrs Garland,' Wexford said. 'I'm here so that you can answer mine. I'm doing you the courtesy of coming here. And I want you capable of answering. Is that clear?' He half-shook his head at Vine who was standing with the glass in his hand and a what-did-your-last-servant-die-of expression on his face. Joanne Garland looked shocked and truculent. 'Very well. This is a very serious matter. I'd like you to tell me when you got home and what you did.'

She said sulkily, 'It was last evening. Well, the plane from Los Angeles gets to Gatwick at half two, only it was late. We weren't through Customs till four. I meant to get the train but I was too tired, I was clapped-out, so I had a car all the way. I was here about five.' She looked hard at him. 'I had a drink – well, two or three. I needed them, I can tell you. I went to sleep. I slept the clock round.'

'And this morning you went down to the shop, found it closed up and looking as if it had been closed up for a long while.'

'That's right. I was mad with Naomi – God forgive me. Oh, I know I could have asked someone, I could have phoned one of my sisters. It never crossed my mind. I just thought, Naomi's screwed it up again – well, like I said, God forgive me. I hadn't got the shop keys, I thought it'd be open, so I shlepped home and phoned Daisy. Well, I reckoned I was phoning Naomi to tear her off a strip. Daisy told me. That poor kid, it must have been hell having to tell me, sort of relive it all over again.'

'The evening you went away, 11 March, you went to see your mother in the Caenbrook Retirement Home between five and five thirty. Would you tell us what you did after that?'

She sighed, cast a glance at the empty glass Vine had placed on the table and passed her tongue across her freshly painted lips. 'I finished my packing. It was the next day I was flying on, the twelfth. The flight didn't leave till eleven a.m. and I was to check in at nine thirty but still I thought, well, I'll go tonight, what if the trains are delayed in the morning? It was just a decision I made on the hop really. When I was packing. I thought, I'll ring up a hotel at Gatwick and see if they'll take me and I did and they could. I'd promised to go up and see Naomi, though we'd actually made all the arrangements during

263

the day. And we weren't going to do the books, Naomi said she'd keep the VAT up to date. But I'd said I'd go just to show willing, you know . . .' Joanne Garland's voice faltered. 'Well, all that. I thought, I'll go to Tancred, have half an hour with Naomi, and then drive home and get myself to the station. It's five minutes' walk to the station from here.'

This fact was well-known to Wexford and he made no comment on it. It was Vine who persisted. 'I don't see why you had to go that night. Not if the plane didn't leave till eleven. Say you had to check in by nine thirty. It's only half an hour in the train, if that.'

She gave him a sidelong aggrieved look. It was evident Joanne Garland had taken against Wexford's sergeant. 'If you must know, I didn't want to run the risk of seeing anyone in the morning.' Vine's expression remained unenlightened. 'OK, don't bend over backwards to understand, will you? I didn't want people seeing me with cases, I didn't want questions, my sisters just happening to phone up – right?'

'We'll leave the magical mystery tour for the time being, Mrs Garland,' said Wexford. 'What time did you go to Tancred House?'

'Ten to eight,' she said quickly. 'I always know the times of things. I'm very time-conscious. And I'm never late. Naomi was always trying to get me to go up there later but that was only her mother flapping. She'd leave these messages on my answering machine but I was used to that, I never played the messages back on a Tuesday. I mean, why shouldn't I be considered as much as Lady Davina? Oh God, she's dead, I shouldn't say it. Well, like I said, I left at ten to eight and got up there at ten past. Eleven minutes past, in fact. I looked at my watch while I was ringing the doorbell.'

'You rang the bell?'

'Over and over. I knew they heard. I knew they were there. God, I mean, I *thought* I knew.' The colour drained from her face and left it paper-white. 'They were dead, weren't they? It had just happened. My God.' Wexford watched her as she briefly closed her eyes, swallowed. He gave her time. She said in a changed, thicker voice, 'The lights were on in the dining room. Oh, God forgive me, I thought, Naomi's told Davina we've done all that needs to be done and Davina's said, in that case it's time that woman learnt not to come disturbing me while I'm having my dinner. She was like that, she would say that.' Again came a vivid recollection of what had

264

happened to Davina Flory. Joanne Garland put her hand up to her mouth.

To frustrate any further calls for God's forgiveness, Wexford said quickly, 'You rang again?'

'I rang three or four times altogether. I went round to the dining-room window but I couldn't see in. The curtains were drawn. Look, I was a bit cross. It sounds terrible to say that now. I thought, OK, I won't hang about and I didn't, I drove home.'

'Just like that? You drove all the way up there and then when they didn't answer the bell you drove home again?'

Barry Vine received a very peevish look. 'What did you expect me to do? Break the door down?'

'Mrs Garland, please think very carefully. Did you pass any vehicle or meet any vehicle on your way to Tancred?'

'No, definitely not.'

'Which way did you come?'

'Which way? By the main gate, of course. That's the way I always went. I mean, I know there's another way, but I've never used it. It's a very narrow lane that other way.'

'And you saw no other vehicle?'

'No, I've said. I hardly ever did, anyway. Well, I think I met John what's-his-name once, Gabbitas. But that was months ago. I definitely met no one on March the eleventh.'

'And going back?'

She shook her head. 'I didn't meet or pass another vehicle when I was coming or going.'

'While you were at Tancred, was there another car or van or vehicle of some kind parked in front of the house?'

'No, of course there wasn't. They always put their cars away. Oh, I see what you mean, oh God . . .'

'You didn't go round to the side of the house?'

'You mean, round the bit past the dining room? No, no, I didn't.'

'You heard nothing?'

'I don't know what you mean. What would there be to hear? Oh – oh, yes. *Shots*. My God, no.'

'By the time you left it would have been – what? A quarter past?'

She said in a low subdued voice, 'I told you, I always know the time. It was sixteen minutes past eight.'

'If it helps, you can have another drink now, Mrs Garland.'

If she was expecting Barry to wait on her she waited in vain. She gave a contrived sigh, got up and went to the drinks cupboard. 'Sure you won't have one?'

It was clear only Wexford was being asked. He shook his head. 'How did you get those bruises on your face?' he said.

The drink cradled in her lap, she sat upright on the sofa with her knees pressed together. Wexford tried to read her face. Was it coyness he saw there? Or embarrassment? Not, at any rate, the memory of some kind of abuse.

'They've almost gone,' she said at last. 'You can hardly see them any more. I wasn't coming home until I was sure they'd faded.'

'I can see them,' Wexford said bluntly. 'No doubt I'm wrong, but it looks to me as if someone punched you in the face pretty savagely about three weeks ago.'

'You've got the date right,' she said.

'You're going to tell us, Mrs Garland. There are a lot more things you're going to tell us but we'll start with what happened to your face.'

It came out in a rush. 'I've had cosmetic surgery. In California. I stayed with a friend. It's usual there, everyone has it – well, not everyone. My friend had and she said to come and stay with her and go into this clinic . . .'

Wexford interrupted with the only term familiar to him. 'You mean you've had your face lifted?'

'That,' she said sulkily, 'and my eyelids tucked back and a peel on my upper lip, all that stuff. Look, I couldn't have had it done here. Everybody would have known. I wanted to get away, I wanted to go somewhere warm and I didn't – well, if you must know, I didn't like the look of my face any more. I used to like what I saw in the mirror and suddenly I didn't – right?'

Things began falling into place very rapidly. He wondered if the time would come when Sheila would want something like this done and feared she would. Could you, anyway, make a mockery of Joanne Garland or disapprove or sneer? She could afford it and it had no doubt achieved what she aimed at. He could understand how she might not want that aggressive gossipy family to know or her neighbours to notice, but would rather present them all with a *fait accompli* to which they might react by attributing her new appearance to good health or the rarely precedented kindness of time.

266

Vague, out-of-this-world Naomi might be allowed to know. Some-one had to be in Joanne's confidence, to hold the fort and run the shop. Who better than Naomi who knew the business inside out and whose reaction to a face-lift might be no more than another woman's to a hair tinting or a shortened hemline?

'I don't suppose you've talked to my mother,' said Joanne Garland. 'Well, why would you? But if you had you'd know why I wouldn't want her getting hold of something like this.'

Wexford said nothing.

'Are you going to let me off the hook now?'

He nodded. 'For the time being. Sergeant Vine and I are going to get our lunch. You'll probably want to have a rest, Mrs Garland. I'd like to see you later. We have an incident room up at Tancred House. I'll see you there at – shall we say four thirty?'

'*Today*?'

'Today at four thirty, please. And if I were you I'd give Fred Harrison a call. You won't want to be driving over the permitted limit.'

More flowers on the gatepost. Crimson tulips this time, about forty of them, Wexford estimated, their stems concealed by the heads of those below, the whole mass of them laid on a pillow of green branches to form a lozenge shape. Barry Vine read the words on the card to him.

'"Hereat the hardest stones were seen to bleed."'

'Curiouser and curiouser,' said Wexford. 'Barry, when I've done with Mrs G. I want you and me to conduct an experiment.'

As they proceeded through the woods, he phoned home and spoke to Dora. He might be late. Oh, no, Reg, not tonight, you mustn't, it's Sylvia's house-warming. Had he forgotten? He had. What time were they due there? Eight thirty at the latest.

'If I can't make it before, I'll be home by eight.'

'I'll go out and buy her something. Champagne unless you've got something more interesting in mind.'

'Only a pillow of forty red tulips but I'm sure she'd prefer champagne. I don't suppose Sheila rang?'

'I would have told you.'

The woods were sheened with green, coming alive with spring. In the long green alleys between the trees white and yellow flowers starred the grass. There an oniony scent from the wild garlic with its

267

stiff jade-coloured leaves and lily-like blossoms. A jay, pink and speckled blue, flew low under the oak branches, uttering its screeching cry. The rain which pattered down filled the woods with a soft rustling susurration.

They emerged into the open parkland, passed through the space in the low wall. A sudden increase in rain power came as a violent cloudburst, water pounding on the stones, streaming down the windscreen and the sides of the car. Through the shivering glassy greyness, Wexford saw Joyce Virson's car back again outside the front door. A sudden premonition which came to him of something momentous in the offing he dismissed as absurd. They meant nothing, those feelings.

He went into the stables, thinking of the sender of flowers, of John Gabbitas who had never mentioned his plans to buy a house, of the defection of the Harrisons, of that strange half-witted woman who listened outside doors. Were any of these anomalies of significance in the case?

When Joanne Garland arrived he took her into the corner where Daisy's two armchairs had been stowed. Since their earlier meeting she had applied pancake make-up and powder to her face. His knowledge of the reason for her trip had made her self-conscious. She looked at him anxiously, sat in one of the chairs, holding her hand up to her cheek in a way designed to hide the worst purple mark.

'George Jones,' he said. 'Gunner Jones. You know him?'

He must be getting naïve. What had he expected? A deep blush? Another collapse into tears? She gave him the sort of look he might have given her had she asked him if he knew Dr Perkins.

'I haven't seen him for years,' she said. 'I used to know him. We were pals, him and Naomi and me and Brian – that's my second husband. Like I say, I haven't seen him since he and Naomi split up. I've written to him a couple of times – is that what you're getting at?'

'You wrote to him suggesting he and Naomi Jones got together again?'

'Is that what he told you?'

'Isn't it true?'

She paused for thought. A scarlet nail scratched at her hairline. Perhaps the invisible mending itched. 'It is and it isn't. The first time I wrote, that's what it was about. Naomi's been a bit – well, wistful, sort of moping. Once or twice she said to me how maybe she should have tried harder with Gunner. Anything was better than loneliness.

So I wrote. He never answered. Charming, I thought. Still, by then I could see it wasn't all that good an idea. I'd been a bit premature. Poor Naomi, she wasn't made for marriage. Well, that applies to relationships in general. I don't mean she liked women. She was best on her own, pottering about with her bits and pieces, her paints and all that.'

'But you wrote to him again, at the end of last summer.'

'Yes, but not about that.'

'About what, then, Mrs Garland?'

How many times had he heard the words she was about to utter? He could forecast them, the precise form of the rebuttal. 'It's got nothing to do with this business.'

He responded as he always did. 'I'll be the judge of that.'

She became suddenly angry. 'I don't want to say. It's embarrassing. Can't you understand? They're dead, it doesn't matter. In any case, there wasn't any – what d'you call it? – abuse, violence. I mean, that's laughable, those two old people. Oh, God, this is so *stupid*. I'm *tired* and it's got nothing to do with any of this.'

'I'd like you to tell me what was in the letter, Mrs Garland.'

'I want to see Daisy,' she said. 'I must go to the house and see Daisy and tell her I'm sorry. For God's sake, I was her mother's best friend.'

'Wasn't she yours?'

'Don't twist my words all the time. You know what I mean.'

He knew what she meant. 'I've got plenty of time, Mrs Garland.' He hadn't, he had Sylvia's party that he had to go to. Let the heavens fall, he had to go to that party. 'We're going to stay here in these two quite comfortable armchairs until you decide to tell me.'

By now, anyway, apart from its relevance to the case, he was dying to know. She hadn't just awakened his curiosity with her prevarications; she had pulled it out of sleep and set its nerves on stalks.

'I gather it's not personal,' he said. 'It's not something about you. You need not be embarrassed.'

'OK, I'll fess up. But you'll see what I mean when I tell you. Gunner never answered that letter either, by the way. Fine father he is. Well, I should have known that, never taking a scrap of interest in the poor kid from the time he scarpered.'

'This was about Daisy?' Wexford asked, inspired.

'Yes. Yes, it was.'

*

'Naomi told me,' Joanne Garland said. 'I mean, you have to have known Naomi to realise what she was like. Naïve's not exactly the word, though she was that too. Sort of not like other people, vague, not having a clue about what goes on. I don't suppose I'm making myself clear. She didn't act like other people, so I don't reckon she really knew how other people did act. Not when they were doing things that were – well, wrong or not on or downright disgusting. And she didn't know when they were doing something – well, successful or clever or special either. Am I making any sense?'

'Yes, I think so.'

'She started talking about this business when we were in the shop one day. I mean, talking about like she might have said Daisy's got a new boyfriend or she was going on some school trip abroad. That's how she came out with it. She said – I'm trying to think of her actual words – yes, she said, "Davina thinks it would be nice if Harvey made love to Daisy. To sort of start her off. Initiate her. That was the word. Because Harvey's a wonderful lover. And she doesn't want Daisy to go through what happened to her." You see what I mean by embarrassing.'

Wexford wasn't shocked but he could see that it was shocking. 'What was your reply?'

'Wait. I'm not done. Naomi said the fact was Davina was too old now for – well, I don't have to spell it out, do I? Sort of physically, if I make myself clear. And it worried her because Harvey – this is what Davina said – was young still and a vigorous man. Yuck, I thought, yuck, yuck. Davina really thought, apparently, that it would be great for both of them and she and Harvey had actually put it to the girl. Well, she told the girl and that same day horrible old Harvey made a sort of pass.'

'What did Daisy do?'

'Told him to get lost, I imagine. That's what Naomi said. I mean, Naomi wasn't indignant or anything. She just said Davina was sex-mad, always had been, but she ought to understand not everybody felt like she did. But Naomi wasn't the way I'd have been – if it was my kid, if I'd had a kid. She just said like she was talking about some difference of opinion we might have had, like whether we were going to show clothes in the gallery or not, she just said it was up to Daisy. I got mad. I said a lot of things about Daisy being in moral danger, all that, but it wasn't any use. Then I got to see Daisy. I met her when

270

she was coming out of school, said my car had broken down and would she give me a lift home.'

'You discussed this with her?'

'She laughed but you could tell she was – well, disgusted. She'd never liked Harvey much and I got the impression she was disillusioned about her grandma. She kept saying she wouldn't have expected that of Davina. She didn't a bit mind me knowing, she was very sweet, she's a very sweet girl. And that sort of made it worse.

'They were all going off on holiday. It really worried me, I didn't know what else I could do. I kept having this picture of old Harvey – well, raping her. It was silly, I know, because I don't suppose he could have and anyway whatever they were, they weren't that sort.'

Wexford had no clear idea what sort she meant but he wouldn't interrupt. All Joanne Garland's initial shame and reticence had gone as she warmed enthusiastically to her tale.

'They were nearly due back when I ran into that chap Nicholas – Virson, is he called? I knew he was a sort of boyfriend of Daisy's, the nearest she had to a boyfriend, and I thought of telling him. It was on the tip of my tongue but he's such a pompous ass I could just picture him going scarlet and sort of blustering out of it. So I didn't. I told Gunner. I wrote him a letter.

'After all, he *is* her father. I thought even bloody Gunner would rise to this. But I was wrong, wasn't I? Couldn't have cared less. I just had to rely on Daisy – well, on her good sense. And it wasn't as if she was a child, not really, she was seventeen. But that Gunner – what kind of a fine bloody father is that?'

Seven gunsmiths in the Yellow Pages for Kingsmarkham, five for Stowerton, three in Pomfret alone, a further twelve in the surrounding countryside.

'It's a wonder we've any wildlife left,' said Karen Malahyde. 'What exactly are we looking for?'

'Someone who had Ken Harrison working for him on a part-time basis and who taught him how to change a gun barrel and lent him the tools.'

'You're joking, aren't you, sir?'

'I'm afraid so,' said Burden.

# 24

Fred Harrison in his taxi passed him as he drove to the main gates. On his way to fetch Joanne Garland, paying her visit of condolence to Daisy, he thought as he returned the man's salute. Condolence? Yes – why not? It was amazing what abuses love survived. You had only to look at battered wives, maltreated children. She had probably kept the old admiring awe of her grandmother, tempered as it was by a real affection, and as for Harvey, she had plainly never cared for him. As to her mother, such people as Naomi Jones, eccentric in their unworldliness, their soft contented passivity, were often very lovable.

What Wexford knew about and Joanne Garland probably did not were the revelations in the letters cited in the *Sunday Times* review. The unconsummated first marriage to Desmond Flory. Those years of living 'like brother and sister', as the euphemism of the time had it, the impossibility in those days and that environment of seeking help. The best years of her sexual life, in anyone's estimation, from twenty-three to thirty-three wasted, lost, perhaps never to be compensated for adequately later on. And towards the end of the war, in whose last days Desmond Flory was to be killed, the meeting with a lover took place, the man who was to be Naomi's father.

The unused energy of those years she had put into the planting of those woods. It was interesting to speculate as to whether the woods would be here now if Flory had not been incapable with his wife. Wexford wondered if Davina Flory's oversexedness wasn't perhaps due to ten years of frustration, if they had always been there in her past, those years, standing empty. She knew that whatever happened in the future they could never be filled, the gap never closed.

From something like that she had wanted to save Daisy. That was the charitable view. Wexford could think of so many other disastrous consequences of a liaison between Daisy and her grandmother's husband that the charitable view came to look like what it was, an empty excuse. She should have known better, he told himself. Good taste and common decency should have taught her better, these and something she claimed to be so keen on, *civilised* behaviour.

Who had the lover been? Who was this man who, like the prince in the story, had ridden up to liberate the woman in the sleeping wood? Some fellow writer, he supposed, or an academic. It wasn't hard to see Davina in the Lady Chatterley role and Naomi's father a servant on the estate.

The rain had stopped. It was damp and misty in the woods but when he left the forest road and was heading towards Kingsmarkham, a late sun had come out. The evening was fine and warm, all those clouds drawn in dense billowing masses to the horizon. The car splashed through a lingering puddle up on to his garage drive. Dora he found on the phone and hope sprang up, to be dispelled by her quick shake of the head. It had only been Neil's father, asking if she wanted a lift.

'What about me? Why shouldn't I want a lift?'

'He assumed you weren't going. People do take it for granted, darling, that mostly you aren't going.'

'Of course I'm going to my own daughter's house-warming party.'

It was unreasonable to be put out of temper by this. Wexford was enough of a psychologist to know that if he was disconcerted, this was due to guilt. Guilt that he took Sylvia for granted, loved her routinely, put her second to her sister, had to make himself think of her lest he came halfway to forgetting her existence. He went upstairs and changed. He had intended putting on a sports jacket and cords but rejected these in favour of his best suit, his only really good suit.

Why did he worry so much about that stupid girl, that ridiculous affected, actressy Sheila? Using those terrible adjectives about her, even to himself, nearly made him groan aloud. Alone in the hall, he picked up the phone and dialled her number. Just on the off-chance. When it rang more than three times and the recorded voice hadn't come on, he felt another resurgence of hope. But no one answered. He let it ring twenty times and then he put the receiver back.

Dora said, 'You look very smart.' And, 'She won't do anything silly, you know.'

'I'd never even thought of that,' he said, though he had.

The house Sylvia and her husband had bought was on the other side of Myfleet, about twelve miles away. A rectory was what it had been in the days when the Church of England thought nothing of putting the incumbent of a benefice into a damp, unheated, ten-bedroomed mansion on five hundred pounds a year. Sylvia and Neil had wanted it, had the late-twentieth century scorn of anything suburban and had hardly been able to wait until they could afford to leave their five-roomed semi-detached. This longing for a 'real house' was one of the few matters they agreed on, as Wexford and Dora had observed in a recent discussion. But no incompatible couple could have striven more earnestly to stay together than these two, accumulating more and more joint possessions, contriving to depend more and more on each other's services and support.

Sylvia, now she had her Open University degree, had a rather good job in the County Education Department. She seemed to like putting impediments in her own way so that she had to rely on Neil's presence and Neil's promises, just as he took on more entertaining and more foreign trips so that he could rely on hers. But buying this house, a further ten miles away from where she worked and in the opposite direction to his grandsons' school, seemed to Wexford to be going too far. He remarked on it to Dora as he drove carefully along the winding lanes to Myfleet.

'Life's hard enough without turning it into an obstacle race.'

'Yes. Has it occurred to you Sheila might be there tonight? She's invited.'

'She won't be there.'

She wasn't. Sylvia told him she wasn't coming – well, she had told her a week ago she wasn't coming – before he could ask. He wouldn't have asked, anyway. From past scenes and shows of bitter resentment, he knew the consequences of asking.

'You're looking very smart, Dad.'

He kissed her, said the house was lovely, though it seemed bigger and starker than he remembered from the one occasion on which he had seen it before, but there was no denying it was a great place to have a party. He walked into the drawing room which was already crowded. The whole place wanted decorating, cried out with icy tears for central heating. A great log-fire in the Victorian mock-baronial fireplace looked good and the heat of fifty bodies would provide the warmth. Wexford said hello to his son-in-law and accepted a glass of Highland Spring, much embellished with ice, lime slices and mint leaves.

274

Everybody knew who he was. It was not exactly unease he could sense as he moved among them so much as caution, a drawing in upon themselves, a perfunctory self-examination. This was truer now than it had once been, with the current campaign against drinking and driving, and he could see men glance at glasses holding an obvious inch of whisky as they wondered whether they could pass it off as apple juice or fall back on the old justification: My wife's driving.

Then he saw Burden. Part of a group that included Jenny and some of Sylvia's fellow educationists, the inspector stood silent, the large glass in his hand really containing apple juice. If it wasn't Mike had gone mad and asked for half a pint of Scotch. He edged his way over, having found a congenial companion for the best part of the evening.

'You're looking very smart.'

'You're the third one who's seen fit to comment on my appearance. In those very words. Am I generally such a ragbag? The head model of the Oxfam cat-walk?'

Burden made no reply but gave Wexford one of his small tight half-smiles accompanied by a little lift of the eyebrows. Himself dressed in charcoal cashmere sweater over a white polo-neck, charcoal washed-silk bomber jacket and designer jeans, he had perhaps not quite achieved the desired effect. Not, at least, in Wexford's eyes.

'Since we're into personal remarks,' Wexford said, 'that get-up makes you look like a trendy vicar. The proper occupant of this house. It's the dog-collar effect.'

'Oh, nonsense,' Burden said huffily. 'You always say something like that, just because I don't invariably look as if I've got "fuzz" stamped all over me. Come in here. Bring your glass. This house is a real warren, isn't it?'

They found themselves in a place that might once have been morning room, sewing room, study or 'snug'. An oil heater burned at one corner, making a smell but not much heat.

Wexford said, 'Look at these things in my glass. They look like marbles. Now what would you call them? Not ice cubes because they're round. How about ice spheres?'

'No one would know what you meant. You'd say "round ice cubes".'

'Yes, but that's a contradiction in terms, you'd have to . . .'

Burden interrupted him firmly. 'The DCC phoned while you were with that Joanne woman. I talked to him. He says it's a farce talking about a "murder room" four weeks after the event and he wants us out of Tancred by the end of the week.'

'I know. I've an appointment to see him. Who calls it a murder room, anyway?'

'Karen does, and Gerry, when they answer the phone. Worse than that. I heard Gerry say, "Massacre room here."'

'It doesn't matter much. We don't have to be there. I feel it's in my grasp, Mike, I can't say more than that. I need one or two things to fall into place, I need one spark of enlightenment . . .'

Burden was looking at him suspiciously. 'I need a whole lot more than that, I can tell you. D'you realise we haven't even got past the first hurdle, that is how they got away from Tancred without someone seeing them?'

'Yes. Daisy made her 999 call at twenty-two minutes past eight. This, she says, was somewhere between five and ten minutes after they had gone. But she doesn't know and this is a very rough estimate indeed. If it was as much as ten minutes, the maximum time I should think, they must have left at eight twelve which is four minutes before Joanne Garland left. I believe that woman, Mike. I think she knows about time like these punctuality addicts do. If she says she left at sixteen minutes past, that's when she left.

'But if they left at eight twelve she must have seen them. That was the time she was walking about the front of the house, trying to see into the dining-room window. So they left later and it took Daisy nearer five minutes than ten to reach the phone. Say they left at seventeen or eighteen minutes past eight. In that case they must have followed Joanne Garland and might well be supposed to be driving faster than she . . .'

'Unless they took the by-road.'

'Then Gabbitas would have seen them. If Gabbitas is guilty of some involvement in this, Mike, it would be in his interest to say he had seen them. He doesn't say that. If he's innocent and he says he didn't see them, they weren't there. But to get back to Joanne Garland.

'When she reached the main gate she would have had to get out of her car and open it. Then she would have to drive through, get out and close it again. Is it conceivably possible that, with the killers' car close behind her, she could have done this and the other car not caught up with her?'

'We could try it out,' Burden said.

'I have tried it. I tried it this afternoon. Only we left three minutes, not two, between the departure of car A and that of car B. I was driving car A at between thirty and forty miles per hour and Barry was in car B, driving as fast as he felt he safely could, forty to fifty, sometimes over fifty. He caught up with me as I got out the second time, to close the gates.'

'Could their car have left *before* Joanne Garland arrived?'

'Hardly. She got there at eleven minutes past eight. Now Daisy says they didn't hear the gunmen in the house until a minute or two after eight. If they left at ten past that allows them nine minutes at most in which to go upstairs and turn the place over, come down again, kill three people and wound a fourth and make their getaway. It could be done – just. But if they got away by the main road through the wood they must have met Joanne coming in. And if they took the by-road road at, say, seven minutes past eight, they would have overtaken Bib Mew on her bicycle, since she left Tancred at ten to eight.'

Burden said thoughtfully, 'You make it sound impossible.'

'It is impossible. Unless there's a conspiracy between Bib and Gabbitas and Joanne Garland and the gunmen, which is patently not so, it's impossible. It's impossible that they left at any time between five past eight and twenty past eight, yet we know they must have done so. We've been making an assumption all this time, Mike, based on a very flimsy piece of evidence. And that is that they came and left *in a car*. In or on some sort of motor vehicle. We've assumed there was a vehicle involved. But suppose there wasn't?'

Burden stared at him. At that moment the door opened and a crowd of people came in, all carrying plates of food, all in search of somewhere to sit. Instead of answering his own question, Wexford said, 'It's supper. Shall we go and get something to eat?'

'We oughtn't to stay in here, anyway. It's not fair on Sylvia.'

'You mean it's the party guest's duty to circulate and thus earn his fizzy water and taco chips?'

'Something like that.' Burden grinned. He looked at his watch. 'D'you know, it's gone ten. We've only got our baby-sitter till eleven.'

'Just time for a sandwich,' said Wexford, who was pretty sure that such favourites of his wouldn't be on offer.

While consuming salmon mayonnaise, he talked to two of Sylvia's colleagues, then to a couple of old school-friends. There was something in what Burden said about doing one's bit as a guest. Dora he could see involved in an amiable argument with Neil's father. He kept half an eye on Burden all the while and edged in his direction when the school-friends went off for more chicken salad.

Burden took up their discussion at the precise point they had left it. 'There must have been some sort of vehicle.'

'Well, you know what Holmes said. When everything else is impossible, that which remains, however improbable, must be so.'

'How did they get there without transport? It's miles from anywhere.'

'Through the woods. On foot. It's the only way, Mike. Think about it. The roads were positively clogged with traffic. Joanne Garland going up and down the main way in. First Bib, then Gabbitas on the by-road. But that doesn't bother them because they're making their way out in perfect safety – on foot. Why not? What had they to carry? A gun and some bits of jewellery.'

'Daisy heard a car start up.'

'Of course she did. She heard Joanne Garland's car start up. Later than she says, but she can hardly be expected to be precise about the time. She heard the car start up after both gunmen had gone and she was crawling to the phone.'

'I believe you're right. And those two could have got away without anyone seeing them?'

'I didn't say that. Someone saw them. Andy Griffin. He was up there that night, bedding down in his hidey-hole, and he saw them. Close enough, I imagine, to know them again. The result of his attempt to blackmail them, or one of them, was that they strung him up.'

After Burden and Jenny's departure, Wexford began to think about leaving himself. They had left it late, their sitter would be obliged to stay on for a further quarter-hour. It was almost eleven.

Dora had gone with a crowd of other women, under Sylvia's leadership, to be shown over the house. They were supposed to keep very quiet, so as not to wake the little boys. Wexford didn't want to ask Sylvia if she had heard from her sister because such a question might provoke a scene of jealousy and resentment. If Sylvia was feeling good about her new house and her present style of life, she would answer his enquiry like a rational person. But if she wasn't –

278

and he couldn't tell what her state of mind was this evening – she would round on him with those old accusations of a preference for her younger sister. He managed to make his way over to Neil and ask him.

Of course Neil had no idea whether Sylvia had recently spoken to Sheila, only vaguely knew that Sheila had been having a relationship with a novelist he had never previously heard of, and was unaware this relationship was over. Without this intention, he made Wexford feel foolish. He said he knew everything would be all right and excused himself to fetch a tray of coffee.

Dora came back, said that if he would like a real drink now she would drive home. No, thanks, Wexford said, he'd found that once you'd had two of these mineral waters, you didn't really fancy alcohol. Shall we go then?

They had both become so delicately careful with this difficult child, bending over backwards not to offend her. But other people were leaving. Only a hard core of nocturnals would linger after midnight. They waited patiently for other people's coats to be brought, for those last-minute pleasantries to be exchanged with departing guests that stand upon their going.

At last Wexford was kissing his daughter and saying good-night, thank you, lovely party. She kissed him back, gave him a nice, warm, unresentful hug. He thought Dora was going a bit far saying, 'Happy house' – what an expression! – but anything that helped along the aim to please.

There were various ways home. Through Myfleet itself or a slight detour north to by-pass Myfleet, or south the long way via Pomfret Monachorum. He took the by-passing route, though that made it sound like a well-lit twin-track highway instead of what it really was, a cat's cradle of lanes in which you had to know how to pick up the right threads.

It was very dark. There was no moon and the stars were hidden by a thick overcast. In these villages the residents had campaigned against street lighting, so that at this hour they appeared uninhabited, every house in darkness but for the occasional square of drawn-curtain gleam, behind which some nightbird stayed up.

Dora heard the wail of sirens a fraction before he did. She said, 'Do your lot have to? At past midnight?'

They were on one of the long stretches of tree-bordered lane between habitations. The banks on either side reared up like

279

defensive walls. In this dark canyon his car lights made a greenish radiance.

'That's not us,' he said. 'That's the fire service.'

'How can you tell?'

'A different kind of howl.'

The volume of sound increased and for a moment he thought the engine was coming this way, would meet them head-on. He had already begun to brake and was edging as close as he could to the nearside, when the wail died again and he knew the engine – appliances, they called them – was on some other road ahead.

The car gathered speed and came up out of the trough of rampart-like banks and dense bushes and sheltering trees, out of the well of darkness. The banks fell away, the road widened and a plain, a spread of downland, opened before them. The sky ahead was red. On the horizon and seeping across the massed clouds was a smoky redness as it might be above some city. But there was no city.

A new wailing began. Dora said, 'It's not in Myfleet. It's this side of Myfleet. Is it a house on fire?'

'We shall soon see.'

He knew before they got there. It was the only thatched house in the neighbourhood. The redness intensified. From a dull smoky rust it grew richer until the glow in the sky was like a fire of coals, like the bright spaces between burning coal. Then they could hear it. A crackling, licking, rhythmic roar.

Already the road was cordoned off. On the other side of the barrier the two appliances were parked. The firemen were hosing with what looked like water but very likely wasn't. The noise the burning house made was like waves of the sea crashing on shingle in a storm, like the rushing tug-back of the tide. It deafened, it made speech impossible, commentary on the blaze, the urgent, streaming flames, silenced by it.

Wexford got out of the car. He went over to the barrier. A fire officer started telling him to get back, to take the Myfleet road, and then he recognised who this was. Wexford shook his head. He wasn't going to attempt shouting above this noise. The heat from the fire reached out here, robbing the air of cold, of damp, blazing like some vast domestic hearth in an abode of giants.

Wexford gazed. He was near enough to imagine it seared his face. In spite of the recent rain, rain that had come too sparsely, the thatch had gone up like paper and kindling. Where it had been, where vestiges of it still were, the blackened roofbeams could be seen through the fierce roaring flames. The house had become a torch but the fire was more alive than a torch flame, animal-like in its greed and determination, its passion to burn and destroy. Sparks spiralled up into the sky, dipping and dancing. A great burning ember, a lump of seething thatch, suddenly blew out of the roof and eddied towards them like a rocket. Wexford ducked and backed away.

When the burning thing was smouldering at their feet, he said to the fire officer, 'Was there anyone in there?'

The arrival of the ambulance saved the man from answering. Wexford saw Dora reversing the car to make room. The fire officer moved the barrier and the ambulance came in.

'It was hopeless attempting anything,' the fireman said.

A car followed. It was Nicholas Virson's MG. The car slowed and stopped, but not as if under control, not as if the driver had braked and gone into neutral and put the handbrake on. It shuddered to a stop and stalled with a jump. Virson got out and stood looking at the fire. He put his hands over his face.

Wexford went back to Dora. 'You can go on home if you like. Someone will bring me.'

'Reg, what's happened?'

'I don't know. I can't imagine it started by chance.'

'I'll wait for you.'

The ambulancemen were bringing someone out on a stretcher. He had expected a woman but it was a man, the fire officer who had made a hopeless attempt. Nicholas Virson turned a stricken face to Wexford. Tears were running out of his eyes.

# 25

The house was in part very old and had been strongly built in that distant past on a timber frame. Two of the main posts survived. They were of oak and nearly indestructible, standing up among the ashes like burnt trees. There had been no foundations and, like trees, these great uprights had been planted deep in the ground.

The blackened site looked more like the leavings of a forest fire than a burnt house. Wexford, surveying the ruins from his car, remembered how he had thought the Virsons' home pretty the first time he had seen it. A chocolate-box cottage with roses round the door and a garden fit for a calendar. The man who did this took pleasure in the destruction of beauty, enjoyed defacement for its own sake. For by now Wexford had no doubt this was a deliberate act of arson.

To wreak death might have been the primary motive, but the lust for spoliation was there as well. It gilded the lily, it iced the cake.

The garage at The Thatched House had contained twenty two-gallon cans of petrol and about half that number of gallon cans of paraffin. These cans had been lined up against the sides of the garage, most of them against the common wall with the house. The thatched roof extended across the garage as well as the house itself.

Nicholas Virson had an explanation. Trouble in the Middle East had prompted his mother to lay in a store. Which particular trouble he couldn't remember but the oil had been there for years, against a 'rainy day'.

The days, Wexford thought, hadn't been rainy enough. A long severe drought had preceded the drizzle of the past few days. Investigators had found little evidence in that garage, there was very little left. Something had ignited those cans, a simple fuse. The discovery of the stub of an ordinary household candle, near-miraculously rolled away and out under the doors, led them to believe this was a vital item in the arson. What the investigator had in mind wouldn't always work but in this case it *had* worked. Soak a piece of string not in petrol, but in paraffin, and insert one end in a can of paraffin. The single can of paraffin would be surrounded by cans of petrol. Tie the other end of the string round a candle halfway down, light the candle and two, three, four hours later . . .

The fire officer was badly burned but would recover. Joyce Virson was dead. Wexford had told the press they were treating it as murder. This was arson and murder.

'Who knew about that petrol, Mr Virson?'

'Our cleaner. The chap who comes to do the garden. I expect my mother told people, friends. I may have told people. I mean, for one thing, I remember a very good friend of mine who'd come over and was very low on juice. I put enough in his tank to get him home. Then there were the chaps who came to patch up the thatch, they went in there, used to have their sandwiches in there at lunch-time . . .'

And a smoke, thought Wexford. 'You'd better let us have some names.'

While Anne Lennox was taking the names down Wexford thought about the interview he had just had with James Freeborn, the Deputy Chief Constable. How many more murders were they to expect before a perpetrator was found? Five people had died so far. It was more than a massacre, it was a hecatomb. Wexford knew better than to correct the Chief Constable, to say something sarcastic, for instance, about hoping there wouldn't be another ninety-five deaths. Instead, he asked for the incident room at Tancred to be maintained just till the end of the week and permission was reluctantly granted.

But no more guards on the girl. Wexford had to assure him that there had been none that week.

'Something like that could go on for years.'

'I hope not, sir.'

Nicholas Virson asked if they were finished with him, if he might go.

'Not yet, Mr Virson.'

'I asked you yesterday, before we had much idea of the cause of this fire, where you were on Tuesday night. You were very distressed

283

and I didn't press the question. I'm asking you again now. Where were you?'

Virson hesitated. At last he made that answer that is never true but nevertheless often given in these circumstances. 'To be perfectly honest with you, I was just driving around.'

Two of those phrases in conjunction. Do people ever 'just drive around'? Alone, by night, in early April? In their home countryside where there is nothing new to see and no beauty spots to discover and go back to see in daylight? On a holiday trip, perhaps, but in their own neighbourhood?

'Where did you drive?' he asked patiently.

Virson was no good at this. 'I don't remember. Just around the lanes.' He said hopefully, 'It was a fine night.'

'All right, Mr Virson, what time did you leave your mother and start out?'

'I can tell you that. Nine thirty. On the dot.' He added, 'I'm telling the truth.'

'Where was your car?'

'Outside on the gravel, and my – my mother's beside it. We never put them in the garage.'

No, you couldn't get them in. There wasn't room. The garage was full of cans of fuel oil, waiting to go up when a flame reached them, running along a piece of string.

'And where did you go?'

'I've told you, I don't know, I just drove around. You know when I got back . . .'

Three hours later. It looked nicely timed. 'You drove around the countryside for three hours? In that time you could have got to Heathrow and back.'

An attempt at a sad smile. 'I didn't go to Heathrow.'

'No, I don't suppose you did.' If the man wouldn't tell him he would have to guess. He looked at the sheet of paper on which Anne had written the names and addresses of those people who knew about the petrol cache: Joyce Virson's close personal friends, Nicholas Virson's friend who ran out of 'juice', their gardener, their cleaner . . . 'I think you've made a mistake here, Mr Virson. Mrs Mew works at Tancred House.'

'Oh, yes. She works for us – er, me, as well. Two mornings a week.' He seemed relieved at the change of enquiry. 'That's how she came to help out at Tancred. My mother recommended her.'

284

'I see.'

'I swear by my life and all I hold sacred,' Virson said passionately, 'I had nothing to do with any of this.'

'I don't know what you hold sacred, Mr Virson,' Wexford said mildly, 'but I doubt if it's relevant in this case.' He had heard the like of this often before, respectable men as well as villains swearing on their children's heads and as they hoped for heaven in a life to come. 'Let me know where I can find you, won't you?'

Burden came up to him after Nicholas Virson had gone. 'I went home that way too, you know, Reg. The place was in total darkness at eleven fifteen.'

'No candle flame glimmering through the chinks in the garage door?'

'The aim wasn't to kill Mrs Virson, was it? I mean, our perpetrator's quite ruthless, he wouldn't care if he killed her or not, but she was incidental, she wasn't his primary quarry?'

'No, I don't think she was.'

'I'm going to get lunch. D'you want some? Today it's Thai or steak and kidney pie.'

'You sound like the lowest form of TV commercial.'

Wexford went outside with him and joined the short queue. From here only the end of the house was visible, the high wall and windows of the east wing. The shape of Brenda Harrison could be dimly seen behind one of these, rubbing at the glass with a duster. Wexford held out his plate for a wedge of pie with mashed potatoes and stir-fry. When he looked up again Brenda had disappeared from the window and Daisy had taken her place.

Daisy was not, of course, polishing the glass, but standing with her hands hanging by her sides. She seemed to be gazing into the distance, into woods and forest and far blue horizon, and to him her expression, as far as he could see, was ineffably sad. She was a figure of loneliness, standing there, and it brought him no surprise to see her put up her hands and cover her face before she turned away.

His head lifted, Burden too had seen. For a moment he said nothing but took his plate of the rather brightly coloured scented food and a can of Coke with the glass upturned over it.

Back in the stables, Burden said laconically, 'He was after her, wasn't he?'

'Daisy?'

'He's always been after her from the first. When he rigged that fire it was Daisy he was after, not Joyce Virson. He thought Daisy would be there. You told me the Virsons had been here to persuade her to come to them on Tuesday night, dinner and stay the night.'

'Yes, but she refused. She was adamant.'

'I know. And we know she didn't go there. But our perpetrator didn't. He knew the Virsons had tried to persuade her and knew too that *they went back in the afternoon to renew their attempt.* Something must have happened to make him certain Daisy would be spending the night at The Thatched House.'

'Not Virson then? He knew she wouldn't be there. You keep saying, "he", Mike. Must it be a "he"?'

'It's something one takes for granted. Perhaps one shouldn't.'

'Perhaps one should take nothing for granted.'

'Bib Mew worked for the Virsons as well as up here. She knew about the petrol in the garage.'

'She listens outside doors,' said Wexford, 'and perhaps hears only imperfectly what is said on the other side of them. She was here on the evening of 11 March. A lot of the – shall we say manoeuvres? – of that night depend on her evidence. She's not very bright but she's sharp enough to live alone and hold down two jobs.'

'She looks like a man. Sharon Fraser said the people who left the bank were all men, but if one of them had been Bib Mew, would she know this wasn't a man?'

'One of the men in the bank stood in the queue with a handful of green banknotes. Since the pound went we don't have green notes in this country. Which country does? Exclusively green banknotes?'

'The United States,' said Burden.

'Yes. Those notes were dollars. Martin was killed on 13 May. Thanny Hogarth is an American who may well have had dollars in his possession when he came here, but he didn't arrive in this country until June. How about Preston Littlebury? Vine tells us he does most of his transactions in dollars.'

'Have you seen Barry's report yet? Littlebury deals in antiques, that's correct, and he imports them from eastern Europe. But his main source of income at the present time is from the sale of East German army uniforms. He was a little shy of admitting it but Barry got it out of him. Apparently, there's a terrific market for that sort of memorabilia here, tin hats, belts, camouflage.'

'But not guns?'

'Not guns, so far as we know. Barry also says that Littlebury has no bank account here. He has no account with that bank.'

'Neither do I,' Wexford retorted, 'but I've got my famous Transcend card. I can use any branch of any bank I like. Besides, the man in the queue with the notes was there simply to *change those notes into sterling*, wasn't he?'

'I've never seen this Littlebury but from what I hear of him he's not the sort to pick up a gun and make off with it. I'll tell you what, Reg, it was Andy Griffin in that queue, with the dollars Littlebury paid him in.'

'Then why did he never change them? Why did we find them in his parents' house?'

'Because he never reached the head of the queue. Hocking and Bishop came in and Martin was killed. Andy picked up the gun and made off with it. He took it to sell it and he did sell it. That was what he blackmailed the purchaser about, possession of the incriminating gun.

'He never changed those dollar bills. He took them home and hid them in that drawer. Because he had a – well, a sort of superstitious fear of being seen with them after what had happened. One day maybe he'd change them but not now, not yet. He'd get far more for that gun than ninety-six dollars, anyway.'

Wexford said slowly, 'I believe you're right.'


The kind hospitable gesture would have been an offer to put Nicholas Virson up. Perhaps Daisy had made the offer and it had been declined. On the same grounds as Virson's refusal to stay the night once before?

Now, though, things were surely different. The man had nowhere to go. But in Daisy's sky this star was setting, no matter how brightly it had once shone, when it had occasioned that wonder and that adoring gaze. Thanny Hogarth had displaced it. What are you when the moon cloth rise?

It was normal behaviour for someone of her age. She was eighteen. But a tradgedy had happened, Nicholas Virson's mother was dead, his house had burned down. Daisy must have offered hospitality and her offer, simply because of the existence of Thanny Hogarth, had been spurned.

Until he found somewhere more permanent, Nicholas Virson had taken a room at the Olive and Dove. Wexford found him in the bar.

287

Where he had acquired the dark suit he wore Wexford couldn't guess. He looked sombre and lonely and much older than when they had first met at the infirmary, a sad man who had lost everything. As Wexford approached he was lighting a cigarette and it was to this act that he made reference.

'I gave up eight months ago. I was on holiday with Mother in Corfu. It seemed a good time, no stress and all that. It's a funny thing, when I said nothing would make me start again, I couldn't have foreseen this. I've been through twenty today already.'

'I want to talk to you about Tuesday night again, Mr Virson.'

'For God's sake, must you?'

'I'm not going to ask you, I'm going to tell you. All you have to do is confirm or deny. I don't think you'll deny it. You were at Tancred House.'

The unhappy blue eyes flickered. Virson took a long draw on his cigarette, like a smoker who has rolled up something stronger than tobacco. After a hesitation he made the classic reply of those he would have defined as of the criminal classes. 'What if I was?'

At least it wasn't, 'I might have been.'

'Far from "driving around", you drove straight up there. The house was empty. Daisy was out and no police officer was there. But you knew all that, you knew how it would be. I don't know where you parked your car. There are plenty of places where it would be hidden from those coming in up the main drive or along the by-road.

'You waited. It must have been cold and boring but you waited. I don't know when they came in, Daisy and young Hogarth, or how they came. In his van or her car – one of her cars. But they came at last and you saw them.'

Virson murmured into his drink, 'Just before twelve.'

'Ah.'

He was muttering now, sullenly. 'She came back just before midnight. There was a young chap with long hair driving.' He lifted his head. 'He was driving *Davina's* car.'

'It's Daisy's now,' said Wexford.

'It isn't right!' He hammered with his fist on the table and the barman looked round.

'What? Not to drive her grandmother's car? Her grandmother's dead.'

'Not that. I don't mean that. I mean, she's mine. We were

288

practically engaged. She said she'd marry me "one day". She said that the day she came out of hospital and came to our house.'

'These things happen, Mr Virson. She's very young.'

'They went into the house together. The fellow had his damned arm round her. A fellow with hair down on his shoulders and two days' growth of beard. I knew he wouldn't come out again that night, I don't know how but I knew. There was no point in waiting any longer.'

'Perhaps it was as well for him he didn't come out.'

Virson gave him a defiant glare. 'Perhaps it was.'

Wexford believed part of it. He thought he could easily believe all of it. Believe but not prove. He was nearly there, anyway, he nearly knew what had happened on 11 March, he knew the motive and the name of one of the two who had carried it out. As soon as he got home he was going to phone Ishbel Macsamphire.

The post had come late, after he had left for work. Among the things for him was a parcel from Amyas Ireland. It contained Augustine Casey's new novel *The Lash* in proof. Amyas wrote that this proof copy was one of five hundred Carlyon Quick were issuing, Wexford's number 350, and he should hang on to it as it might be worth something one day. Especially if he could get Casey's signature on it. Amyas was right, wasn't he, in thinking Casey was a friend of Wexford's daughter?

He suppressed an instinct to hurl it into the log-fire Dora had lighted. What quarrel did he have with Augustine Casey? None. Once Sheila was over the worst, the man had done them all a favour.

He tried the Edinburgh number but no one answered. She was out and might not be in till ten, say, or ten thirty. If someone was out at eight you could be pretty sure she'd be out till past ten. He would while away the time with Casey's book. Even if Mrs Macsamphire said yes to all his questions, it was such a little thing to go on, so thin on its own . . .

He read *The Lash*, or tried to. After a time he realised he had understood nothing, and this wasn't because his attention was elsewhere, he simply found it incomprehensible. A good deal of it was in verse and the rest seemed to be a conversation between two unnamed persons, probably but not certainly male, who were deeply concerned about the disappearance of an armadillo. He had a look at the end, could make nothing of it, and turning the pages back saw that this verse alternating with talk about the armadillo persisted through the pages, apart from one which was covered with algebraic equations and one which contained the single word 'shit' repeated fifty-seven times.

After an hour he gave it up and went upstairs to find Davina Flory's tree book which was on his bedside cabinet. The place he had reached he saw that he had marked with the guide to the town of Heights, Nevada, which Sheila had given him, the town where Casey was to be, doubtless by now had become, writer-in-residence at the university.

At least she was no longer going there. Love was a strange business. He loved her and therefore should have wished for her what she wished for herself, to be with Casey, to follow him to the ends of the earth. But he didn't. He was overwhelmingly glad she was to be denied what she wanted. He sighed a little and turned the pages, looking at the colour plates of forest and mountain, a lake, a waterfall, the city centre with a gold-domed capitol building.

The advertisements were more entertaining. Here was a company which made Western boots to order 'in all the radiant colours of the spectrum, in this world and outer space'. Coram Clark Inc. was a gunsmith in Reno, Carson City and Heights. He sold all kinds of weaponry that made Wexford's eyes open wide. Rifles, shotguns, handguns, air guns, ammo, reloading, scopes, black powder, said the advertisement. The whole spectrum of Browning, Winchester, Luger, Beretta, Remington and Speer. Highest prices paid for used guns. Buy, sell, trade, gunsmithing. You didn't need a licence in some American states, you could carry a gun with you in your car, provided you displayed it openly on the seat. He remembered what Burden had said about students being allowed unrestrictedly to buy guns for self-defence when a serial killer was rumoured to be on some campus . . .

Here was an ad for the finest popcorn in the west and another for personalised licence plates in iridescent colours. He tucked the guide into the back of *Lovely As A Tree* and read for half an hour. It was nearly ten and he tried Ishbel Macsamphire again.

Of course, he couldn't ring her at all much after ten. That was a rule he tried to stick to, that you phone no one after ten at night. Two minutes to ten and someone was ringing the doorbell. The rule about not calling anyone after ten applied equally to calling *on* them, in Wexford's opinion. Well, it wasn't quite ten.

Dora went to the door before he could stop her. He never thought it wise for a woman to go alone to answer the door in the evening. Not a sexist attitude, but prudent, until the day all women went to Karen's trouble and learnt a martial art. He got up and went to the living-room door. A woman's voice, very low. So that was all right. A woman collecting something.

He sat down again, opened *Lovely As A Tree* at the place where the marker was and his eye fell once more on the gunsmith's advertisement. Coram Clark Inc . . . . One of those names he had heard recently in some quite other context. Clark was a common name. But whose name was Coram? *Coram*, he remembered from long-ago school days when Latin was obligatory, meant 'on account of ' – no, 'in the presence of'. There was a mnemonic they learned of prepositions which took the ablative:

*a, ab, absque, coram, de,*
*Palam, clam, cum, ex and e,*
*Sine, tenus, pro and prae,*
*Add super, subter, sub and in,*
*When state, not motion, 'tis they mean.*

Amazing to remember that after all these years . . . Dora came in with a woman behind her. It was Sheila.

She looked at him and he looked at her and he said, 'How marvellous to see you.'

She went up to him and put her arms round his neck. 'I'm staying with Sylvia. I got the night of the party wrong and came yesterday. But, darling, what a fabulous house! And what's come over them abandoning suburbia at last? I'm loving it but I thought I'd tear myself away and sort of pop over.'

At ten o'clock. It was just like her. 'Are you all right?' he said.

'Well, no. I'm not all right. I'm wretched. But I'll be OK.'

He could see the proof of Casey's book lying on one of the sofa cushions. Casey's name wasn't in letters an inch high as it might be on a finished copy but it was plain enough to see. *The Lash by Augustine Casey, uncorrected proof, probable price in UK £14.95.*

'I said a lot of horrible things. Do you want to talk it through?'

Wexford's involuntary shudder made her laugh. 'I'm sorry, Pop, for all the things I said.'

'I said worse things and I'm sorry.'

291

'You've got Gus's book.' There was a look in her eyes that recalled the adoration he had hated to see the slavish spellbound devotion. 'Did you like it?'

What did it matter now? The man was gone. He would lie to be kind. 'Yes, very good. Very fine.'

'I didn't understand a word of it myself,' said Sheila.

Dora burst out laughing. 'For goodness' sake let's all have a drink.'

'If she has a drink she'll have to stay the night,' said Wexford the policeman.

Sheila stayed for breakfast, then went back to the Old Rectory. It was long past Wexford's usual time for going to work but he wanted to speak to Mrs Macsamphire before he left. For some reason, not fully comprehended, he wanted to speak to her from here, not the stables or his own phone in the back of a car.

Just as ten seemed the latest you could phone anyone, so nine was the earliest. He waited till Sheila was gone, dialled the number and got a young woman with a very thick Scots accent who said Ishbel Macsamphire was in the garden and could she call him back? Wexford didn't want that. The woman might be one of those who grudged every penny spent on long-distance calls, who might *have* to grudge every penny.

'Would you mind asking her if she could spare the time to speak to me now?'

While he waited, something strange happened. He remembered quite clearly who it was shared his name with a gunsmith in Nevada, who it was had Coram for a middle name.

# 26

It took him all day because he couldn't start until the late afternoon. All day and half the night because when it was midnight in Kingsmarkham it was still only four in the afternoon in the far west of the United States.

Next day, after four snatched hours of sleep and enough transatlantic phone calls to give Freeborn apoplexy, he was driving along the B 2428 towards the main gate of Tancred. The night had been very cold, laying a sharp silvering on wall and fencepost and a shimmering hoar frost to outline with glitter young leaves and twigs that were still leafless. But the frost was gone now, melted in strong spring sunshine, the sun high and dazzling in a bright blue sky. Much the same as in Nevada.

Every day the trees grew greener. A sheen of green became a mist, the mist a veil, the veil a deep brilliant cloak of it. All the weariness of winter was being covered up by green, dirt and damage concealed as the new growth hid accumulated litter and detritus. A dark grim picture, a grey lithograph, had its spaces gradually filled in by a brush loaded with soft viridian. The forest to the right of him and the woods to the left were no longer dark masses but a variegated shimmering green that the wind stirred, lifting branches and swaying them to let in gusts of light.

A car was parked ahead, by the gate. Not a car, a van. Wexford could just make out the figure of a man, who seemed to be tying something to the gatepost. They approached slowly. Donaldson stopped the car and got out to open the gate, pausing as he did so to examine the confection of blues, greens and violets, of which the latest offering was composed.

The man had returned to his van. Wexford got out of the car and went over to it, necessarily passing behind it in order to speak to the occupant of the driving seat. This viewpoint afforded him the sight of a bunch of flowers painted on the van's side.

The driver was young, no more than thirty. He wound down the window.

'What can I do for you?'

'Detective Chief Inspector Wexford. May I ask if all the flowers on the gate have come from you?'

'So far as I know. Other people may have brought floral tributes but not so far as I know.'

'You're an admirer of Davina Flory's books?'

'My wife is. I don't have time to read.'

Wexford wondered how many times he had heard those two statements before. Particularly in the country, a certain kind of man found it macho to make these disclaimers. Blame it on the wife. Reading, specially fiction, was for women.

'So all these have been tributes from your wife?'

'Eh? You have to be joking. They're my advertising campaign, aren't they? The wife wrote out the bits to put on the cards. It looked like a good place. Constant comings and goings. Whet their appetites and when they're really intrigued, tell 'em where they can order similar for themselves. Right? Now, if you'll excuse me, I've got a date at the crematorium.'

Wexford read the label on this fan-shaped bouquet of irises, asters, violets and forget-me-nots, a peacock's-tail design. No quotation from the poets this time, no apt line from Shakespeare, but: *Anther Florets, First Floor, Kingsbrook Centre, Kingsmarkham* and a phone number.

Burden, when Wexford told him, said, 'Drawing a bow at a venture, isn't it? And a pretty expensive bow. Would it ever work?'

'It has, Mike. I saw Donaldson surreptitiously taking down the address. And you surely remember all the people who said they wished they could get flowers like that. Hinde, for another. You did yourself. You wanted them for your wedding anniversary or something. So much for my sentimental speculations.'

'What sentimental speculations?'

'I'd got as far as imagining this was some ancient who'd been Davina's lover in the dim past. Might even have been Naomi's dad.' He said to Karen who walked by with a clipboard, 'We can get this lot packed up today, ready to move out. Mr Graham Pagett can have

294

his technology back with the grateful thanks of Kingsmarkham CID. Oh, and a polite letter thanking him for doing his bit to fight crime.'

'You've found the answer,' said Burden. It was a statement, not a question.

'Yes. At last.'

Burden looked hard at him. 'Are you going to tell me?'

'It's a lovely morning. I'd like to go outside somewhere, in the sun. Barry can drive us. We'll take the car down through the woods somewhere – and we'll make it a long way from the hanging tree. That gives me the creeps.'

His phone started bleeping.

The small amount of rain that had come had done little to soften the ground. A track indented by the wheels of Gabbitas's Land-Rover showed tyre marks that had probably been made last autumn, penetrating the wood. Vine slid the car along this path, careful not to break down the verges. This was on the north-eastern part of the Tancred woods, the track branching northwards off the by-road, not far from where Wexford had seen Gabbitas and Daisy standing side by side in the evening light, her hand touching his arm.

And as the car followed the winding track through a break in the clustering hornbeams, the great sweep of a green ride opened before them. This grassy road, cut between the central and the eastern woodland, opened a long vista, a green canyon or roofless tunnel, at the end of which was a U-shape of sunlit blue dazzle. At this end and all the way between the walls of the tree trunks the sun lay unbroken on the smooth turf, shadows shortened to nothing at noon.

Wexford remembered the figures in a landscape, the air of something romantic that had pervaded the scene that evening, and he said, 'We'll park here. It's a fine view.'

Vine put on the handbrake and the engine died. The silence was broken by the chattering, tinny, unmusical song of birds in the giant limes, ancient survivors of hurricane. Wexford wound down the window.

'We know now that the killers who came here on 11 March didn't come in a car. It would have been impossible to have done so and to have got away unobserved. They didn't come in a car or a van or on a motorbike. We only assumed they did, but the evidence for doing so was strong. I think I can say anyone would have made that

295

assumption. However, we were wrong. They came on foot. Or one of them did.'

Burden looked up at him sharply.

'No, Mike, there were two involved. And no motor transport or any other sort of transport was used. The time too, we've known that from the beginning. Harvey Copeland was shot at a few minutes past eight, say two or three minutes past, the two women and Daisy at perhaps seven minutes past. The getaway was at ten past or a minute or so earlier, at which time Joanne Garland was still on her way to Tancred.

'She reached the house at eleven minutes past. When the getaway was made she would have been coming in the main drive. While she was ringing and knocking at the door, trying to see in the dining-room window, while she was doing all these things three people were already dead. And Daisy was crawling across the dining-room and hall floors to reach the phone.'

'She didn't hear the bell?'

'She thought she was dying, sir,' said Vine. 'She thought she was bleeding to death. Perhaps she did hear it, perhaps she can't remember.'

Wexford said, 'It would be wrong to put much credence on what Daisy said happened. For instance, it's unlikely anyone suggested the noise upstairs was made by the cat when the cat normally rampaged about at six, not eight. It's very unlikely her grandmother suggested the noise came from the cat. We should also discount everything Daisy said about a getaway car.

'We'll leave these circumstantial things for a moment and enter a more speculative area. The reason for Andy Griffin's murder was certainly to silence him after he had made a blackmail attempt. What was the reason for the murder of Joyce Virson?'

'The perpetrator thought Daisy would be in the house that night.'

'You believe that, Mike?'

'Well, Joyce Virson wasn't blackmailing him,' Burden said with a grin, which he decided was misplaced and changed to a scowl. 'We've agreed he was after Daisy. He must have been after Daisy.'

'It seems a roundabout way of doing things,' said Wexford. 'Why go to the trouble of fixing a timed arson, risk killing others, when Daisy was most of the time totally alone at Tancred and easily accessible? On Freebee's orders she was no longer protected by night and the stables were empty. I have never believed the burning of The Thatched House was designed to kill Daisy.

'It was designed to kill someone but not Daisy.' He paused and looked from one to the other speculatively. 'Tell me, what have Nicholas Virson, John Gabbitas, Jason Sebright and Jonathan Hogarth in common?'

'All male, all young,' said Burden, 'all English-speaking . . .'

'They live round here. Two are American or part American.'

'All Caucasian, middle-class, quite good-looking or very good-looking . . .'

'They're Daisy's admirers,' said Vine.

'That's right, Barry. You've got it. Virson is in love with her, Hogarth is very keen and Gabbitas and Sebright, I think, are considerably attracted. She's an attractive girl, a lovely girl, it's not surprising she should have many admirers. Another one was Harvey Copeland, rather old for her, more than old enough in fact to be her grandfather, but a handsome old fellow for his age and once a "wow on campus". And a real prince in bed, according to Davina.'

Burden was making his Puritan Father face, mouth pulled down, eyebrows drawn together. Laid-back Vine's deadpan look didn't change.

'Yes, I know the idea of old Harvey initiating Daisy sexually is disgusting. It's disgusting and it's also a bit of a joke. Remember there was no coercion probably not even much persuasion. Just a thought wasn't it? You can hear Davina saying it: "It was just a thought, my dear." Only a monomaniac with ideas of revenge very different from most people's would have held it viciously against Harvey Copeland. And who, anyway, would have known?'

'Her father knew,' Burden put in. 'Joanne Garland wrote and told him.'

'Yes. And no doubt Daisy told people. She would have told a man who loved her. She didn't, however, tell me. I had to find it out from her mother's best friend. Let's go to Edinburgh now, shall we?' Burden's involuntary glance out of the window made Wexford laugh. 'Not literally, Mike. I've brought you far enough for one morning. Let's imagine ourselves in Edinburgh at the Festival in the last week of August and the first of September.

'Davina always went to the Edinburgh Festival. Just as she went to Salzburg and Bayreuth, to the Passion Play at Oberammergau every ten years, to Glyndebourne and to Snape. But last year the Book

297

Festival was held as it is every other year and she was due to speak on the subject of autobiographers and also to appear on some literary panel. As a matter of course, Harvey went with her and she also took Naomi and Daisy along.

'This time they took Nicholas Virson as well. An unlikely devotee of the arts but that wouldn't, of course, be his reason for going. He merely wanted to be with Daisy. He was in love with Daisy and took every opportunity of being near her.'

'They didn't stay with Ishbel Macsamphire, an old college friend of Davina's, but they visited her, or Davina and Harvey did. Naomi was ill in the hotel with flu. Daisy had her own occupations. No doubt Davina talked to Ishbel about her hopes for Daisy, mentioning, in what terms we don't know but can guess at, that she had a boyfriend called Nicholas.

'Then one day Mrs Macsamphire saw Daisy across the street with her boyfriend. They weren't near enough to be introduced but no doubt she waved and Daisy waved back. It wasn't until the funeral that they met again. I overheard Mrs Macsamphire say to Daisy that they hadn't seen each other since the Festival "when I saw you with your young man". Of course I thought she meant Nicholas, I have always believed she meant Nicholas.'

'She didn't?'

'Joanne Garland said she met Nicholas Virson in the street at the end of August and thought of speaking to him about this sex initiation business with Copeland. She didn't in fact do this but that's irrelevant here. Virson later told me that he and his mother were in Corfu around the end of August. Now none of this meant much. He could have been in Kingsmarkham and next day he could have been in Corfu, but it did make it unlikely he was in Edinburgh as well at much the same time.'

'You asked him?' Burden said.

'No, I asked Mrs Macsamphire. I asked her this morning if it was a fair-haired man she'd seen with Daisy and she said, no, he was dark and very good-looking.'

Wexford paused and said, 'Shall we get out and walk a bit? I've a fancy to walk the length of this ride and see what's at the end. There's something in human nature, isn't there, always wanting to know what's at the end?'

The scenario he had dreamed about took a new shape. He saw the sequence reform itself as he got out of the car and began to walk along the grassy path. Rabbits had cropped it close so that it resembled mown turf. The air was very soft and mild, scented with something fresh and vaguely sweet. Blossom was coming out on the cherry trees among the uncurling copper-coloured leaves. He saw the table again, the woman lying across it with her head in a plateful of blood, her daughter opposite her in a swoon of death, the young girl crawling, bleeding. Something like rewind mechanism took him back one minute, two, three, to the first sounds in the house, the deliberately created noise as things in Davina's room were over-turned, the jewellery already taken earlier in the day . . .

Burden and Vine walked in silence beside him. The end of this roofless tunnel showed itself slowly approaching but with no opening vista of further woods, further wide green path. It was as if the sea might be beyond, or the termination of the ride a cliff edge, a precipice you would step off into nothing.

'There were two of them,' he said, 'but only one came into the house. He came on foot and entered by the back door at five minutes to eight, well-primed, knowing his way, knowing exactly what he would find. He was wearing gloves and carrying the gun he had bought from Andy Griffin who picked it up in the bank after Martin was shot.

'Perhaps he would never have thought of doing any of this but for the gun. He had the gun so he had to use it. The gun gave him the idea. The barrel he had already changed, he knew all about that, how to do it, he'd been doing it since he was a boy.

'Armed with the gun containing the five cartridges which remained in the chamber, he came into Tancred House and went upstairs by the back stairs to carry out the plan of disarranging Davina's bed-room. The people downstairs heard him and Harvey Copeland went to look, but by that time the man with the gun had come down the back stairs and was approaching the hall along the passage from the kitchen regions. Harvey, on the bottom stair, turned round when he heard footsteps and the gunman shot him, so that he fell backwards over the lowest stairs.'

'Why shoot him twice?' Vine asked. 'According to the report the first shot killed him.'

'I said something just now about a monomaniac with ideas of revenge very different from most people's. The gunman knew what had been proposed for Harvey Copeland and Daisy. He fired two

299

shots into Davina's husband in a passion of jealousy, to be revenged on him for his temerity.

'He then proceeded into the dining room where he shot Davina and Naomi. Lastly, he shot Daisy. Not to kill her, only to wound.'

'Why?' said Burden. 'Why only to wound? What happened to disturb him? We know it wasn't the noise the cat made upstairs. You say the getaway was at ten past or a minute earlier while Joanne Garland was still coming up the main drive, but in a sense there was no getaway at all. Only an escape on foot. Wasn't it Joanne ringing the front-door bell that sent him running for the back way out?'

Vine said, 'If it was her she'd have heard the shots or she'd have heard the last one. He left because he had no more cartridges in the gun. He couldn't shoot her again just because he missed first time.'

The green ride had come to an end and in a way it was a cliff edge, a precipice. The borders of the forest, the meadows beyond, in the distance the downs, rolled away below them. A huge bank of cumulus welled up from the horizon but a long way from the sun, too far away to diminish its brightness. They stood and gazed at the view.

'Daisy crawled to the phone and made her 999 call,' Wexford said. 'She was not only in pain and in a state of terror, of fear for her life, but in mental anguish too. In those minutes she may have been afraid to die, but she wanted to die too. For a long time afterwards, days, weeks, she wanted to die, she had nothing to live for.'

'She had lost her whole family,' said Burden.

'Oh, Mike, that had nothing to do with it,' Wexford said with sudden impatience. 'What did she care for her family? Nothing. Her mother she despised just as Davina despised her, a poor feeble thing who had made a foolish marriage, never got any sort of career together, had been dependent on her own mother all her life. Davina I think she positively disliked, hated her domination of her, those plans for university and travel, even making up her mind what Daisy should study, even arranging her sex life for her. She must have regarded Harvey Copeland with a mixture of ridicule and revulsion. No, she disliked her nearest relations and felt no grief for them after they were dead.'

'She grieved, though. You told me you'd seldom seen such grief. She was constantly crying and sobbing and wishing she was dead. You just said so.'

Wexford nodded. 'But not because she'd seen the brutal murder of

300

her family. She grieved because the man she loved and who she believed loved her had shot her. The man she loved, the only person in the world she loved, and who she thought would risk everything for love of her, had tried to kill her. That's what she thought.

'When she crawled to the phone, in those minutes, the whole world was overturned for her because the man she was passionately in love with had tried to do to her what he had done to those others. And she went on grieving – for that. She was alone, abandoned, first in the hospital, then with the Virsons, lastly alone in the house that was now hers, and he never got in touch, he never tried, he never came to her. He had never loved her, he had wanted to kill her too. No wonder she said to me with great melodrama: "The pain is in my heart." '

As the clouds peaked to reach the sun and the chill came quickly, they turned and began to walk back. It was immediately cold, a hard April breeze cutting the air.

They came to the car, got into it and drove back up the by-road to pass the front of the house. Vine brought the car across the flagstones very slowly. The blue cat was on the stone coping of the pool with one of the goldfish between its paws.

The scarlet-headed fish floundered and flapped, twisting its body this way and that. Queenie patted it pleasurably with the paw that was not holding it down. Vine started to get out of the car but the cat was much too quick for him. She was a cat and he was only a man. She snatched up the flailing fish in her mouth and ran for the front door which was a crack ajar.

Someone inside closed it behind her.

# 27

Most of the technology was gone. The blackboard was gone and the phones. The two men Graham Pagett had sent were carrying out the master computer and Hinde's laser printer. Someone else was carrying a tray of cacti in pots. One end of the stables had been restored to what it had once been, a young girl's private retreat.

Wexford had never seen it this way before. He had never seen what Daisy had here, the taste which had governed the furnishings, the kind of pictures she had on the walls. A Klimt poster, glazed and framed, showed a nude in shimmering, all-revealing gold drapery; another was of cats, a huddle of cuddly Persians nestled together inside a satin-lined basket. The furniture was wicker, white and prettily upholstered in blue and white check cotton.

Was this her taste or Davina's for her? A houseplant, unwatered and the worse for wear, stood drooping in a blue and white Chinese pot. The books were all Victorian novels, their covers pristine, doubtless unread, and works on a variety of subjects from archaeology to present-day European politics, from language families to British lepidoptera. All chosen by Davina, he thought. The only book that looked as if it had ever been taken out of that bookcase was *The World's Greatest Cat Photos*.

He motioned Burden and Vine to sit down in the little sitting-room area that had been created by the impending move. For the last time the caterers' van had arrived outside, but that must wait. He thought once more, angry with himself, how Vine had guessed and spoken up only a day or two after the murders.

'There were two,' Burden said. 'All the time you've insisted there were two of them, but you've only mentioned one. That leaves only one conclusion, as far as I can see.'

302

Wexford looked sharply at him. 'Does it?'

'Daisy was the other one.'

'Of course she was,' Wexford said and he sighed.

'There were two of them, Daisy and the man she loved,' Wexford went on. 'You told me, Barry. You told me at the start and I didn't listen.'

'I did?'

'You said, "She inherits," and pointed out that she'd got the best motive, and I said something sarcastic about supposing she'd got her lover to wound her in the shoulder, and that she wasn't interested in property.'

'I don't know that I was altogether serious,' said Vine.

'You were *right.*'

'It was done for the property then?' Burden asked.

'She wouldn't have thought of it if he hadn't put the idea into her head. And he wouldn't have done it if she hadn't backed him up. She wanted freedom too. Freedom and the place hers and the money, doing what she liked, unconstrained. Only she didn't know what it would be like, what murder *is,* what people look like when they are killed. She didn't know about the blood.'

He thought suddenly about Lady Macbeth's words. No one had bettered them in four hundred years, no one had said anything more psychologically profound. Who would ever think people had so much blood in them?

'She told me very few lies. She didn't have to, she hardly had to act. Her misery was real. It's not hard to imagine what that would be like, trusting someone absolutely, your lover, your accomplice, knowing exactly what he will do and what your own part is. And then it goes wrong and he shoots you too. He's a different person. For a split second before he shoots you, you can see it in his eyes, not love but hatred, you know you've been deceived all along the line.

'So her unhappiness was real – no wonder she kept saying she wanted to die and what would become of her – until one night, when she was here alone with Karen, he came back. He didn't know about Karen and he came at the first opportunity to tell her he loved her, he had only wounded her to make it look real, to put her in the clear. He had always meant to do that and he knew it would be all right, he was a crack shot, he never missed. It was in the shoulder he shot her taking the smallest risk. But he couldn't have warned her, could he?

303

He couldn't have told her in advance, he couldn't have said, "I'm going to shoot you too, but trust me."

'But he had to take risks, didn't he? For the Tancred estate and the money and the royalties, all to be theirs and no one else's. He couldn't phone her, he didn't dare. The first chance he got, assuming she'd be alone, he came to the house to see her. Karen heard him but she didn't see him. Daisy did. He wasn't masked, that was Daisy's own invention. She saw him and no doubt, remembering how he had betrayed her, how he had shot her too, she thought he had come back to kill her.'

Burden objected, 'Shooting her at all was a hell of a risk. She could have taken against him and told us everything.'

'He calculated that she was too deep in it herself for that. Give us a clue as to who he was, arrest him and he would tell us of her part in it. And he counted on her being too much in love with him to betray him. He was right, wasn't he?

'The day after he had come to the house in the dark he came back when she really was alone. He told her why he had shot her, that he loved her, and of course she forgave him. After all, he was all she had. And after that she was a changed girl, she was happy. I've never seen such a transformation. In spite of everything, she was happy, she had her lover back, all would be well. I'm a fool, I thought it was for Virson. Of course it wasn't. She turned on the fountain. The fountain played to celebrate her happiness.

'For a day or two the euphoria persisted – until the memory of that night began coming back.' The red tablecloth and Davina's face in a plate of blood and her harmless silly mother dead and poor old Harvey spread out on the stairs – and that crawl to the phone.

'It wasn't, you see, what she had meant at all. She hadn't known it would be like that. It was a kind of game in the planning and the rehearsing. But the reality, the blood, the pain, the dead bodies, this she hadn't meant at all.

'I'm making no excuses for her. There are no excuses. She may not have known what she was doing but she knew three people would be murdered. And it was a case of *folie à deux*. She couldn't have done it without him but he wouldn't have done it without her. They egged each other on. Kissing the gunner's daughter is a dangerous business.'

'That expression,' Burden said. 'What does it mean? Someone said it to me the other day, I can't think who it was . . .'

'It was me,' said Vine.

'What does it mean? It means being flogged. When they were going to flog a man in the Royal Navy they first tied him to a cannon on deck. Kissing the gunner's daughter was therefore a dangerous enterprise.

'I don't think she knew Andy Griffin would have to be killed. Or, rather, would be killed because this lover of hers saw killing as the way out of difficulties. Someone annoys you? Then kill him. Someone happens to look at your girlfriend? Kill him.

'It wasn't Daisy he was after when he rigged up that candle and string contraption among the petrol cans at The Thatched House. It was Nicholas Virson. Nicholas Virson dared to look at Daisy, dared in fact to think Daisy might actually marry him. Who would have supposed that Virson, who had asked Daisy to stay with him and his mother, wouldn't in fact be home that night but keeping tabs on Daisy up at Tancred?'

'She's more like her grandmother than she knows. Did you notice how few friends she has? Not a single young woman has been to the house all this while – apart from the young women *we* put there. There was just one young woman at the funeral, a granddaughter of Mrs Macsamphire.

'Davina had a few friends from the distant past but *their* friends were Harvey Copeland's. Naomi had friends. Daisy hasn't one young woman to confide in, to be a companion to her now. But men? She's very good with men.' Wexford said it ruefully. He thought for a moment how very good she had been with him. 'Men quickly become her slaves. An interesting point is how short-sighted Davina Flory must have been in believing she would have to provide a lover for Daisy, as if Daisy wasn't ably equipped to provide her own. But they were self-absorbed, both these women, grandmother and granddaughter, and therefore unable to see further than their own noses.

'Daisy met her lover in Edinburgh, at the Festival. We shall find out how eventually. Perhaps at fringe theatre or a pop concert. Her mother was ill and no doubt she escaped from her grandmother whenever she could. She was very sore at the time. Davina's suggestion about Harvey was rankling. Not, I think, because she was shocked or even disgusted, but because she was coming more and more to hate all this interference in her life, this manipulation. Was it going to go on, this arranging her life for her? It wasn't getting better, it was worse.

'But here was a young man who had no regard for her family, no reverence for any of them, someone she must have seen as a free spirit, independent, dashing, bold. Someone like herself, or like she could be if she too was free.

'Whose idea was it? His or hers? His, I think. But perhaps it would never have got off the ground if he hadn't kissed the gunner's daughter. And afterwards he said, All that could be *ours*. The house, the acres, the money.

'It was a simple enough plan and would be simple enough to do. Provided he was a good shot and he was, he was a very good shot. He hadn't a gun and that was a stumbling block. For him, being without a gun was always a stumbling block. It was as if his right arm wasn't complete without a gun in the hand on the end of it. Did they perhaps discuss the possibility of there being a shotgun or a rifle at Tancred? Had old Harvey ever shot birds on the land? Would Davina have allowed that?'

Burden waited a while. Then, when Wexford looked up, 'What happened when they got back here?'

'I don't think *they* did get back here. Daisy did, with her family. She went back to school and perhaps it seemed to her like a dream, a wicked daydream that now would never become real. But one day he turned up. He got in touch with her and they arranged to meet, here, in the stables, where she had her own place. No one saw him, no one came here but Daisy. How about it then? When were they going to do it?

'I don't think Daisy knew whether her grandmother had made a will or not. If there was a will and Naomi and Harvey were dead, she would certainly be the sole beneficiary. If there wasn't a will Davina's niece Louise Merritt might get some of it. Louise Merritt died in February and I don't think it was a coincidence that they waited until after she was dead to carry out their plan.

'Before that, some months before probably, in the autumn, he encountered Andy Griffin in the wood. How it came about I don't know, how many meetings they had before the proposition was put, but Andy offered to sell him a gun and the offer was accepted.

'He changed the barrel, he knew all about that. He'd brought the tools with him.' Wexford explained how he had found the advertisement in the Heights town guide. 'The gunsmith's name was

306

Coram Clark. I knew I'd come across that name somewhere before but I couldn't remember where. All I knew was that it was someone's name and someone connected with the case. It came back to me at last. Right at the start of things, the day after the murders, when the press were up here.

'There was a reporter on the local paper asked a question at the press conference. He hung about outside waiting for me afterwards. He was very cocky, very self-assured, a very young man, no more than a boy, dark, good-looking. He'd been at school with Daisy, he volunteered that information, and then he told me his name. He was talking about what he intended to call himself professionally, he hadn't made up his mind.

'He has now. I saw it on a by-line in the *Courier*. He's calling himself Jason Coram, but his full name is Jason Sherwin Coram Sebright.'

'Sebright had also told me, apropos of nothing in particular, that his mother was American, that he visited his mother in the United States. It was still a long shot.

'He told me that at the funeral. He sat next to me. Later on, he went about interviewing mourners, in a manner which he proudly told me was his US TV technique. He came here to get an exclusive interview out of Daisy the day after the prowler came round the house. I met him coming out and he told me all about it. He was going to call his piece "The Masked Intruder" and perhaps he has, for all I know.

'A handsome dark young man Ishbel Macsamphire had seen her with in Edinburgh. That description might equally have fitted John Gabbitas but Gabbitas is an Englishman with parents in Norfolk.

'Jason Sebright had just left school. He was eighteen, soon to be nineteen. In September he entered the journalism training scheme with a job on the *Courier*. He might easily have gone to Edinburgh at the same time as Daisy was there. I waited until it was ten a.m. in Nevada and put through calls to Coram Clark the gunsmith's in the city of Heights. Coram Clark himself, called Coram Clark Junior, wasn't there but to be found, they told me, at their store in downtown Carson City. Eventually, I spoke to him. He was keen to help. American enthusiasm I find very refreshing. You don't get so much of that "might have been" stuff over there. Had he a young relative called Jason Sebright in this country?

307

'He told me that he was familiar with the technique of changing the barrel of a gun. He told me that the tools for performing such a task would not be bulky and could easily be brought into this country. The Customs wouldn't know what they were for. But he had no young relative called Jason in the United Kingdom or anywhere else for that matter. His daughters, née Clark, were married. He has no sons. He was an only child and has no nephews. He had never heard of Jason Sherwin Coram Sebright.'

'I'm not surprised,' Burden said, not very pleasantly. 'It was about as far-fetched as you could get.'

'Yes. Still, it paid off. Coram Clark had no young relatives in this country or anywhere else. But he gave me a lot of useful information. He said he ran a class in marksmanship at a local shooting range. He also sometimes had students from Heights University working for him, driving, working in the store, even in some cases doing gun repair jobs. Students at American universities do quite frequently work their way through college.

'After I put the phone down I remembered something. An American university sweatshirt with letters on it that had nearly faded or been washed out. But I was sure there had been a capital ST as well as a capital U.

'My friend Stephen Perkins of Myringham University was able to tell me what those letters stood for by the simple expedient of examining the CVs in the applications of prospective creative-writing students. Stylus University, California. They call everything a city over there and Stylus is pretty small for a city but it has a police force and a police chief, Chief Peacock. It also has eight gunsmiths. Chief Peacock came back to me, he was even more helpful than Coram Clark, and he told me firstly that Stylus University had a Military History course on its syllabus and secondly that one of the gunsmiths frequently employed university students to help out in the store on evenings and weekends. I phoned the gunsmiths, one after another. The fourth one I phoned remembered Thanny Hogarth very well. He had worked for him up to the end of his final semester last year. Not because he needed the money. His father was wealthy and making him a big allowance. He loved guns, he was fascinated by guns.

'Chief Peacock told me something else. Two years ago two students at Stylus were shot on campus, both men and with one thing

308

in common. They had, successively, "dated" the same girl. Their killer was never found.'

The bicycle was resting up against the house wall.

'Interior Creators' were inside the house, restoring the dining room. Their van was parked close up against the window Pemberton had broken. Today the fountain was not playing. In the limpid dark water the surviving red-headed fish swam round and round.

The three policemen stood by the pool. 'The second time I went to his house,' Wexford said, 'I saw the tools among a lot of other stuff on a table. I didn't know what they were. I think I even saw a gun barrel, but who knows what a gun barrel is when it's not in a gun?'

Burden said suddenly, 'Why didn't he marry her?'

'What?'

'Before the shootings, I mean. If she'd changed her mind about him he'd have got nothing. She'd only to say she didn't want him any more after what he'd done and he'd be out in the cold.'

'She was under eighteen,' Wexford said. 'She'd have needed parental consent. Can you imagine Davina allowing Naomi to consent? Apart from that, you're an anachronism, Mike, you're out of your time. They're children of today and I daresay marriage didn't occur to them. Marriage? That was for the old people and the Virsons of this world.

'Besides, it sets you apart, this kind of thing, a massacre. Maybe they understood something, that they were marked, that no one else would do for them, they had only each other.'

He went up to the house and was about to pull the sugarstick rod when he saw that the door was slightly ajar, left that way no doubt by 'Interior Creators'. He hesitated, then walked in, Burden and Vine behind him.

They were in the *serre*, the two of them, so intent upon what they were doing that for a second they heard nothing. The two dark heads were close together. On the glass table were a pearl necklace, a gold bracelet and a couple of rings, one a ruby with diamond shoulders, the other set with pearls and sapphires.

Daisy was looking at her own finger, the third finger of her left hand on which Thanny Hogarth had perhaps just placed his engagement ring, a great cluster of diamonds, nineteen thousand pounds' worth of diamonds.

She turned round. She stood up when she saw who it was and, with an involuntary gesture of the diamonded hand, swept all the jewellery on to the floor.

# SIMISOLA

To Marie

# 1

There were four people besides himself in the waiting room and none of them looked ill. The olive-skinned blonde in the designer track-suit bloomed with health, her body all muscles, her hands all golden tendons, apart from the geranium nails and the nicotine stains on the right forefinger. She had changed her seat when a child of two arrived with its mother and homed to the chair next to hers. Now the blonde woman in the tracksuit was as far away as she could get, two seats from himself and three from the very old man who sat with his knees together, his hands clutching his checked cap in his lap and his eyes on the board where the doctors' names were printed.

Each of the GPs had a light above his or her name and a hook underneath it on which coloured rings hung: a red light and rings for Dr Moss, green for Dr Akande, blue for Dr Wolf. The old man had been given a red ring, Wexford noticed, the child's mother a blue one, which was exactly what he would have expected, the preference for the senior man in one case, the woman in the other. The woman in the track-suit hadn't got a ring at all. She either didn't know you were supposed to announce yourself at reception or couldn't be bothered. Wexford wondered why she wasn't a private patient with an appointment later in the morning and therefore not obliged to wait here fidgeting and impatient.

The child, tired of marching back and forth on the seats of the row of chairs, had turned her attention to the magazines on the table and begun tearing off their covers. Who was ill, this little girl or her overweight pallid mother? Nobody said a word to hinder the tearing, though the old man glared and the woman in the track-suit did the unforgivable, the outrageous, thing. She thrust a hand into her crocodile-skin handbag, took out a flat gold case, the function of

313

which would have been a mystery to most people under thirty, removed a cigarette and lit it with a gold lighter.

Wexford, who had been successfully distracted from his own anxiety, now became positively fascinated. No fewer than three notices on the walls, among the exhortations to use a condom, have children immunized and watch your weight, forbade smoking. What would happen? Was there some system whereby smoke in the waiting room could be detected in reception or the dispensary?

The child's mother reacted, not with a word to the woman in the track-suit but by sniffing, giving the little girl a vicious yank with one hand and administering a slap with the other. Screams ensued. The old man began a sorrowful head-shaking. To Wexford's surprise the smoker turned to him and said, without preamble, 'I called the doctor but he refused to come. Isn't that amazing? I was forced to come here myself.'

Wexford said something about GPs no longer making house calls except in cases of serious illness.

'How would he know it wasn't serious if he didn't come?' She must have correctly interpreted Wexford's disbelieving look. 'Oh, it's not *me*,' she said and, incredibly, 'it's one of the servants.'

He longed to know more but the chance was lost. Two things happened simultaneously. The blue light for Dr Wolf came on and the door opened to admit the practice nurse. She said crisply, 'Please put that cigarette out. Didn't you see the notice?'

The woman in the track-suit had compounded her offence by dropping ash on the floor. No doubt she would have ground her fag end out there too but for the nurse taking it from her with a little convulsive grunt and carrying it off into hitherto unpolluted regions. She was unembarrassed by what had happened, lifting her shoulders a little, giving Wexford a radiant smile. Mother and child left the waiting room in quest of Dr Wolf just as two more patients came in and Dr Akande's light came on. This is it, thought Wexford, his fear returning, now I shall know. He hung up the green ring and went out without a backward glance. Instantly it was as if those people had never been, as if none of those things had happened.

Suppose he fell over as he walked the short corridor to Dr Akande's room? Already twice that morning he had fallen. I'd be in the best place, he told himself, the doctors' surgery – no, he corrected himself, must move with the times, the medical centre. The best place

314

to be taken ill. If it's something in my brain, a growth, a bloodclot. . . . He knocked on the door, though most people didn't.

Raymond Akande called, 'Come in.'

This was only the second time Wexford had been to him since Akande joined the practice on Dr Crocker's retirement, and the first visit had been for an anti-tetanus injection when he cut himself in the garden. He liked to believe there had been some sort of rapport between them, that they had taken to each other. And then he castigated himself for thinking this way, for caring, because he knew damned well he wouldn't have involved himself with likings or dislikings if Akande had been other than he was.

This morning, though, these reflections were nowhere. He was concerned only with himself, the fear, the horrid symptoms. Keeping calm, trying to be detached, he described them, the way he fell over when he got out of bed in the morning, the loss of balance, the floor coming up to meet him.

'Any headache?' said Dr Akande. 'Any nausea?'

No, there was none of that, Wexford said, hope creeping in at the door Akande was opening. And, yes, he had had a bit of a cold. But, you see, a few years ago he'd had this thrombosis in the eye and ever since then he'd. . . . Well, he'd been on the alert for something like it, a stroke maybe, God forbid.

'I thought maybe Ménière's syndrome,' he said unwisely.

'I'm no believer in banning books,' said the doctor, 'but I'd personally burn all medical dictionaries.'

'OK, I did look at one,' Wexford admitted. 'And I didn't seem to have the right symptoms, apart from the falling bit.'

'Why don't you stick to the judges' rules and leave diagnosis to me?'

He was quite willing. Akande examined his head and his chest and a few reflexes. 'Did you drive yourself here?'

His heart in his mouth, Wexford nodded.

'Well, don't drive. Not for a few days. Of course you can drive home. Half the population of Kingsmarkham's got this virus. I've had it myself.'

'Virus?'

'That's what I said. It's a funny one, it seems to affect the semi-circular canals in the ears and they control the balance.'

'It's really just that, a virus? A virus can make you fall down like that, out of the blue? I measured my length in the front garden yesterday.'

'It's quite a length to measure,' said Akande. 'Didn't have any illuminating visions, I suppose? No one to tell you to stop kicking against the pricks?'

'You mean visions are another symptom? Oh, no, I see. Like on the road to Damascus. You're not going to tell me that was all Paul had, a virus?'

Akande laughed. 'The received view is that he was an epileptic. No, don't look like that. This is a virus, I promise you, not a case of spontaneous epilepsy. I'm not going to give you anything for it. It'll get right in a day or two on its own. In fact, I'll be surprised if it doesn't get right immediately now you know you haven't got a brain tumour.'

'How did you . . . ? Oh, well, I suppose you're used to patients with irrational fears.'

'It's understandable. If it's not medical books, it's the newspapers never letting them forget about their health for five minutes.'

Akande got up and held out his hand. Wexford thought it a pleasant custom, that of shaking hands with patients, the way doctors must have done years ago when they made house calls and sent bills.

'Funny creatures, people,' the doctor said. 'For instance, I'm expecting someone this morning who's coming on behalf of her *cook*. Send the cook, I said, but that apparently wouldn't do. I've a feeling – without foundation, I must tell you, mere intuition – that she's not going to be too overjoyed when she finds I'm what my father-in-law's boss used to call "a man of colour".'

For once, Wexford was speechless.

'Have I embarrassed you? I'm sorry. These things are always just under the surface and sometimes they bubble up.'

'You haven't embarrassed me,' Wexford said. 'It was only that I couldn't think of anything to say that would be . . . well, a refutation or a consolation. I just agreed and I didn't care to say that.'

Akande gave him a pat on the shoulder, or one that was aimed at the shoulder but landed on his upper arm. 'Take a couple of days off. You should be fine by Thursday.'

Halfway down the corridor Wexford met the blonde woman heading towards Akande's room. 'I know I'm going to lose my cook, I can just see it coming,' she said as she passed him. A miasma that was a mix of Paloma Picasso and Rothman Kingsize hung in her wake. Surely she hadn't meant the cook was going to *die*?

He went jauntily out, pushing open both of the double doors. Only one of the cars in the car park could possibly be hers, the Lotus Elan with the personalized number, AK 3. She must have paid a lot for that, it was one of the earliest. Annabel King, he speculated. Anne Knight? Alison Kendall? Not all that number of English surnames begin with K, but then she certainly wasn't of English origin. Anna Karenina, he thought, being silly.

Akande had said he could drive home. In fact, Wexford would have enjoyed walking home, he loved the idea of walking now he had stopped falling over or being afraid of falling over. The mind was a funny thing, what it could make the body do. If he left the car here he'd only have to come back for it later.

The young woman waddled and the child skipped down the medical centre's shallow steps. Full of good cheer, Wexford wound down his window and asked them if they'd like a lift. Somewhere, anywhere, he was in the mood to drive miles out of his way if need be.

'We don't take lifts from strangers.' To the child she said very loudly, 'Do we, Kelly?'

Snubbed, Wexford withdrew his head. She was quite right. She had behaved wisely and he had not.

He might be a combined rapist and child molester cunningly disguising his nefarious motives by a visit to the doctor. Leaving, he passed a car he recognized coming in, an old Ford Escort that had been resprayed bright pink. You hardly ever saw a pink car. But whose was it? He often had a brilliant eidetic memory, faces and townscapes recorded in full colour, but the names got lost.

He drove out into South Queen Street. It was going to be nice telling the news to Dora and he indulged himself by thinking what might have been, the horror, the communicated dread, the putting of two brave faces on it, if he'd had to tell her he'd an appointment at the hospital for a brain scan. None of that was going to happen. Would he have been brave if it had? Would he have *lied* to her?

In that case he'd have had to lie to three people. Turning into his own garage drive, he saw Neil's car already there, thoughtfully parked on the far left to allow his own passage. Neil *and* Sylvia's car, he had better learn to say, for they had just the one between them

317

now, since hers had been given up when her job went. They might not even be able to afford this one, the way things were now.

I ought to be gratified, he thought, I ought to be flattered. Not everybody's children come flying to the bosom of Mum and Dad when misfortune strikes. His always did. He ought not to have this reaction, this immediate response to the sight of the Fairfax car which was to ask: what now?

Adversity is good for some marriages. The warring couple put aside their strife and stand united against the world. Sometimes. And the marriage has to be in a pretty bad way before this happens. Wexford's elder daughter's marriage had been bad for a long time and it was different from other people's bad marriages chiefly in that she and Neil stayed doggedly together, ever seeking new remedies, for the sake of their two sons.

Once Neil had said to his father-in-law, 'I do love her. I really love her,' but that was a long time ago. A lot of tears had fallen since then and a lot of cruel things been said. Many times Sylvia had brought the boys home to Dora and just as often Neil had taken himself to a motel room on the Eastbourne road. Her educating herself and working for the social services had solved no problems, and nor had their lavish foreign holidays or moves to bigger and better houses. At least, money or the lack of it had never been an issue. There was enough, more than enough.

Until now. Until Neil's father's firm of architects (two partners, father and son) felt the recession, then its bite, then was punched and undermined by it into collapse. Neil had been without work for five weeks now, Sylvia for nearly six months.

Wexford let himself into his house and stood for a moment, listening to their voices: Dora's measured and calm, Neil's indignant, still incredulous, Sylvia's hectoring. He was in no doubt they were waiting for him, had come expecting to find him there, ready to be diverted from his brain tumour or embolism by their catalogue of troubles: joblessness, no prospects, increasing mortgage debt.

He opened the living room door and Sylvia fell upon him, throwing her arms round his neck. She was a big tall woman, well able to embrace him without finding herself clutching his middle. For a moment he thought her affection occasioned by anxiety for his health, his very life.

'Dad,' she said, she wailed, 'Dad, what d'you think we've come to?'

318

I mean, us. It's unbelievable but it's happening. You won't believe it. Neil's *going on the dole.*'

'It won't exactly be dole, darling,' said Neil, using an endearment Wexford hadn't heard on his lips for many a year. 'Not the dole. Benefit.'

'Well, it amounts to the same thing. Welfare, social security, unemployment pay, it comes to the same. It's all unbelievably ghastly, happening to *us.*'

It was interesting how Dora's quite soft voice could penetrate this stridency. It cut through it like a fine wire splitting a chunk of extra strong cheddar. 'What did Dr Akande say, Reg?'

'A virus. Apparently, there's a lot of it about. I'm to take a couple of days off, that's all.'

'What a relief,' Dora said lightly. 'A virus.'

Sylvia made a snorting sound. 'I could have told you that. I had it myself last week, I could hardly keep on my feet.'

'Then it's a pity you didn't tell me, Sylvia.'

'I've got more things to think about, haven't I? I'd be laughing if feeling a bit giddy was all I had to contend with. Now you're back, Dad, perhaps you can stop Neil doing this. I can't, he never takes any notice of what I say. Anybody's got more influence with him than his own wife.'

'Stop him doing what?' said Wexford.

'I've *told* you. Going to the – what's it called? – the ESJ. I don't know what that stands for but I know what it is, the combined dole place and labour exchange – no, they don't call it that any more, do they?'

'They haven't called it that for years,' said Neil. 'The Job Centre.'

'Why should I stop him?' Wexford said.

'Because it's hateful, it's degrading, it isn't the kind of place people like us go to.'

'And what do people like us do?' Wexford asked in the voice that should have warned her.

'Find something in the appointments section of *The Times.*'

Neil began to laugh and Wexford, his anger swiftly changed to pity, smiled sadly. Neil had been studying the situations vacant daily for weeks now, had written, he had told his father-in-law, over three hundred letters of application, all in vain.

'*The Times* don't give you any money,' said Neil, and Wexford could hear the bitterness in his voice, if Sylvia couldn't. 'Besides, I have to know where I stand on our mortgage. Maybe they can do something to stop the building society repossessing the house. *I* can't. Perhaps they can advise me what to do about the kids' schools, if it's only to tell us to send them to Kingsmarkham Comprehensive. Anyway, I'll get money – don't they call it a giro that they send you? One thing, I shall soon know. And I'd better, Reg, I'd better. We've got just two hundred and seventy pounds left in our joint account and that's the only account we've got. Just as well, I expect, since they ask you what savings you've got before they pay out.'

Wexford said quietly, 'Do you want a loan? We could let you have a bit.' He thought, swallowed. 'Say a thousand?'

'Thanks, Reg, thanks very much, but it had better be no. It'll only postpone the evil day. I'm very grateful for the offer. A loan ought to be paid back and I can't see how I'd ever repay you, not for years.' Neil looked at his watch. 'I must go,' he said. 'My appointment with the new claims adviser is for ten-thirty.'

Dora must have spoken without thinking, 'Oh, do they give you an appointment?'

It was odd to see how a smile could sadden a face. Neil hadn't quite winced. 'You see how being unemployed demotes you? I no longer belong among those who can expect social grace. I'm one of the queuers now, the waiters-in-line who are lucky to be seen at all, who get sent home with nothing and told to come back tomorrow. I've probably lost my style and my surname too. Someone'll come out and call, "Neil, Mr Stanton will see you now". At ten to one, though I'm due there at ten-thirty.'

'I'm sorry, Neil, I didn't mean . . .'

'No, of course you didn't. It's unconscious. Or, rather, it's a shift the consciousness makes, an adjustment in the way you think about a prosperous architect with more commissions than he can handle and someone who's out of work. I have to go now.'

He didn't take their car. Sylvia needed it. He would walk the half mile to the ESJ, and later on . . .

'Get the bus, I suppose,' said Sylvia. 'Why not? Half the time I have to. If there are only four a day that's too bad. We have to watch our petrol consumption. I expect he can walk five miles. You used to tell us your grandfather walked five miles to school and five miles back when he was only ten.'

There was a settled despair in her voice Wexford didn't like to hear, much as he deplored her self-pity and her petulance. He heard

Dora offering to have the boys for the weekend so that Sylvia and Neil could get away, if only to London where Neil's sister lived, and he seconded that rather too heartily.

'When I think,' said Sylvia, who was given to doleful reminiscence, 'how I slaved to get to be a social worker.' She nodded to her husband as he left, resumed while he was still in earshot, 'Neil didn't exactly adapt his lifestyle to help. I had to arrange to get the boys looked after. I'd still be working at midnight sometimes. And what has it all come to?'

'Things must get better eventually, dear,' said Dora.

'I'll never get another job with the social services, I *feel* it. Do you remember those children in Stowerton, Dad? The "home alone" kids?'

Wexford thought. Two of his officers had met the parents at Gatwick coming off a plane from Tenerife. He said, 'Epson, weren't they called? He was black and she was white . . .'

'What's that got to do with it? Why bring racism into it? That was my last job as a child care officer before the cuts. Little did I dream I'd be a housewife again before those kids went back to their parents. Will you really have the boys for the weekend, Mother?'

That was the woman he had seen driving the pink car. Fiona Epson. Not that it was important. Wexford debated whether to go upstairs and lie down or defy the doctor and return to work. Work won. As he left the house he could hear Sylvia lecturing her mother on what she called acceptable forms of political correctness.

# 2

When the Akande family had moved to Kingsmarkham a year or so
before, the owner-occupiers on either side of number twenty-seven
Ollerton Avenue put their houses up for sale. Insulting as this was to
Raymond and Laurette Akande and their children, from a practical
point of view it was to their advantage. The recession was at its
height and the houses took a long time to sell, their asking prices
regularly falling, but when the newcomers arrived they turned out to
be nice people, as friendly and as liberal-minded as the rest of the
Ollerton Avenue neighbours.

'Note my choice of words,' said Wexford. 'I said "friendly", I said
"liberal", I didn't say "non-racist". We're all racist in this country.'

'Oh, come on,' said Detective Inspector Michael Burden. 'I'm not.
You're not.'

They were in Wexford's dining room, having coffee, while the
Fairfax boys, Robin and Ben, and Burden's son Mark watched
Wimbledon on television in the room next door with Dora. It was
Wexford who had begun this topic of conversation, he hardly knew
why. Perhaps it had arisen out of Sylvia's accusation when they
discussed the Epsons. He had certainly been thinking about it.

'My wife's not and nor is yours,' Burden said, 'nor our children.'

'We're all racists,' said Wexford as if he hadn't spoken. 'Without
exception. People over forty are worse and that's about all you can
say. You were brought up and I was brought up to think ourselves
superior to black people. Oh, it may not have been explicit but it was
there all right. We were conditioned that way and it's in us still, it's
ineradicable. My wife had a black doll called a gollywog and a white
one called Pamela. Black people were known as negroes. When did

322

you ever hear anyone but a sociologist like my daughter Sylvia refer to white people as Caucasians?'

'As a matter of fact, my mother referred to black people as "darkies" and she thought she was being polite. "Nigger" was rude but "darky" was OK. But that was a long time ago. Things have changed.'

'No, they haven't. Not much. There are just more black people about. My son-in-law said to me the other day that he no longer noticed the difference between a black person and a white one. I said, you don't notice the difference between fair and dark, then? You don't notice if one person's fat and another's thin? What possible help to overcoming racism is that? We'll be getting somewhere when one person says to another of someone black, "Which one is he?" and the other one says, "That chap in the red tie." '

Burden smiled. The boys came in, banging the door behind them, to announce that Martina had won her first set and Steffi hers. Surnames scarcely existed as far as they and their contemporaries were concerned.

'Can we have the chocolate biscuits?'

'Ask your grandmother.'

'She's gone to sleep,' said Ben. 'But she said we could have them after lunch and it's after lunch now. It's the ones that are chocolate *with* chocolate chips and we know where they are.'

'Anything for a quiet life,' said Wexford, and he added gravely, with a hint of scolding in his voice, 'but if you start on them you must finish the whole packet. Is that understood?'

'*Kein Problem*,' said Robin.

After the Burdens and Mark had gone Wexford picked up the booklet his son-in-law had left him to look at, the ES 461. Or rather, the Xerox of the booklet. The original had gone back with Neil to his interview with the Employment Service. Neil, whose method of handling his misfortunes was to wallow in them, with the maximum self-created humiliation, had gone to the trouble of photocopying all nineteen pages of what the Employment Service chose to call a 'form'. He had taken the collection of turquoise blue, green, yellow and orange papers to Kingsmarkham Instant Print where they had a colour copier so that Wexford could see an ES 461 in all its glory (his words) and read the demands a beneficent government made of its unemployed citizens.

A new word had been coined for the first page: 'jobsearch'. There

323

were three pages of notes to be read before completing the 'form' and then forty-five questions, many of them multiple enquiries, which made Wexford's head spin to read. Some were innocuous, some desperately sad, some sinister: Does your health limit the work you can do? asked number thirty, following twenty-nine's, What is the lowest wage you are willing to work for? Sights were set humbly for the enquiry, Do you have any academic qualifications (for example, O Levels, GCSEs, City and Guilds)? Do you have your own transport? asked number nine. Four wanted to know: If you have not worked for the last twelve months, how have you spent your time?

This last made his anger rise. What business was that of these Client Advisers, these small-time civil servants, this *government* department? He asked himself what answers they expected apart from 'looking for work'. Having a fortnight on Grand Bahama? Dining at Les Quat' Saisons? Collecting Chinese porcelain? He pushed the coloured pages aside and went into the living room where Navratilova was still battling it out on Centre Court.

'Move up,' he said to Robin on the sofa.

'*Pas de probleme.*'


Doctors used to tell you to come back and see them next week or 'when the symptoms have cleared up'. These days they are mostly too busy to do that. They don't want to see patients without symptoms, not if they can help it. There are too many of the other kind, the ones that really ought to be in bed and visited at home, but who are obliged to stagger down to the medical centre and spread their viruses round the waiting room.

Wexford's virus had apparently flown away at the moment Dr Akande spoke his magic words. He had no intention of going back for a mere check-up and even disobeyed the doctor in taking no days off. From time to time he thought about that question, the one that asked how the victim of 'jobsearch' had spent his or her time, and he wondered how he would answer. When he wasn't at work, for instance, when he was on leave but hadn't gone away. Reading, talking to grandchildren, thinking, drying the dishes, having a quick one in the Olive with a friend, reading. Would that satisfy them? Or was it something quite other they wanted to hear?

But when Dr Akande phoned him a week later, he was first guilty, then apprehensive. Dora took the call. It was getting on for nine in the evening, a Wednesday in early July, and the sun not yet set. The french windows were open and Wexford was sitting just inside them, reading Camus' *The Outsider*, thirty years after he had first read it, and swiping at mosquitos with the *Kingsmarkham Courier*.

'What does he want?'

'He didn't say, Reg.'

It was just remotely possible that Akande was so thorough and painstaking a general practitioner that he troubled to check up on patients who had been no more than marginally unwell. Or else – and Wexford's heart gave a little hop and a thud – that 'falling sickness' he had had wasn't the minor matter Akande had diagnosed, wasn't the result of a generalized but petty plague, was in fact much more serious, its symptoms the forerunner of . . .

'I'm coming.'

He took the receiver. From Akande's first words he knew he wasn't to be *told* anything but *asked* something; the doctor wasn't dispensing wisdom but coming cap in hand; this time it was he, the policeman, who must make the diagnosis.

'I'm sorry to trouble you with this, Mr Wexford, but I hoped you might help me.'

Wexford waited.

'It's probably nothing.'

Those words, no matter how often he heard them, always caused a small shiver. In his experience, it was nearly always something and, if brought to his attention, something bad.

'If I was really worried I'd get in touch with the police station but it isn't on that scale. My wife and I don't know many people in Kingsmarkham – of course, we're relatively new here. You being my patient . . .'

'What has happened, doctor?'

A small deprecating laugh, a hesitation, and Akande said, using a curious phrase, 'I'm trying in vain to locate my daughter.' He paused. He made another attempt. 'I suppose what I mean is, I don't know how to find out where she is. Of course, she's twenty-two years old. She's a grown woman. If she wasn't living at home with us, if she was somewhere on her own, I wouldn't even know she hadn't come home, I wouldn't . . .'

Wexford cut in, 'Do you mean your daughter is missing?'

'No, no, that's putting it too strongly. She hasn't come home and she wasn't where we expected her to be last night, that's all. But as I say, she's grown up. If she changed her mind and went somewhere else . . . well, she has that right.'

'But you would have expected her to let you know?'

'I suppose so. She's not very reliable about that kind of thing, young people aren't, as you may know, but we've never known her to . . . well, it looks as if she's deceiving us. Telling us one thing and doing another. That's the way I personally see it. My wife, on the other hand, is worried. That's an understatement, she's very anxious.'

It was always their wives, Wexford thought. They projected their emotions on to their wives. My wife is rather anxious about it. It's bothering my wife. I'm taking this step because, frankly, the whole thing is affecting my wife's health. As strong men themselves, *macho* men, they would like you to believe they were prey to no fears, no anxieties, and to no desires either, no longings, no passions, no needs.

'What's her name?' he asked.

'Melanie.'

'When did you last see Melanie, Dr Akande?'

'Yesterday afternoon. She had an appointment in Kingsmarkham and then she was going over to Myringham on the bus to her friend's house. The friend was having a twenty-first birthday party last evening and Melanie was going to it and afterwards to stay the night. They have their majority at eighteen, so what they do is have two parties, one for eighteen and one for twenty-one.'

Wexford had noticed. He was more interested in the suppressed terror he could detect in Akande's voice, a terror the doctor overlaid with a pathetic optimism. 'We didn't expect her home till this afternoon. If they don't have to they don't get up before noon. My wife was working and so was I. We expected to find her at home when we got in.'

'Could she have been in and gone out again?'

'I suppose she could. Of course she has her own key. But she was never at Laurel's – that's the friend. My wife phoned them. Melanie hadn't turned up. And yet I can't see that that's too much to worry about. She and Laurel had had a row . . . well, a disagreement. I heard Melanie say on the phone to her, I can remember her very words: "I'm going to ring off now and don't count on seeing me on Wednesday."'

'Has Melanie a boyfriend, doctor?'

326

'Not any longer. They broke up about two months ago.'

'But there might have been a . . . a reconciliation?'

'I suppose there might.' He sounded grudging. When he said it again he sounded hopeful. 'I suppose there might. You mean, she met him yesterday and they've gone off somewhere together? My wife wouldn't like that. She has rather strict ideas on these matters.'

Presumably, she'd prefer fornication to rape or murder, thought Wexford rather sourly but he didn't, of course, say this aloud. 'Dr Akande, you're probably right when you say this is nothing. Melanie is somewhere where she has no access to a phone. Will you give me a ring in the morning, please? As early as you like.' He hesitated. 'Well, after six. Whatever happens, whether she appears or phones or doesn't appear or phone?'

'I've got a feeling she's trying to get through to us now.'

'In that case let's not occupy the line any longer.'

His phone rang at five past six.

He wasn't asleep. He had just woken up. Perhaps he awoke because he was subconsciously troubled about the Akande girl. As he picked up the receiver, before Akande spoke, he was thinking, I shouldn't have waited, I should have done something last night.

'She hasn't come back and she hasn't phoned. My wife is very anxious.'

I expect you are too, Wexford thought. I would be. 'I'll come and see you. In half an hour.'

Sylvia had married almost as soon as she left school. There had been no time to worry about where she was or what was happening to her. But his younger daughter Sheila had caused him sleepless nights, nights of terror. Home in the holidays from drama school, she had made a speciality of disappearing with boyfriends, not phoning, giving no clue to her whereabouts until, three or four days later, she'd phone from Glasgow or Bristol or Amsterdam. And he had never got used to it. He would tell reassuring stories of his own experiences to the Akandes, he thought, as he showered and put his clothes on, but he would also report Melanie as a missing person. She was female, she was young, therefore they would mount a search for her.

Some days he walked to work, for his health's sake, but it was usually two hours later than this that he started off. This morning was hazy, everything was still, the sun a brighter whiteness in a white

327

sky. Dew lay on the roadside turf high summer had burnt straw colour. He didn't see a soul in the first two streets, then as he turned out of Mansfield Road, he met an old woman walking a minuscule Yorkshire terrier. No one else. Two cars passed him. A cat carrying a mouse in its mouth crossed the road from thirty-two Ollerton Avenue to twenty-five and dived through a flap in the front door.

Wexford didn't have to knock at twenty-seven. Dr Akande was already waiting for him on the step.

'It's very good of you.'

Resisting the temptation to say 'no problem' in one of Robin's polyglot versions, Wexford stepped ahead of him into the house. A nice, dull, ordinary sort of place to live in. He couldn't recall having been into any of the detached four-bedroomed houses of Ollerton Avenue before. The street itself was tree-lined, heavily tree-*shaded* at this time of the year. It would rob the interior of the Akande house of light until the sun came round and for a moment, until he was inside the room, he failed to see the woman who stood at the window, looking out.

The classic stance, the time-honoured position, of the parent or spouse or lover who waits and waits. *Sister Anne, sister Anne, do you see anyone coming? I see only the green grass and the yellow sand. . . .* She turned round and came towards him, a tall slender woman of about forty-five dressed in the uniform of a ward sister at Stowerton Royal Infirmary – short-sleeved navy blue dress, navy belt with a rather ornate silver buckle, two or three badges pinned at the left breast. Wexford hadn't expected someone so handsome, so striking to look at, such an elegant figure. *Why* hadn't he?

'Laurette Akande.'

She held out her hand. It was a long slender hand, the palm corn-coloured, the back deep coffee. She managed to smile. He thought, they always have these wonderful teeth, and then the blood rushed up into his face the way it hadn't done since he was a teenager. He *was* a racist. Why, from the instant he'd walked into this room he'd been thinking, how odd, it's just the same in here as in anyone else's house, same sort of furniture, same sweet peas in the same sort of vase. . . . He cleared his throat, spoke firmly.

'You're worried about your daughter, Mrs Akande?

'We both are. I think we've cause for worry, don't you? It's two days now.'

328

He noted she didn't say it was nothing, she wasn't saying it was just the way young people behaved.

'Sit down, please.'

Her manner was peremptory, a little offhand. She lacked her husband's *Englishness*, perhaps his bedside manner. This was no time, he thought, for tales of the adolescent Sheila's truancy. Laurette Akande spoke briskly, 'It's time we did this officially, I think: I mean, we have to report her missing. Aren't you too high up to take care of it?'

'I'll do for now,' Wexford said. 'Perhaps you'll give me some details. We'll start with the name and address of these people she was supposed to spend the night with. I'll have the boyfriend's name too. Oh, and what was this appointment she had in Kingsmarkham before she was due to leave for Myringham?'

'It was at the Job Centre,' said Dr Akande.

His wife corrected him with precision. 'The Employment Service Job Centre. The ESJ, as it's now called. Melanie was looking for a job.'

'She was trying to find work long before she finished her course,' said Laurette Akande. 'That was at Myringham. She graduated this summer.'

'The University of the South?' Wexford asked.

Her husband answered. 'No, Myringham University, the old Polytechnic that was. They're all universities now. She was studying music and dance, "Performance Arts", it's called. I never wanted her to do that. She got a good history A Level – why couldn't she have read history?'

Wexford thought he knew what the objection was to music and dance. 'They make such wonderful dancers', 'They have these great singing voices. . . .' How often had he heard those seemingly generous remarks?

Laurette said, 'You may or may not know that black Africans are the most highly educated members of British society. Statistics show that. In view of this, we have high expectations of our children, she should have been preparing herself for a profession.' She seemed suddenly to recollect that it wasn't Melanie's education or the lack of it that this crisis was about. 'Well, it doesn't matter now. There were no openings for her in what she wanted to do. Her father had told her there wouldn't be but they never listen. You'll have to retrain in

329

business management or something, I said to her. She went to the ESJ and picked up a form and got an appointment to see a New Claims Adviser there at two-thirty on Tuesday.'

'So when did she leave here?'

'My husband had his afternoon surgery. It was my day off. Melanie took an overnight bag with her. She said she expected to get to Laurel's by five and I remember I said, don't count on it, having that appointment at two-thirty doesn't mean she'll see you then, you could easily wait an hour. She left here at ten past two to give herself plenty of time. I know that because it's a fifteen-minute walk to the High Street from here.'

What an admirable witness Laurette Akande would make! Wexford found himself hoping she would never be called upon to be one. Her voice was cool and controlled. She wasted no words. Somewhere, under the accent of South East England, was a hint of the African country she had come from perhaps as a student.

'You had the impression she was going straight from the ESJ to this place in Myringham?'

'I *know* she was. By bus. She hoped to catch the four-fifteen, which was why I said that about having to wait to see the New Claims Adviser. She wanted to take my car but I had to say no. I needed it in the morning. I was due at the hospital by eight when the day shift starts.' She looked at her watch. 'I am today. The traffic at this hour makes a ten-minute journey into half an hour.'

So she was going to work? Wexford had waited for a sign of that anxiety Dr Akande had been so insistent his wife was prey to. There was none. Either she wasn't worried or she was under an iron control.

'Where do *you* think Melanie is, Mrs Akande?'

She gave a small light laugh, a rather chilling laugh. 'I very much hope she isn't where I think it most likely she is. In Euan's flat – room, rather – with him.'

'Melanie wouldn't do that to us, Letty.'

'She wouldn't see it as doing anything to *us*. She has never appreciated our concern for her security and her future. I said to her: Do you want to be one of those girls these boys get pregnant on purpose and are *proud* of it? Euan's already got two children with two different girls and he's not twenty-two yet. You know that, you remember when she told us about those children.'

They had forgotten Wexford was there. He coughed. Dr Akande said miserably.

'That's why she split up with him. She was just as shocked and upset as we were. She hasn't gone back to him, I'm sure of that.'

'Dr Akande,' said Wexford, 'I'd like you to come down to the police station with me and report Melanie missing. I think this is a serious matter. We have to search for your daughter and keep on searching till we find her.'

Alive or dead, but he didn't say that.

There was nothing Caucasian about the face in the photograph. Melanie Elizabeth Akande had a low forehead, a broad, rather flat nose, and full, thick, protuberant lips. Nothing of her mother's classical cast of feature showed in that face. Her father was an African from Nigeria, Wexford now discovered, her mother from Freetown in Sierra Leone. The eyes were huge, her thick black hair a mass of tight curls. Wexford, looking at the photograph, made a strange discovery. Though she was not beautiful to him, he could see that by the standards of others, of millions of African people, Afro-Caribbean people and African Americans, she might be considered very lovely. Why was it always the white people who set the standard?

The missing persons form, filled in by her father, described her as being five feet seven, hair black, eyes dark brown, and gave her age as twenty-two. He had to phone his wife at the hospital to be reminded that Melanie weighed nine stone two (or 128 pounds) and had been wearing blue denims, a white shirt and a long embroidered waistcoat when last seen.

'You also have a son, I think.'

'Yes, he's a medical student at Edinburgh.'

'He can't be there now. Not in July.'

'No, he's in South East Asia. So far as I know. He went off in a car about three weeks ago with two friends. They were making for Vietnam, but of course they can't be there yet . . .'

'At any rate, his sister couldn't have gone to him,' said Wexford. 'I have to ask you this, doctor. What sort of terms were you and your wife on with Melanie? Were there disagreements?'

'We were on good terms,' the doctor said quickly. He hesitated and then qualified that statement. 'My wife has strict ideas. No harm in that, of course, and there's no doubt we had high expectations for Melanie, which perhaps she couldn't fulfil.'

'Does she like living at home?'

'She really doesn't have much choice. I'm not in a position to provide accommodation for my children and I don't think Laurette would much care for . . . I mean Laurette expects Melanie to live at home until she . . .'

'Until what, doctor?'

'Well, take this idea of retraining. Laurette expects Melanie to live at home while she does that and perhaps not move away until she's earning enough and responsible enough to buy somewhere for herself.'

'I see.'

She was with the boyfriend, Wexford thought. She had met him, according to her father, when they both found themselves in their first term at what was then Myringham Polytechnic, before such institutions were elevated to university status. Euan Sinclair came from the East End of London, had graduated at the same time as Melanie, though by then the quarrel with its anger and insults had divided them. One of Euan's children, now nearly two, had been born when he and Melanie had been going out together for over a year.

Akande knew his present address. He spoke as if it was written in bitterness on his heart. 'We've tried to phone him but the number is unobtainable. That means it's been cut off for non-payment of his bill, doesn't it?'

'Probably.'

'That young man is a West Indian.' Snobbery raised its head in these areas as well, did it? 'An Afro-Caribbean, as we're supposed to call them. Her mother sees him as someone who could potentially wreck Melanie's life.'

It was Detective Sergeant Vine who went to London to seek Euan Sinclair in his rented room in a Stepney street. Akande had told him he wouldn't be surprised if Euan was living there with one of the mothers of his children and perhaps the child as well. This would make it very unlikely that Melanie was there too but Vine didn't say so. Myringham Police had undertaken to send an officer round to the home of Laurel Tucker.

'I shall look in at the ESJ myself,' Wexford said to Burden.

'The what?'

'The Employment Service and Jobcentre.'

'Then why isn't it the ESAJC?'

'Maybe it's really Employment-Service-Job-Centre, all one word. I'm afraid that those civil servants who remodel our language have made Jobcentre into one word as they have "jobsearch".'

For a moment Burden said nothing. He was trying to read, with increasing incredulity, a PR handout from a company guaranteeing to make private cars thief-proof.

'It shuts them up in a metal cage. After two minutes it stops and nothing will start it. Then it makes these blood-curdling howls. Imagine that on the M2 at five-thirty, the obstruction, the safety hazard . . .' Burden looked up. 'Why you?' he said. 'Archbold could do that or Pemberton.'

'I daresay they could,' said Wexford. 'They go there often enough when someone's assaulted an admin officer or started taking the place apart. I'm going because I want to see what it's like.'

# 3

It was going to be a fine day, if you could stand the humidity. The air was still, not so much misty as with a thick feel to it; You wanted to fill your lungs with fresh air but this *was* fresh air, all you were going to get. A hot sun was filtered through meshes of cloud behind which the sky must be a rich dark blue but which looked like a pale opal and was covered with an unmoving thready network of cirrus.

Fumes from traffic were trapped under the cloud ceiling and by the still air. Along the pavement Wexford found himself passing through areas where someone had stopped to talk while smoking. The smell that still hung there was of cigarettes, in one spot a French cigarette, in another a cigar. Though it was still early, not quite ten, a reek of stale seafood swung out from the fishmonger's. To pass a woman from whose skin came light floral scent or musky perfume was a pleasant relief. He paused to read the menu inside the window of the new Indian restaurant, the Nawab: Chicken Korma, Lamb Tikka, Chicken Tandoori, Prawn Biryani, Murghe Raja – all the usual stuff, but you might say that about roast beef and fish and chips. It all depended on the cooking. He and Burden could try it for lunch, when they had a moment. Otherwise, it would be take-away from the Moonflower Instant Cantonese Cuisine.

The Employment Service Jobcentre was this side of the Kingsbrook Bridge, a little way down Brook Road between the Marks and Spencers foodstore and the Nationwide Building Society. Not a particularly sensitive location, Wexford thought, considering this for the first time. The people who came to sign on would be made to wince at anything which reminded them of burdensome mortgages and repossessed houses and hardly cheered by the sight of shoppers coming out of the doors on the other side with carrier bags full of

334

food specialities they could no longer afford. Still, nobody who had a say in it had thought of that and perhaps the ESJ came there first. He couldn't remember.

A car park at the side – 'Strictly ESJ Staff Only' – had access into the High Street. Steps with chipped stone balustrades led up to double doors of aluminium and glass. Inside, the atmosphere smelt stale. It was hard to say what it smelt of, for Wexford could see two notices that forbade smoking ('Strictly Prohibited') and no one was disobeying. Nor was it the smell of bodies. If he were to be fanciful, and he decided he had better not be, he would have said it was the odour of hopelessness, of defeat.

The large room was divided into two sections; one area, the larger, was the Benefit Office, where you went to give proof of life, proximity and continuing unemployed status by signing on; the other offered jobs. On the face of it, an abundance of jobs. One free standing notice board advertised receptionists, another housekeepers and catering, a third shops, managerial, drivers, bar staff and miscellaneous. A closer look showed him that in all cases only the experienced need apply – references were required, CVs, qualifications, skills – yet it was obvious that only the young were wanted. None of the cards actually said, 'Up to age 30', but energy was stressed as a requirement, or a vigorous and youthful outlook.

People sat about on three rows of chairs. All must have been under sixty-five but the older ones looked more. The young ones looked particularly hopeless. The chairs they sat on were a neutral shade of grey and now he noticed there was a colour scheme here, a rather unfortunate combination of a buttery-cream shade, navy blue and this grey. At the end of each row of chairs, on the mottled carpet, stood a plastic houseplant in a plastic Grecian urn. Several doors at the side were marked 'Private' and one, that seemed to lead to the car park, 'Strictly Private'. They had a passion for strictness in here.

Apparently, when you arrived you took a card with a number on it from a kind of ticket machine. When your number and the number of one of the desks came up in red neon you went up and signed your claim. That was the way it looked, a bit like the doctor's. Wexford hesitated between the 'Jobseekers' counter (another new composite word) and the numbered desks. At each one of these someone stood or sat, discussing complications of his or her claim with a staff member. The grey and navy badge the one nearest to him wore on her blouse proclaimed her as Ms I. Pamber, Admin Officer.

The next desk was temporarily free. Wexford went up to Ms W. Stowlap, Admin Officer, and asked politely if he could see someone in authority. She glanced up, said gruffly, 'You have to wait your turn. Don't you know you're supposed to take a card from the machine?'

'This is the only card I have.' She had riled him. It was his warrant card he produced as he snapped, 'Police.'

She was a thin freckled woman with white eyebrows and blushing didn't become her. The pink tide spread to the roots of her pale ginger hair. 'Sorry,' she said. 'You'll want the manager – Mr Leyton, that is.'

While she was away finding him Wexford wondered what the reason could be for all this formality, the 'Ms' and 'Mr' stuff, the initials instead of Christian names. It seemed out of tune with contemporary attitudes. Not that he minded that, recalling the way Ben and Robin called everyone by first names, even Dr Crocker, nearly sixty years their senior.

Discreetly, not staring, he surveyed the people who waited. Quite a lot of women, at least half. Before his wife laid into him, calling him a sexist, a chauvinist and antediluvian as well, Mike Burden had been in the habit of saying that if all these married women didn't take the jobs the unemployment figures would be halved. A black man, someone vaguely South East Asian, two or three Indians – Kingsmarkham was becoming more cosmopolitan daily. Then, in the back row, he spotted the fat young woman who had been in the waiting room at the medical centre. Wearing red and green floral leggings and a tight white tee-shirt, she slumped in her chair with her legs apart, gazing at the poster which, under a drawing of a gaily coloured gas balloon, advertised the 'Jobplan Workshop' and advised candidates for it to 'give your jobhunting a lift'.

It was with unseeing eyes, Wexford thought, that she gazed. She looked as if sledgehammered into apathy, without thoughts, without even resentment, in utter despair. Today Kelly wasn't with her, the little girl who had run along the chairs and torn up magazines. Left with a mother or a neighbour probably, not, he hoped, in one of those toddler farms, where they strapped the infants into pushchairs in front of videos of rampaging monsters. Better that, though, than left alone. Next to her, in fact two empty seats away, a trim handsome girl provided a cruel contrast. Middle-classness stamped her, from her long corn-coloured hair, shining clean and cut as

336

evenly as a curtain hem, her white shirt and blue denim skirt to the brown loafers she wore. Another Melanie Akande, Wexford thought, a new graduate who had found a degree doesn't automatically confer a job . . .

'Can I help you?'

He turned round. The man was about forty, red-faced, black-haired, with big features, the kind who looks as if his blood pressure would be high. To his grey tweed sports jacket was pinned the badge with his name and status: Mr C. Leyton, Manager. He had a harsh grating voice, an accent from somewhere north of the Trent.

'Do you want to go somewhere private?'

Leyton asked the question as if expecting the answer 'no' or 'no, don't bother'.

'Yes,' said Wexford.

'What's all this about then?' He asked it over his shoulder as he led Wexford past the counter and the New Claims booths.

'It can wait till we're in your somewhere private.'

Leyton shrugged. The heavy-set bullet-headed man who stood outside the door moved off as they approached. The Benefit Office was more in need of a security guard than most banks and it was the regular haunt of members of the uniformed branch. Desperation, paranoia and indignation, resentment, fear and humiliation all breed violence. Most people who came here were either angry or afraid.

Rather late in the day the manager said, 'I'm Cyril Leyton.' He closed the door behind them. 'What's the trouble?'

'I hope there won't be any. I want you to tell me if a certain . . . er, claimant came here on Tuesday to see one of your New Claims Advisers. Tuesday, July the sixth at two-thirty.'

Leyton curled his lip and put up his eyebrows. His expression would have been appropriate for the Head of MI5 when asked by some minion, a cleaner or driver perhaps, for access to top secret papers.

'I don't want documentation,' said Wexford impatiently. 'I only want to know if she came here. And I'd like to talk to the New Claims Adviser she saw.'

'Well, I . . .'

'Mr Leyton, this is a police investigation. I suppose you know I could get a warrant in a couple of hours. Is there any point in delaying things?'

'What's her name?'

337

'Melanie Akande. A, K, A, N, D, E.'

'If she came on Tuesday,' said Leyton grudgingly, 'it should be on the computer by now. Just wait a minute, will you?'

His manner was unfortunate, cold, sour, rebarbative. Wexford guessed that the greatest pleasure he got out of life was derived from putting spokes in wheels. What effect must he have on claimants? Perhaps he never saw them, perhaps he was too 'high up' (as Laurette Akande put it) for that.

The room was all grey, lined with filing cabinets. There was a grey chair like those the claimants sat on, a small grey metal desk and on it a grey telephone. The view from the window seemed a riot of colour, though it was only of the shoppers' pickup bay at the back of Marks and Spencers. Cyril Leyton came in, holding a millboard with papers attached to it by an elastic band.

'Your Miss Akande came in for her appointment at two-thirty and brought back her ES 461. That's the form required by . . .'

'I know what it is,' Wexford said.

'Right. The NCA she saw – that is, New Claims Adviser – was Miss Bystock, but you can't talk to her, she's off sick.' Leyton unbent an inch. 'One of these viruses.'

'If she's off sick how do you know it was Miss Bystock Melanie Akande saw and not Mr Stanton?'

'Come on. Her initials are on the claim. See?'

Ostentatiously covering up everything but the bottom right hand corner of the sheet, Leyton showed Wexford the pencilled initials: A.B.

'Did anyone else see her? Any of the other NCAs? The administration officers?'

'Not that I know of. Why would they?'

Wexford said suddenly, with extreme sharpness, 'Don't ask me. It doesn't help to be obstructive.'

Leyton's mouth opened but no sound came.

'Mr Leyton, it is an offence to obstruct the police in their duties. Did you know that? Melanie Akande is missing from home. She hasn't been seen since she left this building. This is a very serious matter. I suppose you read the newspapers? You watch television? You know what happens in the world we live in? Have you some reason for jeopardizing this enquiry?'

The man went a darker red. He said slowly, 'I didn't know. I'd have been . . . well, I had no idea.'

338

'You mean that what I've been treated to is your normal manner?'

Leyton said nothing. Then he seemed to take hold of himself. 'I'm sorry. I'm under a lot of pressure here. Has ... has something happened to her? This woman?'

'That's what I'm trying to find out.' Wexford showed him the photograph. 'Will you ask your staff, please?'

This time he waited outside that stuffy grey room. He thought of the hymn line: 'Frail children of dust ...'. That room was like a cell spun and carved out of dust. He read the other posters, the one advocating work trials, whatever they were, and the one that asked employers: 'Do you always choose the right person to fill your vacancy?' He decided to fill his own vacancy by reading one of the leaflets which lay about.

It was curiously apposite. 'Be alert', it said. 'Be safe when jobseeking.' Inside he read, 'DO – tell a friend or relative where you are going and what time you expect to be back ... arrange to be collected from the interview if it takes place outside working hours ... find out as much as you can about the company before the interview, especially if there are no details in the job advert ... make sure that the interview takes place at the employer's premises or, if not, in a public place. DON'T – apply for a job which seems to offer too much money for very little work ... agree to continue the interview over drinks or a meal, even if it seems to be going very well ... let the interviewer steer the conversation towards personal subjects that have nothing to do with the job ... accept a lift home from the interviewer. ...'

Melanie hadn't been offered a job, she hadn't been sent for an interview – or had she? Cyril Leyton came back with the admin officer labelled Ms I. Pamber, a dark-haired pretty girl with dazzling blue eyes, in her late twenties, wearing a grey skirt and pink shirt. None of the staff wore jeans, Wexford had noticed, everyone was dressed in a neat, rather outdated, way.

'I saw her, this girl you're looking for.'

Wexford nodded. 'Did you speak to her?'

'Oh, no. I'd no call to. I was on the counter. I just saw her go up and talk to Annette ... er, Miss Bystock.'

'Can you remember what time that was?'

'Well, her appointment was for two-thirty and no one's allowed more than twenty minutes. I suppose it must have been twenty to three, something like that.'

339

'If she was able to see Miss Bystock on time. Was she? Or did she have to wait half an hour?'

'No, she couldn't have done. A Claims Adviser's last appointment is at three-thirty, and I know Annette had three to see after her.'

So Laurette Akande had been wrong about that. He asked Leyton for Annette Bystock's address. While the manager was away finding it, he said, 'Did you see her leave the building? Go out through those doors?'

'I just saw her talking to Annette.'

'Thank you for your help, Miss Pamber. By the way, tell me something, in these days of universal first names, why do you all have Ms or Mr and your surname and an initial on your name tags? It seems very formal.'

'Oh, it's not that,' she said. She had a charming manner, he thought, warm and just a touch flirtatious. 'Actually, I'm Ingrid. No one calls me Ms Pamber, not anyone. But they say it's for our protection.'

She looked up at him through long dark eyelashes. Her eyes were the bluest he had ever seen, the blue of a gentian or a Delft plate or a star sapphire.

'I don't follow.'

'Well, most clients are OK, I mean they're nice, most of them. But you do get some nuts – crazy people, you know? I mean, we had someone in here threw acid at Cyril – Mr Leyton, that is. He didn't hit him but he had a go. Don't you remember?'

Vaguely, Wexford did, though he'd been on leave at the time.

'Hopefully, there's very few that would do that. But if we had our full names on our tags, like "Ingrid Pamber", say, they could look us up in the phone book and . . . well, you might get someone who thought he was in love with you or someone – and that's more likely – who hated you. You know, we've got jobs and they haven't, that's what it's about.'

Wexford wondered how many 'I. Pambers' there were in the Kingsmarkham and District telephone directory and guessed at just one. Still, as a safety measure keeping first names a secret was wise. The thought came to him that quite a lot of people might fancy themselves in love with Ingrid Pamber.

Another poster caught his eye, this one warning those seeking jobs not to pay anyone money for finding them work. The system seemed open to many abuses.

With Annette Bystock's address in his pocket, he went out and down the steps. In the half-hour since he had gone in there several young men had arrived to seat themselves on the stone balustrades, two of them smoking, the others staring vacantly at nothing. They took no notice of him. Lying on the pavement where someone, perhaps one of them, had discarded it, was an ES 461, the highly coloured questionnaire form. It was open at page three and when Wexford bent to pick it up he saw that the egregious question four: 'If you have not worked for the past twelve months, how have you spent your time?' had been answered. Carefully printed in the allotted space was the single word, 'Wanking'.

That made him laugh. He began trying to retrace what might have been Melanie Akande's footsteps on leaving the ESJ. According to Ingrid Pamber, she would have been in plenty of time for the three-fifteen bus to Myringham, no more than five minutes' walk away.

Wexford timed himself to the nearest bus stop. These periods of time were nearly always shorter than you anticipated and he found it took him, not five minutes, but three. However, there was no earlier bus she could have caught. He studied the timetable in its frame, somewhat vandalized, with a diagonal crack across the glass, but still readable. The buses went once an hour, on the first quarter. She would have had to wait at least twenty minutes.

It was during that sort of enforced waiting, he thought, that women accepted lifts. Would she have done that? He must ask the parents if she ever, for instance, hitched lifts. Wait, though, until Vine's report came in and there was some information from the Myringham end. Meanwhile, had anyone in the neighbourhood of this bus stop seen anything?

In the dry cleaners he drew a blank. You couldn't see the street from the interior of the wine shop. Its windows were too densely stacked with bottles and cans. He went into Grover's the newsagent. They were his newsagents, the shop that supplied his daily paper and had done for years. As soon as she saw him the woman behind the counter began apologizing for the recent late deliveries. Wexford cut her short, said he hadn't noticed, and anyway he didn't expect some schoolboy or schoolgirl to get up at the crack of dawn to bring his *Independent* by seven-thirty. He showed her the photograph.

Melanie Akande's being black was to their advantage. In a place where there were very few black people, she was known, remembered, even by those who had never spoken to her. Dinny Lawson, the newsagent, knew her by sight but, as far as she knew, Melanie had never been into the shop. As to bus queues, she sometimes noticed them and she sometimes didn't. It was Tuesday afternoon Wexford was talking about? One thing she could tell him was that no one, black or white, got on the three-fifteen to Myringham bus, no one at all.

'How can you be so sure?'

'I'll tell you. My husband said to me, it must have been Saturday or Sunday, he said it was a wonder they went on running that bus in the afternoons on account of no one went on it. Mornings, yes, specially the eight-fifteen and the nine-fifteen, and the ones that come back in the evening, they're busy. So I said, I'll keep an eye open and see. Well, we've kept the shop door open all day this week, it's been so hot, and I could see without even going to the door. And he was right, it's a fact, no one's got on the two-fifteen, the three-fifteen or the four-fifteen Monday, Tuesday or yesterday. My husband said to have five pounds on it and was I glad I didn't take him up on that . . .'

So she had disappeared somewhere between the Benefit Office and the bus stop. No, 'disappeared' was too strong a word – yet. No matter what she told her parents, perhaps she had never intended to take that bus. Perhaps she had arranged to meet someone as soon as her appointment with the New Claims Adviser was over.

In that case, was there a chance she had mentioned this to Annette Bystock? For all he knew, Annette Bystock might be one of those warm friendly people whose effect on others is to invite confidences, and confidences which have no apparent connection with the matter in hand. It was quite possible Annette had asked her if she'd be available for an interview that day and Melanie had said no, she was going to meet her boyfriend. . . .

Or there had been no meeting with a boyfriend, no confidences, nothing to confide, and Melanie had accepted a lift to Myringham from a stranger. After all, Dinny Lawson hadn't said there had been no one in the vicinity of the bus stop all afternoon, only that she had seen nobody get on the bus when it came.

Dora Wexford had got into the habit of preparing large quantities of quite elaborate food for her daughter and her daughter's family when they came to meals. Her husband had pointed out to her that though Neil and Sylvia were unemployed, they weren't poverty-stricken, they weren't on the breadline, but this had little effect. He came home that evening just in time to share in the servings of carrot and orange soup before a main course of braised lambs' kidneys, spinach and ricotta cheese in filo pastry, new potatoes and french beans. Dessert spoons on the table indicated the arrival later of that rarity, that luxury that never happened when the two of them were alone, a pudding.

Pale weedy Neil ate hugely, as if for comfort. As Wexford joined them and sat down, he was describing to his mother-in-law his abortive visit to the Benefit Office. No payments could be made to him because, before losing his work, he had been self-employed.

'What difference does that make?' Wexford asked.

'Oh,' he explained quite carefully. 'As a self-employed person I didn't pay Class One National Insurance contributions during the two tax years prior to the tax year in which I'm making my claim.'

'But you paid them?'

'Oh, I paid them but in another class. He explained that too.'

'Who was it?' Wexford said. 'Ms Bystock or Mr Stanton?'

Neil goggled at him. 'How do *you* know?'

Enigmatically, 'I have my reasons.' Wexford relented. 'I was there today about something else.'

'It was Stanton,' Neil said.

Wexford wondered suddenly why Sylvia was looking so smug. Anxious not to put on weight, she had eaten the kidneys, refused the pastry and had now laid her knife and fork precisely down diagonally across her plate. A little smile lifted the corners of her mouth. One after the other, Ben and Robin asked for more potatoes.

'You promise to eat every bit then.'

'*Problem yok*,' said Robin.

'So what are you going to do? They must do something for you.'

'Sylvia has to claim, if you can believe it. She was only part-time but she got in just enough hours to claim, so she's doing it for herself and me and the boys.'

Having told Ben to chew his food properly and not swallow in lumps, Sylvia said with undisguised triumph, 'I sign on every other Tuesday. It's A to K on Tuesdays, L to R on Wednesdays and S to Z on Thurdays. I get benefit for all of us. *And* they'll pay the mortgage. Neil hates me doing it, don't you, Neil? He'd rather I went out cleaning.'

'That isn't true.'

'It is true. I won't pretend I don't enjoy it because I do. How d'you think I feel after years of my husband telling me first that I wasn't capable of earning and then when I was that what I earned wasn't worth the trouble of working, it'd all go in tax.'

'I never said any of that.'

'It feels *great*,' Sylvia said, ignoring him. 'The whole lot of them depend on *me* now. All the money, quite a lot of it, will be paid to me personally. So much for sexism, so much for chauvinism . . .'

'They won't pay the mortgage,' Neil interrupted her. 'Almost everything you say is wildly inaccurate. They'll pay the *interest* on the mortgage and they're putting a ceiling on the amount of mortgage they'll pay up to. We shall put the house on the market.'

'We shall not.'

'Of course we shall. We have no option. We shall sell it and buy a semi in Mansfield Road – if we're lucky. That looks like Eve's pudding, Dora, one of my favourites. You don't improve the situation Sylvia, by telling a pack of lies as a vindication of the rights of women.'

Ben said, 'You know men have Adam's apples, don't you?'

Silently blessing him for the distraction, Wexford said yes, he did know, he supposed everyone knew.

'Yes, well, d'you know why they're called that? I bet you don't. It's because when the snake gave Eve the apple she could swallow it all right but a lump of it stuck in Adam's throat and that's why men have got that bit sticking out . . . '

'If that story isn't rank sexism, I don't know what is. Are you ever going to eat up those potatoes, Robin?'

'*No pasa nada.*'

'I don't know what that means,' said Sylvia crossly.

'Come on, Mum. Can't you guess?'

Refusing pudding and coffee, Wexford went out into the hall to phone Detective Sergeant Vine.

It had taken Barry Vine a long time to find Euan Sinclair. He had only just got back from London. After he had eaten he was going to write his report. It would be on Wexford's desk by nine in the morning.

'Give me a résumé now,' said Wexford.

'I didn't find the girl.'

Vine had gone first to the address provided by Dr Akande. It was a

fairly large Victorian house in the East End of London, occupied by
three generations of the Sinclair and Lafay families. An old
grandmother, though domiciled there for thirty years, spoke only a
version of the patois. Three of her daughters also lived in the house
and four of their children, though not Euan. He had moved out some
three months before.

Deeply distrustful of the police, the women spoke to him with a
kind of laconic suspicion. Euan's mother Claudine who occupied the
ground floor with her partner and father of her two younger
children, a man called Samuel Lafay, the brother incidentally of the
elder sister's ex-husband . . .

'Oh, get on with it,' Wexford said.

It was clear that Vine was expounding with relish on the
complexities of this intricate family. He seemed to have enjoyed his
day. After asking rhetorically why she should tell him anything about
her son who was a good, clean-living and honourable man, an
intellectual, Claudine Sinclair or Lafay had sent him to a council flat
in Whitechapel. This turned out to be the home of a girl called Joan-
Anne, mother of Euan Sinclair's daughter. Joan-Anne never wanted
to see Euan again, if he came into a million she wouldn't accept a
penny of it in child-support for Tasha, if he went on his knees to her
she wouldn't, she had a good man now who had never been without
so much as a day's work in his life. She gave Vine an address in
Shadwell, home of Sheena ('poor cow, lets him walk all over her')
who was the mother of Euan's son.

Euan had gone to sign on, Sheena told him. Thursday was his day.
After signing on he usually went for a drink with some friends, but
he'd turn up sometime, she couldn't really say when. No, Vine
couldn't wait for him, she couldn't have that. The idea made her
nervous, Vine could see, probably on account of the neighbours. The
neighbours would have identified him in the mysterious way some
people can always spot a policeman and they'd make a note of how
many hours Vine spent in Sheena's flat. All this time Euan's son was
screaming his head off in the next room. Sheena went to attend to
him and came back with a handsome angry boy who already looked
too big for his diminutive mother to carry.

'Oh, stop your noise, Scott, stop your noise,' she said ineffectually,
over and over. Scott roared at her and roared at the visitor. Vine left
and went back at four.

Sheena and her son were still alone. Scott was still intermittently roaring. No, Euan hadn't been back. Phone her? What did he mean, phone her? Why would he? Vine gave up. Sheena gave Scott a bag of salt and vinegar crisps and stuck him in front of a video of what appeared to be *Miami Vice*. When he was quiet, Vine asked her about Melanie Akande but it was plain Sheena had never heard of her. While Vine probed a bit, Euan Sinclair came in.

Tall, handsome, very thin, Euan had the sort of looks that reminded Vine of Linford Christie. His hair was very short, a week's growth, Vine guessed, after a total shave. He walked with the peculiar grace of the young black man, all movement from the hips, the torso erect and still. But it was his voice that surprised Vine. Not Creole English, one generation removed, not East End Cockney, not Estuary but nearer Public School.

Wexford said, half-joking, half-serious, 'So you're a snob as well as a racist, Barry.'

Vine didn't deny it. He said he'd had the impression Euan Sinclair had taught himself to talk like that for some unknown reasons of policy. It suddenly struck him – for the first time – that Euan might deny knowledge of Melanie in Sheena's presence.

'That would have been the first thing I'd have thought of,' said Wexford.

'He didn't, though. That was the funny thing. I could see it was all news to her and she didn't like it. He couldn't have cared less.'

He'd seen Melanie the previous week. At the Myringham graduation ceremonies. They had a talk and she agreed to meet him the following Tuesday in Myringham. By this time Sheena was staring at him with a kind of horror. Melanie was going to Laurel Tucker's party, Euan said, and he could come too.

Vine asked where they were meeting and Euan named a pub in Myringham. At around four. The Wig and Ribbon in the High Street opened from 11.00 am till 11.00 pm. She hadn't turned up, though Euan waited till five-thirty. At this point he saw a man he knew, another alumnus of Myringham University. The two of them got together, went to another pub and then another, and Euan spent the night sleeping on the floor in this man's room.

Sheena could contain herself no longer. 'You told me you were at your grandma's.'

He said to her, in the sort of voice a man uses to say it's raining, 'I lied.'

Sheena stalked to the door. Just before it closed behind her Euan called out, 'You'd better not leave me alone with him. I'm no baby-minder. That's women's work, right?'

'I'll check it out with this bloke he says he met,' said Vine, 'but I believe him. He gave me the fellow's name and address without turning a hair.'

'It looks as if Melanie never reached Myringham,' Wexford said. 'Something happened to deflect her in Kingsmarkham High Street. Somewhere on about two hundred yards of pavement. We have to find out what it was.'

# 4

The Tucker Family, Laurel and Glenda Tucker, their father and stepmother, had little that was new to offer. They were plainly unwilling 'to get mixed up in anything'. It was true that Laurel had expected Melanie on the late afternoon of 6 July and had been displeased when it was clear she wasn't coming. But she hadn't been all that *surprised*. After all, they had quarrelled.

The detective sergeant from Myringham who had been asking the questions said, 'What was that about then?'

Laurel had been at the graduation ceremony, witnessed the meeting between Melanie and Euan Sinclair and seen the two of them go off together. Melanie phoned her next day, said she was thinking of getting back with Euan, he was lonely, there had been no one in his life since they split up, and she'd told him she'd bring him to Laurel's party on Tuesday. I don't want him, Laurel said, I don't like him, I never did. I'm not surprised he hasn't been seeing anyone else – who'd want him? Melanie said if Euan couldn't come to the party she wasn't coming either, and they had a row.

'She did tell her parents she was going to this party,' Burden said to Wexford. 'She was going to the Tucker house first and then on to this party.'

'Well, she wouldn't tell them she had a date with this Euan, would she? They can't stand him, haven't got a good word to say for him. Mother's something of a formidable woman, I'd almost say she'd be capable of locking a daughter up. By this time Melanie had obviously decided she wasn't going to the party. She was going to stick to what she'd said and not go if Euan wasn't also welcome. She was going to meet Euan in the Wig and Ribbon and there's not much doubt she meant to stay with him, spend the night with him.'

348

'Yes, but where? Not at this Sheena's place. People that age don't hire hotel rooms, do they?'

Wexford laughed. 'Not if they're living on the IS they don't.'

'The what?'

'Income Support. If Melanie thought about that aspect at all I expect she thought they'd go to Euan's mother's place in Bow. She'd very likely been there before. And next day she'd come home.'

'Amazing, isn't it?' said Burden, looking down his nose. 'They've got no jobs, they're living on what-d'you-call-it, IS, and they still splash out on drinks and dates with girls and God knows what for train fares.'

'It doesn't matter much, Mike, because we know she didn't go to London. She didn't even go to Myringham. She didn't meet Euan because Euan –' Wexford had another look at Vine's latest report '– spent the evening with someone called John Varcava in the Wig and Ribbon, the Wild Goose and Silk's Club before returning to Varcava's rented room in Myringham at three in the morning. It's all confirmed by a barman, a barmaid, the manager of Silk's and Varcava's landlady, who nearly came to blows with Varcava and Euan Sinclair over the mayhem they were making in her house in the small hours.'

'So what happened to Melanie in those few minutes after she left the unemployment place? The last person she saw, according to you, was this Annette Bystock, the New Claims Adviser. Is there any point in talking to her?'

'She was off sick,' said Wexford. 'She may be back at work by now, though people don't usually go back on a Friday, they take the whole week. But what are we saying, Mike? That Melanie Akande confided the details of some secret appointment to a complete stranger? A woman she'd talked to for fifteen minutes and talked to surely only about filling in a form and job prospects? Come to that, what secret appointment? She'd already got one of those with Euan. Now she's having another with some other chap just an hour before she meets Euan?'

Burden shrugged. 'Well, you said all that. I didn't. My imagination hasn't travelled that far. All I'm saying is, we ought to talk to Annette Bystock, solely on the grounds that she was the last person to see Melanie. . . .' He hesitated.

'You were going to say "alive", weren't you?'

*

349

There but for the grace of God go I, was not a reflection Michael Burden was ever likely to quote. He neither said it to himself when he saw famine victims on television, nor if he passed the half dozen or so homeless who slept on the street in Myringham. He didn't say it now, entering the Benefit Office and contemplating the jobless who sat about waiting on the grey chairs.

That he wasn't among them had nothing to do with God's grace in his opinion, and everything to do with his own industry, determination and hard work. He was one of those who ask the unemployed why they don't get a job and the homeless why they don't find a place to live. If he had been in Paris in the 1780s he would have told the starving who begged for bread to eat cake. Now, wearing his immaculate beige trousers and new jacket of beige linen with a navy fleck – one thing, as Wexford sometimes said, no one would have taken him for a policeman – he contemplated the unemployed and reflected on what a hideous garment the shellsuit was. Marginally worse than the track-suit. It had never occurred to him that these clothes are cheap, warm in cold weather and cool in hot, easy to wash, resistant to creases and very comfortable, and he didn't consider the matter now. He turned his attention to the administrative assistants behind their desks, deciding which one he should approach.

Jenny Burden said of her husband that if he had a choice, he would always enquire of a man rather than a woman, ask a man the way somewhere, go up to a male assistant in a shop, take the seat in a train next to a man. He hadn't liked that, he said it made him sound homosexual, but that wasn't what she meant at all. In the Benefit Office he had a choice, for behind the desks sat a man and three women. The man, however, had a brown skin and wore a label with the name Mr O. Messaoud. Burden, who hotly denied that he was a racist in any degree, nevertheless rejected Osman Messaoud on the grounds (of which he was only subliminally aware) of his skin colour and his name, and went up to freckled, ginger-haired Wendy Stowlap. She happened to be briefly free and this was the reason Burden would have given for choosing her.

'Is it about that girl who's missing?' she asked after he had enquired for Annette Bystock.

'Just routine enquiries,' said Burden blandly. 'Is Miss Bystock back yet?'

'She's still off sick.'

He turned away, almost colliding with Wendy Stowlap's next client, a big heavy woman in a red shellsuit. She smelt powerfully of cigarettes. They can always afford to smoke, Burden said to himself. Two of the boys sitting on the stone balustrade were also smoking, their feet dabbling in a litter of ash and cigarette ends. Burden gave them a long severe look, drawing his brows together. His eyes lingered particularly on the black boy with the Rastafarian hair, a mountainous crest of matted dreadlocks, on top of which rested a woolly cap, knitted in concentric circles of colour. It was the sort of hat he called a tam-o'-shanter, as his father would have done and his grandfather before him.

The boys took absolutely no notice of him. It was as if his body was transparent and their eyes penetrated it to the stonework behind him, the pavement, the corner where Brook Road turned into the High Street. They made him feel invisible. With an angry shrug he went back to the car he had parked in the 'strictly private' area for ESJ staff only.

The address Wexford had given him was in south Kingsmarkham. It was formerly one of the best parts of the town where, in the late nineteenth century, the most prosperous of its citizens had built themselves large houses, each standing in an acre or two of garden. Most of them were still there but partitioned now, and their gardens 'infilled' with new houses and rows of garages. Ladyhall Gardens had come in for this treatment, but the Victorian relics were smaller and each one divided into two or three flats.

Someone had pretentiously named number fifteen Ladyhall Court. It was a gabled house on two floors, built of the 'white' brick which was the fashionable building material here in the 1890s. A screen of copper sycamores hid much of the ground floor from the road. Burden guessed there were two flats on each floor, the two at the rear accessible from a side door. Above the bell for the upper floor a card read: John and Edwina Harris, and above the bell for the lower flat: Ms A. Bystock.

When there was no answer from Flat One, he rang the Harrises' bell. No answer there either. The front door had a lock at the top, a lock in the middle, and a brass knob, now tarnished black. On the off chance Burden tried the handle and to his surprise – and disapproval – it came open.

He found himself in a hallway with plaster scrollwork on the ceiling and uncompromisingly modern vinyl tiles on the floor. The staircase had an iron balustrade and grey marble steps. There was only one door, dark green with the figure 1 painted on it in white. The knocker was brass and so was the knob, but polished brass, and the bellpush bright as gold.

Burden rang the bell, waited. She might be in bed. If she was ill she might well be. He listened for sounds of movement, for footsteps or the creak of a floorboard. He rang the bell again. The little knocker was almost useless, it made a frenzied clack-clack, like a child trying to make its small voice heard.

Probably she was simply not answering the bell. If he was ill in bed, alone in the house, and some unexpected caller rang the bell he wouldn't answer it. There might be someone looking after her, of course, some neighbour perhaps, and that person would have a key.

He knelt down and looked through the letter box. Inside it seemed quite dark, darker than in the corridor. Gradually, through the small open rectangle, he made out a shadowy hallway with red fitted carpet, a small console table, dried flowers in a little gilded basket.

He stood up, rang the bell again, banged on the baby knocker, squatted down and called her name through the aperture: 'Miss Bystock!' and, louder, 'Miss Bystock! Are you at home?'

For one last time he called her name and then he went out of the house and round the side, pushing aside the sycamore branches with their leathery leaves that made everything so dark. This little window would be the kitchen, this one the bathroom. No sycamores here, only waist-high golden rod on either side of a concrete drive. Behind the last window by the side door the curtains were closed. For some reason he looked behind him, the way we do when we think we are being watched. On the opposite side of the street, in a 1900-ish house with a short front garden, someone was looking at him from an upstairs window. A face that looked as old as the house, crinkled, frowning, glaring.

Burden turned back to the window. He thought the drawn curtains a bit strange. How ill was she? Ill enough to need a darkened room to sleep in mid-morning? The thought came to him that perhaps she wasn't ill at all, that she was skiving off work and had gone out somewhere.

He wouldn't have been surprised if the old watcher at the window had come downstairs and crossed the road and tapped him on the shoulder. In the expectation of this he turned round once more. But the face was still there, its expression unchanged, and it was perfectly

352

still, so much so that for a moment Burden asked himself if this was a real person or some sort of facsimile, a wooden cutout of a glaring and evil-countenanced observer, placed there by the occupier as some people keep a painted chipboard cat in their gardens to frighten real ones.

But this was nonsense. He squatted down and tried to see between the curtains but the gap was infinitesimal, the merest line. In defiance of what the watcher over the way might think or do, he knelt down on the concrete paving and tried to look under the hem of the curtains. Here was a gap of perhaps half an inch between curtain hem and lower window frame.

It was dim in there. He couldn't see much. At first he could see scarcely anything. Then, as his eyes grew accustomed to the subfusc interior of the room, he made out the edge of a table, possibly a dressing table, the polished wooden foot of something on blue carpet, a segment of flowered material touching the floor. And a-hand. A hand, which hung down against those printed lilies and roses, a white immobile hand, the fingers extended.

It must be made of china, of plaster, of plastic. It couldn't be real. Or it could be real and she asleep. What sort of sleep was maintained through all that shouting? Almost involuntarily, forgetting possible watchers, he drummed on the glass with his knuckles. The hand didn't move. The hand's owner didn't leap up with a cry.

Burden ran back into the house. Why had he never learned how to pick a lock? Opening this one would be child's play to a lot of men and women he encountered in a day's work. Doors in the movies cave in with ease at the pressure of a shoulder. It always made him laugh angrily when he saw actors on television run up against stout doors and send them crashing in at one shove. It was so silent too, the way they did it. He knew his own efforts would be noisy and very likely bring the neighbours. But it couldn't be helped.

He ran up against the door, applying his shoulder. It juddered and creaked but his action hurt him more than it hurt the door. He rubbed his shoulder, took a deep breath, and hurled himself at it – once and again and once more. This time he kicked it, more of a punch with his foot, and the door groaned. Another foot-punch – he hadn't kicked like that since on the soccer field at school – and the door split and flew open. He stepped over the broken wood and paused to get his breath.

The hallway was tiny. It turned the corner and became a passage.

All five doors were shut. Burden went down it, guessed at the bedroom door, opened it and found a broom cupboard. Next to it must be the bedroom, its door not quite closed, half an inch ajar. First taking a deep breath, he pushed it open.

She lay as if asleep, her head on the pillow, her face turned into it and hidden by a mass of dark curly hair. One shoulder was bare, the other and the rest of her body covered by the bedclothes and the flowered quilt. From the naked shoulder extended her rather plump white arm with the hand he had seen, trailing almost to the floor.

He touched nothing, not the curtains, not the bedclothes, not that buried head, nothing but the hanging hand. One finger he put out to feel it, the back of it above the knuckles. It was stiffening as if frozen and as cold as ice.

# 5

They filled the place, it was so small; the pathologist, the photographers, the scene-of-crime officers, everyone indispensable, each with a specific task. Once the windows had been photographed and the curtains drawn back it was better, and when the body was taken away most of them went with it. Wexford lifted the lower sash in the bay and watched the van bearing Annette Bystock's remains disappear in the direction of the mortuary.

There would have to be formal identification but he had identified her from the passport he found in a dressing table drawer. The passport was a newish one, in the dark red and gold binding of the European Union, issued just over twelve months before. It gave the holder's name as Bystock, Annette Mary, her status as a British Citizen and her date of birth, 22.11.54. The photograph was plainly of the dead woman, clearly identifiable, in spite of the effects on her face of strangulation, the swelling, the cyanosis, the tongue protruding between the teeth. Her eyes were the same. She had stared into the camera with almost the same degree of horrified apprehension as she had looked into her killer's face.

They were round dark eyes. Her hair was dark and fussy, a dense bush of it which must have made a wide frame for her face unless she had somehow confined it. When Burden found her she had been wearing a pink nightdress patterned with white flowers. Across the quilt had lain a white wool cardigan that had evidently done duty as a bedjacket. Thee were no rings on the hands, no earrings in her ears. On the left-hand bedside cabinet were her watch, gold with a black strap, a gold ring with a red stone, probably a ruby, that looked valuable, a comb and a half-empty bottle of aspirins; on the

355

right-hand cabinet were a novel by Danielle Steel in paperback, a glass of water, a packet of throat pastilles and a Yale key.

A bedlamp stood on each cabinet, each one a simple white vase-shaped base with a pleated blue shade. The one on the right of the bed, farthest from the door, was intact. The other had a chip out of its base and its cord torn from the base. This cord, with plug still attached, had gone now, had been removed in a plastic bag by DC Pemberton, but when they first came into the bedroom it had been lying on the floor within inches of Annette Bystock's hanging hand.

'She's been dead at least thirty-six hours,' Sir Hilary Tremlett, the pathologist, had said to Wexford. 'I'll be able to tell you more precisely when I've had a closer look. Let me see, it's Friday, isn't it? On the face of it, I'd say she died on Wednesday night, certainly before midnight on Wednesday.'

He left before the van bearing the body was out of sight. Wexford closed the bedroom door.

'A confident killer,' he said. 'An experienced killer, I'd say. He must have been very sure of himself. He didn't bother to bring a weapon with him, he was sure he'd find one to hand. Everyone has electric leads in their home, but if by chance he couldn't find a suitable one, everyone has knives, heavy objects, hammers.'

Burden nodded. 'Or he was familiar with the place. He knew what was on offer.'

'Must it be a he? Or are you just being politically incorrect?'

Burden grinned. 'Old Tremlett may be able to help us there. I can't somehow imagine a woman breaking into a place and tearing a lead out of a lamp to strangle someone.'

'You're well known for having quaint ideas about women,' said Wexford. 'He or she didn't break in, though, did they? There's no sign of a break-in. They were let in or they had a key.'

'Someone she knew, then?'

Wexford shrugged. 'How's this for a scenario? She started to feel ill on Tuesday evening, went to bed, felt worse in the morning, so she phoned the Benefit Office to say she wasn't coming in and then she phoned a friend or a neighbour and asked them to fetch something in for her. Look at this.'

Burden followed him into the kitchen. It was too small to contain a table but on the narrow counter, on the left side, was a grocer's cardboard box, twelve inches by nine and about nine inches high. The items inside seemed untouched. On top of them lay a supermarket print-out, dated 8 July. Beneath it were a packet of cornflakes, two small pots of strawberry yogurt, a carton of milk, a small wholemeal loaf wrapped in tissue paper, a packet of pre-sliced Cheddar cheese and a grapefruit.

'So the friend that was shopping for her brought that in yesterday,' Wexford said. 'If the friend works, the likelihood is it was yesterday evening . . . Yes, Chepstow, what is it?'

The fingerprint man said, 'I haven't done in here yet, sir.'

'We'll clear out of your way then.'

'There's a key on the bedside table. Why not give the friend a key?' Burden asked as they moved into Annette Bystock's living room. 'The front door was unlocked when I got here. Did she leave her own front door on the latch? Why do that in this day and age?' If Wexford winced Burden didn't notice. 'It's just inviting a burglar.'

'She couldn't give the friend a key if the friend wasn't there, Mike. Man hasn't yet mastered the technique of sending solid objects by phone, radio or satellite transmission. If she didn't want to get out of bed to let him or her in she could only leave the door on the latch. Once the friend had come she could hand over a key.'

'But someone else came in while the door was on the latch?'

'It looks like it.'

'We have to find the friend,' said Burden.

'Yes, I'm wondering if it was a neighbour or if she only made one phone call on Wednesday morning, if she killed two birds with one stone, so to speak. After all, Mike, who are our friends? Mainly, the people we were at school with or trained with or met at work. I think it's very likely the Good Samaritan who brought the yogurt and grapefruit works at the Benefit Office.'

'Karen and Barry are doing the neighbours now, but most of them are at work.'

Wexford had been standing at the window but now he turned round and surveyed the room. He looked at Annette Bystock's pictures on the wall, a bland and innocuous pen and ink drawing of a windmill, a bright watercolour of a rainbow over green hills; at her framed photographs, one in black and white of a girl of about three in a frilly dress and white socks, one of a couple in a suburban garden, the woman with her hair in sausage curls, her dress full-skirted and tight-waisted, the man in floppy grey flannels and pullover. Her mother as a child, Wexford guessed. Her parents newly married.

The furniture was a three-piece suite, a lacquered coffee table, a useless-looking two-tiered table, a bookcase which contained few books and whose middle shelves were used to display china animals. On the bottom shelf were perhaps twenty compact discs and the same number of cassettes. The red hall carpet extended to cover the floor of this room but otherwise the colour scheme was unexciting, mostly beige and brown. Her parents probably had a beige living room and a blue bedroom. There was nothing to show that Annette had been comparatively young, not yet forty, no break-away from convention, nothing minimally adventurous.

'Where's the television?' Wexford asked. 'Where's the video? No radio, no cassette player, no CD player? None of those?'

'That's funny. Maybe she didn't have them, maybe she was some sort of fundamentalist who didn't believe in those things. No, but wait a minute, she had CDs. . . . See that table there? The one with the two tiers. Don't you reckon there's been a TV on the top and a video underneath?'

You could see the marks, a rectangle of dust in the polished surface above and a slightly larger one below.

'It looks as if her invitation to the burglar was accepted,' said Wexford. 'I wonder what else she had. A computer maybe? A microwave in the kitchen, though it's hard to say where it would have fitted in?'

'She was killed for *that*?'

'I doubt it. If our perpetrator killed her for what she had in the flat, he'd have taken her watch and her ring. That ring looks valuable to me.'

'Or it could be that the TV and the video have gone off somewhere to be repaired.'

'Oh, sure, it could be. All sorts of things could be. There's been one single case recorded of successful self-strangulation, so she might be the second one. And she sold the best part of her consumer goods first to pay for her funeral. Come *on*, Mike.'

Returning to the bedroom, now free for any kind of arbitrary examination, Wexford opened the cupboard door and, without comment, though Burden was behind him, eyed the garments inside. Two pairs of jeans, a pair of cords, cotton loons, several not very short miniskirts size twelve and two longer skirts size fourteen, which seemed to indicate that Annette had recently put on weight. Folded sweaters on the shelves, blouses, all of them ordinary, safe, quiet.

Behind the other door hung a navy winter coat, beige raincoat, two jackets, one dark red, one black. Had she never dressed up, gone out in the evenings, been to a party?

Wexford picked the ring off the bedside cabinet and held it out on his palm to Burden. 'A fine ruby,' he said. 'Worth more than all your TVs and Nicam video-plusses and cassette players put together.' He hesitated. 'Which of us is going to be the first to ask the question?'

'It's been on the tip of my tongue ever since I knew she'd been murdered.'

'And mine.'

'OK,' said Burden, 'I will. Is there any connection between this death and the fact that she seems to have been the last person to have seen Melanie Akande alive?'

Edwina Harris came home while they were still there. She pushed the door open, entered the hall, saw Flat One sealed off with yellow tape and was standing staring when DS Karen Malahyde came out to her.

'Did I leave the door on the latch? I mean, I always do when I go out and nothing's ever happened.' She realized what she had said. 'What *has* happened?'

'Can we go upstairs, Mrs Harris?'

Karen broke it to her carefully. It was a shock but no more than that. She and Annette Bystock had been neighbours, not friends, never close. After a few minutes she was able to tell Karen that Annette's parents were dead, she had no brothers or sisters. She thought Annette had once been married but she knew no more than that.

No, she hadn't heard or seen anything untoward in the past few days. She lived in the upper flat with her husband and he hadn't heard anything or he would have told her. In fact, she hadn't known Annette was ill. She wasn't the friend who had brought in the groceries.

'Like I said, I wasn't her *friend*.'

'Who was?'

'She never had any boyfriends to my knowledge.'

'Women friends, then?'

But Edwina Harris couldn't say. She had only once been inside Flat One, but couldn't remember noticing whether or not Annette had television.

'But everyone has TV, don't they? She had a radio, a little white one. I know that because while I was in there she showed it to me. She'd spilt red nail varnish on it and she couldn't get it off, wanted to know what would get it off, and I said remover, but she'd tried that.'

'There's someone lives opposite,' Burden said. It was a bit awkward, he found he couldn't tell whether it was a man or a woman. 'A very old person,' he said carefully, and with equal tact, 'They look as if they'd see everything. Did they know Annette?'

'Mr Hammond? He's never been over here. He hasn't left that room for . . . well, it has to be three years.'

Edwina Harris wasn't prepared to identify the body. She had never seen a dead person and didn't want to start now. Annette had had a cousin somewhere, she had heard her mention a cousin. Jane Something; A birthday card had come from this woman and the postman had put it in her box instead of Annette's. That was when Edwina Harris heard about the cousin, when she took the birthday card over to Annette.

It was Wexford who asked her about the front door to the house. 'It was never left unlocked overnight.'

'Are you sure?'

'Well, I'm sure I never left it unlocked.'

'Strange, isn't it?' said Burden, after they left her. 'Women in ground-floor flats are supposed to be sleepless with dread about intruders. They have alarms, they have bars on all the windows – or that's what I read.'

'Appearance and reality,' said Wexford.

Some time later in the day they found Annette's cousin, a married woman with three children living in Pomfret. Jane Winster agreed to come to Kingsmarkham and identify the body.

Told what had happened, Cyril Leyton at first refused to believe. Incredulously, 'You're having me on,' he had said roughly when phoned, then, 'Is this some sort of trick?' Finally convinced, he repeated over and over, 'My God, my God. . . .'

Tomorrow would be Saturday, but in name only, as Wexford said to Burden. There wouldn't be any time off and all leave would be cancelled. Burden's remarks about women in ground floor flats reminded him of the meeting scheduled for Saturday night at Kingsmarkham Comprehensive. He wondered if he would still be able to take part. The talk he was planning he had given twice before at Women, Aware! meetings and had enjoyed speaking. He wouldn't miss it this time, not unless he absolutely had to; unless, for instance, someone had been arrested for this murder.

The young men – Wexford disliked the word 'youth' and refused ever to use it – were still sitting on the stone balustrade of the Benefit Office steps. Perhaps they weren't the same ones but they looked the same to him. This time he took particular note of them so that he would know them again: a boy with a shaven head in a grey tee-shirt; a boy in a black leather jacket and track-suit bottoms with rats' tail hair tied back in a ponytail; another very short one with fair curly hair and a black boy with dreadlocks and one of those big floppy knitted caps. Assessing them like this, he realized what he had done, what he had told Burden racists did, so he changed the description to: a *boy* with dreadlocks and a knitted cap.

They looked at him with indifference, or three of them did. The one with the ponytail didn't look at him at all. For all that, he expected some muttered remark as he passed them, an insult or a quip, but there was nothing. He went up the steps to find the door locked but a young girl coming towards him behind the glass to open it.

He hadn't seen her before. She was small with pointed features and reddish hair, the label pinned to her black tee-shirt identifying her as Ms A. Selby, Admin Assistant. He said good afternoon to her and something about being sorry to detain them all like this after hours, but she was too shy to reply. He followed her between counters to the back where she opened a door marked not only 'Private' but 'Keep Out' as well.

He hadn't intended it to be like this. Cyril Leyton – for it was surely he who had fixed this up – was evidently a headmaster *manqué*. The chairs, normally those on which clients waited to sign on, were arranged in five rows with grey metal tables in front of each. On these chairs the staff sat. There were more of them than Wexford had realized. He saw to his rather horrified amusement that Leyton had seated them according to rank: the two supervisors, the remaining New Claims Adviser and all Executive Officers, in the first row; administrative officers behind; then the administrative assistants, those who worked on the switchboard, saw to the post, operated the copier, at the back. In the last row, on the extreme left, possibly the seat of the lowliest, was the bullet-headed security officer.

On each table, in front of each member of staff, was a notepad. All that was lacking, Wexford thought, was a blackboard – and perhaps a ferrule for Leyton to hold and use for rapping knuckles. The manager looked busy and important, enjoying himself now the first shock was past. His red face was shiny. Since Wexford had last seen him he had had his hair cut cruelly short and the clippers had left an angry-looking crimson rash on his neck.

'All present and correct, I trust,' he said.

Wexford merely nodded to him. Ridiculous as this regimentation was, the notepads might be useful. So long as they understood they weren't to write down what *he* said but what *they* knew.

'I'll try not to detain you long,' he began. 'You'll all have heard by now of Miss Bystock's violent death. It will be on our local television news at six-thirty and in the papers tomorrow so there's no reason why I shouldn't tell you now that it was a case of murder.'

From somewhere in the audience he heard the sound of an indrawn breath. It might have come from Ingrid Pamber, whose blue eyes were fixed earnestly on him, or the wispy fragile blonde sitting next to her who must have been twenty-five but looked no more than fifteen. Her label was too far away for him to read. In the row in front of them Peter Stanton, the other New Claims Adviser, sat like an important young executive at a seminar, one long elegant leg crossed over the other, ankle on knee, his elbows on the chair arms, his head flung back. He was very good looking in a dark brooding way and he seemed to be enjoying himself.

'She was murdered in her own home, Ladyhall Court in Ladyhall Avenue. We don't yet know when. We shan't know until the postmortem is over and the other forensic tests have been done. We shan't know how she died or when or why. But as far as that goes the help of the people who knew her will be invaluable to us. Miss Bystock had very little family, few friends. The people she knew are the people she worked with and that means *you*.

'One of you or several of you may between you have all the information we need to find Miss Bystock's killer and bring him – or her – to justice. Your cooperation will be invaluable. I should like you all to agree to be interviewed by my officers tomorrow, either in your own homes or at Kingsmarkham Police Station if you prefer. Meanwhile, if any of you has anything to tell me now, anything that might be important or urgent, I shall be in Mr Leyton's office for the next half-hour and I'd be grateful if you'd come to me there and pass this information on. Thank you.'

362

Cyril Leyton said importantly as they walked into the little grey office, 'I can tell you anything you want to know. There's not much goes on here that I don't know about.'

'I've already told everyone that if they have something to tell me that's urgent they should do it now. Have you anything to tell me?'

Leyton grew redder. 'Well, no, not specifically, but I . . .'

'What time did Miss Bystock phone on Wednesday to say she wouldn't be coming in? Can you tell me that?'

'I? No, I can't. I'm not a switchboard operator. I can find someone who will . . .'

'Yes, Mr Leyton,' Wexford said patiently, 'I'm sure you can, but all your staff will be questioned tomorrow. Didn't you hear me say that? I'm asking you what you can tell me.'

Leyton was saved from answering by a tap on the door. It opened and Ingrid Pamber came in. Wexford, who always noticed – as most men do notice – if a woman is specially good looking, had taken good note of this girl. Her looks were the kind that most appealed to him, the fresh wholesomeness of her, her glossy dark hair sleekly held back by a barrette, her fine features and smooth pink and white skin – what his father would have called her 'complexion' – her shapely figure that was slim but a long way from today's anorexic ideal. The clothes she wore were in his opinion the most flattering to any pretty woman: a short straight skirt, a clinging knitted sweater – in this case cream cotton and short-sleeved – low-cut shoes with heels, as unlike a man's shoe as could be.

She levelled at Wexford a rueful smile that was almost laughter through tears. It looked natural but he thought it was calculated. Her eyes were the kind whose irises are such a strong colour that they seem to shed their own blue light.

'I was – I was looking after her,' she said. 'Poor Annette, I was taking care of her.'

'You were friends, Miss Pamber?'

'I was her only friend.'

Ingrid Pamber said it quietly but dramatically. She sat down opposite Wexford, and sat with care, but her skirt was too short not to rise six inches above her knees. The sideways attitude she sat in, knees and ankles close together, seemed designed to show off a woman's legs to best advantage – but a modest woman's, not the Hollywood starlet kind who crosses one leg over the other, extending the toe in its high-heeled shoe. He thought he understood Ingrid

Pamber as a girl whose sexual success depended on a contrived reserve, discreet revelations, an almost shy appeal. In another age she would have managed excellently the manipulation of petticoats to give a sight of ankle or the handling of a shawl that when it slipped allowed a glimpse of cleavage.

'It was you who took the call from Miss Bystock on Wednesday morning?'

'Yes. Yes, it was. She asked the switchboard to put the call through to me.'

'Which was most improper,' said Leyton. 'I shall be speaking to Mr Jones and Miss Selby about that. The call should have come to me.'

'I told you about it,' said Ingrid. 'I told you within about thirty seconds.'

'Yes, maybe, but that's not the . . .'

'Mr Leyton,' Wexford said, 'I'd be grateful if you'd leave us. I'd like to talk to Miss Pamber alone.'

'Look here, this is my office!'

'Yes, I know, and very obliging it is of you to let me use it. I'll see you later.'

Wexford got up and opened the door for Leyton. He had scarcely gone through it before Ingrid Pamber giggled. One of the hardest things we are ever called on to do is feign sorrow when we are happy or pretend happiness when we are in grief. Ingrid remembered too late that, as Annette's only friend, she was supposed to be sad. She looked down, biting her lip.

He waited a moment, then asked her, 'Can you tell me what time this call came?'

'It was nine-fifteen.'

'How can you be so sure of the time?'

'Well, we start at nine-thirty and we're supposed to be in by nine-fifteen.' She opened her eyes wide as she looked at him and he felt the force of that blue beam. 'I've been getting in a bit late lately and . . . well, I was pleased with myself for making it on time. I'd looked at the clock and seen it was nine-fifteen and at that moment the call from Annette came for me.'

'What did she say, Miss Pamber?'

'That she thought she had a bug and felt awful and wouldn't be in and I was to tell Cyril. And she said would I take her in a pint of milk on my way home from work, that was all she wanted, she couldn't eat anything. She said she'd leave the door on the latch for me. It's the kind of door that's got a handle like a door . . . well, an inside-door if you know what I mean.'

Wexford nodded. This then was the friend he had guessed at.

'So I said I would and the minute I put the phone down a man phoned and asked for her. He didn't give his name but I knew who it was.' She gave him a sidelong look, rather a roguish look. 'Anyway, I said she was at home ill.'

'And you did take her the milk?'

'Yes. It was about five-thirty I went in.'

'She was in bed?'

'Yes, she was. I was going to stay for a bit, have a chat, you know, but she said not to come too near in case I caught it. She'd made a list of things she wanted me to get her next day and I took that with me. She said she'd give me a ring at work in the morning.'

'Did she?'

'No, she didn't but it didn't matter.' Ingrid Pamber seemed quite unaware of what she was saying. 'I'd got her list. I knew what she wanted.'

'So she'd given you a key?'

'Yes, she had. I got the things, cornflakes and grapefruit and stuff, and I went in with them at the same time last evening. I left them in the box. I thought she'd put them away.'

'You didn't go in to see her?'

'Last evening? No, I didn't. I couldn't hear anything. I thought she must be asleep.'

He detected the guilt in her voice. Friend she might have been but she hadn't wanted to be bothered with Annette the night before, she had been in a hurry, so she had dumped the box of groceries and left without looking into the bedroom. . . . Or wasn't it like that at all?

'Now when you left the flat on Wednesday evening you had a key, so of course you didn't leave the front door on the latch? It was locked behind you?'

'Oh, yes.'

How blue her eyes were! They seemed to grow bluer, to become neon-like, day-glo peacock eyes, as they gazed earnestly into his. 'So when you returned on Thursday evening, last evening, you found the door locked and let yourself in with your key?'

'Oh, yes. Absolutely.'

He switched to another subject. 'I suppose Miss Bystock had television? A video?'

'Yes.' She looked surprised. 'I remember when she bought the video. It was around last Christmas.'

'Now when you went there on Wednesday and yesterday, did you see the television set?'

She hesitated. 'I don't know, I . . . I'm sure I saw it on Wednesday. Annette said to draw the curtains as I was leaving. She wanted the curtains drawn to stop the sun fading the carpet or something. Funny, wasn't it? I'd never heard of that before. Anyway, I did draw them and I saw the TV and the video.'

He nodded. 'And yesterday?'

'I don't know. I didn't notice.' In too much of a hurry, Wexford thought, in and out, no messing. Something in his look seemed to touch her. 'You don't mean . . . she was dead then, she was already dead . . . you can't mean that!'

'I'm afraid she was, Miss Pamber. It looks very much as if she was.'

'Oh, God, and I didn't know. If I'd gone in there. . . .'

'It would have made no difference.'

'They didn't . . . they didn't kill her for a telly and a video?'

'It wouldn't be the first time such a thing has happened.'

'Poor Annette. That makes me feel terrible.'

Why did he have the distinct impression she didn't feel terrible at all? She spoke the conventional words in the conventional way and her face wore a conventional mask of woe. But those eyes danced with life and vitality and happiness.

'The man who phoned here and asked for her? Who did you think that was?'

She lied again. He marvelled that she thought he couldn't tell. 'Oh, just a friend, one of her neighbours actually.'

'Who did you think it was, Miss Pamber?' he said.

She looked him straight in the eye. 'I don't know, I honestly don't know.'

'You knew who it was just now and now you don't? I'll ask you again tomorrow.'

The light inside her head had gone out. He watched her go, leave the room, let an indignant Leyton back into it. She had lied a great deal, he thought, and he could pinpoint the moment at which the lying began: it was when he first uttered the word 'key'. He looked beyond the greyness at Marks and Spencers loading bay, at a bright green carrier bag the summer wind was tossing to and fro. A woman was lifting carriers from a trolley into her car boot. She belonged to the same type as Annette, dark, stocky with an hourglass figure, a high colour, excellent legs. Why had Ingrid lied about the man who phoned? Why had she lied about the key? And in what respect had she lied?

She had been dead while Ingrid was in the flat on Thursday evening. Ingrid had locked the door behind her. Who then had unlocked it during the night before Burden arrived?

# 6

Those who had jobs and went to them every day were the lucky ones. Looking back a few years, Barry Vine wondered what he would have thought of such a sentiment then. It was true today, no denying it. He was surprised when he found that the occupants of Flat Three and Flat Four in Ladyhall Court all had work.

The Greenalls, however, had not been at their jobs during the previous week; they had been away on holiday, returning home some five hours after the discovery of Annette's body. The occupant of Flat Four, Jason Partridge, a solicitor just six months over the Law Society's exams, had lived there for only a matter of weeks and could not remember ever having seen Annette. Vine, who knew all about how seeing policemen as younger and younger was a sign of middle age, wondered what it meant when solicitors looked like A Level candidates.

On the opposite side of Ladyhall Gardens were an old house divided into three flats, three red brick bungalows and an empty site where six houses like the old one had been demolished. The new ones would be in nineties' trend, a Portmeirion-like arrangement of a Gothic weatherboard house at angles to a brick house, joined to a plaster-rendered Georgian house, all the roofs at different levels, all the windows different shapes. So far only the foundations were there, the 'infrastructure' and walls built to a height of six feet. That limited those likely to have had a view of Ladyhall Court to the bungalows and the old house.

It was Saturday, so the occupants of the bungalows were at home. Vine talked to a youngish couple, Matthew Ross and his partner Alison Brown, but neither of them had so much as looked out of

368

their front windows on the night of 7 July. They knew nothing of Annette Bystock and could not remember ever having seen her.

Next door was shared by two women, Diana Graddon in her mid-thirties, and Helen Ringstead twenty years older. Mrs Ringstead was lodger rather than friend. Diana Graddon couldn't have afforded to live there without her contribution, she frankly said, though since she had lost her own job the Social Security paid her rent. She had once known Annette well. In fact, it was she who, about ten years before when herself a newcomer to Ladyhall Avenue, had told Annette of the flat for sale on the other side of the street.

'We'd lost touch, though,' said Diana Graddon. 'She dropped me, as a matter of fact. I don't know why. I mean, it was silly really, living opposite and all that, but she never seemed to want to know me after she came here.'

'When did you last see her?'

'It must have been Monday. Last Monday. I was going away for a few days. I saw her coming home from work as I was going to get the bus. We just said hello, we didn't really speak.'

She had been away from home until the previous morning, the Thursday morning. Helen Ringstead said she never noticed who came and went across the road.

The wrinkled face that Burden had for a wild moment thought might be a mask or a cutout belonged to a man of eighty-seven called Percy Hammond. It was four years, not three, since he had come down the stairs from his first-floor flat, and most days he remained in the bedroom that overlooked Ladyhall Avenue. Meals-on-wheels were brought to him and twice a week a home help came in. For thirty years he had been a widower, his sons were dead, and his only friend was the tenant of the ground floor flat who, though eighty and blind, made her way upstairs to visit him every day.

It was she who let Burden in. Having introduced herself as Gladys Prior, asked him for his name twice and then made him spell it, she walked up the stairs ahead of him, sure-footed on the treads, her hand touching the banister more from convention than for support. Percy Hammond was in a chair by the window, staring into an empty street. The face that was dinosaur-like in close-up was turned on Burden's and its owner said, 'I've seen you somewhere before.'

'No, you haven't, Percy. You've made a mistake there. He's a

369

police detective that's come to make enquiries. He's called Burden, Inspector Burden, B,U,R,D,E,N.'

'All right. I don't want to write to him. And I *have* seen him before. What do you know? You can't see at all.'

This on the face of it cruel taunt seemed to amuse rather than distress Mrs Prior. She sat down, giggling. 'Where have I seen you?' said Percy Hammond. 'Now *when* have I seen you?'

'Yesterday morning, over on the other . . .' Burden began but was interrupted.

'All right, don't tell me. Don't you know a rhetorical question when you hear one? I know who you are. You were trying to break into the house, or that's what I thought. Yesterday morning. Ten, was it? Or a bit later – eleven-ish? I'm not as good on time as I used to be. I don't suppose you were breaking in, *looking* in, more likely.'

'Of course he wasn't breaking in, Percy. He's a *policeman.*'

'You're naive, Gladys, that's what you are. I suppose Inspector B,U,R,D,E,N was looking through the curtains at our murder.'

That was one way of putting it, if somewhat cold-blooded. 'That's right, Mr Hammond. I really want to know, not if you saw me, but if you saw anyone else. I think you watch the street from your window quite a bit, don't you?'

'Never leaves that window all blessed day long,' said Mrs Prior.

'And how about the night?' said Burden.

'It's light at night this time of the year,' Percy Hammond said, a gleam of pleasure in his hooded eyes. 'Doesn't get dark till ten and it starts getting light again at four. Generally, I get in my bed at ten and out of it at half-past three. That's as long as I can sleep at my age. And when I'm not in my bed I'm at my window, I'm at my watching place. Do you know what Mizpah means?'

'I can't say I do,' said Burden.

'The watching place that overlooked the Plain of Syria. You youngsters don't know your Bible, more's the pity. This window is my Mizpah.'

'And have you seen anything on the . . . er, Plain of Syria these past two nights, Mr Hammond?'

'Not last night but the night before . . .'

'Two tom cats came knocking at the door!' crowed Mrs Prior, laughing.

Percy Hammond ignored her. 'A young chap came out of Ladyhall

370

Court. I'd never seen him before, I knew he didn't live there. I know them all by sight, the ones that live there.'

'What time would that have been?'

'It was dawn,' said Percy Hammond. 'Four. Maybe a bit later. And I saw him again, I saw him come out carrying something, like a big wireless set.'

'Wireless set!' said Gladys Prior. 'I may not have my sight but I do move with the times. They call them tellies and radios.'

'He went in again and came out with something else in a box. I couldn't see what he did with it. If he had a car it was parked round the corner. I thought to myself, he's moving house for someone, getting it done early before the traffic gets bad.'

'Could you describe him, Mr Hammond?'

'He was young, about your age. About your height. Had quite a look of you. It was still darkish, you know, the sun wasn't up. Everything looks black and grey at that hour. I couldn't tell you the colour of his hair . . .'

'He gets confused,' said Mrs Prior.

'No, I don't, Gladys. As I said, it was about four-thirty to five, and I saw him come out and go in again and come out, carrying these boxes, a young chap of maybe twenty-five or thirty, six feet tall, at least six feet.'

'Would you know him again?'

'Of course I would. I'm an observant man. It may have been dark but I'd know him anywhere.'

Percy Hammond turned on Burden the fierce scowl, downturned mouth and heavy dewlaps that was his normal expression, an intense gleam in his saurian eyes.

'Women, learn to be streetwise,' the programme text began. 'Come and hear what the experts have to say about making yourselves aware. In your car, walking home alone after dark, in your home. Do you know what to do if attacked in the street? Can you protect yourself if your car breaks down on the motorway? Can you defend yourself against rape?'

It listed the speakers: Chief Inspector R. Wexford, of Kingsmarkham CID, to talk on 'Crime on the Streets and in Your Home'; PC Oliver Adams on 'Driving Alone and Safe'; WPC Clare Scott, the Rape Adviser, on 'Changed Attitudes to Reporting Rape'; Mr Ronald Pollen, Self-Defence Expert and Judo Black Belt, to show his

371

enthralling and informative video and talk on 'How to Fight Back'. Questions would be invited from the audience which the team of experts would answer. Organizer: Mrs Susan Riding, President, Kingsmarkham Women Rotarians; Chairperson, Mrs Anouk Khoori.

'Have you ever heard of a woman called Anouk Khoori? Curious name, isn't it? Sounds Arabic.'

Dora didn't hesitate. 'Oh, Reg, you never listen to me. I told you all about her coming to the Women's Institute and talking about women's lives in the United Arab Emirates.'

'There you are, I was right. She is an Arab.'

'Well, she doesn't look like one. She's a blonde. Very good looking in a showy sort of way. Very rich, I should think. Her husband owns a lot of shops, Tesco or Safeway or something. No, it's not those, it's Crescent. You know the ones, they're springing up everywhere.'

'You mean those supermarkets you see from motorways that look like palaces from the Arabian nights? All pointed arches and moons on the roof? What's she got to do with not getting raped or mugged? Is she going to tell the women to wear the veil?'

'Oh, she's just there because she wants to get herself in the public eye. She and her husband have built a vast new house where Mynford Old Hall used to be. She's standing for the Council in the by-election. They say she'd like to get into Parliament, but she can't surely, she isn't even English.'

Wexford shrugged. He didn't know and cared less. The task ahead of him, the immediate task, he dreaded and would have avoided if he could. On the way he was going to meet Burden in the Olive and Dove for a drink, but after that – it could be postponed no longer- the Akandes.

The Olive stayed open from and until all hours now. You could drink brandy at nine in the morning if you wanted to, and a surprising lot of European visitors did want to. Instead of being cleared out pell-mell at two-thirty you could drink on through the afternoon and evening till the Olive finally closed its bars at midnight. It was ten past eleven when Wexford got there and found Burden sitting outside at a table in the shade.

There were almost too many tubs, barrels, vases and hanging baskets spilling out fuchsias and geraniums and other unnameable brilliant flowers. But all were scentless and the air smelt of petrol fumes and also of the river, its waters low from drought and scummed with algae. A few yellow leaves had fallen on to the table.

In July they were too early for the autumnal shedding but their presence warned that autumn would come.

Burden had a half of Adnams in a tankard that the Olive called a jug. 'I'll have the same,' said Wexford. 'No, I won't, I'll have a Heineken. I need some Dutch courage.' Returning with it, Burden said, 'The old man definitely saw someone. Those trees don't block the view from up there. He saw the thief of the TV and the video.'

'But not Annette's killer?'

'Not if it was four-thirty in the morning. Annette had been dead five hours by then. He says he'd know him again. On the other hand, he says the man he saw was about my age and then that he was between twenty-five and thirty.' Burden looked down modestly. 'Of course, it wasn't very light.'

'I don't suppose it was, Dorian.'

'Yes, well, you may laugh, but if this character looks like me we may be getting somewhere.'

'It's a killer we want, Mike, not a burglar.' The sun had moved round and Wexford shifted his chair into the shade. 'So – Melanie Akande, where does she come into it?'

'We haven't looked for her body.'

'Where would you start, Mike? In the High Street here? In the cellars of the Benefit Office? If it has a cellar, which I doubt. On British Rail's inter-city line to Victoria?'

'I talked to those layabouts, you know, the ones who hang about outside the Benefit Office. They're always there, always more or less the same ones. What attracts them to the place? They only have to sign on once a fortnight but they're there every day. It would be different if they went inside asking about jobs.'

'Maybe they do.'

'I doubt it. I very much doubt it. I asked them if they'd ever seen the black girl. You know what they said?'

Wexford made a guess. '"I don't know, I might have."'

'Exactly right. That's what they said. I tried to get them to cast their minds back to last Tuesday. Correction, what *passes* for minds with people like that. The way they went about it, I mean the *process*, it was like three very old men trying to recall something. It went something like this, "Well, yeah, man, that was the day I like, you know, I come here early on account of me mum was, you know, going to . . ." mumble, mumble, scratch scalp, and then the next one

373

says, "no, man, no, you got it all wrong, that was Tuesday 'cos I said like . . ."'

'Spare me.'

'The black one, the one with the hair in sort of plaits, only not, sort of matted up, he's the worst, he sounds brain-damaged. You know you can have senile and juvenile diabetes? Well, d'you reckon there's such a thing as juvenile Alzheimer's?'

'I suppose they knew nothing about her?'

'Not a thing. You could have a girl abducted on those steps by three characters from *Jurassic Park* and they wouldn't notice. All I got was that the one with the ponytail says he thinks he saw a black girl on the other side of the street on *Monday*. I'll tell you something, we aren't going to find anyone who saw Melanie after she left the Benefit Office. We'd have done so by now if we were going to. All we've got is the connection between her and Annette Bystock.'

The sun had moved round. Wexford pushed his chair into the shade. 'But what exactly is that connection, Mike?'

'"Exactly" is what I don't know. "Exactly" is what Annette was killed for, to stop her telling. It's obvious, isn't it? Melanie told her something before she left on Tuesday afternoon and whatever it was was overheard. Either that, or some meeting was arranged which the killer of both girls decided must not at all costs take place.'

'You must mean overheard by someone in the Benefit Office, an employee.'

'Or a client,' said Burden.

'But what was it that was overheard? What sort of thing?'

'I don't know and for our purposes it basically doesn't matter. The point is that whoever heard it was worried by it, more than that, felt that his or her life or liberty was endangered by it. Melanie had to die and, because she had passed this secret on, the woman to whom it was spoken had to die too.'

'D'you want another one? The other half for the road before we walk round and see them?'

'*We?*'

'You're coming with me.' Wexford fetched their drinks. When he came back with them he said, 'When someone mentions terrible secrets to me I always need to be given some inkling of what they might be. I'd like an example. You know me, I always want examples.'

They were no longer alone. A number of the Olive's clientele were finding it more pleasant out in the open air. A touring American with a camera posed the other members of his party at a table under a sunshade and began taking shots of them. Wexford moved his chair again.

'Well, this man she was going to meet,' Burden began. 'I mean, she could have told Annette his name.'

'She was going to meet *another* man? That's the first I've heard of it. What was he, a white slaver?'

Burden looked genuinely puzzled. 'A what?'

'Before your time. You've really never heard the term?'

'I don't think so.'

'It must have been used at the beginning of the century and maybe a bit later. A white slaver was a sort of pimp, specifically one who procured girls for prostitution abroad.'

'Why "white"?'

Wexford felt himself approaching dangerous ground. He lifted the 'jug' to his lips and as he did so blinked at the sudden flash. The photographer – not the same one – said something that might have been 'thanks' and dived back into the Olive.

'Because slaves were always thought of as black. It wasn't that long after emancipation in the United States. The girls were taken against their will, I suppose, like slaves, and forced into servitude abroad, again like slaves, only it was brothels for them. Buenos Aires was the favourite place in the popular imagination. Shall we go? Akande's surgery will be over by now.'

It was and he was back at home. The days gone by had aged him. Hair doesn't turn grey in a matter of days from shock or anxiety, whatever the sensation merchants may say, and Akande's was the same as it had been on Wednesday, black with a white sprinkling at the temples. It was his face that had become grey, drawn and gaunt, all the protrusions of the skull showing.

'My wife is at work,' he said as he showed them into the living room. 'We've tried to carry on as usual. My son phoned us from Malaysia. We didn't tell him, there seemed no point in spoiling his trip. He would have felt he had to come home.'

'I'm not sure that that was a good idea.' Wexford noticed what he hadn't noticed before, a framed photograph of the whole family. It stood on the bookcase and it was obviously a studio portrait, posed and rather formal, the children dressed in white, Laurette Akande in

375

a low-cut blue silk dress and gold jewellery, looking beautiful and very unlike a ward sister. 'He might have been able to help. His sister may have confided in him before he went away.'

'Confided what, Mr Wexford?'

'Possibly that there was a man in her life apart from Euan Sinclair.'

'But I'm sure there wasn't.' The doctor sat down and fixed Wexford with his eyes. He had a rather disconcerting way of doing this. Wexford had noticed it when their roles were reversed, when he so to speak was the client and the other man the omniscient adviser, and in his surgery, confronting each other across the doctor's desk, Akande's black penetrating eyes had stared deep into his own. 'I'm sure she had never had any boyfriend but Euan. Apart, that is, from – I'm not quite sure how to say this . . .'

'Say what, Dr Akande?'

'My wife and I . . . well, we wouldn't care for the idea of Melanie taking up with a . . . well, a white man. Oh, I know things are changing every day, they don't even use words like "miscegenation" any more and, of course, there was no question of *marriage* but still . . .'.

Wexford could imagine Sister Akande being as magisterial about this as any county gentlewoman whose daughter was attracted by a Rastafarian. 'Melanie had a white boyfriend, doctor?'

'No, no, nothing like that. It was just that his sister was at the college too, that was how Melanie met him, and she told us they'd had a drink together – with the sister. I mention him because he's the only other boy Melanie told us about apart from Euan. Laurette said at once that she hoped Melanie wouldn't get to know him better and I'm sure Melanie never did.'

How much did he know, this parent, of his children's lives? How much does any parent know? 'Melanie didn't meet Euan last Tuesday evening,' Wexford said. 'That's been established beyond doubt.'

'I knew she didn't. I knew it. I told my wife she'd too much sense to go back to that boy who had no respect for her.' Akande seemed calm but his hands gripped the arms of his chair and the knucklebones showed white. 'Do you . . .' he began. 'Do you have any news for me?'

'We've nothing specific, sir.' Wexford read a lot into that emphatic 'sir', probably a good deal more than Burden was aware of. He heard in the stress a real effort on the inspector's part to treat this man just as he would any other man in the doctor's position. And he could tell that Burden, who had encountered very few black people, was ill-at-ease, not at a loss but nervous, unsure how to proceed. 'We've done all we can to find your daughter. We've done everything that's humanly possible.'

The doctor must have thought, as Wexford did, that this was meaningless. His knowledge of psychology, and perhaps of white men, enabled him to see through Burden. Wexford thought he could detect the ghost of a sneer on Akande's unhappy face. 'What are you trying to say to me, Inspector?'

Burden didn't like that 'trying'. There had been a faintly sarcastic emphasis on the participle. Wexford took over, rather too hastily. 'You must prepare yourself, Dr Akande.'

His short bark of laughter was shocking in that context. It was a single 'Ha!' and then it was gone, the doctor's face wretched again – worse than wretched now, distraught. 'I am prepared,' he said in a stoical voice. '*We* are prepared. You're going to tell me to accept that Melanie must be dead?'

'Not quite that. But, yes, there's a very strong probability.'

Silence fell. Akande put his hands into his lap and forced himself to relax them. He gave a heavy, profound sigh. To his horror, Wexford saw a tear fall from each of those tragic eyes. Akande was unembarrassed. He removed the teardrops with the forefingers of each hand, wiping them across his cheeks, then contemplating the fingertips with bent head.

To keep his face hidden, without looking up, he said quietly, in an almost conversational tone. 'There is something I've wondered about. Since I saw the television news last evening and read this morning's paper. The murdered woman in Ladyhall Avenue, her name is the same as the one Melanie had her appointment with last Monday: Annette Bystock. The paper called her a civil servant and I suppose that's what she was. Is it a . . . coincidence? I've wondered if there could be a connection. As a matter of fact, I was awake all last night thinking about it.'

'Melanie had no previous knowledge of Annette Bystock, doctor?'

'I'm sure she didn't. I remember her exact words. "I have to see the New Claims Adviser at two-thirty," she said, and then, a while later, "a Ms Bystock," she said.'

Wexford said gently that the doctor had not told him that before.

Mrs Akande hadn't told him that on the single occasion he had talked to her.

'Maybe not. It came back to me when I saw the name in the paper.'

Wexford deeply distrusted evidence which 'came back to' witnesses when they saw a name in the paper. Poor Akande said he was prepared, he could accept, but he hoped just the same. Hope may be a virtue but it causes more pain, Wexford thought, than despair. He considered asking the doctor if he knew of anything Melanie might have said to Annette Bystock that would have put both their lives in jeopardy, and then he thought how pointless such a question was. Of course Akande didn't know.

He said instead, 'What is the name of this white boy she had a drink with?'

'Riding. Christopher Riding. But that was months ago.'

Akande, seeing them to the door, struggled not to say it. He lost the fight, wincing before he spoke. 'Is there any . . . is there the slightest hope she may be . . . still alive?'

Until we find her body we can't regard her as dead. Wexford didn't use those words. 'Let's just say you must prepare yourself, doctor.' He couldn't give hope, knowing almost for sure that in a day or two he would snatch it away again.

The women filled the school hall, at least three hundred of them. With ten minutes still to go before the meeting started, they were still arriving and one of the organizers was bringing in more chairs.

'It's not us they're coming for,' Susan Riding whispered to Wexford. 'Don't flatter yourself. And finding out how to blind and maim a rapist is only part of it. No, they've come for *her*. To see *her*. It was a good move getting her in the chair, wasn't it?'

Wexford looked across the platform at Anouk Khoori. He had a feeling he had seen her somewhere before, though he couldn't remember where. Perhaps it had only been a photograph in a paper. She was a big fish in a small pond, he thought, on her way to becoming Kingsmarkham's First Lady. Presumably, that suited her. If it was true that most of these women had come for a sight of her in the flesh, to see what she wore and hear how she talked, their aspirations were not high. In her small way she was like one of those international celebrities whose pictures are always in the papers, whose names are household words and who are favourites for TV chat shows, but of whom it would be hard to say what they *did* and impossible to know what they had achieved.

'She doesn't look Middle Eastern,' he said and immediately wondered if that was a racist remark.

Susan Riding only smiled. 'Her family are from Beirut. Anouk is a French name, of course. We knew them slightly when we were in Kuwait. His young nephew needed a minor op and Swithun did it.'

'They left because of the Gulf War?'

'*We* did. I don't think they ever left. They've a house there and one in Menton and an apartment in New York, or so I've heard. I knew they'd bought Mynford Old Hall so I plucked up my courage and asked her if she'd do this and she was charming about it. Swithun's here, by the way, and it looks as if he's going to be the only man down there. Still, he won't mind, he takes that sort of thing in his stride.'

Wexford spotted the paediatric surgeon sitting one row from the back, looking as urbane as his wife had suggested he would be. Why was it that when women sat with their legs crossed they rested calf on kneecap but when men did it they placed ankle on femur? Out of modesty in the women's case, presumably, but that wouldn't apply now they wore trousers all the time. Swithun Riding was sitting with his ankle on his femur and clasping it with a long elegant hand. Next to him sat a girl with corn-coloured hair so like him she must be his and Susan's daughter. Wexford recognized her. The last time he saw her she had been waiting to sign on at his first visit to the Benefit Office.

'Your son couldn't bring himself to give his father moral support?' said Wexford.

'Christopher's away for a week. He went off to Spain with a bunch of friends.'

So much for another tentative theory.

Across the room Mrs Khoori laughed, a long musical peal. The man she was talking to, an ex-mayor of Kingsmarkham, smiled at her, evidently already smitten. She gave him a light pat on the arm, a delightful and strangely intimate gesture, before moving back behind the table to the central chair. There, she adjusted her microphone with the ease of someone accustomed to public speaking.

'I'll introduce you,' said Susan Riding.

Wexford expected an accent but there was none, only the faintest French intonation, the ends of her sentences rising instead of falling.

379

'How do you do?' She held his hand a little longer than was necessary. 'I knew I should meet you here, I felt it.'

Not surprising, he thought, since his name as a speaker was in the programme. He was a little disturbed by her eyes, which seemed to be assessing him, calculating something about him. It – was as if she was speculating how far she could go with him, at what point she would need to draw back. Oh, nonsense, imagination . . . They were black eyes, and that must be what disconcerted him, such dark eyes in contrast to that creamy-olive skin and very fair hair.

'Are you going to tell us poor creatures how to fight big strong men and protect ourselves?'

Anyone less like a poor creature it would be hard to find. She was at least five feet nine, her body sinuous and strong in the pink linen suit, arms and legs muscular, her skin glowing with health. On the hand he hadn't held was a huge rock of a diamond, a single uncluttered stone on a platinum band.

'I'm not a martial arts expert, Mrs Khoori,' he said. 'I shall be leaving that to Mr Adams and Mr Pollen.'

'But you are going to speak? I shall be so disappointed if you aren't going to speak.'

'A few words.'

'Then you and I must have a chat afterwards. I'm worried, Mr Wexford, I am seriously worried about what is happening to us in this country, child murders, all these poor young girls assaulted, raped and worse. That's why I'm doing this, to do what I can in my small way to . . . well, turn the tide of crime. Don't you think we each and every one of us ought to do that?'

He wondered about that 'us'. How long had she been living here? Two years? He wondered if he was being unreasonable, resenting her claims to Englishness while he honoured Akande's. Her husband was an Arab multi-millionaire. . . . He was saved from making any reply to her earnest, though oddly vague, remarks by a whispered, 'Anouk, we're ready to start,' from Susan Riding.

With great confidence Anouk Khoori stood and surveyed her audience. She waited for their silence, their total silence, holding up her hands, the great ring catching the light, before she began to address them.

An hour later, if he had been asked to give a résumé of what she had said, he couldn't have recalled a word of it. And at the time he was aware that she had that great gift, on which so many politicians have founded their success, of being able to say nothing at length and in a flowing sequence of polysyllabic fashionable words, of talking meaningless nonsense in fine mellifluous phrases with absolute self-confidence. From time to time she paused for no apparent reason. Occasionally she smiled. Once she shook her head and once she raised her voice on an impassioned note. Just when he thought she would go on for half an hour, that nothing but physical force would stop her, she ceased, thanked her audience and, turning to him graciously, began to introduce him.

She knew a lot about him. Wexford heard, to his amusement rather than dismay, his whole *curriculum vitae* reeled off. How did she know he had once been a copper on the beat in Brighton? Where did she find out he had two daughters?

He got to his feet and talked to the women. He told them they must learn to be streetwise but told them too that they must cultivate a balanced attitude to what they heard and read about crime on the streets With a glance of mild displeasure at the *Kingsmarkham Courier* reporter, taking notes from the front row, he said that newspapers were to blame for a great deal of the hysteria over crime in this country. An example would be an account he had read recently of pensioners in Myfleet afraid to leave their homes for fear of the mugger who stalked the village and was responsible for numerous attacks on women and elderly people. The truth, on the other hand, was that one old lady, walking home from the bus stop at 11.00 pm, had had her purse snatched by someone who asked her the way. They must be sensible, avoid taking risks, but not become paranoid. In the rural areas of the police district the chances of a woman being attacked in the street were ninety-nine per cent against, and that they should remember.

Oliver Adams spoke and then Ronald Pollen. A video was shown in which actors simulated an encounter on the street between a young woman and a man with a stocking over his face. When grasped from behind, her attacker's hands at her waist and her throat, the actress showed how to draw the high heel of her shoe down the man's calf and grind it into his instep. This drew delighted cheers and clapping from the audience. They recoiled a little from a demonstration of how to stick your thumbs in an assailant's eyes but shocked gasps soon became sighs of pleasure. Everyone, Wexford decided, was enjoying herself a lot. The atmosphere became grimmer when WPC Clare Scott began to talk about rape.

How many of these women, if raped, would report it? Half, maybe. Once you could have said no more than ten per cent.

Things had changed for the better, but he still wondered if the pictures now coming up on the screen of the comfortable 'suite' at the new Rape Crisis Centre in Stowerton would go far in enticing women to be open about the only crime in which authority often treated the victim worse than the perpetrator.

They were applauding now. They were writing down their questions for the four speakers. In the sea of faces he spotted Edwina Harris and, a dozen seats along from her, Wendy Stowlap. A quarter of an hour, he thought, and he could go home. There was no way he was going to become involved in a chat with Anouk Khoori about crime waves and dangerous Britain.

The first question was for PC Adams. Suppose you hadn't a car phone and your car broke down after dark on an A road where there were no roadside phones? What should you do? After Adams had done his best to answer this WPC Scott, the rape adviser, was asked a difficult question about so-called 'date rape' from someone who sounded like a victim. Clare Scott did her best to answer the unanswerable and Mrs Khoori, having opened the next folded paper, handed it to her. The rape adviser read it, shrugged and after a small hesitation handed it to Wexford.

He read the question aloud. 'If you know a member of your family is a rapist, what should you do?'

There was a sudden silence. Women had been whispering to each other, one or two at the back were gathering their things preparatory to leaving. But now all was still. Wexford saw Dora's face in the second row from the front with Jenny beside her. He said, 'The obvious answer is, tell the police. But you know that already.' He hesitated, then said in a strong voice, 'I would like to know if this question is simply academic or if the member of the audience who wrote this had a personal reason for asking.'

Silence. It was broken by three women in the back row leaving. Then someone broke into prolonged coughing. Wexford persisted.

'You've been told you remain anonymous when you ask these questions, but I should like to know who asked this one. Outside the hall, behind the stage here, there's a door marked Private. I'll be inside that door for half an hour after the meeting with WPC Scott. You only have to come round the side of the hall and knock on that door. I very much hope you will.'

382

After that there were no more questions. The youngest girl pupil at Kingsmarkham Comprehensive came up to the stage and presented Mrs Khoori with a bouquet of carnations. She thanked her effusively, she bent over and kissed her. The audience began filing out, some lingering in groups to talk over what had been discussed.

Although smoking was banned from the hall, Anouk Khoori was evidently unable to wait a minute longer for a cigarette. When Wexford saw her put the kingsize to her lips and bring the lighter to it, he remembered who she was. He recognized her. She had looked very different then, in her track-suit and without make-up, but there was no doubt she was the woman in the medical centre who had come to see Dr Akande about some malady suffered by her cook.

He walked out into the car park, saw Susan Riding step into a Range Rover, Wendy Stowlap toss her holdall into the boot of a tiny Fiat, and then he retreated by the side door into the room at the back, a storeplace for chairs and trestle tables. Clare Scott unfolded a couple of chairs, he sat on one and she on the other. A clock on the wall with a large face and a loud tick gave the time as five past ten. He and Clare talked about the morality of betraying family members in aid of the greater good, whether one never should but keep silent out of loyalty or whether one always should and whether there were exceptions. They talked about the heinousness of rape. Perhaps it was right to betray the perpetrator only in the case of a crime of violence. You wouldn't report your wife's shoplifting, would you? The time went by and no one knocked at the door. They gave it another five minutes, but when they came out of the room at twenty to eleven the hall was empty. There was no one outside. The place was deserted.

# 7

His face looked back at him from the front page of the Sunday paper, a so-called 'quality' Sunday paper. And not only his face. The photograph showed himself and Burden at the table outside the Olive and Dove, only there wasn't much of Burden. Burden would be unrecognizable except to those who knew him well. His, on the other hand, was an excellent likeness. He was smiling . . . well, laughing, to tell the truth, as he raised to his lips the brimming tankard of Heineken. In case there was any doubt, the caption said: *Wexford hunts Annette's killer*, and underneath was the legend: *Chief Inspector in charge of Kingsmarkham murder has time to relax with a pint.*

There hadn't been a moment, he reflected bitterly, when his thoughts hadn't been occupied with Annette Bystock and her death. But to whom could he tell that without seeming absurdly defensive? He could do nothing but pretend he didn't care and thank God the Deputy Chief Constable bought *The Mail on Sunday.*

Things were not improved by the arrival of Sylvia with Neil and the boys. His daughter, having forgotten which newspaper he took, had brought her own copy of the offending one to show him on the grounds that he would 'want to see it.' And no amount of arguing on the part of her mother and her husband could persuade her that there was any irony in the caption. In her eyes it was 'nice', the best photograph she had seen of her father in years and did he think the newspaper would let her have a copy?

Sylvia dominated the conversation at lunch. She was fast becoming an expert on the provisions made by government for its jobless citizens and their dependants. Wexford and Dora had to listen to a lecture on Unemployment Benefit and who was entitled to it, the differences between it and Income Support, and the amenities of something called a 'Job Club' which she was engaged in pulling strings for Neil to join.

'They have all the main newspapers there and free use of the phone, which has to be taken into consideration. And they supply envelopes and stamps.'

'Sounds a breeze,' said her father sourly. 'Somebody once took me to lunch at the Garrick and there weren't any free stamps there.'

Sylvia ignored him. 'After he's been unemployed another three months he can go on a training course. A TFW course might be best. . . .'

'A *what*?'

'Training For Work. And I think I might do one for computers. Robin, be a love, and get the leaflets from my handbag, will you?'

'*Nitcho vo*,' said Robin.

Unable to bear another run-through of the most boring brochures he had ever seen in his life, Wexford made an excuse and resorted to the living room. Sport dominated the television programmes and he baulked at switching to the news in case, mysteriously, his own portrait had found its way to the screen. It was paranoia but he knew no way of conquering it. He even speculated if it could be a journalist's revenge for what he had said the previous night about the press fomenting people's fears of violence.

He was still smarting, though less painfully, when he came into his office very early next morning. His team's reports were already on his desk and no one was going to say a word about that photograph. Burden had seen it. That particular newspaper wasn't his choice but Jenny's.

'Funny how you get used to it,' Wexford said. 'I mean the way the passage of time eases things. I don't feel as bad about it today as I did yesterday, and tomorrow I won't feel as bad as I do today. If only we could live by that instead of just coming to the knowledge afresh each time, if we could be aware at the time that it's not going to matter a lot after a couple of days, life'd be a lot easier, wouldn't it?'

'Hm. You are what you are and that's about it. You can't change your nature.'

'What a depressing philosophy.' Wexford began going through the reports. 'Jane Winster, the cousin, identified the body. Not that there was much doubt. We should get something from old Tremlett today or maybe tomorrow morning. Vine interviewed Mrs Winster at her home in Pomfret but he doesn't seem to have learned much. They weren't close. So far as she knows, Annette had no boyfriends and, oddly, no close woman friend. It sounds a very lonely life. Ingrid Pamber seems to have been the only person she was friendly with.'

'Yes, but would the Winster woman know? She hadn't seen Annette since April. That would be understandable if she lived in Scotland, say, but she lives in *Pomfret* and that's all of three miles. They can't have liked each other much.'

'Mrs Winster says, I quote, "I had my own family to think about". They spoke to each other on the phone. Annette always went to them on Christmas Day and was apparently with them when they celebrated a twentieth wedding anniversary. Still, as you say, it's a bit distant.' He worked through the pages, pausing occasionally to read something twice. 'He also saw that Mrs Harris we talked to – remember? Edwina Harris, the woman upstairs? She heard nothing at night, but she admits she and her husband are heavy sleepers. Another thing she insists on is that she never saw any friend call on Annette or Annette leave the building or come into it with someone accompanying her.

'Neither of the supervisors at the Benefit Office, that's Niall Clarke and Valerie Parker, seems to know anything about Annette, her private life, that is. Peter Stanton – he's the other new claims adviser, the one who looks like the young Sean Connery – he seems to have been very open with Pemberton, told him he took Annette out a couple of times. And then Cyril Leyton told him it wouldn't do. He didn't want staff getting into "intimate relationships".'

'And Stanton accepted that?'

'It doesn't sound as if he was bothered. He told Pemberton they hadn't much in common, whatever that means. Hayley Gordon, she's the young admin officer, the fair one, she hardly knew Annette, she's only been on the staff a month. Karen saw Osman Messaoud and Wendy Stowlap. Messaoud was very nervous. He was born and brought up in this country but he's uneasy around women. He told Karen he didn't want to be interviewed by a woman, he wanted, again I quote, "a police*man*' and he said if Karen questioned him about a woman, Annette that is, his wife would be suspicious. However, he seems to know less than nothing about Annette's life outside the Benefit Office.

'Apart from Ingrid Pamber, Wendy Stowlap appears to be the only member of staff to have been to Annette's flat. She herself lives fairly near, in Queens Gardens. It was a Sunday and she wanted someone to witness a document – doesn't say what kind of document – something she apparently didn't want the neighbours to know about, so she took it round to Annette. Annette was watching a video and told Wendy she'd just bought a new video recorder, some special kind that you punch a code into. That was six or seven months ago. All this circumlocution seems just to prove she did in fact have a video. Now let's have a look at what Barry has to say about Ingrid Pamber . . .'

But at that moment Detective Sergeant Vine came into the room. Vine wasn't really a short man but he looked short beside Wexford, and Burden too towered above him. He had the extraordinary combination of red hair on his head and dark hair on his upper lip. If he was in Barry Vine's shoes, Wexford had often thought, he'd shave off that moustache. But Vine – though this was unexpressed – seemed to enjoy the bicoloured effect, appearing to believe it gave him distinction. He was sharp and watchful and clever, a man with a prodigious memory that he crammed with all kinds of information, useful and otherwise.

'Have you looked at my report yet, sir?'

'I'm reading it now, Barry. This Ingrid really was Annette's only friend, wasn't she?'

'Not exactly. How about this married man?'

'What married man? Ah . . . wait a minute. Ingrid Pamber told you Annette had confided in her she'd been having an affair for the past *nine years* with a married man?'

'That's right.'

'Why didn't she tell me this on Friday?'

Vine sat down on the edge of the desk. 'She said she'd lain awake all night, wondering what was the right thing to do. She'd promised Annette faithfully, you see, that she'd never tell.'

The man who had phoned the Benefit Office, Wexford thought, the man Ingrid had said was a neighbour. 'All right. Yes, I can imagine. Spare us the schoolgirl heart-searching, will you?'

Vine grinned. 'I gave her the usual stuff, sir. Annette's dead, promises to a dead person weren't valid, didn't she want to help find whoever killed her, all that. She told me a bit and then she said she'd tell you. I mean, she'd only tell you.'

'Really? What have I got that you haven't, Barry? Must be age.'

Wexford concealed the mild embarrassment he felt by pretending to read from the report. 'We'll gratify her, shall we?'

'I thought you'd say that, so I asked her if she'd be at the Benefit Office, but no, she won't be. She starts two weeks' leave today and she and her boyfriend can't afford to go away. She'll be at home.'

Burden stepped over the yellow scene-of-crime tape, unlocked the door of the flat and went inside. Starting at the living room, he walked from room to room, slowly studying every object, looking out of the window into reddish-brown foliage, the concrete drive, the red brick side of the house next door. He took down what few books there were and shook their pages in case there were sheets enclosed, but with no particular purpose in mind. In the living room he looked carefully at Annette Bystock's music on a shelf of the bookcase, the compact discs for the missing CD player, the cassettes for the missing cassette player which was also a radio.

Her taste seemed to have been for popular classics and country. *Eine Kleine Nachtmusik*, Bach's *Mass in B Minor* – Burden had heard that this was among the top sellers in classical music – highlights from *Porgy and Bess*, a complete *Carmen Jones*, Beethoven's *Moonlight Sonata*, Natalie Cole's album *Unforgettable*, Michelle Wright, k.d. lang, Patsy Cline. . . . Without Wexford breathing reproof over his shoulder, Burden was quick to notice that Natalie Cole was a black woman and *Porgy and Bess* and *Carmen Jones* operas about black people. Was that significant?

He was trying to find points of connection between Annette and Melanie Akande. There was no desk in the flat. The dressing table up against the bedroom window had served as a desk. Her passport had been taken away. Burden looked at the other papers in the drawer. They were contained in one of those folders made of clear plastic: certificates showing Annette's O and A Level results, a certificate or diploma showing that she had gained a Bachelor of Arts pass degree in Business Studies at Myringham Polytechnic. That was where Melanie Akande had completed her education, only they called it Myringham University now. Burden looked at the date – 1976. Melanie was only three in 1976. Yet there might be a link there. . . .

Edwina Harris had told them she thought Annette had once been married. There was no marriage certificate in the top drawer. Burden tried the bottom one and found a decree of divorce, dissolving the marriage of Annette Rosemary Colegate née Bystock, and Stephen

Henry Colegate, the divorce having been made absolute on 29 June, 1985.

No letters. He had hoped for letters. A brown envelope, eight inches by five, contained a photograph of a man with a high forehead and dark curly hair. Under it was a stack of pamphlets instructing purchasers how to operate a Panasonic video recorder and an Akai CD player. The middle drawer held underclothes. He had already had a good look at the clothes in the wardrobe when he and Wexford came here on Friday. They were safe, dull clothes, the sort bought by a woman who can afford few and must put warmth and comfort before style. Therefore the underclothes surprised him.

They weren't quite what Burden would have called indecent. There were no bras with cut-outs, no crotchless pants. But all the – lingerie, he supposed, was the word – all of it was black or red and most of it transparent. There were two suspender belts, one black, one red, ordinary black bras and black platform bras, one strapless; a thing he called a corselet but Jenny said was a 'bustier' in red satin and lace, several pairs of black stockings, plain, fishnet and lacy, red and black knickers the size of the bottom part of a bikini and a kind of body stocking of black lace.

Had she worn that stuff under those jeans and sweaters, that beige raincoat?

Instead of clearing, as the meteorologists had said it would, the summery mist thinned and turned to rain. A grey drizzle began to fall and cool things down. Vine, driving the car, began speculating as to why rain in England is always cold while in other parts of the world it is warm and why, which he said was more to the point, it doesn't warm up again here afterwards as it does abroad.

'Something to do with being an island, I expect,' said Wexford abstractedly.

'Malta's an island. When I was there on holiday last year it rained but the sun came out afterwards and we were dry in five minutes. Did you see that picture of yourself in the paper yesterday?'

'Yes.'

'I cut it out to show you but I seem to have mislaid it somewhere.'

'Good.'

Vine said no more. They drove in silence to Glebe Lane where Ingrid Pamber lived in two rooms over a pair of lock-up garages with her boyfriend Jeremy Lang. Vine gave it as his opinion that as it was the first day of her holiday and only ten to ten in the morning she would still be in bed.

The neighbourhood was one of the charmless areas of Kingsmarkham. All you could say for it was that beyond the shabbiness, the waste ground and squat buildings, green hills rose skywards, topped with tree rings and behind them the sweep of downs. The district was vaguely commercial or industrial, some of the little houses converted to business premises, a good many buildings of the small factory or workshop kind. Gardens had become yards filled with used cars, scrap iron, oil drums, unidentifiable metal parts. The garages had one door painted black, the other green. At the side, approached by a narrow passage between chain link fencing, was the front door to the flat. There was no shelter from the rain. Vine rang the bell.

After rather a long time, during which there was some banging about and creaking from the upper floor, feet drummed on the stairs and the door was opened by a young man with wild black hair wearing nothing but black-framed glasses and a bath towel round his waist.

'Oh, sorry,' he said when he saw them. 'I thought you were the post. I'm expecting a parcel.'

'Kingsmarkham CID,' said Wexford, who wasn't usually so brusque. 'To see Miss Pamber.'

'Oh, sure. Come up.'

He was a small man, no more than five feet six, and fine-boned with it. The girl was no doubt, as Vine had predicted, still in bed. He closed the door behind them with perfect trust.

'You're Mr Lang?'

'That's me, though I'm mostly known as Jerry.'

'Mr Lang, are you in the habit of letting strangers into your home without question?'

Jeremy Lang peered at Wexford and pushed his right ear at him as if he had been addressed inaudibly or in a foreign language. 'You're police, you said.'

Neither Wexford nor Vine said anything. Each produced his warrant card and held it under Lang's nose. He grinned and nodded. He began to go upstairs, gestured to them to follow him, suddenly yelling at the top of his voice: 'Hey, Ing, you going to get up? It's the cops.'

Upstairs was a surprise. Wexford hardly knew what he had expected, but not this pleasantly furnished clean room with a big yellow sofa, blue and yellow floor cushions on a big brightly coloured woven mat, the walls entirely concealed under draped lengths of cloth, posters, and a huge faded tapestry bedspread. Everything had obviously been perks from a parent or else bought very cheaply but it made a harmonious and comfortable place to be. Houseplants in a yellow-painted wooden trough filled the floorspace between the windows.

The door to the bedroom opened and Ingrid Pamber came out. She too wasn't yet dressed but there was nothing frowsty about her, nothing to suggest she had just risen from a long lie-in. She wore a dressing gown or robe of white broderie anglaise that came to her knees. Her small shapely feet were bare. The satiny dark hair, which had been confined by a barrette when Wexford had talked to her on Friday evening, was now held back by a red Alice band. Without make-up her face was even prettier, the skin glowing, the blueness of her eyes startling.

'Oh, hello, it's you,' she said to Wexford, sounding delighted to see him. On Vine she bestowed a friendly smile. 'Would you like some coffee? If I ask him very nicely, I'm sure Jerry will make us some coffee.'

'Ask me nicely then,' said Jeremy Lang.

She gave him a kiss. A highly sexual kiss, Wexford thought, in spite of being planted in the middle of his cheek and with closed lips. The kiss lingered, she withdrew her mouth an inch, whispered, 'Make us some coffee, my love, please, please. And I'm going to have a huge breakfast, two eggs and bacon and sausages if we've got any and – yes, fried potatoes. You'll cook it for me, won't you, angel? Please, please, mmm?'

Vine coughed. He was exasperated rather than embarrassed. Ingrid sat down on a floor cushion and gazed up at them. She was, Wexford thought, immeasurably more confident and in control here, on her home ground.

'I've already told him a bit of it,' she said, glancing at Vine. 'I've saved the important part for you. It's an amazing story.'

'All right,' Wexford said, and in the manner of Cocteau to Diaghilev, 'Astound me.'

'I never told anyone before, you know. Not even Jerry. I think people should keep their promises, don't you?'

'Certainly they should,' Wexford said. 'But not beyond the grave.'

Ingrid Pamber evidently enjoyed this kind of conversation. 'Yes, but if you'd promised somebody something and they died it wouldn't be right to break your promise and tell their children, would it? Not if it affected their children? I mean, it might be something about them that would ruin their lives.'

'Let's not get on to moral philosophy now, Miss Pamber. Annette Bystock hadn't any children. She had no relatives apart from a cousin. I'd like to hear what she told you about this love affair she was having.'

'He might be affected though, mightn't he?'

'Who do you mean?'

'Well, Bruce. The man. The man I told *him* about.' She pointed a forefinger at Vine.

'Leave that to me,' said Wexford. 'I'll worry about that.'

Jeremy Lang came back with coffee in three cups and on a plate, like a waiter in certain kinds of restaurant displaying to clients the raw materials of their meal, two eggs still in their shells, two rashers of bacon, three pork sausages and a potato.

'Thank you.' Ingrid looked into his eyes and said it again, 'Thank you, thank you, that will be lovely,' the words apparently having some special or secret meaning for the two of them, for the effect on him was to make him roll his eyes while she began to giggle. Wexford coughed. He could manage to get a good deal of reproach into a cough. 'Oh, sorry,' she said, and she stopped laughing. 'I must be good. I shouldn't laugh. I'm really very very sad about poor Annette.

'How long had you known her, Miss Pamber?' Vine asked.

'Since I started working for the ES three years ago. I've *told* you all this. I was a teacher before that, only I wasn't much good. I couldn't get on with the kids and they hated me.'

'You didn't tell me that,' said Vine.

'Well, it's not exactly relevant, is it? I had a place quite near where Annette lived. That was before I met Jerry.' She cast Jeremy Lang a loving look and pursed up her lips in a kissing shape. 'We used to walk home together, Annette and I, and sometimes we'd have a meal somewhere. You know, if we didn't feel like cooking or getting anything in. I went to her flat once or twice but she came to mine much more and I just had a room. I got the feeling she didn't like asking people to her place.

'Then . . . well, I met someone and we started – ' A rueful look this time for Jeremy, who returned it with a pantomime frown. 'We started going about. I didn't live with him or anything,' she added, not making clear what 'anything' might signify. 'That was what made Annette tell me, I think. Or it might have been that one evening when I did go into her place and while I was there the phone rang and it was *him*. That was when she made me promise not to tell anyone what she was going to tell me.

'She'd been so jumpy before the phone rang. I'd guess he'd promised to phone at seven and it was nearly eight. She grabbed that phone like it was . . . well, a matter of life and death. Afterwards she said, "Can you keep a secret?" and I said of course I could and she said, "Well, I've got someone too. That was him," and then it all came out.'

'His name, Miss Pamber?'

'Bruce. His name's Bruce. I don't know Bruce *What*.'

'This was the man you thought had phoned the Benefit Office after Miss Bystock phoned to say she wouldn't be coming in?'

She nodded, untroubled by that earlier lie.

'You know where he lives?' Vine asked.

'My boyfriend and me, we were going to Pomfret one day and we gave Annette a lift. She was going to see her cousin. It was sort of Christmas, the day before Christmas Eve, I think. Annette was sitting in the back and as we passed this house she tapped on my shoulder and said, "Look at that, that house with the window in the roof, that's where you-know-who lives." That was what she said, "you-know-who".

'I don't know the number. I could show you.' Furious faces of discouragement made by Jeremy weren't lost on Wexford. Ingrid saw them and sighed happily. 'I could describe it. I will. You mustn't make silly faces, lovey. Now run away and cook my breakfast.'

'What did you do with the key to Miss Bystock's flat,' Wexford asked, 'when you left on Thursday?'

She answered promptly – too promptly.

Sitting in the car outside number 101 Harrow Avenue, a biggish Victorian house on three floors to which a fourth had been added with a dormer window in the mansard roof, Wexford gave Burden an account of what Ingrid Pamber had told him. They had already been to the house and found no one at home. It was about as far from the street in which Annette lived as was possible and still be in

393

Kingsmarkham. The electoral roll had shown its occupants to be Snow, Carolyn E., Snow, Bruce J., and Snow, Melissa E. Wife, husband and grown-up daughter, Wexford guessed. No hint, of course, was given in the list of those eligible to vote as to how many other children the Snows might have.

'She'd been having this affair with him for nine years,' Wexford said. 'Or so she told Ingrid Pamber, and I can't think of any reason why even a liar like her should lie about that. It was one of those situations in which the married man tells his mistress he'll leave his wife for her as soon as the children are off their hands. Nine years ago Bruce Snow's youngest child was five, so you could say if you were a cynic like me that he was on to a good thing.'

'Right,' said Burden in a heartfelt way.

Wexford cast up his eyes. 'Wait for it. It gets better. They had to meet somewhere but he never took her to an hotel, he said he couldn't afford it. After that trip past the house in the boyfriend's car Ingrid asked her what Bruce had given her for Christmas and Annette said nothing, he never gave her anything, she'd never had a present from him. He needed everything he had for his family. Mind you, according to Ingrid, Annette wasn't resentful, she never criticized him. She *understood*.'

'I take it that after the first confidings there were more on other occasions?'

'Oh, yes. Once she'd started there was no stopping her. It was Bruce this and Bruce that whenever she and Ingrid were alone together. I imagine it was a relief to the poor woman to have someone she could talk to.' Wexford took another look at the house, at the signs of prosperity about it, the evidently recent rooftop extension, the new paint, the satellite dish outside an upper window. 'As I said,' he went on, 'Snow never took her to an hotel and of course they couldn't go to his house. She had her flat but he refused to go there. Apparently, there was some friend or relative of his wife living opposite. So he summoned her to his office after hours.'

'You're joking,' said Burden.

'Not unless Ingrid Pamber is and I doubt if she'd have the imagination. Snow never wrote to her, which is why we found no letters. He gave her nothing, not even a photograph of himself. He phoned, at appointed times, "when he could". But she loved him,

394

you see, and that was why all that was OK, was reasonable in her eyes, was prudent. After all, it would only go on so long as the children were young.'

Burden used his small son's currently favourite word, 'Yuck!'

'I couldn't put it better myself. When he wanted to meet her, or let's say when he wanted his bit on the side . . .' Wexford ignored Burden's pained expression, 'he'd ask her to come to his office. He's an accountant with Hawkins and Steele.'

'Is he now? In York Street, aren't they?'

'In one of those very old houses that overhang the street. The back way has access into Kiln Lane, that sort of alley that comes out in the High Street the other side of St Peter's. There's never a soul about down there after the shops close and Kiln Lane is just an alley between high walls. Annette could sneak down there and he'd let her in by the back door. The best part of this – or the worst part, depending on how you look at it – is that he explained his choice of venue by saying that if his wife phoned the office he'd be there to answer it and she'd know he was working late.'

Lights were coming on in the houses but 101 remained in darkness. Wexford and Burden left the car again and walked up the drive. A side gate was unlocked and they went into the rear garden, a large area of lawn and shrubs whose end was lost in a duster of tall trees, darkening as the dusk came.

'She did that for nine years?' said Burden. 'Like a call girl?'

'A call girl would expect a bed, Mike, and probably a glass of something stimulating. Call girls, I'm told, expect bathrooms. And very definitely to get paid.'

'It explains the underwear.' Burden described what he had found at the flat in Ladyhall Court. 'She'd always be ready for him. I wonder what's going through his mind now?'

'Is he the guy in the photo, d'you think? What I'm wondering is if he's away on holiday.'

'He won't be, Reg. Not if his youngest is only fourteen. He'll wait for the school term to end and that won't be for a couple of weeks.'

'We have to see him and soon.'

Burden considered. 'What makes you say this Ingrid's a liar?'

'She told me she left the key Annette gave her behind in the flat after she left on Thursday. If she did, where is it?'

'It was on the bedside table,' said Burden promptly.

'No, it wasn't, Mike. Not unless she was lying when she said there were two keys there on Wednesday. One of those statements of hers has to be a lie.'

# 8

Only two samples of fingerprints had been found in Annette Bystock's flat. Most were those of Annette herself, the other set of women's prints, on the surface of the grocer's box, the kitchen door, the front door and the hall table, were those of Ingrid Pamber. Not another print had been found in the whole place. It seemed as if Annette's home had not only been her castle, it had been the cell where she passed her solitary confinement.

The thief of the electronic equipment had worn gloves. Her killer had worn gloves. Bruce Snow had never set foot or finger inside the home of the woman who had been his mistress for nearly a decade. No friend, apart from Ingrid, had come there. It was likely, Wexford thought, that Annette had discouraged potential friends. Such visitors might overhear one of her conversations with Snow, might betray her; more to the point as she saw it, might by some indiscretion destroy Snow's carefully planned cover. So, for love's sake, she lived this lonely life. It was the saddest story. . . .

The one friend she had she must have trusted to be discreet. And if Ingrid was to be believed her trust was not misplaced, for Ingrid had told no one until after Annette was dead. It seemed that her death had occurred about seven months after she had first confided in Ingrid, so it was hardly likely to be the result of her divulging the secret or divulging more details.

Wexford sighed. Annette had died in the region of thirty-six hours before Burden found her body on Friday morning. Not earlier than 10.00 pm on the Wednesday and not later than 1.00 am on the Thursday. By the time Ingrid Pamber went into the flat at five-thirty on Thursday, Annette had been dead for a day and half a night. Death was due to strangulation with a ligature, in this case a length

397

of electric lead. He knew that already and such medical details were always incomprehensible. Tremlett offered his opinion that a strong woman might have been the perpetrator. Until her death Annette had been a normal healthy woman with no distinguishing marks, not a scar on her body, no peculiarities or minor deformities. She was of normal weight for her height. There was no disease of any kind present.

The flat had been clean but still a considerable amount of hairs and fibres had been gathered from the bed, the bedside tables and the floor. How helpful it would be, Wexford thought as he often did, if one of the investigating officers had picked up a spent cigarette end in the vicinity of the body, as happened in detective stories. Or if a button torn from the killer's jacket, and obligingly retaining a fragment of tweed on its shank, had been found clutched in poor Annette's lifeless hand. Such clues never came his way. Of course it was true that nobody goes anywhere without leaving a vestige of himself behind and taking a vestige of where he has been away with him. That was only useful if you had a clue who and where he might be. . . .

He was leaving for the local studios to make his television appeal for help from the public when his phone rang. The switchboard said it was the Chief Constable for him, calling from his home in Stowerton.

Freeborn, a cold man, always went straight to the heart of things. 'I don't want to see pictures of you carousing.'

'No, sir. It was unfortunate.'

'It was more than that, it was bloody disgraceful. And in a *good* newspaper too.'

'I can't see it would have been any better in a tabloid,' said Wexford.

'Then that's just one of the many things you ought to see and don't.' Freeborn went on for quite a long time about the need to catch Annette's murderer fast, about the increase in violent crime, about this lovely, safe, once secure, place in which they lived, quickly becoming as dangerous as some inner suburb of London. 'And when you go on TV try not to have a glass in your hand.'

They allowed him only two minutes and that, he knew, would be cut to thirty seconds. Still, it was better than nothing. His appeal would call forth from a public who longed to be important its imagined and

398

fantasized sightings of a killer in the vicinity of Ladyhall Road, confessions to the crime, offers from clairvoyants, claims to have been at school with Annette, at college with her, to have been her lover, her mother, her sister, to have seen her in Inverness or Carlisle or Budapest after she was dead and, perhaps, one genuine and valuable piece of information.

He got to bed late. But he was up early just as the post came. Dora came down in her dressing gown to get his breakfast, an affectionate but unnecessary move as he was only having cereal and a piece of bread.

'One letter and it's for both of us. You open it.'

Dora slit the envelope and drew out a card, deckle-edged.

'Goodness, Reg, she must have taken a fancy to you.'

'Who must? What are you talking about?' Strange that his thoughts ran straight to pretty Ingrid Pamber.

'Invitations to this party are like gold dust, Sylvia says. She'd *love* to go.'

'Let's have a look.' What a fool! Why did he take these fancies into his head at his age? He read aloud what was on the card. '"Wael and Anouk Khoori request the pleasure of the company of Mr and Mrs Reginald Wexford at a Garden Party at their home, Mynford New Hall, Mynford, Sussex, on Saturday, July 17th, at 3pm."' At the foot of the card was the addendum: 'In aid of CIBACT, the Cancer in Babies and Children Trust'. 'They're not giving us much notice. It's the thirteenth today.'

'No, well, that's what I mean. We obviously weren't on the guest list. And then she took a shine to you last Saturday night.'

'I bet Freeborn's on the list,' Wexford said gloomily. 'Everyone will be expected to fork out at least a tenner, which is a bit of a nerve when you consider Khoori's a millionaire. He could underwrite this CIBACT himself without fund-raising bonanzas. Anyway, it doesn't matter since we shan't go.'

'I should like to go,' Dora said as her husband disappeared out of the door. She called after him, 'I said I should like to go, Reg.'

There was no answer. The front door closed quietly.

The inquest on Annette Bystock opened at 10.00 am and was adjourned pending further evidence at ten past. Jane Winster, who was Annette's cousin, though not attending it, was waiting for Wexford when he got back to the police station. Somebody – some fool, he thought – had put her in one of the bleak interview rooms where she sat on a tubular metal chair in front of the chipboard table, looking puzzled and a little alarmed.

'You have something you want to tell me, Mrs Winster?'

She nodded. She looked about her, as well she might, at the cream-painted brick walls, the uncurtained window.

'Come upstairs to my office,' he said.

Someone's head ought to roll for this. What did they take her for, this small middle-aged woman buttoned up in her raincoat, a damp scarf tied round her head? A shoplifter? A bag-snatcher? She looked like a school dinner lady who could have done with a good helping of what she purveyed. Her face was thin and pinched, her hands bony and veined, prematurely aged.

Once in the comparative comfort of his office, carpeted and with seats that were almost armchairs, he expected her to complain of her treatment, but she only gave the room the same wary look. Perhaps all new places overawed her, so sheltered and circumscribed was her life. He asked her to sit down and he repeated what he had said to her downstairs. For the first time she spoke, having seated herself on the edge of the chair, her knees pressed together.

'The policeman who came, there was something I forgot to tell him. It was a bit . . . I mean, I was. . . .'

Vine's briskness had intimidated her, he supposed. 'It doesn't matter, Mrs Winster. You've remembered now, that's the main thing.'

'It was a shock, you see. I mean, we weren't . . . well, we weren't close, Annette and me, but . . . well, she was my *cousin*, my own auntie's daughter.'

'Yes.'

'And having to go to that place and see her . . . well, dead like that, that was a shock. I've never had to do anything like that before and I. . . .'

A woman who left sentences unfinished through self-doubt and perhaps uncertainty that anyone would ever take her seriously. He realized that all this was in the nature of an apology. She was apologizing for having emotions.

'I did tell him we phoned each other. I mean, I said we spoke on the phone but he was . . . well, he was more interested in when I'd last seen her. I hadn't seen her since she came to our wedding anniversary, and that was April, April the third.'

400

'But you had spoken on the phone?'

She was going to need a lot of prompting and of the kind Vine wasn't the man to give. She looked at him appealingly.

'She phoned me on the Tuesday before she . . . last Tuesday, I mean. . . .'

The day Melanie Akande spoke to her. 'Was that in the evening, Mrs Winster?'

'In the evening, about seven. I was getting my husband's meal on the table. He doesn't . . . well, he doesn't like to be kept waiting. I was a bit surprised she phoned but then she said she wasn't feeling too good, she thought she'd go to bed early . . .' Mrs Winster hesitated. 'My husband . . . well, my husband was making signs to me, so I put the phone down for a minute and he said – I know you'll think this sounds awful . . .'

'Please go on, Mrs Winster.'

'My husband – it's not that he didn't like Annette, it's really that's he doesn't care for any outsiders. Our own family's enough for us, he always says. Of course, Annette *was* family in a way but he always says cousins don't count. He said to me, I mean when Annette was on the phone, he said, don't get involved. If she's ill she'll expect you to go over there getting her shopping and all the rest of it. Well, I suppose she did expect that, that's why she phoned, and I felt awful saying I was busy, I couldn't talk then, but I have to put his wishes first, don't I?'

If this was all, he was wasting his time. He had to be patient. 'You rang off?'

'Well, no. Not at once. She said, could she call me back later? I didn't know what to say. Then she said there was something else, something she wanted to ask me about, maybe ask Malcolm too – Malcolm's my husband – it was whether she ought to go to the police.'

'Ah.' This was it then. 'She told you what this was about?'

'No, because she was going to call me back. But she didn't.'

'You didn't phone her?'

Jane Winster flushed. She looked defiant. 'My husband doesn't like me making unnecessary phone calls. And it's up to him, isn't it? He earns the money.'

'Tell me exactly what your cousin said to you about going to the police.'

Wexford was beginning to understand Vine's impatience with her

401

as a witness, even understand whoever it was who had incarcerated her in that grim interview room. His sympathies were fast diminishing. Here was just another person who had rejected Annette Bystock. She was fidgeting with her handbag, pursing her lips; a woman, he guessed, who though an expert at putting herself down would deeply resent anyone else's criticism.

'I can't do the exact words, or I don't . . . well, it was something like, "There was something happened through work and I think maybe I should go to the police but I want to see what you think and maybe Malcolm too." That was all.'

'You mean "at" work, don't you?'

'No. "Through work" is what she said.'

'You never spoke to her again?'

'She never phoned back and I. . . . No, I . . . I hadn't any call to speak to her.'

He nodded. Her cousin having failed her, Annette had called on the slightly more sympathetic Ingrid to come in, do her shopping, pay her the small attentions needed by someone with 'the falling sickness'. As for the police, she had changed her mind, or more likely, postponed the phone call she should have made until she was better. But she was never better, she was much much worse and it was too late.

'Did your cousin ever mention a man called Bruce Snow?'

She looked up with indifference. 'No. Who's he?'

'You'd be surprised to learn he was a married man Miss Bystock had been in a relationship with for several years?'

Jane Winster was more shocked than she had been by her cousin's death, more shocked than when she saw Annette's dead face in the mortuary. 'I'll never believe that. Annette would never have done a thing like that. She wasn't that sort of person.' Astonishment had made her articulate. 'My husband would never have had her in the house if there'd ever been a suspicion of any of that. Oh, no, you've got it wrong there. Not Annette, Annette wouldn't have done that.'

When she had gone, Wexford had a call put through to Hawkins and Steele and asked to speak to Mr Snow. Waiting while a tape played 'Greensleeves', he thought about Snow and wondered how appalling a shock hearing who was calling him would be. Annette, after all, had been found dead on the previous Friday, it had been on television on Friday, in the papers on Saturday. But no one knew of their liaison except Annette and himself, did they? And Annette was dead. He must think he had got away with it. Got away with exactly what, though, Wexford asked himself.

'Mr Snow is on his other line. Will you hold?'

'No, I won't. I'll call back in ten minutes. You can tell him it's Kingsmarkham Police.'

That should stir him up a bit. Wexford wouldn't have been surprised if Snow had called back himself, unable to wait to know the worst, but no call came. He gave it a quarter of an hour before dialling the number again.

'Mr Snow is in a meeting.'

'Did you give him the message?'

'Yes, I did, but he had this meeting straight after he came off the phone.'

'I see. How long will this meeting last?'

'Half an hour. Mr Snow has his next meeting at eleven-fifteen.'

'Give him another message, will you? Tell him to cancel his other meeting as Chief Inspector Wexford will see him in his office at eleven.'

'I can't possibly . . .'

'Thank you.' Wexford put the phone down. His temper had started to rise. He remembered his blood pressure. Then he had a good idea which made him laugh to himself before he picked up the phone again and asked DS Karen Malahyde to come up and see him.

Karen Malahyde was very much the new woman. Young, fairly good looking, she did little to enhance her looks. Her face was always without make-up of any kind, her fair hair was very short as were her fingernails. Many with fewer advantages than she had made themselves into beauties. She could do nothing, however, to disguise the excellence of her figure. Karen was a beautiful shape and had the sort of long legs that looked as if they started at her waist. She was a feminist and almost a radical one, a good police officer but one who had sometimes to be cautioned not to lean too hard on men or favour women.

'Yes, sir?'

'I want you to come with me on a visit to a gallant lover.'

'Sir?'

Wexford told her some of Annette Bystock's love story. Instead of castigating Snow as a bastard, which was what he expected, she said

403

rather gloomily, 'These women are their own worst enemies,' and then, 'did he kill her?'

'I don't know.'

They entered the old house by the front door in York Street. Inside it was poky and low-ceilinged but authentically ancient, the kind of place that is generally said to be full of character. There was no lift. The receptionist left her desk and took them upstairs, up a narrow creaking oak staircase, winding to a passage at the top. She knocked on a door, opened it and said rather cryptically,

'Your eleven o'clock appointment, Mr Snow.'

The man in the photograph Burden had found came up to them with outstretched hand. Wexford pretended not to have seen it. For a moment he thought Snow hadn't been told who his callers were. Surely if he had known he could hardly have been so confident, would hardly have smiled so winningly.

'I'm happy to tell you it's turned up,' he said.

They were evidently at cross-purposes but how and why Wexford couldn't tell. He thought that if he didn't keep a watch on himself he might start enjoying this. It was going to be good.

'What has turned up, sir?'

'My driving licence, of course. There were five places it could have been, I looked in them and there it was in the fifth and last.' Snow realized that something was wrong but he was only disconcerted, not fearful. 'I'm sorry. What did you want to see me about?'

Karen was looking offended at being taken for a traffic cop. Wexford asked, 'What do you *think* we want to see you about, Mr Snow?'

A wariness in his eyes showed that realization was dawning. He put up his eyebrows, his head a little on one side. He was a tall thin man, his bushy dark hair greying, not good-looking but with an air of distinction. Wexford thought he had a mean mouth. 'How should I know?' he said in a voice that was a little shriller than it had been.

'May we sit down?'

Karen, when she was seated, couldn't help showing a lot of leg. Even in those awful brown lace-ups with their Cuban heels, her legs were spectacular. Snow gave them a swift but significant glance.

'I'm surprised you don't know why we've come, Mr Snow,' Wexford said. 'I'd have thought you'd be expecting us.'

'I was. I told you, I thought you were here because I couldn't produce my licence when I was stopped on Saturday.' He knew,

404

Wexford could tell. Was he going to brazen it out? Snow's fingers fidgeted with objects on his desk, straightening a sheet of paper, replacing the cap on a pen. 'So what is it then?'

'Annette Bystock.'

'Who?'

If it hadn't been for those restless fingers, now busy with the telephone lead, those eyes that held a gleam of real panic, Wexford might have doubted, might have thought the dead woman a paranoid fantasist, Jane Winster an oracle and Ingrid Pamber queen of the liars. He glanced at Karen.

'Annette Bystock was murdered last Wednesday,' said Karen. 'Don't you watch television? You haven't seen the papers? You and she had a relationship. You'd been having a relationship with her for nine years.'

'*I what?*'

'I think you heard me, sir, but I don't mind repeating it. You had been having a relationship with Annette Bystock for . . .'

'That is absolute nonsense!'

Bruce Snow got to his feet. His thin face had gone a dark red and a pulse beat in a bluish vein on his forehead.

'How dare you come into my office and make these totally false suggestions!'

For some reason Wexford thought suddenly of Annette coming here, hiding in the alley, tapping on the back door, being brought up that winding stair by Snow to this office where there wasn't even a couch, where there was not the means to produce a drink or even a cup of tea. The phone was there, though, in case his wife called him.

He got up and Karen, taking her cue from him, also rose to her feet.

'No doubt it was a mistake coming to your office, Mr Snow,' he said. 'I apologize.' He watched Snow relax, breathe again, gather up his energy for a final blustering. 'I'll tell you what we'll do. We'll come to your home this evening and talk about it there. Shall we say eight? That'll give you and your wife a chance to have your evening meal first.'

If it hadn't worked it would have shown he was wrong, one or both of the women were fantasists, he'd imagined every sign he'd detected in Snow, and he'd be for the high jump. Freeborn would like this a lot less than newspaper photographs of merry-making.

But it worked.

Snow said, 'Sit down, please.'

'Are you going to tell us about it, Mr Snow?'

'What is there to tell? I'm not the first married man to have a girlfriend. As it happens, Annette and I had decided to break up. It was over.' Snow paused, cleared his throat. 'There is no point in my wife's knowing now. I may as well tell you I went to great lengths to conceal my relationship from my wife. I was anxious not to cause her pain. Annette understood that. Our relationship was, not to put too fine a point on it, purely physical.'

'Then you never intended to leave your wife and marry Miss Bystock once your youngest child was off your hands?'

'Good heavens, no!'

Karen said, 'Where did you meet, Mr Snow? At Miss Bystock's home? At an hotel?'

'I can't see that that's relevant.'

'Perhaps you'd answer the question just the same.'

'At her home,' said Snow uncomfortably. 'We met at her home.'

'That's odd, sir, because we didn't find any fingerprints in Miss Bystock's flat apart from her own and those of a woman friend. Perhaps you wiped surfaces clean of prints.' Karen seemed to rack her brains. 'Or – yes, that would be it – you wore gloves.'

'Of course I didn't wear gloves!'

Snow was growing angry. Wexford watched the beating pulse, the bloodshot eyes. Had he no grief for Annette Bystock at all? After all that time was there no sorrow, no nostalgia even, no regret? And what did the man mean with his 'purely physical' relationship? What did anyone ever mean? That there had been no words exchanged, no endearments, no promises? One at least he had extracted from the dead woman, that she tell nobody. She had very nearly kept it.

'When did you last see her?'

'I don't know. I'll have to think. A few weeks ago, I think it was a Wednesday.'

'Here?' said Karen.

He shrugged, then nodded.

Wexford said, 'I'd like you to tell me where you were between 8.00 pm and midnight last Wednesday. Wednesday, July the seventh.'

'At home, of course. I've always got home by six.'

'Except when you were meeting Miss Bystock.'

Snow winced and coughed as if screwing up his face was a normal preliminary to clearing his throat. 'I got home by six last Wednesday and I stayed at home. I didn't go out again.'

'You spent the evening at home with your wife and – your children, Mr Snow?'

'My elder daughter doesn't live at home. The younger one, Catherine, she's . . . well, she's not often in in the evenings . . .'

'But your wife and your son were with you? We shall need to talk to your wife.'

'You can't bring my wife into this!'

'You have brought her into it yourself, Mr Snow,' Wexford said quietly.

Bruce Snow's 11.15 appointment had been cancelled and now he was obliged to postpone the one he had with a Tax Inspector at 12.30. Wexford didn't think his misery had anything to do with guilt, or rather, with any responsibility for Annette's death. It was terror, the fear of his orderly world falling to pieces. But he couldn't be sure.

'Now you last saw Miss Bystock on a Wednesday some weeks ago. How many weeks, sir?'

'Do you really want me to be precise about it?'

'Certainly I do.'

'Three weeks, then. It was three weeks.'

'And when did you last talk to her on the phone?' Snow didn't want to admit it. He screwed up his eyes like someone in a smoky room. 'It was Tuesday evening.'

'What, the Tuesday before her death?' Karen Malahyde was surprised. 'Tuesday the sixth?'

'I phoned her from here,' Snow said in a rush. 'I phoned her from this office just before I went home.' He rubbed his hands together. 'To make a date, if you must know. For the next night. God, this is my private life you're putting on the line. Anyway, it wasn't important, there was nothing, she just said she wasn't well. She was in bed. She'd got flu or something.'

'Did she mention a girl called Melanie Akande? Did she say anything about giving information to the police?'

This gave Snow a sort of hope. Here was something else. The heat had, at least temporarily, gone off his long and suddenly reprehensible affair with Annette. But he gave a heavy sigh.

'No, I don't – wait a minute, did you say Akande? There's a doctor called that in the same practice as my doctor. Coloured chap.'

'Melanie is his daughter,' said Karen.

'Well, what about her? I don't know anything about her. I don't know him, I didn't know he had a daughter.'

'Annette did. And Melanie Akande has disappeared. But no, of course not, Annette wouldn't have mentioned anything to you because yours was a purely physical relationship, you said, conducted in silence.'

Snow was too wretched to lash back. He did ask when Wexford intended to speak to his wife.

'Oh, not yet, Mr Snow,' Wexford said. 'Not today. I'll give you a chance to tell her yourself first.' He dropped the faintly bantering tone and became serious. 'I suggest you do that, sir, at the first possible opportunity.'

William Cousins, the jeweller, took a good look at Annette Bystock's ring, pronounced it a fine ruby and valued it at two thousand, five hundred pounds. Give or take a little. That was around the sum he would be prepared to pay for such a ring if it was offered to him. He could probably sell it for much more.

Tuesday was one of Kingsmarkham's two market days, the other being Saturday. As a matter of routine, Sergeant Vine cast his eye over the goods for sale on the stalls in St Peter's Place. The stolen stuff either turned up here or at the car boot sales in gardens or on waste ground that had become a regular weekend feature. He generally went round the stalls first, then headed for the sandwich bar to collect his lunch.

Leaving Cousins's, he began his investigation of the market and on the second stall he looked at saw for sale a radio-cassette player. It was made of a hard white plastic substance and across the top of it, just above the digital clock, was a dark red stain someone had tried in vain to eradicate. For a moment or two Vine thought the stain was blood, and then he remembered.

408

# 9

The worst thing, Dr Akande told Wexford, was the way everybody asked them if there was any news of their daughter. All his patients knew and they all asked. At last, unable to keep the truth from him any longer, Laurette Akande had told her son when he telephoned from Kuala Lumpur. Immediately he said he would come home. As soon as he could get a cheap flight he would come back.

'The death of that other girl made me believe Melanie must also be dead,' Akande said.

'I should be raising false hopes if I told you not to think that way.'

'But I've told myself there's no connection. I have to keep hoping.'

Wexford had come to them as he did most mornings on his way to work or evenings on his way home. Laurette, changed out of her navy and white uniform into a linen dress, impressed him with her handsome looks, her dignified demeanour. He had seldom seen a woman with a straighter back. She showed less emotion than her husband, was always under control, cool, steady-eyed.

'I wonder if you can tell me what Melanie did the day before she . . . disappeared,' he said. 'On the Monday. What did she do that day?'

Akande didn't know. He had been at work but it was Laurette's day off. 'She wanted a lie-in.' Wexford got the impression that here was a mother who disapproved of staying in bed late. 'I got her up at ten. It's no good getting into those habits if you want to get on in life. She went down to the shops, I don't know what for. In the afternoon she went for a run – you know, jogging that they all do. She always took the same route, Harrow Avenue, Eton Grove, uphill all the way, horrible in this heat, but it would have been pointless saying so. The world would be a better place if they thought as much about their responsibilities as they do about their figures. My husband came home, we had our meal, the three of us . . .'

'She talked about getting a job,' said the doctor, 'about this appointment she had and the possibility of getting a grant to do business training.' He made an effort at a laugh. 'She got cross with me because I said she'd have to think about working her way through college the way they do in America.'

'Well, we couldn't afford to pay,' Laurette said sharply. 'And she'd had one grant. It wasn't as if her first degree was any good, they do take that into account, I told her. She got sulky about it. We all watched some television. She phoned someone, I don't know who, possibly that Euan, God forbid.'

'My wife,' said Dr Akande, in almost reverential tones, 'had a degree in physics from University College, Ibadan, before she studied nursing.'

Wexford was beginning to pity Melanie Akande, a seriously pressurized young woman. The irony was that it looked as if she had had no more chance of escape from forcible education than a Victorian girl had from its denial. And like that Victorian, she was obliged to live at home for an unforeseeable future.

He referred back to her afternoon's jogging. 'She told you nothing of what she had seen while she was out, anyone who had spoken to her, anything at all?'

'She didn't tell us anything,' said Laurette. 'They don't. They're experts at that. You'd think she'd taken a course in secrecy.'

Wexford got into the car, driving himself, but instead of heading for home, took the Glebe Lane direction. Asking himself if it was possible either of the Akandes was responsible for Melanie's disappearance, perhaps Melanie's death, he had to face the chance that it was. But he still went and talked to them. To allege that Akande might be guilty of such a crime was to presuppose him mad or at least a fanatic. The doctor appeared neither of those things and not at all obsessed about Euan Sinclair's association with his daughter. Wexford had never checked out Akande's alibi, hardly knew if he *had* an alibi. But he could see that there was one car Melanie would have got into while she was on her way from the Benefit Office to the bus stop – her father's.

Then had Akande lied? As Snow had, as surely Ingrid Pamber had? It was strange how he knew she had been lying without

410

knowing what she was lying about. He drove into Glebe Lane, over the cobbles. She came down to let him in and said she was at home alone. Lang had gone to see his uncle, a strange excuse that immediately made Wexford suspicious, though he hardly knew of what. Her eyes met his. It spoke of a sublime self-confidence, or an ability to lie effectively, when someone could look you so boldly in the eye and hold the gaze. She wore a long patterned skirt, blue with paler blue flowers, and a silk sweater. Her dark shiny hair was twisted up on top of her head.

'Miss Pamber, you'll think I have a bad memory but I wonder if you'd tell me all over again just what happened when you called on Miss Bystock last Wednesday? When you took her a pint of milk and she asked you to fetch her some shopping on the following day?'

'You haven't really got a bad memory, have you? You're just testing me to see if I'll say the same things.'

'Perhaps I am.'

The blue she wore made him think all blue-eyed women should wear that shade. She was an ornament to the room so that it seemed to need no other. 'I bought the milk at the corner shop where Ladyhall Avenue crosses Lower Queen Street. Did I say that before?' She must know she hadn't. He said nothing. 'It's easy to park there, you see. It was just a bit after five-thirty when I got to Annette's. The front door to those flats has been unlocked every time I've been there – I don't think that's very secure, do you?'

'Evidently not.'

'I think I said Annette had left her door on the latch. I put the milk straight in the fridge and then I went into the bedroom. I knocked on the door first.' All these details were being given to tease him. He realized that but didn't mind. Any detail, however small, might be relevant in a case like this. 'She said, "Come in". I think she said, "Come in, Ingrid". I went in and she was in bed, sort of half-sitting up, but she looked quite ill. She said not to come near her because she was sure she was infectious, but would I get her the things on this list she'd made. It was a loaf and cornflakes and yogurt and cheese and grapefruit and more milk.'

Wexford listened, deadpan. He didn't move.

'She had two keys on the bedside table. She gave me one – that was the nearest I got to her, I really didn't want to catch it – and she said, now you'll be able to let yourself in tomorrow. So I said I would, yes, I would, and I'd get the things and to get well soon, and she said

411

would I draw the curtains in the living room on my way out. So I did that and I called out goodbye and . . .' Ingrid Pamber looked at him ruefully, her head on one side, 'I may as well come out with it. You're not going to eat me, are you?'

Had he looked as if he wanted to? 'Go on.'

'I forgot to lock the door after me. I mean, I left it on the latch like it was. I just *did*. It was awful of me, I know, but it's easy to do with those sort of doors.'

'So the door was left unlocked all night?'

Before replying, she got up, walked across the room and felt for something behind the books on a shelf. Over her shoulder she smiled at him. Wexford repeated what he had said.

'I suppose so,' she said. 'It was locked when I got there on Thursday. Are you very very angry with me?'

She hadn't seen. She had no realization of what she had done. Her eyes were warm and full of happy light as she handed him Annette Bystock's key.

Carolyn Snow was out. She was taking her son Joel to school, the cleaning woman told Wexford. He decided to take a walk round the block, though 'block' was not the word for it. 'Park' would have been better or 'enclave'. The Snows' house, though twice the size of Wexford's own, was one of the smallest in this neighbourhood. Houses seemed to get bigger and be farther apart as he reached the corner and turned into Winchester Drive. He couldn't remember the last time he was in this part of Kingsmarkham, it must have been years, but he did now recall that he was in the vicinity of the route Laurette Akande said her daughter took when she went running.

The hallmark of desirability in dwelling places is when a suburb looks like a stretch of woodland and no houses are visible, where there are no gates and all that shows that people live somewhere in there are the letter boxes, discreetly positioned in gaps in the hedge. It was very high up, a green thickly treed ridge, beyond which, far below, he could catch glimpses of the winding Kingsbrook. In Winchester Drive green lawns terminated in high hedges or low walls at the pavement and, because you knew it must be there, you fancied you caught the faintest glimpse of mellowed brick between the great grey beech trees, the delicate silver birches and the branches of a majestic cedar.

The presence of two people on one of these lawns, a woman with a basket of shiny dark red fruit, a young man a little over twenty putting a ladder up against a cherry tree, did a little more to damage this image of wooded countryside. Wexford was surprised to identify the woman as Susan Riding, though he hardly knew why he should be. She must live somewhere and was reputed to be well-off. The boy was startlingly like his father with the same straw-coloured hair and Nordic looks, the high forehead, blunt nose, long upper lip.

Wexford said good morning.

She came a little way towards him. If you didn't know who she was and had encountered her away from her own environment, you would have taken her for one of the dossers who slept on Myringham High Street. She wore a cotton skirt with half the hem coming down and a tee-shirt that must have originated with one of her children, for 'University of Myringham' was printed across the faded red material. An elastic band held back her greyish frizzy fair hair.

He thought how her smile transformed her. In an instant she was almost beautiful, beggarwoman into earth mother.

'The birds take most of our cherries. I wouldn't mind if they ate them but they just pick a bit out and drop the rest on the ground.' The boy had gone up the tree, his back towards them, but she introduced him just the same, 'My son, Christopher.' He took absolutely no notice. She shrugged as if this was no more than she had expected. 'You really need to be bird scaring from morning till night. We did last year but I had help then. How do people get staff in this country?'

'I understand it's difficult.'

'Do it yourself is what you're saying, isn't it? That's not so easy when you've got six bedrooms and four children all living at home most of the time. My au pair's just left me too.'

Christopher suddenly let out a string of startling obscenities and the wasp that had been annoying him zoomed out of the tree and headed for Susan Riding. She ducked, flapped at it with her hand. 'I *hate* them. Why on earth did God make wasps?'

'To clean it up, I suppose.' Her puzzled face made him explain. 'The earth.'

'Oh, yes. I really must thank you for giving up your Saturday night to us vulnerable women. I have written to you but I'm afraid I didn't post the letter till this morning.'

413

'Come on, Mum,' said the boy in the tree. 'We're supposed to be picking the buggers.'

Wexford called out to him, 'Do you know a girl called Melanie Akande?'

'*What*?'

'Melanie Akande. You once had a drink with her. Perhaps you saw her more than once.'

Susan Riding laughed. 'What is this, Mr Wexford? An interrogation? Is that the girl that's missing?'

Christopher came down the ladder. 'Is she missing? I didn't know.'

He was at least as tall as Wexford. His hands were big and his feet were big, his shoulders ox-like.

'Melanie disappeared last Tuesday afternoon,' Wexford said. 'Had you seen her recently?'

'Not for months. I went away last Tuesday morning. I can give you the names of the people I went with if I need an alibi. You can see my air ticket or what remains of it.'

'Christopher!' said his mother.

'Well, why ask me? I'm the last person. Can I get on with picking these cherries now?'

Wexford said goodbye and walked on. At the corner he looked back and between a gap in the trees could see the house quite dearly, the back of an Italianate villa, white walls, green roof, a tall turret. He could even see the bars on the ground floor windows. Well, Susan Riding was a Woman, Aware! woman, one who would no doubt be prudent. The place looked as if it contained a lot worth stealing. He turned into Eton Grove and went back down the hill. The Riding house was momentarily clearly visible from the road and then, suddenly, it disappeared behind a dense plantation of shrubs in white blossom. He stepped back to look at it once more and lingered for a while before turning left back into Marlborough Gardens and walking the few hundred yards to Harrow Avenue.

Donaldson in the driving seat of the parked car was reading the *Sun* but folded it up when he saw the boss. Wexford read his own paper for ten minutes. A young man with a camera hung round his neck appeared from round the corner and Wexford put his paper away, although this passer-by was clearly not interested in photographing him, hadn't even noticed him or taken his camera from its case.

'I'm getting paranoid.'

414

'Sir?'

'Nothing. Ignore me.'

The car suddenly appeared from nowhere, driven much too fast, sweeping into the drive of 101 and coming to a stop with a squeal of brakes. He had a good look at her as she left the car and went quickly to the front door, her doorkey on the same ring as the car keys. She was a tall slim woman, fairish, wearing black trousers and a sleeveless top. Two minutes after she had gone inside he went up to the front door and rang the bell. She answered it herself. She was younger than he had expected, probably forty but looking less. It struck him that she looked a lot younger than poor Annette.

No wedding ring. That was one of the first things he noticed and saw too that she had been used to wearing a ring, for there was a band of white skin on that brown finger.

'I've been expecting you,' she said. 'Won't you come in?'

Her voice was cultivated, pleasant, with the sort of accent associated with a select girls' boarding school. Wexford was suddenly and surprisingly aware of how very attractive she was. Her hair was so cut as to transform it into a cap of flaxen coloured feathers. She wore no make-up and her skin was good, smooth, light golden brown, only faintly lined about the eyes. The top she wore was the same sea-blue as her eyes and the brown arms it exposed might have been those of a young girl.

He began to ask himself why a man who had this at home, legitimately and honourably, would chase after Annette, but he knew such questions were always vain. Some of it was due to the legitimate and honourable being less attractive than the illicit and forbidden, and some of it to a strange lusting after the sordid and the naughty, after soft porn made flesh. He would guarantee, for instance, that Mrs Snow didn't wear see-through black and scarlet camisoles, but Calvin Klein briefs and Playtex sports bras.

She took him into a large living room with a green velvet carpet, enough sofas and armchairs to accommodate twenty people, and a fireplace of Cotswold stone with a copper hood over it. It was clear she knew why he had come and that she had her answers ready. She was confident but grim, her movements deliberate, her expression fixed and resolute.

He said carefully, 'I am sure your husband has told you he has been questioned in connection with the death of Annette Bystock.'

415

She nodded. She put her elbow on the arm of her chair and rested her cheek against her hand. It was a pose of controlled exasperation.

'That evening, Wednesday, July the seventh, your husband spent the evening at home with you and your son? Is that correct?'

She delayed answering so long that he was on the point of repeating what he had said. Her reply, when it came, was stiff and cold. 'Whoever gave you that idea? Did he tell you that?'

'What do you mean, Mrs Snow? That he wasn't here?'

The sigh she gave was as heavy and deliberate as the inhaling and exhaling prescribed for the exerciser, a deep intake of breath, a full expulsion of breath.

'My son wasn't here. He, my son, Joel, was upstairs in the playroom. He always is in the week evenings, he has a lot of homework, he's fourteen. We often don't see him between the time he has his meal and bedtime – and sometimes not then.'

Why was she telling him all this? No one was accusing the boy of the crime.

'So you and your husband were alone together? In here?'

'I asked who gave you that idea? My husband wasn't here.' Her expression became unearthly, dreamy, she seemed to gaze into the middle distance as if looking at a perfect sunset, her lips just parted. Suddenly she turned on him. 'He often wasn't on a Wednesday. He worked late on Wednesdays, or didn't you know?'

This was not at all what he had expected. If he hadn't been at home with his wife, why had Snow mentioned her? If his dearest wish was to keep the knowledge of his affair with Annette secret from her, why had he produced his wife as his alibi? Surely because he had no choice . . . the last thing he wanted to do was enlighten Carolyn Snow himself as to her husband's philandering, but it looked as if he would have to. Snow then had chickened out, had lost his nerve, had evaded confession. Or had he?

'Mrs Snow, you have been told of your husband's relationship with Annette Bystock?'

No one can whiten under a tan, but her skin contracted and aged her. It hadn't been a revelation, though. 'Oh, yes. He told me.' She stopped looking at him. 'You understand that I didn't know until yesterday – no, the day before yesterday. I was in the dark, I'd been kept in the dark.' A little cold laugh summed up her feelings about such men as Snow, their values, their cowardice. 'He had to tell me.'

416

'And asked you perhaps to tell me you were with him last Wednesday?'

'He didn't ask me anything,' she said. 'He knew better than to ask for favours.'

There was nothing more to say for the moment. It was all very different from what he had anticipated. Until this moment he had never seriously considered Snow as a suspect, as a candidate for murderer. After all, Snow hadn't been inside the flat at Ladyhall Court. But by that reckoning no one had been in the flat except Annette herself and Ingrid Pamber. There had been no evidence of Edwina Harris's visit or, more to the point, of the thief who came in at some point and took the television, the video and the radio-cassette player. If that thief had worn gloves, so might Bruce Snow have done.

He had spoken to Annette on the Tuesday evening but he might have been lying when he said she told him she was ill and couldn't meet him the following night. She loved him, she never refused him, she put him first. It was one thing not to go to work, to tell Ingrid she would need shopping done for her, but quite another to cancel a longed-for meeting with Snow on the dubious grounds that she might still be ill twenty-four hours later.

But they always met in Snow's office. Always except for just this once? I'm not well enough to go out, she had perhaps said, but you could come here – won't you just for once come here? And he had agreed, had gone there, had stayed and stayed, and quarrelled with her at last and killed her. . . .

Bob Mole had no intention of telling Vine where the radio came from. All he would say at first was that it had been among a job lot saved from a fire. That there were no burn marks on it meant nothing. These rugs, for instance – had Vine even bothered to look at them? – weren't burnt. The three dining chairs weren't burnt. There was plenty of stuff that was and no one was going to buy that from a stall. What did he think, the public were daft?

Where did that stain come from, Vine wanted to know. Bob Mole couldn't account for it. Come to that, why should he account for it and what was Vine getting at? When Vine told him, things changed. It was the word 'murder' that did it, specifically the murder of Annette Bystock, Kingsmarkham's own local murder that was in the daily papers and even on telly.

'It was hers?'

'Looks very much like it.'

Bob Mole, who had gone putty colour, curled back his upper lip. 'Not blood, is it?'

'No, it's not blood.' Vine wanted to laugh but didn't. 'It's red nail varnish. She spilt it. Now tell me where you got it from.'

'It's like I said, Mr Vine. It was what come out of this fire.'

'Sure. I heard you. But who was it rescued it from the flames and put it in your sticky hands?'

'My supplier,' said Bob Mole as if he were a respectable retailer talking about a wholesaler of nationwide repute. 'You're sure it's hers, this Annette that's dead?' He dropped his voice on the name and looked from side to side.

'There's a TV and a video too,' said Vine.

'I never got them, Mr Vine, and that's the absolute honest truth.' With another glance to the right and one to the left, Bob Mole leaned towards Vine and whispered, 'They call him Zack.'

'Does he have another name?'

'If he does I don't know it, but I can tell you where he lives.'

Not an address but a description of a place. Bob Mole didn't know the address. His directions were to go all the way down to the bottom of Glebe Lane, turn down that passage by that place, that sort of church the Methodists used to have but was now a sort of store, go round the back of the used car dump and he lives in the furthest away of the two cottages facing Tiller's paintbrush works.

When Burden heard about it he went on the hunt for Bob Mole's supplier himself, taking Vine with him. He expected something like Ingrid Pamber's place but this back corner of Kingsmarkham made hers look like a smart mews. Confusion could hardly have arisen as to which cottage Zack lived in as the nearer to the lane of the two was derelict, its door and windows boarded up. It scarcely seemed like a dwelling house any longer, but more a shed for neglected animals, a dirty brownish hut, the broken tiles on its roof yellow with stonecrop.

Zack's wasn't much better. Years ago someone had put a pink undercoat on the front door, never painted on top but apparently wiped a brush laden with different coloured paints against its surface. Perhaps this was the work of an employee at the little factory opposite. A broken window had been mended with masking tape.

From a rickety trellis hung the tendrils of a climbing plant that had apparently died some years before.

'The council should do something about this dump,' Burden said crossly. 'What do we pay our rates for, I should like to know.'

The young woman who came to the door was thin and pale, no taller than a child of twelve. She carried on one puny hip a boy of about a year who was crying loudly.

'Yes, what is it?'

'Police,' said Vine. 'Can we come in?'

'Oh, shut up, Clint,' she said to the child, shaking him in a half-hearted way. She looked with a kind of apathetic distaste from Barry Vine to Burden and back again. 'I'll want to see some identification before I let you in.'

'Who are *you*, then?' said Vine.

'Kimberley. Ms Pearson to you. He's not here.'

Warrant cards were produced and she scrutinized them as if to check they weren't forgeries. 'Look at the funny photo of the man, Clint,' she said, pushing the child's head nearly into Vine's chest.

When Clint understood he couldn't have the pictures he began crying even more loudly. Kimberley moved him to her other hip. Burden and Vine followed her into what Burden afterwards called one of the worst tips he'd ever been into. Analyzing the smell, he declared it to be compounded of soiled napkins, urine, fat that chips had been cooked in fifty times, meat kept too long without a refrigerator, cigarette smoke and canned dog food. The linoleum that covered the floor was worn into holes and covered with sticky, hairy patches and dark ring marks. Ashes from last winter's fires were tumbled about the grate which was piled high over them with waste paper and cigarette ends. Two deckchairs faced a huge television set. It was too large to have been Annette's but the video recorder next to it might have been hers.

Kimberley put the child into one of these chairs and gave him a bag of crisps which she produced from one of the many cardboard grocer's boxes that stood about and served as cupboard, sideboard and larder. Another box provided her with a packet of Silk Cut and matches.

'What d'you want him for?' she said, lighting her cigarette.

'This and that,' said Vine. 'Maybe something serious.'

'What's serious mean?' said Kimberley. She had the very pale green eyes of a white cat. Her skin and hair were luminous with grease. 'He

419

never done nothing serious.' She corrected herself. 'He never done nothing.'

'Where is he?'

'It's his signing-on day.'

All ways, as Wexford had thought, led back to the Benefit Office.

'Where did the video come from, Miss Pearson?' Burden asked, refusing to have any truck with that 'Ms' stuff.

'My mum give it me.' Her answer came quick as a flash. That, of course, meant nothing. 'And it's Mrs Nelson.'

'I see. Miss Pearson to him and Mrs Nelson to me. That his name, is it? Nelson?'

She didn't answer. Having finished the crisps, C!int set up a renewed roaring. 'Oh, piss off, Clint,' she said. Taken from his deckchair and placed on the floor, he crawled over to one of the grocer's boxes, pulled himself into a standing position and began removing its contents, item by item. Kimberley took no notice. Apropos of nothing that had gone before, she said, 'They're going to pull it down, this place.'

'Best thing they can do,' said Vine.

'Oh, yes, sure, it's the best bloody thing they can do. What's going to happen to us? You don't think of that, do you, when you say . . .' she mimicked his voice in an exaggerated way, '"it's the best thing they can do".'

'They'll have to rehouse you.'

'You want to bet? In a bed and breakfast maybe. If you want to be re-housed you have to do it yourself. One thing you can say for this dump, the DSS pay the rent. He'll lose that, won't he? He's not had a job in months.'

Outside, Burden inhaled the air, somewhat contaminated though it was with the fumes from paintbrush manufacture. 'Doesn't stop them having kids, does it, being out of work? You'll notice they can always afford to smoke.'

If I lived in that midden I'd smoke myself to death, thought Vine, but he didn't say it aloud.

'Did you see them in the paper, it'd have been around last Christmas? I remember the name, Clint. He had something wrong with his heart and they operated on it at Stowerton Infirmary. There were pictures of him and Kimberley Pearson all over the *Courier*.'

But Burden couldn't remember. He was sure that somehow they would miss Zack Nelson, that he was a genius at slip-giving.

420

Kimberley had no phone, even if it was possible to phone people waiting to sign on. Burden didn't know whether it was or not and he was sure Vine didn't. But when they came into the Benefit Office, Zack was still there.

He was one of a dozen people waiting, sitting on the grey chairs. Burden had made what he thought was an intelligent guess at which one of the seven or eight men he was and got it wrong. The first person he approached, a boy of perhaps twenty-two with a blond crewcut, three rings in each ear and one in a nostril, turned out to be a John MacAntony. The only other man who could possibly be Zack Nelson admitted it first with an exaggerated shrug, then a nod.

He was tallish and of all the men in there, in the best condition. It looked as if he worked out with weights, for his body was lean and hard and he had no need to flex his bare arms to show the large round muscles that stretched the sleeves of a dirty red polo shirt. His long hair, as greasy as Kimberley's, was plaited for an inch or two before being tied with a shoelace. Inside the open neck of his shirt, under the fuzz of dark hair, could be seen the greenish-blue, red and black inks of an elaborate tattoo.

'A word,' said Burden.

'It'll have to wait till my number comes up,' said Zack Nelson without irony.

Burden was baffled, then saw that he referred to the neon signs that hung from the ceiling. When the number on his card appeared he would go up to a desk to sign on.

'How long is that going to be, then?'

'Five minutes. Maybe ten.' Zack made the sort of face at Vine that he himself had made when he smelt the inside of the cottage. 'What's the hurry?'

'No hurry,' said Burden. 'We've got plenty of time.'

They moved away and sat on a pair of grey chairs. Burden fingered one of the leaves of the houseplant in the tub next to him. It had the faintly sticky, rubbery texture of polythene.

Vine said in a low voice. 'He looks like you, you know. I mean, if you grew your hair and didn't wash much. He might be your young brother.'

Incensed by this, Burden said nothing. But he remembered what Percy Hammond had said, that the man he had seen in the night coming out of Ladyhall Court looked like him. If it was true, and

421

here was Vine absurdly confirming it, it said a lot for the old man's powers of observation. It meant that the old man could be trusted.

He looked about the big room. Behind the counter were Osman Messaoud, Hayley Gordon and Wendy Stowlap, this last apparently suffering from an allergy, for she kept wiping her nose on a succession of coloured tissues pulled from a box in front of her. All were occupied with clients. Cyril Leyton stood outside the door of his office deep in conversation with the security officer.

Messaoud's client finished her business and moved away from the desk. A number came up in red neon and the boy with the rings in ears and nose went up. You couldn't see the New Claims Officers from where Burden sat, only the sides of their booths. He got up and began walking about, apparently aimlessly, but avoiding confrontation with Leyton. The new claims officer sitting in the booth next to Peter Stanton's must be a replacement for Annette, but was too far away for Burden to read the name tag he wore. In the light of increased knowledge, Burden made a mental note to subject Stanton to a second interview. After all, the man had admitted to taking Annette out. Was she, in his company, trying to find herself a better option than Bruce Snow? And if so, what had gone wrong?

He was alerted by a woman shouting and he turned round. This was the first instance of 'trouble' there had been since they began calling at the Benefit Office. The woman, fat and unkempt, was complaining to Wendy Stowlap about a lost giro and Wendy seemed to be checking on the computer screen that it had been sent to her. The answer wasn't apparently acceptable and the torrent of complaint became a stream of abuse, culminating in a yell of, 'You're a whore!'

Wendy looked up, unmoved. She shrugged. 'How did you know?'

There came a faint snigger from Peter Stanton who was passing the counter on his way to pick up a leaflet. The woman turned her invective on him and there was a moment when Burden considered intervening. But the staff seemed competent to deal with verbal abuse, and the woman soon deflated.

Zack Nelson's number appeared in red neon at last and he went up to Hayley Gordon. Vine thought her a little like Nelson's girlfriend Kimberley to look at, only cleaner and better dressed and – you had to face it – better fed. Zack would get – what? Nothing here, of course, but when his giro arrived he would collect from the post office unemployment benefit for himself of around forty pounds and

422

the DSS would provide the Income Support for Kimberley and Clint – or did Kimberley herself collect Clint's Child Benefit? It was always the mother, wasn't it? Vine had to confess he didn't know. But no doubt they didn't live in poverty because they liked it.

These were private thoughts which would not affect his attitude to Zack who was a thief, he reflected, and a villain. They weren't permitted to arrest him in here, not unless requested to do so by the ES staff. 'We'll talk in the car,' he said when Zack returned, having assured himself of support for another fortnight.

'About what?'

'Bob Mole,' said Burden, 'and a radio with blood on it.'

It was, as he said to Wexford later, as easy as taking peppermints from a baby who didn't like them. 'That was never blood,' said Zack. He realized immediately what he had said, rolled his eyes and clapped one hand over his mouth.

'Why not blood?' said Vine, leaning close.

'She was strangled. It was on telly. It was in the papers.

'So you admit you were in Annette Bystock's place, that the radio was hers?'

'Look, I . . .'

'We'll go back to the police station, Sergeant Vine. Zack Nelson, you need not say anything in answer to the charge but anything you do say will be taken down and may be given in evidence . . .'

# 10

'Not with murder?' said Zack in the interview room.

Wexford didn't answer. 'What *is* your name, anyway? Zachary? Zachariah?'

'You what? No, it's fucking not. It's Zack. There was some singer called his son Zack that is where my mum got it from. OK? I want to know if you're charging me with murdering that woman.'

'Tell us when you went into the flat, Zack,' said Burden. 'It was the Wednesday night, was it?'

'Who says I ever went in the flat?'

'She didn't bring that radio round to you and give it to you for a birthday present.'

This was a lucky shot on Wexford's part, not even intelligent guesswork. If it had been December instead of July he would have said 'Christmas present.' Zack stared at him in a kind of horror, as he might have at some clairvoyant possessed of proven supernatural powers.

'How d'you know Wednesday was my birthday?'

Wexford held back his laughter with difficulty. 'Many happy returns. What time was it you went into the flat?'

'I want my lawyer,' said Zack.

'Yes, I expect you do. I would in your position. You can phone him later. I mean, you can find one later and phone him.' Zack gave him a suspicious glare. Wexford said, 'Let's talk about the ring.'

'What ring?'

'A ruby ring worth two grand, give or take a bit.'

'I don't know what you're talking about.'

'Was she dead, Zack, before you took that ring off her finger?'

'I never took no ring off her finger! It wasn't on her finger, it was

424

on the table!' Once more he had dropped himself in it. 'Fuck it all,' he said.

'You'd better start at the beginning, Zack,' said Burden. 'Tell us all about it.' Silently he blessed the recording device which had all this on tape. There was no arguing with it.

Zack made a few more attempts at argument before caving in. Finally he said, 'What's in it for me if I tell you what I found in there and what I saw?'

'How about you come up in court tomorrow instead of Friday, you only get one night in a cell and Sergeant Camb'll bring you a Diet Coke for a nightcap.'

'Don't give me that crap. I mean, if I tell you what I know I could help you find her killer.'

'You'll do that anyway, Zack. You don't want a charge of obstructing the police as well as burglary.'

Zack, who had an impressive record of petty offences, the computer had informed Wexford, knew all about it. 'It wasn't burglary. It wasn't dark. I never did no breaking and entering.'

'A figure of speech,' Burden said. 'I suppose you found the door unlocked and just walked in?'

A cunning look came into Zack's face, making it slightly lopsided. There was something sinister about him, something called evil. His eyes narrowed. 'Couldn't believe me eyes,' he said, his tone becoming conversational. 'I tried the handle and the door came open in me hand. I was amazed.'

'I'm sure. Carrying housebreaking tools, were you, just on the off chance? What did you mean just now when you said it wasn't dark?'

'It was five in the morning, wasn't it? It'd been light an hour.'

'Up with the lark, were you, Zack?' Burden couldn't help grinning. 'You always an early riser?'

'The kid woke me up and I couldn't get back to sleep. I went out in the van to clear me head. I was just passing sort of slow – keeping in the speed limit, right? – and the front door was open, so I reckoned I'd pop in and see what was going.'

'D'you feel like making a statement, Zack?'

'I want my lawyer.'

'I tell you what, you make a statement and then we'll get the Yellow Pages and find you a lawyer. How's that?'

Zack yielded quite suddenly. He seemed to collapse without warning. One moment he was truculent, the next he had given in. 'I

425

don't mind,' he said and gave a huge yawn. 'I'm dead tired. I don't never get enough sleep, not with my kid.'

At approximately five am on Friday, 9 July – Zack Nelson's statement ran – I entered Flat 1, 15 Ladyhall Avenue, Kingsmarkham. I had no housebreaking tools and did not break the door or the lock. I was wearing gloves. The front door was unlocked. It was not dark. The curtains were drawn in the living room but I could see. I saw a television set, a video recorder, a CD player and radio-cassette player, and these I removed from the flat, making two trips to do so.

I came back to the flat and opened the door to the bedroom. To my surprise there was a woman in the bed. At first I thought she was asleep. Something in her attitude made me suspicious. It was the way her arm was hanging. I approached nearer but did not touch her, as I could see that she was dead. On the table by the bed was a ring and watch. I did not touch these but left the flat quickly, making sure the door was locked behind me.

I put the television set, the video recorder and the radio-cassette player into the van I had loaned from my girlfriend's father and drove home. I am a dealer in secondhand electronic equipment. I had some of the said equipment salvaged from a factory fire and, included as one lot with some of the salvaged goods, I sold the radio-cassette player to Mr Bob Mole for the sum of seven pounds. The television set and video recorder are at present in my home at 1 Lincoln Cottages, Glebe End, Kingsmarkham.

'I like the virtuous touch about locking the door behind him, don't you?' Wexford said when Zack had been taken to one of the only two cells Kingsmarkham Police Station possessed. 'At least it explains how the door came to be locked when you got there. If anyone from the Employment Service reads an account of tomorrow's proceedings in the magistrates' court, Zack's going to lose his UB. The *Courier* will describe him as a dealer in electronic goods.'

'He won't need it where he's going,' Burden said.

'No, but Kimberley and Clint will. I don't know what happens in a case like this. Do they cut off his dependants' Income Support? Still, he'll not get more than six months and he'll serve four and a bit.' Wexford hesitated. 'You know, Mike, there's something odd in all this, there's something I don't like.'

Burden shrugged. 'Like him finding the door unlocked and the place all open for him? Like him not taking the ring?'

'Well, yes, but not that so much. The front door to the house is usually unlocked and we know Ingrid Pamber left Annette's door unlocked. He says he was afraid of taking a ring and a watch that lay beside a dead body and I believe him. What bothers me is his apparently not knowing anything about the flats or their occupants before going in there. According to him, he just slipped in without bothering to shut the door behind him. He couldn't sleep, but he didn't go out on foot, he went out in his *van*. He just happened to be wearing gloves. In a heatwave in July? According to him, he had no housebreaking tools with him, yet how many people could he count on having feckless friends and leaving their front door unlocked overnight?'

'There are only two flats in there,' Burden said. 'He'd nothing to lose. All he had to do was try Annette's door and then go upstairs and try the Harrises'. If they were both locked he was no worse off than he had been.'

'I know. That's what he says himself. Piece of amazing luck for him, wasn't it, that the first door he tried was unlocked?'

'Maybe it wasn't the first door.'

'He says it was. So we come to the next odd thing. If what he says is true, he had no means of knowing whether there was anyone in the flat or not. What are we to think? That because he'd seen from outside – and remembered, calculated, worked it out – that all the curtains in Flat One were closed, then discovered that the front door was unlocked, he concluded there was no one at home? That would be on the theory that no one would stay in a place overnight with the front door unlocked, but they might go away and forget to lock it. It's all a bit tenuous.'

'He was taking a risk, certainly. But all burglary is risky, Reg.'

Wexford looked unconvinced. He always delved into human motive and the peculiarities of human nature while Burden concentrated on the facts, seldom disputing them however bizarre they might appear. As he made his way back to the Benefit Office, on foot this time, Burden thought of something Wexford had once said to him about Sherlock Holmes, how you couldn't solve much by his methods. A pair of slippers with singed soles no more showed that their wearer had been suffering from a severe chill than that he had merely had cold feet. Nor could you deduce from a man's staring at a

427

portrait on the wall that he was dwelling on the life and career of that portrait's subject, for he might equally be thinking how it resembled his brother-in-law or was badly painted or needed cleaning. With human nature you could only guess – and try to guess right.

He caught Peter Stanton on his way out to lunch.

'Can we have a chat?'

'Not if it stops me eating.'

'I have to eat too,' Burden said.

'Come out this way.' Stanton took Burden out through the door marked 'Private' that led into the car park. It was a short cut to the High Street.

His wife or Wexford would probably have described the man as Byronic. He had those dark piratical good looks women are said to find so attractive, the handsome features allegedly ravaged by dissipations, the dark wavy hair that by Burden's own exacting standards was tousled, the gleam in the eye that may denote a penchant for cruelty or merely greed. Stanton wore a linen suit, stone-coloured and very crumpled, and his tie, which Leyton probably insisted he wear, was loosely tied under the collar of a not very clean shirt whose top button was undone. If it is possible to walk in a laid-back manner, Stanton did so, slouching along, his hands deep in the misshapen pockets of his baggy trousers. At the doorway of a sandwich bar with four empty tables pushed against the wall opposite the food counter, he paused and cocked a thumb.

'I usually come here. OK?'

Burden nodded. The last time he had been in one of these places, of which Kingsmarkham now had three, he had eaten 'prime freshwater shrimps' and the resulting gastroenteritis had laid him low for three days. So when Stanton picked a prawn salad sandwich he stuck austerely to cheese and tomato. He watched without comment while Stanton emptied the contents of a hip flask into his glass of Sprite.

'I want to ask you about the kind of things you say to your clients.'

'Not half what I'd like to.'

Rather coldly Burden said, 'Specifically, I want to know the kind of thing Annette might have said to Melanie Akande.'

'What do you mean exactly?'

'I mean, what happens when a new client brings back a form – is it

428

called an ES something? – and gets given a signing-on day and so on?'

'You want to know what she'd have said to the girl and advised her and all that?'

Stanton sounded deeply bored. His eyes had wandered to the young woman assistant who now emerged from the back regions to join the man behind the counter. She was about twenty, blonde, tall, very pretty, wearing a white apron over a scoop-necked red tee-shirt and the kind of very short tube skirt that is as tight as a bandage.

'Just that, Mr Stanton.'

'OK.' Stanton took a swig of his Sprite cocktail. 'Annette'd have taken a look at the ES 461, seen she'd filled it in right. There are forty-five questions to be answered in all and it's complicated till you know how. Let's say it's . . . well, uncommon for a client to get it right first time on his own. On *her* own, I should say. They've got a funny taste, these prawns, sort of fishy.'

'Prawns *are* fish,' said Burden.

'Yeah, but you know what I mean, sort of strong, like the smell of outside a fishmonger's. Do you reckon I ought to eat them?'

Burden didn't reply. 'Go on about what Annette would have said to her.'

'There's often something a bit off about the food here but the crumpet makes up for it. That's why I go on coming, I suppose.' Stanton caught Burden's basilisk eye. 'Yes, well, once she'd got the form straightened out she'd have given the client, Melanie What's-her-name, a signing-on day. It's alphabetical, that. A to K Tuesdays, L to R Wednesdays, S to Z Thursdays. No one signs on on a Monday or a Friday. What did you say she was called? Akande? She'd have had Tuesday. Once a fortnight on a Tuesday.

'Then Annette'd have explained about how signing-on is to prove you're still in the land of the living, haven't buggered off somewhere or died, that you're available and actively seeking work, and she'd have said how once you've signed on your giro'll be sent to you. That goes to your home address and you cash it at your post office or you can pay it into your bank if you want. Annette'd have explained all that. Then, I suppose, she'd have asked Melanie if she'd any questions. Melanie'd only have a maximum of twenty minutes with Annette, there wouldn't have been time for much.'

'Suppose she'd had a job to offer Melanie? Could she have had? What would have been the procedure?'

Stanton yawned. He had left his second sandwich uneaten. He was now dividing his eye contact between the girl in the bandage skirt and a sandwich maker who had appeared from some nether region. This woman had waist length mahogany-coloured hair and appeared to be wearing nothing but a white chef's cap and a white cotton coat whose hem reached to two inches below her crotch. At a cough from Burden he dragged his stare away, sighing softly. 'There aren't jobs, you know. They're thin on the ground. I suppose Annette just might have had something suitable for this Melanie, client with a degree. Well, once in a blue moon she might have had something.'

'What, in a ledger? A file?'

Stanton gave him a pitying look. 'She'd have run it up on the computer.'

'And if she'd had anything to offer Melanie, what then?'

'She'd have phoned the employer and made an appointment for Melanie for an interview. She didn't, you know,' Stanton said unexpectedly. 'I can tell you that for a fact. Both the New Claims Advisers have the same stuff on their computers and there wasn't anything remotely suitable for a girl of twenty-two with a perform-ance arts degree. You can check it out if you want but I can tell you there wasn't.'

'How did you know her degree was in performance arts?'

'She told me while I was raping and strangling her, of course.' Stanton must have remembered that there is such an offence as wasting police time. He said sullenly, 'Oh, come on. I read it in the paper.'

Burden fetched himself a cup of coffee. 'And that would have been all?' he said. 'No advice? You're advisers, aren't you?'

'That *is* advising, telling her how to sign on, explaining about her giro. What more d'you want?'

Hope had sprung for a moment in Burden's heart. A scenario had begun to take shape of Melanie leaving the Benefit Office on her way to a job interview, from which she had never returned. Only Annette knew where she had gone and why and, absolutely to the point, whom she had gone to see. But his carefully crafted playlet had quickly fallen apart and when he asked Stanton if he could imagine anything confidential, secret or sinister Melanie might have said to Annette, something that was a police matter, he wasn't surprised that the man made a dismissive gesture and shook his head.

'I ought to be getting back.'

'All right.' Burden got up.

'I've got a performance arts degree myself,' Stanton suddenly remarked apropos of nothing. 'No doubt that's why I remember she had. All set to be a great actor, I was, a second Olivier and a bloody sight better looking. That was me fifteen years ago and to this favour have I come.'

Bored by this, unsympathetic, Burden said as they went out into the street, 'Did anyone ever threaten her?'

'Annette? In the office? Bless your policeman's helmet, if you had one, they threaten us all the time. *All the time.* It's worse on the desks. Why d'you think we have a security officer? Ninety-nine per cent comes to nothing, it's vague promises to "get us". Some of them accuse us of keeping their giros for ourselves, losing their ES 461s on purpose, that sort of thing. And then they're going to "get" us or "cut" us.

'Then there's fraud. They know they've been signing on in three or four different names and they think we've reported them to the DSS fraud inspectors, so they're going to get us for that. . . .'

Now Burden recalled Karen Malahyde once being called out to an 'incident' at the Benefit Office, on another occasion Pemberton and Archbold had gone. It hadn't meant much to him at the time. He said suddenly to Stanton, 'You took her out once or twice?'

'Annette?' Stanton became guarded, cautious. 'Twice, to be precise. It was three years ago.'

'Why twice? Why no more? Did something happen?'

'I didn't screw her, if that's what you mean.' Stanton, who had been slouching along, taking long strides, moving slowly, now stopped altogether. He stood indecisively in the middle of the pavement, then sat down on the low wall that bordered an estate agent's courtyard and took a packet of cigarettes out of one of the baggy pockets. 'Cyril the Squirrel called me into his office and said it had to stop. Relationships between staff members of opposite sexes were bad for the image. I asked him if he meant it would be all right for me to fuck Osman but he just said not to be filthy and that was that.'

Burden's look was eloquent of heartfelt agreement with Leyton for once, but he said nothing.

'Not that I was all that sorry.' Stanton took a long draw on his cigarette and expelled the smoke in two blue columns out of his nostrils. 'I wasn't keen on being used as a – how shall I put it? – I don't know, but what it amounts to is she only wanted me around to make this guy she'd got jealous so he'd leave his wife and marry her. Some hopes. She actually told me that, about how she'd tell this chap that I was keen on her and if he didn't want to lose her he'd best get his act together. Charming, wasn't it?'

'You went to her flat?'

'No, I never did. I went to the cinema with her, met her there and we had a coffee after. The next time it was just drinks in a pub and a pizza and we went for a drive in my car. We parked out in the country and there was a bit of how's-your-father but nothing over the top and after that Cyril the doorman put his spoke in.'

They walked back to the Benefit Office together and Burden followed him in. He was talking to the security officer, asking if he could remember any specific threats being made to Annette, when a shrill scream from Wendy Stowlap's counter made him jump and spring to his feet.

'I told you I'd scream if you said that just once more,' the woman shouted. 'If you say that again I'll lie on the floor and scream.'

'What else can I say? You can have dental treatment free if you're on Income Support but you can't get your osteopath's bill paid.'

The woman, who was well dressed and spoke in a ringing actor's voice, got down on the floor, lay on her back and began screaming. She was young and her lungs were strong. The screaming reminded Burden of the noise three-year-olds sometimes make in supermarket aisles. He walked over to her, the security man following. Wendy was leaning over the counter, waving a blue and yellow leaflet with the title 'Help Us to Get It Right and How to Complain'.

'Come along now,' said the security officer. 'Up you get. This won't do, all this noise.'

She screamed harder. 'Stop that,' said Burden. He stuck out his warrant card six inches from the screaming face. 'Stop. You're causing a breach of the peace.'

It was the card which did it. She was middle-class and therefore awed by the police and the suggestion she might break the law. The screaming dropped to a whimper. She got awkwardly to her feet, snatched the leaflet from Wendy's hand and said bitterly to her, 'There was no need to call the police.'

Husband and wife sat side by side, but not too close to each other, in front of the desk in Wexford's office. He didn't want to frighten

432

Carolyn Snow – not yet. Frightening, if needed, would come later. Meanwhile, though the room was hardly equipped as a recording studio, Detective Constable Pemberton was there with an efficient enough device if it was required.

They had arrived separately two minutes apart. And Carolyn Snow quickly explained that they *were* apart, she retaining the house in Harrow Avenue – 'It's my children's *home*' – the husband she had thrown out resorting to an hotel room. Wexford noticed that Bruce Snow was wearing yesterday's shirt. He looked as if he hadn't shaved. Surely his wife hadn't shaved him as well as laundering his clothes and running round at his beck and call?

'We have to clear up this matter of what you were both doing last Wednesday evening, July the seventh. Mr Snow?'

'I've already told you what I was doing. I was at home with my wife. My son was at home too. He was upstairs.'

'Not according to Mrs Snow.'

'Look, this is rubbish, this is all nonsense. I got home at six and I was all evening at home with my wife. We had a meal at seven, the way we always do. My son went upstairs after that, he had an essay to write for his history homework. The War of the Spanish Succession, it was.'

'You have a good memory, Mr Snow, considering you didn't know you'd have to remember.'

'I have been racking my brains, haven't I? I've thought of nothing else.'

'What did you do all evening? Watch television? Read something? Telephone anyone?'

'He didn't have a chance,' said Carolyn nastily. 'He went out at ten to eight.'

'That is a damned lie!' said Snow.

'On the contrary, you know it's true. It was *your* Wednesday, wasn't it? The Wednesday evening every couple of weeks you spent bonking that prostitute on your office floor.'

'Nice language, thank you, that really becomes you, that terminology. A man can take real pride in hearing his wife talk like that, like someone off the streets.'

'Well, you'd know all about those, wouldn't you? First-hand experience. And I'm not your wife, not any more. Two years, just two years, and you'll have to say "my ex-wife", you'll have to explain you're living in a bedsit because your "ex-wife" took you to

433

the cleaners, took the house and the car and three-quarters of your income . . .' Carolyn Snow's normally quiet gentle voice was rising ominously, vibrating with anger, 'just because you were hooked on poking that fat floozie through her red knickers!'

For God's sake, thought Wexford, how much of it has he told her? Everything? Because he thought absolute total confession was his only chance? He gave an admonitory cough which nevertheless failed to stop Snow rounding on his wife and shouting, 'You shut your mouth, you frigid cow!'

Slowly Carolyn Snow rose to her feet, her eyes fixed on her husband's face. Wexford acted. 'Stop this, please. At once. I can't have a matrimonial fracas in here. Sit down, Mrs Snow.'

'Why should I? Why should I be made into some sort of guilty party? I've done nothing.'

'Ha!' said Snow, and he repeated it, reinforced with bitterness, 'Ha!'

'Very well,' said Wexford. 'I thought you might be more comfortable talking to me in here but I see I was wrong. We'll go down to Interview Room Two, DC Pemberton, and with your permission – ' he looked rather sourly at the Snows, making their permission sound like a formality ' – the rest of this interview will be recorded.'

It was rather different down there, some distant resemblance to a prison cell being achieved by white-painted walls of unrendered brick and a window set high up under the ceiling. The electronic devices lining the wall behind the metal table Wexford sometimes thought, and thought uneasily, suggested, if not a torture chamber, the kind of place where they kept you standing all night under bright lights.

On the way down he asked Snow, in seemingly casual fashion and out of earshot of his wife, if it was a fact that a friend or relative of theirs lived in Ladyhall Avenue within sight of the flats. Snow denied it. It wasn't true, he said, and he had never told anyone it was.

In the interview room he placed the Snows opposite each other and seated himself at one end. Burden, back from the Benefit Office, took the other. The austerity of the room, its grimness, quietened Carolyn, as he had known it would. Once in the lift, she had kept up a continuous jibing and carping at her husband while he stood with his eyes shut. Down here she was silent. She smoothed the fair hair back from her forehead and pressed fingers to her temples as if her head ached. Snow sat with folded arms, his chin sagging against his chest.

Wexford spoke into the device. 'Mr Bruce Snow, Mrs Carolyn Snow. DCI Wexford and DI Burden present.' He said to the woman, 'I should like you to tell me exactly what did happen on the evening of July the seventh, Mrs Snow.'

She gave her husband a sidelong look, deliberate and calculating. 'He came home at six and I said, not working late tonight? I'm going back to the office after I've eaten, he said . . .'

'A lie! Another filthy lie!'

'Please, Mr Snow.'

'Joel said he might want his father to give him some help with this essay he had to do and his father said, too bad because I'm going out . . .'

'I did not say that!'

'Because I'm going out, and he did go out. At ten to eight. I didn't suspect anything, mind you, not a thing. Why should I? I trusted him. I do trust people. Anyway, I phoned the office. Joel did want help. I said, we'll phone Dad and you can ask him on the phone. But there wasn't any answer. Not that I had any suspicions even then. I thought he just wasn't answering. I was in bed by the time he got home. It was after half-past ten, nearer eleven.'

'Oh, let her rave.'

'I'm a truthful person, he knows that. Whereas we know the lies *he* tells. Working late! Did you know he screwed her in the office so that if I phoned he'd be there to answer? If she hadn't got her just deserts, getting herself murdered, I could almost feel sorry for the poor fat bitch.'

'May I remind you,' Wexford said wearily, 'that, with your permission, this conversation is being recorded, Mrs Snow?'

'What do I care? Record it! Put it over the public address system all down the High Street! Let them all know, I'll tell them anyway, I've told all my friends. I've told my children, I've let them know what a bastard their father is.'

After they had gone, Burden put on a grave face and shook his head. 'Amazing, isn't it?' he said to Wexford. 'You'd call her a real lady if you met her socially, quiet, well-mannered, refined. Who'd have thought a woman like that would even know that sort of language?'

'You sound like a policeman in a detective novel circa 1935.'

435

'OK, maybe I do, but doesn't it surprise you?'

'They get it out of modern fiction,' said Wexford. 'Nothing to do all day but read. Are we getting anywhere with Stephen Colegate?'

'Annette's ex-husband? He lives in Australia, he's married again, but his mother's in Pomfret and she's expecting him home for a visit on Sunday with his two kids.'

'Have someone check that he really was in Australia, will you? What happened to Zack Nelson?'

'Remanded in custody to the Crown Court. Why are you looking like that?'

'I'm thinking of Kimberley and the child.'

'You don't want to worry about that Kimberley,' said Burden, 'She'll know more about claiming benefit than Cyril Leyton does. She's the kind that's got an honours degree in Income Support.'

Wexford laughed. 'I'm sure you're right. That Snow woman's worn me out.' He hesitated, thought. '"Oh, I am going a long way off, to the island valley of Avilion, where I will heal me of my grievous wound."'

'Blimey,' said Burden. 'And where might that be?'

'Home.'

# 11

'I told her we wouldn't be buying any oriental rugs,' Dora said, 'and I was thinking, chance would be a fine thing, though I didn't say that. Of course, she's quite right, these things are evil and wrong, but it's just that she always throws herself heart and soul into every new project.'

Sheila Wexford had become a life member of Anti-Slavery International. On the phone that evening, just before Wexford got in, she had urged her mother not to buy Middle Eastern or oriental rugs, for these, she said, might well have been woven by children of eleven or twelve or younger. Girls in Turkey went blind from the close work in ill-lit rooms. Children were obliged to work fourteen hours a day and because their parents had put them to this industry as payment of a debt, received no wages.

'I suppose she'll be off to Turkey to see for herself?' said Wexford.

'How did you know?'

'I know my daughter.'

'Why "international", anyway?' enquired Sylvia in a querulous tone. 'International's an adjective. What's wrong with society or association?' Wexford's reference to Sheila as 'my daughter' instead of 'my younger daughter', thus implying in her estimation that he had only one, was what had set her off, he knew. Much she cared about adjectives. 'Sheila wouldn't notice but it's as bad as "collective",' she said and glared at her father.

He was swift to make amends, appending to his question a rare endearment. 'Any sign of a job, darling?'

'Nothing. Neil's got himself into a workshop that could lead to a retraining programme. That's another awful word, "workshop".'

'And "creditable" for "credible",' said her father. It was the kind

437

of conversation he usually had only with Sheila. 'And "gender-related" for male and female and "health problem" for "ill".'

Sylvia was happy again. '*Kanena provlima*, which my son tells me is Greek for his favourite phrase. One good thing about being unemployed is I'll be home with them for the summer holidays. School breaks up next week.'

It was pouring with rain and Glebe End was awash. With no drainage or what there was long dysfunctional, Lincoln Cottages appeared as if floating on a swamp. A great sheet of water engulfed the brick path and came halfway up the tyres of an ancient van, the rear doors of which stood open. A black plastic dustbin bobbed lightly on a puddle by the front door.

Barry Vine had a look inside the van at a damp-looking mattress and an artnchair with no seat cushion while Karen Malahyde knocked on the door. It took Kimberley several minutes to come and open it.

'What d'you want?'

'The stuff your boyfriend nicked,' said Vine.

She shrugged her thin shoulders but she opened the door wider and stood back. Clint was sitting in a high chair, covering his face and the upper part of his body with a glutinous brown mess from a bowl with a crack in it. The high chair, painted white with pictures of rabbits and squirrels, was quite a respectable piece of furniture, gift perhaps of a comparatively affluent grandparent.

Cocking a thumb back the way he had come, Vine said, 'Moving out?'

'What if I am?'

'You gave us to understand you hadn't a hope of being rehoused.'

Kimberley picked up a dirty rag from the top of one of her cardboard boxes and began rubbing at Clint's face with it. The child yelled and struggled. Vine went upstairs and fetched the television set. Karen carried the video out to the car. Lifting Clint on to the ground, Kimberley said, volunteering information for once, 'My nan died.'

Not knowing what to make of this, Vine, who hadn't an unpleasant nature, said, 'I'm sorry to hear that,' and then, because he had cottoned on, 'You mean you've come in for her place or what?'

'That's it. Got it in one. My mum don't want it. She says we can have it.'

438

'When did this happen then?'

'What, my nan dying or my mum saying we could have her place?' She didn't wait for an answer. 'Mum come round Wednesday and I told her about Zack, so she said, you can't stay here, and I said, too right we can't, and that was when she said, you better move in your nan's place. Satisfied?'

'It has to be a change for the better.'

'Clint,' said Kimberley, 'you leave them bottles alone or you'll get a smack you won't like.'

A father and a conscientious one, Vine disapproved of corporal punishment, he had what he called a 'thing' about it, and Clint was very young.

'Is he OK?' he said.

'What d'you mean, OK? You mean he shouldn't be living in this dump? Right, I couldn't agree more. He's moving out, in't he? You a social worker now, are you?'

'I mean,' said Vine, 'is he quite recovered from that op he had?'

'For God's sake, that was a year ago.' She was suddenly furiously angry, her face bright red, her shoulders and arms trembling. 'What the fuck's it got to do with you? Of course he's recovered – look at him. He's bloody marvellous, he's *normal*, he's like he was born that way. Can't you *see*?' She shivered. 'Why don't you and her just take the stuff and fuck off?'

She slammed the door behind them. Vine put his foot in the puddle and cursed.

'I've got another child to see,' Karen said in the car. 'But I'm questioning this one, God help me.'

Wexford found it odious, the whole thing, the idea of asking a young boy for information about his own father. It reminded him, by a roundabout route, of the question he had been handed at the Women, Aware! meeting. Having Karen, a nice-looking young woman with a no-nonsense manner, interview Joel seemed the best way. Presumably, her well-known abrasiveness when questioning men wouldn't extend to boys of fourteen.

He went with her and talked to the mother while she sat with Joel in the quaintly named playroom, a place where there was nothing to play with but plenty of equipment conducive to study. Joel had an impressive collection of textbooks and dictionaries, a computer and a recording device. The posters on the walls were the educational kind, the life of a tree, the human digestive system, a climate map of the world.

Joel looked like his father, dark, thin, already tall, but had his mother's cool manner. Perhaps he too was capable of violent eruptions. He spoke to Karen before she had a chance to speak to him.

'My mother has told me what you've come for. It isn't any good asking me because I don't know.'

'Joel, I only want you to tell me if you were aware of your father going out just before eight. Were you in this room?'

The boy nodded. He seemed relaxed but his eyes were wary.

'You were in this room which is over the garage? If a car went out you'd hear it.'

'My mother keeps her car in the garage. His always stands out.'

'Even so. You've got good hearing, haven't you? Or were you concentrating very hard on your essay?' She had noticed that when the chance came he had not referred to Snow as 'my father'. She took the plunge. 'Your mother has told you what all this is about?'

'Please,' he said. 'I'm not a child. He's been committing adultery and now his woman's been murdered.'

Karen blinked. She was seriously taken aback. She took a deep breath and started again on the car, the garage, the time. Downstairs, Wexford was asking Carolyn Snow if she would care to amend the statement she had made concerning her husband's movements on the evening of 7 July.

'No. Why should I?' She wore no make-up. Her hair looked as if she hadn't washed it since she found out about Annette Bystock. If her clothes were expensive and in good order this was probably because she had no others. She said suddenly, 'There was another one before her, you know. A Diana something. But she didn't last long.' She put her hand up to her hair. 'Is it true that a wife can't give evidence against her husband?'

'A wife can't be *compelled* to give evidence against her husband,' said Wexford. 'It's not the same thing.'

She thought about this and what she thought seemed to please her. 'You won't want to talk to me again, will you?'

'We might. It's a possibility. Not thinking of going away anywhere, I hope?'

Her eyes narrowed. 'Why do you ask?'

He could tell she was thinking of it. 'The schools break up next

440

week. I don't want you going away at present, Mrs Snow.' At the front door he paused. She was standing behind him but left him to open the door himself. 'You have a relative living in Ladyhall Avenue, I believe?'

'No, I haven't. Where did you get that idea?'

He wasn't going to tell her that it had come from her husband or that this person's place of residence was his reason for not going to Annette's flat. 'A friend, then?'

'No one.' She shook her head fiercely. 'My family come from Tunbridge Wells.'

He left, thinking that if Annette had threatened to expedite a marriage between herself and Snow by divulging all to Carolyn, that would be Snow's motive for murder. Carolyn's reaction to learning of her husband's sustained infidelity was all too evident now. She was as unforgiving and as vindictive as Snow had expected her to be. And he would know; there had been another before Annette.

On the other hand, he might have gone round to Ladyhall Court on that Wednesday evening to beg Annette not to tell. He might have promised her all sorts of concessions. Taking her out to dinner occasionally would have been a start, Wexford thought. Or a holiday somewhere with her or just giving her a present. None of it had worked. Nothing else would do but that he leave Carolyn and come to her. They quarrelled, he tore the lead of the bedside lamp out of the wall and strangled her. . . . It was that tearing the electric lead part that didn't ring true, Wexford thought. It would have taken some strength. In the heat of rage, wouldn't he have put his bare hands round her throat?

He crossed the pavement to his car where Karen already waited at the wheel, the only exercise he would get that day. Dr Crocker, and lately Dr Akande, had told him he should walk more (the best kind of cardiovascular exercise, they both intoned) and he was wondering whether to tell Karen to take the car back alone and leave him to do the mile or two on foot, when he saw the doctor coming towards him. Wexford was immediately aware of that craven reaction which makes us want to pretend we haven't seen someone, makes us cross the road and keep our eyes averted, when the prospective encounter may involve reproach or recrimination. He had committed no offence against Dr Akande; on the contrary, he had done everything in his and his force's power to find the doctor's missing daughter, but in spite of this he felt ashamed. Worse than that, he wanted to avoid the society of someone as unhappy and as despairing as the doctor must be. But he made no attempt to do so. A policeman must confront everything or take some other job (retrain, in ES parlance). It was a maxim he had first uttered to himself some thirty years before.

'How are you, doctor?'

Akande shook his head. 'I've been visiting a patient who's only two years short of a hundred,' he said. 'Even she asked me if I had any news. They're very kind, very good. I tell myself it would be worse if they stopped asking.'

Wexford could think of nothing to say.

'I keep thinking about what Melanie might have done, where she went, all that. It's as if I don't think of anything else. It goes round and round in my head. I've even started wondering if we'll ever have her body. I never could understand that, those people who lost sons in war and craved their – their remains. Or just wanted to know where they were buried. I used to think, what does it matter? It's the person you want, the living creature you loved, not the – the outer casing. I understand now.'

His voice had broken on the word 'love' as unhappy people's voices do break on that particular trigger. He said, 'You must excuse me, I try to keep going,' and walked off, as if blindly. Wexford watched him fumbling with the key at his car door and guessed his eyes were thick with tears.

'Poor man,' said Karen, making Wexford wonder if this was the first time she had ever uttered that adjective and that noun in conjunction before.

'Yes.'

'Where are we going now, sir?'

'To Ladyhall Avenue.' He was silent for a moment. Then he said, 'Ingrid Pamber told us something that seems to have got lost in the general shock-horror over Snow's behaviour. Do you know what I'm talking about?'

'Something about Snow?'

'Of course it may not be true. She's a liar and an embroiderer too, I daresay.'

'Do you mean about his wife having some relation living opposite Ladyhall Court?'

Wexford nodded. They turned out of Queens Gardens where Wendy Stowlap lived and passed the corner shop where Ingrid had bought Annette's groceries. A man was banging furiously on the glass side of the phone box in which a woman talked on, unheeding.

A blind woman let them into the house. Her eyeballs, in their baskets of wrinkles, were like glass that has been crazed from too much handling. Wexford spoke gently.

'Chief Inspector Wexford, Kingsmarkham CID, and this is Detective Sergeant Malahyde.'

'She's a young lady, isn't she?' said Mrs Prior, staring into the middle distance.

Karen admitted it.

'I can smell you. Very nice too. Roma, isn't it?'

'Yes, it is. Clever of you.'

'Oh, I know 'em all, all the perfumes, it's how I know one woman from the next. It's no good you showing me those cards of yours, I can't see them, and I don't suppose *they* smell.' Gladys Prior giggled at her own wit. She led them to the staircase and they followed her up. 'What's happened to that young chap B,U,R,D,E,N?' It was evidently some kind of 'in' joke and it made her laugh again.

'He's busy somewhere else today,' said Wexford.

Percy Hammond wasn't looking out of his window. He was asleep. But the light sleep of the very old was easily broken when they came into the room. Wexford wondered what he had looked like when he was young. There was nothing in that creased, pouchy, stretched, puckered face to indicate the lineaments of middle age, still less youth. It was scarcely human any more. Only the white, rosy-gummed dentures, displayed when he smiled, hinted at real teeth, lost fifty years before.

He was dressed in a striped suit with waistcoat and collarless shirt. The knees held up the grey worsted as a frame with sharp metal angles might, and the hands which rested on them were like a pigeon's claws. 'Do you want me to attend an identity parade?' he asked. 'Pick him out from a line of them?'

Wexford didn't. While mentally congratulating Mr Hammond on his quick-witted assumption, he could only tell him out loud that there was no doubt about who had robbed Annette's flat. They already had someone helping them with their enquiries into this matter.

'You couldn't have gone anyway,' said Mrs Prior. 'Not in your state.' She addressed Karen, to whom she seemed to have taken a fancy. 'He's ninety-two, you know.'

'Ninety-three,' said Mr Hammond, thus confirming Wexford's Law that it is only when under fifteen and over ninety that people wish to add years to their true age. 'Ninety-three next week, and I could have. I haven't tried going out for four years, so how do you know I couldn't have?'

'An intelligent guess,' said Gladys Prior with a giggle in Karen's direction.

'Mr Hammond,' Wexford began, 'you've already told Inspector Burden what you saw across the way very early last Thursday morning. Were you looking out of your window on the previous evening?'

'I'm always looking out. Unless I'm asleep or it's dark. Even in the dark sometimes – you can see with the street lights if you turn the light off in here.'

'And do you turn the light off, Mr Hammond?' asked Karen.

'I have to think about the electric bills, missy. My lights were off last Wednesday evening, if that's what you want to know. You want to hear what I saw? I've been thinking about it, going back over it. I knew you'd come back.'

He was blest in such a witness, Wexford thought thankfully. 'Tell me what you saw, will you, sir?'

'I always watch them come home from work. Mind you, a few of them have gone away on holiday. Most of them ignore me but that chap Harris, he always gives me a wave. He got home about twenty past five and ten minutes after a girl came. She had a car and she parked it outside. There's a yellow line there that means you're not supposed to park till six-thirty but she took no notice of that. I'd never seen her before. Pretty girl she was, about eighteen.'

Ingrid would be flattered, for what it was worth. By the time you reach ninety-three, Wexford thought, people of fifty look thirty to you and those in their twenties seem children. 'She went into the flats?'

'And came out after five minutes. Well, seven minutes, it was. I'm no good at guessing time but I timed her, I don't know why. Gives me something to do. I do that sometimes, it's a game I play, I bet on it. I say to myself, ten bob on it, Percy, she comes out before ten minutes are up.'

'The young lady doesn't know what ten bob is, Percy. You're not living in the real world, you aren't. Fifty pee to you, dear, it's twenty years and more since the changeover but it's like yesterday to him.'

444

Wexford interrupted, 'What happened next?'

'Nothing happened. If you mean by that, did any strangers go in. Mrs Harris came out and came back with an evening paper. I had my meal then, bit of bread and butter and a glass of Guinness, the same as I always have. I saw the car come that takes Gladys to her blind club.'

'Seven sharp,' said Mrs Prior. 'And I was back at half-past nine.'

'While you were eating, Mr Hammond,' said Wexford, 'did you sit at the table over there? Did you watch any television?'

The old man shook his head. He pointed at the window.

'That's my telly.'

'Don't get much sex and violence on it, though, do you, Percy?' Gladys Prior became convulsed with laughter.

'So you went on watching, did you, Mr Hammond? What happened after Mrs Prior had gone out?'

Percy Hammond screwed up his already screwed-up face. 'Nothing much, I'm sorry to say.' He gave Wexford a shrewd glance. 'What do you *want* me to have seen?'

'Only what you did see,' said Karen.

'It's around eight I'm interested in, Mr Hammond,' said Wexford. 'I don't want to put ideas into your head, but did you see a man go into Ladyhall Court between five to and a quarter past eight?'

'Only that chap with his dog. There's a man whose name I don't know and Gladys doesn't know, he's got a spaniel. He always takes it out in the evening. I saw *him*. I'd think something was wrong if I didn't see him.'

Something *was* wrong, thought Wexford, something was very wrong. 'No one else?'

'No one at all.'

'Not a man or a woman? You saw no one go in at about eight and come out at between ten and ten-thirty?'

'I said I'm no good with times. But I didn't see another soul until the young chap I told Mr What's-his-name about.'

'B,U,R,D,E,N,' said Mrs Prior with a gale of giggles.

'And it was dark then. I was in bed, I'd been asleep, but I got up – why did I get up, Gladys?'

'Don't ask me, Percy. To spend a penny, I daresay.'

'I put the light on for a minute but it was so bright, I turned it off, and I looked out of the window and I saw this young chap come out with a big box in his arms – or was that later?'

Karen said gently, 'That was in the morning, Mr Hammond. You saw him in the morning, don't you remember? That's the one you asked us about, if you'd have to pick him out in an identity parade?'

'So it was. I told you I wasn't much good with time . . .'

'I think we've tired you out, Mr Hammond,' said Wexford. 'You've been a great help but we'll only ask you one more thing. You and Mrs Prior. Is either of you related to some people called Snow of Harrow Road, Kingsmarksham?'

Two disappointed old faces turned towards him. Both liked excitement, both hated having to deny knowledge. 'Never heard of them,' said Mrs Prior gruffly.

'I suppose you know everyone . . . er, down this street, do you?' Wexford asked her as they were going down the stairs.

'You were going to say "by sight", weren't you? Bless you, I wouldn't have minded. Though it'd be nearer the mark to say "by smell".' She waited till she got to the foot of the staircase before letting her laughter escape. 'There's a lot of old folks down here, the houses are old, you see, and some of them have lived in them for forty years, fifty. Would they be young or old, this person that's related to Mrs What-d'you-call-her?'

'I don't know,' said Wexford. 'I don't know at all.'

# 12

The house was new, just finished, the last coat of paint applied perhaps no more than a week ago. But it still made him feel in a time warp. Not that he saw Mynford New Hall as old but rather that he had gone back two hundred years and, finding himself a character in, say, *Northanger Abbey*, had been brought here to view a brand-new mansion.

It was Georgian, with a pillared portico and a balustrade along the shallow roof, a big house, ivory-white, the windows perfectly proportioned sashes, the columns fluted. In alcoves on either side of the front door stood stone vases hung with stone drapery and with living ivy and maidenhair fern. A gravel sweep would have been better but the carriage drive was paved. The tubs and troughs clustered on it held bay trees and yellow cypress, red fuchsias in full bloom, orange and cream arbutus, pink pelargoniums. By contrast, the flowerbeds were bare, turned earth without a weed showing.

'Give them a chance,' Dora whispered. 'They've only been here five minutes. They must have hired those tubs for the occasion.'

'Where were they before, then?'

'In that place down the hill, the dower house.'

The hill was a gentle slope of green lawns descending towards a wooded valley. A grey roof could just be made out among the trees. Wexford remembered the old hall on the hilltop, a mid-Victorian stucco pile, not old enough or distinctive enough to be listed for preservation. Presumably, the Khooris had encountered no planning difficulties in pulling it down and setting the new hall up.

Their guests thronged the big lawn. In the middle of it stood a large striped marquee. Wexford had referred to it laconically as 'the tea tent', a term Dora obscurely felt to be irreverent or even *lèse majesté*. Her husband hadn't wanted to come. She told him not altogether truthfully that he had promised, then that it would do him good, take him out of himself. In the end he had come for her sake because she had said she wouldn't go if he didn't.

'Do you know anybody here? Because if you don't we might as well go for a walk. I wouldn't mind having a look at the old dower house.'

'No, ssh. Here's our hostess and homing on you if I'm not mistaken.'

Anouk Khoori was a protean creature. He held in his mind the image of her in her tracksuit, her face *au naturel*, hair in a bouncy ponytail; and that other image, the champagne social worker, the ardent campaigner and political aspirant, power-dressed, up on high heels, her jewellery and solitary solitaire.

It was on her hand now but with many companions, flashing white and blue from her fingers as she walked towards them. And she was different again, not simply altered as women always are by change of dress and hairstyle, but altogether unrecognizable. If he had met her off her home ground, if Dora hadn't been there to identify her, he doubted if he would have known Anouk Khoori. This time she was the chatelaine in yellow chiffon and a big straw hat piled with daisies, golden tendrils curling on her forehead and escaping to hang to her shoulders.

'Mr Wexford, I *knew* you would come but I'm delighted just the same. And this is Mrs Wexford? How do you do? Aren't we lucky to have this glorious day? You must meet my husband.' She looked about her, then scanned the horizon. 'I don't seem to be able to see him just at the moment. But come, let me introduce you to some very dear friends of ours that I know you'll love.' As one of those women who never bother much with women, she turned her full gaze on Wexford and her fullest smile, a radiant beaming from lips painted geranium with a fine brush and teeth capped to Wedgwood whiteness. 'And who will love *you*,' she added.

The very dear friends turned out to be an aged man, wrinkled and shrunken, with the face of an ancient guru but dressed in denim and Western boots, and a girl some fifty years younger. Anouk Khoori, a genius at picking up and remembering names and one who swiftly dispensed with surnames, said, 'Reg and Dora, I've been longing for you to meet Alexander and Cookie Dix. Cookie, darling, this is Reg Wexford who is a terribly important police chief.'

Cookie? How on earth did anyone get a name like that? She was getting on for a foot taller than her husband, dressed like the Princess of Wales at Ascot, but with waist-length black hair. 'Is that sort of like a sheriff?' she said.

Anouk Khoori gave a long thrilling peal of laughter and on this laughter, as to a cue provided by herself, floated away. Wexford had astonished himself by his reaction to her, one of physical repulsion. But why should this be? She was beautiful, or many would say so, healthy and strong, extravagantly clean, deodorized, powdered, perfumed. Yet the touch of her hand made him shrink and her scent near him was like a foetid breath.

Dora was making an effort to talk to Cookie Dix. Did she live nearby? What did she think of the neighbourhood? He could make small talk as well as anyone but he could no longer see the point. The shrunken old man stood silent and faintly scowling. He reminded Wexford of a horror film he'd watched one night when he couldn't sleep. There had been a mummy in it which the experimenter had unwrapped, succeeded up to a point in reanimating, and brought along to just such a garden party as this one.

'Have you seen Anouk's diamonds?' Cookie said suddenly.

Dora, who had been talking gently about the weather in July, how it never really got warm in England until July, was surprised into silence.

'The ones she's wearing *now* cost a hundred grand alone. Can you believe that? There's ten times that in the house.'

'Goodness,' said Dora.

'You may well say goodness.' She bent forwards, necessarily stooping in order to push her face close to Dora's, but instead of whispering spoke in her usual clear tones. 'The house is hideous. Don't you think so? Pitiful, really, they think it's based on some Nash design for a house that was never built, but it's not, is it, sweetness?'

The mummy barked. It was exactly what had happened in the horror film, only at this point people had dispersed screaming.

'My husband is a very famous architect,' said Cookie. She extended her neck and pushed her face at Wexford. 'If we were people in a book, me telling you about the diamonds would be a *clue*, there'd be a robbery while we're out here, and you'd have to question all these people. There are five hundred people here, did you know that?'

Wexford laughed. He rather liked Cookie Dix, her naive manner and her metre-long legs. 'At least, I'd say. Still, I doubt if they've left the house unguarded.'

'They have but for Juana and Rosenda.'

Unexpectedly, the mummy began to sing in a cracked tenor, to a tune from the *Mikado*, 'Two little maids from the Philippines, one of them hardly out of her teens . . . '

'I'd have thought they'd have a staff,' Dora said faintly.

'They used to have another one, as a matter of fact she was the sister of our one, but the rich are so mean, haven't you noticed? Well, darling Alexander isn't and God knows he's loaded.' The mummy's face cracked. At just such a ghastly smile the women in the movie had started screaming. 'Mostly they have caterers in,' said Cookie. 'Their servants don't stay. Well, these two do. The money's rotten but they need it to send home.' For some reason Cookie dropped her voice. 'Filipinos do.'

'Filipin*as*,' said the mummy.

'Thank you, sweet. You're such a stickler. I call him my stickler sometimes. Shall we go and have some tea?'

Together they walked down the green slope, deflected from the prospect of tea by the kind of sideshows considered suitable for this type of charity benefit function. A good-looking dark woman in a kind of ankle-length white sweater was conducting a raffle for Fortnum and Mason hampers. A young man in a smock with an easel and palette was doing instant portraits for a fiver a time. Under a long yellow banner with CIBACT on it in black, a man had his twin daughters on display, little fair-haired girls in white frilled organdie and black patent leather shoes with instep straps. Punters were invited to guess the age of Phyllida and Fenella and whoever came nearest to the correct birth date got the child-size white teddy bear that sat on the counter between them.

'Vulgar, you see,' said Cookie. 'That's their trouble. They don't know the difference.'

Dora glanced at the docile children. 'You mean the raffle is all right and perhaps the artist but not the teddy bear thing?'

'Exactly. That's exactly what I mean. Sad, really, when you've got everything.'

At last Alexander Dix expressed himself, otherwise than in song. Wexford thought his voice what a French speaker's would be if he had lived till the age of thirty in, say, Casablanca, and the rest of his life in Aberdeen. 'Nothing else is to be expected when you are a child of the gutters of Alexandria.'

Presumably he was referring to Wael Khoori. Interested, Wexford was about to ask for more when something happened that always happens at parties. A couple appeared from nowhere and bore down upon the Dixes with cries of astonishment and greeting, and as also is always true, their former companions were forgotten. Wexford and Dora were abandoned, still standing in front of Phyllida, Fenella and the teddy bear.

'Better do something for CIBACT, I suppose,' Wexford said, producing a ten pound note. 'What do you say? I'll guess they're five and their birthday was June the first.'

'I don't like to look too closely. They're not animals at Smithfield or something. I see what that Cookie meant. Oh, all right, I'll say they're five but they'll be six in September, September the fifth.'

'Older,' said a voice from behind Dora. 'Six already. Probably six-and-a-half.'

Wexford turned round to see Swithun Riding. His wife looked very small beside him. There was a greater disparity in their heights than that between Wexford and Dora or, come to that, between Cookie Dix and the diminutive architect.

Susan said, 'Do you know my husband?'

Introductions were made. Unlike his son, Swithun Riding responded. He smiled and uttered the usual archaism that was once an enquiry as to another's health.

'How do you do?'

Wexford handed his money to the twins' father and repeated his estimate of their age.

'Oh, nonsense,' said Riding. 'Have you no children yourself?'

The question was uttered in a tone both indignant and arrogant. Good manners had swiftly fallen away. Riding seemed to imply the discovery in Wexford of a wanton and antisocial partiality to total contraception.

'He's got two,' said Dora rather sharply. 'Two *girls. And* he's got a good memory.'

'Well, Swithun's a paediatrician, after all,' said Swithun's wife in mild reproach.

Her husband ignored her. A twenty pound note was handed over, no doubt as a sign of social and perhaps parental superiority, and Swithun Riding offered his estimate as six-and-a-half.

451

'They were six on February the twelfth,' he hazarded but in so firm a voice as to suggest that whatever might be Phyllida and Fenella's official birthday, this was what their natural birthday should be.

The Ridings, joined by the burly Christopher in shorts and polo shirt and a fair-haired girl of about ten, set off in the direction of a plant stall. This was enough to turn Dora in the opposite direction towards the tea tent. Tea was a lavish affair, twenty different kinds of sandwiches, scones with raspberry jam and clotted cream, chocolate cake, coffee and walnut cake, passion cake, pecan pie, eclairs, cream slices, brandy snaps, strawberries and cream.

'Just the kind of thing I like,' said Wexford, joining the queue.

It was a very long queue, a serpent of guests that wound round the inside perimeter of the yellow and white striped tent, and it was the kind of queue seldom seen, as different as could be from a line of dispirited ill-dressed people waiting for a bus or worse, as Wexford had seen recently in Myringham, at a dossers' soup kitchen. The tea tent at Glyndebourne was probably the nearest you'd get to this one. He'd been there once and, uncomfortable in a dinner jacket at four in the afternoon, had lined up for smoked salmon sandwiches just as he was doing now. But there a good many like himself had dressed themselves in ancient evening clothes, dinner jackets just post-war, old women in black lace from the forties, while here it was as if a *Vogue* centrefold had turned into a video. Dora said the woman in front of them was wearing a suit from Lacroix while Caroline Charles dresses were thick on the ground. She added abstractedly,

'Don't eat the clotted cream, Reg.'

'I wasn't going to,' he lied. 'I suppose I can have a bit of pecan pie? And a couple of strawberries?'

'Of course you can but you know what Dr Akande said.'

'Poor devil's got more on his mind at the moment than my cholesterol count.'

All the tables in the marquee were occupied. As he had predicted, the Chief Constable was here, sitting at a table with his thin red-headed wife and two friends. Wexford quickly dodged out of the line of sight and he and Dora took their trays outside. They found themselves reduced to a low wall for seats and the top of a balustrade for a table, and were setting out the food when a voice behind Wexford said, 'I thought it was you! I'm so pleased to see you because we don't know anyone here.'

Ingrid Pamber. Behind her was the wild-haired Jeremy Lang,

452

carrying a tray that sagged under its load of sandwiches, cake and strawberries.

'I know what you're thinking,' said Ingrid. 'You're thinking what on earth are that pair doing here up among the nobs.'

Fortunately, she didn't know what he was thinking. If he hadn't made it a rule long ago never to admire other women while accompanied by his wife, never to do this even in his own thoughts, he would have been dwelling appreciatively on her pink and white skin, that hair as satiny as a racehorse's coat, that figure and the charming tilt to her mouth. As it was, he told himself she was ten times prettier in her white top and cotton skirt than Anouk Khoori or Cookie Dix or the woman who ran the hamper raffle. Then he banished covert admiration and said that though this hadn't been the enquiry he had in mind, how did she in fact come to be there?

'Jerry's uncle's a pal of Mr Khoori. They live next door to each other in London.'

The uncle. So the uncle was real. 'I see.' Since Khoori's London was unlikely to be too far distant from Mayfair, Belgravia or Hampstead, the uncle must be a rich man.

Up to a little more thought-reading but this time with greater accuracy, Ingrid said, 'Eaton Square,' and then, 'May we join you? It's great to have someone to talk to.'

He introduced Dora, who said graciously, 'Share our wall.'

Ingrid began chatting about the happiness of having a fortnight off work, all the places she and Jeremy had been to, some rock concert, the theatre at Chichester. While she talked she managed to mop up a great deal of food. How did the thin eat so much and get away with it? Girls like Ingrid, boys like this bony Jeremy shovelling in scones plastered with their own thickness in clotted cream. They never seemed to think about it, they just ate it.

Better for him anyway to contemplate food and dwell on its effects than about this charming girl who was now with abundant grace and courtesy complimenting Dora on her dress. This afternoon her eyes seemed a brighter blue than ever, almost the colour of a kingfisher's plumage. She wanted to know if they had gone in for guessing the twins' age. Jeremy had said it was silly but she had made him have a go because she did so want to win the teddy bear.

She laid her white hand on Wexford's sleeve. 'I'm mad about cuddly toys. I can't remember – did we go into the bedroom when you came to the flat?'

453

The serpent uncoiling in the garden, that was what it was like. Graceful and courteous she might be, but poison was there too, a tiny sac of it under her tongue. Dora was looking surprised but no more than that. Jeremy, taking the second plate of passion cake, said, 'Of course he didn't go into the bedroom, Ing. Why would he have? There's not room to swing a cat in there.'

'Or a teddy bear.' Ingrid giggled. 'I've got a golden spaniel my dad bought me in Paris when I was ten and a pink pig and a dinosaur that came from Florida. The dinosaur doesn't sound cuddly but he is, maybe the most cuddly, isn't he, Jerry?'

'Not as cuddly as me, though,' said Jeremy and he helped himself to a brandy snap. 'You met my uncle Wael yet?'

'Not yet. We spoke to Mrs Khoori.'

'I suppose I still call him uncle. Don't know really. Until the other day I hadn't spoken to him since I was eighteen. I'll introduce you if you want.'

Neither Wexford nor Dora did much want but could hardly say so. Jeremy brushed crumbs off his jeans and got up. 'You stay there, Ing,' he said kindly, 'and finish up the eclairs. You know how you love eclairs.'

Finding Wael Khoori took a long time and involved walking all the way round the outside of Mynford New Hall. Wexford spotted the Chief Constable, this time heading in the direction of some rather sophisticated coconut shies. It seemed likely that he might avoid an encounter. Jeremy said that when they arrived that afternoon he had expected a house that looked like one of his uncle Wael's Crescent supermarkets with what he called 'minaret things' or else something like Abu Dhabi airport. Instead there was this boring Georgian place. Had Mr and Mrs Wexford ever seen Abu Dhabi airport? While Dora listened to a description of this Arabian Nights extravaganza and tourist snare, Wexford glanced up at the windows of the new house with a vague idea in mind of seeing the face of either Juana or Rosenda looking out.

It was a big house for two young women to manage. Mrs Khoori didn't look the sort of woman to make her own bed or wash up the breakfast things. There must be twenty bedrooms and no doubt bathrooms to go with them. What must it be like to be obliged to travel half across the world in order to feed your children?

The sky was beginning to cloud over and above the downs had dulled to a threatening purple. A little breeze whistled out of the woodland as they began to descend the slope. Wexford disliked the idea of climbing it again, he was growing weary of this hunting for a host who by rights should have sought them out. And he was thinking of saying so, though in politer terms, when Jeremy suddenly looked round and waved to the people behind them.

Three men, two of them walking arm-in-arm. It would have looked less odd, Wexford thought, if each had been in a burnous and galabeah, but all were in western clothes and one was unmistakeably Anglo-Saxon, pink-skinned, fairish, bald. The others were both overweight and tall, taller even than Wexford. Each had the handsome Semite's face, hook-nosed, narrow-lipped, the eyes close-set. Plainly they were brothers, the younger man with a badly pock-marked brown skin, but the other's was no darker than an Englishman's with a tan while his hair, copious and rather long, was white as snow. He seemed about ten years older than his wife but she on the other hand might be older than she looked.

The last thing Wael Khoori wanted at this moment, in the midst perhaps of some business discussion, was to be accosted by this nephew-by-courtesy and introduced to people he didn't want to meet. This was clear from his abstracted and then mildly irritated expression. One thing, he knew Jeremy well, there had been no exaggeration there, though Wexford wouldn't have been surprised if there had been. He called him 'dear boy' like some Victorian godparent.

They were presented to Khoori as 'Reg and Dora Wexford, friends of Ingrid's', which Dora said afterwards she thought a bit much. Khoori behaved as the Royal Family are said to do when meeting strangers. But his manner as he asked his banal questions was impatient rather than gracious, he was in a hurry to get on.

'Have you come far?'

'We live here,' Wexford said.

'Like it, do you? Pretty place, very green. Had tea yet? Have some tea, my wife tells me it's tip-top.'

'Right,' said Jeremy, 'I might have some more.'

'You do that, dear boy. Kind regards to your uncle when you see him.' To Wexford and Dora, he trotted out the old formula, 'Nice to have met you. Come again.'

Linking arms with both companions, neither of whom had been introduced, he steered them away into a shrubbery as dense as a maze. Jeremy said confidingly as they walked back to the marquee,

'Got a funny voice, hasn't he? Did you notice? Estuary English, I suppose, and a hint of cockney.'

'It can't be, though.'

'Well, it can actually. His brother that's called Ismail talks the same. They had an English nanny and *he* says she came from Whitechapel.'

'So he didn't grow up in the gutters of Alexandria?' said Dora.

'Where did you get that idea? His parents were quite aristocratic, Uncle William says, his dad was a Bey or a Khalifa or one of those things, and it was Riyadh. Hi, Ing, sorry we've been so long.'

'They gave the result of the competition,' Ingrid said, 'and I didn't get the bear and nor did you. It was 368 got it. Well, they didn't get it, because no one came up with the ticket. Why do people go in for things and then not look to see if they've won?'

Dora said they must be going and, varying Khoori's formula, that she was very glad they had met. Wexford said goodbye.

'We should have offered them a lift, you know. Jeremy told me they hadn't got their car with them, it's in for repairs.'

'I bet he did,' Wexford said.

That would be a fine thing, driving them back to Kingsmarkham, perhaps be invited in for a cup of tea and then have Dora in her innocence ask them round next week to spend the evening. 'You must meet my daughter Sylvia . . . ' He could imagine it all. He took his wife's arm affectionately. She had got out her ticket and was looking at it as they passed the twins' stall, from which the children had disappeared, though their father – and the teddy bear – remained.

'Three-six-seven,' she said. 'Missed it by one.' She turned to look at Wexford. 'Reg, you must either have three-six-six or three-six-eight.'

He had the winning ticket, of course he had. By some kind of awful intuition he had known it since Ingrid's announcement. The correct answer to the question of the twins' ages was 1 June, on which date Phyllida had been born five years before at two minutes to midnight, and 2 June, birth date of Fenella at ten minutes past. No one had come up with that and Wexford was nearest with 1 June.

'Let me give it back. You can raffle it for the cause.'

'Oh, no, you don't,' said the twins' father nastily. 'I've had as much of that bloody thing as I can stand. You take it or else I chuck it in the river and pollute the environment.'

456

Wexford took it. The teddy bear was as big as a child of two. He knew what he would have to do with it, wanted to do this and didn't want to. Dora said, 'You could . . . '

'Yes, I know. I will.'

They were eating again, taking Khoori's advice and having some more tea. Most people were leaving, so they had acquired the best table, outside the marquee, under the shade of a mulberry tree. Wexford set the teddy bear on the empty chair between them. Ingrid's brilliant eyes were wide, covetous, yearning. How could eyes which absorbed light and never gave it off produce a beam of peacock blue? Or was it of deep ice?

'He's yours if you want him.'

'You don't mean it!'

She had sprung to her feet. 'Oh, you're wonderful! You're so kind! I shall call her Christabel!'

Whoever heard of a female teddy bear? He knew what would happen next. It did – before he could get away. She threw her arms round his neck and kissed him. Dora watched enigmatically. Jeremy continued eating coffee walnut cake. Ingrid's body, which was delightfully and distressingly plump and slim at the same time, clung a little too long and a little too close to his own. He took her hands, removed them gently from his neck and said,

'I'm glad you're pleased.'

Since it wasn't in the nature of things that she should be attracted to him – he wasn't rich like Alexander Dix, young like Jeremy or handsome like Peter Stanton – and nymphomania was a myth, only one possibility remained. She was a flirt. A flirt with the world's bluest glance. 'An hundred years should go to praise shine eyes, and on thy forehead gaze . . . ' He would *not* offer her a lift.

'Maybe he can be a boy after all,' said Ingrid. 'I know – your first name's Reg, isn't it?'

Wexford laughed. He said goodbye again, and over his shoulder, 'It's not available for christening teddy bears.'

A second possibility remained. He thought of it now. She was a liar, he knew that: was she also a murderer? Was she nice to him, or what she thought of as being nice, to get him on her side? They were coming into the field that was a car park, before Dora said anything. The first drops of rain had begun to fall. The breeze had become a serious wind and a woman in front of them in cartwheel hat and diaphanous dress was having to hold her skirts down.

'She was all over you, that girl,' said Dora.

'Yes.'

'Who is she, anyway?'

'A suspect in a murder.' He never told her more than that about his cases. She looked at him quite cheerfully.

'Really?'

'Really. Let's get in the car, shall we? Your hat'll get wet.'

There was a queue to get out but not a long one. The line of cars had to pass through a farm gateway and since Rollses, Bentleys and Jaguars predominated, progress was slow. Only two cars remained ahead of him to squeeze between the gate-posts, when his phone started ringing. He picked up the receiver and it was Karen's voice he heard.

'Yes,' he said, 'yes,' and, 'I see.'

Dora could hear Karen's voice but not distinguish words. The car slipped and bumped through the narrow gap. Wexford said, 'Where did you say?' And then he said, 'I'll take my wife home and come straight there.'

'What is it, Reg? Oh, Reg, it's not Melanie Akande?'

'Sounds like it. I'm afraid it is.'

'Is she dead?'

'Oh, yes,' he said, 'she's dead.'

# 13

Kingsmarkham lies in that part of Sussex that was once the land of a Celtic tribe the Romans called the Regnenses. To its colonists it was simply a desirable place to live, pleasant to look at and not too cold, the indigenous population regarded only as a source of slave labour. Numerous remains of female infants unearthed by archaeologists near Pomfret Monachorum suggest that the Romans practised infanticide among the Regnenses with a view to maintaining a male work force.

As well as this grisly discovery, treasure was found. No one knew how this huge cache of gold coins, figurines and jewellery came to be buried on farmland a mile or two from Cheriton but there was evidence that a Roman villa had once stood there. A rather romantic suggestion was made that early in the fifth century the family who lived there, being forced to flee, had buried their valuables in the hope of coming back one day to retrieve them. But the Romans had never come back and the Dark Ages began.

This treasure was found by the farmer himself, digging up a small piece of land, hitherto part of fields on which sheep grazed, with the intention of growing maize on it for fattening pheasants. It was valued at something over two million pounds, most of which he received. He gave up farming and went to live in Florida. The gold statuette he found of a suckling lioness and twin cubs and the two gold bracelets, one chased with a design of a boar hunt, the other of a stag at bay, can now be seen in the British Museum, where they are known as the Framhurst Hoard.

The result was to encourage prospectors. Looking from a distance as if slowly scouring the heathland and the green valley with vacuum cleaners, they came with their metal detectors and worked patiently

459

and in silence for long hours at a time. Farmers had no objection – there was little arable farming in the area – and so long as they damaged nothing and did not frighten the sheep, they were not only harmless but might possibly be a source of untold wealth. Any successful prospector would be obliged to render up half his loot to the landowner.

So far there had been no more. The cache of which the lioness and the bracelets had been part appeared to have been a one-off. But the treasure-seekers went on coming and it was one of these wandering somewhat outside the favoured area, passing and repassing his detector across an area of chalky scree, who had come upon firstly a coin, then the body of a girl.

It was where the downland began, between Cheriton and Myfleet. A narrow white road, without fence, wall or hedge, ran between the foothills, and it was some twenty yards to the left of it, where the woodland began, on the edge of a wood, that she had been buried. While Colin Broadley was plying his metal detector the weather had been fine, the soil fairly damp from recent rains but not wet. The conditions had been ideal for digging and Broadley, once he had found the coin which had so excited his detector, went on with his excavations.

'When you realized what you'd found,' Wexford said to him, 'why didn't you stop digging?'

Broadley, in his forties, a heavy man with a beer gut, shrugged and looked shifty. He was no archaeologist but an unemployed plumber actuated by greed and hope. It was not he that had called the police but a passer-by who, seeing the extensive excavation in progress and thinking it suspicious, had parked his car and gone to look. This public-spirited citizen, James Ranger of Myringham, was paying for his social conscience by being kept at the scene, seated in his car, where he had been for the past two hours.

'It was a strange thing to do, wasn't it?' Wexford persisted.

'She had to *be* dug up,' Broadley said at last. 'Someone was going to have to do it.'

'That was a job for the police,' Wexford said, and it was true that the police had finished the job. Of course he knew very well what Broadley had been up to. Having found the coin and not being a sensitive or squeamish man, he had dug down, hoping for more money and perhaps for jewellery on what lay beneath.

There had been none. The body was naked. Nor was it possible to

460

say, at this stage, whether or not there was any connection between it and the coin. In the eyes of Broadley, this coin had been the first sample of a Roman treasure, but a closer look told Wexford it was a Victorian halfpenny, bearing the head of the young queen. The hair was done in a style vaguely suggestive of actresses taking part in Ancient Rome movies. Wexford sent Broadley off with Pemberton to sit in one of the police cars.

It was raining steadily. They had put a tarpaulin up over the grave and the trees provided some shelter. Under here the pathologist was currently examining the body. Not Sir Hilary Tremlett nor Wexford's *bête noire* Dr Basil Sumner-Quist, both of whom were away on their holiday, but an assistant or surrogate who had introduced himself as Mr Mavrikiev. Wexford, under an umbrella – there were ten umbrellas at the scene, under the dripping trees – held the coin inside a plastic bag. Not that there was likely to be such a thing as a fingerprint on it after its interment in that fine, chalky, abrasive soil, grains of which clogged the indentations on its surface. Once Mavrikiev was out of there and they had taken the photographs, he was going to have to do what he dreaded: make his way to Ollerton Avenue and tell the Akandes.

He must do it himself, he knew that. He couldn't send Vine or even Burden to do the job for him. Since Melanie had been reported missing he had gone daily to see the doctor and his wife, had missed only the day he had met Akande by chance in the street. He had turned himself into their friend and he knew he had done this because they were black. Their race and their colour merited his special attention, yet this was not as it should be. Ideally, if he truly practised what being unprejudiced was all about, he would have treated them the same as any other parents of a missing child. Later that day the reckoning was coming for him.

Mavrikiev lifted a flap of the tarpaulin and came out. There was some assistant of his at hand to hold an umbrella over him. It was incredible, Wexford could hardly believe his eyes, but the pathologist was going to say nothing to him, was making straight for his waiting Jaguar.

'Dr Mavrikiev!' he said.

The man was quite young, fair, with a washed-out Nordic look. Forbears from the Ukraine probably, Wexford guessed, as he turned round and said,

'Mister. Mister Mavrikiev.'

Wexford swallowed his wrath. Why were they always so rude? This one was the worst of the lot. 'Can you give me an idea when she died?'

Mavrikiev looked as if he might ask for Wexford's credentials. He pushed out his lips and scowled. 'Ten days. Maybe more. I'm not a magician.'

No, you're a real bastard . . . 'And the cause of death?'

'Nobody shot her. She wasn't strangled. She wasn't buried alive.'

He ducked into his car and slammed the door. Didn't like being called out on a wet Saturday night, no doubt. Who did? Wouldn't like doing a postmortem on a Sunday either, but that was too bad. Burden came stumbling across the slippery wet scrub, his coat collar turned up, his hair dripping, no umbrella for him.

'Have you seen her?'

Wexford shook his head. He didn't feel anything any more about looking on the dead who have met their death by violence, not even on the decomposing dead. He was used to it and you can get used to anything. In some ways fortunately, his sense of smell wasn't what it had once been. He ducked under the tarpaulin and looked at her. No one had covered her, she wasn't even decently covered with a sheet, but lay sprawled on her back, still in a reasonable state of preservation. The face, particularly, was very nearly intact. Even in death, after days of death and interment, she looked very young.

The black patches on her dark skin, notably the sticky black mass on the side of her hair, might have been decay or they might have been bruises. He didn't know but Mavrikiev would. One of her arms lay at an odd angle and he wondered if it could have been broken before death. Out in the rain again he drew a long breath.

'He said ten days or more,' said Burden. 'That would be about right.'

'Yes.'

'Back to Tuesday week's eleven days. If whoever brought her here came in a car they didn't bring the car in here off the road. Of course she may have been alive when she got here. He may have killed her here. Want me to attend the postmortem? He says nine in the morning. I will if you like. I just shan't speak to Mavri-whatsit unless he speaks to me.'

'Thanks, Mike,' said Wexford. 'I'd rather go to the PM than do what I've got to do tonight.'

*

Ten minutes to nine and still light in that grim hopeless way only a wet summer evening in England can be. It was hard to tell whether it was rain falling or just water dripping from the trees. The air was still and heavy and the humidity hung as a cold whitish vapour. No lights were on in the house but that meant nothing. Dusk had barely come. Wexford rang the bell and almost immediately a light came on in the hall and another in the porch above his head. The boy who opened the door he recognized at once as the Akandes' son who had been in the photograph with Melanie.

Wexford introduced himself. The boy being there made things worse, he thought, but better perhaps for the parents. One child was left to comfort them.

'I'm Patrick. My mother and father are in the back, we're finishing supper as a matter of fact. I only got home today and I've been sleeping. I didn't wake up till an hour ago.'

To forewarn him or not? 'I'm afraid the news is bad.'

'Oh.' Patrick looked at him, then away. 'Yes, well, you must see my parents.'

At the sound of their voices Raymond Akande had risen from the table and was standing there, looking towards the door, but Laurette remained where she was, sitting very upright, both hands lying on the cloth on either side of a plate with orange segments on it. Neither of them said anything.

'I have bad news for you, Dr Akande, Mrs Akande.'

The doctor drew in his breath. His wife silently turned her head in Wexford's direction.

'Will you sit down, please, doctor? I expect you can guess what I've come to tell you.'

The tiny tremor of Akande's head signified a nod.

'Melanie's body has been found,' Wexford said. 'That is, we are as certain as we can be without a positive identification that this is Melanie.'

Laurette beckoned her son. 'Come and sit down again, Patrick.' Her voice was quite steady. She said to Wexford, 'Where was she found?'

How much he had hoped they wouldn't ask! 'In Framhurst Woods.'

Leave it there, don't ask any more. 'Was her body buried?' Laurette asked relentlessly. 'How did they know where to dig?'

Patrick put his hand on his mother's arm. 'Mum, don't.'

463

'How did they know where to dig?'

'People go up there with metal detectors looking for treasure like the Framhurst Hoard. One of them found her.'

He thought of the bruises and the broken arm, the matted blackness on the skull, but she didn't ask the question so he had had no need to lie. Instead, 'We knew she must be dead,' she said. 'Now we really know. What's the difference?'

There was a difference and it lay in the presence of hope and its absence. Everyone in the room knew that. Wexford pulled out the fourth chair from the table and sat down on it. He said, 'It is probably no more than a formality but I must ask you to come and make an identification of the body. You'd be the best person, doctor.'

Akande nodded. He spoke for the first time and his voice was unrecognizable. 'Yes. All right.' He went over to his wife and stood by her chair but he didn't touch her.

'Where?' he said, 'And what time?'

Now? Let them try to get a night's sleep first. Mavrikiev would want to do the postmortem early but it might take a long time. 'We'll send a car for you. Say one-thirty?'

'I should like to see her,' said Laurette.

You would no more say to this woman that it was better not, that it was an anguish no mother should be put through, than you'd say it to Medea or Lady Macbeth. 'Just as you wish.'

She said nothing more to him but turned her face towards Patrick, who must have read there some rare sign of weakness or sensed an early warning that her control would break. He put his arms round his mother and held her tightly. Wexford left the room and let himself out of the house.

If those stripped raw features had been less unmistakeable, he would have failed to recognize the pathologist. And this had nothing to do with the grisly disguise supplied by a green rubber gown and cap. Mavrikiev was a changed man. Such violent mood swings are rare in normal people and Wexford wondered what cataclysmic event had so soured him the evening before or piece of good fortune recently cheered him up. One of the oddest things was that he behaved at first as if he had never encountered either policeman before.

'Good morning, good morning. Andy Mavrikiev. How d'you do? I'm not anticipating this being a long job.'

464

He got to work. Wexford wasn't inclined to watch closely. The sound of the saw on a skull, the sight of the removal of organs, though not sickening to him, were not particularly interesting. Burden watched everything, as he had watched Sir Hilary Tremlett's operations on Annette Bystock, and asked a stream of questions, all of which Mavrikiev seemed happy to answer. Mavrikiev talked all the time and not only about the remains on the table.

Although he scarcely offered it as an explanation of his contrast in mood, it *was* an explanation. At five on the previous morning his wife had gone into labour with their first child. A difficult delivery was expected and Mavrikiev had hoped to be with her throughout, but the call to Framhurst Heath had come just as the question was being debated: continue to wait and hope for a normal delivery or perform a caesarean?

'I wasn't best pleased, as you can imagine. Still, I was back in time to see Harriet made comfortable with an epidural and a healthy baby delivered.'

'Congratulations,' said Wexford. 'What was it?'

'A nice little girl. Well, a nice big girl, nearly ten pounds. You see this? Know what it is? It's a ruptured spleen, that's what it is.'

When he had finished, the body on the slab – or rather the face, for the poor empty body was now entirely concealed under plastic sheeting – looked a good deal better than when first unearthed. It even appeared as if decomposition was less advanced, for Mavrikiev had done an undertaker's job as well as a pathologist's. The dreadful confrontation awaiting the Akandes would be less harrowing.

He pulled off his gloves. 'I'll revise what I said last night. I said ten days or a bit more, didn't I? I can do better than that. Twelve days at least.'

Wexford nodded, not surprised. 'What did she die of?'

'I told you her spleen was ruptured. There's a fracture of the ulna and a fracture of the radius on the left side – that's the arm, the left arm. She didn't die of that. She was very thin. Could have been a bulimic. Contusions all over her body. And a massive cerebral embolism – bloodclot in the brain to you. I'd say the chap beat her to death. I don't think an instrument was used, just his fists and maybe his feet.'

'You can kill someone with your fists?' said Burden.

'Sure. If you're a big strong guy. Think of boxers. And then think

465

of a boxer doing to a woman what he does to an opponent, only without gloves. See what I mean?

'Oh, yes.'

'She was just a kid,' said Mavrikiev. 'Late teens?'

'Older than that,' said Wexford. 'Twenty-two.'

'Really? You surprise me. Well, I must get out of this gear and be on my way as I've a luncheon date with Harriet and Zenobia Helena. It was nice meeting you gentlemen. You'll get my report pronto and soonest.'

Burden said when he had gone, 'Zenobia Helena Mavrikiev. What does it sound like?'

The question was rhetorical but Wexford answered it. 'A maid-servant in one of Tolstoy's stories.' He cast up his eyes. 'Bit better than last night, wasn't he, but what an insensitive-bugger! My God, it got up my nose a bit, him on about *his* daughter and the Akandes' daughter's ruptured spleen all in the same breath.'

'At least he doesn't make sick jokes like Sumner-Quist.'

Wexford found himself incapable of eating any lunch. This departure of appetite, rare for him, seemed to please Dora who was always trying by subtle or direct means to make him eat less. But it excited wondering comment from Sylvia and her family who had invited themselves to lunch, as was increasingly their habit on a Sunday. Today he could have done without their company.

Now that the novelty of being, so to speak, the family's breadwinner was starting to wear off, Sylvia had fallen into the irritating habit of pointing out one thing after another on the table and various objects in the room, such as flowers and books, as being beyond the means of those living on seventy-four pounds a week. This was the sum total of UB and IS granted the Fairfaxes by the Employment Service and the Department of Social Security. How quickly she had seized upon that weapon of the disadvantaged most calculated to wound the sensibilities of the better off! Her father sometimes wondered where she had picked up such a catalogue of maddening habits.

A tinkly laugh preceded most of these comments. 'That's clotted cream, Robin, to put on your raspberries. Make the most of it. You're not likely to get it at home.'

Robin, of course, said it was no problem. *'Koi gull knee.'*

'I shouldn't have any more wine, Neil. Drinking is just a habit and it's not a habit you can afford the way things are.'

466

'If it isn't there I can't drink it, can I? But it is *here* and I'm making the most of it like you told the boys to do with the clotted cream. Right?'

'*Mafesh*,' said Robin in a heartfelt way.

Wexford felt he was spending his life escaping from things, uncomfortable situations, people's misery, unhappy occasions. It was raining again. He drove himself down to the mortuary, having resisted a masochistic temptation to fetch the Akandes himself.

The car brought them, both of them, at ten past two. Masterful for once, Akande said to his wife, 'I'll go in first. I'll *do* it.'

'All right.'

Laurette was hollow-eyed. Her features seemed to have got bigger and her face smaller. But her glossy hair was still carefully dressed, coiled and pinned to the back of her head. And she was still well dressed. In the black suit and black blouse, she looked as if she was going to a funeral. Raymond Akande's face had been grey for a long while now and he had been losing weight steadily since his daughter first disappeared. That fortnight had made him ten pounds lighter.

Wexford took him into the mortuary, the chilly abode now shared by the bodies of two dead women. He lifted the edge of the sheet in both hands and exposed the face. Akande hesitated a moment, then came forward. He bent over, looked at the face and sprang back.

'That's not my daughter! That's not Melanie!'

Wexford's mouth went dry. 'Dr Akande, are you sure? Look again, please.'

'Of course I'm sure. That's not my daughter. Do you think a man doesn't know his own child?'

467

# 14

Shock suspends everything. There is no thought, only automatic reaction, movement, mechanical speech. Wexford followed Akande out of the mortuary, his mind a blank, his body obeying motor instructions.

Laurette had her back to them. She had been talking, or doing her best to talk, to Karen Malahyde. At the sound of their footsteps she got up, but slowly. Her husband went up to her. His walk was a little unsteady and when he put out his hand to her he seemed to clutch her arm for support.

'Letty,' he said, 'it isn't Melanie.'

'*What?*'

'It isn't her, Letty.' His voice shook. 'I don't know who it is but it isn't Melanie.'

'What are you saying?'

'Letty, it's not Melanie.'

He was very close to her. He bowed his head against her shoulder. She put her arms round him and held him, she held his head against her breast and stared at Wexford over his shoulder.

'I don't understand.' She was cold as stone. 'We gave you a photograph.'

The enormity of what had happened, realization of that enormity, was beginning to take over from shock. Wexford said, 'Yes,' and 'Yes, that's right.'

Her voice began to rise. 'This dead girl, she's black?'

'Yes.'

Karen Malahyde, who had seen Wexford's face, said, 'Mrs Akande, if you'd just . . .'

468

Softly, as if it was a baby she held, so as not to disturb the baby, Laurette Akande whispered, 'How dare you do that to us!'

'Mrs Akande,' said Wexford, 'I am extremely sorry this has happened.' He added, with what must have been a lie, 'No one regrets it more than I do.'

'How dare you do that to us?' Laurette screamed at Wexford. She forgot the baby at her breast. Her hands had ceased to nurse him. 'How dare you treat us like that? You're just a damned racist like the rest of them. Coming to our house patronizing us, the great white man condescending to us, so magnanimous, so liberal . . . !'

'Letty, don't,' Akande begged her. 'Please don't.'

She ignored him. She took a step towards Wexford, both fists up now. 'It was because she was black, wasn't it? I haven't seen her but I know, I can see it all. One black girl's just the same as another to you, isn't she? A *negress*. A *nigger*, a *darkie* . . .'

'Mrs Akande, I'm sorry. I am deeply sorry.'

'*You* regret it. You damned hypocrite! You don't have prejudice, do you? Oh, no, you're not a racist, black and white are all equal in your eyes. But when you find a dead black girl it's got to be *our* girl because we're black!'

Akande was shaking his head. 'Not a bit like her,' he said. 'Not a bit.'

'Black, though. Black, isn't she?'

'That's the only way she's like her, Letty. She's black.'

'So we don't get a wink of sleep all night. Our son sits up all night and what's he doing? He's crying. For hours and hours. He hasn't cried for ten years but he cried last night. And we tell the neighbours, the nice white liberal neighbours who are big-hearted enough to feel sorry for parents whose daughter's been murdered, *even though she was only one of those coloured girls, one of those blacks.*'

'Believe me, Mrs Akande,' Wexford said. 'it's a mistake that's been made many times before and the dead have been white.' It was true but still she was right, he knew she was right. 'I can only apologize again. I'm very sorry this has happened.'

'We'll go home now,' Akande said to his wife.

She looked at Wexford as if she would have liked to spit at him. She didn't do this. The tears she hadn't shed when she thought the body in there was her daughter's now streamed down her cheeks. Sobbing, she hung on to her husband's arm with both hands and he led her out to the waiting car.

A salutary lesson. We think we know ourselves but we don't, and self-discovery of this particular kind of ignorance is bitter. What he had said to Laurette Akande about a similar confusion sometimes occurring between the bodies of white people was factually accurate. It was scarcely true in spirit. He *had* assumed a black girl's body was that of a missing black girl and he had done so *because she was black*. The photograph he had of Melanie Akande had not been referred to. The known heights of the missing girl and the dead girl had not been compared. With a wince, he remembered how only that morning, only about three hours before, Mavrikiev had expressed surprise that the age of the body on the table was twenty-two and not eighteen or nineteen. Now he recalled something learned long ago from a forensic report, that certain important bones in the female anatomy have fused by the age of twenty-two. . . .

The worst thing for him was that it had shown him he was wrong about himself. This error had occurred through prejudice, through racism, through making an assumption he could never have made if the missing girl were white and the body white. In such a case he would merely have thought it likely the lost girl had been found, but he would have done a lot more rigorous research into appearance and statistics before summoning the parents to make an identification. Laurette's reproaches were valid, if violent.

Well, it was a lesson and that was how it must be viewed. There was no question of ceasing his visits to the Akandes. The first one, but only the first one, would be uncomfortable for all of them. Unless, of course, they saw to it that the first was the last. He had apologized, and more humbly than he usually did to anyone. He wouldn't say he was sorry again. It came to him, and brought him a wry amusement, that the lesson was having its results already, for from tomorrow he was going to begin treating the Akandes not as members of the disadvantaged minority worthy of special consideration, he was going to treat them as ordinary human beings.

But since the dead girl wasn't Melanie, who was she?

A black girl was missing and a black girl's body had been found but there was no apparent connection between the two.

Burden, untroubled by Wexford's scruples and sensibilities, said it ought to be easy enough to identify her now that the police had a national register for missing persons. It would be easier because she

470

was black. Whatever might be the situation in London or Bradford few black people lived in this part of southern England and still fewer went missing. By this time, however, halfway through Monday, he had already discovered that nowhere in the area of the Mid-Sussex Constabulary had the police a missing person approximating to this girl's description on their computer.

'There's a Tamil woman been missing since February. She and her husband had the Kandy Palace restaurant in Myringham. But she's thirty and though I suppose technically she's black, they're very dark those Tamils . . . '

'Let's not get into that one again,' said Wexford.

'I'll get on to the national register,' Burden said. 'I suppose she could have been brought here, dead or alive, from some place like South London where I've no doubt girls go missing every day. And what happens now to our theory that Annette was killed because of something Melanie told her?'

'Nothing happens to it,' Wexford said slowly. 'Finding this girl has nothing to do with Melanie. It's irrelevant, it's something else. We still have the *status quo*. Melanie does something or says something her killer doesn't want known and he kills Annette because Annette, and presumably Annette alone, has been told what that is. After all, this girl being dead doesn't mean Melanie's alive. Melanie is dead too and we just haven't yet found her body.'

'You don't think this girl – what shall we call her? We'd better give her a name.'

'Yes, OK, but for God's sake don't come up with something from *Uncle Tom's Cabin*.'

Puzzled, Burden said, 'I've never read it.'

'Sojourner, we'll call her,' Wexford said, 'after Sojourner Truth, the "Ain't I a woman?" poet. And maybe . . . well, I somehow see her as impermanent, homeless, alone. "I am a stranger with thee and a sojourner", you know.'

Burden didn't know. He wore his deeply suspicious uneasy look. 'Sodgernah?'

'That's right. What were you going to say. You said that this girl . . . ?'

'Oh, yes. You don't think *this* girl – I mean what's-her-name, Sojourner – you don't think *she* said something significant to Annette?'

Wexford looked interested. 'At the Benefit Office, d'you mean?'

471

'If we don't have a clue who she is she's just as likely to be signing on or be a new claimant as not. It's a way of identifying her, see if they've got someone answering her description among their claimants.'

'Annette was killed on Wednesday the seventh, Sojourner certainly before that, maybe on the fifth or sixth. It fits, Mike. It's a good idea. Clever of you.'

Burden looked pleased. 'We can also check what immigrants are registered with us. I'll go down to the Benefit Office myself. Take Barry with me. By the way, where is Barry?'

Sergeant Vine tapped on the door and was in the room before Wexford had time to answer. He had been in Stowerton, talking to James Ranger. Ranger was retired, a widower, a solitary man, who had been on his way to spend Saturday evening baby-sitting his grandsons when from his car he spotted Broadley digging up a grave.

'He says he won't do that again,' said Vine. 'Apparently, his daughter and her husband missed their dinner dance. He says next time he sees some peasant, I quote, desecrating the environment he's going to accelerate and drive right on past. D'you know what he thought Broadley was up to? You won't believe this. He thought he was digging up orchids! Apparently there's some rare orchid grows up there and he's its self-appointed guardian.'

'Ranger by name and ranger by nature,' said Wexford. 'Bit unusual, though, wasn't it, quiet elderly chap like him, champion of endangered species, baby-sitter, owner of a ten-year-old but immaculate 2CV, bit odd him having a carphone, isn't it? What does he have it *for*? To call the botanical police when he sees someone pick a primrose?'

'I asked him that. He said it was as well he *did* have it, so he could ring us.'

'Not an answer to your question, though.'

'No. When pressed, he said – wait for it – it was in case he broke down on the motorway at night.'

Vine laughed. 'I've got him high on my suspect list. I was coming away from his place, had to park the car half a mile away as usual, when who do I see coming out of that block of flats in the High Street, Something Court, Clifton Court, but Kimberley Pearson.'

'Did you speak to her?'

'I asked her how she was getting on in her new home. She had Clint with her all dressed up in a brand-new baby tracksuit sitting in a very smart buggy. She'd tarted herself up a good bit too, red leggings and one of those bustier things and shoes with heels like that.' Vine held up thumb and forefinger five inches apart. 'A changed woman. She'd told me she was moving into the home of her late grandma. It didn't seem that sort of place. I mean, quite a smart block of newish flats.'

Burden gave Wexford a sidelong look. 'That'll set your mind at rest,' he said not very pleasantly. 'You were getting worried about their fate.'

'"Worried" is a strong word, Inspector Burden,' Wexford snapped. 'Most people not entirely callous would be concerned for a child living in those circumstances.'

There was a short uncomfortable silence. Then Vine said, 'She seems to be getting on all right without Zack. Glad to see the back of him, I expect.'

Wexford said nothing. He had another date with the Snows. Did the death of Sojourner affect his approach to them? Did it perhaps entirely change his attitude? He felt suddenly as if lost in a dark wood. Why had he bitten Mike's head off like that? He picked up the phone and asked Bruce Snow to come to the police station at five.

'I shan't be done here till half-past.'

'Five, please, Mr Snow. And I want your wife here too.'

'You'll be lucky,' Snow said. 'She's going away tonight, taking the kids and going to Malta or Elba or somewhere.'

'No, she isn't,' said Wexford. He dialled the number of the house in Harrow Avenue and a young girl's voice answered.

'Mrs Snow, please.'

'This is her daughter. Who wants her?'

'Chief Inspector Wexford, Kingsmarkham CID.'

'Oh, right. Hang on.'

He had to hang on a long time and felt his temper rising. When she finally came to the phone she had regained her coolness. The ice maiden was back in occupation.

'Yes, what is it?'

'I'd like you to come down to the police station at five, please, Mrs Snow.'

'Sorry, but that won't be convenient. My flight to Marseille is at ten to five.'

'It will be leaving without you. Have you forgotten I asked you not to go anywhere?'

473

'No, I haven't, but I didn't take it seriously. It's so absurd – what has all this to do with me? I'm the injured party. I'm taking my poor children away from it all. Their father's behaviour has broken their hearts.'

'Their hearts can wait a few days to be mended, Mrs Snow. I don't suppose you'd like to find yourself on a charge of obstructing police enquiries, would you?'

He knew better than to believe he could understand people. Why, for instance, did this woman need to lie? She was, as she had just told him, the injured party. Deceiving a wife with a mistress over a period of *nine years* was to do her a serious injury, for it humiliated as well as hurt her, it made her feel a fool. As for Snow, Wexford knew he would never understand the man's conduct. He would hardly have believed it had someone told him that here, in England, in the nineties, a man could enjoy a woman's sexual favours for years on end without paying her, without giving her presents or taking her out, without the use of a hotel room or even a bed, in his office, on the floor, so as to be within reach of his wife's voice on the phone.

And if he couldn't understand that, why should he understand any other aspects of Snow's behaviour? It seemed absurd to him that the man might have killed Sojourner because, say, Annette had told her about their affair. But *all* Snow's transactions were incomprehensible to him. So might he have beaten her to death and buried her out there in Framhurst Woods? Kill Annette, kill the woman Annette had told, and all to stop it reaching his wife's ears? Well, they all now knew what happened when it did reach his wife's ears. . . . Sojourner could have been blackmailing him. Perhaps only in a small way. It wouldn't hurt him to give her a bit of money from time to time to keep her from telling his wife. And then she asked for more money, perhaps for a lump sum. Wexford found he disliked thinking this way. Somewhere in his mind, not quite consciously, he had made Sojourner into a good person. Sojourner was the innocent victim of wicked men who exploited and abused her, while she was herself virtuous and gentle, a keeper not a betrayer of secrets, a fearful, simple, trusting soul.

Of course he was sentimentalizing her. Where now was the lesson he should have learned and thought he had learned from that business with the Akandes? He knew nothing about the girl, not her real name, her country of origin, her family if any, not even her age. And Mavrikiev's forensic report, when it came, would tell him very little of that. He didn't even know if she had ever so much as set foot in the Benefit Office.

Bruce Snow sat in Interview Room One with Burden. His wife was with Wexford in Interview Room Two. Putting them in the same room last time had resulted in the slanging match Wexford didn't want to see repeated. He faced a sulky Carolyn Snow across the table, Karen Malahyde standing behind her and wearing a look of unconcealed distaste – for everything concerned with Mrs Snow, Wexford guessed, her lifestyle, her status as wife without a job or personal income and, unfortunately, her new position as a betrayed, deceived woman.

'I'd like to put it on record,' Carolyn was saying, 'that I think it outrageous I'm being stopped from going on holiday. It's an unjustified interference with my liberty. And my poor children – what have they done?'

'It's not what they've done but what you've done, Mrs Snow. Or, rather, not done. You can put what you like on record. For all your boasts that you don't tell lies, you haven't been truthful with me.'

In the other room Burden was asking Bruce Snow if he would like to amend his statement at all or add to it in any way. Would he, for instance, care to tell Burden what he was doing during the evening of the seventh of July?

'I was at home. I was just at home. Reading, maybe, I don't remember. Sitting with my wife. I watched television. But it's no use asking me what I watched, I don't remember.'

'Have you ever seen this girl, Mr Snow?'

Burden showed him a photograph of Sojourner's twelve-days-dead face. It had been skilfully taken but still it looked like the picture of a dead face and a battered one too. Snow recoiled.

'Is that Akande's daughter?'

That mistake again. . . . But Burden wasn't going to let it pass. 'What makes you say that?'

'Oh, for God's sake. I've never seen her before anyway.'

Her eyes as tragic as if she had suffered a bereavement, Carolyn Snow was asking Wexford to let her go on holiday. Her trip had been booked six months before. When it was made Snow would have been going too but his elder daughter had agreed to take his place. The hotel wouldn't be able to take them next week, there would be no places on flights, the travel agent's fee wasn't refundable.

'You should have thought of all that before,' said Wexford, and he showed her the picture of Sojourner, the closed eyes, the bruised skin, the bare patches on the forehead and temples where the hair had begun to fall. 'Do you know her?'

'I've never seen her before in my life.' Instead of flinching, Carolyn peered more closely. 'Is she coloured? I don't know any coloured people. Look, I've missed my plane but the travel agent says she thinks she could get us on the one tomorrow morning that goes at ten-fifteen.'

'Really? Amazing, isn't it, how much more accommodating to passengers' needs air services have become?'

'You make me bloody sick! You're just a sadist. You're enjoying this, aren't you?'

'There's considerable job satisfaction attached to what I do,' said Wexford, wondering if the Employment Service would make 'job satisfaction' all one word. 'I have to get something out of it.' He looked at his watch. 'All these long hours, unpaid overtime. I'd rather be at home with my wife than stuck in here trying to get the truth out of you.'

'Have a good marriage, do you, Chief Inspector? All this has wrecked mine, I hope you know that.'

'Your husband has done that, Mrs Snow. Revenge yourself on him if you like. You won't get revenge on us.'

'What do you mean, revenge?'

Wexford drew his chair closer and put his elbows on the table. 'Isn't that what you're doing? You're revenging yourself on him for his affairs with two women. Deny he was at home that evening, insist he went out at eight and was out two and a half hours, and maybe you won't only get your house and a big chunk of his income out of him, you'll have the added satisfaction of seeing him on a murder charge.'

He had got it exactly right, he could see it in her eyes.

'Was she blackmailing you, Mr Snow?' said Burden on the other side of the wall.

'Forget it. I've never seen her.'

'We know what happens when your wife finds out about your

infidelity. We've seen. She's not a forgiving woman, is she? I think you'd have willingly paid up to keep her from finding out and perhaps paid over a long period.' Overstepping the bounds once more, he said, 'What on earth did Annette Bystock have to make you go on and on with it?' There was no answer, only a scowl. 'Still, you did go on. Did you get tired of paying? Did you see there'd never be an end to paying, even if you ended things with Annette? Was killing your blackmailer the only way?'

Beyond the partition, Carolyn Snow said, 'Everything I've said was true but, yes, I'd like to see him come to grief – why not? I'd like to see him pay for those two women with years in prison.'

'That's frank,' said Wexford. 'And what about yourself, Mrs Snow? Do you fancy paying for your revenge?'

'I don't know what you mean.'

'You seem to be looking at things upside-down. You've supposed throughout that we've been questioning you to confirm or deny what your husband says were his movements. That it is your *husband* who is the suspect, your *husband* who is the only possible candidate for Annette Bystock's killer. But you're quite wrong. There is yourself.'

She said it again, but anxiously this time. 'I don't know what you mean.'

'We have only your word for it that you knew nothing about Annette's role in your husband's life until after she was dead. I think we know what your word is worth, Mrs Snow. You had a better motive than he for killing her, you had a better motive than anyone.'

She stood up. She had gone quite white. 'Of course I didn't kill her! Are you mad? Of course I didn't!'

Wexford smiled. 'That's what they all say.'

'I swear to you I didn't kill her!'

'You had motive. You had means. You have no alibi for that Wednesday evening.'

'I didn't kill her! I didn't know her!'

'Perhaps you'd like to make a statement now, Mrs Snow. With your permission we'll record your statement. And then I can go home.'

She sat down again. She was breathing in short fast gasps, her forehead furrowed, her mouth puckered. Clenching her fists and digging the nails into her palms brought back some of her control. She began to tell the recording machine what had happened, how she

477

had been alone in Harrow Avenue but for her son upstairs, how her husband had gone out at eight and returned at ten-thirty, but she broke off and spoke directly to Wexford.

'Can I go away tomorrow now?'

'I'm afraid not. I don't want you leaving the country. You can have a few days in Eastbourne, I've no objection to that.'

Carolyn Snow began to cry.

*Tuesday, 20 July*

In the past Sergeant Vine had spent many a long hour sitting at one of these desks in the area at the back, trying to look like an administrative assistant while he waited for a certain person to show up and sign on. Someone he was after for a spot of petty crime, it usually was, and this was a sure way of running him to earth. Whatever their income from theft, from bag-snatching, receiving, shoplifting, they all wanted their UB as well.

So while Wexford and Burden were as newcomers to the Benefit Office, it was familiar territory to Vine. No one got on well with Cyril Leyton while Osman Messaoud was generally unapproachable, but he had an easy relationship with Stanton and the women. Burden, closeted with Leyton and the security officer, left him to get on with it. Waiting till Wendy Stowlap was temporarily free, he surveyed the waiting claimants and spotted two he knew. One of them was Broadley, the discoverer of Sojourner's body, the other Wexford's elder daughter. He was still trying to think of her name, it must begin with a letter between A and G, when Wendy Stowlap's client moved away from the desk.

She looked up. 'All these foreign people coming in here, Italians, Spanish, I don't know what. Why should we keep them on our taxes? The European Union's got a lot to answer for.'

'Surely you don't have a lot of black claimants, though, do you?' he said to her. 'I mean, not out in this neck of the woods.'

'Out here in the boondocks, is that what you're saying?' Wendy was a native of Kingsmarkham and fiercely proprietorial of her home town. 'If you don't like it here why don't you go back to Berkshire or wherever you come from that's so lively and sophisticated?'

'OK, sorry, but do you?'

'Have claimants who are coloured people? You'd be surprised. We've more than we did two years ago. Well, we've got more

478

*claimants* than we had two years ago, a lot more. The recession may be ending but unemployment's still very serious.'

'So you wouldn't specially notice a black girl?'

'Woman,' Wendy corrected him. 'I don't call you a boy.'

'I should be so lucky,' said Sergeant Vine.

'Anyway, I never noticed any black *woman* speaking specially to Annette. I never noticed that Melanie, as you know. Frankly, I've got enough on my plate here on the counter without watching what everyone else is doing.' Wendy pressed the switch that made the next neon number come up. 'So if you'll excuse me I can't keep my clients waiting any longer.'

Peter Stanton wanted to know if Sojourner was good looking. He said frankly that he often fancied black women, they had such fantastic long legs. He liked their long necks, like black swans, and narrow hands. And the way they walked, as if they carried a heavy jar on their heads.

'I only saw her when she was dead,' said Vine.

'If she made a claim – that is, if she completed an ES 461 – we can find her for you. What's her name?'

Hayley Gordon also asked Sojourner's name. The two supervisors asked a lot of pointless questions about whether she was claiming UB or Income Support, had she ever worked, and what kind of job was she looking for. Osman Messaoud, off the counter this week and doing his stint at the very desk where Vine had been used to sit and wait, said he closed his mind and sometimes his eyes to young women claimants. If he caught sight of them he forced himself not to look.

'Your wife doesn't trust you as far as she can throw you, is that it?'

'It is proper for a woman to be possessive,' said Osman.

'That's a matter of opinion.' An idea came to Vine. He felt around it, trying to put the question delicately. 'Is your wife . . . er, Indian like yourself?'

'I am a British citizen,' said Osman very coldly.

'Oh, sorry. And where's your wife from?'

'Bristol.'

The man was really enjoying this, Vine thought. 'And where did her family come from?'

'I am asking myself what all this can be leading up to. Am I perhaps a suspect in the murder of Miss Bystock? Or perhaps my wife is.'

'I only want to know . . . ' Vine gave up and said brutally, 'if she's coloured too.'

Messaoud smiled with pleasure at the corner into which he had driven the sergeant. 'Coloured? What an interesting term. Red perhaps or blue? My wife, Detective Sergeant Vine, is an Afro-Caribbean lady from Trinidad. But she is not on the dole and she has never set foot in this office.'

Eventually Vine was able to extract from the combined Benefit Office staff, at the sacrifice of political correctness on everyone's part, that a total of four of their claimants were black. They were two men and two women and all of them were over thirty years old.

# 15

Did he know, Sheila asked on the phone, that the BNP had put up a candidate for the Kingsmarkham borough by-election?

'But that's next week,' Wexford said, trying to remember who or what the BNP were.

'I know. But I've only just heard about it. They've already got one borough council seat.'

Memory returned. The BNP were the British National Party, committed to a white Britain for the white man. 'That's in East London,' he said. 'It's a bit different out here. It'll be a Tory walkover.'

'Racist attacks in Sussex increased sevenfold last year, Pop. That's fact. You can't dispute statistics.'

'All right, Sheila. You don't suppose I want a bunch of fascists getting on the council, do you?'

'Then you'd better cast your vote for the Liberal Democrat – or Mrs Khoori.'

'She's standing, is she?'

'As an Independent Conservative.'

Wexford told her about his encounters with Anouk Khoori and about the garden party. She wanted to know how Sylvia and Neil were getting on. For the first time for many years Sheila was without a man in her life. This lack seemed to have made her a calmer, sadder woman. She was to be Nora in an Edinburgh Festival production of *A Doll's House*. Would he and Mother think about coming? Wexford thought about Annette and Sojourner and the missing Melanie and said he was afraid not, he was very much afraid not.

Visiting the Akandes for the first time since that scene in the

481

...ward, to face them, he had
...r all that he couldn't eat any
...e but nothing more. Some lines
...mind: 'There is an old Greek saying
...by things themselves but by what they
mortuary, he to...could tell if he was thinking in the right
acted in g...of the weekend, warmer less stuffy weather had
breat...it was hot today, the air glass-clear, the sky a bright
...ink and white lilies had opened in the Akandes' front
...ie had been able to smell their funereal scent before he even
...d the gate. Laurette Akande came to the door. Wexford said,
'Good morning,' and waited to have it slammed in his face.

Instead, she opened it wider and asked him to come in, though not
very graciously. She seemed chastened. The house was quiet. No
doubt the son Patrick wasn't up yet – it was only just after eight. The
doctor was in the kitchen, standing up by the table, drinking tea out
of a mug. He put the mug down, came up to Wexford and for some
reason shook hands with him.

'I'm sorry about what happened on Sunday,' he said. 'Obviously it
was a genuine mistake on your part. We hoped it wouldn't mean
you'd not come and see us any more, didn't we, Letty?'

Laurette Akande shrugged and looked away. Wexford thought he
might make it one of his laws – he had a mental catalogue of
Wexford's first law, second law, and so on – that if after the first two
or three expressions of regret you stop apologizing to someone you
have offended, they will soon start apologizing to *you*.

'As a matter of fact,' said Akande, 'oddly enough, it's rather
cheered us up. It's given us hope. The fact that this girl wasn't
Melanie has really given us grounds for hope that Melanie's still
alive. Perhaps you think that's foolish?'

He did, but he wasn't going to say so. They were in the worst
position parents could be in, worse than that of those whose child is
dead, worse than Sojourner's parents, if she had any. They were the
parents whose child has disappeared and who may never know what
her end was, what torment she suffered and what was the nature of
her death.

'I can only tell you I've no more idea of what may have happened
to Melanie than I had two weeks ago. We shall continue to look for
her. We shall never give up looking. As for hope . . . '

'A waste of time and energy,' said Laurette harshly. 'Excuse me, I have to go to my work now. Patients don't stop needing nursing just because Sister Akande's lost her daughter.'

'You mustn't mind my wife,' the doctor said after she had left. 'All this is a terrible strain on her.'

'I know.'

'I'm just thankful I've got this quite illogical feeling that Melanie's alive. It may be ridiculous but I could almost say I *know* I'll come home from my rounds one afternoon and find her sitting in there. And she'll have a perfectly reasonable explanation for where she's been.'

Such as what? 'It would be wrong of me to encourage you to hope,' said Wexford, remembering his resolve to treat the Akandes just like anyone else. 'We've no grounds for believing Melanie is still alive.'

Akande shook his head. 'Do you know who the . . . the other girl is, the one you thought might be Melanie? I suppose I shouldn't ask, any more than you'd ask me about a patient.'

'I was about to ask you. I was going to ask if you'd ever seen her before.'

'You didn't have much chance, did you? We should have been relieved but we were only angry. I'd never seen her before. Surely it won't be hard to find who she is? After all, there aren't many people like us down here. Only one of my patients is black.'

Whether they were connected or not, this second death inevitably meant that all the possible witnesses in the first case must be questioned again in reference to the second. If one of them had seen Sojourner in any connection, recognized her face, remembered her however tenuously, this might provide the link they were looking for. It might go some way to establishing her identity. The worst scenario he could construct was the one in which Sojourner's body had been brought by car hundreds of miles, perhaps from some northern place where inner-city prostitutes were as likely to be black as white, had no past, certainly no future, and whose disappearance might pass unnoticed.

He found he was once more thinking of her tenderly and the forensic report did nothing to mitigate his tenderness. Mavrikiev established her age as no more than seventeen. Her injuries were frightful. As well as the arm, two ribs were fractured. Bruising to the inner thighs, old, healed lacerations of the genitals indicated some previous violent sexual assault and on more than one occasion. The pathologist calculated that a violent blow of the fist had sent her sprawling and that in her fall she had struck her head on some hard, sharp object. This it was that had caused her death.

Fibres found in the head wound had gone to the lab for analysis. Mavrikiev expressed his opinion that these were wool from a sweater, not from a carpet, but would commit himself no further on this subject which was not his speciality. Wexford read a lab report which confirmed this. The fibres were Shetland wool and mohair, typical components of a knitting yarn. More of this mixture had been found under her fingernails, along with grains of the soil in which she had been buried. But there was no blood under the nails. She had scratched no one in putting up a fight for her life.

Embassies, High Commissions, African countries all had those. It was a line of enquiry and he put Pemberton on to it. Karen Malahyde set up enquiries at the places of education, many of them closed by now, so that meant contacting head teachers, school administrators, college principals and accommodation officers. If Sojourner was only seventeen she might have been still at school. The chances of her having stayed in an hotel immediately prior to her death were slight, but enquiries had to be made at all of them, from the Olive and Dove at one end of the scale to the Glebe Road humblest bed-and-breakfast at the other.

Annette had told her cousin that she had something she ought to tell the police, and Wexford asked himself why she hadn't said those same words to Bruce Snow when he phoned her that same Tuesday evening, the evening before her death. He thought of the relative in Ladyhall Avenue whose existence both Snows denied. And he wondered what a girl as young, as vulnerable and, it seemed, as unwanted as Sojourner could have done to make someone beat her to death. Could he be looking at things back to front? Could the case be, not that Annette had been killed because of what she was told, but that Sojourner was killed because of what Annette said to *her*? Was Annette herself the repository of some secret, unknown to Snow or Jane Winster or Ingrid Pamber?

Meeting Burden outside the Nawab, he said, 'I couldn't face breakfast this morning and now I'm feeling that not unpleasant emptiness which is the silent luncheon gong of the soul.'

'That's P. G. Wodehouse.'

Wexford didn't say anything. This must have been the first time Burden had ever guessed the source of one of his quotations. It was a heart-warming experience, over which the Inspector immediately poured a stream of cold water. He said in the crabbed voice he sometimes used, 'Messaoud's got a West Indian wife.'

'I've got an English wife,' said Wexford inside the restaurant, 'but that doesn't mean she knew Annette Bystock.'

'It's different. You know it's different.'

Wexford hesitated, took a piece of *nan* from the plate in front of him. 'OK, yes, I do know. It is different. I'm sorry. And, incidentally, I'm sorry about yesterday. I shouldn't have spoken to you like that.'

'Forget it.'

'Not in front of Barry I shouldn't. I'm sorry.' Wexford remembered his new law and changed the subject. 'I like Indian breads, don't you?'

'Better than Indians. Sorry, but that fellow Messaoud is really bad news. But I'll go and talk to his wife, shall I?'

The businessman's special they had ordered, the 'Quickie Thali', arrived quite quickly. It consisted of practically everything you thought of as Indian food put round the edge of a big plate with a pile of rice in the middle and a *poppadom* on the side. Wexford poured himself a glass of water.

'I wish that picture we've got didn't make her look so dead, so *long dead,* but it can't be helped. It won't do any harm to show it around in Ladyhall Avenue. We shall try it on the shopkeepers in the High Street and the shopping centres, the supermarket checkouts.'

'The station,' said Burden, 'and the bus station. Churches?'

'Black people go to church more than white people, so yes – why not?'

'Stowerton Industrial Estate? They'd be glad to have someone go missing up there – wouldn't have to make them redundant. Sorry, a sick joke. It's worth trying, isn't it?'

'Everything's worth trying, Mike.'

Wexford sighed. By 'everything' he hadn't meant talking to every black resident of the British Isles. He had really meant proceeding as they would have if Sojourner had been a white schoolgirl. But he knew suddenly that he couldn't do that, that this wasn't the way, however apparently ethical.

A quick glance at the fax from Myringham Police awaiting him on his desk told him none of the descriptions matched Sojourner's details. The missing women were categorized according to their ethnic origin, but wasn't such classification inevitable in a case such as this? He remembered a conversation he had once had with Superintendent Hanlon of Myringham CID on the subject of political correctness.

'As far as I'm concerned,' Hanlon had said, 'PC means police constable.'

Four women whose forebears were from the Indian sub-continent and an African were on the list. Myringham, with its industry, though now depleted, had attracted far more immigrants than Kingsmarkham or Stowerton, and its two universities were attended by students from all parts of the world. Melanie Akande was not the only alumna of the former Myringham Polytechnic to have gone missing. Here on the list was Demsie Olish from the Gambia, a sociology student, whose home was in a place call Yarbotendo. One of the Indians, Laxmi Rao, was a graduate student at the University of the South. There had been no sign of her since Christmas but it was known she had not returned home. The Sri Lankan Burden had already mentioned to him as the missing restaurateur. The Pakistani, Naseem Kamar, a widow, had been employed as a seamstress in a garment factory until the company which owned it went into receivership in April. With the loss of her job Mrs Kamar disappeared. Darshan Kumari, Myringham Police were nearly sure, had run off with the son of her husband's best friend. They suspected that Surinder Begh had been killed by her father and uncles for refusing to marry the man of their choice, but they had no evidence to support this theory.

These women's next-of-kin would have to be fetched to the mortuary and try to make an identification. Well, not Mrs Kamar's. She was thirty-six. And the age of Laxmi Rao, twenty-two, was an unpleasant reminder of the mistake he had already made. The most likely candidate was Demsie Olish. She was nineteen, had gone home to the Gambia in April and returned, had been seen by her landlady, by the two other students living in the house, by numerous students in her year at Myringham – and then, after 4 May, was seen no more. It was a week before she was reported as missing. Everyone who knew her thought she must be somewhere else. The drawback to her being Sojourner was her height, which was given as five feet five. Once these women had been eliminated, they would spread the net further afield. . . .

He called a conference at five for a pooling of discoveries and offered up Demsie Olish himself. A girl who had been her friend and whose home was in Yorkshire was coming to look at the body next day. To be on the safe side, if no identification was made, Dilip Kumari would be asked to attempt it. His wife was only eighteen.

Claudine Messaoud had been as helpful as her husband was obstructive. It sounded as if Burden had liked her, which was something of a triumph for race relations. Though she knew of no black woman between sixteen and twenty who might have gone missing, she put Burden on to the church she attended and which was also attended by other black people. These were the Kingsmarkham Baptists. The minister told Burden that most of Kingsmarkham's black families had a representative there, usually a middle-aged woman. Even so, they were few.

'Laurette Akande goes there too,' he said. 'So that only leaves four families. I've seen one of them but they're young and their children are only two and four. I thought Karen might feel like talking to the rest.'

'Karen?' said Wexford, turning to her.

'Sure. I'll do that tonight. But I suspect I've already seen two of them, that is the ones that have kids at the Comprehensive. Two girls of sixteen and a boy of eighteen, all currently at home and available and seen by me.'

'That will leave the Lings, I should think,' said Burden. 'Mark and Mhonum, M, H, O, N, U, M, in Blakeney Road. He's from Hong Kong, runs the Moonflower restaurant, she's black, and the age of their kids isn't known, or if they have any. She's the one who is Dr Akande's only black patient.'

Pemberton had talked to someone at the Gambian High Commission. They were aware of the disappearance of their national, Demsie Olish, and were 'keeping a close eye'. The numerous other African embassies had even less to offer him. He had narrowed down the women on the national register who came closest to matching Sojourner's description to five. Next-of-kin and, failing that – that often did fail – friends, would have to be fetched to Kingsmarkham for the weary work of attempting identification.

Wexford had calculated that, as far as he could tell, eighteen black people lived in Kingsmarkham, perhaps half a dozen more in

Pomfret, Stowerton and the villages. That number included the three Akandes, Mhonum Ling, nine people comprising three of the church-going families, the two male clients at the Benefit Offfice, a mother and son who were the other Kingsmarkham Baptists, Melanie Akande who was one of their female clients, and the sister of one of the Baptists who was the other.

The Epsons, who lived in Stowerton, were the family whose children Sylvia had taken into care. He was black, she was white. A year ago they had gone on holiday to Tenerife, leaving their nine-year-old in charge of their five-year-old. Now it appeared they were away again but when Karen phoned, a child-minder answered. The woman sounded jittery and harassed but knew of no missing black girl aged seventeen.

'Those boys, young men, that hang about outside all the time, I don't suppose it's always the same lot, but the day I went there after we found Annette's body, one of them was black. Dreadlocks and a big knitted cap. We seem to be locating and pigeon-holing every black person in Kingsmarkham, I don't like it but no doubt it has to be, so what about him? Where does he fit in?'

'He wasn't there today,' said Barry, and to Archbold, 'He wasn't there, was he, Ian?'

'I didn't see him. You've got a mother and son on the list – he may be the son.'

'He's probably my eighteen-year-old,' said Karen.

'Not if yours is still at school, he isn't. Not unless he's a full-time truant. He'll have to be found.' Wexford glanced from one to the other, suddenly feeling ages older than any of them. The rest of what he was going to say was on the tip of his tongue, but he said it to himself. It's not so easy, is it? Not all their mothers go to church. Most of them don't stay on at school or go on to further education. As for embassies, we forget, we always forget, that most of these people are British, are in the law as British as we are. They aren't on record, they have no dossiers, no cards of identity. And they slip through the net.

She was very young and though dark, with an olive skin and long black hair, looked fragile. This was Demsie Olish's college friend, Yasmin Gavilon from Harrogate, who seemed uncertain what was expected of her, whose shyness was extreme. Wexford would have preferred someone else to take her in there, but this was a task he couldn't delegate. Still fresh in his mind was what had happened last time. And this girl looked so young, looked far less then her twenty years.

He had explained three times now that what she was to see might not be Demsie, was even very probably not Demsie. She must only look and tell him the truth. But looking down into her trusting puzzled face, so seemingly innocent, so untouched by experience, he very nearly told her to go home, get the next train back, and he would find someone else to look at Sojourner's body.

The smell of formaldehyde was like a gas. The plastic cover was folded back, the sheet withdrawn. Yasmin looked. The expression on her face changed no more than it had done when she was brought into Wexford's office and introduced to him. Then she had murmured, 'Hallo,' and now she murmured, 'No. No, it isn't.' The tone was the same.

Wexford escorted her out. He asked her again. 'No,' she said. 'No, that isn't Demsie,' and then, 'I'm glad it isn't.' She tried to smile, but her face had taken on a greenish pallor, and she said quickly, 'I want to go to the toilet, please.'

When she had been given hot sweet tea and taken away in a car to the station, Dilip Kumari arrived. If Wexford had seen him in the street, had not been told his name or heard his voice, he would have taken him for a Spaniard. Kumari spoke in the sing-song Welsh-sounding but perfect English of the Indian who is Indian-born. He was the assistant manager of the NatWest Bank in Stowerton High Street and he looked all of forty.

'Your wife is very young,' said Wexford.

'Too young for me? Is that what you are saying? You are right. But it didn't seem so at the time.' He was philosophical, fatalistic, almost jaunty. It was quickly apparent he was as certain as he could be, without having seen her, that Sojourner was not Darshan Kumari. 'To the best of my belief, she has run off with a boy of twenty. Of course, if this is she, which I doubt extremely, I will not have the trouble and expense of divorcing her.'

He laughed, perhaps to show Wexford he was not entirely serious. They went inside and Sojourner was once more exhibited. 'No,' he said. 'No, indeed,' and outside once more, 'Better luck next time. Do you happen to know if you can divorce a woman you can't find? Perhaps only after five years, alas and alack. I wonder what the law is on this matter? I shall have to find out.'

Which particular net had she slipped through? The same one perhaps as the boy with dreadlocks in the coloured cap who wasn't outside the Benefit Office when Wexford got down there ten minutes later. The shaven-headed boy was there, this time in a tee-shirt so faded that the dinosaur on it was a ghost of its former self, and the ponytailed boy in tracksuit pants, chain smoking. And with them was a very short stout boy with golden curls backcombed to make him look taller and a nondescript spotty boy in shorts. But the black boy with dreadlocks wasn't there.

Two sat on the chipped, stained, rough-surfaced balustrade on the right side and two on the left where there was also a small rubbish tip of empty, caved-in coke cans and crushed cigarette packets. The ponytailed boy was smoking a cigarette he had rolled himself. The spotty boy sat with his feet in a sprawl of cigarette stubs, his toes in the black canvas lace-up boots desultorily making a pattern of circles and loops in the ash. He was chewing the cuticles round his fingernails. His opposite neighbour with the pale dinosaur on his chest, just as Wexford approached, hit on the diverting idea of throwing pieces of gravel, of which he had a handful, at the stack of cans, his aim perhaps being to dislodge the top one and send it rolling into the area below.

He took no notice of Wexford. None of them did. He had to say who he was twice before getting anyone's attention, and then it was the short boy who looked up at him, possibly because he was the only one not otherwise occupied.

'Where's your friend?'

'You what?'

'Where's your friend? The one in the striped hat?' That was one way of not having to identify him by ethnic origin. Wexford told himself for God's sake to stop being needlessly sensitive. 'The black one with the plaits?'

'Don't know what you're talking about.'

'He means Raffy.' A stone found its target, the can wobbled and fell. 'He has to mean Raffy.'

'OK, I do. D'you know where he is?'

No one answered. The smoker smoked, concentrating as if it was a study he was engaged in, involving memory and even powers of deduction. The cuticle-biter bit his cuticles and made more rings with his toes in the smoker's ash. The stone-thrower threw his handful of gravel over his shoulder and produced a packet from which he took a cigarette. Having given Wexford the kind of look one might give a dangerous dog, at present quiescent, the fat golden-haired boy got off the wall and went into the Benefit Office.

'I asked you if you know where he is?'

'Might do,' said the stone-thrower in the dinosaur tee-shirt.

'So?'

'Might know where his mum is.'

'That'll do for a start.'

It was the cuticle-biter who gave him the information. He spoke as if only a madman, living in a self-created world of schizophrenic fantasy, could be ignorant of this fact. 'She sees the little kids across at Thomas Proctor, don't she?'

This sentence, though seemingly obscure, immediately told Wexford, without his having to pause and decipher, that Raffy's mother was the lollipop lady who, at 9.00 am and 3.30 pm, conducted the children who attended the Thomas Proctor Primary School across the road.

He asked the stone-thrower, 'Has he a sister?'

The thin shoulders rose and dropped again.

'A girlfriend?'

They looked at each other and started laughing. The golden-haired boy came out and the cuticle-biter whispered something to him. He too laughed and the infectious laughter soon had them all convulsed. Wexford shook his head and walked off the way he had come.

# 16

A full moon loomed behind the distorted branches of a cherry tree on which the blossoms were an improbable shade of bright pink. This picture, painted on a bamboo scroll, was repeated all round the walls of the Moonflower Takeaway's waiting room. It was the only place he'd ever been to, Wexford had once said, where they kept the radio and the television on at the same time. The clientele, waiting for their fried rice and lemon chicken, never looked at the moon and cherry blossom pictures and they only looked at the television when sport was on.

This lunchtime the radio was playing Michelle Wright singing 'Baby, Don't Start With Me', and the television was showing a re-run of *South Pacific*. Karen Malahyde walked into the Moonflower just as Mitzi Gaynor, the fierce competition with the country singer, had started to wash that man right out of her hair. Karen went up to the counter where a woman was dispensing orders as they came through from the back.

It was a semi-open plan arrangement and Mark Ling could be seen in the gleaming steel kitchen as he conjured with half a dozen woks, while his brother stood talking to him and decanting a sack of rice.

Mhonum Ling was a small sturdy woman whose skin was the colour of a coffee bean and whose straightened hair, still faintly crinkled, had the glitter of a seam of coal. Wearing a white coat like a doctor's, she was dispensing foil containers of chow mein and sweet and sour pork to customers whose numbers came up in red neon above her head. It was a bit like a happier version of the Benefit Office, though the Moonflower's clients sat on cane chairs, reading *Today* and *Sporting Life*.

When Karen told her what she wanted, Mhonum Ling beckoned

rather peremptorily to her brother-in-law and cocked her head in the direction of the counter. He came at once.

She looked at the picture. 'Who's this?'

'You don't know? You've never seen her before?'

'No way. What she done?'

'Nothing,' said Karen carefully. 'She's done nothing. She's dead. You've not seen anything about it on TV?'

'We got work to do,' said Mhonum Ling proudly. 'We've no time for watching that.' With a long plum-red fingernail, she prodded her brother-in-law, who was gossiping with a customer and had failed to see an order of fried rice and bamboo shoots come up behind him. She gave the clients a severe glance. 'No time for reading papers either.'

'OK, so you don't know her. There's a boy, maybe eighteen, with Rasta hair, always wears one of those floppy cap things, he's the only person that looks like that round here, he's not your son, is he?'

For a moment Karen thought Mhonum was going to say she'd had no time for having children. But, 'Raffy?' she said. 'That sounds like Raffy. Don't forget the fortune cookies, Johnny. They don't like going without their fortune cookies.'

'Is he a relative, then?'

'Raffy?' she said. 'Raffy's my nephew, my sister's son. He left school two years ago but he's never had work. He never will, there aren't the jobs. My sister Oni, she wanted Mark to give him a job here, just a job helping in the kitchen she said, you could do with another pair of hands, but what's the use? We don't need no other two hands and we're not in the charity business, we're not aid workers in Africa.'

Karen asked where Mhonum's sister lived and was given an address. 'But she won't be home, she'll be working. *She's* got work.'

On the chance of finding Raffy at home, Karen went round to Castlegate, Kingsmarkham's only tower block, where Oni and Raffy Johnson lived at number twenty-four. It wasn't much of a tower, a mere eight storeys high, local authority housing which the borough council would have liked to sell off to its tenants, if those tenants had been prepared to buy. Wexford had predicted that soon they would have no option but to pull it down and start afresh. Twenty-four was on the sixth floor and the lift was, as usual, out of order. By the time she got up there Karen was sure Raffy wouldn't be at home. She was right.

493

What made Wexford think this Raffy could help them? He had no grounds to go on, not the least evidence, just a hunch. You could call it intuition and sometimes, she knew, he intuited spectacularly. She had to have faith and tell herself that if Wexford thought Raffy was worth hunting down because the answer lay with Raffy, it quite possibly did. Sojourner – somehow, in some perhaps tenuous way – was connected to this boy his aunt spoke of so contemptuously.

She got back just as Kashyapa Begh's Jaguar swept on to the forecourt in front of the police station and Wexford asked her to take him into the mortuary. Kashyapa Begh was a shrivelled elderly man with white hair who wore a pinstriped suit and snow-white shirt. The pin in his red silk tie was a large ruby and two small diamonds. He put Karen's back up by asking her why he was being escorted on this serious business by a woman. She said nothing, remembering that in all likelihood this man and his male relatives had murdered a girl to stop her marrying the man of her choice. Glancing at the body with no attempt to conceal his distaste, Kashyapa Begh said in an outraged tone,

'That was a complete waste of my time.'

'I'm sorry about that, Mr Begh. We have to work on a process of elimination.'

'Process of folly,' said Kashyapa Begh and strutted off towards his car.

It was scarcely out of sight before a police car brought Festus Smith, a young Glaswegian, whose seventeen-year-old sister had been missing since March. His reaction to the body was much the same as Begh's, though he didn't say travelling 400 miles to see it had been a waste of his time. After him came Mary Sheerman from Nottingham, mother of a missing daughter. Carina Sheerman had disappeared on her way home from work on a Friday in June. She was sixteen and she had gone missing once before just before her fourteenth birthday, but she wasn't the dead girl in the mortuary.

On his way to see Carolyn Snow, Wexford told himself that Sojourner was a local girl, she had lived within the town or its environs. It was not that she had slipped through a net but that her disappearance had never been reported. Because it wasn't known? Or because whoever would know wanted to keep her absence concealed, as they had once wanted to conceal her existence?

Carolyn Snow was in the back garden, sitting on a striped sun lounger and reading just the sort of example of modern fiction from which, he had told Burden, her knowledge of obscenities derived. It was Joel who took him out there. Wexford thought it a long time since he had seen such a look of desperate bewildered misery on an adolescent's face.

Carolyn Snow barely looked up. 'Yes?' she said. 'What is it now?'

'I thought I would give you an opportunity to tell the truth at last, Mrs Snow.'

'I don't know what you're talking about.'

Another of Wexford's laws was that no truthful person ever makes this remark. It is exclusively the province of liars.

'I, however, know very well that you weren't telling me the truth when you said your husband went out in the evening on July the seventh. I know he was here all the evening. But you told me he went out and, moreover, you encouraged your son, a boy of fourteen, to support you in this lie.'

She laid the book face down on the seat beside her. Wexford remained standing. She looked up at him and a faint flush came into her face. The twitch of her lips was almost a smile.

'Well, Mrs Snow?'

'Oh, so what?' she said. 'To hell with it. I've given him a few sleepless nights, haven't I? I've punished him. Of course he was at home that evening. It was just a joke saying he wasn't, and it was pretty easy too to fool everyone. I told Joel all the details of what he'd done *and* I told him about that Diana, and he would have done anything to support me. There are *some* people who care about me, you know.' Her smile was a real one this time, a broad, sunny, slightly mad, smile. 'He's in an awful state, he really thinks he could be done for murdering that bitch.'

'He won't be,' said Wexford. 'It's you I'll be charging with wasting police time.'

He had made himself Australian and already had a marked Australian accent. Vine had scarcely shaken hands with him, had said no more than, 'Good morning, Mr Colegate,' before the man was off on a diatribe against the Royal Family and the virtues of republicanism.

His mother, whose house in Pomfret this was, put her head round the door to ask Vine if he would like tea. Stephen Colegate said, not tea, please, what was wrong with coffee, for God's sake?

495

'Nothing for me,' said Vine.

Two children hurtled into the room with a Scottie dog at their heels. They jumped on to the sofa, arms up, screaming. Colegate looked at them with satisfaction. 'My daughters,' he said. 'I got married again in Melbourne. Wife couldn't come, she's got a high-powered job. But I'd made a promise to my mother I'd make it to the UK this year and when I say something I stick to it. Take the doggie in the yard, Bonita.'

'So you didn't come over for your former wife's funeral?'

'Good God, no. When I got shut of Annette that was for keeps.' He gave a loud laugh. 'In life, in death and beyond the grave.'

It occurred to Vine that Annette Bystock had had an unfortunate taste in men. The two little girls leapt off the sofa and fled, the younger aiming a kick at the dog as they passed it.

'When did you arrive in this country, Mr Colegate?'

'Now why the hell would *I* kill Annette?'

'If you would just tell me when you got here, sir.'

'Oh, sure. I've nothing to hide. It was last Saturday. I came on Qantas, wouldn't touch a Pom airline with a six-foot pole, rented a car at Heathrow, the kids slept all the way. I can prove all this. You want to see my air ticket?'

'That won't be necessary,' said Vine and he showed him Sojourner's picture but it was clear from the indifferent glance Colegate gave it that he had never seen her before. The coffee came, brought by an apprehensive woman who was unused to making it.

Stephen Colegate said, 'I never got here till Saturday, did I, Mum?'

'More's the pity. You told me you were coming on the sixth, I still don't know why you changed your mind.'

'I *told you*. Something came up and I couldn't get away. If you say that sort of thing he'll think I came over earlier and hid out somewhere so as I could throttle Annette.'

Mrs Colegate gave a little shrill scream. 'Oh, Stevie!' She drew breath while her son, wrinkling his nose, skimmed floating grains off the surface of the thin brown liquid in his cup. 'I know it's wrong speaking ill of the dead,' she said, and was still doing so, dismembering Annette's character and, by extension, that of her parents, when Vine quietly took his leave.

It was far from usual practice in Kingsmarkham local elections to display posters with photographs of the candidate on them. That's because they're so ugly, Dora had said uncharitably, and Wexford had to agree. The bull-necked, red-faced representative of the British National Party, with his head of grey stubble and small piggy eyes, was no beauty, and the vulture-faced Lib Dem with beaky nose and hooded eyes not much better. Anouk Khoori, on the other hand, in most people's opinion, would be an ornament to any office she might hold and her poster the best advertisement she could have contrived for herself.

Wexford paused to look at the one displayed on a hoarding in Glebe Road. It was all photograph but for her name and her political status. She smiled down at him and judicious air-brushing had removed the lines such smiling must have created. For the photograph her hair had been done in the ringleted mode. Her eyes were limpid, sincere, earnest. The Thomas Proctor School would be a polling station next week, and this poster was just near enough to it for that face to linger in the mind.

He was early, but cars were already parked at the pavement, waiting to pick up departing children. It was said to be a good school, the choice of certain affluent parents more likely to have opted for private education. His quarry came round from the side of the school, carrying her stop sign. She was evidently also Karen Malahyde's quarry. By some different route from his, Karen must have been led to this school and this crossing, for he suddenly saw her leave a car he had at first taken for that of a Thomas Proctor parent and begin walking towards the woman who had reached the pavement.

She turned when she saw him. 'Great minds, sir,' she said.

'I hope the great minds think wisely as well as alike, Karen. Her son's called Raffy. Do you know the surname?'

'Johnson. She's Oni Johnson.' She risked asking the question. 'Why do you think Raffy might identify her?'

He shrugged. 'We've no more reasons to think Raffy knew her than that old villain Begh did. Or Dr Akande, come to that. It may be because I think of them both as . . . well, outcasts. Expendable people that no one cares much about.'

'And it's our last chance?'

'There's no such thing as a last chance in our work, Karen.'

The school doors opened and the children started coming out. Most of them were carrying bags and packages as well as satchels. It was their last day until school started again in September. Oni

Johnson was a stocky black woman, about forty, her navy skirt tight on her, wearing a day-glo yellow jacket over her white blouse and a navy peaked cap on her head. She stood at the pavement edge like a shepherd who must gather in her flock without a dog to help her. But the children were obedient sheep, they had done this before, they had done it every day.

She looked to the right, to the left, to the right again, and then she marched into the road, holding up her stop sign. The children streamed after her. Wexford noted the youngest Riding child, the girl who had been at the garden party with her brother. Further up the pavement a black-haired girl with gold earrings was hauled into a car driven by a woman that Wexford thought might be Claudine Messaoud. He was seeing black people everywhere these days. That was always the way. This time it was a boy of eight or nine opening the door of a car he recognized as the Epsons' but driven by someone whose face he couldn't see. Not exactly black this child, though, light brown with light brown curly hair, black only in the world's uncompromising categorization.

Oni Johnson held up her hand at the fresh throng of children waiting on the pavement. She walked back to them, taking slow deliberate steps, and back on the kerb, beckoned to the traffic to proceed. The Riding girl jumped into her parents' Range Rover. The car that might have been the Messaouds' passed southwards and a stream of traffic followed it. Wexford went up to Oni Johnson, showed her his warrant card.

'Nothing to worry about, Mrs Johnson. Just routine. We'd like to talk to your son. Will you be going home when you've finished here?'

Alarm flashed in her eyes. 'My Raffy – what's he done?'

'Nothing, so far as I know. We want to talk to him about something else, some information he may have.'

'All right. I don't know when he be home. He come in for his tea. I be going straight there when I'm done here.' She let a car pass and then, holding up her stop sign, she marched into the road, but this time, Wexford thought, less confidently.

The first of the cars that waited while she shepherded the children over was, he saw, being driven by Jane Winster. She looked at him and looked away. The child sitting next to her was all of sixteen and must have been fetched from some other school, the Comprehensive probably.

He wasn't far from home. A quick cup of tea in his own house, he thought, and then he'd meet Karen at Castlegate. The last car to pass was a Rolls Royce driven by Wael Khoori.

Sylvia was there with her sons, sitting round the kitchen table with Dora. For Ben and Robin this too was the last day of term. 'I'm thinking of doing a training course. It's to be a counsellor in a medical centre.'

'Enlighten me,' said her father.

'They have one at Akande's, Reg.' said Dora. 'Haven't you seen "Counsellor" on the door when you go down the passage to his surgery?'

Robin was temporarily distracted from his video game. 'A counsellor is what they call lawyers in America.'

'Yes, well, it isn't here. I'll have patients referred to me for counselling as a better option than handing out tranquillizers, that's the idea. And don't try to say something else clever, Robin. Just get on with your puzzle.'

'*Ko se wahala,*' said Robin.

Long ago the members of his family had stopped asking Robin any questions about his 'no problems'. Sylvia's theory was that if ignored, he would grow out of it. As phases went, this one had lasted a long time and showed no sign of coming to an end. It was months since parents, grandparents and brother had laughed or commented or enquired but now Wexford said, 'What language is that, Robin?'

'Yoruba.'

'Where do they speak it?'

'In Nigeria,' said Robin. 'Sounds good, don't you think? *Ko se wahala.* Better than *nao problema,* that's practically the same as English.'

'Did you get it from someone at school?' Wexford asked, hopeful but of what he hardly knew.

'Yep. I got it from Oni.' Robin seemed very pleased to have been asked. 'Oni George. She's next to me on the register.'

So Oni was a Nigerian name . . . Raymond Akande was Nigerian. He was suddenly sure, for no good reason but instinct, that Sojourner was too. The other Oni, Oni Johnson, had said she would be home by five. He had a strong feeling, an almost excited intuition that he was on the brink of finding it all out, of finding who Sojourner was, what connection there was between her and Annette and why they had both been killed. The boy was the answer, the boy

499

called Raffy in the coloured cap, who had nothing to do all day but observe, notice, record – or go blindly through his empty days?

Karen was waiting for him when he got to Castlegate at five past. The hoarding outside the block was covered with posters of Anouk Khoori, no fewer than ten of them, pasted up side by side. He and Karen picked their way across the broken concrete forecourt. A dog, or fox, or even, these days, a human being, had torn open one of the black plastic rubbish bags piled by the front entrance and left behind a scattering of chicken bones, takeaway containers, frozen vegetable packets. It had become a lot warmer as the day went on and an almost chemical smell of decay emanated from the bags.

Wexford could remember when a Victorian Gothic house with turrets and crenellations had stood on this spot, not very beautiful, grotesque rather, but interesting. And its garden had been an arboretum of rare trees. All of it went in the sixties and, in spite of universal disapproval, petitions and even a demonstration, Castlegate had been built on the site. Even those who would otherwise have been homeless disliked it. Wexford pushed open the entrance doors and the cracked glass in them rattled.

'The lift's not working,' said Karen.

'Now she tells me. How many flights up is it? If the boy's not home we may as well wait for him here.'

'It's only six flights, sir. But if you'd like me to go up and find out I...'

'No, no, of course not. Where are the stairs?'

The walls were concrete, painted cream and peeling, the floor laid with grey composition tiles, crazed by wear to the colour of coal dust. A graffitist had spray-painted 'Gary is a scumbag' on the wall that contained the broken lift.

'They're going to pull the place down,' Karen said as if it was her responsibility to apologize for the shortcomings of Castlegate, for its Inner London-style sleaze and dilapidation. 'Everyone's been rehoused but the Johnsons and one other family. Round here, sir. The stairs are on the left.'

She checked a cry. Her hand flew to her mouth. A split second and Wexford too saw what she had seen.

At the foot of the concrete staircase a woman, or a woman's body, lay spread on the tiles. Her head was in a pool of blood. Oni Johnson had never reached home.

# 17

In the Intensive Care Unit at Stowerton Royal Infirmary, Oni Johnson lay all night between life and death. In that small world she was the responsibility of Sister Laurette Akande, who had been in charge of this ward for the past year. Not all Oni's injuries came from falling downstairs, though it seemed she had fallen and rolled down all six flights. A bruise on her head was on the left side while it was the right which had struck the floor, so there was a policeman stationed outside her door day and night and Wexford was treating the case as one of attempted murder.

Murder, if she died. Laurette Akande told him she doubted if Oni Johnson would survive her injuries. Both legs were broken and the left ankle, there was a fracture of the pelvis, of three ribs and the right radius, but the most serious injury was a depressed skull fracture. Cranial surgery was essential if her life was to be saved and an operation was performed by Mr Algernon Cozens, the neurosurgeon, on Friday afternoon. The boy who had sat by her bed for hours on end, who had sat there staring, unchecked tears trickling down his face, had signed the form of consent with slow deliberation like a robot whose mechanism is wearing out.

'But why was the attack just before we got there?' Karen asked Wexford.

He shook his head.

'Do we know what the weapon was?'

'Bare hands perhaps. Whoever did this waited round the corner at the top of the stairs and when she appeared, struck her a blow in the face with his fist which sent her rolling down those stairs. All he had to do was run down after her, kick her down probably, and make his escape ten minutes before we got there.'

'Bare hands were used on Sojourner,' said Burden. 'I'll never forget that, Mavrikiev telling me how to kill with your fists.'

'Yes. It's the only link we have and it's not much of one.'

'Where was the boy?'

'When all this happened? He never seems to know where he is at any given time. One thing, he wasn't at Castlegate. That crowd that hang about outside the Benefit Office say he was with them for part of the afternoon but they don't know which part. They wouldn't. He drifts about. He begs.'

'He *begs*?'

'They all do, Mike, if they see a likely benefactor. That's what he took me for. I suppose I should be flattered. We were looking for him – remember? – when his mother was taken to hospital and I met him coming along Queen Street towards Castlegate. He stuck out his hand and said, "Got the price of a cup of tea, mate?" When I told him who I was and what had happened I thought he was going to faint.'

Three hours after that he and Raffy Johnson had had their talk. But Raffy had never seen any black girls in Kingsmarkham. 'Only old women,' he told Wexford. How about Melanie Akande, Wexford asked, had he ever seen her?

A curious look, part humiliation, part scorn, came into Raffy's face, and Wexford understood before he spoke that these children of immigrants were already infected with the English disease. Their blackness had not saved them.

'It's like, she's a different class, in't she?' said Raffy. 'Her dad's a doctor and all that.'

Race and poverty and a hierarchical system had condemned him to a lonely celibacy, for it seemed never to have crossed his mind to speak to, let alone try to befriend, a white girl.

'Your mother is from Nigeria, isn't she?'

'Right.'

He looked blankly at Wexford. Raffy had apparently, never asked his mother about her native land and no information had been given him unasked. He knew only that she had come here with her sister when they were very young and after her sister had married a Chinese man. Wexford had no interest in the identity of Raffy's father, if indeed the boy knew it. He seemed to know so little, to be without interests or skills, ambition or hope, but to live from day to day, his only wish to stay alive to wander the streets of the town that had given him nothing.

'I asked him,' Wexford said, 'if he knew why anyone would try to kill his mother. I expected indignation, I expected shock. What I didn't expect was a sort of nervous smile. He looked at me as if I was having him on. He was almost embarrassed.'

'But he takes it seriously now?'

'I don't know. I tried to make him understand that someone had attempted to murder his mother. God knows, he must see murder on television every day of his life, but for him telly is fantasy and life is reality – just what they're supposed to be, only we're always being told that young people confuse the two.'

Karen said tentatively, 'The perpetrator couldn't have been confused, could he? Mistaken Oni Johnson for Raffy? It wasn't very light up there.'

'Even if it was dark no one could mistake Oni for her son. He's six inches taller, for one thing. He's as skinny as a rake and she's rather plump. No, it was Oni our killer meant to attack and I haven't the faintest idea why.'

The only other people who lived in Castlegate, a married couple, had been at work at the time. No one had been about in the empty parking areas which surrounded the block. It was as if it had already been abandoned to the demolition squad, the fact that four people still lived in it almost forgotten. Oni Johnson's attacker could hardly have found a more propitious place to attempt a silent secret murder.

Karen's suggestion had its final dismissal next day when someone made a second attempt on Oni Johnson's life.

Archbold was outside her door all night and Pemberton took over from him in the morning. Nobody could have gone in without being seen by them but they had seen only the hospital staff, doctors, nurses, technicians, and Raffy.

It was the staff nurse who told Wexford, a young woman called Stacey Martin. He came into the ward at nine and she met him when he reached the door of Oni's room where Pemberton was already waiting.

'Would you come in here, please?'

She took him into the office with 'Sister' on the door. 'I came on at eight this morning,' she said. 'The night to day changeover is at eight.

503

Sister had already come on. I went straight in to look at Oni and I thought it was funny, the sheet was pulled up over her hand.'

'I don't follow you,' said Wexford.

'It's hot in here, as I expect you've noticed. We keep it hot so patients don't need bedclothes over them. The sheet was covering the back of her hand where the IV line goes in. Well, I pulled it back and the line wasn't going in. It had been taken out and a clip put on to stop it leaking all over the bed.'

He looked at her and saw shock still on her face. 'You say "someone" took it out. Could she have done it herself?'

'Hardly. I mean, I suppose it's just possible . . . but why would she?'

Before he could answer, if he could have answered, the door opened and Laurette Akande came in. She eyed him like a headmistress with a troublesome pupil. He realized for the first time how deeply she disliked him.

'Mr Wexford,' she said in frosty tones. 'Can I help you?'

'You can tell me what goes through the . . . er, drip on Oni's arm?'

'The intravenous line? Drugs. Quite a cocktail of medication. Why do you want to know that? Oh, I see. Staff Nurse Martin's been passing on her ridiculous suspicions, has she?'

'But the line was pulled out, wasn't it, Mrs Akande?'

'Sister. Unfortunately, it was. That is, it *came* out. No harm was done, there was no setback in Mrs Johnson's condition . . .' She changed her tune abruptly, sending a beaming smile in Stacey Martin's direction, 'thanks to Staff Martin's prompt action.' The tone became mildly satirical. 'We must all be very very grateful to her. Come along now, I'll take you in to see Mrs Johnson.'

She was alone in the room, wearing a white gown, covered only to the waist by a sheet and propped up, not lying flat. One of Raffy's comics was on the bed table but Raffy wasn't there.

'Is she conscious?' Wexford asked. 'Can she talk?'

'She's asleep,' said Laurette Akande.

'Could the boy have done it?'

'Nobody did it, Mr Wexford. Nothing has been done. The IV line came out. It was an unfortunate accident but no harm was done. All right?'

There would be a hospital enquiry, he thought, if he told anyone else of this, if Staff Martin did. It was clear Sister Akande had no intention of telling anyone, for her job would be on the line. And what was the point now?

'I would like to stay here,' he said. 'Inside this room.'

'You can't do that. You've an officer outside, that's the usual procedure.'

'I'll be the best judge of the usual procedure,' he said. 'There are curtains round that bed. If there are things to be done it would be improper for me to see, you can draw the curtains.'

'I've never in all my years of nursing heard of a policeman sitting inside a room in an ICU.'

'There's always a first time,' said Wexford. He forgot about being polite, sensitive to this woman's feelings, he even forgot his terrible blunder in the mortuary. 'I shall create a precedent. If you don't like it you'll have to lump it or I go to Mr Cozens for permission.'

She compressed her lips. She folded her arms and looked down at them, controlling the temper of which he had had a previous sample. Then she advanced a step to the bed and peered closely at Oni Johnson. She agitated the IV line for a second or two, eyed the monitor on the wall and stalked out without looking at him again.

Either he or Burden must stay there, he thought. Barry Vine, perhaps, and Karen Malahyde. No one else. Until she talked and told them what it was she knew she must never be left on her own. He sat down on the uncomfortable chair and after half an hour a nurse he hadn't seen before, a Thai or Malaysian woman, brought him a cup of tea. They drew the curtains round Oni in the late morning and at one o'clock Algernon Cozens came in with a retinue of housemen, registrars, Staff Nurse Martin and Sister Akande.

No one took any notice of Wexford. Laurette Akande must have given some prior explanation for his presence but he would have betted anyone anything it wasn't the correct one. He called Burden on his cellphone and at three the inspector came in to take over, entering the room simultaneously with a very smartly dressed Mhonum Ling. Her tight high-heeled shoes gave her an added four inches and, with her hair elaborately piled on the top of her head, she had become quite a tall woman.

In time-honoured fashion, she had brought grapes, useless to Oni who was still fed intravenously. She seemed glad to see Burden, it was someone to talk to and share the grapes with, though Burden shook his head when they were offered.

She had no idea, she said, why anyone would want to kill her

505

sister. Like Raffy, she seemed embarrassed by the question, and glossed over it as soon as she could to begin on a catalogue of Oni's misfortunes and mistakes, how ill-luck had dogged her since their arrival in Britain, how she always seemed one of life's victims. She didn't know how her sister managed always to stay so cheerful. Mhonum had no children and perhaps this was why she cited Raffy as the chief of her sister's troubles, a problem since the day he was born – since *before* he was born, since his father disappeared as soon as Oni told him she was pregnant. Raffy had been hopeless at school, had been a chronic truant. He could do nothing, could barely write his name. He would never have a job, would live on benefit all his life. The hard-working and prosperous Mhonum shook her head over Raffy, remarking that the only good thing she could say about him was that he wouldn't hurt a fly.

'Does your sister have any enemies?' Burden asked, rephrasing his question.

Mhonum popped a grape into her mouth. 'Enemies? Oni? She don't even have friends.' She glanced over her shoulder at the sedated woman as she spoke. 'There's only Mark and me and we're busy people. We've a business to run, right?' Her voice went down to a whisper. 'Oni had this boyfriend but he was soon gone, she scared him off. Oh, she was so possessive, you wouldn't believe, want to own him, right? But he run off like Raffy's daddy, it's the same old story all over again.'

'Can you think of any reason why anyone would want to kill Mrs Johnson?'

She licked the tips of her fingers delicately. Burden observed her clothes, what he calculated was five hundred pounds' worth of turquoise silk trouser suit and cream-coloured Bruno Magli shoes. 'No one want to kill her,' she said. 'They just *kill*, a person like that. They're made that way. She was there and they kill, that's all.'

As if he didn't know, as if he needed instruction in that particular field.

Barry Vine took over from Burden in the evening. He brought with him a computer game belonging to his son and a Spanish exercise book. He was learning Spanish when he managed to make it to the evening class. In response to a peremptory summons Wexford drove himself to Stowerton to see the Chief Constable. The traffic was at its worst in the early evening and he found himself in a slow line approaching the roundabout. In his rear mirror he saw the Epsons' pink car behind him but no more than a pale glimmer of the driver's face. It took him all of a further fifteen minutes to get to Freeborn's house.

He had described it to Burden as the only even moderately attractive house in ugly little Stowerton. Once it had been the rectory, a sprawling place with several acres of garden.

'How long is this going to go on, Reg?' Freeborn wanted to know. 'Two girls dead and now this woman at death's door.'

'Oni Johnson is recovering,' Wexford said.

'More by luck than your activities. Come to think of it, she's only in the state she is because of your activities.'

Wexford thought that hard. He could have rejoined that if he and Karen had been less prompt she would soon have died, lying there in her own blood on Castlegate's concrete floor. He didn't. A quite arbitrary date came into his head and he said he would have worked the whole thing out by the end of next week. Just give him a week.

'No one been taking any more mugshots of you, I trust?' Freeborn laughed unpleasantly. 'I'm scared to look in the paper these days.'

Barry sat all night in Oni's room and Wexford took over from him in the morning. Sitting there, he watched a doctor come in and draw the bed curtains, a new staff nurse shake the IV line. How could he tell who meant harm to Oni? How would he know if the injection administered by the surgical registrar was beneficial to Oni – or lethal? All he could do was *be* there and hope the time would soon come when she could talk to him.

Raffy came in at mid-morning, as usual wearing his knitted cap, though it was a hot day and hotter in the ward. He looked at the pictures in his comic, got out his cigarettes and, perhaps realizing smoking would be the ultimate solecism, put them away again. He sat there for half an hour before creeping out. Wexford heard him running down the corridor outside. Karen took over in the afternoon, her arrival timing with Raffy's return. He walked in eating chips out of a greasy paper bag.

'If she comes round, if she talks, let me know at once.'

'Of course I will, sir,' Karen said.

It happened on Sunday while Vine was in the ward. Raffy was the first person Oni's opening eyes alighted on. She put out her hand, secured his and held it. Wexford found them like that, the boy looking puzzled and somewhat at a loss, Oni clutching his long fingers in her plump stubby ones. She smiled at Wexford and she started talking.

Once she had begun, she spoke a lot, about the room she was in, the nurses, the doctors, she spoke to Raffy about the chances of getting a job as a hospital porter. Of what had happened to her at the top of the stairs in Castlegate she had no memory at all.

It was only what he had expected. The mind is kind to the body and allows it to heal without the setbacks painful and terrible memories may induce. But he dared not leave her until she had told him everything she knew. If only she knew what it was she knew! God help her if what she knew seemed to her trivial or insignificant or, worse, she had forgotten it. She had emerged as a cheerful and co-operative woman, willing to talk about herself and her life and her son but whose memory now held two segments of recollections, those of the hospital that went back to her waking in the ward on Saturday, and those of her previous life which ended abruptly as she entered Castlegate on Thursday afternoon, walked past the dysfunctional lift and began to climb the stairs.

'That lift always out of order,' Oni said. 'But, you know, I always hope. Always I say to myself, Oni, I say, maybe today they mend it and up you go, sailing up like a bird. But no way and I have to go on my own two feet. These things are sent to try us, I'm telling myself, and then all go black and the floor come up in my face and I wake up in here.'

'Before you went into the building, can you remember seeing anyone about? Was there anyone about outside?'

'Not a soul. He was up there, wasn't he, waiting to bop me with his great boxer fist.'

'And you've no idea who "he" might be?'

She shook her head under its thick white bandage. Her own phrase 'great boxer fist', which she had used several times, always made her laugh. She had that curious habit, common to Africans and Afro-Caribbeans too but almost incomprehensible to Europeans, of laughing merrily at tragic or terrifying events. Her laughter shook the bed and Wexford looked round, anxious not to alert a nurse who might take Oni's excitement as a sign to terminate their talk for another day.

'Has anyone threatened you? Have you quarrelled with anyone?'

508

His questions elicited giggles, then a casting up of eyes. She looked as her son had looked when asked who would want to kill his mother: embarrassed, suspicious of mockery, determined to treat the situation lightly. Sudden inspiration made Wexford ask,

'Have you had any quarrel or argument with a car driver, someone you've stopped on the crossing?'

It was mad to think of attempting to kill for such a reason, or he would once have thought it mad. Now he knew people did such things. Sane-looking, ordinary men drove the streets of this town and any other, who if reproved by a traffic warden would think nothing of taking savage revenge – especially if it was a woman who had dared upbraid them. Especially if it was a black woman. But there had apparently been no such violent paranoiac in Oni Johnson's past.

Like her sister, she said, 'He's a killer, right? Don't have to have no reason. He kill, he made that way.' And her brisk summing up of man's senseless iniquity brought so much fresh cause for laughter that this time the nurse did come over and say that was quite enough for today.

It was possibly quite enough for ever. Leaving Barry Vine in the ward and walking back to the lift down the corridor, Wexford asked himself if there was anything more to be got out of Oni, or if she and Mhonum Ling could be right and this was a virtually unmotivated attack by some psychopath; someone who took against black residents or women or mothers or dwellers in tower blocks or even just other people. Perhaps it had nothing to do with Raffy, nothing to do with the Benefit Office and Annette, perhaps there was no connection between Oni and Annette or, come to that, Oni and Melanie Akande. Perhaps Raffy had plucked the IV line out himself because it frightened him or he thought Oni was hurt by it or he was merely trying to shake it the way he had seen done by the hospital staff. Weren't most killings, after all, committed from motives incomprehensible to ordinary men or from no apparent motive at all?

He had been so deep in thought that he missed his way but, finding a staircase ahead of him, walked down it. Here, however, he was really lost, in a part of the hospital he had never been before. He had just registered the words, Department of Paediatrics and Diseases of Children, lettered above the open double doors ahead of him, when a door opened on his left and Swithun Riding, his white coat open over a fawn fuzzy sweater, came out of it with a baby in his arms.

Wexford expected to be ignored, but Riding instead gave him a cordial smile and remarked that he was glad to see him, he had intended, next time he did see him, to congratulate him on guessing the correct age of those twins at the garden party.

'My wife told me. So much for *my* expertise, she said. What do you do with the teddy bear, have a childhood regression and cuddle up to it at night?'

Wexford was too interested in Riding's manner with the baby to think up a clever rejoinder. He said merely, 'I gave it away,' and marvelled at the tender way the paediatrician held the child, with such delicacy for one so big, with such gentle firmness, each of his huge hands large enough to contain it like a cradle. And Riding's expression, normally so elevated and arrogant, the lofty look of the proud possessor of superior intellect and physique, grew soft and almost feminine as he looked down into the tiny round face, the wide blue eyes.

'Nothing wrong with him, I hope?' Wexford hazarded.

'Nothing worse than an umbilical hernia and we've seen to that. Not a him, by the way. A lovely little lady. Don't you adore them? Aren't they gorgeous?'

It might have been a woman talking, and the words, uttered in a strong baritone, which should have been grotesque, sounded only charming. Riding was transformed, he was for a moment a 'nice' man. And Wexford felt it would be possible to ask the way out without risking some crushing put-down.

'Oh, back the way you've come and turn left,' said the paediatrician. 'And now I must take this little sweetheart back to Mother or she'll be fretting and no wonder.'

Telling Dora about it later, Wexford was rather surprised to hear it was no surprise to her.

'Sylvia was referred to him with Ben, don't you remember? When Ben broke his arm and had those complications. Oh, it must have been three years ago, soon after the Ridings came here.'

'One judges people on the strength of a single unfortunate encounter. It's a pity but there it is.'

'She said he was wonderful with Ben and Ben had quite a crush on him.'

Three years ago when Sylvia had a job and Neil had a job and

510

Dora complained they never saw them. 'We're not expecting them tonight, I hope. I mean, any of them.'

'No. We're not *expecting* them, for what that's worth. We oughtn't to talk about our child like that, ought we? It's wrong of us. I always think I'm tempting Providence and something awful will happen and then think of the guilt I'll feel.'

Wexford was starting to say that Providence had been tempted enough times by now to have learned how to resist, when the doorbell rang. Sylvia had a key but she also had the sensitivity not to use it when she came unexpectedly. 'I'll go,' he said, thinking on his way to the door of another evening of counsellor-training, job club and polyglot 'no problems'.

But it wasn't Sylvia and family. It was Anouk Khoori.

Again he had to look twice to be sure it was she. Her blonde hair was severely drawn back, her make-up light and she wore the female politician's favoured pearl ear studs. The skirt of her dark blue linen dress came well below the knee. Her manner was simple and disarming. At first it appeared the best, the least pompous technique a woman of her sort and her appearance could have used. She stepped inside without waiting to be asked. 'You'll have guessed. I've come to ask you to vote for me.'

He had guessed but only a matter of seconds before. She reminded him suddenly of Ingrid Pamber, a sophisticated and highly accomplished version of Ingrid. And this was strange because she was far from attractive to him, while Ingrid . . . To his surprise, to his distaste, Anouk Khoori tucked her arm into his and led him through his own house unerringly to where Dora was.

'Now Dora, my dear,' she said. 'I've the whole of this street to do tonight and all the next one – politics is *hard* work – but I've come to you first, the very first, because I feel we three have something special, we're what everyone but the English calls *sympathetic*.'

The look on his wife's face he knew well, the smile, the rapid blinking of her eyes, and then only the smile with lips closed, the lifted head. Pretentiousness evoked it and an assumption of intimacy on the part of virtual strangers. Anouk Khoori's hand on his arm, a beige-coloured hand with purple vein branches, purple varnish on the long nails, lay there, in his fancy like some exotic crustacean. It was as if his arm, immersed in water, had come up with this thing attached to it, this pentapod or tentacled actinia. If he had indeed attracted such a creature while swimming he could have shaken it

511

off. No such recourse was open to him here and his earlier aversion from this woman, his senseless repulsion, returned to him with a shudder.

But she had to sit down and this she could hardly do while clamped to him. Dora offered her a drink, a cup of tea if she preferred. Anouk Khoori, refusing with a smile and an inordinate show of gratitude, launched into her appeal. At first it seemed an exclusively defensive campaign. The idea of fascism, which these days meant racism, coming to a place like Kingsmarkham was horrible in the extreme. She herself was a relative newcomer to the borough but she felt so at home here that it was almost as if she was a natural Kingsmarkhamian, so profound was her sympathy with the hopes and fears of its residents. Racism appalled her and any ideas which might be prevalent of aiming at a white Kingsmarkham. The British Nationalist must be kept off the council at all costs.

'I wouldn't call electing you an action to take "at all costs", Mrs Khoori,' Dora said smoothly. 'I was going to vote for you anyway.'

'I knew it! I knew you'd feel that way. In fact, I said to myself as I came to your door – before going to anyone else, if you remember – I said to myself, I'm wasting my time, they don't need this, they're my supporters already, and then I thought, but I need their boost and *they* need . . . well, just to see me! Just to know that I appreciate them and I *care*.'

She turned the full radiance of her smile on Wexford and, unable to resist the flirtatious gesture, lifted one hand and smoothed her sleek sweep of hair. In spite of what she had said, her raised eyebrows and enquiring tilt of the head implied the expectation of a like support from him. But Wexford had no intention of committing himself. The poll was secret and his vote private. He asked her what positive moves she had in mind should she be elected and was rather amused by signs of ignorance.

'Don't worry,' she said. 'The first thing I shall work for will be the demolition of that terrible Castlegate where that poor woman was attacked. And then we shall build good new local authority housing on the site from the proceeds of private sales.'

Wexford corrected her gently. 'Local councils' assets from private sales are frozen and look like being so for some time to come.'

'Oh, I ought to know that, I do know it really.' She was not a whit put out. 'I can see I've a lot of homework to do. But the great thing is to get me there first, don't you agree?'

This Wexford refused to do. Pressed – the hand was back on his arm as he showed her out – he said that he was sure she also really knew his vote was a private matter between himself and his conscience. She entirely agreed, but she was tenacious, she was confrontational, her husband said, it was part of her nature not to shirk the truth, however unpalatable. By this time, Wexford had no idea what she meant but he managed a fairly gracious goodbye with the usual rider of its having been delightful to see her.

Later on she must have given a similar treatment to the Akandes, for when Wexford called on them next morning, Laurette so far unbent as to complain about the candidate's remarking that black people were her special friends and asserting her affinity with them. 'Do you know what she said to me? "My skin is white," she said, "but oh, my soul is black." You've got a nerve, I thought.'

Wexford couldn't help laughing but it was discreet gentle laughter. Mirth had no place in that house. But Laurette seemed to have forgotten their altercation in the matter of the IV line. She was more cordial than he had ever known her, for the first time offering him something to drink. Would he like coffee? Or she could easily make tea.

'Mrs Khoori won't get very far if that's her manifesto,' said the doctor. 'There can't be more than half a dozen of us in the place.'

'Eighteen precisely,' said Wexford. 'That's not families, that's individuals.'

He drove himself to the Infirmary and parked his car in the only available space, next to the library van. The car on the other side was a curious purplish colour and this brought to mind the Epsons' car. Suddenly Wexford understood what had been teasing the back of his mind since driving to the Chief Constable's house. The pink car behind him was being driven by a white man. He hadn't been able to see his face but he had seen that the man was white. The Epsons were a mixed-race couple – no doubt candidates for Laurette Akande's disapproval – but it was *Fiona Epson who was white and her husband black*. Did that mean anything? Was it significant? He had often remarked that everything was significant in a murder case. . . .

The library service was a private concern run by volunteers and last year Dora had persuaded him to donate to it a dozen of his books which she called 'superfluous'. To his surprise he saw Cookie

Dix step down from the driving seat of the library van. It was rather more astonishing that she recognized him.

'Hello,' she said. 'How are you? Wasn't that a wonderful party at the Khooris? Darling Alexander adored it, he's been quite bearable to live with ever since.'

She spoke as if they were old, intimate friends, and all the details of her no doubt problematic married life common knowledge between them. Wexford asked her if he could help her load the books on to her trolley. Though nearly as tall as he, she looked fragile with her stick limbs, fairy face and stream of black hair.

'You're terribly kind.' She stood back to let Wexford lift the trolley out from the back of the van. 'I hate Monday and Saturday mornings, I really do, but these are the only good works I ever do and if I give them up my life will be one of pure unbridled hedonism.'

Wexford smiled and asked her where she lived. 'Oh, don't you know? I thought everyone knew the house that Dix built. The glass palace with the trees inside? The top of Ashley Grove?'

One of the town's monstrosities, one of the places all the visitors stared at and asked about. He helped her load books on to the trolley, enquired where they came from and who selected them. Oh, she did, all her friends gave her books. He should bear her in mind when next he had a clear-out.

'Everyone thinks of romances and detective stories,' she said as he parted from her inside the entrance, 'but I find horror the most popular.' She gave him a beaming smile. 'Mutilation and cannibalism actually. That's the stuff if you're feeling really low.'

Vine had been with Oni Johnson all night. She was sleeping now and the curtains were drawn round her bed. Wexford said quietly,

'I know you're going off duty but there's just one thing. Three times now Carolyn Snow has told me Snow's former girlfriend was called Diana. If it rings any bells with you, think about it, will you?'

Half an hour after he had taken Vine's place Raffy came in, gave his mother a kiss which woke her up and sat down to look at the pictures in his comic. Today must have been Laurette Akande's day off and the ICU sister was a red-haired Irishwoman. She brought tea which Raffy looked at suspiciously and asked if he could have a coke.

'My goodness, you go down and fetch that for yourself out of the machine, young man. Whatever next!'

'I like him here beside me,' said Oni when Raffy had gone outside, having first helped himself to coins from her purse on the bedside table. 'I like to know what he's doing.' But Wexford remembered her sister's words about Oni's possessiveness. 'What we going to talk about today?'

'You're looking a lot better,' Wexford said. 'I see you've got a smaller bandage.'

'Small bandage for a small brain, huh? Maybe my brain smaller now that doctor been cutting it around?'

'Mrs Johnson, I'll tell you what we're going to talk about today. I want you to think back a few weeks, say three weeks, before last Thursday, and tell me of anything strange that may have happened.'

She looked at him without speaking.

'Anything odd or different at home, at work, anything about your son, any new person you met. Don't hurry, just think about it. Go back to the beginning of July and try to remember any unusual thing.'

Raffy came back with a can of coke. Someone had switched on the television and he moved his chair closer to it. Oni couldn't reach his hand. She let hers rest on his arm. She said to Wexford, 'You mean, like someone talking to me at the crossing? Like coming to the front door? Like seeing a stranger?'

'All that,' said Wexford. 'Anything.'

'There was someone draw a thing on our door but Raffy clean it off. Like a cross with turning corners.'

'A swastika.'

'That was the day the Job Centre had a job for Raffy and he go for the interview but it was no go. Then Mhonum, my sister, she had her birthday, she forty-two, though she don't look it, and we go to Moonflower for birthday dinner. I got another job – you know that? School cleaner, three times a week. There was one day I'm cleaning and I find a ten pound note, they get lot of pocket money these kids, and I hand it in to the teacher. Thought I might get a reward but no way. These things are sent to try us, you know? This the kind of thing you want?'

'Exactly the kind of thing,' said Wexford, though he had hoped for something more illuminating.

'This is all the start of July, right? On Sunday the lady come to the door, lady with long blonde hair, saying you vote for me in council elections, but I say maybe, I don't know, I think about it. Though

515

maybe that was the next Sunday. It was a Monday the day after, I know that, what was the date of the first Monday?'

July the fifth?'

Raffy was laughing at something on the television. He put his empty coke can on the floor. His mother said, 'Come here, Raffy. I like to hold your hand.' The boy shifted his chair a fraction without taking his eyes from the screen. Oni made a grab for his hand and gripped it, though this meant stretching her arm to its fullest extent.

'What happened on that Monday?' said Wexford.

'Not so much. The only one thing was in the afternoon and I am at the crossing. Maybe not that Monday but the next. All I am sure is the day after the election lady come. I thought, pity Raffy not here. He take you there, poor girl, you won't lose your way if Raffy take you.'

Wexford was lost. 'I don't quite follow you, Mrs Johnson.'

'I'm telling you, I stand at the crossing before the children come out of school, I just stand there, and a girl come along and stop in front of me, right on the pavement, right in front of me, and she talk to me in Yoruba. I am so surprise you could knock me over with a feather. I never hear Yoruba in twenty years but from my sister and she too proud for it. But this girl is from Nigeria and she say to me in Yoruba, what way is it to where they give you jobs? *Mo fé mò ibit'ó gbé wà* I want to know where it is.'

# 18

Four hours of deep sleep and Barry Vine was up, had taken a cold shower and phoned Wexford. The Chief Inspector said something incomprehensible to him in an African language. The translation was enough to send him straight off to the Benefit Office.

Ingrid Pamber's holiday was over and she had been back at work for two days, at the desk between Osman Messaoud and Hayley Gordon. She turned the blue beam of her eyes on Vine and smiled at him as if he were a departed lover returned from the wars. Deadpan, he showed her the photograph of Sojourner's dead face and a photograph of Oni Johnson that Raffy had managed to produce from the flat in Castlegate. Sojourner meant nothing to her; Oni she recognized.

Vine's indifference to her charms and smiles made her petulant. 'The lollipop lady, isn't she? I'd know her face anywhere. I think she's got it in for me. I only have to be late for work coming down Glebe Road and she's bound to stick that lollipop sign of hers up in front of me.'

'Did Annette know her?'

'Annette? How should I know?'

Ingrid alone of the Benefit Office staff failed to ask what had happened to Oni and why he wanted to know. On the other hand, she was the only one who recognized her. No one, to the best of their recollection, had ever seen Sojourner before. It was Valerie Parker, one of the supervisors, who voiced what the others perhaps had hesitated to express in words.

'I'm afraid all black people look much alike to me.'

Osman Messaoud, passing her on his way to one of the computers, said nastily, 'How peculiar. All whiteys look alike to black people.'

517

'I wasn't talking to you,' said Valerie.

'No, I don't suppose you were. You keep your racist remarks for like-minded individuals.'

A momentary hesitation – should he stand up and be counted? Should he hotly deny the imputation? – and Vine had left them to an argument that was developing into a low-voiced hissing match. Niall Clarke, the other supervisor, a would-be sociologist, said, 'I don't think white people do know black people in a society like this. I mean, in a place like Kingsmarkham, a country town. After all, up until about ten years ago there weren't any black people here. You'd turn round and stare if you saw one in the street. When I was at school there weren't any black pupils. I doubt if we've got more than three or four blacks signing on here now.'

Valerie Parker, routed by Messaoud and rather pink in the face, said, 'What was her name?'

'I wish I knew.'

'I mean we could try checking with the computer if we knew her name. I mean, there are probably hundreds with the same name but we could . . .'

'I don't know her name,' Vine said, and he had a feeling he was never going to find out.

Even without a name, it should be easy to identify and locate a lost black girl in a town like Kingsmarkham where whites overwhelmingly predominated, but it wasn't. She had been directed to this place, presumably she started on her way to this place, but somewhere along the line she had vanished. Or she had reached here but no one had noticed her. Privately, Vine thought she had never got here, he would want to know more from Oni Johnson before he pursued this line. On his way to the door he passed the booth where Peter Stanton was advising a new claimant and he saw that the claimant was Diana Graddon.

Until now he hadn't made up his mind whether to talk to her or not. It seemed unnecessary, even prurient. Of course Wexford's remark had rung a bell and of course he had thought about it, before falling asleep and from the moment he awoke. But what was it to him, or to any of them, if this woman had once been Snow's girlfriend, and been superseded by Annette Bystock? What was its relevance to this case of two murders and one attempted murder? But now he had seen her Vine sat down on one of the grey chairs next to a plastic pot with its plastic peperomia and waited.

What sort of an impression did that Stanton make on women, eyeing them like that, his eyes rolling? Of course Diana Graddon was quite attractive but Vine had the feeling that all that would ever matter to Stanton was that she was youngish and a woman. He pulled a leaflet called 'Income Support, See If You Are Entitled' out of the rack and read it to pass the time.

It took Burden no more than twenty minutes to arrive at the Infirmary with the photograph of Sojourner. Oni Johnson recognized her at once.

'That's her. That's the girl spoke to me outside Thomas Proctor.'

It must have been July the fifth, Wexford thought. She was dead by the evening. Mavrikiev had said she died at least twelve days before she was found on the seventeenth. Oni Johnson had spoken to her a matter of hours before she died.

'I don't suppose she told you her name?' Burden asked.

'She never said her name. Why should she? Never said where she come from, no way. She say to me where she going, to the Job Centre, to get a job. That all she say. *Mo fé mò ibit'ó gbé wà?*'

'Can you describe her?'

'Someone been beating her, that I do know. I seen *that* before. Her lip's been cut and her eye, you don't get no bruises like that walking into doors, no way. So I tell her where ESJ is, down the road and right and right again, between Nationwide and Marks and Spencers, and then I say to her, who been beating you?'

'You said that in English or in Yoruba?'

'In Yoruba. And she say to me, *bí ojú kò bá kán ẹ ni, ṁ bá là ọ̀ràn náà yé ẹ.* I tell you what that mean. "If you are not in a hurry, I would like to explain to you."'

Wexford's heart did a little bounce. 'And did she?'

Oni shook her head vigorously. 'I say, yes, I have the time, the children not coming out for five minutes, ten minutes, yet, but then, when I am saying this, a car pull up right by where I stand, a mother driving a car, right? She come to fetch her child and I say to her, no, you can't park here, you go further down road, and when I am done with all this I turn round but that young girl, she gone.'

'What, gone out of sight?'

'I could see her, long way away, long way off down the road.'

'Tell me what she was wearing.'

519

'Had a cloth round her head, a kind of a blue cloth. A dress with flowers, white with pink flowers, and shoes like Raffy wear.'

Both policemen looked at Raffy's feet, twisted round the chair legs. Black canvas lace-up half-boots with rubber welt and soles, perhaps the cheapest footwear obtainable in Kingsmarkham's most down-market shoe shop.

'Can you remember which direction she came from, Mrs Johnson?'

'I never see her till she's there, talking in my ear. I don't see her coming from the High Street, so maybe she come from other end. Maybe she come from Glebe Lane end where there's fields. Maybe she drop from helicopter into field, huh?'

'She talked to you in Yoruba,' said Wexford. 'But she could speak English?'

'Oh, sure. Little bit. Like me when I come here. I say to her, you go down there, long way down, and you in High Street, you turn right and after little way right again and there's ESJ between Nationwide and Marks and Spencers. It all English words so I say it in English. And she nods her head like this...' Oni Johnson nodded her bandaged head vigorously, 'and say what I say, down here and right and right again, and here it is between Nationwide and Marks and Spencers. And then I ask her who been beating her.'

'Mrs Johnson, can you remember anything about her manner? The way she was? Was she out of breath? Had she been running? Was she happy or sad? Was she nervous?'

The smile which had come back into Oni's face slowly faded. She frowned a little and nodded again, but less energetically. 'It was like someone is after her,' she said, 'someone chasing after her. She was frightened. But after she gone I watch and the place empty, no one is after her, no one chasing. But I can tell you, she very frightened.'

'We can discount being dropped from a helicopter,' Wexford said in the car. 'Though the idea does have its attractions. She came from somewhere in the neighbourhood, Glebe Road, Glebe Lane, Lichfield Road, Belper Road ... ' He considered, seeing the topography in his mind's eye, 'Harrow Avenue, Wantage Avenue, Ashley Grove ... '

'Or across the fields beyond Glebe End.'

'What – from Sewingbury or Mynford?'

'Why not? Neither of them are that far.' Burden considered. 'Bruce

520

Snow lives in Harrow Avenue, or he used to. He was living there on July the fifth.'

'Yes. But if you can think of some reason for Bruce or Carolyn Snow to be chasing a terrified black girl down Glebe Road at three-thirty in the afternoon, you're a better scenario-maker than I am. Mike, this isn't a very big place even now. She could have come from anywhere north of the High Street and that includes your house and mine.'

'And the Akandes,' said Burden.

'Those shoes – is there any point in asking around the shoe shops to see if a black woman bought those sort of shoes recently?'

'It can't do any harm,' said Wexford, 'though she's not likely to have left her name and address on their mailing list, is she?'

'Meanwhile, we've got all this new stuff but we're no nearer knowing who she was, are we?'

'We probably are but we don't know it yet. For instance we know the motive behind the attack on Oni. Someone wanted to stop us getting that information about Sojourner out of her.'

'Then why not do it two weeks ago?' Burden objected.

'Very likely because although he, whoever he is, knew Oni Johnson had that information, he never supposed we would run her to earth. He never imagined we'd get to speak to someone whose tenuous connection with Sojourner was merely that she happened by chance to ask her the way in the street. But last Thursday he realized he was wrong. *He saw Karen and me talking to Oni outside the Thomas Proctor.*'

'He?'

'He or she, or let's say, his or her agent. Someone in the know saw us. The rest was guesswork and he had just about an hour in which to get to Castlegate and wait at the top of those stairs. We're going to do a house-to-house, Mike. We're going to question every house-holder in Kingsmarkham north of the High Street.'

At the Benefit Office they found themselves asking the same questions that Barry Vine had asked an hour before. But Barry had only conjectured that Sojourner had been there without knowing when; Wexford was almost positive that she had come, into the building on Monday, 5 July, no later than four o'clock in the afternoon.

'Looking for work,' he said to Ingrid.

'Aren't they all?' Ingrid turned the blue beam of her eyes on him and lightly lifted her shoulders. 'I *wish* I'd seen her, I really do.' The implication was that she wished it for his sake, so that she could please him. 'But I *would* remember on account of seeing Melanie Akande next day. I'd have thought when I saw Melanie, wow, look at that, how odd, another black girl I've never seen in here before.' She gave him a rueful smile. 'But I didn't see her.'

'She may have lived near you,' Wexford persisted. 'In Glebe Lane or at Glebe End. If you didn't see her in here that day, do you think you ever saw her near where you live? In the street? Looking out of a window? In a shop?'

She looked as if she pitied him. He had this onerous task to perform, this quest to make, this job to do, and she was so sorry . . . If only she could help, if only there was something she could do to make his burden lighter. Her head was a little on one side, a characteristic gesture. He thought how it would be if he were, say, twenty-five again, and there was this girl that he was obliged to keep meeting, a girl who was spoken for in a way, but only in a way, and he wondered how he would have gone about cutting Jeremy Lang out. Not 'if' but 'how', for he was sure he would have attempted it, if only for the bluest eyes on earth. . . .

'I've never seen her in all my life,' Ingrid said and, suddenly brisk again, she pressed the buttons on her machine that would light up the next client's number above their heads.

Deep in thought, Wexford made his way back through the Job Centre area and the free-standing advertising on which potential employers offered what situations were vacant. Most of them gave no names and no locations, stating only pitifully low wages and curious trades, some of which he had never before heard of. He was momentarily distracted and let his eye run down the ranks of cards. In fact, there were few jobs here that anyone, however desperate, would want to apply for and a phrase came into his mind: 'needy nothing trimmed in jollity. . . .' Inadequate salaries were offered to those willing to care full time for three children under four or combine twenty hours a week assisting in a boarding kennels with keeping house for a family of five.

He didn't know why an advertisement for a children's nanny (no previous experience required) while the parents were abroad on business seemed to ring a bell in his mind. But he knew his intuition was usually sound and he was searching back in his memory, trying to find a link, when he went outside to find Burden.

The boys sitting on the wall outside had already been shown Sojourner's photograph by Barry Vine. 'That other one', was how the short boy with the golden hair described him. The boy with the ponytail seemed to be doing his best to get through his packet of twenty cigarettes by lunchtime, for eleven stubs lay in the ash round his feet. Burden pinned his hopes on their ability now to be more specific.

'On a Monday afternoon,' he said. 'The first Monday of July. At about four.'

The shaven-headed boy with the range of tee-shirts – he was in a faded red one today with Michael Jackson's face on it – looked at the photograph and, armed with these new details, said as if squeezing the statement out, as if it was the result of tremendous intellectual effort, 'I might've.'

'You might have seen her? You might have seen her go into the Benefit Office?'

'The other one asked me that. I don't mean that. I said I never see her go in there.'

Wexford said quickly, 'But you did see her.'

A glance at ponytail and, 'What d'you reckon, Danny? It's a long time back.'

'I never seen her, man,' said Danny, stubbing out his cigarette and coughing. With nothing to do with his hands, he began picking at the skin round his fingernails.

The boy with the golden hair said, 'I never seen her neither. D'you reckon you saw her, Rossy?'

'I might've,' said the one in the tee-shirt. 'I might've seen her across the road. Standing over there looking. There was me and Danny and Gary and a couple of other kids, don't know what they call them, we was all on the steps like now, only more of us, and she was over there looking.'

He had said so before. Burden remembered now. In the early days of the hunt for Melanie Akande, he had mentioned seeing a black girl on the Monday. 'And that was on July the fifth in the afternoon?' he asked, full of hope.

But if it had been that Monday he had now forgotten. 'Don't know about that, don't know the day or the time. It was hot, I do know that. I took me top off to get a bit of sun and this old bat come along and says to me, that's the way to get skin cancer, young man. I told her what she could do, silly old cow.'

'The girl on the other side, do you think she wanted to go into the Benefit Office?'

Danny spoke while still picking bits of his cuticles, 'If she'd wanted to, why'd she never cross the road? She'd only to cross the road.'

'But you didn't see her, did you?' Burden asked.

'Me? No, I never see her. But it stands to reason, she'd only to cross the road.'

'She never did,' said Rossy, and losing interest, 'Give us one of your fags, Dan.'


Half an hour before, standing on the same spot, Diana Graddon had said to Vine, 'Do you mind if I smoke?' They were about to get into his car.

'I'd rather you waited till we've got you home.'

She shrugged and compressed her lips. He was fascinated by her resemblance to Annette Bystock. They might have been sisters. This woman was the younger by a few years and she was slimmer than Annette, less voluptuous, but they had the same dark curly hair, similar bold features, big mouth, strong nose and round dark eyes, only Annette's had been brown and this woman's were a bluish-grey.

Asked about Snow, she had made no attempt to deny the relationship, though she showed considerable surprise. 'It was ten years ago!'

'D'you mind telling me if it was you introduced him to Annette Bystock?'

Surprise was renewed. She was incredulous. 'How could you possibly know?'

Vine, of course, was well-practised in parrying such enquiries. 'The relationship hadn't lasted long, I'd guess.'

'A year,' said Diana Graddon. 'I found out he'd got children. The youngest was only three. Funny, how it all comes back. I haven't thought about any of this for years.'

'But you didn't split up then?'

'We started having rows. Look, I was only twenty-five and I didn't see why I should settle for him sneaking round for an hour in the evening and then not hearing a word for a week and then a phone call and another bang-bang, thank you very much, sir. He did take me out but only once in a blue moon. I didn't want him permanently either, I mean I wasn't thinking marriage or anything like that. I was young but I wasn't daft. I could just envisage what that'd be, living with a guy who'd got three kids and a wife to keep and a possessive wife by all accounts.' She drew breath and Vine, drawing up outside the house in Ladyhall Road, was wondering how much more of this he wanted to hear when she said, 'He came round one evening when Annette was there. Oh, I knew he'd come, he always phoned first, but I thought, so what? We'll have a *social* evening for once, we'll actually manage to meet without having sex, see what he thinks about that, though I could imagine. Funny how it all comes back, isn't it? Annette didn't know who he was or . . . well, what we were to each other, if you see what I mean.' An unpleasant thought seemed to strike her. 'You don't mean you think he did it? Killed her, I mean?'

Vine smiled. 'Can we go into the house, Miss Graddon?'

'Oh, yes, sure.' She unlocked the door. Helen Ringstead appeared not to be at home. They went into the living room. 'I mean,' she said, 'he and Annette, they hardly knew each other. I don't suppose they ever met again.'

So she didn't know . . . he was amused. Odious though Snow might be, you had to hand it to him, he had it all worked out. Vine was going to ask another question but he didn't have to.

'He broke things off soon after that. He told me his wife had found out. Someone she knew had seen us together in a restaurant on one of the *rare* occasions he gave me dinner. This woman had heard him call me Diana. He confessed it all to her, threw himself on her mercy, or so he said.'

'Was it about then that you told Annette there was a flat for sale opposite?'

'It must have been. She'd got divorced a little bit before that. We were still friends then.' Diana Graddon lit the cigarette Vine had denied her in the car. She drew in a long inhalation. 'The fact is, I don't know why we stopped being friends. You'd think we'd have been in and out of each other's houses, living more or less opposite, but we sort of drifted apart, and I think it was her doing. She sort of withdrew into herself. And what's more, I don't think she's had a boyfriend since she split up with Stephen. But I'm just amazed when you say you suspect Bruce.'

He hadn't said it. Vine marvelled at Snow's structure of deceit and double-dealing. However much as a human being he deplored

525

Snow's behaviour, as a man he could not fail to admire his chicanery. He had kept his affair with Diana a secret from Annette and his affair with Annette a secret from Diana, and if he had not succeeded in keeping Diana a secret from his wife he had lulled Carolyn for nine years into the belief that her marriage was inviolable. Had Annette's move to Ladyhall Gardens, opposite Diana, dismayed him? Or had it rather given him the perfect reason for his new relationship to remain on the level of a simple sexual transaction, continually repeated? It was obviously unwise to entertain a girlfriend in a restaurant and indiscreet to go to her home, so he was protected against closer involvement.

What had he said to Annette? Don't be too friendly with Diana, she knows my wife? Or even, she's quite capable of getting in touch with my wife? The best liars stick as close to the truth as mendacity allows.

'I mean, Bruce would have had to know her,' Diana persisted. 'He'd have had to have a motive, wouldn't he? Believe me, I'd have seen him if he'd ever been to see her here and I never did. I mean, I saw everyone Annette knew, I must have seen everyone who ever called there.' She hesitated, coughed a little. The cigarette trembled in her fingers. 'It's funny, but I was sort of fascinated by her. I wonder why that was? I don't know why I'm asking you, you're not a psychologist, but I wonder if a psychologist would say it was because she . . . well, she rejected me really, didn't she?'

Vine, who knew Wexford's methods, waited in silence. He might not be a psychologist but he knew what psychotherapists did. They put the patient or client or whatever on a couch and they listened. A word uttered at the wrong time might be fatal. He would listen, though he didn't know what he was listening for. Nor did Freud, he thought.

'I suppose I resented that. I used to say to myself, who does she think she is, giving me the cold shoulder? I saw her come in with that pretty girl sometimes, the one from the employment office that she worked with, and she was a bit pally with Edwina What's-her-name. But, d'you know, that was all. Well, I saw her cousin there once or twice, a Mrs Winster, I can't remember her first name. Joan, Jean, Jane. No man ever set foot in the place, it was like a nunnery. I mean, the idea of Bruce going in there, it's a laugh really.' She smiled a little at the absurdity of the notion. 'Old Bruce,' she said. 'What's he up to

526

these days? Apart from murdering women he doesn't know?' The smile split into laughter.

Disappointment slumped Vine's shoulders. She had nothing to tell him. It was all over. He thought of revealing all to her in the hope that disbelief, the slow dawning of enlightenment, the subsequent rage, would bring forth revelations. But if there were no revelations to deliver? He said idly, preparing to go,

'You told me you last saw her on the Monday evening?'

'Yes, I was going away to stay with my boyfriend in Pomfret.' She gave a sidelong smile, glad of the opportunity to tell him Snow had a successor. 'It was always a bit awkward, you can imagine, Annette and me, we sort of avoided each other, but we happened to look across the road at the same time. She said hello and I said hello and then I remembered I'd left a sweater I wanted behind, so I went back.

'When I came out again – oh, it was no more than two minutes, if that – she'd gone into the flats and there was this girl standing outside the door, the front door of Ladyhall Court, I mean. Well, Annette must have gone straight into her living room to open the window. She leaned out and saw the girl and the girl – she was a black girl, incidentally – she went over to the window and said something and that . . . well, that was the last time I ever saw Annette.'

# 19

Which way is it to find work? She had asked Oni Johnson this in an obscure language because there was something about Oni that told her this woman was Nigerian too.

And Sojourner had done what she was told and walked on, southwards to the High Street, fearful of some pursuer, but reaching there unscathed, reaching the Benefit Office too. Instead of going in, she had waited on the other side of the street, staring. Why hadn't she crossed the road, as Rossy suggested, and gone in?

'Men,' said Wexford. 'She was scared of men. Yes, OK, I know Rossy and Danny and Co don't seem very intimidating to us, but neither you nor I is a seventeen-year-old and, I suspect, extremely unsophisticated black girl. She's got an inbuilt fear and distrust of whites anyway. Some man had been beating her and she was going to tell Oni about it but just at that moment those kids had to come out of school.

'Men are more frightening to women than other women are. Yes, they are, Mike, whether you like it or not. And here are this lot, one of them stripped down to nothing but his jeans, sitting there, more of less barring the door. And to crown it all, when a woman comes along and speaks to one of them he shouts at her, gives her some obscene instruction, calls her a silly old cow – or worse. That's what he tells *you* he calls her.'

The house-to-house enquiries had begun. With a street plan of north Kingsmarkham in front of him, Wexford was beginning to see how the town had expanded since first he came there. Estates as big as villages had been built on the northern outskirts. In the inner areas old houses had been pulled down, as in Ladyhill Avenue, and each one replaced by a dozen small ones and yet another block of flats.

528

The ward in which he would vote in the council election had once comprised the whole town; now it was a small section of it. He looked up from the map as Burden said,

'So Sojourner hangs about on the opposite pavement – what for? Just in the hope that they'll go away?'

'Or that someone will come out. She'll have seen clients go in and come out again but no one after about three-thirty, remember. No one signs-on on a Monday and the New Claims Advisers have their last appointment at three-fifteen. So anyone who comes out at four-thirty is going to have to be working there.'

'You're saying she followed Annette home?'

'Why not?'

'You mean it was just chance she picked Annette?'

'Not quite,' said Wexford. 'Most of the other people that work there have cars parked in the car park at the back. They wouldn't come out the front way.'

'Stanton doesn't take his car to work,' Burden objected. 'And nor does Messaoud. His wife has it in the day.'

'They're men. Sojourner wouldn't have followed a man.'

'All right, she follows Annette across the High Street, down Queen Street over there ... ' as if Wexford hadn't a street plan in front of him, 'along Manor Road and into Ladyhall Gardens. It's then that Diana Graddon sees her. Or, rather, she sees Annette and when she comes out a second time, she sees Sojourner at the front door of Ladyhall Court.'

'To be precise, she sees Annette leaning out of the window talking to Sojourner. Did Annette let her into the house? Did she want to be let in?'

'Annette must have told her that if she wanted work, or wanted the dole, her only course was to come to the Benefit Office next day, the Tuesday. Maybe she said to ask for her and gave her her name but didn't let her in. She wasn't very free about letting people into her flat.'

'So what did Sojourner say that made Annette wonder if she should tell the police?'

'You think that's what it was? It was Sojourner that told her that, whatever it was? This was twenty-four hours, more than twenty-four hours, before she spoke on the phone to cousin Jane on Tuesday evening.'

'I know, Mike. I'm guessing. But look at it this way. Sojourner said something to Annette that she didn't like or made her suspicious. What it was we don't know, very likely what she was going to tell Oni but never did, something about the man who beat her and maybe where he lived. However, we do know that Sojourner never took the advice Annette presumably gave her, to come to the Benefit Office next day.

'When she didn't come, don't you think it likely that Annette became uneasy? Perhaps she wanted to discuss whatever it was with Sojourner before she took any steps. But by that time Annette was feeling unwell. She went home, went to bed, was ill enough to tell Snow she couldn't see him next day but was still worried enough to pass her worries on to her cousin.

'As to why I think the something the police should know came from Sojourner, well, she *died* that night, didn't she, she was murdered that night. She couldn't go to the Benefit Office because she was dead. And her failure to come must have compounded Annette's fears – only with that virus, believe me, for the time being you're not thinking about anyone but yourself.'

'So on the Monday evening, Annette just sent Sojourner back home, wherever that was?'

'She behaved, no doubt, as anyone would in the circumstances. Probably she didn't give any advice at all beyond telling her to come to the Benefit Office. Unfortunately, tragically, Sojourner had nowhere else to go but home. What happened next we've no idea, but we can make a reasonable guess that someone at home, father, brother, husband even, some male relative, shall we say "punished" her for running away?'

'The person she was afraid was pursuing her?'

'Oh, yes.'

'How did he know about Oni Johnson? How did he know about Annette?'

'She told him, don't you think?'

Burden looked as if he would like to ask why but he didn't. 'You said Sojourner "told him". Told who? Her father? Her brother? Husband? Boyfriend?'

'Husband or boyfriend, it would have to be. We know all the black people here, Mike, we've found them all, we've talked to them. But she may have had a white boyfriend.'

All the while Wexford talked he had been thinking, inescapably, of Dr Akande. It sometimes seemed to him that all roads led back to the

530

Akandes and that, conversely, every route he took he found one or other of the Akandes there. He picked up the phone and asked Pemberton to come up.

'Bill, I want you to get on to Kimberley Pearson's family and find out everything you can about them.'

Pemberton attempted to disguise his incomprehension and failed. 'Zack Nelson's girlfriend,' said Burden.

'Yes. Oh, sure. What, parents, d'you mean? Where are they?'

'I don't know. I haven't the faintest, somewhere within a radius of twenty miles, say. There is, or was, a grandmother. I want to know where she lived and when she died. And Kimberley's not to know. I don't want a hint of this reaching Kimberley.'

With a flash of insight that surprised Wexford and pleased him, Pemberton said, 'Do you reckon Kimberley's life's in danger, sir? Is she the next girl he's after?'

Wexford said slowly, 'Not if we keep away from her. Not if he – or she – thinks we've done with her. I'm going back to the hospital. I want to talk to Oni again.' He added, remembering what Freeborn had accused him of, 'But I'm not even going to drive down Stowerton High Street, I'll go the long way round.'

Mhonum Ling was there. If there were to be a competition for the most over-dressed woman in Kingsmarkham, Wexford thought, it would be hard choosing between Oni's sister and Anouk Khoori. Mhonum's ankle-length pink skirt was just short enough to disclose her jewelled sandals. The tee-shirt she wore was a far cry from Danny's; it had sequins on it. He held Oni's hand for a moment and she gave him one of her tremendous smiles.

'I'm going to take you through all that again,' he said.

She made a face of mock-horror but he thought she enjoyed it really. Raffy walked in, carrying a ghetto-blaster, mercifully not on. Wexford he was used to by now but he gave his aunt the sort of look more likely to be on the face of someone who has seen a lioness on the loose. When Oni repeated the things Sojourner had said in Yoruba, Mhonum shrugged her shoulders and turned her head to look Raffy up and down.

'When she'd gone out of sight,' Wexford said, 'did the children start coming out? Or did a lot of parents arrive before that?'

'Mothers and father, mostly mothers, they start coming five, ten minutes before children come out. That one in the car parked right

531

by my feet, the one I moved on, she was the first. Then all the others start coming.'

'I'd like you to think carefully about this, Mrs Johnson. Did you get the impression she ran away from you because she was afraid of *one of the parents seeing her?*'

Oni Johnson tried to remember. She screwed her eyes tight shut with the effort of concentration. Mhonum Ling said, 'You know her name yet?'

'Not yet, Mrs Ling.'

'What you bring that radio in here for, Raffy?' she said to her nephew and, without waiting for an answer, 'You go down the drinks machine and fetch a Diet Fanta for auntie and one for your mummy.' She produced a handful of change from her pink patent-leather bag. 'And have yourself a coke, good boy, hurry up now.'

Opening her eyes, Oni said, 'No good, I don't know. I never did know. She frightened, she in big hurry, but I don't know what she frightened of.'

He went down the stairs with the silent boy pattering along in front of him. Raffy stopped at the drinks machine, stared hopelessly at the keys and the pictures above them. Diet Coke he could wrest from it. Fanta presented more of a problem. Wexford put out a finger as he passed, tapped the relevant key and walked on out to the car park. At least a hundred cars had arrived since he left his. He was remembering how he had told the Chief Constable and a good many other people besides that he would have this case solved by the end of the week. Early days, though, it was only Tuesday.

Turning out of the hospital gates and into the roundabout, he nearly took the first exit. Then he remembered he had to avoid the High Street and drove round to the third. Perhaps he was being over-scrupulous. No one was following him, the idea was ridiculous, it wasn't as if he intended to stop outside Clifton Court, still less call on Kimberley Pearson, but he took the third exit just the same. He might have saved Oni Johnson's life but he had terribly endangered it first.

This devious route took him along Charteris Road and into Sparta Grove. He hadn't been along that street since the little Epson boys were taken into care, and he had only gone there then to say a few words into the television cameras about parents who went off on holiday and left their children at home unattended. Now he tried to remember which of this three-storey Victorian row was their house. Not a slummy house at all, the Epsons weren't poor, if they didn't want their children with them they could easily have afforded to pay a child-minder.

He was driving slowly. Ahead of him a man came out of one of the houses, closed the front door behind him and got into a pink car parked at the pavement edge. Wexford pulled in and switched off the engine. The man was tall and heavily-built, fair-haired, young, but he had his back to him and Wexford couldn't see his face. He wasn't Epson. He was too young and Epson was black, a Jamaican.

The car moved off, gathering speed very rapidly, tearing round the corner into Charteris Road. He had seen that man in that car very recently and he had an idea the circumstances were somehow distasteful or that he wanted to avoid thinking about them. That, no doubt, was the reason he couldn't remember.

He sat there for a moment or two but memory had deserted him. His route home took him through the industrial estate, a stark and deserted place, half the factories boarded-up or to let. A narrow country lane led back on to the Kingsmarkham road and ten minutes later he was in his own house.

The answer to things had sometimes in the past come to him, directly or indirectly, from Sheila; from a remark she made or her latest interest or passion, or something she had given him to read. Whatever it was, it had set him on the right road. He needed her now, a word or two from her, a pointer.

But it was his other daughter visiting him this evening with Ben and Robin, having arranged to meet Neil in her parents' house after his job club session. Her indulgent mother had invited them all to stay for supper. Even as he digested this, Wexford thought how much Sylvia would hate being termed, even in his secret mind, his 'other daughter'. No father ever struggled so hard not to show the preference he felt and no father, he thought, so signally failed. As soon as he walked in the door he had realized he must resist phoning Sheila while Sylvia was there, or at least while Sylvia was in earshot.

The evening was warm. They sat outside, a ring of chairs round the sunshade table, and Sylvia's suggestion that they eat there was met, inevitably, by a version of her older son's favourite phrase.

'*Mushk eler.*'

'Well, it's a problem for me,' said Wexford. 'You know I can't stand al fresco eating, all those mosquitos. It's the same with picnics.'

The boys and their grandmother immediately engaged in argument about the merits and demerits of picnics. Sylvia, ignoring them, lay

533

back in her chair, half-closed her eyes, and began to talk about her counselling course, how completely different was the approach from when she did her social sciences degree, how the emphasis here was on people, on human interaction, on enabling and personal interdependence . . . It was ridiculous, Wexford thought, the way he was behaving, afraid to phone Sheila secretly, lest she had her answering machine on and would therefore ring back after an hour or two. How soon would Sylvia and family go? Not for hours. Neil wasn't expected for an hour.

Dora took the boys with her into the house. Robin was to lay the table, she said. The expected response didn't come, presumably because it *was* a problem.

'Wouldn't you like a drink?' he said to Sylvia, as much to stem the tide as because he wanted one.

'Sparkling water. Mostly we'll be dealing with depression and anxiety states. But there's always a lot of domestic violence and you have to bear in mind the secrecy imperative in creating confidence in the client. We shall counsel each other, I mean, of course, initially . . .'

When Wexford came back with her water and his beer she was still talking. She seemed to have reached the physical abuse by strong people of other, weaker people. Her eyes were shut now and she was staring up through her closed lids at the blue summer sky.

'Why do they do it?' said Wexford.

He had interrupted her in mid-flow. She opened her eyes and looked at him. 'Do what?'

'Men beat up their wives, people mistreat their kids.'

'Are you really asking me? Do you really want to know?'

A pang, a guilty wince, was the effect on him of these questions. It was as if she was amazed that he wanted to know anything she could tell him. She would talk, she would assert herself, on and on, relentlessly, but not to entertain or inform. To get back at him, to show him. Now he sounded as if he really wanted to know. Her tone was one of incredulity – you're asking *me*?

What he really wanted was to find a way of escape and phone Sheila. Instead he said, 'I'd like to know.'

She didn't answer directly. 'Have you ever heard of Benjamin Rush?'

'I don't think so.'

'He was the Dean of the Medical School at the University of

534

Pennsylvania. Oh, nearly two hundred years ago. He's known as the father of American psychiatry. Of course there was slavery then in the United States. One of the things Rush maintained was that all crimes are diseases and he thought not believing in God was a mental disease.'

'So what's he got to do with physical abuse?'

'Well, I bet you've never heard of this before, Dad. Rush made up something called a Theory of Negritude. He believed being black was a disease. Black people suffered from congenital leprosy but in such a mild form that pigmentation was its only symptom. Do you see what holding a theory like that means? It justifies sexual segregation and social maltreatment. It means you've got a reason for ill-treating people.'

'Wait a minute,' said Wexford. 'What you're saying is that if someone is an object of pity you're going to want to use physical violence against them? That seems cock-eyed. It's the contrary of everything social morals teach us.'

'No, listen. You *make* someone into an object of – not so much of pity as of weakness, sickness, stupidity, ineffectiveness, do you see what I mean? You hit them for their stupidity and their inability to respond, and when you've hurt them, marked them, they're even more sick and ugly, aren't they? And they're afraid and cringing too. Oh, I know this isn't very pleasant, but you did ask.'

'Go on,' he said.

'So you've got a frightened, stupid, even disabled person, silenced, made ugly, and what can you do with someone like that, someone who's unworthy of being treated well? You treat them badly because that's what they deserve. One thinks of poor little kids that no one can love because they're dirty, covered in snot and shit, and always screaming. So you beat them because they're hateful, they're low, they're *sub-human*. That's all they're good for, being hit, being reduced even further.'

He was silent. She mistook his silence for shock, not at the content of what she had said but because she had said it, and quick to make amends, said, 'Dad, it's horrible, I know, but I do have to know about these things, I have to try to understand something about the doer as well as the done-to.'

'No,' he said, 'It's not that. I know that. I'm a policeman, remember? There was something else you said, it struck a chord. One word. I can't remember . . .'

'"Sub-human"? "Ineffectiveness?"'

'No. It'll come to me.' He got up. 'Thank you, Sylvia. You don't know how you've helped me.' Her look went to his heart. For a moment she looked like her son Ben. He bent over and kissed her forehead. 'I know what it was,' he said, half to himself. 'It's come back to me.'

Upstairs, at his bedside as yet unread, were the leaflets and brochures Sheila had sent him, the literature of her latest passion. He would read them as soon as Sylvia had gone. But he had also remembered something about the man who came out of the Epsons' and had been driving the Epsons' car. He hadn't seen his face. And he hadn't seen the face of whoever was driving that car when a little boy had come out of the Thomas Proctor gates and got into it.

Wexford could see that little boy quite clearly, a brown boy with brown curly hair, who could have been that man's son but only if his mother was black and only if he had fathered him when he was a boy himself.

Was this the man Sojourner had been running to escape a fortnight before?

No, Wexford thought, that wasn't the way it was at all . . .

# 20

The usual call on the Akandes must be postponed. If Wexford's guess was right, he would be in no mood to face them with this at the forefront of his mind. And what was there to say? Even the common pleasantries, weather commentary, enquiries after their health, would come stiltedly. He thought of how he had tried to prepare them, telling them to abandon hope, and he remembered Akande's optimism, flaring one day, dying the next.

He drove himself to work, passing the Akandes' house but keeping his eyes on the road ahead. Reports awaited him on the progress of the house-to-house enquiries but they were negative, they had yielded nothing apart from racism among unlikely householders and an unsuspected liberal attitude where prejudice was most anticipated. When it came to human beings, there was no knowing. Malahyde, Pemberton, Archbold and Donaldson would keep on all day, ringing doorbells, showing the photograph, asking. If Kingsmarkham produced nothing, they would begin on the villages, Mynford, Myfleet, Cheriton.

Wexford took Barry Vine with him to Stowerton. They avoided the High Street and went by way of Waterford Avenue where the Chief Constable's house was. The neighbourhoods changed very quickly in Stowerton and it was a long stone's throw to Sparta Grove. Wexford smiled to himself as they passed the house, thinking how near Freeborn had been to it all, this . . . well, conspiracy, wasn't it? – going on under his nose.

The pink car was parked in the road, back where he had frst seen it the night before. In the broad daylight of a sunny morning it looked very dirty. A finger graffitist had written 'Clean me now' in the dust on its boot lid. Not a window in the house was open. It seemed empty – but the car was there.

The doorbell wasn't working. Vine banged smartly on the knocker and remarked, looking up at the closed windows, that nine in the morning was early for some people. He knocked again and was about to bellow through the letter box when the sash of an upstairs window was raised and the man whose back Wexford had seen the evening before and had been unable to identify, put his head out. It was Christopher Riding.

'Police,' said Wexford. 'Remember me?'

'Should I?'

'Chief Inspector Wexford, Kingsmarkham CID. Come down and let us in, please.'

They waited a long time. Scuffling noises came from inside and the sound of something made of glass being dropped and broken. A string of muffled curses was followed by a dull thump. Vine suggested wistfully that it would be a good idea to kick the door down.

'No, here he comes.'

The door was opened cautiously. A child of about four put his head round it and giggled. He was peremptorily pulled back and the man whose face had appeared at the window stood there. He wore shorts and a heavy, very dirty, Aran sweater. His legs and feet were bare.

'What d'you want?'

'To come in.'

'You'll need a warrant for that,' said Christopher Riding. 'You're not coming in here without one. It's not my property.'

'No, it's the property of Mr and Mrs Epson. Where are they this time? Lanzarote?'

He was a little disconcerted, enough to step back. Wexford, who had the edge on him as far as height went, if not youth, gave him a shove with his elbow and pushed past him into the house. Vine followed, shaking off Riding's detaining hand. The child began to wail.

It was a house of numerous little rooms, a steep staircase climbing up its centre. In the middle of the staircase stood an older child, a grubby soft toy trailing from one hand. It was the brown boy with brown curly hair Wexford had seen come out of Thomas Proctor. When he saw Wexford he turned tail and fled upstairs. The sound of

538

a radio came from behind a closed door. Wexford opened it quietly. On all-fours on the floor, a girl was picking up broken glass – no doubt the remains of the object which they had heard dropped – and putting the pieces on to a folded newspaper. She turned her head at the sound of his careful cough, sprang to her feet and let out a cry.

'Good morning,' Wexford said. 'Melanie Akande, I presume?'

His coolness belied his true feelings. Extreme relief at finding her alive and well and living in Stowerton fought in his mind with anger and a kind of appalled fear for her parents. Suppose Sheila had done this? How would he have felt if his daughter had done this?

Christopher Riding leant against the fireplace, a cynical half-amused expression on his face. Having looked at first as if she was going to cry, Melanie had controlled her tears and now sat in an attitude of despair. In her surprise she had cut her finger on one of the pieces of glass and it bled unheeded. Blood trickled on to her bare feet. From upstairs one of the Epson children began to wail.

'Go and see what he wants, will you?' Melanie spoke to Riding as if they had been married for years and not too happily.

'Christ.'

Riding shrugged his shoulders with great drama. The younger boy got hold of his jeans and hung on, burying his face in the back of the man's knees. Christopher walked off, dragging the child behind him, and banged the door.

'Where are Mr and Mrs Epson?' Wexford said.

'Sicily. They're coming back tonight.'

'And what were you planning to do?'

She sighed. 'I don't know.' The sight of her finger brought the tears back once more to her eyes. She started wrapping a tissue round it. 'See if they'll keep me on, I suppose. I don't know, God knows, sleep on the streets.'

She was dressed exactly as, according to the missing person description, she had been on the day she vanished, in jeans, a white shirt and a long embroidered waistcoat. The look on her face was one of utter disenchantment with the life she found herself in.

'Do you want to tell me about it here or shall we go to the police station?'

'I can't leave the kids, can I?'

Wexford thought about it. There was a funny side which he might come to see later on. Of course she couldn't leave the kids. The

Epson children were on the Social Services register and had been since their parents were given suspended prison sentences for leaving them in the house alone for a week. But he didn't fancy fetching out a child care officer, getting a care order made, setting the whole machinery in motion for the sake of removing Melanie Akande for one day. No doubt the Epsons, considerably frightened by what had happened last time, had more or less properly engaged her to look after their two sons.

'What did you do? Answer an ad in the Job Centre?'

Melanie nodded. 'Mrs Epson, she said to call her Fiona, she was in there. I'd been talking to the New Claims Officer and when I was done I sort of wandered over into the jobs part and there was this woman standing by the board that advertises jobs for nannies and minders and whatever. I'd never thought of that sort of work but I was looking at it and she said did I want to come and work for her for three weeks.

'Well, I knew you weren't supposed to go with people who offer you jobs like that but a woman seemed different. I mean, it's because of sexual harassment, isn't it? She said, why not come and see, so I went with her. She had a car in the car park and we went out the side door – that car you saw outside.'

'That's why those boys outside never saw you leave,' said Vine.

'Maybe.' A thought struck her. 'Have my parents been looking for me?'

'The whole country's been looking for you,' said Vine. 'Didn't you see the papers? Didn't you see the telly?'

'The TV broke down and we didn't know who to get to come and see to it. I never saw a paper.'

'Your mother thought at first you were with Euan Sinclair,' said Wexford. 'She *feared* it was possible. Then she thought you were dead. Mrs Epson brought you here, then? Just like that? She didn't ask if you wanted to go home first, if you wanted to fetch your things?'

'They were going away the next day. They'd more or less decided they'd have to take the kids. I can understand they didn't want to. They're *awful* kids.'

'Not surprising, is it?' said Vine, the conscientious father.

Melanie lifted her shoulders. 'I said to Fiona that I could stay if she wanted. I'd got my things with me, you see . . . well, I'd got enough on account of I'd been going to Laurel's. But I didn't want to go

540

there. I had a date with Euan first but I didn't want to meet him, I didn't want to hear any more of his lies. This house and being here was just what I wanted. Anyway, I thought so. I'd earn some money that wasn't a grant or *pocket money* from Dad. I thought I'd be alone and that was what I wanted, to be alone for a bit. But you're not alone with kids.'

'Christopher Riding wasn't with you all the time?'

'I don't know where he was. I didn't know him very well – not then. It was – it was after I'd been here about a week. I was nearly giving up, those kids are so terrible, I had to drive the big one to school, that's why they left me the car, and Chris saw me, he recognized me, and then he – he followed me back here.'

After she had been there about a week, Wexford thought. That would have been the day or the day after he had talked to Christopher Riding and asked him about Melanie. At least he had been telling the truth then.

'He thought it was funny,' Melanie said. 'I mean, the whole set-up. It sort of fascinated him. He stayed a bit.' She looked away. 'I mean, he came and he went. He helped me with the kids. They *are* awful kids.'

'And were you an awful kid, Melanie?' said Vine. 'It's a pretty awful daughter, isn't it, that goes off, disappears, without a word to her parents? Lets them think she's dead? She's been murdered?'

'They couldn't have thought that!'

'Of course they did. What stopped you making one phone call?'

She was silent, looking down at the blood-soaked tissue on her finger. Wexford thought of all the people who must have seen her and who did nothing about it, who did nothing because she was always with two black children they took to be her children. Or saw her with Riding, that they took to be the father of the children with them. Wexford had thought a missing black girl should be easy to find because black people were rare here, but the reverse was true. It was for that very reason that she had failed to be recognized.

'They wouldn't have let me stay here,' Melanie said in a voice not much above a whisper. Christopher, who had come back into the room, got a sidelong unhappy look. 'My mother would have called it being a servant. My father would have come and fetched me home.' Her voice rose and there was a hysterical edge to it. 'You don't know what it's like at home. No one knows.' She gave Christopher a bitter look. 'And I can't get away if I haven't got a job and a – a roof.' She said to Wexford, picking him for some reason, 'Can I talk to you alone? Just for a minute?'

A shattering scream split the air. It came from upstairs but it might have been in the same room. The scream was followed by a violent crash. Melanie shouted, 'Oh God!' and 'Go and see what he's doing, Chris, *please*.'

'Go yourself,' said Christopher, laughing.

'I *can't* go. They want me here.'

'For Christ's sake, I've had enough of this. I don't know what the attraction was in the first place.'

'I do!'

'It's wearing thin now at any rate.'

'I will go,' said Barry Vine in stern admonitory tones.

Wexford said to Melanie, 'We'll go into one of the other rooms.'

A bleak place that no one seemed to use with a dining table and chairs round it and a bicycle in one corner. A green window blind was pulled down to its fullest extent. Wexford motioned the girl to a chair and sat down opposite her.

'What did you want to say to me?'

'I thought of having a baby,' she said, 'just so that the council would give me a place.'

'More likely put you up in one of their famous bed and breakfasts.'

'That would be better than Ollerton Avenue.'

'Really? What's so bad about it?'

She relaxed quite suddenly. She put her elbows on the table and gave him a look that was conspiratorial, secrets-sharing. Her wry smile made her enormously attractive. She was at once pretty and charming. 'You don't know,' she said. 'You don't know what they're really like. You just see the hard-working kindly GP and his beautiful efficient wife. They're fanatics, those two, they're obsessed.'

'In what respect?'

'They're probably better educated than almost anyone in this place. That's for a start. My mother got a science degree before she started nursing and she's just about everything you can be as a nurse, she's got qualifications in *everything*. Medical and psychiatric, you name it, she's got it. When we were kids, Patrick and me, we never saw her, she was off all the time getting more certificates. Our gran and our aunties looked after us. My father may be just a GP but he's a surgeon too, he's a Fellow of the Royal College of Surgeons, he can

542

do all sorts of surgery, not just take out an appendix. He could easily be as good as Chris's dad.'

'So they were ambitious for you?'

'Are you kidding?' said Melanie. 'You know what they call people like them? The Ebony Elite. The black *crème de la crème*. Our futures were all mapped out for us before we were ten. Patrick was to be the great consultant surgeon, a brain surgeon probably – yes, really, that's not funny to them. And it's all right for him, that's what he wants, he's heading that way. But me? I'm not all that bright, I'm just average. I like singing and dancing, so I did my degree in that, but my parents *hated* it because it's what successful black women do, you see. They were glad when I couldn't get a job, they wanted me to go back to college so long as I could live at home. Or I'd be permitted to get office work and study for business management in the evenings *from home*. They talk about careers and training and degrees and promotion *all the time*. And they're too civilized to actually say it, but they're both bursting with pride because they found out that the people who wouldn't live next door to us both left school at sixteen.

'If I got away they thought I'd get back with Euan or someone like him.' She twisted her mouth into a bitter shape. 'And maybe I will now. I can't have a baby if I haven't got a man, can I? I wouldn't let Chris go that far, though that's what he came for, whatever he says. He only fancies me because I'm black. Charming, isn't it? I've had to fight him off.'

'Your parents shouldn't be kept in ignorance any longer. Not for an hour. They've been through a lot. Nothing they've done could justify that. They've suffered intensely, your father has lost weight, he looks an old man, but they've carried on with their work . . .'

'They would.'

'I'll tell them you're safe and then you must see them. Bring the children with you, you haven't much choice.' He thought of the waste of police time and resources, the cost of it all, the misery and pain and abuse, her brother's recall from his Asian journey, his own shame and self-justification. But he relented. Mawkish and sentimental it might be, but he was sorry for her. 'When do the Epsons get home?'

'She said nine or ten.'

'We'll send a car for you at six.' He got up, preparing to leave, but remembered something. 'One good turn deserves another. I'll want to talk to you again. All right?'

'Yes.'

'I suppose it was you talked to my officer on the phone when we rang up to enquire about the dead girl?'

She nodded. 'It gave me a fright. I thought that was *it*.'

'You'd better see to that finger. Have you any plasters in the house?'

'Thousands. That's top priority. Those kids are always wounding themselves and each other.'

Two reports from Pemberton were on his desk waiting for him. The first told him that the Kingsmarkham shoe shop which sold black cloth and rubber half-boots kept close records of their sales. In the past six months four pairs had been sold. An assistant remembered selling one pair to John Ling. She knew him because he was one of only two Chinese men in the town. Another pair had gone to someone she described as a 'bag lady', who had come into the shop carrying two bulging carrier bags and looked as if she slept on the street. The purchasers of the other pairs she couldn't remember.

Wexford gave the second report a quick glance and said, 'I want Pemberton here too.'

The phone in his hand, Burden said, 'You've gone quite red in the face.'

'I know. It's excitement. Listen to this. Kimberley Pearson's grandmother did die at the beginning of June but she didn't leave any money, still less any property. She'd been living in one of those council bungalows in Fontaine Road, Stowerton. Mrs Pearson, who was her daughter-in-law, knows nothing about any money coming to Kimberley, not family money that is, there *is* no family money, they're all as poor as church mice.'

'Clifton Court, where Kimberley moved after Zack was put on remand, is a block of rented flats – or apartments, as Pemberton mysteriously calls them. And who do you think the company is who owns the freehold of the block?'

'Just cut the suspense and tell me.'

'None other than Crescent Comestibles, or in other words, Wael Khoori, his brother and our local council candidate, his wife.'

Pemberton came in. 'You can rent those flats with an option to buy,' he said. 'Forty pounds a week and they claim that when the transfer's made mortgage repayments will amount to the same. Of course, I haven't talked to Kimberley, I asked her mother not to say a word about any of this. Her mother says she went over to Clifton Court the minute Zack was banged-up, put down a deposit and fixed up to move in next day. She's bought a whole lot of furniture since then.'

'Is she going to buy?'

'According to mother, she's already got a solicitor doing the conveyancing. They were squatting in that cottage at Glebe End, by the way, only nobody cared. It's no use to the owner, is it? It needs fifty thousand spent on it before anyone would buy it.'

'And Crescent Comestibles own that block of flats?'

'So the managing agents told me. It's no secret. They're building all over Stowerton, wherever there's a bit of land going or an old house knocked down. It's the same process everywhere. The flats are cheap by today's standards. You pay rent while you're waiting for your mortgage to come through and the mortgage is a hundred per cent with no deposit. Your mortgage repayments are the same as your rent.'

'In accordance with Mrs Khoori's own political standpoint,' said Wexford slowly. 'Help the disadvantaged to help themselves. Don't give it to them but give them the chance to be independent. Not a bad philosophy, I suppose. I wonder if the day will come when someone starts a political party called Conservative Socialists.'

The doctor was told between seeing patients at the medical centre, his wife called to the phone in Intensive Care. Wexford came to the house as Dr Akande arrived home and the pain in his face was as bad as when he thought his daughter was dead. It would be worse if she were dead, immeasurably worse, but this was very bad. To learn that your child is prepared to put you through this, is indifferent as to whether you go through it or not, that is made bearable only when filtered through anger and Raymond Akande wasn't angry. He was humiliated.

'I thought she loved us.'

'She acted impulsively, Dr Akande.' He hadn't said anything about Christopher Riding. Melanie could do that.

'She was in Stowerton all the time?'

'It looks like it.'

'Her mother works just down the road. I was there making my rounds.'

545

'The Epsons left them a car to do the shopping and take the child to school. I don't suppose she went out much on foot.'

'I ought to be down on my knees thanking heaven for all its mercies, I ought to be in a seventh heaven – is that what you're thinking?'

'No,' said Wexford, and boldly, 'I know how you feel.'

'Where did we go wrong?'

Before he could answer – if he had felt able or inclined to answer – Laurette Akande walked in. Wexford's first thought was that she looked ten years younger, his second that she was brimming with happiness and his third that she was the angriest woman he had seen in years.

'Where is she?'

'A car will bring her at six. She'll have the children with her. It was either that or making some care arrangement and since the Epsons return tonight . . .'

'Where did we go wrong, Laurette?'

'Don't be silly. We didn't go wrong. Who is this woman, this Mrs Epson, who leaves her children in the care of a totally unqualified person? I hope someone's going to prosecute her, she should be prosecuted. I am so angry I could kill her. Not Mrs Epson, Melanie. I could kill her.'

'Oh, don't, Letty,' said the doctor. 'We thought someone *had* killed her.'

The car brought Melanie and the boisterous Epson boys a couple of minutes after six. She walked defiantly into the room, her head held high. Her parents, who were sitting down, remained seated, but after a moment or two of silence her father got up and came towards her. He put out a hand and took hers. He pulled her a little towards him and kissed her cheek tentatively. Rather than responding, Melanie allowed this.

'I'll leave you,' Wexford said. 'I'll see you here tomorrow, Melanie, nine in the morning.'

None of them took any notice of him. He got up and went towards the door. Laurette found a strong determined voice. She no longer seemed angry but only decisive.

'Well, Melanie, we'll hear your explanation and then we'll say no more about it. I think you'd better apply to do a degree in business studies. You might get in in October if you're quick about it. The University of the South do a good course and that would mean you

546

can live at home. I'll send away for the forms for you tomorrow and meanwhile Dad might let you temp for the receptionist at the. . . .'

The younger Epson boy began screaming. Wexford let himself out.

# 21

In the seclusion of the booth he made a cross on his voting paper. There were three names: Burton K.J., British National Party; Khoori A.D., Independent Conservative and Sugden M., Liberal Democrat. Sheila said the Lib-Dem didn't stand a chance and the only way to keep out the BNP was by drumming up big support for Anouk Khoori.

But Wexford now had serious reasons against voting for Mrs Khoori and he made his cross next to the name of Malcolm Sugden. Maybe it was a wasted vote but he couldn't help that. He folded his paper in half, turned round and dropped it through the slot in the ballot box.

Since he went into the Thomas Proctor Primary School some five minutes before, Anouk Khoori had arrived in a car driven by her husband, a gold-coloured Rolls Royce. Burton of the BNP was already there, standing on the asphalt forecourt, surrounded by ladies in silk dresses and straw hats, the former vanguard of the Conservatives, seduced away by the attractions of the far right. He was smoking a cigar, the fumes of which hung heavily and reached distantly, on this warm still morning. Mrs Khoori stepped from the car like a royal personage. She was dressed like one, but of the younger set, in a very short white skirt, emerald green silk shirt, white jacket. Her hair hung like a yellow veil from under her white hat brim. When she saw Wexford she put out both hands to him.

'I knew I should find you here!'

He marvelled at the confidence which enables someone who is almost a stranger to speak in the tones of a lover.

'I knew *you* would be among the first to vote.'

Her husband materialized behind her, smiled a big broad studied smile and thrust his hand in Wexford's direction. The thrust was strong, like he imagined a boxer's might be, but the handshake was limp and it was as if his own hand held a wilted lily. He withdrew it and remarked that they had a fine day for the poll.

'So English,' said Mrs Khoori, 'but that's what I love. Now I want you to promise me something, Reg.'

'What would that be?' he said, and even in his own ears his voice sounded off-puttingly grave.

She was quite undeterred. 'Now that County Councils are disappearing, this authority of ours is going to expand and become very important. I am going to need an adviser on crime prevention, on public relations, on my approach to the *people* of this sleepy old town – right? You will be that adviser, won't you, Reg? You'll help me? You'll give me the support I'm going to need more than I've ever needed support all my life. What do you say?'

Wael Khoori was grinning all over his face, as well he might, but this was a genial empty smile directed at whoever passed. Wexford said, 'You'll have to get in first, Mrs Khoori.'

'Anouk, *please*. But I am going to get in, I know it, and when I'm there you'll help me?'

It was absurd. He smiled but said nothing, avoiding the direct snub. The time was five to nine and Raymond Akande's morning surgery started at eight-thirty. Laurette would have left in time to start the day shift at eight. In the five minutes it took him to drive to Ollerton Avenue, Wexford thought of all those visits he had paid to this house, the doctor's misery, the boy's tears. He remembered taking those parents to the mortuary and Laurette's hysterical rage. There was nothing to be done about all that. He could hardly charge any more people with wasting police time as that itself was a waste of police time.

The chances were he would never come here again. This was his last visit. Even after yesterday, after identification and explanation, it was a shock to see the photographed face, the dead face, alive. She opened the door to him and for a moment he was silenced by the very fact of her, her existence.

'There's no one here but me,' she said.

'Christopher would hardly be welcome, I suppose?'

'He's gone back home. I don't ever want to see him again. It was his sister that was my friend, it was Sophie, not him.'

Wexford followed the girl into the living room whose walls had heard her parents ask if there was any hope of her being alive. She smiled at him, tentatively at first, then serenely.

'I'm feeling happy, I don't know why. It must be getting shut of the Epson kids.'

'How much did they pay you?'

'A hundred. Half before they left and the other half last night.'

Wexford showed her the photograph of the dead Sojourner.

'Have you ever seen her?'

'I don't think so.'

This expression, of course, means no, but a not entirely unqualified no.

'Sure?'

'I've never seen her. Are you allowed to take photographs of dead people and show them around?'

'What alternative would you suggest?'

'Well, records kept of everyone with photos and fingerprints and DNA and whatever, a central computer with details of everyone in the country on

'Our job would be a lot easier if we kept records like that but we don't. Tell me what you did the day before you went to the Benefit Office and met Mrs Epson.'

'What do you mean, what I did?'

'How you spent the day. Your mother said you went for a run.'

'I go for a run every day. Well, I couldn't when I had those kids to look after.'

'All right. You went for a run – where?'

'My mother doesn't know everything, you know. I don't always go the same way. Sometimes I go up Harrow Avenue and along Winchester Drive and sometimes I take Marlborough Road.'

'Christopher and Sophie Riding live in Winchester Drive.'

'Do they? I've never been to their house. I've told you, I'd only seen him a couple of times before he followed me back to the Epsons'. I knew Sophie at college.'

If she had been happy five minutes before, she now looked disproportionately distressed. He wondered what would become of her, if the bullying tactics of that domineering mother would drive her to seek out Euan Sinclair again. He eased the subject back to the route she had taken while out running.

'So which was it that day?'

Melanie seemed pleased to cross him. 'I didn't go there at all that day. I went across the fields to Mynford. By the footpaths.'

He was disappointed, though he hardly knew why. By asking these questions, whose significance he felt rather than knew, he had hoped to intuit something.

She fixed her eyes on him the way her father did. 'I went nearly to Mynford New Hall. It gave me a bit of a shock, seeing the house. I didn't know I was so near it.' Her gaze bored into him mesmerically. 'That was the day I went to the Benefit Office. You are talking about that, aren't you?'

'It's the day before you went to the Benefit Office I want to know about.' He tried to keep his patience. 'The Monday.'

'Oh, the Monday. I'll have to think. I went along the Pomfret road on Saturday, and then on Sunday – it was the same Sunday and Monday, along Ashley Grove, up Harrow Avenue, along Winchester Drive and into Marlborough Road. It's nice up there, nice air, and you can look down and see the river.'

'While you were out on these runs you never saw this girl?'

He had the photograph out again and she looked at it again, but quite dispassionately this time.

'My mother said you got them to identify a corpse as me, only it wasn't me. Was it her?'

'Yes.'

'Wow. Anyway, I never saw her. I hardly ever saw anyone on foot. People don't walk, do they? They go in cars. I bet you'd be suspicious, wouldn't you, if you saw someone walking up there? You'd stop them and ask what they are doing.'

'It hasn't come to that yet,' said Wexford. 'You never saw her face at a window? Or saw her in a garden?'

'I've told you, I never saw her.'

It was hard to remember Melanie Akande was twenty-two. Sojourner at seventeen, he was sure, would have seemed older. But Sojourner, of course, had suffered, had been through the mill. The Akandes had kept their daughter a child by treating her as an irresponsible person, fit only to be controlled and directed by others. It made him shudder to think of her having a baby in order to escape.

The house-to-house was over. Nothing had come out of it, so when he said that they were off to Ashley Grove, Burden wanted to know what was the point of that.

'We are going to pay a visit to an architect,' he said to Burden when he had told him of the interview with Melanie. 'Or perhaps an architect's wife before she goes out doing good works in the parish.'

But this was not Cookie Dix's day for taking reading matter to the sick. She was at home with her husband, though it was neither of them that admitted Wexford and Burden to the house.

And what a house! The hall, which was circular and from which a white staircase arced up, bulging like the prow of a sailing ship, had a marble floor on which lemon trees in pots flowered and fruited simultaneously. Other trees grew in the soil itself, of which beds had been created, ficus with rustling leaves and feather-leaved alders, pen-thin cypresses and silver willows with distorted trunks, all reaching up to the light from the glass dome high above them. The maid, black-haired, black-eyed and sallow, kept them waiting under the trees while she went away to announce their presence. She was back within thirty seconds and led them through a pair of double doors – Wexford had to duck under a branch – through a kind of ante-room, stark black and white, and another pair of doors, into a yellow and white sun-flooded dining room where Cookie and Alexander Dix sat eating their breakfast.

In a reversal of the usual order of things, Cookie got to her feet while her husband remained seated. He had *The Times* in one hand and a piece of croissant in the other. In response to their good morning he said nothing but called out to the departing servant, 'Margarita, bring some more coffee for our guests, will you?'

'We are rather late getting started this morning,' said Cookie. If she had been questioned the day before by Pemberton or Archbold she said nothing about it. She was wearing a dark green satin garment, more like a dressing gown than anything else but not much like one, being extremely short and tied round the waist with a jewelled cummerbund. Her long black hair was fastened on to the top of her head where it sprouted in fronds rather like the top of a frost-blackened carrot. 'Do sit down.' She waved a vague hand at the other eight chairs ranged round the glass-topped table with its verdigris encrusted legs. 'We were out on the toot last night . . . well, at a party. It was the small hours – the tiniest of hours – when we got home, wasn't it, darling?'

Dix turned the page and started reading Bernard Levin. Something made him laugh. His laughter was the sound sappy wood makes when burning, a crackling and spitting. He looked up, still smiling, watched Wexford sit down, then he watched Burden, and when they were in chairs opposite each other, said, 'What can we do for you gentlemen?'

'Mr and Mrs Khoori are friends of yours, I believe?' Wexford said.

Cookie glanced at her husband. 'We know them.'

'You were at their garden party.'

'So were you,' said Cookie. 'What about them, anyway?'

'At that party you said Mrs Khoori had a maid who had recently left her and that she was the sister of your maid.'

'Of Margarita, yes.'

Wexford felt a pang of disappointment. Before he could say any more Margarita came back with the coffee on a tray and two cups. It was impossible to imagine her and Sojourner being related, still less sisters. Cookie, who was very quick off the mark said something to her in rapid fluent Spanish and the answer came back in that language.

'Margarita's sister went home to the Philippines in May,' Cookie said. 'She wasn't happy here. She didn't get on with the other two maids.'

Having poured the coffee and held out the milk jug and sugar basin to each of them in turn, Margarita stood passively, her eyes downcast.

'They came over together?' Wexford asked and at Cookie's nod said, 'On the six months' stay allowance or for twelve months because their employers were living here?'

'Twelve months. That's renewable – I mean, the Home Office – is it, darling? They'll – what will they do, Alexander?'

'She will apply to have her stay extended by successive periods of twelve months and after four years, if she wants to remain longer, she can apply to stay indefinitely.'

'How did you and the Khooris come to have sisters working for you?'

'Anouk went to an agency and told me. There's this agency that recruits women in the Philippines.' She said something in Spanish and Margarita nodded. 'She can speak English quite well if you want to talk to her. And she can read it. When she and her sister came into this country they had to be interviewed by the entry clearance officer and they were given a leaflet explaining her rights as a – what is it, darling?'

'Domestic entering the United Kingdom under the Home Office Immigration Act 1971,' said Dix without looking up from Levin.

Overnight Wexford had read it all up from Sheila's literature. He said to the waiting woman, 'Was there anyone else working with your sister apart from . . . ?'

'Juana and Rosenda,' said Margarita. 'Those two not nice to Corazon. She cry for her children in Manila and they laugh.'

'But no one else?'

'No one. I go now?'

'Yes, you can go, Margarita. Thank you.'

Cookie sat down and helped herself to coffee from the new pot. 'My head's a bit rough this morning.' Wexford would never have guessed it. 'Corazon has four children and an unemployed husband at home. That's why she came to work here, for money to send home. Margarita hasn't children and she isn't married. I think she came . . . well, to see the world, don't you, darling?'

Dix's laughter might have derived from her rather inane enquiry or from the article he was reading. He reached over and patted her hand with a scaly claw of the kind usually seen in the Natural History Museum. Cookie shrugged her green satin shoulders.

'She gets around a bit, has herself some fun. I think she's found a boyfriend, hasn't she, darling? We don't exactly keep her locked up like some do.'

There was a pause. 'Such as the Khooris,' said Alexander Dix with devastating timing.

Burden set his coffee cup back in its saucer. 'Mr and Mrs Khoori keep their servants locked up?'

'Darling Alexander does exaggerate, but yes, you could call them rather restrictive. I mean, if you live at Mynford Old Whatsit, you can't drive and there's no one to drive you – *ever* – and you've got the whole of that huge house to keep spick and span – what on earth do those words mean, I wonder, "spick" and "span"? – never mind, we all get the sense of it. If you live like that, what can you do if you *are* let out, but walk across the fields into the outermost reaches of Kingsmarkham?'

Involuntarily Burden glanced at Wexford and Wexford glanced at him. Their eyes met for an instant. 'They've had no other servants?'

'Not so far as I know,' Cookie said, wavering.

'Margarita would know,' said Dix, 'and she says not.'

'But Margarita never actually went there, darling.' Cookie pursed her lips and gave a silent whistle. 'Are you looking for someone shut up in the house? A sort of madwoman in the attic?'

'Not quite that,' said Wexford and he said it sadly.

Dix must have picked up the note in his voice, for he said in a hospitable way, 'Is there anything else we can get you?' He surveyed the table and found it wanting. 'A biscuit? Some fruit?'

'No, thank you.'

'In that case, perhaps you'll excuse me. I have work to do.' Dix got up, a very small diplodocus on its hind legs. He made a small bow to each of them, then to his wife. He would perhaps have clicked heels had he not been wearing sandals. 'Gentlemen,' he said, and, 'Cornelia,' thus answering one of Wexford's unspoken questions.

Cookie said confidingly when he was out of earshot, 'Darling Alexander is so excited, he's starting a new business. He says we're about to see the dawn of a new Renaissance in building in this country. He's found this marvellous young man who's going into partnership with him. He advertised and this brilliant person answered just out of the blue like that.' She smiled happily. 'Well, I do hope I've been of help.' Wexford marvelled at her disconcerting habit of seeming to read his thoughts. 'You won't find Anouk at home today, you know. She'll be riding about on a float, *exhorting* the populace to vote for her.'

From the front drive they looked back at the house, an intricate arrangement of glass panels, black marble panels and sheets of what looked like wafer-thin alabaster.

'You can't see in,' said Burden, 'you can only see out. Don't you think that's claustrophobic?'

'It would be if it was the other way about.'

Burden got into the driving seat. 'That woman, Margarita I mean, she seemed happy in her work.'

'Sure. There's no objection to people employing servants if they treat them properly and pay them what they're worth. The labourer is worthy of his hire. And the Act's all right, Mike, as far as it goes. In fact, on the surface it looks very good, it looks as if it deals with all contingencies. But it's open to terrible abuse. Domestic workers coming into the country aren't given immigration status independent of the household they work for. *They may not leave and they may not take up any other form of work.* That's what we're looking for, something of that sort.'

Instead of Anouk Khoori, it was the BNP's float which passed them as they came back into the High Street. Ken Burton, the candidate, unselfconscious in black jeans and a black shirt – was its significance largely lost on observers? – rode standing up where the passenger seat should have been, blasting out his manifesto through a megaphone. He might be of the *British* Nationalists but, with some subtlety, it was England for the *English* that he was promoting in this sweet warm corner of Sussex.

Posters plastered over the back of the van not only exhorted the electorate to vote for Burton but also to join the march of the unemployed which was scheduled to take place from Stowerton to Kingsmarkham on the following day.

'Did you know about that?' Burden asked.

'I've heard rumours. The uniformed branch have it sewn up.'

'You mean they're expecting trouble? Here? *Here*?'

'In this green and pleasant land? Well, Mike, there *are* a lot of people out of work. It's much higher than the national average in Stowerton, about twelve per cent. And tempers do run high.'

'It's time to pay a visit to Mynford New Hall, I think.'

'She won't be there, sir. She's out drumming up defaulters.'

'So much the better,' said Wexford.

'You mean we talk to the servants?'

'It's not a servant we're looking for, Mike,' Wexford said. 'We're looking for a slave.'

# 22

This was the long way round, by the road that took in Pomfret and Cheriton. You could walk it across the fields from Kingsmarkham in forty minutes or run it in twenty-five, it was only about two miles, but seven this way. Burden, who was driving, had never seen Mynford New Hall before. He asked if it was as old as it looked but, on hearing building had barely been completed at the time of the garden party, lost interest.

Wexford had expected election posters, even though Mynford was outside the ward for which Mrs Khoori was standing. But there was nothing on the gate-posts and nothing in the windows of the mock-Georgian house. Someone had planted full-grown, fully-blooming geraniums in the beds that had been bare a fortnight ago. A bell-pull had been added since his first visit and a pair of the biggest and most elaborate carriage lamps he had ever seen.

But he doubted if the bell-pull was connected, either that or there really was no one at home. It was Burden who looked up and saw the face looking down at them, a pale oval face and head whose black hair was invisible in the blackness behind it. Wexford, who had rung that bell four times, called out,

'Come down and let us in, please.'

Obedience was not prompt. Juana or Rosenda continued to stare impassively for some moments. Then she gave a little nod, a bob of the head, and disappeared. And when the door was finally opened it was not she who opened it but a woman with brown skin and Mongolian features. Wexford had not exactly expected a uniform but he was surprised by the pink velour track-suit.

It was very cold in the house, with the same feel that you get when entering the chilled food area in a supermarket. Perhaps they had the same air conditioning system as that installed in the perishable food departments of Crescent Stores. He and Burden produced their warrant cards. The woman looked at them with interest, apparently deriving some amusement from a comparison between photographs and the living men.

'You got old since this one,' she said to Wexford with a scream of laughter.

'What's your name, please?'

The laughter was switched off and she looked at him as if he had said something very impertinent.

'Why you want to know?'

'Just give us your name, please. Are you Juana or Rosenda?'

The change from affront to sullenness was rapid. 'Rosenda Lopez. That one Juana.'

The woman whose face had stared down at them had come silently into the hall. Like Rosenda she wore white trainers but her track-suit was blue. Her accent was the same as Rosenda's but her English was better. She was younger and might almost have given justification to Dix's *Mikado* parody that the Khooris' maids were barely out of their teens.

'Mr and Mrs Khoori are not at home.' Her next words sounded like a phone answering machine. 'Please leave a message if you would like to.'

'Juana what?' said Burden.

'Gonzalez. Now you go. Thank you.'

'Ms Lopez,' said Wexford, 'Ms Gonzalez, you have a choice. You may either talk to us here and now or else come with us back to Kingsmarkham to the police station. Do you understand what I'm saying?'

It was necessary to repeat this several times, for him to repeat it and for Burden to put it into slightly different words, before there was any sort of response. Both women were mistresses of the art of silent insolence. But when Juana suddenly said something in what he took for Tagalog and both broke into giggles, Wexford thought he could understand the misery of Margarita's sister Corazon who had been laughed at for missing her children.

Juana repeated the incomprehensible words, then apparently translated them. 'No problem.'

'OK. All right,' said Rosenda. 'You sit down now.'

There seemed no need to penetrate further into the house. The hall

was a vast chamber, pillared, arched, alcoved, the walls panelled and
with recessed colums, very much the kind of room guests must have
been welcomed into at a Pemberley or a Northanger Abbey. Only
this was new, all new, barely finished. And even in the early
nineteenth century, even in winter, no great house would have been
as cold inside as this one. He sat down on a pale blue chair with
spindly gold legs but Burden remained standing as did the two
women, side by side, enjoying themselves.

'Did you work for Mr and Mrs Khoori when they were in the
Dower House?'

Burden had to take them to a window and point out the woods in
the valley, the invisible roofs. Nods encouraged him.

'And again, of course, when they came here in June?' More nods.
He remembered what Cookie Dix had said about shutting people up.
'Do you go out much?'

'Go out?'

'Into town. Go and see friends. Meet people. Go to the cinema. Do
you go out?'

From the vertical, their heads moved horizontally. Juana said,
'Don't drive car. Mrs Khoori go shopping and we don't want
cinema, have TV.'

'Was Corazon with you at the Dower House?'

His very anglicized pronunciation of the name had them in giggles
again and the way he said it repeated by each of them. Then, 'She
was cook,' said Juana.

Memory returned. The medical centre and a woman who broke
the no smoking rule. 'She had to have the doctor? She was ill?'

'Always ill she was. Homesick. She went home.'

'And that left the two of you,' Wexford said. 'But there was
another servant, at the same time as Corazon or perhaps after?'

It was hard to tell if they were blank or wary. He sought political
correctness, saying carefully, 'A young girl, seventeen or eighteen,
from Africa.'

Almost shivering from the cold, Burden showed them the photograph. The effect was to stimulate more laughter. But before
Wexford could decide whether they were laughing from race
prejudice, simple wonder that anyone could suspect them of an
ability to identify this girl or from a kind of pleasurable horror –
Sojourner's face seemed to look more deeply dead each time he
produced the photograph – the front door opened and Anouk

Khoori came in, immediately followed by her husband, Jeremy Lang and Ingrid Pamber.

'Reg,' she said, not a bit discomposed, 'how lovely! I had a feeling I might find you here.' She held out both hands to him, one of them holding a cigarette. 'But why didn't you let me know you were coming?'

Wael Khoori said nothing. His was invariably the manner of the highly successful millionaire businessman who puts on a genial, smiling, silent front, while seeming to be quite elsewhere, preoccupied by distant things, high finance, perhaps the Hang Seng index. He smiled, he was patient. He stood waiting.

'We have come home for lunch,' said Mrs Khoori. 'Electioneering is very hard work, I can tell you, and I'm famished. Isn't it lovely and cool in here? Of course you must stay to lunch, Reg, and you too, Mr . . . ?' She addressed Rosenda in exactly the same friendly rather breathless way, 'I do hope you can put on something delicious and *quick*, please, as I have to get back to the *fray*.'

Khoori spoke. He ignored everything his wife had said. She might not have said a word. 'I'm quite aware of what you're here for.'

'Really, sir?' said Wexford. 'We'll talk about it then, shall we?'

'Yes, of course, after lunch,' said Anouk. 'Come along, into the dining room everyone, and quickly because Ingrid has to go back to work.'

Again she was ignored. Khoori simply stood his ground while she swept up Jeremy and Ingrid, an arm round each of them, and propelled them across the hall. Ingrid, pinched and pale in her sleeveless dress, nevertheless turned to give him one of her flirtatious looks, arch, tantalizing. But she was changed, the blue glance had lost its power. Her eyes had lost their colour and for a moment he wondered if he had imagined that brilliant azure, but only for a moment, for Khoori was saying,

'Come with me. In here.'

It was a library but a quick glance round showed him it was not of the kind one would use for reference or wish to spend much time in. The Khooris had perhaps said to a firm of interior decorators, put shelves all over the walls and fill them with suitable books, old ones with handsome bindings. So *The Natural History of the Pyrenees* in seven volumes had been supplied and Hakluyt's *Voyages* and Mommsen on Rome and Motley on the Dutch Republic. Khoori sat down at a reproduction desk. Its green leather inlay had been made to look as if quill pens on parchment had been scratching at it for centuries.

'You don't seem surprised to see us, Mr Khoori,' said Wexford.

'No, I'm not, Mr Reg. Annoyed but not surprised.'

Wexford looked at him. This was very different from Bruce Snow's assumption that they were traffic police. 'What do you suppose this is about?'

'I suppose, I *know*, that those women or one of them have not applied to the Home Office for an extension of their stay. This, despite their extreme desire to stay and my having had the applications typed for them. And their knowledge that they can only stay under the provisions of the Immigration Act of 1971. All they have to do is sign the letter and take it to the post. I know because this is what happened last time, when they first came to us and had been granted an initial stay of six months. You have to keep a constant eye on these people and I haven't the time to be as vigilant as I should be. So, very well, that's that. What do we do to put matters right?'

A little subterfuge would do no harm, Wexford thought. 'Simply reapply, Mr Khoori. A mistake was made but made in good faith, apparently.'

'So I reapply and this time make sure the application gets to its destination?'

'Right,' said Burden, transforming himself into an Immigration official. He began inventing with a facility Wexford could only admire. 'Now, this woman Corazon, we understand she wanted to change her employment, which is of course illegal. Under the provisions of the Act she's only permitted to work for the employer whose name is on the stamp in her passport.'

'There was some story about the other servants ill-treating her . . . well, being unkind to her. She was always in tears.' Khoori shrugged. 'It wasn't very pleasant for myself and my wife.'

'So, understanding she wasn't permitted to work elsewhere, she went home? When would that have been?'

Khoori put up one hand and smoothed his casque of white hair. It fitted him like a wig but it plainly was not a wig. The hand was long, brown, exquisitely kept. He frowned a little while he thought. 'About a month ago, maybe less.'

And it was exactly four weeks to the day since Wexford had first encountered Anouk Khoori at the medical centre. She still had a cook then, a servant who had perhaps fallen ill through homesickness and the cruelty of others.

'Would you mind telling me, sir,' Wexford said, 'where the money came from for her return flight?'

'I paid, Mr Reg. I paid.'

'Very generous of you. Just one other thing. I'd like you to set me right on this question. Would you say it was true that in the Gulf States the labour laws don't recognize domestics as workers but treat them as family members?'

Suspicion that this might be a trap flicked in Khoori's eyes. 'I'm not a lawyer.'

'But you're a Kuwaiti national, aren't you? You must be aware if this is so or not, if it is in fact taken for granted.'

'Broadly speaking, I suppose it's so, yes.'

'So that families from the Gulf States do bring in servants *as family members or friends*, having no status as domestics and therefore no protection from abuse? And although it's clear they are coming in not on holiday but to work they are allowed to stay as visitors.'

'Possibly. I've no experience of it.'

'But you know it happens? And that it happens because refusing entry to domestics either as workers tied to one employer and restricted to twelve-month stays, or as family members or friends and ostensible visitors, might discourage wealthy investors like yourself from coming here at all?'

Khoori gave a loud braying laugh. 'I'm damned if I'd be here if I had to wash my own dishes.'

'But you have never personally brought anyone in under those special circumstances?'

'No, Mr Reg, I have not. You can ask my wife. Come to that, you can ask Juana and Rosenda.'

He led them into a vast cold dining room with ten windows down one wall and a painted ceiling. Some ten feet under the depicted cherubs, cornucopias and lovers' knots Anouk, Jeremy and Ingrid sat at a mahogany table big enough for twenty-four, eating smoked salmon and drinking champagne.

'We are celebrating my victory in advance, Reg,' said Anouk. 'Do you think that a very foolhardy thing to do?'

Her husband whispered something to her. It evoked a tinkle of laughter, not however a happy sound. The repulsion she held for

Wexford came back and he turned instinctively to look at Ingrid, beautiful fresh young Ingrid whose hair was still crisp and smooth and skin glowing with health but whose eyes had become as dull as stones. As he looked she took a pair of glasses from her bag and perched them on her nose.

If she had changed, it was nothing to the change that had come over Anouk Khoori. Under the make-up she had gone bright red and her features seemed to knot up with tension.

'It's that girl who was murdered, isn't it? That black girl? We've never seen her.' Her carefully modulated voice grew shrill. 'We know nothing about her. We've never had anyone working for us here but Juana and Rosenda and that Corazon who left and went home. I think it's awful this happening today. I will not have anything like this happening to spoil my chances!'

As her voice rose on to a high note of panic, Juana and Rosenda both came into the room, the former with a carafe of water on a tray, the latter carrying a fresh plate of brown bread and butter. Their employer's vexation, the sudden angry distress that Wexford at any rate had never witnessed before, caused them a mirth they could barely conceal. Juana had to hold her hand tightly over her mouth while Rosenda's lips twitched as she stood staring.

Wexford had scarcely anticipated her inspired guesswork. Or was it less guesswork than genuine guilt?

'You tell them,' Anouk shouted, 'you tell them, you two. We never had anyone here like that, did we? You love it here, don't you? No one ever hurt you, you tell them.'

Juana's laughter broke free. She was beyond controlling it. 'He crazy,' she said, gasping. 'We never see no one like that, do we, Rosa?'

'No, we never see no one, no way.'

'No way we don't. Here your bread and butter. You want more lemon?'

'All right,' Wexford said. 'Thank you. That's all.'

Evidently remembering that he had already voted, Anouk shouted at him, 'You can get out of my house! Now! Both of you, get out!'

With a little gasp, Ingrid had got up, clutching her napkin. 'I shall have to go. I must get back to the office.'

Rosenda was holding the dining room door open, murmuring, 'Come on, come on, you got to go now.'

'You'll give me a lift, won't you?' Ingrid said to Wexford.

It was Burden who answered. 'I'm afraid not.'

'Oh, but, surely . . .'

'We're not a taxi service.'

Behind them in the dining room Anouk had given way to a crisis of nerves, uttering little staccato cries. Khoori said to no one in particular that it might help to bring the brandy. Wexford and Burden made their way across that desert of a hall to the front door, escorted by both giggling women. The heat outside met them in a wave, a positive sensuous pleasure. They were barely in the car when Ingrid came out followed by Khoori who handed her into the car they had arrived in.

'I'll bet that's the first time a Rolls like that has ever brought anyone to the Benefit Office,' said Burden, starting the engine. 'Looks a bit different without her contact lenses, doesn't she?'

'You mean that blue was *lenses*?'

'What else? I suppose she got allergic and had to leave them off.'

Perhaps it was from the scent of his after-shave, but Gladys Prior knew it was Burden before he spoke. She even spelt his name out before he spoke, persisting with the joke that afforded her so much amusement. Wexford's enquiry brought fresh gales of laughter.

'Is he in? Bless you, he hasn't set foot outside in four years.'

Percy Hammond was at his Mizpah, looking out across his Plain of Syria. Without turning round, identifying them by their voices and their footsteps, he asked, 'When are you going to catch him, then?'

Wexford said, earning a surprised and perhaps admonitory glance from Burden, 'Tomorrow, I should think, Mr Hammond. Yes, we'll catch . . . er, them, tomorrow.'

'Who's going to have that flat opposite?' said Mrs Prior unexpectedly.

'What, Annette Bystock's flat?'

'That's the one. Who's going to have it?'

'I've no idea,' said Burden. 'It'll probably go to the next-of-kin. Now, Mr Hammond, we'd like a little more help from you . . .'

'If you're going to catch him tomorrow, eh?'

Burden's expression showed all too plainly what he thought of Wexford's wild boast. 'What we want you to do, sir, is go back over what you saw from this window on July the eighth.'

'And, more importantly,' said Wexford, 'what you saw on July the seventh.'

It would have been unprecedented, he would never have done it, not actually done it, but Burden *nearly* corrected Wexford. It was on the tip of his tongue to murmur, you don't mean that, not the seventh, he saw no one on the seventh but that girl with the blue lenses and Edwina Harris and a man with a spaniel. It was all in the report. Instead of saying it, he coughed, he cleared his throat just a little. Wexford took no notice.

'On the Thursday morning, very early, you saw this young chap who looked a bit like Mr Burden here come out of the house with a big box in his arms.'

Percy Hammond nodded vigorously, 'About four-thirty it was, a.m.'

'Right. Now on the previous night, the Wednesday night, you went to bed and to sleep but you woke up after a while and got up . . .'

'To spend a penny,' said Gladys Prior.

'And naturally you looked out of your window – and you saw someone come out of Ladyhall Court? You saw a young man come out?'

The old wrinkled face was distorted even more by the effort of remembering. He clenched his hands

'Did I say that?'

'You said it, Mr Hammond, and then you thought you'd made a mistake because you definitely saw him in the morning and you couldn't have seen him twice.'

'But I did see him twice . . .' Percy Hammond said, his voice dropping to a whisper. 'I *did*.'

Wexford took it gently, moving with care. 'You saw him twice? In the morning – and the night before?'

'That's right. I knew I did, whatever they said. I saw him twice. And the first time, he saw me.'

'How do you know?'

'He wasn't carrying a box that first time, he wasn't carrying anything. He came to the gate and he looked up and looked straight at me.'

It was the last visit he would pay to Oni Johnson. She had nothing more to tell him. By her openness she had saved herself and next day she would leave Intensive Care for a room to be shared with three other women in Rufford Ward.

565

Laurette Akande came out to meet him. She looked at him and spoke as if the past month had never been. She had never lost a daughter and he hadn't found that daughter, there had been no anguish, no suffering and no joyful reunion. He might have been a sympathetic stranger. Her manner was light, her voice brisk.

'I wish someone could get that boy of hers to have a wash. His clothes and his hair smell, not to mention the rest of him.'

'He'll be gone when his mother goes,' said Wexford.

'It can't be soon enough for me.'

Oni looked pretty, sitting up in bed wearing a pink satin quilted bedjacket over the bandages, much too hot for the temperature, the obvious gift of Mhonum Ling. Mhonum was on one side of the bed, Raffy on the other. It was true that he smelt unpleasant, his curious hamburger and tobacco odour battling, and winning the battle, against his aunt's Giorgio eau-de-toilette.

'When you going to catch him then?' said Oni.

He was fated, it seemed, to be that afternoon the butt of eveyone's laughter. Oni laughed and then Mhonum laughed and Raffy joined in with a sheepish snigger.

'Tomorrow.'

'Are you kidding?' said Mhonum.

'I hope not.'

It was developing into a pattern. Sylvia drove the children and Neil into Kingsmarkham, Neil went to his job club, promising to meet them later, and Sylvia homed on her parents. Or, more often, her mother. Wexford never asked how long she had been there by the time he got home, he didn't want to know, though later Dora sometimes told him, always qualifying these grumbles with a prefatory 'I really shouldn't talk like this about my own child . . .'

'I don't suppose you've any objection,' Sylvia said when he walked in, 'if I take part in the unemployed march tomorrow?'

He was surprised to be asked – and just a little touched. 'It won't be the kind of event in which arrests are made. There'll be no setting fire to property and no overturning of cars.'

'I thought I ought to ask you,' she said in a tone that implied long-suffering dutifulness.

'Do as you like as long as you don't frighten the horses.'

'Will there be *horses*, grandad?'

Wexford laughed. He thought he was due for a spot of laughter

566

whose meaning eluded the others. The doorbell rang suddenly. No one ever came to their door and rang it in the Colonel Bogey mode: da-da-di-di-di-pom-POM. Such jauntiness was wholly unexpected. Wexford went to answer it. His son-in-law was on the doorstep, grinning widely, insisting on shaking hands with him.

'Can I have a drink? I need one.'

'Of course.'

'Whisky, please. I've had a wonderful afternoon.'

'I can see that.'

Neil took a swig of his drink. 'I've got a job. And in my own line. I'm going into partnership with this old architect, terribly distinguished man, and he's funding it, I'm . . .'

'I do think,' said Sylvia, 'that it's outrageous you coming out with that in front of everyone instead of telling me first.'

Her father was inclined to agree but he said nothing. He had a drink too. 'Alexander Dix,' he said, when the whisky struck home.

Neil had taken his younger son on his knee. 'That's right. The one offer I answered that was taken up. How did you know?'

'I doubt if there's more than one rich old distinguished architect in Kingsmarkham.'

'We're starting with a rather ambitious plan for the Castlegate site. A shopping mall, if that isn't to degrade what it will ultimately be. A thing of beauty, an asset to the town centre, crystal and gold, with a Crescent supermarket as the pivot of the whole thing.' He caught his father-in-law's eye and misinterpreted the gleam he saw there. 'Oh, without the moons and minarets, don't worry. It's part of this new government policy to restore commerce to town centres.' He said laconically to Sylvia, 'You can stop signing on as from Tuesday.'

'Thanks very much. That's for me to decide, I think.'

'You might say you're pleased.'

'I don't specially want to be part of the kind of society where the woman is indoors and the man comes home and says he's got a lucrative new job, so she says, Oh goody, can I have a pearl necklace and a fur coat now?'

'You shouldn't wear fur,' said Ben.

'I don't, I can't afford it, and never will be able to.'

'*Walang problema*,' said Wexford in Tagalog.

Robin, in his headset, looked up at him pityingly from the screen

567

in his hand. 'I don't do that any more, grandad,' he said. 'I'm into first day covers with celebrity autographs now. Do you think you could get me Anouk Khoori's?'

# 23

The march of the unemployed was due to begin at eleven in the morning, the marchers asked to assemble in Stowerton marketplace with their banners and the column would form up from the steps of the old Corn Exchange. It was going to be even hotter, but with rain later and the chance of thunder. The local news, that Wexford watched intermittently while getting dressed, told him all this, but it was Dora, who had got it from Sylvia, who supplied the details of the route. The march would proceed through Stowerton to the round-about, pass along the bleak streets of the industrial estate, rejoin the Kingsmarkham road and enter the town by the Kingsbrook Bridge. Its final destination was Kingsmarkham Town Hall.

He had to go back to the news for results in the council election. Voting, however, had been so close between the Liberal Democrat and the Independent Conservative that a recount was taking place. Ken Burton was out, having secured a mere fifty-eight votes. Wexford wondered whether to phone Sheila and tell her the news, but decided against it. She probably had her own means of knowing, anyway.

'Guess what,' said Dora. '*We're* invited to Sylvia's for Sunday lunch.'

But Wexford only said obscurely, 'I hope it's all right,' and added, 'Neil's job, I mean.'

The day was still and sultry, heat hanging under a sky of veiled blue. It was like the beginning of the month when he had been reading by the open french windows and Dr Akande had phoned with the first mention of Melanie. The air this morning had a scalding feel, and Burden said he'd known cooler steam come out of a kettle. Inside the car the air conditioning was as efficient as that at Mynford

New Hall and Wexford told Donaldson to turn it off and open a window.

'We're very quick to dismiss old people's statements of fact, aren't we?' Wexford said. 'If there's the slightest doubt we immediately assume they're senile or their memories are useless or even that they're no longer quite sane. Whereas with a younger person we'd at least listen and even encourage while they sort things out.

'Percy Hammond said he went to bed on that Wednesday evening, went to sleep, but woke up, got up and "put the light on for a minute". He turned if off "because it was so bright". I think we all know that feeling. He looked out of the window and saw "this young chap come out with a box in his arms". "Or was that later?" he said.

'We didn't ask him to think about it, we didn't say "think carefully, try and remember the times", Karen just confirmed that it must have been later, this was in the morning, he saw the "young chap" in the morning. I was just as much to blame, I let it go too. But, Mike, the fact was that the old man *saw Zack Nelson twice*.'

Burden looked at him. 'What d'you mean?'

'He saw him at eleven-thirty or thereabouts on Wednesday and he saw him *again* at four-thirty the following morning. There was no real doubt in his mind about that. The only doubt was whether Zack was carrying the "box" at night or in the morning. And that first time, on the Wednesday night, Zack saw *him*. He saw a face looking at him from the window. D'you see what that means?'

'I think so,' Burden said slowly. 'Annette died after 10.00 pm on the Wednesday and before 1.00 am on the Thursday. If Percy Hammond saw him for the first time at . . . But that means Zack killed Annette.'

'Yes, of course. The doors were open. Zack went in at, say, eleven-thirty, and found Annette asleep in bed. She was weak, she was ill, she was probably running a temperature. He looked around for something with which to do the deed. Perhaps he had something with him, a scarf, a cord. But the lamp lead was better. He pulled it out of the lamp, strangled Annette – who was too feeble to put up much of a fight – took nothing and left. There's not a light on anywhere but a street lamp, there's no one to see him, he's in the clear – until he looks across the road and sees, pressed against the glass, old Percy Hammond's face staring out at him.'

'But then surely, the last thing he'd do would be to go back five hours later?'

'Are you sure of that?'

'The last thing he'd want was to draw attention to himself.'

'No, that's exactly what he did want. He wanted to draw attention to himself or someone else wanted him to. This is what I think happened. It's guesswork but it's the only possible answer. Zack was scared stiff. The possessor of what is, after all, putting it brutally, quite a frightening face, had seen him, had stared long and hard at him. He panics, he needs advice. He realizes fully the enormity of what has happened.

'Who can advise him? Obviously, only one person, the man or woman who has put him up to this, the instigator whose paid hitman he is. It's the middle of the night but never mind that. He's doubtless been told never to contact this person, but never mind that either. He makes his way down the road to the corner shop, outside which is a phone box. He makes his call and the advice comes back from a far cleverer perpetrator than Zack could ever be: go back, steal something, make sure you're seen. Make sure you're seen a second time.'

'But why? I don't get it.'

'He, whoever he is, must have said, They will know the time she died. If you go back at four or later *they will know she must have been dead before you got there.* You will be in the clear as far as murder goes. Of course you'll go to prison for the theft but not for long and it's worth it, isn't it? It was an elderly person saw you, you say? They'll take it for granted an elderly person was confused about the time.'

'We did,' Burden said. 'We did take it for granted.'

'We all do it. We all patronize the old, and worse. We treat them as if they were small children. And we'll be on the receiving end of that one day, Mike. Unless the world changes.'

The place was strangely like the interior of the cottage at Glebe End. Kimberley had transported all her possessions in cardboard boxes and plastic carriers and in these containers they remained. They were still to her what cupboards and drawers are to other people. But she had bought furniture: a huge pneumatic three-piece suite of purple and grey tapestry with gold braid and gold swags, a crimson table inlaid with gilt, a television set in a white and gold cabinet. There was no carpet, there were no curtains. Clint, who had learned to walk since Burden had last seen him, staggered about the room, wiping the chocolate biscuit he had sucked on any tapestry surface he came into contact with. Kimberley was dressed in black leggings, stiletto heeled white shoes and a strapless red bustier. She gave Burden a belligerent look and said she didn't know what he meant.

'Where did it all come from, Kimberley? All this? Three weeks ago you were wondering what'd become of you if you lost that cottage.'

She maintained her sullen glare, but taking her eyes from his face, gazing down at her own feet, her toes turned in.

'It came from Zack, didn't it? It didn't come from your grandmother.'

She said to her feet, 'My nan did die.'

'Sure she did but she didn't leave you anything, she'd nothing to leave. What was it, paid to Zack in cash, was it? Or did he open a bank account for you and him and have it paid in there?'

'I don't know nothing about this, you know. It don't mean nothing to me.'

'Kimberley,' said Wexford. 'He murdered Annette Bystock. He didn't just steal her TV and her video. He murdered her.'

'He never!' She looked up and sideways, her shoulder hunched, as if trying to protect her face from a coming onslaught. 'He nicked her things, that's all he done.' The child, back at his favourite occupation of removing articles from one cardboard box and putting them into another, now fished out an unopened packet of teabags and trotted over to his mother with his find in his hands. She snatched him up and set him on her lap. It was as if she made him into a shield for herself. 'He told me, he just nicked her telly and stuff. If he's got money in the bank, why shouldn't he have? OK, it was his family it come from, not mine. He said to say my nan, on account of she died. But it was his family it come from. His dad's got money. Don't tear that open, Clint, you'll have the tea all out.'

The child took no notice. He had torn the cardboard and found the teabags. He was immensely content. Kimberley held him tightly, her arm clamped round his waist. Her voice was fierce, 'He never done no murder. Not Zack. He never would.'

She was telling the truth, Wexford thought, insofar as she knew it. He was almost sure she didn't know. 'Zack told you there'd be money in the bank, did he, before he went away?'

She nodded vigorously. 'In *my* account. He put it in there for me.'

572

Clint had a teabag gripped in both hands, his face growing red with the effort of tugging at it.

'Why this flat, Kimberley?' said Burden.

'It's nice, in't it? I liked it, I fancied it, in't that enough for you?'

'Wasn't it because you didn't have to make any effort? It belongs to Crescent Comestibles, doesn't it, and that's Mr Khoori? You didn't have to do a thing. Mr Khoori put you in here and gave you the money to get what you wanted.'

It was plain to Wexford that she had no idea what Burden meant. She was no actress. She was simply ignorant and these names signified nothing to her. The child on her lap had succeeded in his endeavour, had split open the teabag and was scattering tea over her leggings and the floor. But she was oblivious to it. She stared in bewilderment and said at last, 'You what?'

Wexford saw no point in explaining. 'What did happen, Kimberley?'

She brushed the blackish grains off her legs and gave Clint a half-hearted shake. 'I was walking down the High Street here with him in the buggy and I saw that written up about flats and mortgages and whatever and I thought why not, there's all that money Zack says is mine now, and I went in and saw this feller and said I got the money, I could give him the cash or a cheque and when could I move in. And that's what I done, moved in. And I don't know nothing about any Mr Coo-what you said, I've never heard of him.'

Of course, she must know that the source of this unexpected accession of cash was suspect. Legitimately earned money, no doubt many thousand pounds, does not find its way miraculously into the bank accounts of such as Zack Nelson. Families such as the Nelsons have no private fortunes, set up no trusts, to assist their humbler scions. She knew that as well as they did. But Wexford was aware she would never come out with it, she would never say she knew this gain must be ill-gotten but her desire for better accommodation was so great that she conveniently overlooked that fact. She would only come up with wilder explanations and excuses.

'The main thing,' he said to Burden when they were outside in Stowerton High Street, 'is that she doesn't know where it came from. Zack Nelson, in his wisdom, never told her. Or, rather, he told her a lie which he knew she would know was a lie but would accept. He meant her to be safe and she is safe. We needn't have made detours to avoid the High Street.'

573

'*He* knows, though.'

Wexford shrugged. 'And do you think he'll say? At this stage? OK, we can go along to the remand centre and ask him and he'll trot out all that stuff about Percy Hammond being senile and Annette being dead long before he ever went into Ladyhall Court. And that's what we can't prove, Mike. We'll never prove Percy Hammond saw Zack twice. If Zack keeps his mouth shut now, and he will, the worst that can happen to him is he'll go down for six months for burglary.'

They were walking along the street, just walking and quite aimlessly, the heat making for slow idle steps, yet they were at the Market Cross almost before they knew it. Banks are always together in whatever part of a town is given over to them and passing first the Midland, then the Natwest, made Burden say,

'This bank account Zack opened. He must have done that before killing Annette. As soon as he agreed to do it, on the Tuesday or the Wednesday at the latest. We can find out whose cheque or banker's draft or whatever was paid in to that a couple of days later.'

'Can we, Mike?' Wexford said it almost wistfully. 'On what grounds are we going to take a look at a bank account in Kimberley Pearson's name? She hasn't done anything. She hasn't even been charged with anything. She doesn't know where the money came from but she's probably convinced herself by now that it came from Zack's rich old grandad. She's innocent in the eyes of the law and no bank is going to let us breach her right to privacy.'

'It beats me why Zack Nelson drew attention to himself by having Bob Mole sell that radio in full public view like that, in the market that we make a point of keeping our eye on.'

Wexford laughed. 'Just for that, Mike. For that reason. It was the same as when he went into Annette's flat, the same drawing attention to himself. That's what he wanted to do, to get it over, get himself charged with theft and banged-up, out of harm's way. He even chose the most easily identified item among the stolen goods, that radio with the red stain on it.'

They stopped in the square and were about to turn round and retrace their steps, as people do who have been walking aimlessly, when Wexford's attention was caught by the crowd which had gathered outside the Corn Exchange. It was a Victorian building, its pillared entrance approached by a flight of steps. These steps some of the people who were waiting treated like seats in an amphitheatre, sitting or lounging on them. Up by the entrance half a dozen seemed

574

to be working on a banner, which suddenly unfurled and stretched out read, 'Give Us the Right to Work'.

'It's the start of the unemployed march,' said Burden. 'Who would have thought that could ever happen here? I mean, you could imagine it in Liverpool, say, or Glasgow. But here?'

'Who could imagine slavery would ever happen here? But Sojourner was a slave.'

'Not exactly that, surely.'

'If someone works without wages, or without accessible wages, cannot leave her employment, is not allowed out, is beaten and abused, what is she but a slave? "Slaves cannot breathe in England, if their lungs Receive our air, that moment they are free; They touch our country and their shackles fall." I got that out of a book, I don't suppose it'll stay in my memory for long. The point is, it may have been true once, it isn't any more.' Wexford took a piece of paper from his pocket. 'I copied this down. It's a case history and it didn't happen in the eighteenth century or the nineteenth but six years ago.

'"Roseline,"' he read, '"is from Southern Nigeria. At the age of about fifteen she was 'bought' for £2 from her impoverished father who was led to believe he would be paid that sum regularly every month to help feed his other five children. Roseline, he was told by the couple, was to stay as their guest and be taught domestic science. They brought her to Sheffield where the husband worked as a doctor. She was kept as a servant, not allowed out, slept on the floor, and was made to kneel on the floor for two hours if she fell asleep before being allowed to go to bed. Her working day started at 5.30 am and lasted for eighteen hours. She cleaned and washed for her employers and their five children. She was caned and kept short of food. On one occasion, in desperation, she wrote a note intended for the next-door neighbour offering sex for a sandwich. The note was discovered and she was further punished. In September 1988, while her abusers were away for a week, she gathered enough courage and spoke to a regular passer-by who had often seen her staring out of the window, and beckoned to her. This neighbour helped her to escape, and she took her former employers to court. She was awarded £20,000 in damages. However, she had only been given leave to stay for three months, and her employers had kept her for over three years. She was an illegal overstayer and thus liable to immediate deportation."'

Burden was silent for a moment. Then he said, 'Sojourner tried to escape and was further punished – is that what you're saying?'

'They went too far with their punishment. No doubt, they were afraid of the publicity and of having damages awarded against them. They made sure that wouldn't happen. They made very thoroughly sure by killing Annette, who perhaps had it in her power to reveal their identity and whereabouts, and tried – twice – to kill Oni who might have been told where they lived.'

'You think she was allowed in like this Roseline as a visitor? She was allowed three months or six months but overstayed?'

'Who's to know if she's never allowed out and no one sees her? If visitors to the house never see her? In fact, an employer has only to say to her that if she's discovered she'll be deported to wherever it is, the Gulf probably, for her to collude in this breaking of the law.'

'If conditions are that bad for her wouldn't she want to be deported?'

'That depends on what awaits her. There are a good many parts of the world where all that's left for a homeless destitute woman is prostitution. In any case, Sojourner only colluded so far. She is supposed to have been told her rights *before* she left to come here, she's supposed to have been given the pamphlet to read, explaining the Immigration Rules Concession and what to do if she's ill-treated. But that's good only so far as it goes. If, as I think, Sojourner came in as a visitor with the family, as a *guest,* she wouldn't have any rights and, for all we know, she can't read. She very likely can't read English, anyway.

'Probably she knew very little about the outside world, this England, Kingsmarkham. She was black but she never saw another black person. And then, one day, looking out of a window, she saw Melanie Akande out running . . . '

'Reg, that's pure fantasy.'

'It's intelligent conjecture,' Wexford retorted. 'She saw Melanie. Not once only but many times. Nearly every day from the middle of June onwards. She saw a black girl like herself out there, a Nigerian like herself, and maybe she sensed Melanie's African origins.'

'Allowing that that's true, which I'm not sure I can, so what?'

'I think it gave her confidence, Mike. It showed her that escape might be possible and the world wouldn't be entirely alien. So she ran away, in the dark, knowing nothing else . . . '

'No, that won't do,' Burden said. 'That can't be so. She *knew about the ESJ.* She knew it was where you went to find work or get money if there was no work . . . Look . . . the march is starting.'

A hundred of them? Like most people, Wexford wasn't much good at calculating numbers from a rapid glance. He would have to see them in sets of four or eight before he could tell. They were forming up now, four abreast, with a chosen two in the vanguard, holding the banner, both men and both middle-aged. Burden thought he recognized one of them from frequent visits to the Benefit Office. It was then that he had his first sight of the two officers from the uniformed branch, two of whom had suddenly appeared on the Corn Exchange steps.

They were a procession now and they began to move. What signal set them off was hard to know. A whispered word perhaps, travelling down the line from one to another, or the banner suddenly up-raised. The two officers on the steps went back to their car, parked on the market square flagstones, a white Ford with the scarlet stripe and eagle crest of the Mid-Sussex Constabulary.

'We'll follow them too,' said Wexford.

They stood back to let the column pass. Marching was rather slow, as it always is at the start. Speed would pick up when they came out into the main road to Kingsmarkham. Nearly everyone wore jeans, a shirt or tee-shirt, trainers on the feet, the ubiquitous uniform. The oldest person there was a man well into his sixties who could not have hoped for work and must be marching out of public-spiritedness or altruism or even for the fun of it. The youngest was a baby girl in a pushchair, her mother a twin of Kimberley Pearson before she came into a fortune.

A second banner brought up the rear: 'Jobs for All. Is It Too Much to Ask?' Two women carried it, a pair who looked so much alike they must have been mother and daughter. The column proceeded up the High Street, the police car crawling behind it. Wexford and Burden got back into their car and Donaldson moved out behind the white Ford.

'Someone must have told her,' said Wexford stubbornly, answering Burden's rebuttal as if there had been no break in their conversation. 'There must have been someone who went there or someone she met who told her the ESJ was the place.'

'Like who?' Burden was very sure of his ground. 'And if so, why didn't this person tell her where it was? Help her to escape, come to that? Tell her how to have recourse to the law?'

577

'I don't know.'

'If this person told her about jobs and benefit and how to get away, why hasn't he or she come to us?'

'These are minor things, Mike. These questions will be answered. At the moment we don't know where this beating up happened, where her death happened. But we do know why. Because, getting no help from Annette, she had no choice but to go home. Where else could she go?'

The column turned left into Angel Street and, picking up speed, came to the roundabout. The first exit was for Sewingbury, the second for Kingsmarkham, the third led to the industrial estate where Wexford had been two days before. After passing between the factory sites, it would rejoin the Kingsmarkham road at the pub called the Halfway House.

'Not much point in that,' said Burden. 'Half the industry's closed down.'

'I expect that is the point,' Wexford said.

The sun which had shone quite brightly while they were in Stowerton marketplace had gone in, retreating behind a thin veil of cloud. It had grown white and distant, a mere puddle of light, and the cloud was breaking, the little clouds were edged with darkness. But the heat remained, the heat even increased, and two of the young men among the marchers shed their shirts and tied them round their waists.

Reinforcements awaited them on the corner of Southern Drive, half a dozen men and a young woman with a banner of their own, obscurely proclaiming: 'Yes to Euro-Work'. There is perhaps no more dismal sight in social terms than a row of empty factories. Boarded-up shops have nothing on it. The factories, two of them brand new, had their windows all closed in the heat, their front doors padlocked and signs either offering the buildings to let or for sale planted in lawns on which untended grass grew long. The members of the column, again at some signal, turned their heads as one to acknowledge these monuments to joblessness as they passed, like a regiment honouring a cenotaph.

Not all the factories were closed. One that manufactured machine parts had remained open and another producing herbal cosmetics seemed to be flourishing, while Burden remarked that the printers on the corner of Southern Drive and Sussex Mile had reopened and its presses were once more operating. It was a good sign, a sign of recession ending and prosperity returning, he added. Wexford said nothing. He was thinking, and not just about economic problems. In accordance with its previous behaviour, the column should have cheered but it kept silence. Its members seemed not to share Burden's optimism. Up the long shallow hill the column went. The distance was a mile, at least a mile, and Wexford would have asked Donaldson to pass and go on ahead but passing was impossible. The road became a narrow country lane, a white pathway between high hedges and giant trees.

They met only one car before they reached the turn into the Kingsmarkham road. It stopped and the white Ford stopped too. But before the officer had his door open, the column's members had shifted, had converted themselves into a single line, the banners held back flat against the hedge. Slowly the car came on and as its occupants came into focus Wexford saw that the driver was Dr Akande, his son beside him in the passenger seat. Akande nodded and raised one hand in the classic gesture of thanks. The hand went down before he saw Wexford, or it might have been that he didn't see him. The boy next to him had a sullen injured expression. That was a family who would never forgive him for warning them to prepare for a daughter's, a sister's, death.

Traffic on the Kingsmarkham road wasn't at its heaviest at Friday lunchtime but it wasn't light either. The white Ford went past the marchers and took up its new position at the head of the column. More joined at the point where the Forby road turned in and they stopped to let a dozen cars coming this way from Kingsmarkham pass by. It was close on a hundred and fifty people now, Wexford calculated. A good many seemed to have decided that this stretch was the place to attach themselves to the marchers, whole families who had abandoned their cars on the grass verges, women with three or four children who looked on this as a fine day out, boys in their teens that Burden said could only be there because they were looking for trouble.

'We'll see. Maybe not.'

'I meant to tell you. All this slavery stuff put it out of my head. Annette did make a will and who do you think she left her flat to?'

'Bruce Snow,' said Wexford.

'How did *you* know? That's too bad, I was going to astound you.'

'I didn't know. I guessed. You wouldn't have been so dramatic if it had been the ex-husband or Jane Winster. I hope he's grateful. He'll

579

have somewhere to live after his wife's taken him to the cleaners. Won't be very comfortable with Diana Graddon on the other side of the street.'

The column was coming up to the outskirts of Kingsmarkham. Like most English country towns, it was approached by roads lined by big houses dating from the mid- and late-nineteenth century, 'villas' with high hedges and old-fashioned gardens, a subtly different atmosphere from Winchester Avenue and Ashley Grove. Wealth hid inside the walls of these houses instead of flaunting itself, concealed under an indifference that almost amounted to shabbiness.

A woman came running out of one of the houses, down a long flagged path, to join the march. She might have been employer, employee or employed, it was impossible to tell from her jeans and sleeveless shirt. Would Sylvia stay at home now the need had gone? Or would she join the march, generously campaigning for others? Burden, who had been lost in thought, suddenly said,

'That case history of yours, does it give the nationality of the employer?'

'No. Presumably, the family were British.'

'They might be, but Nigerian too.' Burden was struggling and Wexford didn't help him. 'I mean they might have been Nigerian *before* they were British.' He gave up. 'Were they black?'

'It's PC, it doesn't say.'

Up ahead of them the bridge over the Kingsbrook had come into sight. A massive resistance to the introduction of roundabouts had kept Kingsmarkham town centre, at least to a superficial eye, much as it had always been. But the bottleneck caused by the narrow bridge had resulted in so many traffic hold-ups that the bridge had been widened two years before. It was no longer the shallow stone arch featured on many postcards, but an uncompromising affair of grey-painted steel, overlooked by the motel extension to the Olive and Dove Hotel. The trees were mostly still there, the alders and willows and giant horse chestnuts.

It was the favoured beat of teenage boys who ran among traffic stopped by a red light to clean windscreens. The boys were there today but they gave up their thankless and often unwelcome labours to join the march. This side of the bridge a knot of people, perhaps a dozen, joined the tail of the column. Among them was Sophie Riding, the girl with the long corn-coloured hair Wexford had first seen waiting her turn in the Benefit Office and whose name he had learned from Melanie Akande. She and a woman with her were carrying a red silk banner, skilfully made and with the words 'Give Graduates a Chance' cut out in white and stitched to the silk.

The column waited. The policeman on duty waved on the three cars waiting at the lights and when they had passed beckoned the marchers on to the bridge. Wexford saw the drinkers at the tables outside the Olive get to their feet and crane their necks to see the lengthening procession go by. Burden said, 'By the way, something else I forget to say, Mrs Khoori got in.'

'Nobody ever tells me anything,' said Wexford.

'With a majority of seven. What you might call a close-run thing.'

'D'you want me to follow them, sir?' Donaldson asked.

The marchers intended to turn into Brook Road. The banner-carriers at the head of the column stopped on the far side of the bridge and one of them held up his hand, pointing to the left. Some consensus of opinion, an invisible wave, must have passed along the quadruple line of people, for the message reached him and the column turned, snaking to the left like a train negotiating a sharp curve in the rails.

'Park opposite the Benefit Office,' Wexford said.

Ahead of them, the marked police car did this too. On the walls between which the steps ran up sat Rossy, Danny and Nige, and Raffy with them. Raffy, without his hat for once, displayed the huge helmet of dreadlocks that crowned his head and tumbled in a cascade down his back. As the procession approached and came to a straggling halt, Danny got down off the wall and stubbed out his cigarette.

'What happens now?' Burden said.

'Some gesture will be made.'

As Wexford spoke, Sophie Riding gave up her end of the 'Give Graduates a Chance' banner to the man next her. She detached herself from the column and walked up the steps. In her hand she held a sheet of paper, a petition perhaps or statement. Rossy, Danny, Raffy and Nige stared after her as she disappeared into the Benefit Office.

She was inside no more than fifteen seconds. The paper had been handed over and a point had been made. Within moments of her absorption back into the column, the double doors of the Benefit Office opened and Cyril Leyton appeared. He looked from left to right, then directly at the column, which was no longer a column, which had lost its shape and become an amorphous scattered crowd. Leyton scowled. He seemed about to say something and perhaps would have done if he had not, in that moment, caught sight of the police car on the opposite side of the road.

The door swung and swung again behind him as he went in. It was the kind that is made, no doubt wisely in the circumstances, to be unslammable. Apparently at no word of command, like a flock of birds whose leader directs them by silent unknown means, the crowd formed into fours once more, swung round – those in the vanguard had no intention of giving up pride of place – and headed back the way it had come.

The boys from the wall joined on the end. Sophie Riding took up one end of her banner and the woman with her the other end. As the column turned into the High Street, the clock on St Peter's church began striking noon.

# 24

The heat was like the inside of a rain forest now, or like a sauna. There was no breath of wind. The sun was lost under banks of frothy whiteness that overlaid a sky of dark grey cloud. Thunder had begun to roll but so distantly that its rumblings were lost behind the throb and beat of traffic noise.

The march occupied the left-hand lane of Kingsmarkham High Street. Here the High Street was fairly wide and there was room for Stowerton-bound cars to creep past, but those heading for Stowerton were diverted into Queen Street and the long serpentine southern route. The column passed St Peter's church as the final note of the midday clock chimes died away, and proceeded northwards close to the churchyard wall. At the point where the diversion began two police officers, a man and a woman, cleared space for the column to pass. It had picked up more people at the churchyard gate and, outside the biggest of the High Street supermarkets, a man and a girl who had taken a trolley from the rank on the forecourt abandoned it and tagged on to the end of the procession instead.

The police car with the stripe down its side and the crest on its door had turned back and been replaced by an unmarked Vauxhall, driven by PC Stafford from the uniformed branch with PC Rowlands beside him. Wexford and Burden had left theirs on a vacant meter outside the offices of Hawkins and Steele where Bruce Snow worked, but when Stafford put his head out and offered a lift, Wexford shook his head and said they would follow the column on foot. Sophie Riding, who had handed in the petition at the Benefit Office, was two people ahead of them. They were sandwiched between her and her banner and the unmarked police car. That was how they came to witness so entirely what was about to happen.

The Range Rover was parked on the right-hand side and facing right on a broken yellow band fifty yards or so ahead of them outside Woolworths. It was an inconvenient place to have parked on this morning of all mornings but its positioning broke no traffic rule. Wexford didn't recognize the Range Rover, any more than he did the white van behind it and the car in front of it, but he did note the behaviour of its driver and the behaviour of the other drivers in leaving vehicles on that particular spot as antisocial. He noted too its olive green colour and a memory came into his mind of the Women, Aware! meeting and a note passed to him. More interesting at that moment was the sight, far ahead, only accessible to someone as tall as he, of Anouk Khoori crossing the greensward outside the council offices, her arms outspread. She wore a loose flowing garment and she was holding out her arms like a royal personage returning from a goodwill tour, greeting the children from whom she has been parted for a month.

Wexford was remarking to Burden that he wondered if she would tell the marchers that she knew they would come, she had had a feeling they would, when the nearside door of the Range Rover opened and Christopher Riding stepped down on to the pavement. The Range Rover was now no more than a car-length ahead of where Wexford and Burden were. Its offside door opened and Christopher's father got out. Things happened very quickly then.

Christopher edged round the front of the Range Rover as his sister Sophie came alongside. He and Swithun Riding in a concerted swift movement seized her by the arms and she dropped the banner with a cry. They lifted her off her feet, threw back the car door and slung her inside. Both tall and powerful, with big hands and muscular arms, they swung her in the air, her bright swatch of corn-gold hair flying out, before throwing her into the back seat.

The marchers in the immediate vicinity fell back, fanning out. A woman screamed. Someone picked up the banner. The column ahead of the girl marched on, unaware of what had happened, but those at its tail stopped to stare. Now Swithun Riding was back in the driver's seat, his son squeezing himself between the bonnet of the Range Rover and the car in front of it. There must have been a central locking system, for Sophie couldn't unlock the door and escape. She was beating her fists against the window, she began to scream.

Wexford looked back at the unmarked Vauxhall and cocked his head at Stafford. He lunged forward and grabbed the rear door handle, but finding the door locked as he expected, hammered on the glass. Stafford and Rowlands had both left the Vauxhall. This was not what they had expected, this was unprecedented, this in *Kingsmarkham*?

The driver of the car ahead of the Range Rover, knowingly or unwittingly, now reversed an inch or two. It was a dangerous move and made Christopher let out a bellow of rage and fear. The reversing car nearly crushed him, but the driver had braked just in time. Christopher found himself trapped between its rear bumper and the Range Rover's front fender. The two vehicles made a man trap which pinned his legs. He stood struggling, waving his arms and shouting, 'Go forward, go forward, you bastard!'

The front of the column, still unaware of the fracas at the rear, marched on, unperturbed. Like a pantomime horse whose hind legs have given up the game, it broke into an ungainly trot for the last final hundred yards of its progress. The rearguard had scattered into a crowd of fascinated spectators. Burden, with a quick nod to Wexford, slipped round the back of the Range Rover and in front of the white van behind it, walked past the imprisoned screaming girl, and wrenched open the passenger door Riding had unlocked for his son.

'Go back, go back!' the boy was yelling now.

Riding started the engine and had begun to move the shift when Burden put his foot on the step and climbed into the passenger seat. Riding had never seen him before and must have taken him for an interfering member of the public. Without hestitation, he did at once the utterly unexpected, drawing back his right arm like a discus thrower and letting fly with a savage punch to Burden's jaw.

The passenger door swung open. Burden reeled backwards through the empty space. He broke his fall by clutching at the door frame but still half-tumbled to the pavement. The girl screamed more loudly. His passenger door swinging, Riding reversed into the white van, hitting it with a reverberating crash. Then he saw the uniformed policemen. He saw Wexford.

Wexford said, 'Open that door.'

Riding only stared at him. Half the crowd had moved round the Woolworths side of the van. Someone picked Burden up. He staggered, dazed, put a hand up to his head and sat down heavily on the low wall in front of the store. Wexford pushed the boy out of the

585

way and, moving between the Range Rover and the car ahead, stepped up inside the swinging door.

'Don't try the same thing with me, will you?' he said.

He unlocked the nearside rear door and helped the girl out. Her face was awash with tears. She held on to him, her hands gripping his sleeves. A stream of invective pouring from Riding made her tremble. He thrust his face at the open door, shouting in Burden's direction, 'What's it to you if I stop my own daughter making a foul exhibition of herself? What business is it of yours, for Christ's sake?'

The girl shook. Her teeth had begun to chatter. Christopher, now free and rubbing his crushed legs, stood up and put out one hand to her in a gesture of appeasement. She screamed at him, 'Get away from me!'

Wexford said, 'All of you are coming to the police station *now*.'

Blood was running down Burden's face. He mouthed something, while holding on to his head. The howling siren of an ambulance, summoned by Stafford, sent the crowd falling back, splitting now into two distinct groups, one solidly behind Burden, the rest spectators by the churchyard wall. The ambulance came out of York Street and blocked the road, parking where the column had marched. Ahead the marchers had gone out of sight and with the appearance of the paramedics, two of them with a stretcher Burden scowled at, the first drops of rain began to fall.

Riding had unlocked his driver's door. His face dark red, he stepped down and said to Wexford. 'Look, what I did was entirely justifiable. I told my daughter I'd stop her if she joined the march, she knew what was coming to her. That chap seemed to think he was making some sort of citizen's arrest . . .'

'That chap is a police officer,' Wexford said.

'O God, I didn't . . .'

'If you'll get into the car we'll go to the police station. You can do your explaining there.'

The girl was tall and strong and straight. She looked what she was, the product of twenty-two or -three years of top-grade feeding, fresh air, care and attention, the best of schools. Wexford didn't know when he had seen a more vulnerable face. There was no bruising on it but still it looked bruised. The skin was soft beyond belief, almost transparent, the eyes puffy, the lips chapped and that in high summer. Her hair, the colour of the ripe barley they had been cutting in the fields up at Mynford, looked unnatural framing that suffering face, it looked like false hair worn by an actress miscast for her part.

She said to Karen Malahyde, 'I can go home if they're not there.'

'Well,' said Karen, but she said it kindly, 'just at the moment you aren't going anywhere. Would you like a cup of tea?'

Sophie Riding said she would. Carefully, Wexford said to her, 'We won't go in the interview room. They aren't very pleasant places. We'll go up to my office.' Suddenly, he thought of Joel Snow and he knew Karen was thinking of him too. This was different, of course it was – wasn't it? Joel too had been unwilling while this girl knew it was the only way. He said to her in the lift, 'It won't take long.'

'What do you want me to do?'

'Something I wish I'd been able to ask you to do two weeks ago.'

They went into his office. The rain was heavy enough to blind the windows and make it dark. Karen put on lights and the sky outside the window turned to a streaming twilight. She gave Sophie a chair.

Wexford sat down behind his desk. 'It was you sent me that question about a rapist at the Women, Aware! meeting?'

She was eager to talk but she was afraid too. 'Oh, yes! I wanted to come round afterwards, like you said. I would have done if I could, I hope you believe me.'

Suddenly, preceding the thunder by seconds, a brilliant zig-zag of lightning expelled everything, seeming to hold the streaming water suspended, making the dark sky invisible, until the crash came and the world went on. Sophie shuddered and made a little sound, like a protest. There was a tap at the door and Pemberton came in with tea. She covered her face with her hands for a moment, then took them away to show the tears flowing down her cheeks. Karen pushed the box of tissues at her.

'I believe you,' Wexford said. 'I understand what stopped you coming to me.'

Sophie took a tissue. 'Thanks.' She said to Wexford, 'What do you want me to do?'

'Make a statement. Tell us about it. It won't be difficult, practically speaking. It may be difficult emotionally.'

'Well,' she said, 'I can't go on like I have been. It has to stop. I can't go another day, not another minute.'

He said fairly, 'There are other ways. We'll manage without your statement. You don't have to do it. But if you don't, I'm afraid . . . well, there may be more . . .'

Karen said into the recording device, 'Sophie Riding at Kingsmark-ham Police Station on Friday, July twenty-ninth. The time is 12.43pm. DCI Wexford and DS Malahyde are present . . . '

When it was over and he had heard it all, Wexford went downstairs to where Sophie's father sat in Interview Room One with DC Pemberton. He looked chastened. His face had resumed its normal colour. The twenty minutes he had waited down here had no doubt brought him to regret his hasty behaviour. A man who has hit another man is always aghast to discover that the other is a policeman.

He got up when Wexford came in and began to apologize. His reasons for behaving as he had came out with easy fluency and they were the excuses of the man who has always been able to buy or talk his way out of trouble.

'Mr Wexford, I can't tell you how sorry I am about all this. Needless to say I wouldn't have struck your officer if I'd had any idea. I took him for a member of the public.'

'Yes, I expect you did.'

'This doesn't have to go any further, does it? If my daughter had been reasonable and got into the car – after all, she'd completed the best part of that damn fool march – if she'd done that none of this would have happened. I'm not a harsh father, I adore my children . . . '

'Your treatment of your children isn't in question,' Wexford said. 'Before you say any more I should warn you that anything you do say will be taken down and may be given in evidence . . . '

Interrupting, Riding shouted, 'You're not charging me with hitting that chap!'

'No,' said Wexford. 'I'm charging you with murder, incitement to murder and attempted murder. And when I have done that I shall go into the room next door and charge your son with rape and attempted murder.'

'Without Sophie Riding's statement,' Wexford said, 'I doubt if anything could have been made to stick. We have no evidence and no proof, no more than conjecture.'

Burden's face was swollen like a Victorian cartoonist's image of a man with toothache. 'Assault on a police officer is the least of his worries, I suppose. Odd, isn't it, I was the one most impressed by what Mavrikiev said about killing someone with your fists and it was me who really had it brought home to me.

'It's a funny thing, you see these characters in films, westerns and that sort of thing, they knock each other around but it never seems to have any effect, they get a great swinging blow to the jaw but they're up again in a flash and hammering away at the other one. And you see them in the next scene with not a mark on them, all spruced up with a girl on their arm, taking her out for a night on the town.'

'Hurts, does it?'

'It's not so much that it hurts. It feels so enormous. And it doesn't feel as if it'll ever *work* again. At any rate he left me all my teeth. So, are you going to tell me about it?'

'Freeborn'll be here in half an hour and I'll have to tell *him*.'

'Well, you can tell me first,' said Burden.

Wexford sighed. 'I'll play you the tape of Sophie Riding's statement. You realize, of course, that Sojourner knew of the existence of the Benefit Office through Sophie. She'd heard Sophie talking about it, about going there and signing on and so forth, though she didn't know where it was.'

'What, talking about it to her parents?'

'And her brothers and her little sister, no doubt. Sojourner waited on them, she'd always have been in and out, though never out of the house.'

'How did they get her into the country in the first place?'

'Sophie doesn't know. She wasn't there, she was already at Myringham Polytechnic that's now Myringham University and before that she'd been at boarding school here. But she'd seen Sojourner at their home in Kuwait when she was there in the holidays and she remembers when Sojourner first came. Her idea is that she was brought here as the boy's girlfriend. In a hideous kind of way, she *was*, if "girlfriend" is one definition of the woman you have forcible sexual intercourse with.'

'*That* was going on?'

'Oh yes. The father too, I daresay, though I don't know – yet. Listen to Sophie.'

Wexford wound the tape on, pressed 'play', reversed and got the point in the statement he wanted. The girl's voice was soft and plaintive, yet outraged too. It came over as a cry for help, yet there was no appeal in it.

589

My mother told me a Kuwaiti man bought her from her father in Calabar, Nigeria, for five pounds. He meant to educate her and treat her like a daughter but he died and she had to be a servant. My mother talked as if we'd done her a great favour, as if it was the best thing in the world for her finding a 'good home' with us. 'Good home' is the expression they use about dogs that get rescued, isn't it? I think she was about fifteen then.

I never thought much about it. I know I should have but I wasn't at home with them very much. I liked it here in England, I was always longing to get back to England. When the Gulf War started they came home. It wasn't a problem for my father, he could work anywhere, he's a brilliant paediatric surgeon. I don't like saying it, I wish I didn't have to, but it's true. He loves babies, you should see him with a baby, and he loves all of us, his family, his children. But we're different, as far as he is concerned, we're what he calls the upper crust. He says some people are destined to be hewers of wood and drawers of water. I think that comes from the Bible. For him some people are born to be slaves and wait on others.

I must have been very naive. I didn't know what the bruises on her were . . . well, the bruises and cuts and all the other marks. In Kuwait I'd thought she was pretty to look at but she wasn't pretty in England. I'd graduated and I was home all the time and it was all a mystery to me. I never saw anyone hit her but I could tell she was frightened of my father and my brother. And my other brother David when he was at home, though mostly he wasn't, mostly he's away at college in America. The bad part – for me, that is – the bad part was that I thought she was stupid and clumsy, I could even see what my mother meant when she said she wasn't fit to sleep in a proper bedroom.

The machine on pause, Wexford went on, 'Psychologists say that someone ugly and dirty is a ready candidate for abuse. That your own abuse has resulted in the ugliness makes no difference. The reasoning behind it seems to be that ugliness deserves punishment and dirt and neglect of personal hygiene even more so. It got to a point where Sojourner was being beaten and struck for every small fault. She worked twelve or fourteen hours a day but that wasn't enough. Susan Riding told me herself they had six bedrooms in that house but that didn't mean they had one for Sojourner. She slept in a small room off the kitchen. All the rooms on the ground floor at the back have bars at the windows, to keep out burglars no doubt, but very convenient if you want to prevent someone escaping.

'I've just been to the house, I've seen it. It used to be a dogs' room and they've got a dog in there now. Susan Riding says it was more "appropriate", her word, for Sojourner to be in there, "in case they wanted her to do anything for them in the night." The mattress on the floor was apparently "what she'd been used to", she "wouldn't know what to do with a bed." Here's Sophie again.'

The girl's voice sounded clearer and more confident this time.

I needed a job, so I did the obvious thing, I went to the Job Centre and I signed on, only it wasn't the obvious thing to my parents. My father said it was a disgrace, that was for the working classes. He was quite prepared to keep me. Education wasn't *for* anything, he said, it was to make you a finer, better person. He'd make me an allowance. Hadn't he always kept me? My mother actually said they would keep me *until I got married*. We argued about this a lot and that poor girl overheard. Her English was never brilliant but she'd have understood that. She'd have known there was a place nearby you could go to and ask them to find you work and if there wasn't any work they'd give you money.

It was the beginning of July, the first or the second, when my brother Christopher asked her to wash his running shoes for him . . . well, told her to. They were white trainers. She made a mess of it, I don't know what she did, but she was terrified. Anyway, he beat her up for it. That was when I first realized what went on. It sounds absurd, I know, that I didn't know before, but I suppose I just didn't want to believe that of my own brother. I love my brother, or I did love him, he's my twin, you know.

I saw Christopher go into her room and come out again after about twenty minutes. I'd have gone in but she didn't make a sound, not through all that beating she never made a sound.

But when I saw her next day I knew. I asked my brother and he denied it. She was clumsy, he said, I should know that, she always had been, she wasn't really fit to live in a civilized house. He made a lot of remarks about mud huts and he said she couldn't cope with furniture, she was always knocking into furniture. Well, I wasn't satisfied, I told my father but all that happened was he flew into a rage. If you haven't seen him in a rage you can't know what

I mean. He's terrifying. He accused me of being disloyal to my family, he wanted to know where I'd 'picked up these ideas' and was it from my 'Marxist' friends I'd met at the Job Centre.

I know I should have done more. I have a lot of guilt about that. Somehow, then, I knew what I'd been hiding from myself all this time, that Christopher had raped her too, over and over, there had been all the signs I pretended not to see. All I did was send you that question at the meeting and that was worse than useless.

On the Monday after the beating she disappeared. My father was at the hospital and Christopher was in London at a job interview of all things. I guessed she'd run away and my mother thought she had, but we didn't know what to do, and in the evening my mother had to go out to a committee preparing for that Women, Aware! meeting. She left a note for my father. I said we ought to tell the police but my mother got into a panic at that. Of course I can understand why now. I had a date and when I got in at about eleven-thirty my mother was in bed and Christopher was out but my father was there. He said he didn't know what we were in a flap about, he'd told my mother. He'd sent the girl home, she was worse than useless and it made him sick seeing her about the house. He said he'd sent her back to Banjul on British Airways but there isn't a BA flight to Banjul on a Monday, the only flights are on Sunday and Fridays, I checked. My brother was out all evening and my father told me and my mother he was driving her to Heathrow but he can't have been because there wasn't a flight.

I didn't believe any of it. For some reason I thought she'd be in her room. They'd have beaten her up when she came back and she'd be in there lying on her mattress. I tried the door but it was locked. Well, you know, in a house like ours – a house like *theirs* – all the inside keys fit all the locks. I got another key and unlocked the door and everything was gone. She hadn't got much, just the two dresses that were my mother's cast-offs from years back and those awful black lace-up canvas boot things my mother bought her, the cheapest you can get. But it was all gone, all but the mattress and her headcloth. I don't know why they didn't find it when they cleaned the blood up but they didn't. It was on the mattress and the mattress was sort of red and blue. Well, the cloth was blue and red – red with the blood on it.

I've kept it. It was like a kind of madness, keeping it. I longed to throw it away but I couldn't. Even then it didn't occur to me that she might be dead. My brother was out that night for hours. I heard him come in, it must have been two-thirty or three, and he went off on his holiday to Spain next morning, so I never had a chance to talk to him. Anyway, I was afraid to talk to him, this wasn't my brother, this wasn't Chris that had been closer to me than anyone. Then I found his sweater in the wash with blood all over it.

I thought maybe my father had got her taken to hospital secretly because my brother had gone too far. My father has a lot of influence, I don't know if he could do that, but I thought he could. All I could think of then was my brother raping her, my brother raping *anyone*. I didn't blame my father much then, I thought maybe he was just protecting his own son, I went to the Women, Aware! meeting with him and I wrote that question to you on an impulse. My father didn't see what I'd asked. I told him I'd asked whether it was legal to carry a CS gas canister. But I couldn't come up afterwards and explain, I couldn't get away from him.

Chief Constable Freeborn seemed to have forgotten about Wexford's 'carousing' picture in the paper. If the three weeks it had taken to catch the murderer of the two women still rankled, he gave no sign of it. He was all affability. To the old 'snug', a tiny room containing a table and three chairs, in the deepest recesses of the Olive and Dove, a barmaid brought the three beers he had ordered. Wexford sat down in the chair with the arms. He thought he deserved it.

'You have to remember,' he began, 'that she knew nothing about what rights she had under the Immigration Act, she didn't know there *was* an Immigration Act. She knew she wasn't allowed to work, but "work", it had been explained to her long ago, was what you got paid for and she was never paid, she was simply given "a good home". Susan Riding called her the "au pair" – or that's what she called her to me after Sojourner was dead. To do Mrs Riding justice, and I suppose everyone merits justice, I don't think she knew much about Sojourner's fate. She let her sleep on a mattress on the floor in the "dog's room" because she's that sort of woman, the kind that used to talk about the poor keeping coal in the bath if you gave them bathrooms. In buying Sojourner the cheapest footwear she could get, she probably thought she was being very bountiful. I wonder what she'd say if she knew the shop assistant put her down as a bag lady who slept on the street?

'But she knew nothing about the rape or the violent assaults, and if she suspected she shut her eyes to it, told herself not to let her imagination run wild. That evening when she came home from the committee meeting, her husband told her he'd sent the girl home and Christopher was out driving her to the airport. According to Mrs Riding, Sojourner had become "dirty and lazy" and was worse than useless. Except that she needed help in the house, she was glad to see the back of her.

'What had in fact happened was that Sojourner ran away on the Monday afternoon. Riding was out, the boy Christopher was in London and the young sister was at school. She didn't know where to go, she had never been out before, not out of their grounds, that is, but she knew there was a place where you went to find a job. She must have reasoned that anywhere she could find work couldn't be worse than what she'd left behind.'

Freeborn interrupted. 'You say she didn't know where to go. Winchester Avenue's a good way from the – what-d'you-call-it – ESJ, how did she know the way?'

'She didn't, sir. Perhaps she followed the river. You can see the Kingsbrook if you look down from there over the gardens. Melanie Akande liked to look at it while she was out running. Maybe some instinct led Sojourner towards the river, downhill, maybe she knew a town is often on a river. Her instinct led her to Glebe Road and she encountered Oni Johnson who directed her to the Benefit Office. The rest you know, how she followed Annette home and, failing to get the help she wanted from her, she had no choice but to return to where she had come from.'

'Pity this Annette didn't send her to us,' said Freeborn.

The understatement of all time, Wexford thought, but of course he didn't say so. 'She doesn't seem to have gone home at once or perhaps it took her a while to find her way back. At any rate, she didn't get there until Susan Riding and Sophie had gone out. Let us take it that she went in the back way and into her room where Swithun Riding found her.

'I don't say he meant to kill her. There seems no reason why he would. He asked her where she had been and when she told him he asked if she had spoken to anyone. Yes, the woman who takes the children across the road and this woman from the place where they give you jobs or they give you money. What's her name and where does she live? She tells him and it all comes out. Riding's daughter

594

has described his rages. He flew into one then and set about her with his fists. Mike knows what his fist feels like and she was a young girl, thin and frail. They fed her pretty badly. Even so, she didn't die from his fists but from striking her head against the steel frame round the window bars. When you're in that room you can see how it happened.'

'So he got his son to help him dispose of her,' said Burden. 'Young Christopher took the body to Framhurst Woods and buried it, did he?'

'That was when he was supposed to be driving their erstwhile slave to Heathrow. I doubt if he knew where to do the deed, just drove out into the country until he found somewhere suitable. The road isn't busy and he'd have waited till dark.'

'And after that Riding had to make up his mind what to do about Annette and Oni.'

'I don't think he meant to do anything about Oni. After all, the Oni connection was a bit tenuous. Oni wouldn't go to the police, she had nothing to go *with*, but Annette was different. He must have gone nearly mad wondering what Sojourner had told Annette. He wouldn't have got much sleep that night. Just after Annette made her phone call to the Benefit Office next day a man phoned and asked for her Ingrid Pamber thought it was Snow but it wasn't, it was Riding. And he got an answer that gave him a little breathing space. Annette was at home ill in bed.'

'How did he know her name?' Freeborn wanted to know.

'Sojourner got it off the plate above the bell at Ladyhall Court. His next move was to get hold of Zack Nelson. Nelson owed him one, you see. It was Riding who performed the operation on Zack's son when the child was found to have some kind of heart malformation at a few weeks old. No doubt, Nelson had made extravagant promises at the time – "Anything in the world I can do for you, doc, any time, you only have to ask," – you can imagine the kind of thing.

'Zack needed money too. He needed somewhere for his girlfriend and their child to live. But Zack botched it up, he let Percy Hammond see his face and he had to go back on Riding's instructions for a somewhat less venal offence – burglary. He knew he'd go down for that, he *wanted* to go down for that, so he got Riding to pay the blood money into an account he opened for Kimberley Pearson.

'So it looked as if Riding and his son were in the clear, until that is

595

our treasure-seeking plumber dug up the body. Even then it must have been clear to Riding no one had the faintest idea who Sojourner was. The real fear started when he was picking up his younger daughter from the Thomas Proctor School and he saw me homing on Oni Johnson.

'I saw the Range Rover pull away from outside the Thomas Proctor the day of the attack on Oni but of course I didn't make the connection. I thought it was her son Raffy we wanted to talk to, not Oni. Riding easily got to Castlegate before she got home – or else his son went: Christopher may also have seen me, for he was there in the Epsons' pink Escort, picking up the Epsons' older child. By the way, unpleasant though it is to contemplate, I think Christopher followed Melanie to Stowerton on that previous occasion because he had acquired a taste for black girls, it was black girls he fancied. Luckily for her, Melanie didn't fancy *him* and he was no doubt afraid to attempt the rape of a free and independent young woman.

'I don't yet know which of them made the attempt on Oni's life. We shall find out. I do know that it was Riding who went into the Intensive Care Ward next day and – with very little time or privacy at his disposal – pulled the IV line out from Oni's arm. It didn't work but it was worth a try.'

'Who picked the Riding child up from school the day Sojourner ran away?' Burden speculated. 'Not Riding or his wife obviously. A friend probably, they very likely had a rota system. Because if he'd done it or his wife had done it they'd have caught Sojourner before she got to Annette or Oni and none of it would have happened. I wonder if he thinks of that now?'

Freeborn, who had finished his drink in one single long swig, said irritably, 'Why do you call her that? What does it mean?'

'I didn't fancy Miss X. We hadn't a name for her.'

'Well, you know it now, presumably?'

'Oh, yes.' said Wexford. 'I know it now. If she ever had a surname no one seems to remember it. Sophie never forgot the first name she gave them when she was handed over from the man who died, but the others had forgotten it. She was called Simisola.' He got up. 'Shall we go?'

# Acknowledgement

The author is grateful to Bridget Anderson for permission to quote in this novel passages from her book *Britain's Secret Slaves* published by Anti-Slavery International and Kalayaan.

# ROAD RAGE

To the Chief Constable and Officers of the Suffolk Constabulary.

My thanks are especially due to Chief Inspector Vince Coomber of the Suffolk Constabulary who gave me good advice and corrected my mistakes.

# 1

Wexford was walking in Framhurst Great Wood for the last time.
That was how he put it to himself. He had walked there for years, all
his life, and walked as well as ever, was as strong, and would
continue to be so for a long time yet. Not he but the wood would
change, the wood would scarcely be there. Savesbury Hill would
scarcely be there or Stringfield Marsh, and the River Brede, into
which the Kingsbrook flowed at Watersmeet, that too would be
unrecognisable.

Nothing would happen yet. Months must pass first. For six
months the trees would remain and the uninterrupted view over the
hill, the otters in the Brede and the rare Map butterfly in Framhurst
Deeps. But he didn't think he could bear to see it any more.

> And that will be England gone,
> The shadows, the meadows, the lanes,
> The guildhalls, the carved choirs.
> There'll be books, it will linger on
> In galleries; but all that remains
> For us will be concrete and tyres.

He walked among the trees, chestnuts, great grey beeches with
sealskin trunks, oaks whose branches had a green coating of lichen.
The trees thinned and spread themselves across the grass that rabbits
had cropped. He saw that the coltsfoot was in bloom, earliest of
wildflowers. When he was young he had seen blue fritillaries here,
plants so localised that they were seen only within a ten-mile radius
of Kingsmarkham, but that was a long time ago. When I retire, he
had told his wife, I want to live in London so that I can't see the
countryside destroyed.

601

A defeatist attitude, she said. You should fight to keep it. I haven't noticed fighting keeping it, he'd said. She was on the committee of the newly formed KABAL, Kingsmarkham Against the Bypass And Landfill. They had already had one meeting and had sung 'We Shall Overcome'. The Deputy Chief Constable had got to hear of it and said he hoped Wexford wasn't thinking of joining as there was going to be trouble, trouble of a peace-disturbing and possibly violent kind, in which the Chief Inspector might well be, at least peripherally, involved.

A little breeze had got up. He came out of Framhurst Great Wood on to the open land and looked up at the ring of trees crowning Savesbury Hill. From here not a roof or tower or silo or pylon could be seen, only birds flying in formation towards Cheriton Forest. The road would pass through the foundations of the Roman villa, the habitat of Araschnia levana, the Map butterfly, found nowhere else in the British Isles, cross the Brede and then the Kingsbrook. Unless the impossible happened and they made a tunnel for it or put it on stilts. Araschnia and the otters would like stilts about as much as they liked concrete, he thought.

Kingsmarkham wasn't the only town in England whose bypass had been swallowed up in building and so become just another street. When that happened a new bypass had to be built, and when that too was engulfed, another perhaps. But he would be dead by then.

With this gloomy thought he returned to his car that he had left parked in Savesbury hamlet. He always came to his walk by car. Would he be prepared to give up his car for the sake of England? What a question!

He drove home through Framhurst and Pomfret Monachorum in pessimistic mood and therefore noticing all the ugly things, the silos like iron sausages up-ended, the sheds full of battery hens, electricity substations sprouting wires and looking like newly landed aliens, bungalows with red-brick garden walls and wrought-iron railings, Leylandii hedges. Nietzsche (or someone) had said that having no taste was worse than having bad taste. Wexford didn't agree. On a happy day he would have observed newly planted well-chosen trees, roofs rethatched, cattle in the meadows, ducks paddling in couples, looking for nesting sites. But it wasn't a happy day, not, that is, till he came into his house.

His wife's habit was to come out of wherever she was to meet him when something good had happened, something she couldn't wait to tell him. He bent down to pick up the card which had been dropped through the letter-box, looked up and saw her. She was smiling.

'You'll never guess,' she said.

'No, I won't, so don't keep me in suspense.'

'You're going to be a grandfather again.'

He hung up his coat. Their daughter Sylvia already had two children and a shaky relationship with her husband. He risked spoiling Dora's pleasure. 'Another scheme for keeping the marriage going?'

'It's not Sylvia, Reg. It's Sheila.'

He went up to her, put his hands on her shoulders.

'I said you'd never guess.'

'No, I never would have. Give me a kiss.' He hugged her. 'It's turned into a happy day.'

She didn't know what he meant. 'Of course I wish she were married. It's no good telling me one out of every three children is born out of wedlock.'

'I wasn't going to,' he said. 'Shall I phone her?'

'She said she'd be in all day. The baby's due in September. She took her time telling us, I must say. Give me that card, Reg. Mary Pearson told me her son got a holiday job delivering those cards for this new car-hire firm, Contemporary Cars, and he's taking one to every house in Kingsmarkham. Every house – can you imagine?'

' "Contemporary Cars"? No one'll be able to pronounce it. Do we need a new car-hire firm?'

'We need a good one. *I* do. You've always got the car. Go on. Phone Sheila. I hope it's a girl.'

'I don't care what it is,' said Wexford, and he began dialling his daughter's number.

# 2

The route planned for the Kingsmarkham Bypass was to begin at the arterial road (an A road with motorway status) north of Stowerton, pass east of Sewingbury and Myfleet, cut across Framhurst Heath, enter the valley at the foot of Savesbury Hill, bisect Savesbury hamlet, cross Stringfield Marsh and rejoin the main road north of Pomfret. The minimum of residential area was to be disturbed, Cheriton Forest avoided and the remains of the Roman villa just circumvented.

Probably the first remark on the subject to appear in a newspaper was that made by Norman Simpson-Smith of the British Council for Archaeology. 'The Highways Agency says this road will pass through the periphery of the villa,' he said. 'That is like saying an access road being built in London would only cause minor damage to Westminster Abbey.'

Until then the protest had simply taken the form of representation by various bodies at the inquiry held jointly by the Departments of Transport and the Environment. Friends of the Earth, the Sussex Wildlife Trust and the Royal Society for the Protection of Birds, were the obvious ones. Less expected presences were those of the British Council for Archaeology, Greenpeace, the World Wide Fund for Nature, KABAL and a body that called itself SPECIES.

But after Simpson-Smith's comment the protests came, as Wexford put it, not in single spies but in battalions. The environmental groups, whose members numbered two million, sent representatives to look at the site.

Marigold Lambourne, of the Royal Society of Entomologists, was there on behalf of both the Scarlet Tiger Moth and the Map butterfly. 'Araschnia is found thinly distributed in north-eastern

France,' she said, 'and in the British Isles solely on Framhurst Heath. There are probably two hundred specimens extant. If this bypass is built there will soon be none. This is not some minuscule fly or bacterium invisible to the naked eye we are talking about but an exquisite butterfly with a two-inch wingspan.'

Peter Tregear of the Sussex Wildlife Trust said, 'This bypass is a project dreamed up in the seventies and approved in the eighties. But there has been a revolution in global thinking since then. It is all utterly inappropriate for the end of the century.'

A woman wearing a sandwich board with *No, No, No to Rape of Savesbury* painted on it appeared on the hill when the tree-fellers moved in. It was June, and warm, and the sun was shining. She took off the sandwich board and revealed herself entirely naked. The tree-fellers, who would have cheered and whistled if she had been young or had been sent to one of them as a strippergram, turned away and set to even more busily with their chain-saws. The foreman called the police on his mobile. Thus the woman, whose name was Debbie Harper, got her photograph – her large, shapely body wrapped by then in a policeman's jacket – in all the national papers and on to the front page of the *Sun*.

That was when the tree people came.

Perhaps Debbie Harper's picture alerted them to what was going on. Many of them belonged to no known official body. They were New Age Travellers, or some of them were, and if they arrived in cars and caravans, none of these vehicles were parked on or near the site. Debbie Harper had disrupted the tree-felling and only four silver birches had so far been cut down. The tree people drove steel bolts into tree trunks at a height calculated to buckle a chain-saw blade when felling began. Then they began building themselves dwellings in the tops of beeches and oaks, tree-houses of planks and tarpaulin and approached by ladders which could be pulled up once the occupant was installed.

That was June and the site of the first of the tree camps was at Savesbury Deeps.

Debbie Harper, who lived with her boyfriend and three teenage children in Wincanton Road, Stowerton, gave interviews to every newspaper which asked her. She was a member of KABAL and SPECIES, Greenpeace and Friends of the Earth, but her interviewers weren't much interested in that. What they liked about her was that she was a Pagan with a capital P, kept ancient Celtic festivals and worshipped deities called Ceridwen and Nudd, and posed for *Today* wearing just three leaves, not fig-leaves but rhubarb, these being more appropriate for an English summer.

'We're unhappy about the spiking of the trees,' Dora said on her return from a meeting of KABAL. 'Apparently the chain-saws can come apart and maul workmen's arms. Isn't that an awful thought?'

'This is just the beginning,' her husband said.

'What do you mean, Reg?'

'Remember Newbury? They had to get in six hundred security guards to protect the contractors. And someone cut the brake pipe on a coach carrying the guards to the site.'

'Have you talked to anyone who actually wants this bypass?'

'I can't say I have,' said Wexford.

'Do you want it?'

'You know I don't. But I'm not prepared to give up driving a car. I'm not happy about sitting in traffic jams and feeling my blood pressure go up. Like most of us, I want to eat my cake and have it.' He sighed. 'I daresay Mike wants it.'

'Oh, Mike,' she said, but affectionately.

Wexford had broken his resolution not to go back to Framhurst Great Wood. The first time he went was to watch wildlife experts building new badger setts (with ramps and swing doors like cat flaps) in the heart of the wood. The tree-houses in the second camp were already being built, which was perhaps enough to drive the badgers to their new homes. The second time was after the tree-fellers refused to endanger their lives by using chain-saws on trees whose trunks were embedded with nails or bound with wire. A few felled trees lay about. The Highways Agency was seeking eviction orders against the tree dwellers but meanwhile another camp took shape at Elder Ditches and then another on the borders of the Great Wood.

Wexford climbed up Savesbury Hill, again, he told himself, for the last time, from where the four camps could clearly be seen. One was almost at the foot of the hill, one half a mile away at Framhurst Copses, a third on the threatened verge of the marsh and the fourth and furthest away half a mile from the northernmost reaches of Stowerton. The countryside still looked much as it always had, except that a field in the neighbourhood of Pomfret Monachorum was packed with earth-moving equipment, diggers and bulldozers. These things were almost always painted yellow, he reflected, a dull, dead yellow, the colour of custard that had been kept in the fridge too long. Presumably yellow showed up better against green than red or blue.

He walked downhill on the far side, then wished he hadn't, for he found himself up to his thighs in stinging nettles. Their hairy pointed leaves failed to sting through his clothes but he had to keep his arms and hands held high. The nettles filled an area as big as a small meadow and Wexford was thinking that if the road had to go somewhere it would be no bad thing for it to pass through here, when he saw the butterfly.

That it was Araschnia levana, he knew at once. Among all the tens of thousands of words that had been written lately about Savesbury and Framhurst, he remembered reading that Araschnia fed on stinging nettles in Savesbury Deeps. He advanced a little until he was a yard from it. The butterfly was orange-coloured, with a chocolate-brown pattern and flashes of white, and the underwings had a sky-blue river-like border. You could see why it was called the Map.

It was alone. There were only two hundred of them, perhaps now not so many. When he was a child people had caught butterflies in nets, gassed them in killing bottles, attached them to cards on pins. It seemed appalling now. Only a few years ago people who opposed bypasses were looked on as cranks, loony weirdos, hippie dropouts, and their activities on a par with anarchy, communism and mayhem. That too had changed. Conventional figures of the Establishment were as determined in their opposition as that man he could now see peering out between canvas flaps through the fork in a tree branch. Someone had told him that Sir Fleance and Lady McTear had marched in a demonstration organised by supermarket millionaires Wael and Anouk Khoori.

Like most Englishmen, he had his reservations about the European Union, but here, he thought, was one instance when he wouldn't mind an absolute veto coming from Strasbourg.

Towards the end of the month, the British Society of Lepidopterists created a new feeding ground for Araschnia, a stinging-nettle plantation on the western side of Pomfret Monachorum. A journalist on the *Kingsmarkham Courier* wrote a satirical but not very funny piece about this being the first time in the history of horticulture anyone had been known to plant nettles instead of pulling them up. The nettles, naturally, flourished from the start.

The badger movers set about a similar reversal of the usual order of things. Instead of preserving habitats, they were obliged to destroy them. In opening and sealing up a sett that, if it remained in occupation would have been in the direct path of the new bypass, they had first to cut away a dense mass of brambles. The growth of brambles had been vigorous, indicating it was new this year, springing from heavily pruned stock, and the prickly trailing runners were heavy with green fruit. They lifted the cut mass with gloved hands and found something lying beneath that made them recoil, one of them shout out and another retreat under the trees to vomit.

What they found was the badly decomposed body of a young girl.

Kingsmarkham police had no real doubts as to who this was. But they made no announcement of their guess as to identity. It was the newspapers and television who named her, with few reservations, as Ulrike Ranke, the missing German hitchhiker.

She had been nineteen, a law student at Bonn University, the only daughter of a lawyer and a teacher from Wiesbaden, and she had come to England in the previous April to spend Easter at the home of a girl who had been an au pair in her parents' house. The girl's family lived in Aylesbury and Ulrike had set out to make her journey on the cheap. It had never been quite clear why. Her parents had supplied her with enough money for a return air ticket to Heathrow and her train fare. However, Ulrike had hitched across France and taken the ferry to Dover. That much was known.

'I don't find it at all mysterious,' Wexford had said at the time. 'I would have if she'd done what her parents told her to do. That would have been astonishing, that would have been a mystery.'

'What an old cynic you are,' said Inspector Burden.

'No, I'm not. I'm a realist, I don't like being called a cynic. A cynic is someone who knows the price of everything and the value of nothing. I'm not like that, I just don't like mealy-mouthed hypocrisy. You've had teenage children, you know what they are. My Sheila used to do that stuff all the time. Why spend good money when you can do it for free? That's their attitude. They need the money for music and the means of playing it, black jeans and prohibited substances.'

It seemed he was right, for on the girl's body, in the pocket of her Calvin Klein black jeans were twenty-five amphetamine tablets and a packet containing just under fifty grammes of cannabis. There was nothing on her to show that she was Ulrike Ranke and no money. Her father identified her. The man who had raped and strangled her two months before either had not recognised the contents of her pocket for what they were or had no use for them. The money which she had carried on her in notes, all five hundred pounds of it, was gone.

Framhurst Copses had not previously been searched. None of the countryside round Kingsmarkham had come under scrutiny. There was no reason to suppose Ulrike Ranke had passed this way. Kingsmarkham was miles from the route she might have been expected to take from Dover to London. But someone had put her body in a woodland declivity and hidden her under the fast-growing tendrils of blackberry bushes. In the opinion of the pathologist and forensic examiners the body had not been moved, she had been killed where she lay.

Because there had been no search there had been no inquiries either. But immediately the identity of the dead girl was announced, William Dickson, the licensee of a public house named the Brigadier (he called it an hotel) phoned the police with information. Once he had seen photographs of Ulrike Ranke in the *Kingsmarkham Courier* he recognised her as the girl who had come into his saloon bar in early April.

The Brigadier was on the old Kingsmarkham bypass, one of those roadhouses put up in the late thirties, pseudo-Tudor, thickly half-timbered, apparently huge but in fact only one room deep. A car park behind was overshadowed by a very large prefabricated building, designed as a dance hall (Dickson called it a ballroom). The car park was surfaced in macadam but all round the house and the area in front was gravelled. Very unpleasant to walk on, as Vine remarked to Burden, worse than a shingle beach.

'It was just before closing time on Wednesday April the third,' Dickson said when the two policemen came in.

'Why didn't you say so before?' said Burden.

He and Detective Sergeant Vine were sitting up at the bar. Alcohol had been offered and refused by both. Vine was drinking mineral water which he had paid for.

'What do you mean, before?'

'When she went missing. Her picture was all over the papers then. And the TV.'

'I only look at the local,' said Dickson. 'All I ever see on the telly is sport. Folks in the bar trade don't get a lot of leisure, you know. I'm not exactly overburdened with quality time.'

'But you recognised her as soon as you saw her in the *Courier*?'

'Nice-looking chick, she was.' Dickson looked over his shoulder, reassured himself of something and grinned. 'Very tasty.'

'Oh, yes? Tell us about April the third.'

She had come into the bar at about ten-twenty, a young blonde girl 'dressed like they all dressed' in black but with some sort of jacket. An anorak or parka or duffel, he didn't know, but he thought it was brown. She had a shoulder-bag, a big overstuffed shoulder-bag, not a backpack. How could he remember so well after nearly three months?

'I've got a photo, haven't I?'

'You what?' said Vine.

'There was a hen party going on,' said Dickson. 'Girl getting married at Kingsmarkham Register Office on the Thursday. She asked the wife to take their picture, her and her friends round their table, and she handed her this camera, and just as the wife took their picture this German girl came in. So she's in the picture, in the background.'

'And you've a copy of this photograph? I thought you said it wasn't your camera?'

'The girl – the bride, that is – she sent us a copy. Thought we'd like to have it, seeing as it was in the Brigadier. You can see it if you want.'

'Oh, yes, we want,' said Burden.

Ulrike Ranke was well behind the group of laughing women and out of the brightest lights, but it was plainly she. Her coat might have been brown or grey, or even dark blue, but her jeans were unmistakably black. A string of pearls could just be glimpsed lying against the dark stuff of her blouse or sweater. The canvas and leather bag on her right shoulder looked overfull and heavy. She wore an anxious expression.

'When I saw that picture in the *Courier* I said to the wife to find that photo and the minute I set eyes on it I realised.'

'What did she come in here for? A drink?'

'I told her she couldn't have a drink,' Dickson said virtuously. 'I'd called for last orders. It wasn't a drink she wanted, she said, she wanted to know if she could make a phone call. Comical way of talking she had, like an accent, couldn't get her tongue round some words, but we get all sorts in here.'

It never ceased to surprise Burden that the British, the vast majority of whom can speak no language but their own, are not above mocking those foreign visitors whose command of English is less than perfect. He asked if Ulrike had made her phone call.

'I'm coming to that,' said Dickson. 'She asked to use the phone – called it a "telephone", long time since I've heard that expression – and said she wanted a taxi. That's who she'd be phoning, a taxi firm, and did I know of one. Well, naturally, we get a lot of call for taxis out here. I said she'd find a number by the phone, we got a card stuck up on the board by the phone. I said she'd have to use the pay-phone, I wasn't having her using the one in the office.'

'And did she?'

'Sure she did. She came back in here. The clientele was all gone by then and the wife and I was having a clear-up. She started telling us how she'd hitched a lift from Dover in a lorry. The driver'd said he'd take her as far as he was going and dropped her off here, he was parking for the night in a lay-by. I said to the wife I reckon she was lucky he *did* drop her off, good-looking young kid like that.'

'She wasn't lucky,' said Burden.

Dickson looked up, startled. 'No, well, you know what I mean.'

'She called a taxi? D'you know which one?'

'It was Contemporary Cars. It was their card stuck up by the phone. There was other numbers on a bit of paper but that was the only card.'

'And the taxi came?'

For the first time Dickson looked less than proud of himself, the picture of rectitude and earnest integrity slipping slightly. 'I don't rightly know. I mean, she said they'd said fifteen minutes, they'd said it'd be Stan in fifteen minutes, and when I went up to bed like half an hour later I looked out of the window and she was gone, so I reckon he turned up all right.'

'Are you saying,' said Burden, 'that she didn't wait for him in here? You sent her outside to wait for him?'

'Look, this is a hotel, not a hostel . . .'

'This is a public house,' said Vine.

'Look, the wife had gone to bed, she'd had a heavy day, and I was clearing up. We'd had a hell of a day. It wasn't that cold out. It wasn't raining.'

'She was nineteen years old,' said Burden. 'A young girl, a foreign visitor. You sent her out there to wait in the dark at eleven o'clock at night.'

Dickson turned his back. 'I'll think twice,' he muttered, 'before I phone you lot with information next time.'

Later that day, after hours of questioning, Stanley Trotter, a driver for Contemporary Cars and a partner with Peter Samuels in the company, was arrested for the murder of Ulrike Ranke.

# 3

Sheila Wexford intended to have her baby at home. Home births were fashionable and Sheila, her father said with a kind of fond sourness, had always been a dedicated follower of fashion. He would have liked her to go into the world's best obstetrics hospital, wherever that might be, some four weeks before the birth was due. When labour began he would have preferred the top obstetrician in the country to be present, along with a couple of caring medical assistants and a troop of top-of-their-finals-year midwives. An epidural must be administered after the first contraction and, should labour continue for more than half an hour, a Caesarean be performed – a keyhole one if possible.

That, at any rate, was what Dora said his preference would be.

'Nonsense,' said Wexford. 'I just don't like the idea of her having it at home.'

'She'll do what she likes. She always does.'

'Sheila isn't selfish,' said Sheila's father.

'I didn't say she was. I said she did what she liked.'

Wexford considered this contradiction in terms. 'You'll go up and be with her, won't you?'

'I hadn't thought of it. I'm not a midwife. I'll certainly go after the baby's born.'

'Funny, isn't it?' said Wexford. 'We've come a long way in sexual enlightenment, the equality of women and men, got rid of the old shibboleths. Men are present at the births of their children as a matter of course. Women breast-feed in public. Women talk publicly about all sorts of gynaecological things they'd once have died before mentioning. But you can't imagine that there's anyone who wouldn't balk, to say the least, at the idea of a father being present when his daughter gives birth, can you? You see, I've shocked you. You're blushing.'

'Well, naturally I am, Reg. Surely you don't want to be present at Sheila's . . . ?'

'Lying-in? Of course I don't. I'd probably pass out. I'm only saying it's an anomaly that you can be there and I can't.'

Sheila lived in London with the father of her child, an actor called Paul Curzon, in a mews off Welbeck Street. The baby would be born there. Wexford, whose knowledge of London was shaky, checked it out on his *Geographer's Atlas*, and found that Harley Street was near enough for comfort. Harley Street was full of doctors, as everyone knew, and hospitals too probably.

Contemporary Cars was housed in a prefabricated building of temporary appearance on an otherwise empty lot in Station Road. It had once been the site of the Railway Arms, a pub which was less and less frequented, its one-time customers finding beer prices exorbitant and drink-driving laws draconian. The Railway Arms closed down, then was pulled down. Nothing else was built and there were those in Kingsmarkham who called the windswept, litter-strewn site, fringed with nettles and surrounded by spindly trees, an eyesore. In their eyes, the arrival of the converted mobile home hardly improved matters, but Sir Fleance McTear, Chairman of both KABAL and the Kingsmarkham Historical Society, said that in view of the projected bypass it was the least of their worries.

Peter Samuels, the self-styled chief executive of Contemporary Cars, told everyone his business would soon be moving into permanent premises, but so far there had been no sign of this. The old Railway Arms site offered plenty of parking space for taxis and very convenient exits and entrances into the station approach. It was in these trailer-like offices with their stowaway tables, shower cabinet and pull-down beds from former days on the road that Burden first interviewed Stanley Trotter.

At first Trotter denied all knowledge of Ulrike Ranke. His memory jogged by Vine's quoting from William Dickson and mentioning the German girl's accent, Trotter eventually recalled taking Ulrike's phone call – taking the call, not driving out to the Brigadier. He had intended to do that himself, he said, but was due to pick up someone off the last train from London, so passed the job on to one of the other drivers, Robert Barrett.

The difficulty there was that when questioned, Barrett had no recollection of his movements on the night of 3 April beyond being sure that he had fares throughout the evening, it was a busy evening. The whole week had been busy – something to do with Easter, he thought. But he was sure of one thing: he had never, in the five months he had worked for Contemporary Cars, picked up a fare from the Brigadier.

Burden asked Stanley Trotter to come to Kingsmarkham police station. By then he had discovered that Trotter had form, previous convictions of no inconsiderable kind. His first offence, committed some seven years before, was breaking and entering shop premises in Eastbourne, his second, far more serious, was robbery, a definition which implied assault. He had punched a young woman in the face, knocked her to the ground, kicked her and taken her handbag. She was walking home along Queen Street, quite alone, one midnight. For both these offences Trotter had gone to prison, and would have served a much longer sentence for the second if his victim had suffered more than a bruise on her jaw.

But it was enough, or almost enough, for Burden. He had got Trotter to confess that he did in fact drive out to the Brigadier at ten-forty-five on 3 April. Originally, he said, he had been too scared to admit it. He drove there, reaching the pub just before eleven, but the fare wasn't waiting. If she had been there once she was gone by then.

At this point Trotter demanded a lawyer and Burden had no choice but to agree. A sharp young solicitor from Morgan de Clerck of York Street arrived promptly and when Trotter said he couldn't recall whether or not he had rung the bell at the Brigadier, told Burden his client had said he couldn't remember and that must be sufficient.

Outside the interview room Vine said, 'Dickson said she was out in the street. Trotter wouldn't have had to ring the bell.'

'No, but he didn't know she'd be out in the street, did he? He'd have thought – anyone would have thought – she'd be inside the pub and have rung the bell as a matter of course. Are you telling me he'd have shown up at the pub at eleven at night and finding no one there just turned round and gone back to Station Road?'

'That's what *he's* telling you,' said Vine.

They went on questioning Trotter. The solicitor from Morgan de Clerck took them up on every small point, while providing his client with an unending supply of cigarettes, though not a smoker himself.

Trotter, a round-shouldered, thin and unhealthy-looking man of about forty, got through twenty by the end of the afternoon and the atmosphere in the interview room was blue with smoke. The solicitor interrupted everything by incessantly asking how long they intended to keep Trotter and finally asked if he was to be charged.

Recklessly, Burden, hardly able to breathe, gasped out a yes. But he didn't charge him, he just kept him at Kingsmarkham police station. When Wexford got to hear of it he was dubious about the whole thing, but Burden got a warrant and Trotter's home in Peacock Street, Stowerton, was searched for evidence. There, in the two-roomed flat over a grocery market kept by two Bangladeshi brothers, Detective Constables Archbold and Pemberton found a string of imitation pearls and a holdall of brown canvas bound in dark-green plastic.

To Wexford it wasn't much like the shoulder-bag in Dickson's photograph, nor did it conform to the description of his daughter's bag Dieter Ranke had given the police. This one was an altogether cheaper affair and brown and green instead of brown and black. The Rankes were comfortably off, both parents professionals with significant jobs, and Ulrike, an only child, had wanted for nothing. Her pearls were a cultured string, carefully matched, an eighteenth-birthday present for which her mother and father had paid the equivalent of thirteen hundred pounds.

'That poor chap will have to take a look at the bag,' Wexford said, meaning Ranke and thinking of himself and his daughters. 'He's still in this country for the inquest.'

'It won't be so bad as identifying the body,' said Burden.

'No, Mike, I don't suppose it will.' Wexford didn't want to pursue that, he might say something he'd be sorry for afterwards. 'I'm told the Department of Transport are applying to the High Court for leave to evict the tree people.'

Burden looked pleased. The idea of the bypass had always been attractive to him, largely because he thought it would put an end to traffic congestion in the town centre and on the old bypass. 'No one made all this fuss in the old days,' he said. 'If government decreed a road was to be built people accepted it. They took the entirely proper view that if they voted their representatives into parliament they'd done their democratic duty and they must abide by government decisions. They didn't build tree-houses and – and *streak* – is it called streaking? They didn't do criminal damage and cripple tree-fellers who are only doing their job. They understood that a road such as this is being built *for their own good*.'

' "He didn't know what the world was coming to",' said Wexford. 'That's what they'll put on your tombstone.' He gave Burden a sidelong look. 'Big demonstration tomorrow. KABAL, the Sussex Wildlife Trust, Friends of the Earth and Sacred Globe, the whole lot led by Sir Fleance McTear, Peter Tregear and Anouk Khoori.'

'It will just make more work for us. That's all it'll accomplish. They'll still build the bypass.'

'Who knows?' said Wexford.

He didn't question Trotter himself. Burden, harassed by Damian Harmon-Shaw of Morgan de Clerck, succeeded in getting an extension of twelve hours to the time he was allowed to keep Trotter. He knew that when that time was up he would either have to charge him or let him go, as the Magistrates' Court was unlikely to be persuaded by the evidence to issue a warrant of further detention.

The three Vauxhalls and the three VW Golfs used by Contemporary Cars were all examined. Peter Samuels put up no objection. The cars had each been cleaned inside and out at least ten times since 3 April and had each carried hundreds of fares. If there had ever been traces of Ulrike Ranke's brief occupancy of one of them, a hair perhaps, a fingerprint, a thread from her clothes, these had long ago been removed or obliterated.

'You haven't any evidence, Mike,' Wexford said after he had listened to the tape. 'All you have are his previous convictions and the fact that he went to the Brigadier and finding no one there, turned round and went home again.'

'He knows Framhurst Great Wood. He's admitted going to the picnic area when his kids were young.' Trotter's desertion of his wife and small children, and his subsequent divorce, remarriage and very rapid second divorce, were other factors which had prejudiced Burden against him. 'He knows the lane into the wood and he knows all about parking at the picnic place. The body was found two hundred yards from there.'

'Half the population of Kingsmarkham knows that picnic area. I used to take my kids there, you used to take yours. One might say it was pretty open of him to admit knowing it. He wasn't obliged to.'

Burden said coldly, 'I know he's guilty. I know he killed her. He killed her for that string of pearls, the most easily disposable of all jewellery, and for the five hundred pounds she was carrying.'

'Do you know he was short of money?'

'His sort is always short of money.'

Dieter Ranke came to Kingsmarkham two hours before Burden's extension was up. In the meantime he and Detective Sergeant Karen Malahyde had questioned Trotter again but made no progress. Ulrike's father rejected the brown canvas bag after a cursory glance. The cheap pearl necklace found in Trotter's flat provoked an outburst of anger. He shouted at Barry Vine, then apologised, then wept.

'You will now allow my client to go,' said Damian Harmon-Shaw in a very smooth voice and smiling condescendingly.

Burden had no choice. 'He's got off scot-free,' he said to Wexford, 'and I know he killed her. I can't bear that.'

'You'll have to bear it. I'll tell you what really happened, if you like. When that miscreant Dickson had turned her out into the street Ulrike wasn't at all happy being on that road with no other house in sight. If the pub lights were put out there wouldn't have been any light, it would have been very dark indeed out on the bypass. She waited for the taxi, but before it came another car stopped and the driver offered her a lift. A car or a lorry – who knows?'

'And she'd take it, in spite of the dangers?'

'Individual instances are quite different, though, aren't they? People think themselves judges of character. They think they can tell what someone's like from a face and a voice. It's dark, it's late, she's cold, she's no idea where she's going to sleep that night, if she's going to sleep anywhere, she doesn't know when she'll get to Aylesbury. A man comes along in a car, a warm, well-lit car, and he's a nice man, not young, a fatherly man who doesn't make personal remarks, who doesn't ask her what's a lovely girl like her doing out on a dark night, but just says he's on his way to London and would she like a lift. Maybe he says more, that he's on his way to pick up his wife in Stowerton and drive her to London. We don't know, but we can imagine. And Ulrike, who's tired and cold and knows a decent older man when she sees one . . .'

'Great scenario,' said Burden. 'There's only one objection. Trotter did it.'

But next day Stanley Trotter was back at work, busy along with Peter Samuels, Robert Barrett, Tanya Paine and Leslie Cousins in

618

picking up from the station and driving to the meeting point the hordes of bypass demonstrators who arrived from London.

Some walked. It was only a mile. The young and the poor were obliged to walk. Some of the activists were virtually penniless. A comfortably off élite, most of the Wildlifers, a few Friends of the Earth and a large number of independent but dedicated conservationists, formed a long queue outside the station waiting for taxis from Station Taxis, All the Sixes (named for its phone number), Kingsmarkham Taxis, Harrison Brothers and Contemporary Cars.

The meeting point was the roundabout on the road between Stowerton and Kingsmarkham. Something over five hundred people gathered there, members of a Group called Heartwood carrying tree branches felled the day before, so that, as Wexford put it, they looked like Birnam Wood coming to Dunsinane.

They marched through the town, heading for Pomfret and the site that would be the start of the new bypass. Councillor Anouk Khoori, joint managing director with her husband of the Crescent supermarket chain, had dressed herself from head to toe in appropriate green, even to green eyeshadow and green fingernails.

The dying leaves on Heartwood's green branches dropped off along the route, leaving a trail down the middle of the road. Debbie Harper was there in her sandwich board but this time it was apparent she was adequately clothed underneath it in blue jeans and green T-shirt. Dora Wexford, having met with no opposition from her husband – 'I wish I could join you,' he'd said – marched in the orderly ranks of middle-class KABAL. Its members had all rather ostentatiously eschewed green garments and, indeed, anything in the nature of the gear that might associate them with the New Age.

Wexford, who watched the march from his office window (and waved to his wife who didn't see him) noted some newcomers. Their banner proclaimed them as members of SPECIES. He amused himself for a while trying to think of what this could be an acronym for – Save and Protect Environmental Culture In Ecological Something or Sanctuary for the Preservation of Earth Co-operation and Integration Something Something.

At their head marched a commanding figure. He was tall, at least as tall as Wexford himself and he exceeded six feet by a good three inches. He carried no banner, waved no flag, and his clothes were very different from the uniform that was a mixture of denim and medieval pilgrims' gear. This man, whose head was shaved, wore a great cloak of a pale sand colour that flapped and rippled as he walked. Wexford saw with something of a shock that his feet were bare. His legs appeared to be bare too, as much as could be seen of them. The swinging folds of the cloak hid so much.

If he hadn't been concentrating on this man, staring at his profile of huge forehead, Roman nose and long chin, he might have seen one of the marchers throw a stone through the window of Concreation's offices on the Pomfret Road.

This converted Georgian house, which housed the company building the bypass, was separated from the roadway by a lawn and drive-in. No one seemed to know who had thrown the stone, though there was a lot of speculation, the more conservative partakers in the demonstration suggesting a member of either SPECIES or Heartwood. Wexford asked Dora later, but she hadn't seen the stone thrown, only heard the crash and turned to look at the smashed window.

The rest of the demonstration passed without incident. Three days later eviction notices were issued on people living in the four camps on the bypass route. But before the Under Sheriff of Mid-Sussex could begin carrying out the evictions, building had begun on two new tree camps, one at Pomfret Tye, the other at Stoke Stringfield, 'under the auspices', as the announcement to the press rather grandly had it, of SPECIES.

The crime tape round the area where Ulrike Ranke's body had been found came off and the badger movers returned to their task. The British Lepidopterists announced that eggs of Araschnia levana had been seen on nettles in the new plantation, though no larvae had yet been hatched.

It was August, and the tree-felling had resumed, when the masked raiders came into Kingsmarkham by night and made their onslaught on the premises of Concreation.

# 4

They invaded the building, smashing windows, computers, fax machines, phones and copiers. They pulled open the drawers of filing cabinets and either tore up the contents or slung them in the shredders. The police got there very quickly but while arrests were being made, another group had occupied the headquarters of Kingsmarkham Borough Council. A third rampaged about destroying High Street shops.

Some of those arrested were tree people, but the hooded ones, wearing black stockings over their heads with eye and mouth holes, were newcomers to the town. They had come in during the day and set up a new camp on the bypass route, this one making the seventh. Yet more eviction orders had been applied for.

The day after what became known as the Kingsmarkham Rampage, Mark Arcturus, a spokesman for the campaigns section of Friends of the Earth, appealed for the protest to remain law-abiding. 'Everything we can accomplish,' he said, 'will be lost if the public associates the protest with violence and criminal damage, and we shall lose the public support we have enjoyed, which has been so heartening to us. Until yesterday the action was peaceful and civilised. Let us keep it that way.'

Sir Fleance McTear said that KABAL was dedicated to peaceful protest. 'We do not condone violence even in so good a cause.'

The *Kingsmarkham Courier*, but no other newspapers, carried a statement from a man called Conrad Tarling to the effect that desperate situations called for desperate measures and what choice had the public when government ignored the voice of the people? Tarling described himself as the King of the Wood and the leader of the SPECIES representation on the bypass site. Wexford recognised

621

him from the picture accompanying the story. He was the cloaked man who had marched in the procession.

A team of workers were brought in under guard to remove spikes and wires from tree trunks. The tree people in the camps watched them at work and bided their time until the guards, who for a while kept up a round-the-clock shift system, eventually went home.

Patrick Young, of English Nature, announced in *New Scientist* the discovery in the River Brede of a rare caddis, Psychoglypha citreola, its larva a tiny worm in a mosaic-like cast, the adult form a yellow-winged fly, about an inch long. As a result the government's conservation advisers considered whether parts of the river should be designated as an area of special scientific interest.

'Under the European Habitats and Species directive,' Young said, 'super-reserve status gives the highest level of protection. Psychoglypha could still save this unparalleled area of beauty and rare species. Its discovery highlights the Department of Transport's failure to carry out an adequate environmental assessment of the Brede and Stringfield Marsh.'

One of the tree-houses in the camp at Elder Ditches caught fire on a hot afternoon towards the end of the month. Its occupants, a man and a woman, were leading lights in SPECIES. The tree-house and its tree were both destroyed but after some initial alarm it was decided that the fire was an accident, caused by a spirit stove used for tea-making falling over.

'These people,' said Burden to Wexford, 'destroy more of the environment than they save.'

'One tree. You're ridiculous.'

'Being right often seems ridiculous at first,' said Burden sententiously. 'How's Sheila?'

'She's fine. The baby's due in three weeks. I'd feel a lot better if she'd have it in hospital.' Wexford went on, principally to rile the inspector, 'One of her friends has joined the protest. He's called Jeffrey Godwin, he's an actor, owns the Weir Theatre.'

'That converted mill at Stringfield? He ought to know better.'

'He's got the Weir to stage a protest play, opening next week. It's called *Extinction*.'

'Sounds a bundle of laughs,' said Burden. 'I for one shan't be buying any tickets.'

On the last Monday in the month Concreation shifted its earth-moving equipment from the meadow at Pomfret Monachorum and the first digger plunged its great spiked shovel into the green hillside.

Wexford had been mildly worried for six months, waking up in the night sometimes and imagining the icy emptiness, the great yawning abyss opening at his feet, if Sheila should die in childbirth. He had never known of childbirth death, since the sole occurrence of this in his own life had happened to an aunt of his when he was only four, but he was still worried. The coming child he thought of too, not especially about it, but about the effect on Sheila if it should be less than perfect, about her grief which would in the natural course of things be his grief too.

But he knew during those months that the anxiety he suffered would be nothing to what he would suffer when Sheila's due date arrived, in the days that followed that due date, for first babies, they say, are never on time, and – unbearable to contemplate – once he knew labour had begun. This worry, though, was yet to come, not to start until 4 September. He told himself not to be a fool, to banish it from his mind, at least until that due date, for there is no point in worrying twice, once for real and once about the prospect of future worry. 'Most of the things you have worried about,' he said to Dora on the evening of 1 September, 'have never happened.'

'I know,' she said, 'I taught you that axiom,' and as she spoke the phone rang.

He picked up the receiver.

'Hi, Pop,' said Sheila. 'I just had the baby.'

He had to sit down. Fortunately, the chair was there.

'Can you hear me, Pop? I had the baby and she's fabulous. She's called Amulet. She's got black hair and blue eyes. And do you know, it wasn't half as bad as I expected.'

'Oh, Sheila . . .' he said, and to Dora, 'Sheila had the baby.'

'Well, aren't you going to congratulate me?'

'Congratulations, darling.'

'She weighs three point four four kilos. I don't know what that is in pounds, you'll have to find conversion tables. I could have phoned you when labour started but I knew it would only worry you and then things happened so fast . . .'

'Here's your mother,' he said. 'Tell your mother all about it.'

Dora talked for fifteen minutes. When she finally put down the phone she said to Wexford that she'd be going to London in two days' time. 'She asked me to come tomorrow.'

'Why not go tomorrow?'

'Too many things to see to here. I can't just up sticks and go off like that. Besides, I think I should give her a day or two. Let her get used to the baby. It's not as if there'll be anything for me to do there except be with them. She's got a private nurse.'

'Amulet,' said Wexford. 'I expect I shall get used to it.'

'Don't worry. She'll be called Amy.'

SPECIES and the tree people swarmed over the earth-moving equipment during the night, removing metal parts, cutting cables, immobilising engines and mixing iron filings with diesel. A number of arrests were made, a guard was put on the diggers and James Freeborn, the Assistant Chief Constable of Mid-Sussex, appealed for a government grant of £2.5 million for policing the bypass.

Wexford asked for a meeting with him to discuss the outbreak of shop-breaking and petty thieving in Sewingbury and Myfleet. Four hundred security guards, hired by the Highways Agency, were housed in decaying huts on the former Army base at Sewingbury. Local residents put the blame on them, complained that they were responsible for pub brawls and that the buses which transported them to the bypass site caused traffic congestion, noise and pollution.

'An irony, isn't it?' Wexford said to Dora. 'Who shall have custody of the custodian? But thanks to this meeting I shan't be able to drive you to the station.'

'I shall get a taxi. If I weren't carrying all this stuff, all these presents you insist on, I'd walk it.'

'Phone me this evening. I want to hear all about this child. I want to hear her *voice*.'

'The only voice they have at that age,' said Dora, 'is crying, and we'll have as little of that as possible, I hope.'

He left the house at nine for his meeting. Before he went he meant to tell her not to phone Contemporary Cars. It wasn't particularly important but he didn't care for the idea of Stanley Trotter driving his wife. Of course it might not be Stanley Trotter, it might be Peter Samuels or Leslie Cousins, and even if it was Trotter the chances were he wouldn't mention Wexford, or his arrest, or Burden's unfounded suspicions. That really depended on whether Trotter was paranoid or aggrieved, or just relieved to have been released when he

624

was. Anyway, he hadn't warned her, but at the time he hadn't said a word to her about Trotter so if the worst came to the worst she could justly plead ignorance.

His meeting ended without any firm policy being agreed on, but his presence there seemed to put ideas into Freeborn's head. If he hadn't anything better to do that afternoon perhaps he would like to accompany the Deputy Chief Constable on a tour of the conservation sites. It was being undertaken prior to the environmental assessment of the Brede and Stringfield Marsh and the bodies represented would include English Nature, Friends of the Earth, the Sussex Wildlife Trust, KABAL and the British Society of Entomologists.

Wexford could think of a lot of better things to do. He couldn't imagine why Freeborn's presence was required, still less his own, and he remembered rather sadly his resolve not to go near Framhurst Great Wood again, a decision that had already once been broken.

Of course he said he would come, he hadn't much choice. It was no good being an ostrich about these things, he must confront the prospect like everyone else. Perhaps he could even tell the Entomologists of his sighting of the Map butterfly. He was thinking about this and about how animals and insects and even some plants dislike the moving of their habitats, even when this is no more than a mile or two, when the call came in to Kingsmarkham police station from Contemporary Cars.

Not Trotter but Peter Samuels. It was a little after noon. He had come back to the offices in Station Road to find his receptionist bound and gagged and tied to a chair, the place turned over and the petty cash stolen.

Barry Vine went down there with Detective Constable Lynn Fancourt. The door to the mobile home was open and Samuels was standing on the steps.

Inside, it was a squeeze for the four of them. Tanya Paine, whose job it was to answer the phones, the one for the cars and the one for potential fares, sat on the pull-down bed rubbing her wrists. The cord that tied her had been tightly bound round wrists and ankles. A pair of tights had been used as a gag and another to blindfold her. She wasn't hurt but she was frightened and shaken, a young woman in her early twenties, white-faced under the heavy make-up, her elaborately done long hair coming down from its chignon where the gag and blindfold had been tied.

'I'd been driving a client to Gatwick,' Samuels said. 'I was on my way back. Couldn't make out why I hadn't had a call from Tanya here. I mean, it was unheard-of, an hour going by without a call. I thought maybe the phone was down. So I come back here. I mean, I never come back here, not till my dinner-time, but being as I hadn't had a call not in all of an hour and a half . . .'

'All right, sir, thank you very much,' said Vine. 'Let's hear from Miss Paine. Just one man, was it, Miss Paine? Did you get a look at him?'

'There was two,' said Tanya Paine. 'They had black masks on with holes for their eyes and mouth. Well, not masks, hoods. It was like the pictures in the paper of that lot that broke into the bypass builders' place. And one of them had a gun.'

'Are you sure of that?'

'Of course I'm sure. I was scared. I was dead terrified, actually. They opened that door and came up the steps and shut the door and the one with the gun pointed it at me and said to get in here. So I did – well, I wasn't going to argue, was I? They made me sit in that chair and one of them tied me up. At gunpoint. I hadn't got no choice, it was at gunpoint.'

'What time would that have been?'

'Ten-fifteen, ten-twenty, something like that.'

'And you were gagged and blindfolded?' said Lynn Fancourt.

'I don't know why. I couldn't see their faces anyway, not with them masks. They blindfolded me and I couldn't see a thing. I heard them moving about. Then they shut the door on me, that door, and I couldn't hear either. Oh, well, I heard the phone ring a few times, I could hear that. They was here a good while after they tied me up, a long time, I don't know how long it was before I heard the door bang.'

The room where they were had originally been the bedroom of the mobile home. To the built-in furniture, pull-down bed, hanging cupboard and two foldaway tables, had been added a fireside chair and two Windsor wheelback chairs, to one of which Tanya Paine had been tied. Beyond the door was the kitchen, equipped with microwave, fridge and cupboards with counters, and beyond that the living area, currently used as the office. With both interior doors shut not much of what was going on in the office could have been heard by a gagged and blindfolded woman shut in the bedroom.

Vine and Lynn Fancourt looked it over. 'Contemporary' as a title for this company was something of a misnomer. The two telephones were the only evidence of modern technology. There was no computer and no safe.

'We don't need no safe,' said Samuels. 'Twice a day I bank the takings, once at dinner-time and once at three.'

'So what was in the petty cash box?' asked Vine, holding up an empty tin that long ago had contained cream crackers. He held it in a clean handkerchief between thumb and forefinger, though whatever fingerprints might have been there had by then been irrevocably smudged by Samuels' and Tanya Paine's handling of it.

'Maybe five quid,' said Samuels, 'and that'd be pushing it. I'd got my takings on me and the same would go for Stan and Les. They'd bring them in round about midday and I'd bank the lot.'

Vine shook his head. It was a long while since he had heard of anything so slapdash.

Tanya Paine came out, her hairdo reassembled, her lipstick renewed. 'I thought you'd want to see me the way they left me,' she explained, 'before I repaired the damage. There was three pounds forty-two in that cash box, Pete. I checked it out on account of thinking I'd pop out for a capuccino and a Mars bar when Stan came back and I'd not got no change myself. Three pounds forty-two exactly.'

They had taken it. But had they been looking for something else? A drawer had been pulled out from under the counter where the phones were. A book of receipt stubs was on the floor. The VAT book had been opened and left face-downwards. But policemen get to know when a place has been ransacked or conversely, made to look as if it has been ransacked. This effort to deceive had not even been whole-hearted. The two masked men had come for something Contemporary Cars had but, as Vine said to Lynn on the way back to the police station, it wasn't three pounds forty-two and it wasn't some vital document among the VAT inputs.

'What were they doing then for what she calls a long time after they'd left her tied up in there?'

'I don't know,' said Vine. 'The chances are though that it wasn't the long time she says. She was scared, understandably so, and it seemed like a long time. It was probably a couple of minutes.'

'So they tied her up, shut the two doors on her, took the petty cash and dropped a few things on the floor to make it look like a search? And they had a *gun*?'

627

'That'll have been a toy or a replica. No one was hurt, it's a small sum that's missing, there was no damage – and we're never going to find those two, you know that.'

'That's a bit of a defeatist attitude, Sergeant Vine,' said Lynn, who was twenty-four, new from her training and ardent.

'You watch it, young Lynn. I don't mean we're not going to check the place over and see if the prints are those of any villain known to us. We shall observe the usual routine but there's been rather a lot of this sort of thing lately, though I'll admit the masks and the gun are novelties.'

When Burden heard of it he immediately seized on the fact that one of Contemporary Cars' drivers was Stanley Trotter. One of the two intruders could even have been Stanley Trotter.

'Tanya Paine would have recognised him,' said Vine. 'Anyway, why would he need that? He was on the spot or could be. He could look for whatever it was without tying the girl up.'

'Where is he now?'

'Down there, I reckon. They all come in at midday with their takings. They're all there. Well, not Barrett, he's away on his holidays.'

Burden went down to Station Road, accompanied by an enthusiastic Lynn Fancourt. Tanya Paine was back on her phones, apparently none the worse for wear. She sent them through to the kitchen area, where Trotter was sitting in front of the black-and-white television set, eating a hamburger and with a plate of chips on his knees.

'Maybe you'd like to tell me where you were between ten and midday,' Burden said.

Trotter took a bite out of his hamburger. 'The station trade,' he said with his mouth full. 'And when that come to an end after the ten-nineteen'd come and gone, I got a call from here to fetch a fare from Pomfret. Masters Street, Pomfret, number fifteen, to be precise, which I took to the station, picked up a fare as was waiting and drove them to Stowerton, and by then it'd have been half-eleven, so I had my tea break. I was back in the cab by ten off twelve and I hung about down by the station, but when I never got no more calls from here, I thought, funny, that's very funny, that's never happened before.'

'What then?'

'I come back here, didn't I?'

'I'd like the name of the fare you picked up in Pomfret.'

628

'I don't know his name. Why would I? Tanya said to go to fifteen Masters Street, Pomfret, and that's what I done.'

Burden asked Tanya Paine for the fare's name. Presumably she kept a record. She looked at him blankly.

'I'd have to write them down.' She spoke as if writing by hand was comparable to mastering some difficult language, Russian, for instance. 'Pete's thinking of getting a computer,' she said, 'if he can pick one up second-hand.'

'So you've no idea how many calls come in or who from?'

'I never said that. I know how many. I sort of jot it down.'

She showed him a sheet of paper on which perhaps thirty or forty dashes had been made in pencil.

'What about the fare you picked up at the station after that?' Burden asked.

'I took him to Oval Road, Stowerton. Number five or it might have been seven. He'll remember me and so will the Pomfret chap.'

Trotter fixed Burden with a stony glare. He didn't look guilty, though. He looked as if he had nothing to hide. Burden was unable to imagine how the incidents of the morning at Contemporary Cars could have any connection with the murder of Ulrike Ranke, but that was what police work was about, discovering connections where none seemed to exist. He went back to the office where Tanya Paine had retreated. Squinting into a small hand mirror, she was applying violet-coloured mascara, her lips pursed and her nostrils narrowed.

'Is it possible,' he said, 'that one of the two men who tied you up could have been one of the drivers here?'

'Pardon?' She turned round and passed her tongue wetly across her lips.

'The two men' – he rephrased it – 'could one or both of them have been known to you? Did you have any sort of feeling of familiarity?'

She shook her head, stunned by this new turn the inquiry was taking.

'Did they speak?'

'One of them did. He said to keep quiet and I'd be OK. That's all.'

'So you didn't hear the other one's voice?'

Again that amazed shake of the head.

'The other one, then, he was masked and you didn't hear his voice. You can't really say he couldn't have been known to you, can you? If you couldn't see his face and didn't hear his voice, it could have been someone you knew very well.'

'I don't know what you mean,' said Tanya Paine. 'I'm confused now. They tied me up and gagged me and it was *horrible* and I want counselling. I'm a victim.'

'We can arrange that, Ms Paine,' said Lynn sympathetically.

Burden took Lynn Fancourt down to Stowerton with him where they established that no one from number five Oval Road had been brought by taxi from the station that morning. Nobody was at home at number seven, so they had either gone out again or Trotter was lying, an alternative Burden preferred to believe. A woman at number nine told them her neighbour was called Wingate, but she had no idea whether he had been fetched from Kingsmarkham station that morning or where he was now.

The Pomfret fare, if he existed, might still be in London or Eastbourne or wherever the train had taken him, but more than three hours had elapsed, so it was equally likely he was back again. Lynn rang the bell at fifteen Masters Road, a between-the-wars bungalow with a view over the bypass site.

The woman who answered the door had been doing some interior decorating. She had magnolia gloss paint on her hands, her jeans and shirt, and streaks of it in her hair. She looked cross and hot. No, she hadn't got a husband. If Burden meant her partner, he was called John Clifton, and yes, he had gone to London that morning on the ten-fifty-one. A taxi had taken him to Kingsmarkham station but she hadn't heard him phone for it, she hadn't seen it come and she had no idea which firm it was or who was driving the car. John had called out goodbye and said he was off and . . . 'What's happened to him?' she said, suddenly alarmed.

'Nothing, Miss . . .'

'Kennedy. Martha Kennedy. You're sure nothing's happened to him?'

'It's the taxi driver we're interested in,' said Lynn.

'In that case, perhaps you'll excuse me. I want to finish these bloody doors before John gets back.'

Burden said they would call again later. The door was shut rather sharply in his face. On the way back to Kingsmarkham they passed Wexford who was driving himself to Pomfret Tye for his meeting and tour with the Deputy Chief Constable and the conservationists.

The day, which had started dull and misty, was such a one as all lovers of the countryside should be given for their viewing of natural

630

wonders. Or perhaps should not be given, should be denied, lest the soft air, the sunshine, the blue sky and the rich green of vegetation give too painful and nostalgic an edge to a pastoral loveliness that must soon pass away. Better for all, Wexford was thinking, if the day were dull and cold, and the sky the colour of the concrete soon to spread itself across these hills, these deeps and marshes, and bridge on stark grey pillars the rippling waters of the Brede.

Today the butterflies would be out, the tortoiseshells and fritillaries as well as Araschnia, and wild bees on the eyebright and the heather. There were goldcrests in the fir trees of Framhurst Great Wood. He had seen a pair of them once when on a picnic with Dora and the girls, and he and Sheila had looked, though looked in vain, for the nest that is like a little hanging basket. Dora – he had meant to phone her at lunch-time, in spite of what he'd said about her phoning him in the evening. But he hadn't, he'd decided to wait. By now she would have seen the new child, his granddaughter Amulet. Alone in the car, he laughed out loud over the name.

Freeborn hadn't yet got there, much to his relief. If the Deputy Chief Constable had arrived first he would have had something snide to say about it, even if Wexford himself had been on time, even if he had been early. Somewhat to his dismay, Anouk Khoori, chairperson of the Council's Highways Committee, a woman with whom he had crossed swords in the recent past, was representing the local authority. She was fetchingly dressed in a yellow T-shirt with green jodhpurs and green wellies, her bright blonde hair tied up in a black-and-yellow bandanna, and she was exercising her wiles on Mark Arcturus of English Nature, smiling into his eyes, one scarlet-tipped hand resting on his sleeve. All smiles ceased when she became aware of Wexford's presence and she gave him a very brief, frosty glance.

Wexford said in his best stolid-policeman voice, 'Good-afternoon, Mrs Khoori. A fine day.'

The Entomologists introduced themselves and Wexford told them about Araschnia. Anecdotes on the theme of rare butterflies spotted in unlikely places were interrupted by the arrival of Freeborn accompanied by Peter Tregear.

The Deputy Chief Constable took it upon himself, like a primary school head teacher, to count heads. 'If we're all here we may as well begin.'

'We're surely not going to walk, are we?' said Anouk Khoori.

Wexford couldn't resist. 'They haven't built the road yet.'

631

'And let us hope they never will,' said Arcturus, as if the earth-moving equipment wasn't busy a couple of miles on the other side of Savesbury Hill even while they spoke. 'Let us be positive. Let us remember hope is one of the cardinal virtues.'

It wasn't a very long walk that the party undertook. They took the footpath across the meadows from Pomfret Tye and at Watersmeet, where the Kingsbrook flowed into the Brede, Arcturus was able to point out, under the clear, golden water, clinging to a round, gleaming pebble, the mosaic cylinder of the yellow caddis. Mrs Khoori was disappointed. It wasn't big enough for her taste.

Half a mile along the river, perhaps not so much, Wexford could see the old mill building that Jeffrey Godwin had converted into the Weir Theatre. Dora wanted to see that play, *Extinction*, and no doubt Sheila would come down for it . . . He switched his mind from that train of thought. Janet Braiswick, of the English Entomologists, was walking with him and he told her about the goldcrests, and about seeing scarlet tiger moths when he was a boy. She told him how as a child in Norfolk she had once, but only once, seen a swallowtail in the fens.

They came to the nettle plantation at Framhurst Deeps, treading softly now, even Anouk Khoori silent and anxious. The sun was hot, it was butterfly weather, and they waited and watched almost reverently, but no Map butterfly appeared. No butterfly at all rose from the long grass and the ox-eye daisies that whitened the meadows like summer snow.

The dismantled badger setts were studied, for here at this point the bypass would run, through Araschnia's nettles, through the outskirts of the wood and into Stringfield Marsh. In the distance Wexford could see the latest camp, the cluster of houses put up by tree dwellers. Eviction notices had been applied for but not yet issued. Meanwhile the tree dwellers had spiked every oak, ash and lime in a half-mile stretch. Perhaps Sir Fleance McTear wanted to avoid the controversy these spikes might evoke or the indignation of Mrs Khoori, who was known to disapprove of all protest that was not a matter solely of the written or spoken word, for he suggested they turn back and make a small detour to take in the area designated for the new badger setts.

They were too far away to hear, still less see, the diggers working at the start of the site. Much too far to see the guards brought in by bus to protect the construction workers, the watching tree people, the witnesses. This was no more than a nature walk, Wexford thought, reminiscent of distant schooldays when Kingsmarkham infants were brought to these meadows to see the dragonflies and the water beetles. He asked Janet Braiswick when she had last seen tadpoles in an English pond but she couldn't remember, only that it was at least thirty years, when she had been a small child.

At five they were all back in Pomfret. Sir Fleance suggested tea in a local teashop, at least a cup of tea if no one wanted to eat, but this proposal met with no enthusiasm. They were all depressed by what they had seen, they were saddened. Even Freeborn, Wexford noticed, was subdued. He and Anouk Khoori were country dwellers who never went out into the country, who had been obliged to do so today, and had in some strange way been frightened by what they saw, by its existence and its ephemerality.

> And that will be England gone,
> The shadows, the meadows, the lanes . . .

They would rather not have seen it and then they could have pretended it wasn't there, just as he had thought he wouldn't go back so that he also could pretend. Avoid that place, don't pass that way, avert the eye, until there were no more ways to pass or places to be in . . .

And now he might as well go home. He remembered then that he would be alone at home. Well, he had plenty to read. He could start on those George Steiner essays everyone said were wonderful. And at some point there was always television, accompanied by a small single malt. Dora would probably phone about seven. She wouldn't expect him to be home much before seven, but she would phone then because whoever cooked for Sheila, and there was certain to be someone, would put dinner on the table at half-past.

The house was hot and stuffy. Today it had felt more like July than early September. He opened the french windows, drew a chair up to the garden table, went back into the house for beer from the fridge and the book of essays: *No Passion Spent.* Was it necessary to begin at the beginning or could he dip? He thought it would be fine to dip.

The french windows blew shut. He wouldn't hear the phone but Dora wouldn't phone before – well – ten to seven. At a quarter to seven he considered eating. What should he eat? When Jenny Burden went away she left her husband home-made frozen dinners in the freezer, one for every day of her absence. Wexford wouldn't submit his wife to such slavery, but he didn't like cooking, the fact was he couldn't cook. Bread and cheese and pickles for him, and maybe a banana and ice-cream. Soup first, Heinz tomato. Burden said that this was every man's favourite soup . . .

When it got to ten-past seven and Dora hadn't phoned he began to wonder. Not to worry; to wonder. She was a punctual, meticulous woman. Perhaps they had people round for drinks and she couldn't just slip away. He would postpone eating until he'd spoken to her and he turned off the gas under the soup.

The phone rang at seven-fifteen.

'Dora?' he said.

'It's not Dora, it's Sheila. Where have you been? I've been phoning and phoning. I phoned your office and you weren't there, I phoned home over and over.'

'I'm sorry. I didn't expect a call till seven. How are you? How's the baby?'

'I am fantastic, Pop, and the baby is perfectly fine, but where is Mother?'

'What do you mean?'

'Mother. We expected her by one at the latest. Where is she?'

# 5

He had done all the things one does in these circumstances: phoned hospitals, checked at the police station what road accidents there had been that day – only a car going into the back of another on the old bypass – phoned next door and talked to his neighbour.

Mary Pearson hadn't seen Dora since the afternoon of the day before but she had seen a car parked outside that morning. At about ten-forty-five, she thought it was. Maybe a few minutes earlier.

'That would be for the eleven-o-three,' said Wexford.

'She was allowing herself a lot of time.'

'She always does. Was it a black taxi?'

'It was a red car, I don't know the make, I'm afraid I don't know about cars, Reg. I didn't see her get in it.'

'Did you see the driver?'

Mary Pearson hadn't. She sensed at last that something was wrong. 'You mean you don't know where she's got to, Reg?'

If he admitted it the whole street would be talking within the hour. 'She must have told me but it's slipped my mind,' he said, and added, 'Don't worry,' as if she would worry and he wouldn't.

Kingsmarkham Cabs used black taxis, so Dora hadn't gone with them. And she couldn't have used Contemporary Cars because they were out of action from about ten-fifteen until just after midday. So much for the caution he'd forgotten to give her, yet for which there had been no need . . .

He phoned All the Sixes, Station Taxis, and every local company he could find in the phone book. None of them had picked up Dora that morning. He was beginning to have that feeling of unreality which comes over us when something utterly unexpected and potentially terrible happens.

635

Where was she?

Now he wished he had been discreet, had told Sheila some lie as to her mother's whereabouts, for he had to phone her again and say he had no idea what had happened, he had no clue. Holding old-fashioned ideas about post-parturitive women, he thought shocks would be dangerous, a shock would dry up her milk, fear would delay her recovery. It was too late now.

Sheila wailed down the phone at him, 'What do you mean, you don't know what's happened, Pop? Where is she? She must have had some ghastly accident!'

'That she has not had. She'd be in hospital and she's not.'

He could hear Paul saying soothing things. Then the baby began to cry, strong, urgent staccato screams.

It can't be true, was what he wanted to say, this can't be happening. We are dreaming the same dream, nightmaring the same nightmare, and we shall wake up soon. But he had to be strong, the paterfamilias, the rock. 'Sheila, I am doing everything I can. Your mother is not injured, your mother is not dead. These things I would know. I'll phone you as soon as I find out more.'

He went into the kitchen and poured the soup down the sink. It was nearly half-past eight and dusk, darkness coming. An oval orange moon was climbing up behind the roofs. He asked himself what he would think if this were someone else's wife. The answer was easy: that she'd left him, gone off with another man. Women did it all the time, women of all ages, after many years of marriage or a few. As a policeman, he'd ask that husband if such a thing was possible. First he'd apologise, say he was sorry but he had to ask, and then he'd inquire about her friends, any particular man friend.

The husband would be affronted, indignant. Not my wife, my wife would never . . . And then he would think, remember, a chance word, a strange phone call, a coldness, an unusual warmth.

But this was Dora. *His* wife. It wasn't possible. He realised he was reacting just like the husband of his experience, his small fantasy. My wife would never . . . Well, Dora *would* never and that was all there was to it. It was insane to think like that and he was ashamed of himself. He had no strange phone calls to remember, devious behaviour, unguarded coldness, feigned warmth. It wasn't just that she was Caesar's wife, she wouldn't want to.

He poured himself an inch of whisky, then returned it to the bottle.

He might have to drive somewhere. Instead he picked up the phone and dialled Burden's number.

It took Burden seven minutes to get to him. Wexford was grateful. He had a funny thought: that if they'd been Italians or Spaniards or something, Burden would have put his arms round him, embraced him. Of course he didn't do that, just looked as if the thought had crossed his mind also.

Wexford made them tea. No alcohol tonight, just in case. He told Burden the whole story and described what he had done, the hospitals, the taxi companies, checking the road accidents.

'It's hopeless going to the train station,' Burden said. 'There's never anyone there. The days are gone when there was someone to check your ticket and watch you go through. I suppose she'd even get her ticket out of the machine?'

'She always does. They've got a new one that takes credit cards.'

'What does Sylvia say?'

Wexford hadn't even thought about his elder daughter. It would be true to say that for the past two or three hours he had forgotten her existence. A flood of guilt swamped him. Always he tried desperately to pay her the same attention he did to Sheila, to need her as much, to love her as well. Sometimes this had the effect of making him pay her *more* attention and give her more consideration, but now in a crisis, all that had fled, had disappeared as if he had made no such resolve, and he had behaved like the father of an only child. He said abruptly, 'I'll phone her.'

It rang and rang. The answering machine came on, Neil's voice with the usual formula.

Exasperated, Wexford wasn't going to give his name and the date and time of day – what nonsense! – but just said, 'Please phone me, Sylvia. It's urgent.'

Dora must be with *them*. Everything was coming clear. Some dreadful thing had happened, an accident, or one of the children had been taken ill. He hadn't asked hospitals about Sylvia's children. Dora had been told before she could phone for a taxi and had gone to them – yes, been fetched by one of them. Sylvia had a red car, a scarlet VW Golf . . .

'Would she have gone like that?' Burden asked. 'Without telling you? If she couldn't get you, wouldn't she have left a message?'

'Perhaps not if it was' – Wexford looked up at him – 'bad enough.'

637

'You mean, she'd have wanted to spare you? What are you thinking, Reg? Someone terribly injured? *Dead*? One of Sylvia's boys?'

'I don't know . . .'

The phone rang. He snatched it up.

'What's so urgent, Dad?' Sylvia was cool, pleasant, sounding more contented than usual.

'Tell me first if you're all all right?'

'We're fine.'

He couldn't tell whether his heart sank or leapt. 'Have you seen your mother?'

'Not today, no. Why?'

After that he had to tell her.

'There must be some perfectly simple explanation.'

He had heard those words a thousand times, had even uttered them. He said he would call her back as soon as he had news.

'Thanks for not asking if she could have left me,' he said to Burden.

'It never crossed my mind.'

'I'm wondering if she decided to walk to the station after all.'

'In that case, what about the red car?'

'Mary just saw a red car. She didn't know it was a taxi. She didn't see Dora get into it. It might have been any car parked outside.'

'What are you saying? That she set out to walk to the station and something happened to her on the way? She collapsed or . . .'

'Or she was attacked, Mike. Attacked, robbed, left there. There have been a lot of strange goings-on in this place lately: that masked lot on the rampage, the breaking into Concreation, that business at Contemporary Cars this morning.'

'D'you want to go out and follow the route she'd have taken?'

'I think I do,' Wexford said.

His daughters would phone in his absence, but he couldn't help that. Burden drove. The only route Dora could reasonably have taken was along roads that were built up all the way. There was no stretch of open country, no area of waste ground, no alley to pass through and only one footpath to take as a short cut. It had been a misty morning but the sun had come through bright and strong by ten-thirty. People would have been about, in the street, in their front gardens.

Before they came to Queen Street Burden parked and they

explored the footpath. It led between the backs of shop yards and of gardens, was overhung with trees on both sides. A couple of teenagers were standing up against a garden gate kissing. There was no one else, nothing else. Burden drove across the High Street, entered Station Road, the station approach.

'It's not possible, is it?' Burden said, turning round outside the station.

'I ought to be relieved.'

'Let's say she walked it, and I reckon she must have done if none of the taxi firms took her, could she have met anyone on the way who gave her some sort of news so grave or so important as to distract her from going to London?'

'That's the idea I had about Sylvia all over again really, isn't it?'

'Well, could she?'

Wexford thought about it. He looked at the houses they passed, some of whose occupants he and Dora knew, well or slightly, but none were friends. The United Reformed Church, the Warren Primary School, a row of shops, then roads that were purely residential. Some acquaintance comes running out of one of these houses, calls out to Dora, rushes her indoors, pours her heart out, appeals for help . . . Denies her the use of a phone? Frustrates her visit to a new grandchild, the longed-for granddaughter? Compels her attention for *eleven hours*? 'No, Mike, she couldn't,' he said.

All the stories he had ever read of people going missing, all the cases of missing people he had ever come across . . . He thought of them now. The woman who had gone into a supermarket with her boyfriend, left him waiting at the fish counter, to go herself to the cheese counter, and was never seen again. The man who went out to buy cigarettes but never returned. The girl who checked into a Brighton hotel in the evening but who wasn't in her room in the morning, was nowhere. All those others who just weren't where they should have been at some given time, who had disappeared without clue, without trace.

Still, it was only eleven hours. A day, he thought, a whole lost day. In his house the phone was ringing. Sheila. No, he had no news. He told her – absurdly – what he had told Mary Pearson, not to worry.

'Don't say there must be some perfectly simple explanation, Pop.'

'That's what your sister said. Maybe she's right.'

Burden offered to stay the night with him.

'No, you go home. I shan't sleep anyway, I don't suppose I'll go to bed. Thanks for coming.'

He didn't say aloud what he was thinking. He let Burden go, watched him depart and went back into the dark house, switching lights on. She must be dead, he said to himself, then said it to the empty room.

'She must be dead.'

He amended it to: she must be dead or badly hurt. And not found. Somewhere she lay. There was no other explanation for her not phoning him or one of the girls, or somehow getting a message to him. Then he thought of the note that might have been left for him, the note that blew off the mantelpiece or fell down behind the furniture. He crawled about the floors, looking for the scrap of paper that would explain everything, tell all. Of course there was no note. When had Dora left him notes?

The small whisky he had poured back into the bottle he poured out again. Someone else could drive him if need be. The need wouldn't be tonight, he knew that by some kind of intuition.

Everyone knew. Because of his phone calls of the previous night and because Burden got in first, they all knew. They didn't expect him but he went in because he didn't know what else to do.

He had slept in the armchair for about an hour. Then he got up, had a shower, made himself a mug of instant coffee. You can phone hospitals at any hour, so he phoned a few, all ones he had phoned the evening before. No Dora Wexford had been brought in. He phoned both daughters and found that they had been talking to each other half the night. Sylvia was going to London to give Sheila support once she had found someone with whom to leave her sons, school being still out for the summer holidays. Would Dad like Neil to come and stay with him?

Dad would not, but he said it politely: 'No, thank you, my dear. You're very kind.'

He had been at the police station for an hour, not doing anything, sitting at his desk, when Barry Vine came in to say there had been a phone call from someone wanting to report a missing boy, a teenager. Vine, who wouldn't normally have been anxious to regard a boy of fourteen, six feet tall, gone from his grandmother's house for twenty-four hours as missing, thought the circumstances justified special attention.

'What circumstances?' said Wexford.

'This boy was going to London. He was going to the station in a cab.'

'My God,' said Wexford softly.

'Do I get the grandmother down here, sir?'

'We'll go to her.'

Rhombus Road was two streets from Oval Street where Burden had come with Lynn Fancourt on the previous day to check on the fare Trotter said he had fetched from Kingsmarkham station. Since then Wingate had confirmed Trotter's statement: he had been picked up from the station at about eleven, having come off the ten-fifty-eight train, and deposited in Oval Street at eleven-twenty. Wexford and Vine passed his door, turned left and left again and parked outside seventy-two Rhombus Road.

It was a street of small terraced houses, put up at the end of the nineteenth century, as so many in Stowerton had been, to accommodate workers in the chalk quarries and their families. All were now owner-occupied, affordable by young couples and first-time buyers. Most front doors were painted various bright colours, flowery window-boxes attached to sills and front gardens concreted over to give room for one parked car.

No car stood in front of seventy-two, which though not shabby, retained its original glass-panelled front door and sash windows, had flower beds full of chrysanthemums and Michaelmas daisies and a gravel path. The door was opened by a woman who looked far too young to be the grandmother of a fourteen-year-old. She had frizzy dark hair, pulled back with two slides from a pale, freckled face that appeared as if make-up had never touched it. Denim dungarees were loose around her waist and over the check shirt. Her eyes were frightened, too wide open.

'Come in, please. I'm Audrey Barker. Ryan is my son.'

They went into a small, exquisitely tidy living-room that smelt of lavender polish. The woman who had got up from her armchair was in her seventies, plump, white-haired, in a heather-and-green tweed skirt and a twinset the colour of the scent.

Wexford said, 'Mrs Peabody?'

She nodded. 'My daughter came this morning. She came as soon as she knew about the muddle we'd got in. She's not well, she's just got out of hospital, that's why Ryan was staying with me, because she was in hospital, but as soon as we didn't know – I mean, as soon as we knew . . .'

'Why don't you sit down, Mrs Peabody, and tell us about it from the beginning?'

It was Audrey Barker who answered him. 'Basically, my mother thought Ryan was going home yesterday and I wasn't expecting him till today. We should have phoned and checked but we didn't. Ryan himself thought yesterday was the day.'

'Where do you live, Mrs Barker?'

'In south London, Croydon. You get the train from Kingsmarkham and change at Crawley or Reigate. You don't have to go into Victoria. Ryan had done it a good few times. He's nearly fifteen and he's tall for his age, taller than most grown men.' She evidently thought they were condemning her, though their faces were quite blank. 'He could have walked to Kingsmarkham station,' she said.

'It's over three miles, Audrey. He had his bag to carry.'

Vine steered her back to the previous morning. 'So Ryan was going home, Mrs Peabody, and you thought he ought to have a taxi to the station. Is that right?'

She nodded. Slowly she clenched her fists and held them in her lap. It was a controlling gesture, a way of containing panic. 'The stopping train is the eleven-nineteen,' she said. 'The bus would have got him there an hour ahead of time and the next one would have been too late. I said why not have a taxi. I'd give him the money, it would be my treat. He'd only once been in a taxi before and that was with his mum.' Her voice slipped a bit. She cleared her throat. 'He didn't know what to say so I phoned up. It was a bit before half-past ten, five-and-twenty-past ten. I asked the man for a taxi for a quarter to eleven. That was to give Ryan time to buy his ticket. A nice bit of time, I don't like rushing. Oh, I wish I'd gone with him – why didn't I, Audrey? I was just too stingy to pay the fare back again.'

'That's not being stingy, Mum. That's common sense.'

'Who did you phone, Mrs Peabody?'

She thought. One hand went up and briefly covered her mouth. 'I said to Ryan to do it. Phone up, I mean. But he wouldn't, he said he didn't know what to say, so I didn't push it. I said, find me the number in the book, the local Yellow Pages book, and I'll do it. He gave me the number and I did it.'

'Wrote the number down, do you mean? Or brought you the phone book and pointed at it, or what?'

642

'He just said it. I put the phone on my lap and he said the number and I dialled it.'

'Can you remember it?' Wexford asked, knowing how hopeless this was, registering her bemused shake of the head. 'It wasn't double six, double six, double six, was it?'

'It was not,' she said. 'I'd remember that.'

'Did you see the car? The driver?'

'Of course I did. We were waiting in the hall, Ryan and me.'

They would be, Wexford thought, they would be there on the spot waiting, these two inexperienced taxi takers, the old woman and the boy, he could picture them. Mustn't keep the driver waiting, have you got the money ready, Ryan, and a fifty-pee piece for his tip? Here he is now. You want to go to the station, that's all you have to say to him, now give Nan a nice kiss . . .

'He came on the dot,' said Mrs Peabody, and Ryan picked up his bag and that bag they all wear on their shoulders, a back-something, and I said lots of love to Mum and to give me a kiss and he did. He had to bend right over to kiss me and he gave me a big hug and off he went.'

She began to cry. Her daughter put an arm tightly round her shoulders. 'You're not to blame, Mum. Nobody's blaming you. It's just all so mad, there's no explanation.'

'There must be an explanation, Mrs Barker,' said Vine. 'You didn't expect Ryan till today, you said?'

'They start back at school tomorrow. I thought he was coming the day before they started but him and my mother, they thought it was two days before. We should have phoned, I don't know why we didn't. I did phone when I got home from hospital. That was Saturday and I was sure Ryan said it was Wednesday he was coming home, but now I reckon what he said was I'll be home all day Wednesday or something like that.'

'So you weren't worried when he didn't turn up?' said Wexford.

'I wasn't worried till first thing this morning. I phoned Mum to check up on his train. It was a shock, I can tell you.'

'It was a shock for both of us,' said Mrs Peabody.

'So I got the next train down here. I don't know why, it was just instinctive, to be here with Mum. Look, where is he? What's happened to him? He's not what you'd call big but he's very tall, he's not stupid, he knows what he's doing, he wouldn't go with some man who offered him something. I mean, money, sweets, he's *fourteen* for God's sake.'

Dora's a grown woman, Wexford thought, a middle-aged woman who knows what she's doing, who wouldn't go with any man who offered her anything . . .

'Have you got a photograph of Ryan?'

On the verges of Framhurst Great Wood men worked all day, under the supervision of a tree expert, at extracting metal spikes from the trunks of oaks, limes and ashes, at chain-saw-felling height. One of them injured his left hand so badly that he had to be taken as a matter of urgency to Stowerton Royal Infirmary where it was feared at first he would lose two fingers. The tree people in the high branches were peaceful and silent, but those in the tree-top camp at Savesbury Deeps bombarded the workmen with bottles, empty Coke cans and sticks. From the top of a noble sycamore someone poured a bucket of urine on to the head of the tree expert.

Clouds had been gathering since lunch-time and the rain began at three. It descended delicately at first, pattering on a million tired summer-weary leaves, increasing in volume until it became a deluge. The Elves, as some called them, retreated into their tree-houses, drew up their tarpaulins, while some of them descended into the tunnel they had dug to link Framhurst Bottom with Savesbury Dell. Lightning lit up every Elves' nest in the high branches and a great gust of wind shook the trees so that their trunks swayed like the stems of flowers.

Over the whole panorama of woods, hills and green valleys (as seen from the air) the wind, weighted with heavy rain, flew in great silvery grey sweeps that glittered when the lightning came. The thunder rolled, then clattered with a sound like trees falling or heavy objects flung down on top of each other from a great height.

The workmen and the tree expert went home. Down in Kings-markham, Wexford also went home: a brief visit to check on his forlorn hope that there might be something significant or even vital on his answering machine.

He found both his daughters there.

The three-day-old Amulet lay in Sylvia's lap. Sheila leapt up and threw herself into his arms.

'Oh, Pop darling, we thought we ought to be here with you. We both thought that simultaneously, didn't we, Syl? We didn't hesitate,

we didn't *think*. Paul drove us down. I didn't even bring the nurse –
well, I couldn't, could I? Where would we put her? And I don't really
know anything about babies, but Syl does, so that's OK. And poor,
poor you, out of your mind about Mother, you must be!'

He bent over the child. She was a pretty little girl with a round
rose-petal face, tiny prim features and hair as dark as Sylvia's was
and Dora's once had been. 'Lovely blue eyes,' he said.

'They all have blue eyes at that age,' said Sylvia.

He kissed her, said, 'Thank you for coming, dear,' and to Sheila,
'You too, Sheila, thank you,' though he didn't want them, they were
an added complication and his heart had sunk when he saw them,
ungrateful devil that he was. Many people would give all they had
for the devotion of not just one daughter but two. 'I have to go back
for a couple of hours,' he said. 'I only came home to see if there was a
message.'

'There's nothing,' said Sheila. 'I checked. It was the first thing I
did.'

When one has children one has no privacy. They take it for
granted that what is yours is theirs, personal things and the secrets of
your heart, as well as possessions. He ought to be used to it by now.
But how kind they were, his daughters, how good to him.

'Surely you're not indispensable at a time like this?'

It was a remark characteristic of his elder daughter. He ignored it,
though looking at her kindly. How different they were, the two of
them. Most of the time he didn't see it but now, inescapably, he saw
her mother in Sylvia, the same features, the same almond-shaped
dark eyes, hardened in Sylvia's case just as Sylvia was taller and
altogether a bigger woman. But the likeness . . . It made him gasp
and turn his gasp to a cough.

Sheila took his arm, looked into his face. 'What can we do for you,
darling? Have you had lunch?'

He lied, said he had. She was so absolutely the successful young
actress who has just had a baby, she was it and playing it in her
muslin tunic and white trousers, strings of beads, fair hair loose and
flowing, soft, fruit-coloured make-up. Yet Sylvia in jeans and loose
T-shirt, looking down with unusual tenderness at the baby on her
knees, seemed more the child's mother.

'I'll see you both later,' Wexford said and plunged back through
the torrents to his car.

They had mounted a hunt for his wife and Ryan Barker, mainly

645

concentrated on inquiries in and around Kingsmarkham station. Every taxi company had been investigated. The drivers had no more knowledge of Ryan than they had of Dora and the station staff, such as they were – three ticket clerks and four platform staff – remembered nothing of either.

By five, Vine and Karen Malahyde with Pemberton, Lynn Fancourt and Archbold had come up with only one certain thing: neither Dora Wexford nor Ryan Barker had reached Kingsmarkham station on the previous morning. Somewhere between their points of departure and the station they had been spirited away.

It was Burden to whom the Roxane Masood phone call was relayed at five in the afternoon.

'I want to report my daughter missing.'

Something cold touched the back of his neck and flickered down his spine. He nearly said that he supposed she'd taken a taxi to the station the morning before. But it was his caller who said that.

'Pomfret, you said? We'll come.'

It was a cottage at the end of the short High Street where the shops came to an end, an ancient lath-and-plaster dwelling with eyelid gables and tiny latticed windows. Rain streamed off the eaves of the thatched roof. Pools of water lay on the path and inundated the tiny lawn. Wexford and Burden had to stand inside on the doormat and shed dripping raincoats, so heavy had the downpour been between car and front door.

She was in her early forties, thin, intense-looking, with big dark eyes and chestnut hair hanging in a shaggy mane to her shoulders. She wore a garment that in any other time in history would have been called a night-gown, white, diaphanous, floor-length, with flounces and bits of lace. The ethnic painted beads round her neck removed any such illusion.

'Mrs Masood?'

'Come in. It's my daughter that's called Masood, Roxane Masood. She uses her father's name. I'm Clare Cox.'

The interior looked as if it had been decorated and furnished in the early seventies and then frozen. Indian and African artefacts littered the place, the walls were hung with strips of Indian printed cotton and brass bells on strings, and there was a heavy odour of sandalwood. The only picture was framed in dark polished wood inlaid with mother-of-pearl.

It was a photograph of a young girl, the biggest photograph

Wexford thought he had ever seen, and she was almost too beautiful to be real. When you looked at it you could understand those fairytales in which the prince or the swineherd is shown the likeness of some girl unknown to him and falls instantly in love. 'This portrait is of magical beauty, such as no eyes have seen before,' as Tamino sang. Her face was a perfect oval, her forehead high, her nose small and straight, her eyes huge and black with arched eyebrows, her hair a gleaming black veil, long, centre-parted, water-straight and fine as silk.

Wexford reflected upon these things afterwards. At the time he quickly turned away from the portrait and having ascertained that this was Roxane herself, asked Clare Cox to tell him what had happened on the previous day.

'She was going to London. She had an appointment at a model agency. She's got a fine arts degree but she wasn't interested in that, she wanted to be a model and she'd tried everything, all the agencies. Mostly, they didn't want to know; she was too beautiful, they said, and not thin enough, but she's *extremely* thin, believe me . . .'

'Yesterday morning, Ms Cox,' Vine prompted her.

'Yes, yesterday morning. She was going to London to this agency and then to see her father. He's got a business in Ealing, he's done very well for himself and he takes her out to some very grand places, I can tell you.' She caught Vine's eye and collected herself. 'She didn't turn up. Anyone else would have phoned to find out why not but not him, of course not. He thought she'd changed her mind, if you please.'

'How do you know then . . . ?

'He did phone. An hour ago. Some pal of his thought he could get her modelling work. I hope it's bona fide, I said, you hear such terrible things, porno rings and whatever, and I said why don't you ask her yourself and he said, put her on, and that's when it came out. He hadn't seen her.'

'Did you check with the modelling agency?'

She put out her hands, raised her shoulders. Her voice was a thin scream. 'I don't even know where the bloody place is!'

'So yesterday morning,' said Wexford, 'she went to Kingsmarkham station by taxi? Which taxi?' He was sure she wouldn't remember. 'Did you hear her make the call?'

'No, but I know when it was and who it was. She always had taxis, her father makes her an allowance and it's liberal, I can tell you. She'd always used the same company since they started. She phoned just before eleven. She knew the girl who worked for them, answered the phone, I mean. Tanya Paine. They were at school together.'

'Roxane can't have gone to Contemporary Cars yesterday, Ms Cox,' said Burden. He thought of how to put it. 'Their phones were down. They were out of order. She must have called another company.'

'Well, she didn't,' said Clare Cox. 'I was up in my studio, painting. That's what I do, I'm a painter. She came in and said the cab was coming in fifteen minutes and she'd catch the eleven-thirty-six. I don't know why I said it, but I did, I said, right, and then I said, how's Tanya, and she said, I don't know, I didn't talk to Tanya, it was some guy answered.'

'You mean she phoned Contemporary Cars at – what? Ten-thirty? And they answered?'

'Of course they did. And the cab came for her at ten to eleven. I saw her get in it and that was the last I saw of her.'

648

# 6

Wexford finally got home to his daughters and his granddaughter at ten at night. But he was glad to have been busy, up to a point to have been distracted. Sylvia's insistence that he must be exhausted irritated him, though he gave no sign of annoyance. Her emphasis on the unfairness of it, on the way he had to do everything himself if he wanted it done, sent him to the dining-room in quest of a small whisky. Upstairs Amulet was screaming the place down.

'My posterity is driving me to drink,' he said to himself.

Then he thought how wonderful it would be to have Dora here to say it to. It was years since he had actually thought, in positive words, that to see his wife would be wonderful. How quickly, he reflected, disaster or potential disaster disturbs that which we accept as normal, shifts the aspect, makes us see the truth. You could so easily understand those who said, I will never be rough with her again, never offhand, never take her for granted, if only . . .

Earlier, once they had left Clare Cox, he and Burden, with Vine and Fancourt, had moved in on Contemporary Cars. They had gone over the place once again and then fetched Peter Samuels, Stanley Trotter, Leslie Cousins and Tanya Paine down to the police station.

Burden was looking at Trotter rather in the way a Nazi-hunter might have looked at Mengele if he had found him lying low in a suburb of Asunción: with satisfaction and vengefulness and something like glee.

Who had driven Roxane Masood to the station? Who had driven Ryan Barker?

'I've told you enough times,' Peter Samuels said. 'We never got no calls between half-ten and twelve midday. We couldn't have on account of Tanya here being out of action.'

Tanya Paine was becoming aggressive. 'I didn't make it up, you know. I didn't tie myself up. I'm a victim and you're treating me like a criminal.'

'I'll need the name or at any rate the address of the fare you drove to Gatwick,' Burden said to Samuels. 'I don't understand how you all just accepted not getting any calls for an hour and a half. Didn't it occur to you to go back and find out why not?'

'We was busy,' said Trotter. 'You know where I was, going from Pomfret to the station and then to Stowerton, you know all that. It was a *relief* to me there weren't no calls, I can tell you.'

'Anyway, it wasn't all that abnormal,' Leslie Cousins said. 'I can think of dozens of times when it's been slack.'

Burden rounded on him. 'I'll have the addresses of the fares you took, please.' He said to all of them, 'I want you to think. Have you any idea, even a suspicion, who it could have been that came into the place and tied Tanya up? Anyone you've talked to? Anyone who knew no one ever went back there before twelve noon?'

Peter Samuels asked if they minded if he smoked. He was a stout, heavy man with three chins and split veins on his cheeks, probably no more than forty but looking older. He had the cigarette packet out before anyone replied.

Burden said rather unpleasantly, 'Not if it helps your concentration.'

Trotter didn't ask if anyone minded his smoking. The moment their cigarettes were lit Tanya Paine began an artificial coughing. Cousins, the youngest of them and Tanya's contemporary, grinned and cast up his eyes. He said that any of their fares might know they never went back there before midday.

'A regular fare might notice. I mean, one of us could have said. Why not? No harm in that, is there? I mean, one of us only has to say we're busy, none of us never goes back to the office before twelve.'

At last Samuels said he sometimes had occasion to tell a fare he hadn't a radio link with the office but worked a car-phone system. That was if the fare asked. Sometimes a fare wanted to be picked up when he came back on the train, for instance. Could he call directly from the train on his mobile? 'That's when I'd tell him. I'd say to call the office and Tanya'd get through to one of us, depending on who was likely to be available.'

'So you're saying that anyone you've ever driven might know?'

'Not *anyone*,' said Samuels. 'Only them as asked.'

It was after this that they were allowed to go home and Vine, with Lynn Fancourt and Pemberton, started house-to-house inquiries in the vicinity of Kingsmarkham station. Only there weren't many houses. Contemporary Cars' office stood on half an acre of waste ground overlooked by nothing much, bounded on one side by the blank brick wall of the bus station and on the other by a tall, thin building that housed a shoe repairer on its lowest level and an aromatherapist, photo-copying agency and a hairdresser on the upper floors. Outside, and for a few feet inside, the chain-link fencing which bounded the land, thin, straggling trees, poplars and elders, grew out of six-foot-high nettles.

Opposite, beyond a row of cottages, was a pub called the Engine Driver, then a cash-and-carry hardware store, then the station car-parks.

Two hours later they knew very little more than when they started. Housewives, shoppers, drivers bent on catching trains, pub patrons, don't notice two men parking a car and mounting the steps of a mobile home unless they have reason to do so. The men could easily have put on masks once they had entered Contemporary Cars' office, for they would not have been seen by Tanya Paine until they had opened a second door.

Wexford pondered on how much more *noticeable* women were than men. If the intruders had been women someone might well have noticed them. Would this change as the equality gap between the sexes narrowed even more? Would women dressed like men, women in jeans, dark jackets, short-haired, without make-up, be as easily ignored?

He went to bed, then got up again when all was quiet. Sleep was impossible, unthinkable. Sheila's bedroom door was ajar and he stood in the doorway for a moment, watching her sleeping, the baby also sleeping beside her, in the crook of her arm. Such a sight would once have given him intense pleasure. For the first time in his life he understood what it was to want to roar aloud one's misery and terror. The thought of his children's reaction if he actually did that, their panic and fear, almost made him smile. He sat downstairs in an armchair in the dark.

Reading was as impossible as sleep. He thought of the Contemporary Cars business, knowing now for certain what had happened. The two men, with several accomplices, were arranging the taking of hostages. They had immobilised Tanya Paine in order to have

651

uninterrupted access to the phones for an hour and a half – or as long as it took. Very likely they weren't particular as to who their hostages were. They only had to be three people who phoned Contemporary Cars for a taxi between ten-thirty and eleven-thirty. The three they got were enough.

Ryan Barker, or his grandmother representing him, had phoned from Stowerton at ten-twenty-five for the eleven-nineteen, Dora from Kingsmarkham at ten-thirty for the eleven-o-three, Roxane Masood at ten-fifty-five for the eleven-thirty-six. Why was there a gap of twenty-five minutes before they responded to another call? Because no calls came in? Because none came in from one person alone and they felt unable to handle two passengers? (He winced at that, at that word 'handle'.) Because they had only two drivers working with them? It was possible too that one of them was one of the drivers, leaving the other to deal with the phone . . .

And then what? Ryan Barker might not have been too sure of the way to the station. His driver might have taken him almost anywhere within, say, a five-mile radius, before he realised. But Roxane Masood would have known within five minutes, Dora much sooner. Wexford didn't think his wife would simply have accepted, have wept, have pleaded. She would have tried to do something. Not to the extent of jumping out of the car, not that.

He clenched his fists, squeezed his eyes shut. Verbal protest, no doubt. A threat to leave the car. They must have taken steps to guard against such an eventuality. There must have been an accomplice waiting at, say, the first stop, red traffic light, halt sign, road junction. Then the rear door is opened, the accomplice enters, another one of those toy or replica guns is brandished . . .

Yes, that was how it was done in each case. But why?

Look at the alternative. Kidnap three people picked out of the street in broad daylight? It would have to be in daylight because there was never anyone about after dark. These days there never was. People stayed at home in front of the television or if they went out, went in cars. They even drank at home and pub after pub was closed. Like the Railway Arms. Beer was expensive and you couldn't go to a pub by car anyway, not with the current laws as to driving over the permitted limit. This way, the way the kidnappers had done it, there was no suspicion, no resistance, no struggle, until the route became unfamiliar, and then, with the accomplice at hand, it would have been too late.

Another reason for that twenty-five minute gap might be that they wanted women because women were physically less strong. And, even in Ryan Barker's case, it was a woman who had made the call. If she told them the fare would be a fourteen-year-old boy that wouldn't be enough to deter them. So they had a girl, a teenage boy and a middle-aged woman as their hostages, and the last-named happened to be his wife.

They must *be* hostages, surely? There couldn't be any other reason.

Another why remained. None of the three had any money, not real money. He and Dora were more or less comfortably off, Roxane Masood's father was prosperous, but Wexford doubted if he was in the millionaire league, and Ryan Barker's family seemed in straitened circumstances, if not positively poor. What ransom therefore could they be looking for?

Sometime during the night he made himself a cup of tea and fell asleep in the chair for an hour. A bit later he brewed coffee, went to the front of the house and watched the dawn come. The dark sky began to grow pale at the horizon, a rim of lightening that was not quite light. Upstairs Amulet gave one cry before Sheila silenced and comforted her with the breast. Dark clouds shifted and positive light, pale-green and gleaming, showed clear and cold.

With the coming of dawn over the bypass site, the Under Sheriff for Mid-Sussex, Timothy Jordan, moved in on the Savesbury Deeps camp with his bailiffs. It was the largest of the camps and its occupants had been served with eviction notices some time before.

The protesters were either in the seven tree-houses on the site or sleeping in hammocks strung between the oak, ash and lime trees which predominated in this area. Before the sun came up Jordan had them corralled inside a circle of yellow-coated policemen. He woke them by announcing with the aid of an amplifier that he had a court order granting him possession of the land and that they should vacate it. The amplifier was essential because the forest birds' dawn chorus was so loud: jug-jug, tweet-tweet, tu-witta-woo.

Meanwhile, in Sewingbury, the fleet of buses were picking up security guards from the old Army camp and ferrying them to the site north of Stowerton where the earth-moving would begin in half an hour. In Framhurst Great Wood, inside the secret tunnel, whose existence they supposed unknown to all but the members of

653

SPECIES, six people who regularly slept there were rousing themselves from sleep. The other end of the tunnel came out near the foot of Savesbury Hill.

The last of the six to emerge were a self-styled professional protester called Gary and the woman who had been his companion since they were both fifteen and whom he called his wife. No one knew her name but everyone called her Quilla. Gary had never trimmed his blond beard and it hung nearly to his waist. His clothes would have been more appropriate, and have attracted less comment, if the date had been 1396. He wore breeches, cross-gartered, and a brown canvas tunic, and Quilla a long cotton gown. They turned back for blankets because the morning was chilly and came face to face with a German Shepherd dog. At the Savesbury end the bailiffs and police had penetrated the tunnel mouth.

Once Gary and Quilla were out, Timothy Jordan sent a tunnelling expert known as the Human Mole into the tunnel to check it was empty and then put a guard on each end. Another bailiff, called the Human Spider, shinned up the tallest tree towards the house in its top branches. A rain of chopped wood, tin cans and bottles descended on him, for a while impeding his progress. On the ground Jordan's men began pulling people out of the bender tents and emptying them of their contents, before ripping the structures apart.

Somehow the quieter and more organised bands of protesters had got to know about it and a growing number of them assembled outside the security line: KABAL, SPECIES and Heartwood. When they saw one of the big rough-coated dogs come out from the tunnel mouth they began a low angry chanting. Up in the tree the Human Spider encountered a woman on the threshold of her tree-house and as the two of them struggled with each other fifty feet up, the crowd chanted, 'Shame, shame, shame!'

Patiently and in silence, Gary and Quilla assembled their property which had been flung out of the tunnel. They looked as if about to go on a pilgrimage to Canterbury with a Pardoner and a Wife of Bath. Neither of them would have touched, still less owned, anything made of plastic, so they stuffed their clothes, their blankets, their pots and pans, into old-fashioned jute sacks. Quilla began to sing the madrigal 'April is in my mistress' face' and the other dispossessed protesters joined in, with the tune if not always the words.

Up in the tree the woman whom the Human Spider had laid hands on had either fainted or, more probably, staged a faint, and hung limp between the two men who supported her. They began to lower her down the ladder, a perilous exercise, as her passive resistance gave them no help.

'Shame, shame, shame!' chanted the crowd.

Gary and Quilla sang:

> 'April is in my mistress' face,
> And July in her eyes hath place.
> Within her bosom lies September,
> But in her heart a cold December.'

By now the sun had risen, a fiery ball between black rails of cloud. The birds' calling was more subdued. Jug-jug, tu-witta-woo . . . A sharp gust of wind blew through the tree-tops.

On reaching the ground the woman who had appeared to faint sprang from the arms of the men who had brought her down. She was dressed in rags, some of which flowed and others which wrapped her like a mummy's bandages, and now, as she stood there and raised her arms to the crowd in a gesture of triumph or encouragement, her tattered garments streamed and fluttered in the wind. She ran to Quilla, embracing her and crying.

'We'll go to the Elder Ditches camp,' said Gary. 'I've had it with tunnels. You can show us how to build a tree-house, Freya. We'll build a big tree-house for the three of us.'

'I am a tree,' cried Freya, once more spreading out her arms.

'We're all trees here,' said Gary.

While Wexford's daughters made the kind of breakfast for him that he never ate, fussed over him and begged him to rest, Burden went in to work half an hour earlier than he need have done. His mind was full of Stanley Trotter. No amount of argument was going to convince him Stanley Trotter wasn't involved in this up to his neck and deeper. The man had murdered Ulrike Ranke and now he was engaged in a conspiracy to kidnap. It was probably a perverts' ring. The German girl had been raped before she was strangled and Burden believed this was developing into some sort of elaborate sex crime.

He had been at his desk ten minutes when a call was put through to him from the front desk. 'The editor of the *Kingsmarkham Courier* to speak to someone in authority. The governor's not in yet.'

'I suppose I'll do,' said Burden.

'He said you failing the governor.'

The editor, who had been there for some years now, was a man called Brian St George. Burden had met him once or twice, often enough, apparently, for St George to feel justified in calling him by his Christian name in full.

'I've received a funny sort of letter, Michael. Came in the post just now. It was the first one my personal assistant opened.'

If St George had a PA, Burden thought, he was Sherlock Holmes. 'What do you mean, a funny letter?'

'Maybe it's a hoax, but somehow I don't reckon it is.'

Trying to keep sarcasm out of his voice, Burden suggested St George tell him the letter's contents.

'Or do you think you'd better come down here, Michael?'

'Tell me what's in it first.' Suddenly Burden had a warning feeling, what Wexford called *fingerspitzen*-something. 'Don't handle it too much. Read it to me without handling it if you can.'

'OK, Michael. Will do. Funny, isn't it? A letter in these days. I mean, a phone call, a fax, e-mail, whatever, but a letter! Wonder it wasn't brought round by a guy on horseback.'

'Could you read it?'

'Right. Here goes. "Dear Sir, We are Sacred Globe, saving the earth from destruction by all means in our power. We are holding five people: Ryan Barker, Roxane Masood, Kitty Struther, Owen Struther and Dora Wexford . . ." They have to be wrong there, don't they? I mean, that's your boss's wife, isn't it? Since when's she been missing?'

'Go on.'

'OK. ". . . Owen Struther and Dora Wexford. They are safe for the moment. You will not find them. We will be in touch today to tell you our price for them. Inform all national newspapers and Kingsmarkham police for maximum publicity. We are Sacred Globe, saving the world." '

Burden said quietly as Wexford came into the room, 'We'll come to you now and take possession of that. In the meantime tell no one. Is that understood? No one.'

# 7

The sheet of paper was A4 size, Wexford guessed, 80 grammes weight, plain white, the kind you can buy by the ream from any office supplier. Once the letter would have had to be handwritten, later typed – and typing was almost as great a giveaway as handwriting. Now, with computers, detection was nearly impossible. The expert would probably be able to say which software had been used, which word-processing program, and that was all. No spelling mistakes any more, no capitals in error for lower case, no slipped letters, no chipped digits.

There might be fingerprints but he doubted it. The writer had folded the sheet once and then, in the same direction, once more. The envelope it had come in lay beside it. Laser printers are unable to print envelopes but a program is available for printing envelope labels and this facility had been used. It was, he thought, dreadfully anonymous.

They sat round Brian St George's desk, the letter lying in the middle of the leather inlay. St George was immensely pleased with himself, a complacency he had stopped trying to deny. He kept smiling wonderingly, amazed at the plum of a story which had come his way.

He was a cadaverous grey man with a hatchet face and a big belly that hung like a half-filled sack from his bones. His pale-grey chalk-striped suit was in serious need of dry-cleaning. A woman may wear a crew neck or an open-collared shirt under a suit but on a man this gives the appearance of his being half dressed and it was a long time since St George's sweatshirt had been the white it was when it started life. He could hardly keep his hands off the letter. They strayed towards it and he pulled them back, like a boy teasing an insect. 'I suppose I can photo-copy it?' he said.

'You can have that PA of yours in here to copy it by hand,' said Burden. 'But it's not to be touched.'

'They're not used to copying by hand.'

'Do it yourself then.' Wexford had never previously encountered the editor of the *Kingsmarkham Courier* that he could remember and he didn't much like what he saw. 'Which national newspapers did you have in mind to release this to?'

'The lot,' said St George, suddenly nervous, fearing the worst.

'You can do that but with the strict embargo that nothing is to appear until we give the go ahead. That goes for the *Courier* too, naturally.'

'Yes, but hold hard a minute, publicity's the best thing out in a case like this. You want publicity. You've a lot more chance of finding these people if everyone knows what's going on.'

'Nothing at all till we give the go ahead. I hope that's understood. This is a very serious matter, the most serious you're ever likely to be involved in. Mr Vine will stay here with you to see my instructions are carried out.'

'It is your wife, isn't it?'

Wexford didn't reply. He had read the letter on the desk: '. . . Ryan Barker, Roxane Masood, Kitty Struther, Owen Struther . . .' and then, when he reached his wife's name, the four syllables had come at him and struck him like a blow; black, hard letters leaping off the sheet. His eyes had closed involuntarily. He hoped now he hadn't recoiled, actually stepped back, but he feared he had. Feeling the blood recede from his face, as if it retreated like a withdrawing tide into the centre of his body, he had had to sit down suddenly.

His voice had deserted him but it was back now, deep and strong. 'Who beside yourself has seen this letter, Mr St George?'

'Call me Brian. Everyone does. No one but my PA, Veronica, has actually seen it.'

'Keep it that way. Mr Vine will speak to Veronica. At present silence is absolutely imperative. You will speak to these national newspapers and we will have a meeting with their editors later today.'

'OK, if that's the way you want it. It seems a crying shame but I bow to the inevitable.'

'We shall ask British Telecom to put a trace on your phones,'

Burden said, lifting the letter in gloved fingers and slipping it between plastic. 'How many lines are there?'

'Only two.' St George said it in the tone of a man who would like to have said 'twenty-five'.

'These Sacred Globe people have expressed their intention of making contact again today. Everything that comes over the phone into these offices must be recorded. I shall send you an officer to take Mr Vine's place in due course.'

'By God, you're taking things very seriously,' said St George, still smiling.

Wexford got up. He said, 'I expect you know it's an offence to attempt to pervert the course of justice.'

'No need to look at me. I'm a law-abiding sort of chap, always have been, but I suppose I'm allowed to express an opinion, and in my opinion you're making a grave mistake.'

'I'll be the judge of that.'

Wexford could think of half a dozen nastier things to say but he hadn't the heart for any of them. Going down the stairs they passed a young woman coming up. She had black curly hair hanging to her waist and a scarlet skirt that measured about nine inches from waist to hem. The personal assistant, probably.

'I'm not going to hang about,' Wexford said. 'I'm going straight to the Chief Constable. Meanwhile we'll need a trace on all our phones.'

'Yes. I wonder how many BT can do. It won't be an unlimited number. Who are these Struthers, Reg? Kitty and Owen? Why weren't they reported missing?'

Donaldson opened the car door and they got in the back. Wexford punched out one of the numbers of the Mid-Sussex Constabulary headquarters in Myringham, then asked for the Chief Constable's extension. He seldom saw the Chief Constable, most of his dealings being with Freeborn, the Deputy. Montague Ryder was a distant, lofty figure who suddenly seemed approachable when, in response to Wexford's insistence on urgency, he came to the phone and agreed instantly to a meeting as early as possible.

'I'll go over there now, or once we've dropped you. I don't think it's odd the Struthers haven't been reported missing, Mike. They're probably a married couple living alone. I expect they intended going away on holiday. I've been wondering about the interval between Dora calling for a car at ten-thirty and Roxane at ten-fifty-five, but this accounts for it. There wasn't an interval, these Struthers called for a car around ten-forty-five. The probability is they phoned Contemporary Cars to catch one of those trains between the eleven-nineteen and the twelve-o-three . . .'

'Or to go to Gatwick. If it was a holiday they might have been going by air.'

'True. But whatever it was, if they left an empty house behind them, who would know they were missing? If a family member was there, he or she wouldn't expect to hear from them. It would be odder if they *had* been reported missing. What is peculiar is that there were two of them and one could be a man maybe in the prime of life.'

'You mean, it's harder to abduct such people than . . .' Burden tried to be tactful, failed abysmally '. . . well, one on his – her – his own.'

'Yes.'

'Maybe he's an elderly man. They could both be in their seventies for all we know. I'll have them checked out. The phone book may be enough. Struther's not a common name in this neck of the woods. Are we going to say anything about this to the boy's mother and grandmother and the girl's mother?'

'Not yet.'

'What do they want, Reg? What's this price of theirs?'

'I think I know.'

Wexford turned his face away and Burden said no more. He got out of the car and went into the police station. There, though there were others to do it for him, he looked up Struther in the phone directory himself. There were two Struths, fifteen Strutts but only one Struther: O. L. Struther, Savesbury House, Markinch Lane, Framhurst.

He punched out the number. Four double rings and then, of course, one of those damned answering machines. Burden hated them. At least the greeting message on this one wasn't facetious, not the kind that said, 'Call me back if there's money in it,' or 'If you want to take me out to dinner I'm on.' A man's voice, which could have been middle-aged or old, but certainly wasn't young. The English it used was very correct, even pedantic. Courteously, it named the woman first.

'Neither Kitty nor Owen Struther is available at present to answer

660

your call. If you would like to leave a message, please do so after the tone, giving your name, the date and the time. Thank you.'

Burden thought it worth a try. He left a message, asking whoever might be there – a slim chance but a possibility – to contact Kingsmarkham police as a matter of urgency. Then he got on to British Telecom.

The Regional Crime Squad's Major Crime Unit, consisting of a detective chief inspector, one inspector, six detective sergeants and six detective constables, all specially trained, was housed in an unpretentious building in Myringham. Once it had been a set of auction rooms. It was built of brown bricks with vaguely Gothic windows and a door round the side. Through these windows computer screens could usually be seen, with people staring into them.

Wexford had passed it on his way to the Constabulary headquarters, an altogether more impressive place put up in the eighties when architecture was beginning to take a turn for the better after the lamentable previous ten years. The headquarters, out on the Sewingbury Road, had an ambitious roof, a kind of terraced mansarding, with a large square tower in the middle, curved wings and a pillared portico. On the lawn in front stood a statue of Sir Robert Peel, who, as well as being the founder of the police force, was said to have occupied a house at Myfleet for ten months between the autumn of 1833 and the summer of 1834.

The Chief Constable had a suite in the tower. An ante-room was full of the usual computer operators. One of them left her machine and took him through, knocking on a brass-fitted mahogany door. Wexford had that feeling of the heart rising into the throat, though he wasn't in the least nervous of Montague Ryder. It was rather that, at present, every happening seemed fraught with foreboding, every moment in passing time pregnant with dread.

The room was huge, like a lounge in a good country hotel, with armchairs, sofas, low tables, a big bowl of dahlias and Michaelmas daisies standing on an antique cabinet. Windows, designed less for opening and letting in light than for viewing panoramas, afforded the sight of green hills, deep valleys and the distant rolling downs.

Montague Ryder got up from where he had been sitting at a desk and came to Wexford with outstretched hand. 'I've been talking on the phone with Mike Burden,' he said. 'I think he's pretty well filled me in. You did right to hesitate but we must tell those parents at once. Anything else isn't feasible.'

He was a small man, slight but strong-looking, many inches shorter than Wexford. Abundant uniformly pale-grey hair covered his head like a neat cap and his eyes were the same clear dove-grey. 'This is a bad business about your wife.'

Wexford nodded. 'Yes, sir.'

'Won't you sit down?'

A green leather sofa accommodated them both, one at each end, facing one another. On the desk, a few feet away, stood a framed photograph of a pretty fair-haired woman with a child of maybe ten and another of eight. Wexford found he couldn't look at it. He said, 'These people, this Sacred Globe, will make contact again today. How or where we don't know.'

'Burden told me. You were quite right to embargo newspaper coverage. I shall set up a meeting with newspaper representatives for later today myself. I shan't need you at that.'

Wexford hesitated, then said, 'I hardly suppose you're going to need me at all, are you, sir? I mean, once I've given you the facts. You won't want me on the case.'

Ryder got up. He was recognisably the kind of person who never sits still for long, a pacer, a fidget, a man with too much energy for the ordinary uses of daily life and one whom exhaustion probably hit at the end of each day. He said, 'Would you like coffee? I'll have it sent in.'

'Not for me, sir, thank you.'

'Right. I drink too much of the stuff anyway.' He perched on a chair arm. 'You mean, of course, that I'd take you off the case because of your wife's involvement. In other circumstances that would be so, but I can't here.' Perhaps for the first time ever, he essayed Wexford's first name. 'I can't, Reg. We'll call in the Regional Crime Squad, but even so I don't have enough senior officers to dispense with you. I need you to lead this investigation. I'm putting you in charge of it.'

The first call from a national newspaper came in at ten-thirty. They wasted no time, Burden thought, referring the speaker, and the two others who called within minutes, to the Chief Constable's office at Myringham. As far as he was concerned, the sooner they got on with that restraining press conference the better.

Where would it come to, the phone call from Sacred Globe? He presumed it would be a phone call. The post, after all, had come and there was no second delivery. A message by fax or e-mail would be too dangerous to send, its very existence a clue to the transmitter. So a phone call it would be. To the police station? To the *Courier*? Somehow he didn't think so. One of those insistent national newspapers perhaps, or the local authority, the mayor's office, even the Constabulary headquarters. No, not that last. It would be somewhere they would least suspect, yet to someone certain to pass it on . . .

To one of Wexford's daughters?

He'd see about a trace on Wexford's home phone. And then he was going to take Karen Malahyde and the two of them would go up to Savesbury House, home of the Struthers. If his message had been received it hadn't been answered. Probably there was no one there. He couldn't place the house, couldn't see it in his mind's eye, but big country houses were two a penny round here, he'd probably know it when he saw it. If the Struthers had neighbours there was a good chance of one of them having seen something.

Facially, Karen looked like a dedicated police officer. She had been promoted to detective sergeant the previous year. Her expression was serious, her dark eyes steady, but her face was too scrubbed-looking, her hair too grimly cropped, for her to be considered good-looking. That was above the neck. Below, she had all the attributes of a catwalk model, perfect figure, and legs, as Burden's son John had once said, to die for. Burden himself didn't think of women in those terms and had been congratulated on this negativity by Wexford who, perhaps ironically, praised his political correctness. Karen herself was almost too PC for Kingsmarkham, particularly in her dealings with men. He didn't care whether she liked him or not, yet he rather fancied she did.

She was an excellent driver and it was she who drove the two of them. In Savesbury Lane they were stopped by the police cordon, for the bailiffs were still busy breaking up tree-houses and clearing occupants. When the sergeant in his yellow coat realised who it was he would have made an exception and let them through, but Karen good-humouredly turned round and took an alternative route via the Framhurst byroad.

The village of Framhurst would be the most badly affected of all conurbations in the Kingsmarkham neighbourhood. 'Conurbations' was a Highways Agency word which had made Wexford laugh grimly, for Framhurst was no more than a village street, a crossroads, three shops and a church. The school, built in 1834, had long since been converted into a house that its occupants whimsically called Lescuela.

Of the shops, one was an old-fashioned family butcher's to which customers came from all over the neighbourhood, another a general store, newsagent and video library, and the third a teashop with a striped awning and tables on the pavement outside. Framhurst had traffic lights at the point where the Kingsmarkham road crossed the one that passed between Pomfret and Myfleet. No one was sure how much of the new bypass would be visible from the houses which lined the village street, but there was no doubt about the coming destruction of the view from the hill to which that street led. The whole valley lay spread out below, woods, marsh, round, tree-capped Savesbury Hill, and the River Brede threading through the light-green and the dark-green like a long, crinkly strand of white silk.

Burden looked down on it. Of course you couldn't see any of those people from here. You couldn't see the pilgrims transformed into refugees, moving on with their bundles to pastures new. One day, not far off now, a twin-track road, three lanes each side, would change the entire face of that panorama, like a white bandage covering a long never-to-be-healed wound.

They found the house with some difficulty. It was concealed in shrubbery and tall trees, and was invisible from the road. Its nearest neighbour was a cottage on the outskirts of Framhurst village. They went past the house, realised they had gone too far and turned round. A sign on the gatepost was overgrown with tendrils of wild clematis. Karen had to get out and pull away the leaves to disclose a name: Markinch Hall in almost obliterated letters with Savesbury House printed boldly over the top of it.

'Interesting,' said Burden. 'I wonder if what-are-they-called, Sacred Globe, had problems finding the place.'

'Mr and Mrs Struther probably gave directions over the phone.'

The gates were open so they drove in and up a gravelled drive bordered by cypresses with tall alders and sycamores making a backdrop behind them. Brick and timbered walls gradually appeared as the trees thinned, and the varied colours, red, yellow and purple, of a well-tended garden replaced much of the green. The house looked like two houses joined together, the one ancient and picturesque, gabled and lattice-windowed, the other a tall Georgian building with portico. The whole must be very big, Burden thought, big enough for several families and with outbuildings or even wings behind.

There are gardens and gardens, his wife said. Most of them are full of stuff from the local garden centre, but the other kind, the rare kind, contain plants you hardly ever see, plants her father called 'choice', the ones that only have Latin names. The gardens of Savesbury House came into this latter category. Burden would have been hard put to it to name a single one of these flowers, these bedding plants and climbers, but he could tell the effect was very pleasing. The sun which succeeded the rain of the day before brought out a subtle sweet scent from whatever it was that spread its blossoms over the Georgian façade.

A Gothic front door on the older part of the building, black and worn, arched and studded, looked as if it hadn't been opened since Queen Victoria's Golden Jubilee. Burden was approaching it, his eye on a curly iron bell-pull, when a man came round from the side of the house. He glanced at Burden, curled his lip at Karen, eyed Burden again and said, 'What d'you want? Who are you?'

It was the kind of accent that the majority of the British people laugh at and Americans can't understand, a plummy drawl that is never acquired by public school alone but requires parental back-up and preparatory education from the age of seven.

Burden had no incentive to be nice. He said, 'Police' and produced his warrant card.

The man, who was young, no more than in his mid-twenties, looked at Burden's photograph and back at the original as if he seriously expected a hoax. He said to Karen, 'Have you got one too or are you just along for the ride?'

Karen exhibited warning signs, familiar to Burden, though not perhaps to her questioner. Her eyes snapped, then stared unblinking. 'Detective Sergeant Malahyde,' she said and put her card in his face.

He stepped back a little. He was tall, well-built, in riding breeches and hacking jacket over a white T-shirt, his features copyable by an artist or photographer as the archetype of the English upper class: straight nose, high cheek-bones, tall forehead, firm chin and the kind of mouth that was once called clean-cut. His hair, of course, was

665

straw-blond and his eyes steel-blue. 'All right,' he said. 'What have I done? What misdemeanour have I committed? Have I driven without lights or subjected some young lady to sexual harassment?'

'May we go inside?' Burden said.

'Oh, I don't really think so, do you?'

'Yes, I do think so, Mr Struther. It is Mr Struther, isn't it? The son of Owen and Kitty Struther?'

He was temporarily disconcerted and returned Burden's look in silence. He walked up to the front door and pushed at it. The door came open with a long, drawn-out groan. Over his shoulder he said, affectedly casual, 'Has something happened to my parents?'

Burden and Karen followed him into the house. The hall was low-ceilinged, half-timbered, a huge, sprawling place with a stone-flagged floor on which black carved furniture stood about, the kind that looks as if Elizabeth I might have sat on it or eaten off it. They all had to duck under the lintel to get through the doorway into a living-room. Here were floral chintz, Indian rugs, arts-and-crafts tables, and all was exquisitely clean and sweet-smelling.

'Do you live here, Mr Struther?' They hadn't been asked to sit down but Burden did so.

'I look the sort of guy who would live at home with Mummy, do I?'

'May I know where you do live?'

'London. Where else? Fitzhardinge Mews, West One.'

He *would* have a West One address, Burden thought. 'Then I suppose you are here to take care of the house while your parents are away on holiday?'

That did surprise him. He looked at Karen's legs, pursed his lips. 'Something like that,' he said. 'It's scarcely a hardship to come here on my own holiday. My mother fears burglars, my father has some phobia about an inefficient drain, ergo . . . ! Now can we come to the point?'

'You were here yesterday morning,' Karen said, 'when a driver from Contemporary Cars came to collect your parents and drive them to Kingsmarkham station?'

'Gatwick airport, actually. Yes, why?'

'Where were they going?'

'You mean, where are they now. Florence. A city more familiar to you as Firenze, no doubt.'

'If you make a phone call to their hotel, Mr Struther, you will find

666

that they are not there. They never went there.' Burden had been about to say that Kitty and Owen Struther had been abducted but he waited. The man's hostility was almost tangible. 'If you make that phone call you will find that your parents are missing.'

'I am not hearing this. I do not believe this.'

'It is true, Mr Struther. May I know your first name, please?'

'Not to call me by it, I beg. I'm old-fashioned about things like that. My *Christian* name is Andrew. I am Andrew Owen Kinglake Struther.'

'You do know where your parents are staying, Mr Struther?'

'Certainly I do and I consider that question impertinent. You've had your say, I've registered your absurd news and now I'd like your space.'

Burden decided to give up. He was under no obligation to make this man believe in his parents' abduction. He had done his best. Later in the day, no doubt, Andrew Struther would be on the phone to Kingsmarkham police station, having had what he had been told confirmed at Gatwick and in Florence, but instead of showing contrition and asking for more facts, demanding to know why the whole story hadn't been imparted to him earlier.

But as they entered the hall once more and crossed the stone flags there was a sound of running footsteps from above and a girl came down the staircase, followed by a German Shepherd dog. She was about Andrew Struther's age, a white-faced, red-lipped girl with a mass of untidy mahogany-coloured hair, wearing jeans and what looked the top half of baby-doll pyjamas. The dog was young, black and tan, not unlike the bailiff's dogs, with a dense, glossy coat. At the bottom the girl stopped, holding on to the carved banister post.

'Cops,' said Andrew Struther.

'You're kidding.'

'No, but don't ask. You know how low my boredom threshold is.'

The dog sat at the foot of the stairs and stared at them. Burden and Karen let themselves out but the front door slammed behind them before they could close it. Burden made no comment to Karen and she drove in silence. The sun had gone in and a light rain splashed the windscreen, too scanty for wipers to be needed. He thought of the various places Sacred Globe might phone, the places they would know about, a group practice surgery, a hospital, a high-street shop. Once they had done that the story would be out and there would be no way to stop it, never mind high-level newspaper conferences.

Somehow he knew they would phone somewhere he hadn't thought of and couldn't cover. British Telecom were obliging, but they couldn't put a trace on every possible phone and no one else but BT was permitted to do it.

Karen found a parking space almost outside Clare Cox's cottage, just where the double yellow line ended, and tucked the car behind a black Jaguar of last year's registration. Its owner – Burden guessed it before he was told – opened the door to them. He was a small, neat man, improbably dressed in a denim suit. His skin was waxen-cream, his hair and moustache inky black and Burden thought he looked like a not very old artist's rendering of Hercule Poirot.

'I am Roxane's father. Hassy Masood. Please come in. Her mother isn't feeling too good.'

Though obviously Asian, or of Asian parentage, Masood spoke with the accent of west London. The background, created by Clare Cox, of Indian artefacts and vaguely central-Asian rugs and hangings, suited his appearance but not his voice, manner or, apparently, his taste. In the living-room he shook his head disparagingly, cast up his eyes and, gesturing with his hands, exclaimed, 'This junk! Can you believe it?'

'We'd like to see Ms Cox if that's possible,' said Karen.

'I'll fetch her. You've no news of my daughter, I suppose? I came down here last night. Her mother was in a rare old state.' He smiled tightly, wrinkling up his eyes. 'So was I, in point of fact. Families should be together at a time like this, don't you think?'

Burden said nothing.

'I'm not staying here, of course. One gets used to big places, large rooms, don't you find? I should feel stifled here. I'm staying at the Kingsmarkham Posthouse. My wife and our two children and my stepdaughter will be joining me later today.'

'Ms Cox, please, Mr Masood.'

'Of course. Please sit down. Make yourselves at home.'

They found themselves both staring at the portrait. Roxane was the offspring of two not specially good-looking people whose genes cunningly combined to produce a rare beauty distant from either of them. Yet it was her father's black, liquid eyes that looked down from the wall and his thick, smooth skin like whipped cream that covered those fine cheek-bones, that rounded chin, those perfect arms.

'That photograph,' Clare Cox said, entering the room and seeing them looking. 'It's not good of her, not really. I tried painting her but I couldn't do her justice.'

'No one could,' said Masood. 'Not even ...' he sought for a suitable name, came up with one highly inappropriate '... Picasso could.'

Clare Cox was a pitiful sight. Perpetual crying had soaked and swollen her face and made her voice hoarse. The tears still lay on her red, puffy cheeks. She collapsed into a chair that was swathed in a red-and-purple shawl and lay back in an attitude of absolute despair. Burden, who had begun to have doubts after the Andrew Struther experience, now felt that telling the parents must be right. Hope, even vain hope, was better than this.

Karen told them what had happened, the bare facts, that at any rate at the moment, Roxane was safe. Roxane wasn't dead or injured, or the victim of a rapist. All Masood and Roxane's mother could do for a moment was stare in stupefaction.

Then Masood said, 'Abducted?'

'It seems so. Along with four others. As soon as we know anything we'll keep you informed. I promise you that.'

'But at the moment,' Karen said, 'we don't know any more. We'd like to have a trace put on your phone.'

'You mean you ... someone will come and ... an engineer?'

'No. BT can do it without coming here.'

'But they – these *abductors* – could phone *here*?'

'We don't know where or when the phone call will come, but yes, we think it will be by phone.'

Quietly, Burden explained how important it was to have their silence. No one must be told. 'Not your wife and children, Mr Masood. No one. As far as they are concerned, Roxane is simply missing.'

He gave the same injunction to Audrey Barker and her mother in Rhombus Road, Stowerton. They too were asked for their permission to have Mrs Peabody's phone monitored. Audrey Barker's reaction to the knowledge that her child was missing had been quite different from Clare Cox's. There were no signs of tears but her face was whiter than ever, her eyes seemed larger and she looked as if she had lost even more weight off her thin, stringy frame. Burden remembered that she had been ill, had recently left hospital. She looked as if she needed to be back there.

Mrs Peabody was simply confused. It was all too much for her.

She took her daughter's hand and held it in both of her own. Over and over she kept saying, 'But he's a big boy, he's big for his age. He wouldn't get into a stranger's car.'

'He didn't think it was a stranger, Mother.'

'He wouldn't have got into it, he's too big for that, he knows better, he's big for his age, Aud, you know that.'

'Can I see the other mother?' Audrey Barker said. 'Can we meet? You said there was a young girl taken too. We could form a support group, the other mother and me, and maybe the other women – have they got family?'

'That wouldn't be wise just at present, Mrs Barker.'

'I don't want to do anything out of turn but I just thought . . . well, it helps to talk about it, to share your experience.'

You haven't had an experience yet, Burden thought grimly, and let's hope to God you won't have. Aloud, he repeated what he had already said, that it was better not at present.

'They won't want you interfering, Aud,' said Mrs Peabody.

'These people who've got my son, what do they want?'

'We hope to know that today,' said Karen.

'And if they don't get it what will they do to him?'

At the police station they waited for Sacred Globe to call. They waited at the *Kingsmarkham Courier*, Barry Vine's vigil having been taken over by DCs Lambert and Pemberton. It was still only noon.

It was an ill-assorted group who had been taken away and imprisoned somewhere, Wexford thought. He thought in this way to distract himself from terrible ideas, from actually picturing Dora and imagining how she must feel. A twenty-two-year-old potential model who looked like an Arabian Nights princess, an over-tall schoolboy of fourteen, a married couple who, if Burden wasn't exaggerating, belonged to that county set of an anachronistic but still surprisingly powerful élite – and his wife.

She would get on better with the boy and the girl, he thought, than the two whose horizons were perhaps bounded by the hunt, paternalistic good works and pre-Sunday-lunch sherry parties. Then he reminded himself that, after all, the Struthers had been going to *Florence*. There must be something redeemable about a couple who would spend a holiday there instead of on a Scottish grouse moor.

Dora would be all right. 'Your mother will be all right,' he had said hollowly to his daughters. And they believed him, as they always did when he spoke, as it were, *ex cathedra*. The doubts were all inside himself. He knew the wickedness of this world as they didn't. But he knew Dora too. She would be sensible, practical, she had a great sense of humour and she would make it her business to comfort those young people. If they were all together, the five of them. He hoped they were together, not each in solitary confinement.

Would they know who she was? She wasn't the sort of woman to say, 'Do you know who I am?' Or even, 'Do you know whose wife I am?' Would they recognise the name? Not unless she told them, he was sure of that. Only those he had had dealings with knew his name. But if she had told them, then it might well be to his house that the call would be made. They would expect him to be there, not here. They would ask Dora and she would tell them he would be at home, waiting to hear about her.

At one o'clock he and Burden sent out for sandwiches. He tried to eat but he couldn't. Having one's wife abducted was a fine way of losing weight, except that he'd prefer obesity. Once the rejected sandwiches had been removed he went down to check the progress being made in setting up an incident room.

Some five years before, an annexe to the police station had been fitted up as a gym. This was at the height of the great fitness craze when it was thought advisable, at least for the younger members of the force, to work out as often as possible on exercise bikes, treadmills, skiers and stair-steppers. Wexford had read somewhere that most people who start exercising keep it up for a maximum of six weeks and this proved to be the case. Recently the gym had been used entirely as a badminton court but, as Burden had said, not really intending a pun, that would have to be shuttled out of the way.

The inevitable computers were going in, the modems, the phones. He walked about, looking at things, not seeing, aware that eyes were on him in a new and curious way.

He had become a victim.

Now her son was at school, Jenny Burden had gone back to teaching history at Kingsmarkham Comprehensive. It was a pity, as far as she was concerned, that the continental system didn't operate here and schools start at eight and finish at two. Perhaps that would eventually come about through the European Union, a body her husband had no time for but which Jenny tended to think of as a good thing. As it was, she had to find someone to look after Mark between the time he stopped at three-thirty and the time she finished at four.

But things were different on Thursdays, not just this Thursday, the first day of term, when her last class ended at twelve-thirty and she could go home. The nicest thing about it was being there when her friend who did the afternoon school run brought Mark home at three-forty, when he ran in and jumped into her arms. In the meantime, having eaten the one lunch she got all week that didn't have chips or pizza in it, she was curled up in an armchair reading Roy Jenkins' *Gladstone*.

The phone ringing slightly annoyed her. People shouldn't phone during these lovely quiet two and a half hours, her only alone time. But she answered it, she had never managed to get into the way of letting a phone ring. 'Hallo?'

A male voice. Absolutely ordinary, she said afterwards, as accent-free as a voice could be, somewhat monotonous, impossible to say if young or middle-aged. Not old, she could say that. A dull voice, perhaps purposely geared to be without a regional note or a peculiarity of pronunciation.

'This is Sacred Globe. Listen carefully. We have five hostages: Ryan Barker, Roxane Masood, Kitty Struther, Owen Struther and Dora Wexford. I will tell you our price for them in one moment. Naturally, if the price is not paid, they will die one by one. But you know that.

'Our price is that you stop the bypass. All work on the Kingsmarkham Bypass must be discontinued and not resumed. That is our price for these five people.

'We will be in contact again. Another message will be sent before nightfall. We are Sacred Globe, saving the world.'

# 8

'Did you guess right?' Burden said.

'I'm afraid so.'

Wexford was reading the transcription Jenny had made, as accurately as she could, of Sacred Globe's phone message. There was nothing in it to surprise him, it was in fact routine stuff, but the threat to kill the hostages if the 'price' was not paid still reared up off the page at him.

His new team had come into the room and it would shortly be time to address them. As well as Burden from Kingsmarkham there were Detective Sergeants Barry Vine and Karen Malahyde with the four DCs, Lynn Fancourt, James Pemberton, Kenneth Archbold and Stephen Lambert. The Regional Crime had sent him five officers from their complement of fourteen: DI Nicola Weaver, DS Damon Slesar paired with DC Edward Hennessy, and DS Martin Cook paired with DC Burton Lowry.

Nicola Weaver, Wexford had met for the first time ten minutes before. A woman had still to be very good to have risen to where she was at her age. She couldn't have been more than thirty. Hers was a sturdy figure, not very tall. She had strong features, black hair severely cut, the fringe at right angles to the sides, and she wore a wedding ring. Her eyes were a clear turquoise-blue and though she seldom smiled, when she did she showed perfect white teeth. She had shaken hands with him, a firm handshake, and said as if she meant it, 'I'm very glad to be here.'

Slesar was dark, handsome in a strained, bony way, one of those tall, skinny people who can eat anything without putting on weight. His very short hair was a dull lamp-black, his skin the olive of the Welshman or Cornishman. Wexford had a feeling he had seen him somewhere before, met him, but for the moment he had no recollection of where. DC Hennessy was his opposite, thickset, of medium height, with a pudgy face, reddish hair and light-hazel eyes like a ginger cat's. The other sergeant was thickset and heavyish, with bright, sharp eyes. DC Lowry was black, skinny and elegant, like a cop in a television serial.

Karen Malahyde greeted DS Slesar like an old friend – or something more? At any rate she didn't favour him with the short, cool look and tight nod she gave most male newcomers, but smiled, whispered something and sat down next to him. Could he have encountered Slesar in her company? Was that the solution? Somehow he didn't think so. It was something of a mild joke among them all that Karen never seemed to have a boyfriend.

He began by telling them what some but not all of them knew already, that his wife was among the hostages. Nicola Weaver, who evidently didn't know, said something to her neighbour, Barry Vine, and raised her eyebrows at his answer.

Wexford told them about the two messages, beginning with the one to the *Courier* which had resulted in the Chief Constable's press conference and an undertaking secured from all national newspapers that they would print nothing until he lifted the embargo. The second message, he said, had been received by Inspector Burden's wife at their home and he had a copy of Jenny's transcript shown on the screen.

'I think and hope this may be an instance of someone being too clever – and in his opinion amusing – for his own good. We might have expected the message to come to my house, since my wife may well have told her captors who she is and who I am. To choose Inspector Burden's home took us by surprise as was the aim. We must try to avoid being taken by surprise again.

'But in being clever he may also have been unwise. How did he know about Mike Burden? How did he know of his existence? Perhaps because Mike had had dealings with him and it's unlikely these were of a – how shall I put it? – a social nature.' A ripple of laughter made him pause. 'That is something we have to go into,' he went on. 'No doubt Sacred Globe found his phone number in the book, but we have to investigate how he knew whom to look up.

'The hostages were taken at random. We know that. Therefore there's little point in much investigation of their backgrounds. That isn't going to help us find where they are or who has them. We have to begin from the other end, with Sacred Globe itself. That's our starting point and getting on with it is imperative. This means contact with all the pressure groups protesting currently at the building of the bypass.

'Most of them – a couple of days ago I'd have said all of them – are legitimate groups of sincere people protesting against what they see as an outrage in a peaceable way. But in these instances there are always the others, those in it for the pleasure of causing disruption, for example, the rioters who invaded Kingsmarkham one Saturday night a month ago and many of whom, perhaps like our hostage takers, were masked and seemingly unidentifiable.

'Someone in these groups, in SPECIES or KABAL, is going to be able to help us. Even someone with Sussex Wildlife or Friends of the Earth, both legitimate, concerned societies, may well have come in contact with very different elements while on other protests. These people have to be talked to and any clues they may give us quickly followed up. The tree people and those in the camps have to be talked to. They may be our most valuable sources of information.

'I've said that the hostages' backgrounds aren't apparently of much significance but, on the other hand, I would draw your attention to a connection between Tanya Paine, Contemporary Cars' receptionist, and the hostage Roxane Masood. Miss Masood and Miss Paine appear to have been acquaintances if not close friends. They knew each other, which is the principal reason for Miss Masood's calling that particular taxi firm. This may mean nothing, it's probably no more than coincidence, but it is a tiny lead that shouldn't be neglected.

'The Chief Constable is at present with the Highways Agency. What will come of that meeting I don't know. I do know, as sure as I have any certainties about this business, that the government isn't going to say, "OK, forget about the bypass, let the hostages go and we'll build it somewhere else." Nothing like that is going to happen. That isn't to say there won't be some sort of interim compromise. We must wait and see what he has to say when he returns from his meeting.

'Meanwhile, because time is very important, we all have to get going on the lines I've just laid down. Principally, to find out who Sacred Globe are, their members, their leaders. We have to wait too for the message we are told will be sent before nightfall.

'Are there any questions?'

Nicola Weaver got to her feet. 'Is this to be classified as a terrorist incident?'

675

'Doubtful,' Wexford said. 'Not at any rate at this stage. As far as we can tell, Sacred Globe isn't attempting to overthrow the government by force.'

'Wasn't there a group or an individual who planted bombs on new housing estates?' This was Inspector Weaver again. 'I mean, bombed them to discourage new building? They're a possibility, I should think.'

'What about the guy who made concrete hedgehogs and put them on motorways?' This was DC Hennessy's contribution. He added, 'The idea being simultaneously to avenge squashed hedgehogs and wreck cars.'

'Anyone like that can be a lead,' Wexford said.

Turning with a slight frown from Karen Malahyde, who had apparently been whispering information to him, Damon Slesar asked, 'I understand Inspector Burden's wife is a schoolteacher at a local school. Could one of these Sacred Globe folks have been in her class at school or be a parent of such a child?'

'It's a good point,' said Wexford. 'Good thinking. That way he might know whose wife she was.' At once, as he uttered those words, his own wife came powerfully into his mind, seemed to stand before his eyes. He blinked, resumed, 'This is another lead to look into as soon as you leave this room. Talk to Inspector Burden and find out where his wife taught up till five years ago and where she has begun teaching now. Right. That's all. I hope you're all happy to work late tonight.'

It was still only four o'clock. Before nightfall, Wexford repeated to himself, before nightfall the third message would come. Now, in early September, night didn't fall until eight o'clock, if by the term one meant after sunset and when dusk has begun. In the next four hours that message might come to almost anyone. The same options as earlier applied and earlier they had been wrong.

Jenny had, with commendable presence of mind, immediately punched out the number 1471 that summons a recorded voice telling the subscriber the caller's number. But the caller had, prior to the call, put in the number that negates this procedure, so there was no result. These days any call could be traced if the caller's number was known, except that a call box was almost certainly being used and this time it would be a different one. Were they in the vicinity, he wondered, or a hundred miles away? Were the hostages together or held separately.

He asked himself, knowing he shouldn't ask, shouldn't touch it, shy away from this, whom they would kill first? If things didn't go the way they wanted – and how could they? – who would be first?

The only call to come in during the next hour in connection with the hostages was from Andrew Struther, son of Owen and Kitty Struther, of Savesbury House, Framhurst.

Burden was rather surprised to hear the voice of a reasonable man using reasonable words, even apologising. 'I'm sorry, I'm afraid I was a mite discourteous. The fact was this tale of my parents being missing seemed to me so totally incredible. However – I've phoned the Excelsior in Florence and they're not there. They've never been there. I'm not exactly worried . . .'

'Perhaps you should be, Mr Struther.'

'I'm sorry, I don't entirely follow . . . Hasn't there simply been a mistake?'

'I think not. The best thing would be for you to come down here and we'll give you the facts as we know them. I'd have done so this morning, but you were' – Burden endeavoured to be polite – 'not particularly receptive.'

Struther said he would come. He didn't know the whereabouts of Kingsmarkham police station and Burden had someone give him directions. Pass through Framhurst, over the crossroads, keep straight on, follow the signs for Kingsmarkham . . .

DCs Hennessy and Fancourt had gone to the bypass site to interview tree people at the Elder Ditches and Savesbury camps, where Burden was to join them. Detective Inspector Weaver was with the KABAL hierarchy and Karen Malahyde, with Archbold, was researching SPECIES, where their headquarters was, how many members they had nation-wide, what they did and if it ever involved breaking the law.

A phone call came to Wexford from Sheila to say Sylvia was going home. Neil had been in touch with the news that their younger son, Robin, had chicken-pox. She was going home, but would be back next day, as soon as she was certain she couldn't carry the chicken-pox virus or bacterium back to Amulet. Wexford had given up arguing, protesting, telling them both to go home. He just uttered, 'yes, darling, that's fine, anything you like,' adding that he didn't know when he'd be back. The message wouldn't come to his home anyway. Sacred Globe would know very well he wouldn't see much of the inside of his house at the moment.

A promise had been extracted from Peter Tregear of Sussex Wildlife to be with him by five-thirty, when Andrew Struther arrived, accompanied by his girlfriend whom he introduced as Bibi. Both wore sun-glasses, though it wasn't a bright day. The girl's were the mirror kind that you can see your own face in. She wore a red-and-white-striped Breton top, so skimpy that every time she moved an inch of tanned midriff showed. She seemed highly conscious of her good looks and allure, fidgeting her body into provocative poses. Wexford left them to Burden. He felt Burden was owed an apology, though he doubted if it would come.

Perhaps because Burden had told him he should be worried, Struther had brought with him a photograph of his missing parents. They were standing in snow in bright sunshine on some ski slope. Both were smiling and screwing up their eyes. It would have been hard to identify the originals from this, but Burden didn't think he was going to have to. He saw a tall man in a dark-blue ski suit, a rather shorter woman in red. From what could be seen of it under woolly hats, both had fair hair fading to grey, light eyes and were strong, straight and lean. Owen Struther might have been fifty-five, his wife a few years younger.

'I must ask for your silence,' Burden said. 'We are taking a very serious view of this. I don't think I'm overstepping the mark if I say that a leak to the press will result in prosecution for obstructing the police in their inquiries.'

'What is this?' said Struther.

Burden told him. He didn't name the other hostages. A reluctance to name Wexford's wife had seized him.

'Unbelievable,' Struther said.

The girl gave a shriek. She sat up awkwardly, forgot to be provocative, took off her glasses. Hazel eyes, verging on the golden, had the look of an animal's, empty of emotion, though greedy and purposeful.

'Why them?' Struther asked.

'Chance. A random selection. There have been threats. Threats to kill unless conditions are met.'

'Conditions?'

Burden saw no reason why not to tell him. All the next-of-kin of the hostages would have to be told. Much as he would have preferred to shy away from it, he said, 'That the building of the bypass be stopped.'

678

Struther said, 'What bypass?'

He lived in London, he might not read the papers, watch television. There were such people. 'I rather think the proposed route can be seen from the windows of your parents' house.'

'Oh, that new road? The one people keep demonstrating about?'

'That one.' Wexford watched Struther digest this information, nod, put up his eyebrows. 'Thank you, Mr Struther,' he said. 'We'll keep you informed. Remember what I said about not speaking to anyone about this, won't you? It's of the greatest importance.'

Dazed now, as if in a dream, Struther said, 'We won't say anything,' and then, 'Christ, it's just beginning to hit me. Christ.'

Peter Tregear must have passed him going out as he came in. The secretary of the Mid-Sussex Wildlife Trust was not to be told of the abductions, only of a subversive group called Sacred Globe. What did he know of them? Had he even heard of them?

'I don't think so,' Tregear said. 'There are so many of these groups and splinter groups. It's never simple. Have you ever read a book about the French Revolution?'

Wexford looked at him in astonishment.

'Or the Spanish Civil War, for that matter. I mention those world-shaking events because in both of them, and the Russian Revolution too, it was so far from simple and straightforward. Not just two sides, I mean, but dozens of splinter groups and factions, almost impossible to follow. Human nature's like that, isn't it? Can't keep things simple, people always have to have a lot of internecine squabbles; one little thing they don't agree with and they're off forming a collective of their own. Give me animals every time.'

'So you think the members of Sacred Globe were part of one of the other groups but they disagreed with the rules or the aims or whatever, maybe wanted more action, less talk, more violence even, so they broke away and formed their own.'

'Or didn't break away,' said Tregear. 'Stayed *and* formed their own group.'

'Before Mark was born,' Jenny said, 'I'd been teaching first at Sewingbury High School as it then was, and later at Kingsmarkham Comprehensive. Oh, and I did a bit of part-time at that private school, St Olwen's, when Mark was three and going to that nursery in the mornings.'

Wexford had found her in her husband's office where she had been

679

since receiving the call. Her little boy was with his school friend, siblings and parents.

'I've told half a dozen people everything I can remember about that phone call,' she had said when Wexford came in. 'And soon I'll be telling them what I *can't* remember.'

'Don't do that,' he had said. 'We've picked your brains enough on that. Now we want to know how he came to phone you.' He listened in silence to the enumeration of her teaching experience. 'Did your pupils – sorry, you call them students now, don't you? – did they know who Mike was, what Mike did?'

'I suppose so. Some of them did. Kids aren't like they used to be when we were young, Reg.' She was flattering him there, he thought, considering she was getting on for twenty years his junior. She smiled at him. 'We'd never have asked teachers personal questions. We'd have got short shrift if we had. It's different now. For one thing they genuinely want to know. They're interested in people the way we weren't. Or I wasn't. At the Comprehensive they call me by my Christian name.'

'And they'd ask you about your husband? What he did?'

'Oh, all the time. The ones I taught five years ago, ten years ago, and the ones now. Except that now *every one* of them knows he's a policeman.'

'And back then? Say seven years ago? I'm thinking of seventeen- and eighteen-year-olds at that time. Is there anyone you can think of who specifically asked?'

'I think pretty well everyone knew then, Reg. They were all interested in my wedding – you remember what a big, showy wedding we had, all my mother's doing – and it was in the local paper then what Mike did.' She looked at him doubtfully. 'Where's Mike now?'

'Somewhere at the bypass site. Why do you ask?'

'I hoped he'd be coming home. But he won't, will he, not for hours? Can I go, Reg? I need to fetch Mark.'

Not for hours . . . It would have been the end of a normal day, but Burden knew that for him it was only half over. Eyes peering at you from forest depths and forest trees was an image constantly recurring in children's literature. He was always reading such descriptions to his son, but the eyes in the child's book belonged to animals and these were human. He was aware of them from the branches above him and the scrubby coverts beneath. A sacking curtain was pulled aside at the entrance to one of the tree-houses and a man stepped out, saying nothing, staring down, his face impassive.

They had left the car in a lay-by on the lane and walked first along the green ride, then taken the path that wound its way through groves of man-high birch saplings. Lynn Fancourt knew the way better than he did, a good deal better than Ted Hennessy who trod warily, rather as if he was being taken on a tour of an unexplored rain forest. Twittering birds gathered in the tree-tops, preparing to roost. Burden thought he could hear the sound of a guitar ahead of them, but soon the music and the keening voice stopped and all that could be heard was the birds' tuneless murmuring.

Then, as the birches were left behind and the great trees began, he saw the eyes. Their approach had been heard, their footfalls on the twigs and leafmould and dry grass, and that was why the guitar had been put away. Everyone in the trees prepared to watch for them. Burden had been used to believing that it was only animal eyes that shone in dark places, but these gleamed in exactly the same way. He had just taken in the fact that their arrival had interrupted the activities of three people who seemed to be involved in the building of a new tree-house, when the man on the platform spoke.

'Can I help you?'

He said it like someone serving in a shop, with the same degree of friendly politeness, but he wasn't much like a shop assistant, more a leader of men, tall with a commanding air, a cloak wrapping him. He might have been a general surveying the battlefield before the fighting starts.

Archbold said very correctly, 'Kingsmarkham Crime Management. We'd like a word.'

'What are we supposed to have done now?'

'We're making inquiries,' Burden said. 'That's all. We'd just like to talk to you.' He moved his hand, a half-wave. 'Nothing to do with this camp. It won't take long.'

'Wait.'

The cloaked man disappeared into his tree-house. There wasn't much he could do about it, Burden thought, if he didn't come out again. And there were fewer eyes staring now. He looked up at the tree-house which was in process of being built. A wooden framework had been constructed on the firm foundation made by the two huge limbs and lopped-off trunk of a long-ago pollarded beech. A woman in an awkward-looking long dress clambered down the trunk and began searching for tools in a canvas bag on the ground. She passed a hammer up to the man with the long fair beard who had come halfway down for it. At that moment their leader – Burden somehow knew he was that – came out from behind the curtain, his cloak left behind, and shinned down his ladder, suddenly transformed into a normal person in jeans, sweatshirt and trainers.

Not quite a normal person perhaps. For one thing, this man was exceptionally tall, exceptionally long-legged, with long-fingered, attenuated hands. His head was shaved, his features like those Burden had seen in pictures of Native American chiefs, harsh, razor-sharp, fleshless bones and skin. 'Conrad Tarling.' He nodded as he spoke, a kind of substitute for a handshake. 'They call me the King of the Wood.'

Burden could think of no rejoinder.

'Would you prove your identities, please?'

A glance at the warrant cards and the nod came again.

'We've been through a lot, had a good deal of trouble,' said Conrad Tarling in the tone of someone who has spent six months in a refugee camp. 'What is it you want to ask about?'

Lynn Fancourt told him. While she was explaining, the hammering started. The man building the tree-house had begun attaching lengths of timber to the beam construction. Lynn raised her voice. She had to shout above the noise and Burden went over to where the woman in the long dress was standing.

'Would you mind stopping that for the time being?'

'Why?' the man in the tree said.

Burden had never seen such a long beard except in illustrations to children's books: the wizard, the woodcutter. He didn't know why he kept on thinking of children's books. 'Police,' he said. 'We have some inquiries to make. Just hold off for ten minutes, will you?'

For answer, the hammer was flung out of the tree. Not, however, in Burden's direction or anywhere near him. The woman in the long dress picked it up and scowled at him. He heard Lynn Fancourt ask Tarling in her normal voice if he had ever heard of Sacred Globe or knew anyone in the camp who might have, when a girl in mummy-like wrappings and draperies appeared, running from nowhere, from a tree-top or out from among the trees perhaps, but who erupted into the midst of them, shouting and throwing out her arms.

'You turn us off our land, you drag us out of our homes, and now you come here and ask us to betray each other. It's not enough that you wreck this country, this world, you've got to wreck the people too. Not just their bodies, not just the way you carried me unconscious down a ladder at dawn this morning, not just that, though I might have fallen and been disabled for life, not only that, but you'd wreck our souls too. You'd make us betray our friends and when you do that you smash the spirit!'

There was a silence which Burden broke. 'Your friends?' he said.

'She's upset,' Tarling said. 'And no wonder. I don't suppose it was you, was it? It was the bailiffs. But you all get tarred with the same brush and who's to blame for that?'

'As you do, Mr Tarling, and who's to blame for *that*?'

Tarling began a lecture on environmental issues, the destruction of ecological balance and the danger of what he called 'emissions'. Burden nodded once or twice, then left him and went home, from where he phoned in to the old gym and announced where he would be that evening. They had agreed to keep each other constantly informed of whereabouts.

'They weren't exactly co-operative,' he said to Jenny while eating a fast supper at the table with his son. 'I got started on the wrong foot, I suppose. This Quilla – how does a woman get to be called Quilla? What's it short for or long for? – she gave me a name. And the other one, the Freya one, softened up a bit and gave me a place. I strongly suspect neither exists.'

'I suppose you're going out again?' Jenny said it neutrally, not at all in a tone of exasperation.

'Well, what do you think? That we're going to have a nice evening watching a detective series on telly?'

'Mike,' said Jenny, 'I've remembered something – well, someone. At the Comprehensive before Mark was born.'

He stopped eating.

'I don't want to remember it in a way because it's so – well, isn't it awful in our society, the way people with morals and high ideals and courage get labelled as subversives and terrorists? The way that happens and other people who never did a thing in their lives for peace or the environment or against cruelty, they're the ones that are respected?'

'No one's talking about terrorists,' said Burden.

'You know what I mean. Or I bloody well hope you do. I've made you see things a bit more my way, haven't I?'

'Yes, love. I'm sorry. I'm a bit tired.'

'I know. Mike, there was a boy at school – it would be six years ago, he was seventeen then, so he'd be twenty-three now, he was an animal rights person when animal rights were mostly about being against the fur trade and saving endangered species. He was an idealist and I don't think he'd have hurt anyone, though when I come to think of it he never seemed to care much for *people's* rights. He left school and went up north somewhere and later on, it was after Mark was born, someone, one of the teachers, I happened to meet her, told me he'd been convicted of stealing a lot of animals or maybe birds from a pet shop and releasing them somewhere. And the thing was, he asked for ten other offences of that kind to be taken into consideration. So I thought . . .'

'Why did you never tell me?'

'You wouldn't have been interested.'

Burden said quietly, 'No, you thought I'd say, serves him right, or, these people are a menace to society, and perhaps I would have. What was his name?'

'Royall, Brendan Royall.'

His little boy was beginning to read. Burden had never before come across a child who, instead of being read to, now wanted to read to the parent who had done so for him night after night for four years. But he hadn't known a parent like that before or many children, come to that. He kissed his wife and for a moment laid a loving hand on her shoulder.

' "I really couldn't eat mouse pie," ' read Mark. 'Mummy, you're not listening.'

Mouse pie, said Burden to himself, mouse pie. The things these writers thought of. Upsetting to an animal rights activist, that would be, a source of distress no doubt to this Brendan Royall . . . He drove himself to Clare Cox's. The Jaguar was still outside. Hassy Masood had returned with his second family, for the front door was opened by a young girl in a sari.

The tiny living-room was full of people. Masood, who had changed his denim suit for one of dark-grey broadcloth, proceeded to introduce them. 'My wife, Mrs Naseem Masood, my sons, John and Henry Masood. My stepdaughter, Ayesha Kareem, who is Mrs Masood's daughter by her first marriage to Mr Hussein Kareem, now alas dead. Roxane's mother, Miss Clare Cox, you of course already know.'

684

Burden said good-evening. Something about Hassy Masood made him feel tired before he got started. Unlike her daughter, Naseem Masood wore western dress, a very tight red suit with a short skirt, a great deal of expensive costume jewellery, gold with red stones, high-heeled white shoes. Her black hair, teased into tendrils, was nearly as long as Gary the tree man's beard. Her daughter was tall and willowy, had coppery skin, strangely light-brown eyes, long nose and curved lips, the look of a girl from Omar Khayyám. She made Burden think of the only bit of poetry he knew and the lines about bread and wine and thou beside me in the wilderness, came back to him. The little boys, pale, neat, black-haired, stared at him in a way he wouldn't have cared for his own son to stare at anyone.

On the sofa Clare Cox lay with her feet up, her eyes closed. She made a gesture to him with her hand, a movement of greeting possibly, or more likely, despair. She wore the same night-gown-like garment he had always seen her in, reminding him of Quilla, for it was soiled now, stained down the front, perhaps with her tears.

'I am sorry to disturb you, Miss Cox,' he began, 'but I know you understand that in the circumstances . . .'

Masood interrupted him. 'Now what can we get you in the way of refreshment, Mr Burden? A drink? A sandwich? I doubt if you have had time today for much in the way of sustenance. I don't of course touch alcohol myself but having seen fit to provide Miss Cox with supplies in the way of wine and brandy, I can with no trouble at all . . .'

'No, thank you,' said Burden. 'Now, Miss Cox, this won't take a moment.'

She opened her eyes. 'Do you want to speak to me alone?'

'That won't be necessary.'

After he'd said it he realised he might have relieved her of the rest of them, but he wasn't thinking fast enough. He thought only that if Hassy Masood had been obedient his wife would not know about Sacred Globe, but the questions he needed to ask could have been asked of the parent of any missing person.

She sighed. The girl called Ayesha turned on the television, lowered the sound to a murmur and sat on the floor staring at it, six inches away. Mrs Masood took her sons by the hand, then put an arm round each of them and pulled them to her. Masood, who had left the room, came back into it with glasses of what looked like orange squash on a tray.

Sticking to his refusal to drink, Burden said, 'What can you tell me about your daughter's friendship with Tanya Paine?'

'Nothing. She just knew her.'

Clare Cox had turned her face away, pushing it into a cushion. The girl on the floor drank her orange squash noisily, with slurps.

Burden said, 'Were they at school together?'

For a moment he thought she wasn't going to answer. Then she turned over and half sat up. 'They were at Kingsmarkham Comprehensive, but they weren't close friends, they just knew each other. Roxane's cleverer than her. She was in the top group for art and English.'

'I don't suppose he wants to know that,' said Naseem Masood to no one in particular.

Clare Cox spoke rapidly. It was a way of getting it over quickly, of getting rid of him. 'Roxane had a job – well, it started as a holiday job – working in the instant print place in York Street and she ran into Tanya who had a job next door and they'd got into the way of having a coffee together. Then Tanya went to work for Contemporary Cars and Roxane left to be a model, but when she wanted a car she'd always go to Tanya.'

As she was speaking the eyes of everyone in the room apart from the girl on the floor had turned to the portrait on the wall. The beautiful face looked back at them.

Mrs Masood was the first to remove her gaze. Having derived the maximum from this interview, she had apparently decided she had had enough. She got up, smoothing and pulling down her skirt. 'We should be getting back to the hotel now, Hassy,' she said. 'The boys want their dinner and Ayesha's a growing girl.' She addressed Burden. 'That Posthouse is a very good hotel for a place like this.'

He asked Clare Cox if she had Tanya Paine's address and was given the name of a block of flats in Glebe Road. Tanya, Clare Cox seemed to think, shared with three others. He waited until the Masood family had left, Ayesha, in spite of her height and her grown-up clothes, tearful and stamping her foot at being taken away from the silent screen.

'Have you no one to be with you overnight?' he asked.

'God,' she said, 'give me the chance to be alone.' She wiped her eyes with her fingertips, though there had been no tears in them. 'Mr Burden? It is . . . er, Burden, isn't it?'

'That's right.'

'I wanted to tell you something about Roxane. Oh, it isn't helpful, it isn't anything, but it's worrying me so . . .'

'What is it?'

'It's . . . do you think they're keeping her somewhere like a – oh, God – a small room, a cupboard even, I mean. She's claustrophobic, you see. I mean, she's really claustrophobic, seriously, not the way people just say they are when they don't like going in lifts. She can't be shut in anywhere, she can't stand it . . .'

'I see.'

'This is quite a small house but she's all right here when the doors are open. She always leaves her bedroom door open. I shut it once by mistake, I forgot, and she got in an awful state . . .'

What could he say? A couple of soothing sentences that offered very little comfort. But her question remained with him as he got into the car and drove back to Kingsmarkham. Sacred Globe weren't likely to be keeping the girl in some spacious apartment with french windows open on to lawns and terraces. The probability was somewhere small and confined, and he thought about cases he had known or read of, people kept in sheds or tanks or chests or car boots. How was Dora Wexford about claustrophobia? Did any of the rest of them have phobias or, come to that, allergies, special dietary requirements? It seemed to serve no useful purpose to find out . . .

He found Tanya Paine by herself, her flatmates all out. Solitary evenings she evidently devoted to beauty treatments, for her head was wrapped up in a towel, her nails were newly painted and there was a powerful foul smell in the room of some kind of depilatory.

At first she took his visit as that of a concerned social worker checking up on whether she had been given the counselling she had asked for. He recognised her as a total solipsist, with no interest in anyone but herself or in anything but her immediate concerns. In a way, this was an advantage, because telling her about the abductions would be out of the question.

Almost anyone else would have asked. She remained unsurprised by his questions, confirmed what Clare Cox had said, but volunteered no further information. To her, it appeared, Roxane Masood was just a girl she knew, not a girl who had affected her much; a mate to have a laugh with (as she put it), someone to meet for a coffee and a Danish. As soon as she could she steered the conversation back to her counsellor, a woman whom she had seen once, but who was not giving her the satisfaction she hoped for. 'She never asked me what sort of childhood I had. Don't you reckon that's funny? I was all geared up to tell her a few bits about my mum and dad and she never even asked.'

The phone ringing saved Burden from making any answer. Afterwards he had no idea how he knew, how the sense of what it was, of who was making this call, came to him in an inspiring flash, almost from the moment she picked up the receiver.

Perhaps it was the tone in which she said, 'What?' or the expression on her face, her lower lip dropping, her eyes widening. He got up, was across the room in two strides, met her eyes and took the phone from her. She seemed relieved to be rid of it, dropping it into his hands like a snake or a hot coal.

A couple of sentences had already been uttered. Burden concentrated on listening as he had never listened before.

'. . . Globe. You know the hostages we have. You know our price.'

It was as Jenny had said, a dull, accentless, monotonous voice.

'By morning we need a public assurance of cessation of work on the Kingsmarkham Bypass. We are not exigent, we are not draconian. A moratorium will suffice. Stop the work for the time being while we negotiate.

'But a public assurance via the media we must have and by nine tomorrow morning. If not, the first of the hostages will die and the body be returned to you before nightfall.

'Pass this message on to the police and the media.'

Burden didn't speak. He knew it would be useless and, in any case, he didn't want the possessor of this voice to know it wasn't Tanya Paine listening to him.

'I repeat, pass this message to the police and the media. The embargo on publicity is not of our doing. Remember that. Publicity is what we desire.

'We are Sacred Globe, saving the world. Thank you.'

The phone was put down, the burr began and Burden turned round to see Tanya Paine staring at him, open-mouthed and with clenched fists.

# 9

The second meeting was at nine that night and it was in the old gym. The Chief Constable and the Deputy were both there, but Wexford presided. His team had brought in a mass of information but the most useful, it appeared, came from Burden who had discovered a positive lead in Brendan Royall and, by the purest coincidence, been present when Sacred Globe's phone call came to Tanya Paine.

'Why her?' Nicola Weaver wanted to know.

'That's been puzzling me,' Burden said, 'and those words he used, "draconian" and "exigent" and "moratorium". I'm not sure I know what "draconian" means myself. She's not what you'd call bright.'

The message, rendered as accurately as he could by Burden and put on the word processor, was up on the screen in front of them in a hugely magnified version.

'But it doesn't matter, does it?' Damon Slesar said. 'The sense is what matters, the crux of it, that unless there's a public announcement by nine one of the hostages . . .' He had been going to say, 'get the chop' and, apparently remembering Wexford's wife, quickly changed it to '. . . one of the hostages' life is endangered. She'd pass that on all right.'

'Still, it was a piece of luck for us you were there, Mike,' said the Chief Constable. 'Or could they have known you were there?'

'I don't think so, sir. I told no one.'

'How about the voice, Mike?' Wexford asked.

'Possibly the same voice as the one that delivered the earlier message to my wife. On the other hand, she thinks the voice she heard was accent-free and not disguised, while I'm pretty sure the one I heard was. All those long words but a hint of a cockney accent. You know how you sometimes hear an actor talking cockney on TV

689

and it sounds good – they learn it from tapes and they've learnt well – but at the same time it's not genuine, it's not the real thing, it's telly cockney that we've got used to and accept. Well, that's what this voice was like, someone who'd learnt his cockney from a tape, and dropped his voice and took the inflections out of it. Altogether too much of a good thing, if you get my meaning.'

Lynn Fancourt and Archbold then had something to say about the name they had picked up at the Elder Ditches camp. A woman called Frances, known as Frenchie, Collins arrested in Brixton for being involved in an affray, was put forward by Freya, the dispossessed tree woman, though she spoke of her with such vindictiveness that Lynn suspected she was attempting revenge or settling a score. But it would have to be followed up.

Karen Malahyde, making inquiries at Framhurst Copses camp, was on to two leads which directed her to a house at Flagford that had long been a commune of activists of various sorts. Slesar and Hennessy were working on the Brendan Royall angle and Barry Vine was set for a renewed interrogation of Stanley Trotter.

The Chief Constable told them what he had achieved that day. Against everyone's will – but they had no choice – Sacred Globe's condition would be complied with and publicly announced.

'It goes against the grain,' Montague Ryder said. 'You know that. You all feel that. But "moratorium" is the word, a good word, and that's all it will be. That bypass is going to be built.'

The atmosphere in the gym was very different from what it would have been if the hostages had not included Dora Wexford. If the rest of them only sensed or intuited that, her husband knew it. However serious the matter, in other circumstances there would have been a degree of light-heartedness, a grim humour, a derisive profanity. As it was, they were wary, even embarrassed, and each one of them, in his or her own way, was afraid.

Not a single face was lit by a grin, no witticism or crack was exchanged, as they parted. The Chief Constable and his Deputy left together. Damon Slesar, departing with Karen, the two of them side by side, made a point of saying good-night to Wexford, and saying it very respectfully. 'Good-night then, sir.'

They made for one car between them, but not looking into each other's faces or speaking. Burden made the expected offer of accompanying Wexford home, staying the night if he wanted it, and Wexford again refused, though giving him heartfelt thanks.

690

Nicola Weaver caught up with him as he came into the car park. He thought how tired she looked. Someone had told him she had two children under seven and a not very co-operative husband. Her eyes were a curious shade of dark, bluish green, the same colour as the malachite in the ring she wore. 'There's something I thought you should know,' she said to him. 'You probably know already, but in case not – in this country the vast proportion of kidnap victims, more than a majority, turn up unharmed. With kids it's different but adults, getting on for a hundred per cent.'

'I did know, but thanks, Nicola.' He wasn't going to tell her she was the fifth person to impart these facts to him that day.

'Nicky,' she said. 'What good would it do them, anyway, to kill someone? It's an empty threat.'

'I'm sure you're right,' he said. 'Good-night.'

She got into her car and he got into his. The night was dark and moonless. He could see some tiny stars, infinitely distant pinpricks in black velvet. Lines came into his head and he repeated them as he drove home.

> 'Setebos, Setebos and Setebos,
> Thinketh he dwelleth in the cold of the moon,
> Thinketh he made it, with the sun to match,
> But not the stars,
> The stars came otherwise.'

A white sports car was parked on his drive. He recognised it as belonging to Paul Curzon, Amulet's father, and when he went upstairs he saw that Sheila's bedroom door was shut. The two of them were in there and their baby with them. Instead of causing him pain, it pleased him, gave him a tiny idea of peace, if not comfort.

If he was going to get any sleep it was better to get it not immediately but later in the night. Sleep that came at once would vanish after an hour and leave him wakeful and a prey to every kind of dreadful anxiety for the long hours to come. But sleep came, he lost himself in it after a short struggle, and slipped into a dream of Dora, of Dora and himself when young.

Why is it always our younger self in dreams, and even more so, the younger selves of those close to us? No book had ever offered him the answer to that, no dream expert analyst, for dreams are not expressive of our wishful thinking or surely they would all be happy and optimistic. In his dreams his daughters were children, his wife a

691

young woman, and he, though unseen by himself, the dreamer, *felt* young. This time he had come up to a tower, like a castle rising out of a great empty plain, and she was leaning out of an upper window, extending her arms to him.

Her hair was very long, as it had been in the early years of their marriage. It hung over the window-sill and down the stonework of the tower like Rapunzel's in the fairy story, only Dora's hair was dark, black as a raven's wing. He came close to the tower and took hold of the hair in his two hands, not intending to climb it, of course – even in the dream he knew real people didn't do that and in any case he was far too heavy to attempt it. She still smiled down but suddenly a terrible thing happened. The weight of her hair was too much for her, or his hold on it was too much, and with a cry she toppled forward and plunged from the window. He awoke, uttering a continuation of that cry, shouting as if they were calling out a protest together.

No one came. His room was far enough away from Sheila's for her to hear nothing. Besides, like most dream shouts, it had come out strangled and muffled. He lay for a while in the dark, then got up and walked about. We are all mad at night, someone had said. Mark Twain, maybe. It was true – or, in his case, was it? Didn't he have something to go mad about?

In the morning that announcement would come. Presumably via radio and television, later in the newspapers. But what if it didn't come? What if the assurance given Montague Ryder came to nothing because some higher decision affected it, because someone – the Home Office? The Department of the Environment? – thought it would smack of giving in to the demands of terrorists?

Nicky Weaver had told him what he already knew, that it was highly unlikely the hostages would come to harm. On the other hand, her assumptions were based on statistics of the kind of kidnapping carried out solely for monetary gain. These Sacred Globe people were fanatics, money didn't come into it with them. If they killed, whom would they kill first?

Stop it, he said to himself, stop it. They'll kill no one. It wouldn't be Dora, anyway, if it was the youngest or the oldest they chose. He looked at the time, then wished he hadn't. It wasn't yet two. If he must think he ought to be thinking of possible connections between this suspect and that, this suspect and that place – only there were no

692

suspects. As for the place, maybe that was an angle they had neglected up till now and should neglect no longer.

He was at a loss. Where did you start? With the people always. Find a suspect and you were a good way to finding a place. If that announcement didn't come ... The Chief Constable had given a guarantee it would come. He put the light on and tried to read. It was a history of the American Civil War, lent him by Jenny Burden, well-written, exhaustively researched, containing many descriptions of the carnage in that terrible conflict, of wounds, of slow death.

He kept seeing Dora afraid. She was strong, but she would be afraid. Anyone would be. His mind was partially distracted by a thought for that girl, Roxane Masood, whose mother had said she was claustrophobic. Confinement in a tiny room wouldn't bother Dora any more than confinement in a banqueting hall, but the claustrophobe ...

At about four he fell into a jerky, fitful sleep. Waking just before six, reflecting on the events of the evening before, he remembered where he had previously encountered Damon Slesar. It was that 'Good-night then, sir' that brought it back to him. That spurious word 'then', inserted like an apology.

It had been at a conference he had attended more out of curiosity than anything, for its subject was the differences between British and continental European police practice. There had been speakers from France and Germany and Sweden. Nothing strange about Slesar's being there, of course, except that most of the others had outranked him. In many ways it was admirable to see a man of his age and rank so wisely putting himself in the picture. On the Saturday night Wexford saw him again, this time in the local pub, where he was dining with a *commissaire* he knew from an investigation that had once taken him to the South of France. Slesar and some cronies sat at the next table, drinking whisky.

Afterwards, having stuck meticulously to fizzy water Wexford, with Commissaire Laroche, was making for his car when he saw Slesar heading for his. It hadn't occurred to him that after drinking as he had been Slesar would attempt to drive. But, accompanied by the two friends he had sat with, he was unlocking the driver's door.

Wexford had spoken almost involuntarily. 'Better not.'

Slesar looked at him, his eyes glazed. There was a loose, uncoordinated look to his face, the muscles out of control. He said, 'I'll be fine.'

693

By now there must have been half a dozen people around them. Wexford kept his voice light, almost jovial. 'Come with me. I'll drive you back. Someone can fetch your car in the morning.'

Slesar seemed to realise how many witnesses to all this there were. His dark face reddened. You could see it clearly in the lamplight. 'You're right, sir,' he said, and then, 'Jim'll drive me.' He touched the man behind him on the shoulder with more perhaps of a stagger than a touch, holding on to the car for support. He looked at Wexford and said, 'Good-night then, sir.'

A sensible man. A man who could take reproof and remain cheerful. Wexford was glad he had remembered, as far as he could be glad about anything, and pleased to have Slesar on his team. He got up and went downstairs in his dressing-gown, a dark-red affair more like velvet than towelling, which Sheila had given him for his birthday. Paul was in the kitchen, making a cup of tea, the baby, awake but not crying, in the crook of his left arm.

Wexford asked himself if it was good for an actor to be quite so good-looking these days. Paul Curzon had perhaps been born half a century too late. Amulet's black hair was his, or perhaps it was Dora's . . . Wexford put out his arms for the child, for he wasn't best pleased to see someone holding a baby and boiling a kettle at the same time.

'How are things?'

How much did Paul know? Only that Dora was missing? 'Just the same,' Wexford said.

The first local news, Newsroom South-East, would be just before seven. There might be something on the radio before that. He didn't want to hear it – or not hear it – in anyone else's company, he wanted to be alone.

'You didn't mind me staying the night, did you? I miss them – well, I miss Sheila and I rather want to get to know that baby so that I can miss her too.'

Wexford managed a sort of laugh. 'I'm glad you did.' An idea came to him. 'You know, Paul, I wish you'd take her home, take *them* home.'

'But you need her here. She says you need her. She says she doesn't know what would happen to you if she wasn't here.'

Wexford shook his head. Misunderstandings always depressed him. It was even worse when they happened between people who were close, who thought themselves knowledgeable of the other's

694

mind. He would have to be tough. 'Frankly, it only adds to my worries having her here. Don't look like that. She's very important to me, I love her dearly and that's an understatement, but while she's here on her own with the baby I keep wondering about her, if she's all right, what she's doing, and I can do without that, Paul. I never see her, you know. I'm never here except at night. Take her home. Please.'

Paul passed him a cup of tea. 'Sugar?'

'No, thanks. Take her up a cup and tell her you're taking her home.'

'OK. I'd love to. There's nothing I'd like more. If you're sure . . .'

'I'm sure.'

He had forgotten how simply comforting it was to carry a baby about. A stupid feeling came over him that if only he could walk about the house like this for hours with this warm, cuddly child held close against his chest, things would be better, he would worry less, he would be less prone to terrible fancies. The large blue eyes looked calmly up into his own. Did such young babies normally have eyelashes of that length and thickness? Her skin was like cream and like mother-of-pearl too.

He carried her into the living-room and looked out of the window at the sun coming up and into the dining-room out of the french windows at the garden full of long shadows. She pursed her mouth and blinked when he told her he was waiting for Newsroom South-East, that an hour had never passed so slowly before.

Paul came back and took her from him. 'Breakfast,' he said, and to Wexford, 'She only woke once in the night.'

'What did Sheila say?'

'She'll come home with me, but she won't promise to stay.'

Radio Four had nothing to tell him. He left it on because it was better to have voices and music and a weather forecast than silence. It occurred to him that a way of using up the time would be to shower and shave and get dressed, so he did all those things. By the time he was done – and he had tried to dawdle – it was still only a quarter to seven.

He put on the television as well as the radio. They only talked about money and business at this hour, and the inevitable sport. He heard the letter-box as the daily papers came through. Nothing on the front pages of either of them, nothing inside either. He reminded himself that to the vast majority of the population of the British Isles this wasn't really news. You only cared if you lived nearby – or if you were a fanatic. It would be news all right if they *knew*. If they had been told of the hostages and the demands and the conditions. That would drive the Lebanon and European Monetary Union off the front pages and prime time.

Newsroom South-East, here it was now: the pretty, dark young woman talking first about a visit Princess Diana would be paying to a Myringham hospital, and then . . .

'The Highways Agency announced last night that all work on the Kingsmarkham Bypass is to be suspended. This is due to an environmental assessment of the River Brede and Stringfield Marsh which must be carried out under a European Habitats and Species directive before work can continue.

'Though certain to be no more than a temporary suspension, it may last for some weeks. We talked to Mark Arcturus, of English Nature. Is this good news for the protest groups, Mr Arcturus, or is it only . . . ?'

Wexford switched it off. A great wave of something more than relief, something like happiness, had flooded him. He put his hand up to cover his mouth, the way children do not only when they have said something injudicious but when they have thought it. That he could be *relieved* at these people's victory! That he could be filled with joy!

It was all nonsense anyway. What was he thinking of? Dora was still in their hands. All the hostages were still in their hands, and he was nowhere nearer finding who Sacred Globe were and where their headquarters was than he had been twenty-four hours ago.

The news travelled fast. When Burden, with Lynn Fancourt, began his inquiries at the camp at Pomfret Tye, the tree dwellers were already celebrating. Someone – Sir Fleance McTear's name was suggested – had supplied them with a good imitation of champagne. A fire had been made on the edge of the heath and they were sitting round it, singing 'We shall overcome' and drinking sparkling wine.

'It's strictly in contravention of a by-law,' Burden said sourly to Lynn, 'lighting bonfires. These so-called nature lovers, ecologists or whatever, they're always the worst.'

He recognised the couple whose tree-house had burnt down back in the summer, admonished them for the fire and started on his questions. They asked him if he didn't think it was great news, man, and didn't he reckon that word 'suspension' was a nonsense? What they really meant, man, was that they were giving up on the bypass altogether and 'suspension' was just a way of saving face, didn't he agree?

Neither Lynn nor he got very far with rooting out clues to Sacred Globe and they moved on to Framhurst Great Wood. There, to Burden's surprise and considerable dismay, they found Andrew Struther and the red-haired Bibi sitting on a log in conversation with half a dozen tree people.

Struther jumped up, looking guilty. 'I say, I know what you must be thinking, I'm frightfully sorry but it really isn't that way. I haven't actually disclosed a thing.'

'Come over here, will you, Mr Struther?'

Bibi seemed to take his departure as an excuse for getting to know the tree people better. She got up off the log and followed a young man in nothing but a pair of shorts and a big straw hat to where a ladder was placed up against the trunk of a massive chestnut. He indicated to her to go ahead of him and went up close behind her as she took her first upward steps, giggling wildly.

Burden said, 'May I ask what you're doing here, Mr Struther? You have friends among these people? Yesterday you indicated to us that you didn't even know a bypass was planned.'

'That was yesterday.' Struther had gone rather red. 'You can actually learn quite a lot in twenty-four hours, Inspector, if you put your mind to it. I thought I'd better learn something, considering what's happening to my parents.'

'I hope you've said nothing to any of these people about that.'

Now it was an aggrieved look that Burden got. 'No, I haven't. I was bloody careful about that. I made a point of it. I was told not to and I haven't.'

'Then what exactly are you doing here? I don't suppose *you're* making an environmental assessment.'

'I thought if I talked to them one of them might give me a clue about who would do a thing like that, who's likely to be . . . well, a sort of terrorist.'

Precisely, in fact, what he and the rest of the team were doing. It sounded strangely feeble on Struther's lips.

'I'd leave that to us, if I were you, sir,' Burden said. 'It's our job, you see. Leave it to us and get off home. Someone will be along to see you later.'

'Really? What will that be about then?'

'I'd prefer to leave that till later, Mr Struther, as I've said.'

The girl had disappeared inside a tree-house. Struther looked wildly about for her, began shouting, 'Bibi, Bibi, where are you? We're going home, darling.'

The tree people watched him impassively.

Karen Malahyde had run the woman called Frenchie Collins to earth at her mother's home in Guildford. Nicky Weaver, Damon Slesar and Edward Hennessy were working on flimsy material given them by the SPECIES cadre and Archbold and Pemberton were tracing, by phone and computer, environmental activists nation-wide. Wexford had a meeting scheduled for two-thirty. He had already spoken to the Chief Constable and his Deputy and talked on the phone to Brian St George.

The editor of the *Kingsmarkham Courier* sounded indifferent and Wexford thought he knew why. If he had been allowed to use the story when the letter first came from Sacred Globe on the previous morning, he would just have got it into this week's edition of his newspaper. Now, on Friday, it was too late. As far as he was concerned he would have been happiest if nothing more had been heard from Sacred Globe, the hostages or the police until the following Wednesday evening. 'I still think you're making a mistake,' he said. 'When something like this happens the public have a right to know.'

'Why do they?' said Wexford rudely. 'What right? Who says so?'

'It's a first principle of journalism,' said St George sententiously. 'The right of the public to know. Muzzling the press never did anyone a mite of good. Not that it's any skin off my nose, I couldn't care less, only I don't mind it going on record that I think you're making a grave mistake.'

But the Chief Constable said, 'We're going to keep it dark, Reg, as long as we can. Frankly, I'm surprised we can. But since we can, let's keep at it.'

'It's Friday now, sir. I've a hunch the press isn't going to be all that interested. They'd think of it as a waste, using a piece of news like that at the weekend.'

'Really? I hadn't thought of it like that.'

'What they'd like,' said Wexford, 'is to have the embargo lifted on Sunday evening. Great stuff for Monday morning's papers.' He suppressed a sigh. 'If you approve, sir, I'd like to tell the hostage families of the . . . well, the conditions and the threat. I think we ought to. I'll do it myself.'

Audrey Barker and Mrs Peabody first. He would go to Stowerton on his own, then to Clare Cox in Pomfret, finally to Andrew Struther, as soon as the meeting was over. The Chief Constable seemed to think it a good idea. You could keep it from the press but not from those families, not in fairness and humanity.

His own family were just as much involved as the Masoods, Barkers and Struthers, and saying goodbye to Sheila that morning he had promised to phone her whether there was news or not. He would keep in touch daily, twice daily. Before he left he phoned Sylvia, told her that her sister had gone back to London, that he was all right, he was fine, but there was no news.

They were all assembled in the old gym ten minutes before time, all, that is, except Karen Malahyde who was still off somewhere in pursuit of Frenchie Collins, and Barry Vine who was beginning to share Burden's view of Stanley Trotter. Wexford walked in and everyone stopped talking. It wasn't just respect and courtesy, he knew that. They had been talking about him among themselves, and about Dora. For the first time he found himself wishing that what he had thought would happen had happened, that the Chief Constable had put someone else in charge of this business.

Nicky Weaver, looking a lot less tired and enervated than on the previous evening, looking brisk and energetic, had a good many leads to talk about from SPECIES and KABAL. A SPECIES officer, now apparently a reformed character, had once, quite a long time ago, been sent to prison for attempting to sabotage a nuclear power station. This man had given her a comprehensive list of names of people he said were anarchists.

'Why did he tell you?' Wexford wanted to know.

'I don't know. Probably because he's currently only in favour of peaceful resistance. Someone took him on a tour of the power station at Sizewell and he was so impressed he completely changed his tune.'

'It looks as if we've done all we can at the camps,' Wexford said. 'The computer can deal with all the names we've come up with and make cross-references, if any. With this suspension of work on the bypass we've bought ourselves time and that's important. There should be, some time today, another message from Sacred Globe.'

'They haven't promised it. There was no undertaking in last

night's message that another would follow, but something will come. We have traces on as many Kingsmarkham, Pomfret and Stowerton phones as BT can provide us with. BT have done us proud and there are no complaints in that area. But Sacred Globe are vain people, they're arrogant. Such people always are. They'll want to congratulate us on having the good sense to fall in with their demands. They'll phone or get in touch by some means or another. It won't have escaped their notice that the suspension is temporary. It's a suspension, a postponement if you like, not a full stop.

'Unless I'm much mistaken they are going to want a full guarantee that the Kingsmarkham Bypass is cancelled. And that, of course, we can't give them. That we can never give them, come what may.'

Nicky Weaver raised her hand.

'Nicky?'

'This guarantee – it's struck me that this is something no one, no authority, would, could, ever give. For instance, such a guarantee could be given, the hostages would be released and an immediate reneging on the undertaking could follow. Or even if their intention was sincere, even if they promised not to build this bypass, once there was a change of government, even a change of the Secretary for Transport, it could be built. So how are Sacred Globe ever to get round that?'

'I suspect they live for the moment,' said Wexford. 'Get a guarantee and if it lasts five years they've done well. If a bypass is proposed later – well, maybe they start again. Nothing is certain in this world, is it?'

He thought he saw a shiver run through her, but perhaps it was his imagination.

# 10

From Stowerton Dale to Pomfret Monachorum silence prevailed over the bypass route. It was rather cold for early September, windy with a touch of Siberia in the breeze, and from time to time a sharp shower of rain rattled down. Birds which had sung tweet-tweet, pu-wee, jug-jug at dawn were silent now and would make no sound until roosting time. In the camps the early euphoria had subsided, it was anticlimax time and the tree people were discussing, thinking, planning and, above all, wondering.

The heavy earth-moving equipment had been returned to the meadow where it had first been assembled. The buses that carried the security guards to the site had not run that day and the guards in their dilapidated air-base huts talked among themselves about the chances of being laid off.

Stowerton children, hitherto kept away by the guards, clambered over the heaps of earth, playing at guerrilla warfare in a mountainous region. KABAL called an emergency meeting at which a decision was reached. Lady McTear and Mrs Khoori were to draw up a petition to the Department of Transport for all members (and any other supporters that could be found) to sign that, in the light of a need for environmental assessment under an EU directive, and the unique ecological phenomena present at the site, work should never be resumed on the bypass.

When Mrs Peabody was young you tidied up the bedroom and put the child into a clean night-dress before the doctor came. If anyone in authority was coming you cleaned the whole house. Going shopping 'into town', you dressed up in your best. These habits die hard and it was plain that a kidnapped grandson wasn't enough to deflect Mrs

Peabody from her conditioning. She was the kind of woman who would put clean sheets on her own deathbed.

He felt deeply, painfully, sorry for her in her pink twinset and pearls, her pleated skirt and shiny shoes. She even had on lipstick. All the cushions in the living-room were plumped up and magazines were set out in a fan shape on the little table. She could powder her face but not summon up a smile for him, just managing a subdued, 'Good-afternoon.'

Her daughter, from a generation who saw things quite differently, from Clare Cox's generation, looked as if she hadn't washed herself or combed her hair since she heard. He knew all about pacing, he had done plenty of it himself these past days and nights, and he thought she paced this house for long hours. It was apparent she couldn't keep still, though she looked ill, in need of a long convalescence.

'I have to be here, on the spot,' she said to him. 'I ought to go home, I've just left everything, but it would be even worse at home.' She sprang up, walked across the floor to the window, stood there clenching and unclenching her hands. 'You said on the phone you had something to tell us.'

'It isn't bad news?' Mrs Peabody was a marvel of self-control, he thought, and wondered what her nights were like, when the bedroom door was shut. 'You did say it wasn't bad.'

He told them of the condition, that work on the bypass must stop. Audrey Barker walked across the room again, nodding, silent and nodding, as if she had thought of this or as if she wasn't surprised. But Mrs Peabody looked as bewildered as if he had told her the hostages would be released only if the entire population of Kingsmarkham agreed to learn Swahili or pilot helicopters.

'What's our Ryan got to do with that? That's the government.'

'I quite agree with you, Mrs Peabody,' Wexford said, 'but that's the condition.'

'They *have* stopped,' Audrey Barker said, coming up close to him; her hands working once more. 'It was on the TV. Is that why they've stopped?'

'There's been a suspension of work, yes.'

Mrs Peabody seemed overawed. He could see her digesting what had been said, interpreting it into a form she could understand. 'And all on account of our Ryan?' she said. 'Well, and the rest of them. Our Ryan and the rest of them.'

702

She shook her head in wonderment. This was fame, this was to be lifted out of obscurity, get into the newspapers, have one's name on television. 'Our Ryan,' she said again.

Her daughter glanced angrily at her. She said to Wexford, 'If the work's stopped, why hasn't he come back?'

Why hadn't he? Why hadn't any of them? It was now four in the afternoon, nine hours after that announcement of suspension had been made. Not another word had been heard from Sacred Globe. The message Burden had happened to receive was the last one and had been made twenty hours before.

'I don't know. I can't tell you because I don't know.'

She had forgotten that his wife was among the hostages. 'But what are you doing to find them? Why aren't you out there now looking for them? There must be ways.' She was tearing at her hands now, as if to pull them off the wrists. They were marked already with self-inflicted bruises. 'I'd go and look myself only I don't know how. You know how, you must do, it's your job. What are you doing for them? They could kill Ryan, they could torture him – Oh God, Oh Christ, what are you doing?'

Aghast, Mrs Peabody laid a small wrinkled hand on her daughter's arm. 'You mustn't speak like that, Aud. No good can come out of being rude.'

'There's no question of torture, Mrs Barker.' At least, that was something he could be sure of, especially if he didn't let himself think too much about it. 'And I don't think any of the hostages will be killed. If Sacred Globe kill them they lose their bargaining power.' Every word he uttered was a jab of the knife. He almost gasped. 'I'm sure you can understand that.'

She turned away, then rounded on him once more. 'Then why haven't they come back to you now the bypass has stopped?'

It was the same question. Clare Cox had asked it half an hour before when he had been with her in Pomfret. Alone, the Masood family having – incredibly – 'gone out for the day' to do the tour of Leeds Castle, she had been trying to paint to distract herself. At any rate, there were smears of paint on the smock she wore over one of her flowing dresses.

'Why haven't they done what they said they would?' she had asked him.

It wasn't then but now that he repeated to himself the words delivered to Tanya Paine that Burden had remembered: *Stop the work for the time being while we negotiate. But a public assurance via the media we must have by nine tomorrow morning. If not, the first of the hostages will die and the body be returned to you before nightfall . . .*

While we negotiate . . . But no overture of negotiation had come, no request for any kind of talk. And the message said nothing about returning the hostages, only about killing them if work on the bypass wasn't suspended. There had been nothing at all about what must be done before the hostages could come back.

'We'll keep you informed as soon as anything happens,' he said to Audrey Barker.

The phone rang as he was speaking. She picked up the receiver and was instantly calmed by the voice at the other end. A little colour came into her face. She spoke in monosyllables but gently, almost sweetly. It occurred to him as he left and set out for Framhurst that he knew less about her and her son than about any of the hostages. There was something about her and her mother that inhibited asking, and this was increased by their plight.

Who and where, for instance, was Ryan's father? Was there anyone else at home in Croydon? Probably Mrs Peabody was a widow but he didn't know that. Audrey Barker had been in hospital for an operation but he didn't know what for or how serious it was or even if she was fully recovered now. Who was the caller that she had talked to on the phone? Perhaps it didn't matter, any of it, perhaps these things were simply their private business that in the circumstances no one should inquire into.

Hadn't he told his team himself that the backgrounds of the hostages should be of no particular interest to them or their operation?

Rain had begun to fall more heavily as he entered that part of the country now inevitably associated with the bypass. Here, the apocryphal visitor from Mars would have suspected nothing, have received no hint of destruction, pollution, environmental damage. The deep lanes wound between overgrown banks and high hedges, the wind sighed in the high branches of beech trees, the woods slept quietly under the soft patter of rain and a few still-green leaves fluttered down.

In Framhurst a dozen or so tree people sat on the pavement under the teashop's striped awning, drinking Coke and one of them a cup of tea. Robin Hood's Merry Men probably looked rather like that,

Wexford thought, not in the orange knee breeches and fringed green tunics of cartoon film but a medieval version of denim with brown cagool-like garments on top, bearded, dirty, but strangely the representatives now of those who cared about preserving England. But why did they always look like this? Why weren't they ever men in grey suits? He slowed as he passed them, then quickly drove on to Markinch Lane.

Savesbury House was impressive. Burden had described it as half barrack, half architectural hotchpotch, but Wexford saw the mixture of styles as charming, as essentially English. The drive ran deep between groves of tall trees, their branches reaching for the sky. Then the lawns opened out and the flower beds were displayed with their rare unnameable herbaceous plants. If you stood on the edges of those lawns and parted the foliage with your hands you could doubtless see the whole great panorama of Savesbury and Stringfield, and the river winding below you.

A dog padded from the side of the house as he left his car. The animal approached him with stealthy, silent menace, a shaggy black German Shepherd, behaving in the intimidating way such dogs sometimes do, curling its upper and lower lips back about an inch to show a trim double row of bright white teeth.

Wexford's father had been one of those people of whom it is said that they can 'do anything with dogs'. He hadn't quite acquired that art himself but some of his father's talent had come to him, by association or by genes – perhaps he just wasn't afraid – and he put out his hand to this creature and said a casual hallo. He didn't like dogs, he had never liked the various dogs Sheila had foisted on him and Dora to 'mind' while she was away, but they liked him. They fawned on him, as this one did, stuffing its nose into his coat pocket when he bent down to it.

The white-faced girl called Bibi, a cigarette hanging from her mouth, opened the door. He had seen her before but in the distance, just as he had seen Andrew Struther, when the two of them came to see Burden at the police station. Her face, that Burden and Karen Malahyde had simply found good-looking, reminded him of a cartoon character the artist wants to look beautiful and evil, the Snow Queen perhaps or Cruella De Vil. That red hair was a most peculiar colour, nearer crimson than mahogany, and he didn't think it was dyed.

She grabbed the dog by its collar, cooing at it, 'Come here,

Manfred, come to mother, sweetheart,' as if he had been sticking pins into it.

Burden had said the interior of Savesbury House was beautifully furnished and 'squeaky' clean. Two days in the care of Andrew Struther and Bibi had changed all that. A plate of Chum or some such stood almost in the middle of the hall floor with a bowl of water alongside it. Manfred had been chewing bones between meals and Wexford nearly tripped over half a femur that lay on the drawing-room threshold. In there, cups and glasses stood about on shelves and table tops, a plate with a half-eaten sandwich sat on the seat of an armchair. Several large ashtrays had been filled to overflowing. The place was stuffy and there was an unpleasant smell compounded of cigarette smoke and old marrowbones.

Andrew Struther, entering the room, also nearly fell over the femur. Before uttering a word to Wexford he said crossly to the girl, 'Can't you put that bloody Manfred in kennels? You said you would. You absolutely promised when I agreed to have him here *for no more than two days*. Right? Remember?'

The face he turned to Wexford was sullen and aggrieved, a very handsome marble-hewn face though, lightly tanned, a shade darker than the butter-coloured hair. He and the girl were today both dressed like tree people in elegant green and brown – Elves who shop at Ralph Lauren. His parents, Wexford thought, were by far the richest of the hostages. They made Dora look poor and the others on the breadline.

'Chief Inspector Wexford, I think you said?'

'That's right. I believe you already know the condition these people have imposed.' He remembered the elucidation that had come to him while he was at Mrs Peabody's. 'Sacred Globe, as they call themselves, have not undertaken to release the hostages on suspension of work on the bypass, only to negotiate. However, there has so far been no move made by them towards negotiation.'

'Why do you say that?' the girl asked in a petulant voice. ' "As they call themselves" – why do you say that?'

Wexford said stoutly, 'People who commit acts of this kind aren't deserving of respect or dignity, do you think?'

Bibi didn't answer but Struther rounded on her. 'I just hope to Christ you aren't starting to feel *sympathy* with a bunch of shits who have kidnapped my mother and father.'

His pale-brown face had become bright red. Wexford had seldom

706

seen calmness so swiftly transformed into violent rage. Struther took a step towards the girl and for a moment he thought he would have to intervene, but Bibi stood her ground, put her hands on her hips and stared insolently up into his face.

'Oh, what's the use!' Andrew Struther shouted. 'But I want that dog out of the house first thing tomorrow. Is that understood? And this place cleared up. My mother will be coming back – do you realise that? My mother will soon be back. Isn't that right, Chief Inspector?'

'I very much hope so.' Wexford remembered his caution about the private lives of the hostage families being of no interest, but he disobeyed it again. 'What is your father's occupation, Mr Struther?'

'Stock market.' Andrew Struther spoke shortly. 'Same as me,' he added.

Manfred, in the hall, was chewing a chair leg. Whether it had mistaken the leg for a bone or just liked reproduction Chippendale Wexford didn't know and wasn't staying to find out. He drove slowly down the drive between the trees. The rain had stopped while he was inside Savesbury House and a pale, misty sun appeared in the blue triangle among the clouds. His car thermometer told him the outside temperature in Celsius and Fahrenheit: 13 and 56, not brilliant for the time of year.

Five minutes later he was in Framhurst village street. Most of the tree people had gone from outside the teashop but two remained. The teashop owner had rolled up the awning, perhaps when the rain had stopped, and optimistically placed more tables and chairs out on the pavement. On two of these, with a single teacup between them on the table, sat a man with the longest beard Wexford had ever seen, a golden beard like a skein of embroidery silk, and beside him a bedraggled young woman in the kind of clothes Clare Cox favoured, a dirty cotton gown with a spotted scarf tied around the waist.

He saw them so clearly and observed so much because the teashop was on a corner of a crossroads, one turning leading to Sewingbury, the other to Myfleet, and boasted Framhurst's single set of traffic lights. The light had turned red as he approached. He had already identified the man (from Burden's description) as Gary and the woman as Quilla, when she suddenly sprang to her feet, jumped off the pavement and placed herself in front of him in the middle of the road. Wexford shrugged, wound down the window.

'What do you want?'

707

She seemed taken aback that he wasn't angry and hesitated, both hands up to her face. He waited. There was no traffic behind him, none ahead. She brought her face up to the car window.

'You're a policeman, aren't you?'

He nodded.

'Not one of the ones who came talking to us at the camp?'

'Chief Inspector Wexford,' he said.

She seemed taken aback or shocked, shaken anyway. Perhaps it was only his rank, a higher one than she had expected.

'Can I talk to you?'

He nodded. 'I'll park the car.'

There was a space round the corner on the Myfleet road. He walked to where she was now sitting at the table with the bearded man. 'Your name is Quilla,' he said, 'and you're Gary. Shall we have a cup of tea?'

They seemed astonished that he knew their names, almost superstitiously affected, as if a name taboo were in existence and he had broken it. He explained, it was simple. Gary smiled diffidently. You could have sat there till Doomsday, Wexford said, before anyone would come out to serve you. He went into the shop and presently a girl of about fifteen came out to take their order.

'I could do with something hot inside me,' Quilla said. 'You're always cold in our business. You get used to it but a hot drink's a welcome thing.'

'Would you like something to eat?'

'No, thanks. We all had some crisps when the others were here. That was when we saw you go through and the King said you were a policeman.'

'The King?'

'Conrad Tarling. He knows everybody – well, he knows them by sight. The others went back to the camp, but I said I'd wait and see if you came back and Gary waited with me.'

'You want to tell me something?'

The tea came, three cups and saucers, a large pot, synthetic sweetener in packets and the kind of liquid in plastic cups that looks like milk but never originated in a cow. Wexford thought it was disgraceful in the midst of the countryside and said so.

'Take or leave it,' said the girl. 'That's all there is.'

'We campaign to stop that sort of thing too,' said Gary. 'We're against everything that's unnatural, everything that's synthetic, pollutant, adulterated. We've dedicated our lives to that.'

Instead of saying that it was extremely difficult in modern life to sort out the natural from the unnatural, if indeed anything natural remained, Wexford asked them how long they had been professional protesters.

'Since I was sixteen and Quilla was fifteen,' Gary said. 'That's twelve years ago now. I'm in the building line but we've never had jobs – well, paid jobs. The work we do is pretty hard.'

'How do you live then?'

'Not on the benefit. It wouldn't be right to be kept by a government and taxpayers when we're opposed to everything they think and everything they live by.'

'I don't suppose it would,' said Wexford, 'but it's a novel viewpoint.'

'We don't need much. We don't need transport often and we make the roof over our own heads. We do itinerant farmwork when we can get it. I do the odd building job. I cut grass. She makes straw dollies and sells them and she makes jewellery.'

'A hard life.'

'The only possible one for us,' said Quilla. 'I heard – well, I don't know how to say this.'

'What did you hear? That we were looking for names?'

'Freya said. Freya's the woman the bailiffs nearly dropped out of a tree yesterday. She said you were looking for a terrorist.'

Wexford drank the last of his tea. The undertaste of non-lactic soymilk creamer ruined it. 'That's a way of putting it.'

'What's he supposed to have done?'

'I can't tell you that.'

'OK. But if you're looking for someone who doesn't care that for human life, who'd do anything, abominable things, to save a beetle or a mouse, I can tell you who you want. Brendan Royall, he's called. Brendan Royall.'

# 11

It was the only name to have come to them twice, from two completely separate sources. Brendan Royall was Jenny Burden's ex-pupil, the boy who had 'never seemed to care much for people's rights' but had committed eleven offences in connection with the theft and subsequent liberation of animals.

To Quilla – her surname was Rice, Wexford discovered – Brendan Royall was the enemy, the activist who not only got protest a bad name but did things in the course of his campaigning that were opposed to all she stood for. It was her indignation over the very case Jenny had mentioned, he thought, which had led her to speak to him.

'They died, all those creatures he *liberated*. The birds didn't know how to fly and he didn't know what to feed them on. He was carrying the animals in the back of a van down the motorway and the back doors came open. It was carnage, it was abominable. I don't believe he cared, it was done for the principle, he said.'

'I'm surprised he's not here,' Gary said. 'I've been expecting him to turn up ever since we came and the first camp started. It's his sort of thing, you see.'

Quilla nodded eagerly. 'Not the spoiling the countryside so much as those insects and whatever. The Map butterfly and the yellow caddis. He'd kill a hundred people to save a stick insect. I once heard him say people weren't necessary, they were just parasites.'

Wexford offered them a lift back to the tree camp. They refused at first, they could walk, they wouldn't be beholden, but the rain started again and Wexford said it seemed a shame when he was going that way anyway. Quilla said she didn't know where Brendan Royall was at present. He ought to have been *here*, putting up some sort of demo along the Brede and she couldn't understand why he wasn't. When

710

Gary had last heard of him he had been in Nottingham, but Quilla said she had come across him later than that, in some connection with making a tunnel for weasels under the A134 in Suffolk. The difficulty was that, like them, he never really lived anywhere.

'His parents are round here somewhere,' said Quilla. 'I've got an idea he may have gone to school here.'

'That's right,' said Gary. 'He did. I don't know about living round here but he told me his grandad used to have a big house near a place called Forby and it should have been his, only his dad cheated him out of it.'

'He *would* say that.'

'He wanted to turn it into a sanctuary for animals that had been illegally imported. It was a great big place with a lot of grounds. Only his dad came in for it and sold it. His dad gave Brendan some of the money but that wasn't good enough for him. He wanted the house or all the money for the cause.'

It was almost six when Wexford got back to the station. Nothing more had been heard from Sacred Globe. They would have reached him on his mobile if it had, but still he'd hoped . . .

'This Brendan Royall is the most positive lead we've got so far,' he said to Burden. 'He's just the sort we're looking for, obsessed with what they all call Nature with a capital N, and with a total disregard for human life.' He winced when he said that part, but Burden pretended not to notice. 'Gary Wilson says he can't understand why he's not here, protesting with them, but I can. I hope I can.'

'You mean because he's one of those Sacred Globe people? He's not in a tree camp because he's somewhere else holding the hostages?'

'Why not? I want everyone to stop whatever they're doing and go out after Brendan Royall. Someone – you, if you like – should talk to Jenny and see if she can remember where the Royall parents lived. Or live. It's only six years ago, the fellow's only twenty-three now. Then there's the house that was the grandfather's. Someone in Forby is bound to know. It shouldn't be hard. Let's get the team in here, Mike, and brief them.'

The third meeting of the day was at six-thirty. Everyone was back from what had proved largely fruitless searches. Karen Malahyde had been to the council flat in Guildford, had been redirected by a tired old woman who said she never wanted to see her daughter again and finally found Frenchie Collins ill in bed in a dirty room in Brixton. She had been in Africa, had picked up some infection and

711

was still far from recovery. Karen saw no reason to doubt this, nor to disbelieve her when she said she had lost four stone in weight.

Barry Vine had been talking to KABAL and DS Cook with his DC to the Heartwood collective, whose leader, a bold young woman, had asked Burton Lowry if he was doing anything that evening. Lowry replied coolly that he was hunting hostage takers, so she said some other time and gave him a long, heavily charged look. None of that was passed on to Wexford. He told them about Brendan Royall, the parents, the grandfather's house, the eleven offences.

'You can sort it out among yourselves how you do it. I'm going to talk to Mrs Burden again but you can proceed as you like. I don't need to tell you that there's been no more word from Sacred Globe.

'One last thing. Make a start tonight. But don't keep at it too long. The great thing is to prepare the ground for tomorrow. We're all under a good deal of pressure and must have our sleep. Needless to say again, all leave is cancelled and we're all coming in tomorrow bright and early. So let's try and get some sleep tonight. That's all.'

He caught a flash from Nicky Weaver's blue-green eyes. It seemed to him, perhaps erroneously, full of empathy and compassion. She attracted him. She wasn't the sort of woman he had ever admired, she was a frightening departure from those sweet, young, pretty girls, and it was all the worse for that. Why did he have to feel this now, to bring him guilt and remorse, when all he really wanted in the world was to have Dora back? Inescapable, though, this appalling feeling of how wonderful it would be to have Nicky come home with him, drink with him, listen while he talked, take his hand – and then?

Someone had told him she adored her husband, a man who had nagged her to give up work when the children were very young and since then punished her for not agreeing by doing nothing himself. She had to employ a nanny for the evenings because Weaver, though not in general averse to staying at home, refused to do so if it might involve minding his own children. But Nicky would never hear a word against the man . . .

'Wake up,' said Burden. 'You're coming back to have a bit of supper with me and pick Jenny's brains – remember?'

'I know. I'm coming.'

'Brendan Royall or no, I'm convinced that Trotter's involved in this somehow. I talked to him again this morning, Vine's talked to him, in that pigsty he lives in. I know he murdered that girl, Ulrike Ranke, and I've a theory he's set himself up as a hit man. You can

712

understand that, a man kills once, he gets used to it, he'll kill again, but for money this time . . .'

'Trotter didn't murder the girl, Mike.'

'I wish I could be as sure as you.'

'No, you don't. You don't wish that at all. What you wish is that I'd listen seriously to all this rubbish about Trotter and the girl, only you know damn well I won't. As for his other calling, where does a hit man come into all this? No one's been killed yet.' Wexford was aware of Burden watching him carefully, almost with tenderness. 'Don't bloody look at me like that! I'll say it again, no one's been killed yet, and if they are it won't be Trotter that's responsible. Trotter was just like all the rest of that Contemporary Cars lot, a fool who knows about as much about running a business as I do about Psychoglypha citreola and as little about the environment as my granddaughter Amulet. So forget him, will you? Stop wasting your time on him. We've other things to do.'

Jenny put her arms round him and kissed him sweetly. It took your wife being abducted to make women really nice to you, he thought wryly. He sat down in the Burden living-room and let Mark read to him. At any rate he'd never been read to by a five-year-old before. Life was full of new experiences.

It was *The Wind in the Willows*, old-fashioned stuff but none the worse for that, and when he had finished Mark said very politely, 'I hope you don't mind, Mr Wexford, but Badger reminds me of you.'

He didn't mind. Mike brought him a stiff whisky and he accepted it because it had been preceded by an offer to drive him home.

They ate salmon mousse, chicken casserole and blackberry-and-apple crumble. No doubt it had been put on in kindness to him because he thought it unlikely Burden ate like that every night. Jenny told him all she could remember about Brendan Royall, every word he had ever uttered to her, every principle and theory of life he had aired. More to the point, she now recalled mention of Royall's grandfather's house, a paranoid rambling on about Royall's being cheated out of his inheritance and vague threats – which she, as his teacher, had tried to discourage – of getting even.

'The Royalls lived outside Stowerton somewhere, north Stowerton, I do remember that. A smallholding or a . . . I do believe it was some kind of wildlife sanctuary. In a small way, that is.'

'Now it'll have a fine view of the bypass approach road.'

'I expect they moved after the grandfather's house was sold.

713

Brendan used to say that he would get even with his father and then he boasted that he was going to get half the proceeds – as soon as he got it he was going to leave school.'

'Did he show any particular concern for animals when he was at school?'

'Not that I know of, Reg. But then they didn't practise vivisection in the biology class.'

'All right. I asked for that. You said his parents had an animal sanctuary, so I wondered.'

'I honestly can't remember. But I think it was more like a . . . do they call them petting zoos? Rabbits and a pony and a couple of goats.'

Wexford smiled. 'Did he get money from the sale of his grandfather's house?'

'I don't know. But he did leave when he was seventeen.'

Wexford got on the phone to Nicky Weaver with this new information, but Nicky already knew most of it. The grandfather had lived in some style at a house near Forby called Marrowgrave Hall and the sanctuary or petting zoo had become something more in the nature of a theme park.

'Don't keep it up too long, Nicky,' Wexford said. 'Remember what I said about sleep.'

'I know. I'll get off home now. My kids are alone or they will be in ten minutes.'

'You'd better remember about sleep too, Reg,' Burden said, catching his last words. 'It's nearly ten. I'm going to drive you home in your car and Jenny will follow us to drive me back.'

'Have I really had that much?'

'Who's counting? But, if you must know, it was two double whiskies and three glasses of burgundy.'

'You drive me, Mike. And thanks.'

He ought to have felt swimmy but he was stone-cold sober. He let himself into his house, closed the door behind him and stood in the dark for a moment, making himself aware of the silence, the emptiness. Sylvia was gone, Sheila was gone. He was alone now. He walked into the living-room and sat down in an armchair, still in the dark.

The members, or whatever you called them, of Sacred Globe would go to prison for years for abduction, for threats, for holding people against their will, depriving them of liberty, he couldn't remember the words of the charge. They wouldn't be inside for much longer if they killed the hostages. On the other hand, if they killed them there would be no one alive to describe their captors.

He thought of Roxane Masood, the claustrophobe, of the questions Audrey Barker had asked and of the couple who had been going on holiday to Florence. But he couldn't think about Dora, not now, he would have cried aloud if he had allowed himself to do that.

Why do we always go to bed at night? Most of us do. When the time comes, even if we aren't tired. Why don't we sleep in chairs, vary bedtimes, think, now is the time, fall into bed, slip into sleep? Because there must be a routine to life, a framework to hang life on. Routines were what kept you sane, gave you something to do at this moment and at that, definite places to go, positive things to do. Abandon it and that way madness lies.

He went upstairs. He got into his pyjamas and the crimson velvet dressing-gown and lay down on top of the bedclothes. The Civil War book was on the bedside cabinet and he thought how much he would like to pick it up and throw it through the closed window. The sound of the glass shattering would be satisfying in a curious, brief sort of way. Only it was Jenny's book.

Jenny . . . Her story of Brendan Royall matched Gary Wilson's. That didn't mean Royall need be involved with Sacred Globe. Gary and Quilla could be involved with Sacred Globe and have told him about Royall as a diversionary tactic. Suppose no outsiders were involved with Sacred Globe, suppose they stood alone. It had been taken for granted that activists in other peripheral or ancillary fields would know about or even be attached to Sacred Globe, but there was no rule about that. They could be a group of people who were individually opposed to environmental damage and had linked up as the result of a word spoken, a passion shared, a spontaneous decision.

But no. Because normally law-abiding people don't behave like that. And amateurs would need one person, or more than one, to organise them into this form of active violent protest. But the truth might well be that they were a mix of ardent amateurs and ruthless professionals, which brought him back to where he started: that someone up in those trees, or someone in KABAL or SPECIES, or in any organisation represented in Kingsmarkham to fight that bypass, must know or have a clue or a tenuous connection.

Why hadn't Sacred Globe sent another message? Why the silence, a silence that was now more than twenty-four hours long?

They had sent a letter. They had been in contact twice by phone. Short of the methods obviously closed to them because of ease of identification, what means of communication was left?

The personal one, the face-to-face contact. They had talked last time about negotiation and now, he thought, they meant to send a representative. Next time the message would be brought to them by word of mouth. What, by someone who just walked in wearing a Sacred Globe T-shirt? Carrying a white flag of truce? Anyone who was sent must face immediate arrest and yet . . .

He must stop thinking about it. He must sleep. Revolving these things in his mind was the worst way of aiming for that. Better try one of the recognised methods that were variations on counting sheep. He took off the dressing-gown, turned over and started repeating to himself all the names of houses in Jane Austen: Pemberley, Norland, Netherfield Hall, Donwell Abbey, Mansfield Park . . .

Trying to think what Lady Catherine de Burgh's house was called, he fell asleep. It was the drink and sheer weariness. Even as he slipped into it he knew it wouldn't last long.

The moon that had been covered on the previous night rose into spaces between the thin cloud, into a clear sea of darkness. It was a white full moon with a greenish iridescence, the light from it very bright and cold. Wexford thought it was the moonlight, a shining path of it in the gap between his half-closed curtains, that awakened him. A strip of moonlight lay across his face and neck, like a white arm.

He got up and pulled the curtains till they met. If he had only done that before he went to bed perhaps he wouldn't have wakened. The hour of sleep he had had might be all he was going to get for the night. He looked round the bedroom in the greyish pearly light. Dora's things were everywhere. Hairbrushes and a bottle of perfume on the dressing-table, a scarf hanging over the back of a chair, on her bedside cabinet a box of tissues and her other watch, the one she wasn't wearing. In closing the cupboard door he had inadvertently caught up the stuff of one of her skirts in it. The pale, silky material, a handful of it, gleamed in the half-dark. He opened the door, pushed the material in, moved a hanger along the rail, smelt her scent and closed the door again.

He was back in bed when he heard the sound and immediately knew he had heard it before, one minute before, and it was that which had awakened him, not the moonlight.

Sitting up, he listened. It came again. A crunch, made and repeated, footsteps on the gravel of the path. He got out of bed and reached for the clothes he had taken off, just the trousers and socks. Over the back of a chair was a round-necked sweater. He pulled it over his head, stepped softly to the bedroom door and opened it silently. From down below came another sound, a different sound, a click, a screwing, a release. Someone was trying the back door.

It was bolted on the inside. What did they think he was, a policeman who'd leave his back door unlocked all night? This was Sacred Globe, he had no doubt about it. As he had thought, they had sent a representative and to him, to his home, in the night. The digital clock on Dora's side told him it was twelve-fifty-two.

The moonlight hadn't penetrated the thick curtains at the landing window and it was darkish. His eyes grew accustomed to it as he waited. He could see the outlines of windows now and the moon's pale ambience, over the banisters to the hall, the window there, the open door into the living-room. Below the landing window, at the side of the house, there came another footfall, then another. They had tried the back door and were returning to the front. Tap, tap, quite light footfalls, but loud too. They weren't making silence a priority, that was for sure. Whoever they were, whatever they wanted, they weren't afraid of him.

How would they make him let them in? By ringing the doorbell, presumably. Yet why had they tried the back door first? It came to him suddenly. *They would have Dora's keys.*

They would have a key to the back door and one to the front door, and for some reason they had tried the back first, but it had been bolted on the inside.

Now for the front door.

He didn't want to be seen straight away. He went to the front of the house, into the front bedroom, and looked out of the window, but the porch overhang blocked his view. Padding back, he heard a key turn in the front-door lock. The door opened and someone entered the house. The door was softly, almost stealthily, closed.

The last thing he expected was light. He heard a switch click without realising what it was, then light streamed up on to the landing. He marched out of the bedroom to the head of the stairs, prepared to confront them.

Dora was standing in the hall, looking upwards.

717

# 12

He held her in his arms. He was afraid to slacken his hold in case she
vanished again. It couldn't be a dream because she was the age she
really was and he was his real age too. She laughed weakly when he
told her that in his dreams he and she were always young, but her
laughter broke raggedly and she began to cry. He held her and
pressed her wet face against his cheek.

'What can I do for you? What would you like? Shall I carry you
upstairs? I used to be able to do that. Shall I try?'

'Like Rhett Butler,' she said through her tears. 'Oh, Reg, don't be
so silly.'

'I'm a fool. I know. Oh God, I'm so happy.'

She said drily, but with a break in her voice, 'I'm not exactly down
in the dumps myself.'

'A drink,' he said, 'a stiff one. Have you had proper food? I won't
ask you anything about what's happened, not tonight. The entire
Mid-Sussex Constabulary will want to ask you tomorrow, but not
tonight.'

She stepped back a little from him, looked into his face. 'Why
weren't you in bed, Reg? What's happened?'

'I thought you were a representative of Sacred Globe and I wasn't
going to meet them in that cardinal's robe.'

'Is that what they call themselves? I suppose I am in a way,' she
said, 'though not what you'd call an official one. I don't know why I
was released. No one said. They just put that foul hood over my head
again and drove me here.'

'You don't have to talk about it now. My God, no one was ever so
happy to see someone else since the world began . . . What would
you like? Tell me.'

718

'Well, most of all I'd like a bath. Washing facilities weren't all they might have been. I'd like a bath and you to bring me a very stiff gin and tonic in the bath, and then I'd like to go to sleep.'

When he came back with her drink he found all her clothes in a heap on the bedroom floor. The first time she had ever done such a thing, he thought. And grinning to himself, then actually laughing aloud with happiness, he picked up every garment and dropped them all into a large, sterile plastic bag.

Six-thirty in the morning was too early to call the Chief Constable but Wexford called him.

Montague Ryder sounded as if he had been up for hours and had already run twice round Myringham Common. 'I am sure you know, I don't have to tell you, that we are going to have to talk exhaustively to your wife and she is going to have to tell us all she knows. It must be taped and probably gone through twice, with a time interval in between, to make sure nothing gets missed out.'

'I know that, sir, and she knows it.'

'Right. Good. Time is of the essence and the sooner we get started the better. But don't wake her, Reg. Let her sleep till nine if she can.'

She had been fast asleep when he crept out of the bedroom to make his phone call. He hadn't slept much himself, getting only fitful bursts of sleep, because he kept waking to see if it was real, if she was really back and there in bed beside him. Down in the kitchen he made tea, squeezed orange juice, then brewed coffee as well for good measure. The time passed like a flash. He thought of the previous morning when he had been walking Amulet about, waiting for the news, and time had dragged, had seemed to stand still. Time travels in diverse paces with diverse persons. I'll tell you who Time ambles withal, who Time trots withal, and who he stands still withal . . .

Sylvia was the first daughter he phoned because he wanted to phone Sheila first.

'You should have called me last night,' Sylvia complained.

'No, I shouldn't. It was one o'clock. She's asleep now but you can come over and see her tonight.'

Sheila answered the phone in a tearful tone. He told her.

'Oh, Pop,' said Sheila, 'how absolutely amazingly wonderful, darling. Shall I bring Amulet and come over now?'

When he went upstairs at half-past seven Dora was awake and sitting up. She put out her arms and hugged him. 'I got plenty of

719

sleep in that place, so I wasn't tired. There was nothing to do but encourage the others and sleep.'

'Do you know where you were?'

'I haven't a clue,' she said. 'Of course I knew that would be the first thing you'd all want to know – and so did they. They were scrupulously careful about that from the very first.'

He brought up her breakfast and she chose coffee. He had a shower, singing bits of Gilbert and Sullivan at the top of his voice. She was laughing at him and he loved that.

'But, Reg, tell me something,' she said when he came back into the room in the crimson dressing-gown, 'who's in charge of this? It can't be you, they wouldn't have had that, not with me being one of the hostages.'

'It was. It is.'

He explained why and she said, 'poor you' and then she said, 'Last night you said you expected their representative and I said I was one in a sort of way. They gave me a message, you see. That was the only time any of them spoke. They handcuffed me, they brought me out and put the hood on.' She shivered a little. 'One of them spoke. It was quite a shock. Up till then it had been as if they were dumb or deaf mutes. He called it "the next message". Does that make sense?'

He nodded.

'Well, he said they'd noted the suspension but suspension won't be enough. They want cancellation. Negotiations start on Sunday, he said.'

'How do negotiations start?' Wexford asked.

'I don't know.'

'They didn't say any more?'

'That was all.'

Wexford, Burden and Karen Malahyde. Not an interview room. Everyone but Dora jibbed at that, she said she wouldn't have minded, she rather liked being the centre of attention and she'd never seen the inside of an interview room except on television. But they had the recording equipment taken to the old gym and four armchairs too, to make it more like a party and less like an interrogation. The Chief Constable came over specially, shook hands with Dora and told her she was a brave woman.

'Where do you want me to start?' she said when she was sitting

720

down with her third cup of coffee of the day beside her. 'At the beginning, I suppose?'

'I don't think so,' said her husband. 'As you said yourself, the most important thing at the moment is where. Tell us what you can about the place you were held in.'

'But you know I don't know where it was.'

'We must hope to find where it was from what you tell us.'

'That almost means beginning at the beginning because it was the journey that took me there. But I don't know which way he went or how long it took, you don't when you've got a hood over your head. But I'd guess we were driving for an hour, not more, and for some of the time we were on a big road, possibly a motorway.'

'Could it have been in London?' Karen asked. 'London or just outside London?'

'I suppose it could have been the southern suburbs, Sydenham, Orpington, somewhere like that, but I don't know, I haven't a clue really. I wasn't in the car long enough for it to have been north London. It could have been almost anywhere in Kent or Hampshire, it could have been the coast.'

Dora was very pale, her husband thought. And in spite of having slept heavily, she had had less than six hours and she looked tired. He had wanted to drive her straight to Dr Akande at the medical centre but she had refused, she had almost laughed at him. They shouldn't delay, she had said, she was all right. But when she was dressing he had seen her stagger and have to catch hold of a chair.

Disapproval was no uncommon feeling for Burden to have and he disapproved of the whole thing. Dora should have seen the doctor, been given a thorough examination and probably a tranquilliser if not a sedative. He had no time for counselling himself – though giving lip service to the whole counselling theory because it was police policy – but he firmly believed in the principle of shock hitting victims a good deal later than one would expect. Shock would hit Dora and then she'd have a breakdown.

She had dressed in a grey skirt and grey-and-yellow-checked blouse, oldish clothes, comfortable and familiar. When she left to go to Sheila she had been wearing a new suit, caramel-coloured linen. She had worn it for four days, it had got crumpled and creased as linen does and now she never wanted to see it again. The other clothes in her suitcase she hadn't seen since that hood was first put over her head, for they had taken the case away and, for all she

721

knew, still had it in their possession. She had been allowed to bring her handbag back with her but not the suitcase, nor the presents she had been taking with her to Sheila.

She had paused to drink her coffee and when she began again seemed to realise for the first time that she was being recorded. Her voice grew more stilted and became slower.

'The hoods we wore – we all had them on sometimes – were like small sacks with eyeholes and the sacking had been sprayed, I think, with black spray paint. Or soaked in paint. My hood was quite thick and heavy. They didn't take it off till I was inside.'

'Talk naturally,' Wexford said. 'Forget the machine.'

'I'm sorry. I'll try.'

'No, it's OK, you're doing fine.'

'Well, then, you're going to want to know inside what and that I can't tell you.' She gave the recorder a glance, cleared her throat. 'But it was on the ground floor and I think partially below ground. I went down two steps to get into it. Like a basement but not like a cellar. Am I explaining that properly?'

'I think that's perfectly clear,' said Burden.

'I want you to know that I took pains to notice everything from the start, to note the size and shape of everything and all the time to try and pick up clues to where I was. I thought it might be necessary and it has been.'

'Good for you, Mrs Wexford,' said Karen. 'You're a marvel.'

Dora smiled. 'Wait till you hear. The results didn't match up to the intention. The boy was already there when I arrived. Ryan Barker he's called but I suppose you know that. He was in the room, sitting on one of the beds. He was just sitting there, staring. The room was quite big, about a third the size of this gym, and oblong, but there was only one window and that was on one of the shorter walls and quite high up. Not all that high up, though, because the ceiling was rather low. I'd say not seven feet. Reg wouldn't have bumped his head on it but he'd have been scared of doing that. I can't do the room measurements in metres but I'd say it was about thirty feet by eighteen to twenty.

'There was the door I came in by and another door that led into a very tiny washplace with a lavatory and basin. There were four beds in the room, narrow, single, foldaway beds. Later on they brought in another one and I think it was because they only intended to take four hostages but in fact took five . . .'

722

'What makes you think that?' Karen asked.

'You don't want me having opinions, do you? Well, if you think it could be useful. I had a feeling they thought there'd be only one of the Struthers when in fact it was both. And later on Owen Struther said his wife had phoned for a car, so they thought they'd be picking up a woman on her own. Anyway, they brought in a fifth bed. The beds were the only furniture apart from two kitchen chairs.'

'What sort of a room was it?' Wexford asked.

'You mean, how old, in what state of decoration, was it a sort of kitchen room or a sort of living-room, don't you? Well, it definitely wasn't a living-room. The walls were uneven, with peeling white-wash, and the electrics were rather primitive, all the cables showing. Under the window there was an old sink, a large butler's sink, but there were no taps. There were rough wooden shelves all along one of the longer walls but there was nothing on them. It was rather like a garage except that there was no garage door for a car to come in by. It could have been a workshop. I thought about that aspect of things a lot and came to the conclusion it could once have been a small factory.'

'Did you look out of the window?' This was Karen.

'The first chance I got. A sort of box had been built round the outside of it. I can only describe it by saying it was like a kind of rabbit hutch in which the rabbit wouldn't have got much light. You could open the window – or you could have if it hadn't been locked – I mean it was openable, and outside, fixed over it, there was this structure, this contraption of wood and wire netting that was more like a chain-link fence. I climbed up on the sink that first day and tried to have a look out and I could see green. Green and brickwork and a lump of concrete like a broken step, and that's all. It might have been the country or a suburban garden. All I can say is that it wasn't an outlook on to some inner city place.'

'Could you tell which way the window faced. Its orientation?'

'The sun came in in the afternoons. It faced west. I'd say due west. I've said there was a little room to wash in with a loo. Well, that was quite interesting because it was new. I mean, it had never been used before. The walls were painted white and the basin and lavatory pan were absolutely new, only there was no lavatory seat or lid. There was no window either. It looked as if it had been a cupboard which had just been converted and done as cheaply as possible, as if it had been done for *us*, I mean, on purpose to accommodate the hostages.

723

'We stayed in the main room for three nights and four days. Or I did. And Ryan did. The others were moved after a while. Shall I go back to the beginning now?'

'We'll take a break,' said Wexford.

'Are you sure?'

'I'm quite sure. I'm going to pass on what you've told us to the rest of the team and see if it sparks off any ideas. We'll start again in an hour.'


Three children from Stowerton arrived at the police station at eleven with a bagful of bones. They had discovered them, they told the duty sergeant, in one of the heaps of earth, now temporarily abandoned, at Stowerton Dale. One of them put forward the opinion that the bones were Roman, the others that they were of recent origin, the detritus of a serial killer's massacre.

'Sounds like Manfred's been busy,' said Wexford when he heard about it, and explained about Bibi's German Shepherd.

'They'll have to go for analysis,' said Burden despondently.

'I suppose so. Anyone can see most of them are spare ribs and the rest are what's left over from an oxtail stew.'

'What did they mean about negotiations starting on Sunday?'

'I wish you hadn't asked me that question.'

Karen Malahyde sat with Dora drinking coffee. She thought Mrs Wexford shouldn't have another cup, she had already had three, and told her so very kindly and politely. Dora said all right and please to call her Dora, she couldn't be doing with that Mrs Wexford stuff, and did Karen think there might be any orange juice available? If she wasn't expecting the freshly squeezed kind, Karen said, something could be rustled up, the sort they called 'made from concentrate'.

Dora fell asleep in the quite comfortable armchair but woke up when Karen came back. Why did Karen think they hadn't sent her suitcase back with her? And those presents she had been taking to Sheila, babyclothes and a kimono and books? What possible use could they be to them?

'I think we ought to wait and talk about that when Mr Wexford and Mr Burden come back, Mrs . . . er, Dora.'

'I'm sure you're right. You only know orange juice is the real thing when it's got bits in it, don't you?'

Wexford and Burden came back together and Burden started the recorder.

724

'I was asking about my suitcase,' Dora said. 'It doesn't matter all that much. In a way nothing matters but that I'm back and so far the other hostages aren't, but why would they want it? It's just an ordinary medium-sized fibre case, dark-brown, with my initials on it. And there were the other things I was carrying, presents for Sheila and the baby.'

'It's possible,' said Burden, 'that in their haste to get rid of you they simply forgot.'

'Can we go back to the beginning now?' Wexford shifted his chair out of a shaft of sunlight coming through one of the gym's long windows. 'Can we start at last Tuesday morning?'

'Right.' Dora sat back, curled her legs up under her. 'I had to phone for a car. There is a taxi firm called All the Sixes and I phoned them because their number's easy to remember. It was getting on for half-past ten. I wanted to catch the eleven-o-three, which was allowing plenty of time. Anyway, what I got from All the Sixes was one of those recordings that are so maddening. You know, "Please hold the line" and the voice goes up on the "please" and up again on the "line". And then it goes, "Your call will be answered as soon as possible" and then a burst of *Eine Kleine Nachtmusik*. So I found that flyer they'd sent us and called Contemporary Cars.'

'The voice that answered,' Karen said. 'What was it like?'

'A man's. Ordinary, rather flat and dull. No accent. Quite young. It was exactly ten-thirty, by the way. I happened to look at the digital clock on the video while I was talking. He came very promptly – about seven minutes later, I should think.'

'Can you describe him?'

'Not very precisely. I've thought a lot about it. I can only say he wasn't very tall, maybe five feet eight, he was thickset and he had a beard. He walked a bit stiffly, he was bandy-legged. Oh, and he smelt. There was a peculiar smell about him.'

'D'you mean BO? Sweat? A sweetish fried-onion smell?'

'No, not that. More like nail varnish remover. Acetone, is it called?' She looked from one to the other of them, suddenly much livelier, her tiredness driven away by the excitement of talking about it all. 'Like nail varnish or remover, not exactly unpleasant, just odd.

'The doorbell rang and I fetched my case and the parcels – well, carrier bags, from the living-room before I answered the door. The idea, you see, was that he'd carry them to the car for me. But when I opened the door he was standing at the front gate with his back to me. I suppose I should have called to him to take the case but I didn't, I just said good-morning or hallo or something and he nodded. I put the case and the parcels outside the door on the mat, pulled the door shut after me and locked the deadlock.

'He was in the car by then, in the driver's seat. I didn't think it was odd, I just thought he was rather rude. He hadn't even opened the car door for me. I did just glance at his profile before I got into the car, but most of his face was covered by this black curly beard. The car was full of his smell. He had longish, thick, dark curly hair and a pullover or sweatshirt on that was a sort of greyish-blue.'

'What sort of car was it?' Burden asked.

'Small, red, a VW Golf, I think. Anyway, it was like my daughter Sylvia's.' Dora added drily, 'If I were a detective with reason to be suspicious I'd have taken the number, but I'm not and I didn't.'

Burden laughed. 'Were you wearing a seat-belt?'

'What a question! Of course I was wearing a seat-belt. Remember whose wife I am.' Dora shook her head, exasperated. 'I had the suitcase in the car with me, on the seat beside me, and the parcels on the floor. He drove the usual route to the station but he did a sort of detour in Queen Street. There was a bit of a hold-up, there mostly is, and I didn't think anything of it. Taxi drivers go all sorts of odd ways these days to avoid traffic.

'We stopped at a red light on the junction of York Street and Old London Road. The light there is a pedestrian crossing that's operated on a button. Now, of course, I know it was deliberate that he drove to that particular crossing. The lights are pedestrian-controlled. Someone waiting there pressed the button as the car approached, the light turned red and we stopped. The nearside rear door was opened and this man got into the car.

'It all happened so quickly, I couldn't have struggled or cried out. For one thing I was trapped in the seat-belt and, you know, it takes a moment or two to extract oneself from a strange seat-belt, it's not like the one in one's own car. And I didn't get a look at him either, no more than a fleeting glimpse of someone young and tall with a stocking over his face.'

'You mean he was standing at the lights with a stocking over his face?'

'There was no one else about,' Dora said, 'but I think, I have the impression, he pulled a stocking over his face with one hand while he opened the car door with the other. It meant I couldn't see his face at all, only that it looked rubbery. But that would be the effect of a stocking on anyone's face, wouldn't it?

'He pulled a hood over his own head and one over mine. I couldn't see anything for a moment, I was struggling and trying to shout, and I was aware of handcuffs going on. It wasn't pleasant. No, much worse than that, it was . . . it was terrifying.'

'Would you like to take another break, Dora?' Wexford asked.

'No, I'm fine. I expect you can understand that I was very frightened. I suppose I was more frightened than I've ever been in my life. After all, I haven't been in that many frightening situations; I suppose I've been sheltered. And there was nothing I could do. It was a bit better when I could see. He had adjusted the hood, pulled it down.

'I could see outside for a moment and that we were on the old bypass. He pointed to the floor, indicating I was to get down there. So that I couldn't be seen from outside, I suppose, or see out. I obeyed him, of course I did, and sat on the floor.

'I think I was in the car for about an hour. It might have been longer but I don't think it was less than an hour. I didn't struggle any more because it wasn't any use. I was terribly afraid. It's not much point saying that now, so I won't go into it. I was afraid I'd lose control of myself in various ways and I wanted to avoid that more than anything. I tried to stay calm, to breathe deeply, but that wasn't easy sitting on the floor with the hood on.

'The car turned in somewhere, through a gate or just into a narrow street or even round the back of a factory or warehouse, I just don't know. But it went much more slowly and it kept taking bends to the right and left. Then we stopped. The hood was still turned so that the eyeholes were at the back. I think he'd only adjusted it at the beginning to show me it did have eyeholes. Anyway, I couldn't see a thing, just a stuffy blackness, and my hands were handcuffed in front of me.

'My arms were taken by one of them on each side of me. I think it was the driver on the right-hand side because he didn't seem all that much taller than me and his arm felt quite thick and pudgy. And the smell of him . . . The one on the other side held my arm very hard, you could call it an iron grip. I had the impression of long, thin, strong fingers. He didn't smell of anything. I can't say if it was country air or town air and it was the same sort of temperature as at home.

'I sensed, I heard, a heavy door being unlocked, then opened, and I was taken inside. I wasn't pushed in or flung in or anything, just walked down the steps and in, brought to one of the beds and helped to sit on it. They took the hood off me first, then the handcuffs, but they kept their own hoods on. He had stubby brown hands and the other one had long fingers. That was when I saw Ryan. They went away, closed the door and locked it behind them.'

'We'll break for lunch,' Wexford said, 'and then I'll want you to have a rest.'

The best thing would have been to take his wife out to lunch. Wexford kept reverting in his mind to ways of doing this, even if it meant having Burden and Karen Malahyde along as well. But he really knew he couldn't do it. Not today, not in these circumstances, not the Olive and Dove's new La Méditerranée restaurant, a nice bottle of wine, salades de crevettes, sole meunière and crème brulée. Another time. Next week but not today. He sent out for assorted sandwiches, smoked salmon, cheddar and pickle, ham and tongue.

She was looking a bit better. The talking must be doing her good. Of course, tiredness and shock notwithstanding, it *would* do her good. That was what psychotherapy was about, talking to people who not only listened but wanted more than anything else to listen. It was much better for her than keeping it all inside, lying in bed stuffed full of Akande's sedatives.

He let her have another cup of coffee. A lot of nonsense was talked about coffee, about its speeding effects and its caffeine, but you never heard of anyone who actually came to harm through drinking it. She put cream in hers and sugar, which she never would have done at home. The rest he had tentatively said she should have she had rejected.

Burden started the recorder. It was he who asked the first question. 'You were alone in the room with Ryan Barker, is that right?'

'For a while, yes. He was very frightened, he's only fourteen. I talked to him. I told him not to worry too much. If they were going to hurt us they would already have done so. I think I realised by then that we were hostages, though I'd no idea what the ransom could be. Ryan said he knew he ought to be brave – being a male, I suppose was what he meant – and later he said his father had been a soldier who'd died in battle, in the Falklands – but I said, no, he didn't have to be, he could bawl the place down if he liked and that would fetch them back and we could ask them why we were there. Mind you, I was scared stiff myself, but having him there was good for me, because I couldn't show it in front of him.

'Anyway, we weren't alone for long. Roxane was brought in. I'm taking it you do know Roxane Masood is one of the hostages?'

'Roxane Masood and Kitty and Owen Struther are the others,' Karen said.

'That's right. Roxane was a good deal less passive than I was, I can tell you. She was struggling as they brought her in and when they took the hood and the handcuffs off her she tried to fly at them.'

'Who brought her in?'

'The driver and another man. Another tall one, taller than the driver, but not as tall as the one who was in the car with me. As far as I could tell, in his late twenties, maybe thirty. It was he took the handcuffs off Roxane and the driver took the hood off her.

'Roxane made for their eyes with her fingernails even though they had hoods on. The thin man fetched her a great blow across the head and she fell over. She fell on the bed and I think she passed out for a while. I went to her and held her and she came round and started to cry. But that was only because he'd really hurt her. It wasn't crying like Kitty Struther.

'They brought the Struthers in about half an hour later. He was the stiff-upper-lip sort. He reminded me of Alec Guinness in *The Bridge on the River Kwai*. You know, very stiff and straight and *English*, refusing to have any dealings with his captors, that sort of thing. The other man that brought me, the one with the rubbery face, he brought Kitty in. She spat at him when the hood came off her. He didn't do anything, just wiped it off.

'I once read in a book how amazed someone was to hear a really refined ladylike woman use foul language in a situation that was . . . well, like this one. They wouldn't have believed she'd known it. Well, that was how I felt about Kitty Struther. The spitting and then the words she used. I suppose it was hysterics, but she screamed and yelled and pounded on the mattress with her fists. After a bit Owen tried to calm her down, so she started punching him. I don't think she knew what she was doing, but she screamed for a very long time. The rest of us just sat there, appalled. And then she began this soft, awful weeping. She curled up like a foetus and buried her face, and at last she fell asleep.'

Dora stopped, sighed, slightly lifted her shoulders. 'I expect you'd like me to tell you what I can about the rest of the people who were holding us.'

'Would you have a look at this, please, Dora.' Burden had produced a photograph which he held out to her. 'Could the dark one, the driver, be this man? Forget the beard, beards can come off and go on at the drop of a hat. Could this be your driver?'

Dora shook her head. 'No. I'm sure not. He's thin, this man, and older. Somehow I know the driver wasn't very old, and he was heavier.'

When Karen had taken her away to get a cup of tea, 'Who is it?' Wexford asked.

Burden put the photograph away. 'Stanley Trotter,' he said. 'He also smells. We had a bit of news in today. I haven't bothered you with it, you had enough on your plate. It's from the police in Bonn, Bonn in Germany.'

Wexford thought. 'Where Ulrike Ranke was at university?'

'That's it. You remember the pearls? The eighteenth-birthday present of matched cultured pearls for which her parents paid thirteen hundred pounds?'

'Of course I do.'

'Well, she sold them. Needed the money rather than jewellery, I reckon. The Bonn police have found it and the jeweller who gave her seventeen hundred Deutschmarks for it.'

'Not generous,' said Wexford, having done his mental arithmetic.

'No. Did she buy herself another string for twenty, something to show the parents if need be? Certainly she bought one because we know she was wearing a string of pearls in the Brigadier photograph. And was that the one . . . ?'

'It's not Trotter, Mike,' said Wexford. 'He's not her killer and he's not Dora's driver.'

# 13

The signboard, planted in the grass verge, read: Euro-Fun, The Only International Theme Park in Sussex. The lettering was white on a blue ground and underneath it someone had painted, not very expertly, a small deer or chamois, a windmill and what might have been the Leaning Tower of Pisa. Damon Slesar swung the car in through the open gates, or rather, the one open gate, the other being off its hinges and leaning against the fence, and up a track that would be two ruts of mud in winter.

The theme park had been arranged as a series of paddocks, through which the track wound in a haphazard way. Its distant appearance was slightly redeemed by an abundance of trees which hid some of Euro-Fun's worst excesses, though most of these were revealed as prospect became foreground. Each section bore the name of the country represented there, lettered on a swinging sign suspended from tall pillars rather like barbers' poles. The whole had grown shabby with the years and there were few visitors. Five people, three adults and two children, were walking about in bemused fashion in the area labelled Denmark, dubiously eyeing a wooden dolls' house with a green roof and a plastic facsimile of the Little Mermaid seated on the edge of a stagnant pond lined with blue polythene.

What precisely visitors to the place were supposed to do wasn't clear. Perhaps only walk, look and wonder. A man and a woman were doing that, especially from their expressions the wondering part, among rain-damaged wax tulips in the shadow of a monstrous red-and-white plastic windmill, while a couple of pre-teens sat on the steps of a chalet staring at a cuckoo clock. The cuckoo had come out in front of the clock face and, the mechanism breaking down at this

731

point, stayed out, silent, its beak permanently frozen open in the cuckooing position.

'You ever brought your kids here?' Damon Slesar asked.

'Please,' said Nicky Weaver, 'do me a favour. Oh, look at the Parthenon! Can you believe it?'

It looked as if made of asbestos but was probably plasterboard, the pillars whitewashed drainpipes. A figure, that properly belonged in a shop window but was now dressed in white pleated skirt and black jacket, stood in front of the Acropolis strumming at a stringed instrument. Next door was Spain with a papier-mâché bull and matador, and then came the ticket office and car park. Adjacent to the car park stood a sprawling bungalow in need of a paint.

The man who came out was middle-aged, in cable-knit pullover and grey cord trousers. He was one of those men who have practically no hair on their heads and a great deal on upper lip and cheeks. In his case it was grey and shaggy, a thick, drooping moustache and slightly curly side whiskers.

'Will that be two, then, madam? Car park straight on.'

'Police,' said Nicky, showing him her warrant card instead of the expected cash. 'I'm looking for Mr or Mrs Royall.'

He was no stranger to police inquiries. Nicky could tell. The police can. He thumped his chest with his fist, said, 'James Royall at your service, ma'am. What can I do for you?'

Nicky knew that 'ma'am' wasn't politeness or deference, but intended as a joke, a parody of the style policemen use when addressing a senior female officer. James Royall was being funny.

'I'd like to talk to you about your son. Brendan – is that right?'

'Now I can't leave my post, can I, ma'am?'

Damon Slesar turned his head, craning from side to side. 'I don't see any rush, do you? They're not exactly queuing up.'

'We'd like to talk to you *now*, Mr Royall,' Nicky said. 'Whether you leave your post or find someone else to man it is immaterial to me.'

The little office or hut had an inner room. Nicky opened the door to it, walked in and beckoned to James Royall. There were two kitchen chairs and a table doing duty as a desk. The walls were lined with shelving on which stood dozens, perhaps hundreds, of artefacts from the theme park: figurines, plastic animals, sections of tree, dolls' house, boat, all broken, all apparently awaiting repair.

Royall picked up the phone, said into it, 'Mag, can you get down

732

here. Something's come up.' He looked towards Damon, 'What about his nibs, then?'

'We're anxious to get in touch with your son, Mr Royall. Do you know where he is?'

'Ask me another.' Royall shrugged his shoulders. 'You've come to the wrong shop, you know. Him and me and his mum, we're what you might call *estranged*. In other words, not exactly on speaking terms.'

'And what accounts for that, Mr Royall?'

He transferred his glance to Nicky whose appearance and tone, and perhaps also her rank and profession, he seemed to find amusing. A small smile lifted the corners of his mouth under the drooping moustache. 'Well, ma'am, I don't know that that's any business of yours, but speaking as an easygoing man, I'll tell you. In the first place my son Brendan thought for some mysterious reason, unfathomable to me, that when I came into my old man's property I should pass it over lock, stock and barrel to him. Nice expression that, don't you think? Lock, stock and barrel. Refers to guns, of course. But you'd know all about that, ma'am. The twenty K I did give him from the sale of said property wasn't enough, oh dear, no. So he kept coming back for more. But he didn't care for our Euro theme. The bull and the matador, they were among what he took exception to . . .'

'And the moles, dear,' said a woman's voice from the doorway.

'Oh, and the moles, Mag. You're right. Not wanting this place to resemble the Alps, being as we already had our Swiss area, we had the cheek to call in the mole exterminator without consulting his nibs first and that, you might say, cooked our goose.'

Mrs Royall, called to the receipt of custom and now perhaps unwilling to relinquish it, hovered in the doorway, continually glancing over her shoulder lest a car or party should slip past her unawares. She said to Nicky in a rather helpless way, 'I'm Brendan's mother.'

'Can you tell us your son's whereabouts, Mrs Royall?'

'I only wish I could. It's been a cause of great sadness to me being cut off from my only child and all over this passion he's got for animals. We love animals too, I said to him, only you have to be practical in this world.'

Royall made the sound usually written as 'pshaw!'. 'It's not animals, it's money. And you know damn well where he is. Keeping

733

an eye on his future prospects. Sucking up to them as are in his grandad's shoes.'

'And where might that be, sir?'

'Marrowgrave Hall, *ma'am*. As I sold to my cousin, Mrs Panick, some seven years ago and passed on a fair whack of the proceeds to that greedy, grasping monkey-lover . . .'

'Oh, Jim!' wailed Mrs Royall.

They left as another car arrived, this time with Austrian registration plates. Nicky wondered what its occupants would think of the section devoted to their motherland with its gilt-caparisoned plastic horse, bust of Mozart and musical box which played Viennese waltzes on the insertion of a ten-pee coin.

'It wasn't the same people who brought Roxane or Kitty and Owen in,' said Dora. 'Or, rather, I'm not sure about the tall one, it might have been him, but the driver, it wasn't him this time. This man was taller, though not so tall as the tall one, and he was thinner, and I think he was younger.

'The tall one, his was the only face I ever saw, and I saw it through a tan-coloured stocking. A fairly thick stocking, twenty denier, if you know what that means. He was white, Caucasian, as they say, his features might have been sharp or they might actually have been rubbery. I couldn't identify him. If you showed me photographs I could say he looks a bit like that or that or that, but I couldn't positively say. I've no idea what colour his eyes were. There was only one of them whose eye colour I actually saw.

'The driver I've told you about. I don't think I can add to that. I never saw his eyes. I never heard any of them speak, they never spoke to us. The third one, the one who helped bring Roxane in – there was a fourth but he didn't appear till the next day – the third had a tattoo on his arm.'

'A *tattoo*?'

Wexford and Burden had the same thought. This is the detective story clue, even the old-fashioned detective story clue, the ineradicable mark that is the perfect giveaway. But now, today, in reality?

'He had a tattoo on his arm?' Wexford said. 'Are you sure?'

'I'm sure. I didn't see it till next day. Not till the Wednesday. It was a butterfly tattoo, red and black, but I suppose all tattoos are. I'll tell you more about it when I come to that, shall I?'

'Right.'

734

'I said there was a fourth man,' she went on. 'He was one of those who brought our breakfast next day. He was another tall one, the same height as the first tall one, and I honestly don't know what to say about him. He even wore gloves, so I don't know what his hands were like. He was just a tall, masked figure, thin, straight, with an athletic stride, frightening really, though I'd stopped being frightened by then. I got angry, you see, and that kills fear. I couldn't identify any of them and I don't think the other hostages could.'

'But you didn't see this fourth one, the gloved one, till the next day, the Wednesday?'

'That's right. I shouldn't have got on to him now. I shouldn't have got on to the tattoo. You're telling me off in the nicest possible way, aren't you?'

'I wouldn't dream of it!' Karen Malahyde laughed. She hesitated, then said, 'Why did they let you go?'

'I don't know.'

'You said one of them spoke to you?'

'It was yesterday evening. About ten. I was alone by then with Ryan, just the two of us. The others had been taken away. The tall one who wore gloves came in with the tattooed one. I was sitting on my bed – I mostly was. They motioned me to get up and hold out my hands and I did. And then they put handcuffs on me.'

Wexford made a sound, turned it into a cough. He clenched his fists and unclenched them. She looked at him, made a rueful face.

'They took me outside. I didn't struggle or protest. I'd seen what they did to those who did that – well, to one who did that. I didn't even say goodbye to Ryan. Well, I thought I'd be coming back. Then they put the hood on me. That was when the tattooed one spoke to me. It was only about a minute after I'd been led out but – well, that was a bad minute. I thought they were going to kill me. Still, let's pass on. It was a shock hearing his voice.'

'What was it like?'

'His voice? Cockney, but not natural. I mean, it was like cockney that's been learned.'

Burden caught Wexford's eye and nodded. The man who had phoned Tanya Paine had a cockney accent he thought sounded as if learned from tapes. He said to Dora, 'What exactly did he say?'

'I'll try and remember accurately. Now then – "Tell them the suspension has been noted. Suspension isn't enough. Work has to stop permanently. Tell them negotiations start on Sunday." Then he

735

told me to repeat it and I did. I'd lost my voice from nerves but it came back because if they were giving me a message I knew they must be sending me home.'

'They put you in a car? Did you see the car?'

'Not then. They turned the hood round so that I couldn't see anything. I couldn't see any more of the place where we were than when I arrived. They put me in the back seat of a car and fastened the seat-belt on me. The drive took about an hour and a half. I'd have moved the hood round so that I could see out but what with the seat-belt and the handcuffs I couldn't. When the car stopped the driver opened the door, came round and took off the hood. It was dark but I could see it was the same man who had brought me, the short, dark, bearded man. The one who smelt. He still smelt. He'd put on dark glasses. Shades, do they call them?

'He took off the handcuffs, undid the seat-belt and helped me out. He gave me my handbag – it was the first I'd seen of it since Wednesday. He didn't speak, I never heard his voice. The car was parked alongside the cricket field, which is about a quarter of a mile from our house. I think he parked there because it's just field on one side and the Methodist church and graveyard on the other. No one to see, I suppose.

'It was past midnight and all the street lamps were out. He got back into the car, leaving me there. I tried to see the registration but it was too dark. As for the make and colour, it was lightish, it could have been any of those creamy-grey colours or greyish or light-blue. He didn't put his lights on until he was a good fifty yards away. The number started with an L and ended with a five and a seven.

'After that I walked home. My house keys were in my bag. I tried to let myself in the back way but the door was bolted on the inside, so I went round to the front. But you asked me why they let me go. I'm sorry, I never really answered that. Just to deliver the message? It couldn't be just that. I honestly don't know why.'

'All right,' said Wexford, 'that's enough for today. You can talk some more to me at home, if you like, but that's an end of the formal stuff for now. You've given us plenty to go on.'

It was as ugly a house, as only the Victorians in their later architectural phases could build. The remarkable thing, as Hennessy said to Nicky Weaver, was that it had evidently been intended as a dwelling house and not an institution. The principal building

736

material was brick of a yellowish khaki, the sickly colour occasionally broken by lines of red tile. Eight sash windows were close up underneath the shallow slate roof. There were eight more below, these slightly deeper, but on the ground the three on either side of a front door that stood plumb in the centre were set in pointed Gothic arches. It had a mean, squat front door without benefit of panelling, with no porch, not even set in a recess. Still, Marrowgrave Hall was an enormous place, as Damon Slesar saw when he walked round the side, for the whole front edifice was repeated on the back, the roof merely taking a kind of dip in the middle.

The only outbuilding was a garage, a prefabricated affair that stood separate from the house. Hennessy looked through the single window at the back but there was nothing inside except a pile of empty sacks. Nicky rang the doorbell. It was answered by a woman of enormous girth, one of those people who are so hugely fat that it is a wonder they can bear the daily heaving of this mass of flesh from place to place. She was probably still in her forties, with a pale moon-face and loose mouth, a little thin, reddish hair. A floral tent enveloped her, reaching to her heavily bandaged knees and shins.

'Mrs Panick?' said Nicky.

'You're the police, dear. We've been expecting you. We had a call.'

'May we come in?'

The smell was of food. It was quite a nice smell, especially if you happened to be hungry, a compound of vanilla and burnt sugar and something fruity. An occasional whiff of cheese joined in as they were led down a dour corridor, then frying bacon, finally as they entered a cavernous kitchen a heady amalgam of the lot, rich, hot, almost succulent. Their progress was necessarily slow as Patsy Panick lumbered ahead of them with difficulty. In the kitchen she stood, hanging on to a chair, getting her breath.

An elderly man was sitting at a long pine table, eating a meal, presumably his lunch, though it was not much past eleven-thirty. He was nearly but not quite as fat as his wife. Women and men put on weight differently and while his wife's was distributed more or less evenly all over her, Robert Panick's had rested, accumulated, swelled and become mountainous, only on his stomach. Slesar remarked afterwards, when they were on their way back through Forby, that he had read somewhere about Thomas Aquinas having to have a great ellipse cut out of the table at which he worked, to accommodate the Angelic Doctor's huge belly. Robert Panick could have done

737

with an ellipse cut out of this one, but no one had thought of it and he was obliged to sit some two feet back from the table and bend as far forward as his girth allowed to eat his food.

It had apparently been a plateful of fried meat, liver and bacon perhaps, with chips, peas and fried bread. More of the same sizzled in two pans on the stove. A plate of Mrs Panick's half-eaten meal was also on the table and, approaching it, she absent-mindedly lifted a forkful to her mouth.

'Give them something to eat, Patsy,' said Panick, who hadn't otherwise seemed to notice their presence. 'Some of those chocolate biscuits with the jelly in or we've got some frozen Mars in the freezer.'

'No, thanks,' said Slesar for all of them. 'Very good of you, but no thanks all the same. We wanted to ask you about the house. You bought it off a Mr James Royall about seven years ago, I believe?'

'That's right, dear. Only it was six years. Jimmy's my cousin. His daddy that lived here was my uncle. We'd always loved this house, hadn't we, Bob? It's a lovely old house, a real lovely antique, and when we got the chance to have it – well, Bob had done ever so well in business and just sold up, and why not blow some money on the house of our dreams? That's what we said.'

Her husband nodded and, having finished up the last scrap of fried bread, passed his plate to her for a refill. Most of the contents of the two pans went on to it. Mrs Panick sat down in front of her own plate and the chair emitted a long, painful creak.

'You don't mind if I go on with my meal, do you? I wish you'd have something yourselves. A nice piece of Victoria sponge? I made it myself this morning. Well, all right, if you're sure. Our needs are very modest, dear, as you see, and we don't run a car, there's a very nice delicatessen in Pomfret that delivers twice a week, so we felt we could afford the place and the upkeep, and we manage quite OK, don't we, Bob? Mind you, I think my cousin Jimmy made a special price for us, us being family.'

'The son, Brendan,' Nicky said. 'I suppose you know him too?'

'Know him? He's more like a son to us. I mean, first cousin once removed, that's a laugh. He's like our own. And he won't have anything to do with Jimmy and Moira, dear. Says his dad's cruel to animals as well as cheating him out of his inheritance and it is true my uncle John often said Brendan could have the place when he went. His dad did give him a bit of the money we paid over but he

738

spent most of it on his Euro theme. Still, I said to Brendan, don't you worry, dear, it'll be yours one day.'

'Meaning?'

'That we'd leave it to him in our wills.'

'So you see him?'

'See him? He always pops in when he's down this way. I say to Bob, Brendan's made us his parents since his own was so unsatisfactory. We're – what's the term I want? – yes, surrogate. We're surrogate parents for Brendan. And I think he knows he'll always get a good meal here. Now you've eaten all the rest of that fry-up, Bob, I'm going to have to find myself something else.'

'There's a pudding, isn't there?' said Panick in the tone of someone asking a bank manager if it can possibly be true his account is in the red.

'Of course there's a pudding. When have I served you a meal without a pudding? Not in all our married life. But I've got an empty corner wants filling now and I reckon I'll have to attack the Camembert the way the French do, before the dessert, right?'

'Do you know where Brendan is now, Mrs Panick?'

'Well, he won't be with his mum and dad, dear. That's for sure. Nottingham maybe? He was down here a couple of weeks back, no, I tell a lie, more like a month, something to do with butterflies or frogs. He loves animals, does Brendan. That's his work, you know, saving animals, a bit like the RSPCA. And he came in to see us and we happened to be having pheasant that night, frozen of course, the season not starting till next month, but none the worse for that, and I did bread sauce and orange sauce though that's not strictly the thing with pheasant, and oven chips and a suet roll to fill up and a chocolate roulade with clotted cream.

'He came rolling down our drive as happy as a lark at just on five and parked the caravan right outside the kitchen window, so that he could get the cooking smells, he said.'

'He lives in a caravan?' said Hennessy, trying not to sound too aghast.

'Well, a Winnebago is the correct term, dear. He's always on the move, you never know where he is from one moment to the next.'

'He hasn't a fixed address?'

'Not what you'd call fixed. Not unless you count this one.'

'We'd appreciate it if you'd let us know if he turns up here.'

'You can be sure of that,' said Patsy Panick, which wasn't at all what Nicky expected.

'Where are you hiding that pudding, Patsy?' said Bob.

Driving back through Forby, once designated (or damned) as the fifth prettiest village in England, Nicky Weaver said, 'Didn't you think they were too good to be true?'

'No one's too good to be true,' said Hennessy, after the manner of Wexford, whom he admired. 'What are you suggesting, ma'am, that they were acting?'

'I suppose not. The way they were going at that food, Brendan Royall won't have too long to wait for his inheritance.'

'Isn't it too bad, him living in a Winnebago?' said Damon. 'Just our bloody luck.'

'What, you mean you're envious because you want a Winnebago or sick because it means he's always on the move?'

'Both,' said Damon.

Four men, one of them tattooed, one smelling of acetone, one wearing gloves. A red Golf, a basement room, a newly converted washroom, masks of spray-painted sacking, handcuffs, a light-coloured car, registration L something something five seven. A man with a learned cockney voice. These were what Wexford presented to those of his team who were not in Nottingham or Guildford at a meeting in the old gym at four. They told him about a paranoid man who had quarrelled with his parents and a Winnebago Nicky Weaver had begun tracing.

'I'd very much like to know if Brendan Royall has a tattoo,' he said. 'Presumably, his parents could tell us.'

'Or Mrs Panick might know,' Nicky Weaver said.

Rather shyly, Lynn Fancourt said she didn't want to appear ignorant, but what was a Winnebago? Burden explained that it was a luxury mobile home, not far removed from a bungalow on wheels. Royall could range the country in it, parking in lay-bys overnight if he chose.

Then Wexford played the tapes to them. The Chief Constable arrived unexpectedly after the first one had been running for five minutes. He sat and listened. When it was over he accompanied Wexford up to his office.

'Your wife must have a lot more to tell us, Reg.'

'I know she has, sir, but I'm a bit afraid . . .'

740

'Yes, I know what you mean. And so am I. Would it help her to have counselling, do you think?'

'Frankly, sir, talking to me *is* her counselling. Just talking and having me listen. We shall talk more this evening.'

The Chief Constable looked at his watch, the way people do when they are going to talk about time. He said, 'Do you remember saying to me the newspapers wouldn't be all that interested if the embargo on this story was lifted on a Friday or a Saturday? That what they'd like best would be to have it late on Sunday?'

Wexford nodded.

'Then we'll lift it tomorrow.'

'All right. If you say so.'

'I do. We'll have the whole pack of them down here, we'll have phone calls pouring in all day with sightings of the Struthers in Majorca and Singapore, we'll have people who know the basement room is in the house next door, but nevertheless, we may also get help. And we need more help now, Reg.'

'Yes, sir. I know we do.'

'Sometimes I think it would be better if we adhered more to the continental system, like they have in France, for instance. Kept investigations secret, made them more in the nature of undercover operations, low-profile stuff, not all this sharing everything with the public. Keep the press, the public and the victims' families at arm's length while the investigation goes on. Once you recruit the public, the pressure on us increases.'

Shades of that conference on continental methods . . . 'They expect instant results,' said Wexford.

'That's right. And then mistakes are made.'

After that, Wexford went home. As he drove down the High Street he passed a straggling line of tree people, laden with packs, heading for the best places to hitch lifts to somewhere, anywhere. They were leaving, or some of them were. While the environmental assessment went on they were off to protest elsewhere.

The red Golf parked outside his house made his heart lurch. But, of course, it was Sylvia's. He was so involved in all this he couldn't recognise his own daughter's car. He let himself into the house and found not one but both daughters there. Dora was holding Amulet in her arms. He had to remind himself that this was the first time she had seen the baby.

'I'll be staying the night with Syl, Pop,' Sheila said. 'Just in case you're feeling aghast.'

'I could never feel anything but delight at seeing you,' he said untruthfully and, with a smile at Sylvia, 'both of you.'

'Don't strain yourself.' Sylvia got up. 'We're going. We just had to see Mother. Don't you think we've been good, not saying a word about this to anyone? I mean, Sheila knows masses of journalists, she could easily have let something out, but we've been *clams*.'

'You've been magnificent,' said Wexford. 'You can talk all you like on Monday.' He gave Sheila a severe look. 'I never heard of a woman junketing about the countryside with a week-old baby the way you do. Now give me a kiss, both of you, and get out of here.'

After they had gone he hugged Dora and felt her heart beating fast. He was aware that the hand which reached up to rest on his shoulder was shaking.

'Do you want a drink? Something to eat? I'll take you out to dinner if you like. It's late but not too late for La Méditerranée.'

She shook her head. 'I started to shake when I got home. Karen drove me home and came in with me and made me a cup of tea, but once she'd gone the shaking began. Then the girls came. Sheila had a hired car all the way from London. I don't want to start shaking again, Reg. It's very disconcerting.'

'Would it help to go on talking? I mean, about that place and those people?'

'I think perhaps it would.'

'I'll have to record it.'

'That's all right,' she joked, her laugh a little ragged. 'I'm spoilt now. I'll never want to have an ordinary conversation unless I know it's gone on tape.'

# 14

'If they didn't speak,' he asked her, 'how did they find out who you all were?'

There were dark smudges under her eyes and lines round her mouth he didn't think had been there before. But the shaking had stopped. Her thin hands lay calm in her lap. And her voice was steady.

'After the Struthers were brought in Tattoo came back and gave us each a bit of paper. They were torn-off scraps of a lined writing pad. He didn't say anything, but as I've said, none of them ever did. Kitty Struther was lying on the bed crying and moaning that she wanted to go away on her holiday. It was bizarre. There we were in that awful situation and she kept whining about her holiday that had been ruined. Tattoo just put her bit of paper beside her, but her husband picked it up and filled it in for her.

'It just said, "name", which we took to mean they wanted our names. Owen Struther said they were criminals and terrorists, and he wasn't doing anything to gratify criminals, but when Roxane told him how they'd hit her – she had a great bruise on the side of her face by that time – he did it all the same. He said he'd compromise for his wife's sake. We all wrote our names down and after a while Tattoo came back and collected them.'

'You didn't tell him who you were?'

She looked at him inquiringly. 'I wrote down Dora Wexford, if that's what you mean. Oh, I see. I didn't say I was married to you. I suppose I thought they'd know that – but no, maybe not.'

How many people would recognise his name? Not all that many. True, in the past he had several times appeared on television in connection with previous cases, to appeal for witnesses, for help

743

from the public, but no one remembers the names of policemen in these broadcasts, or of those who get their pictures in the papers.

'Remember they never spoke to us, Reg,' she said. 'And on the whole we didn't speak to them much. Well, Roxane spoke to them. And the first time they brought us food Kitty said thank you and that made Roxane laugh, only Tattoo got hold of her by the shoulders and shook her till she stopped. But the rest of us hardly said a word to them. I don't think they ever knew the investigating officer was my husband.'

They did by Friday afternoon, he thought, they found out, and that's why they let her go. It was too much for them, the idea of having his wife among the hostages, a hassle they could do without. It must have come as a shock to them. Besides, releasing her was a sure way of getting their message to him. But how had they found out?

'You've said how Tattoo struck Roxane Masood when she tried to attack him and Rubber Face, right? Why didn't he or they strike Kitty Struther?'

Dora considered. 'Kitty didn't attack him, she only screamed and yelled.'

'She spat at him. Most people would find that pretty inflammatory. Later on Tattoo got hold of Roxane and shook her, and that was only for laughing when Kitty thanked him for the food.'

'Well, I don't know, Reg, I can't answer that. I know they didn't like Roxane. You see, she was trouble from the start. Owen Struther talked a lot about not doing anything conciliatory, "not giving any quarter to the enemy" was his phrase, he wasn't old enough to have been in the Second World War, though he talked as if we were all prisoners of war, but it was Roxane who put up more resistance than any of us. Not that first time but the second evening we had food brought, it was The Driver and Rubber Face, she took one look at it and said, "What's this filth?" and threw it on the floor. It was cold baked beans and bread, quite edible, really, if you're hungry and we were, but she threw it on the floor. Rubber Face hit her again and she was going to fight back. It was horrible, but this time Owen Struther intervened and they stopped. He didn't do much, just told them to stop and put his hand on Roxane's shoulder. Anyway, I suppose he had an authoritative manner or something and it was effective. Kitty started crying again and he sat with her, stroking her head and

744

holding her hand. Then Tattoo came in and cleared up the mess on the floor.'

'You all slept in the basement room that night?'

'At about ten Rubber Face and Tattoo came in, switched off the light and took the bulb out of the socket. Oh, and they did the same in the washroom. They always came in pairs, by the way. After all, we were five, although I don't suppose Kitty or I could have done much. It was very dark in there, though after a while a little light filtered in through the rabbit hutch on the window.'

'Artificial light, you mean?'

'Light that might have been from a street lamp or the outside light on a house or a porch light. Not the moon, though we did get moonlight on the Thursday night. There was a blanket on each bed but no pillows. It wasn't cold. We none of us took our clothes off – how could we? Well, I took off my skirt and jacket. One thing that will make you laugh . . .'

'Really?' he said. 'I doubt it.'

'It will, Reg. I'd got a toothbrush in my handbag. They took my bag away next day but I had it then. I'd bought three new tubes of toothpaste the day before and it was one of those offers you get everywhere now, buy three and you get a free toothbrush with a small tube of toothpaste, all in a plastic case for travelling. Well, I don't know why, but I'd put this in my handbag and there it was. We all shared it. If anyone had ever told me I'd share my toothbrush with four strangers I'd never have believed them.

'We all lay there in the dark and Owen Struther started talking about its being the first duty of a prisoner to escape. There was no way out of the washroom, so the main door remained and the window with its bars and its rabbit hutch, but he said the window was a possibility. In the morning he'd examine the window.

'Ryan Barker had hardly said a word while the light was on, but he seemed to gain a bit of courage in the dark. Anyway, he said he'd like to try and escape and he'd help. Owen said, "Good man," or something equally daft and Ryan said his dad had been a soldier. It was as if he was talking to himself in the dark. He said his dad had been a soldier in some war, he didn't say which war then, and had died for his country. It was quite strange hearing him say that in the dark. "My dad died for his country."

'Anyway, Kitty was crying again. She wanted Owen to "hold her", she said, which was a touch embarrassing for the rest of us, and anyway he couldn't. Those beds were only two feet wide. She lay there moaning that he had to care for her, he had to look after her, she was so alone, she was so frightened.

'I didn't think I'd sleep but I did. After a while. I was trying to work out how they'd done it, managed the Contemporary Cars driving, I mean. With four of them it could quite easily be done. Anyway, there were more than four and I'll come to that. Working that out must have sent me to sleep, but the bed next to me shaking woke me up. It's funny – or perhaps it's not – but talking to you like this has stopped *me* shaking. I feel quite reasonably OK.

'I didn't shake in there but Roxane did. It was Roxane's trembling making the bed shake. I put out my hand to her and she clutched it and said she was sorry but she couldn't stop, it wasn't fear, I mean fear like Kitty's, it was claustrophobia.'

'Ah,' said Wexford. 'Yes.'

'You mean you knew?'

'Her mother told me she was claustrophobic and that it was a severe form she had.'

'It was. It is. She whispered to me that it was all right in the light but in the dark it affected her badly. It would have been all right if the door had been open, but of course it never was.

'She was really a very sensible girl, Reg, in many ways, only she was too brave for her own good. We pushed our beds a bit closer together. Holding her hand seemed to help, so I went on doing that and after a time we both went to sleep.

'In the morning our breakfast was brought in by Gloves and Rubber Face. That was the first time we'd seen Gloves. He had a gun.'

'He had a gun?' Wexford said. 'A handgun?'

'If that's the name for a pistol or a revolver, yes. It might have been a toy or a replica, I wouldn't know, and Owen, who surely would know, said afterwards that it wasn't real. So probably the gun Rubber Face had in the car wasn't real either.

'The gun got used later. Oh, don't look like that, no one was hurt.' Dora reached out and took hold of his hand. 'They didn't put the bulbs back, they never did. It wasn't very light in there, though the sun was shining outside. Light never really penetrated through the bars and the rabbit hutch. Gloves unlocked the window and opened it. That wasn't as generous a move as I've made it sound because the bars made it impossible to squeeze anything thicker than an arm between them. At any rate, we got some air into the room.

'Our breakfast was slices of white bread – you know, Mother's Pride or something, pre-sliced – an orange each and a cake each, a sort of dry muffin thing, jam in small containers, the kind you get in hotels, five mugs of instant coffee and three plastic pots of non-lactic soymilk stuff. I suppose we got such a big meal because we weren't to have anything else till the evening. Owen talked a lot of nonsense about sharpening the one spoon that came with it and turning it into a screwdriver – he was thinking of unscrewing the door hinge – but Rubber Face came back and checked on everything before taking the trays. Shall I tell you about the rest of the day now?'

'No, my dear, I'm going to send you to bed. I'll bring you up a hot drink. More talk tomorrow.'

He sat there alone for a while, trying to think what it was that she had said which rang such a jangling of bells in his mind. It came to him at last. The non-lactic soymilk, that's what it was, the milk substitute the hostages had been brought for their breakfast. He had had it in the tea he had with Gary and Quilla on the previous afternoon and it had left an unpleasant taste in his mouth. It all seemed a hundred years ago now, so much had happened since.

But those two had known he was a policeman though not his name. He had told them he was called Wexford and, now he looked back, he remembered how Quilla had seemed to start at the name. At his rank, he had thought then, but suppose it had been at the name?

At around five-thirty on Friday afternoon outside the Framhurst teashop he had told Quilla and Gary his rank and his name. Four hours later preparations were under way for releasing Dora.

It was strange ground for him, all unfamiliar, new, untried. Some of the time he felt as if he was finding his way through a dark wood where all the trees were exotics, the obstacles unidentifiable and the wild animals threatening in an indefinable way. The taking of hostages, the demanding of a ransom that was of a political nature, all that was something he never expected to have to handle and if asked would have suggested its handling by some different, even remote, authority.

So on this Sunday morning he seemed to have reached an impenetrable part of the wood, but one which he must penetrate. He hardly knew what his next move should be. The computers now held a mass of information, details of every lead that had been followed, background – curricula vitae, if you like – of every person named in the investigation, coincidental and cross-matched activities, possible sites and 'safe houses', transcribed interviews. Then there were the tapes. There was the letter to the *Kingsmarkham Courier* and the versions of the later messages. In it all he could see nothing concrete, nothing to make him feel the time was approaching when he could order a certain place to be pinpointed and one or more persons to be targeted.

He had sent DS Cook and DC Lowry to find Quilla and Gary and bring them to Kingsmarkham police station. If they were still at the Elder Ditches camp, he thought, if they hadn't departed the day before with so many others. Dora had still been asleep when he was preparing to leave and he was wondering what to do when Sheila phoned. Sheila, who had spent the night at Sylvia's, would come in on her way home, now or as soon as the hire car arrived, and stay with her mother until he returned. He had left, feeling one anxiety lifted.

Blind in the dark wood, he had nevertheless come to a decision. All the hostages' families should be fetched in, assembled in the old gym with those of his team who were available and told the present state of things, told, too, that the story would break on Monday morning. Whatever the Chief Constable might say about continental practice, they had involved the hostages' families and must continue to do so. Now, as he looked at them all sitting there, he wondered if he had done the right thing – but how did you know the right thing when there was no precedent?

He remembered how Audrey Barker had asked him if she could be put in touch with the other mother and form a support group. He had refused, largely to reduce to a minimum the chances of a breach of secrecy. They could do it now if they wanted to, perhaps discussion would be a comfort to them, but he had noticed that now the opportunity had come each sat isolated, silent, giving no more than an occasional suspicious glance at the others.

Mrs Peabody hadn't come, so her daughter was the only member of the group without support. Hers was a lonely figure, her head bowed, her hands folded in her lap, her face paper-white. Despair seemed to enclose her, a misery that the news of her son's safety had done nothing to dispel. By contrast, Clare Cox had a hopeful air. She looked practical, resolute, above all she looked *different*. A jacket and skirt, a pair of black pumps, transformed her appearance. Her hair was tied back with a black silk ribbon. Masood, in a smart dark suit with a purple sheen, had accompanied her but without his second family. Wexford noted with as much amusement as he was capable at present of summoning up for anything that they were holding hands.

Whispering from time to time in Bibi's ear, Andrew Struther looked tired and strained. The girl wore white shorts and a red tank top which left her midriff bare. But he was formally dressed in a white shirt and tie, linen jacket and dark trousers. They too were holding hands but in a far more demonstrative way than Roxane's parents, an almost libidinous way. Bibi's hand enclosed his caressingly and moved it to rest on her pale-golden thigh. Distress hadn't touched her, but then why should it? It wasn't her parents who had been kidnapped.

Wexford got up on the impromptu platform and began talking to them. He told them how the facts of the case which had been presented to the press on the previous Wednesday would no longer be embargoed after this evening. The media would be free to use them with the other more recent information which Kingsmarkham CID would pass on to them today.

He believed they already knew that Sacred Globe had released his wife. It was she who had been able to give them so much information about the present condition of the hostages and to tell them that on Friday when she left all were alive and well. She had also carried with her the message that Sacred Globe would begin negotiations today, Sunday, but no word had yet been received as to what they might have in mind. Nor, he said, could he say that these putative discussions were of a kind into which the police – or, come to that, the hostages' families – would be prepared to enter.

They listened. He asked them if they had any questions. He knew he hadn't been entirely open with them or perhaps he hadn't been entirely open with himself. That 'alive and well' business – how true was that? Now he thought he had forborne to question Dora any more, had postponed further questioning, because there were things about Roxane Masood particularly, and the Struthers to a lesser extent, he hadn't wanted to hear before he spoke to these people. Their fears were somewhat allayed. Was there any point in giving rise to more fear at this juncture?

Audrey Barker put up her hand like a child in a classroom – or a child in a classroom in his day.

'Mrs Barker?'

Her eyes, her strained, stretched face, had the look of someone who has just witnessed something terrifying. Seen a ghost, perhaps, or a bloody motorway pile-up. 'Can you tell me a bit more about Ryan?' she asked. It was the voice of a woman on the edge of tears. 'How he was, I mean, how he's taking it?'

'He was fine on Friday evening. His spirits were good.' Wexford didn't add that from then on the boy would have been alone. 'The hostages appear to be adequately fed, there is no problem there. They have washing facilities, beds and blankets.'

Don't ask me if they are all together, he prayed silently. Don't ask where the girl is. No one did. Clare Cox seemed to take it for granted that Roxane was also in that room when Dora left it.

Masood, having disengaged his hand from hers, had been writing something in a small leather-bound notebook. He looked up and asked, 'Can you please tell us who's looking after them?'

'There appear to be five men or four men and a woman.'

'And perhaps by now you have a clue as to where they are?'

'We have clues, yes, many clues. Leads are being followed all the time. As yet we have no firm knowledge of where the hostages are being held, only that it's somewhere within a radius of about sixty miles. Tomorrow's publicity may be of considerable help to us there.'

The question was bound to come. It always did. Andrew Struther asked it.

'Yes, all right, that's all very well, but why haven't you done more to find them? It's how many days now? Five? Six? What exactly have you been doing?'

'Mr Struther,' Wexford said patiently, 'every officer in this area is working all out to find your parents and the other hostages. All leave has been cancelled. Five officers from the Regional Crime Squad have joined them.'

'Miracles we do at once,' said Masood, as if the aphorism was witty or new. 'The impossible will take a little longer.'

'We must hope it won't prove impossible, sir,' Wexford said. 'If there are no more questions perhaps you'd like to confer among yourselves for a while. There has been talk of forming a support group that might be helpful at the present stage.'

But they hadn't quite done with him. The other question he had

750

almost believed wasn't inevitable was suddenly put by, of all people, Bibi.

'Bit funny, wasn't it, I mean, a bit peculiar, that your wife was the one to be released? I mean, how do you account for that?'

The kind of rage he must never show welled up inside him, the kind that made hypertension an actual physical sensation, blood pressure pounding. He drew breath, said calmly and at that moment with perfect truth, 'I can't account for it. I can only hope that the truth about that and everything else will soon emerge.' Another long, deep breath and he added, 'You will of course all be prepared for a good deal of media attention. As far as the police are concerned, no restriction will be placed on anything you may choose to say to the press or any interviews you give.' He raised his head and looked at them all. 'Keep your spirits up. Be optimistic.' They stared back as if he had insulted them. 'Thank you for your attention,' he said.

He stepped down from the platform, feeling a strong desire, which must not be indulged, to get away from these people. They stood about, rather, he thought, as if they expected refreshments. Then a strange thing happened. The two mothers gravitated towards one another. Until then he could have sworn there had been no rapport between them, scarcely recognition of a shared plight, but now, as if the things he had said had brought home to them their common anxiety, they approached each other, eye meeting eye. And as if following stage directions on the same script, each reached out and they closed together in an embrace; they fell into each other's arms.

Men would never do that, he thought. So much of awkwardness, of embarrassment, had been left out of women. He was aware of a certain degree of embarrassment even in himself, something that surprised and very nearly amused him, while Masood looked the other way and Struther said something to the girl that made her giggle.

Wexford coughed tactfully. They would keep in touch, he told them, and to remember that all this would break in the media by the morning.

Dora, fetched by Karen, sat in his office, a pleasanter place than the old gym. A good night's rest had improved her appearance, taken away that tired, drawn look. Some of her natural vivacity was back and she had dressed herself carefully in a skirt and top he hadn't seen before, blue and beige, flattering colours for her.

751

Burden was also in the room and the recorder had just been switched on. At first a little stiff and inhibited by the device, Dora now spoke as freely as if it hadn't been there.

'Chief Inspector Wexford has entered the room,' said Burden, 'at ten-forty-three.'

That seemed to amuse Dora who smiled. 'Where was I? Had I got to the first morning?'

'The morning of Wednesday, September the fourth,' Burden said.

'Right. I'll go on calling them The Driver, Gloves, Rubber Face and Tattoo, if that's all right.' Their smiling nods encouraged her. 'Oh, and the fifth one, the – what's the word? – not transvestite. Oh, yes, hermaphrodite.'

'What?' said Burden. 'You're not serious?'

'I don't know if it was a man or a woman. No faces, you see, and no voices. It was wise of them not to speak, wasn't it?'

'Clever villains don't speak,' Burden said. 'We know all about that round here. Go on, Dora.'

'The others wore black trainers but The Hermaphrodite wore those big clumping shoes with heavy tops and thick soles – are they Doc Marten's? – and I did wonder if that was to make the feet look bigger – if it was a woman, that is. He/she moved like a woman, a bit more graceful than the others, less deliberate, lighter – oh, I don't know, does one know?

'As soon as we were left alone that morning Owen Struther got hold of Ryan – well, sat beside him and started talking to him. It was this doctrine of escape of his and I think he picked on Ryan because although he wasn't yet fifteen, he was the only other male there. And Ryan is six feet tall. I didn't like it because, after all, he may be the size of a man but he's only a child still in many ways.

'Owen kept telling Ryan to be a man. It was up to them to defend us women because they were men, that was part of their role in life, and the most important thing was for Ryan never to show fear, and a lot of other rubbish like that. I left them to it, went into the washroom and did my best to wash myself all over. I spent a good deal of time in there trying to keep clean, and apart from anything else it was a way of passing the time.

'Roxane washed herself too and we both used my toothbrush. I told Kitty the washroom was free but she barely took any notice of me. She'd paced about earlier, pounded her fists on the walls and all that, but then she'd collapsed on to her bed, she'd had some coffee

752

but no breakfast, and she seemed simply to have succumbed to despair.

'It was strange, her husband so active and determined and full of energy, so much the audacious officer in an old war film, and she as feeble as if she were actually going through a nervous breakdown. Well, there was the spitting and the bad language, but that was momentary and all in the past by then. You couldn't understand how two people who were married to each other and presumably had been for years and years, could have such different attitudes to life.'

'What were these escape plans?' Wexford asked.

'I'll come to that. I spent the morning talking to Roxane. She told me about her parents, her father is this quite rich entrepreneur. He was born in Karachi but came here as a child and worked his way up from nothing. She's very proud of him, but more sorry for her mother than proud. Her mother would never marry Mr Masood, though he wanted her to. Roxane could remember him still pressing her mother to marry him when she was ten years old. But Clare – she calls her Clare – put her career first and said marriage was obsolete, though apparently her career never amounted to much. Then Mr Masood married someone else and had more children. Roxane minds a lot about that, she's jealous, she doesn't like her stepmother, I'm afraid she gets a tremendous kick out of her stepmother being overweight while she, of course, is slim as a reed.

'She told me about wanting to be a model and her father helping her, and then we got on to her claustrophobia. She said it came from her grandmother – that is, Clare's mother – shutting her in a cupboard as a punishment when she was a toddler. I mean, if that's true it's quite terrible – one can hardly understand such a thing – but I did wonder myself if it could really be the cause. These psychological things are always more complex than that, aren't they?

'Anyway, I mustn't go on about her. She was claustrophobic, but she could just about manage in that room, only it did make me wonder how she'd get on if this modelling got off the ground and she had to stay in small hotel rooms. But maybe she'll be another Naomi Campbell and only stay in suites.

'They didn't bring us any lunch. They didn't come near us for hours. Owen Struther examined the whole room, taking Ryan round with him, paying particular attention to the window and the door. The window was open but it was still impossible to see much, only the greenness and that grey something that was a sort of concrete

753

step, and it was virtually impossible to reach out of it either. Owen's arm was too thick to get between the bars, but Ryan could squeeze his out. Not that there was any point in it. He put his arm through the bars as far as he could and managed to touch the wood of the rabbit hutch. He said he felt rain on his hand but we could already see it was raining . . .'

'Could you hear the rain?' asked Slesar.

'You mean, drumming on the roof? No, nothing like that. I had the impression there was at least one and probably two storeys above the basement room. It wasn't a barn or a free-standing garage.

'I'll come back to Owen Struther. His idea was that the only possible method of escape would be while they were inside feeding us or fetching our tray and the door was unlocked. Closed but unlocked. He and Ryan would do it with Roxane to help them. I don't think he thought much of any potential strength I might have and, of course, his poor wife was hopeless.

'Roxane was to distract the attention of one of them. I don't know what he had in mind at that point, maybe make another attack and we all knew what that resulted in. But I don't think he'd have cared. He was obsessed. They would pick a time when The Hermaphrodite was one of the pair because he/she would be easier to handle. Incidentally, that would have been all very well if they'd been in and out every few minutes, but as I've said we hadn't seen them for hours. Still, the whole escape plan wasn't very practical. While Roxane was busy with one of them – being beaten up, I suppose – he would handle the other and Ryan would make his escape by way of the door.

'I intervened then and asked him if he realised Ryan was only fourteen. For one thing, he couldn't drive a car. What did he think he was going to do out there in the middle of God knows where? So the plan was changed and he was to go out through the door while Ryan and I handled the other one.

'In the event it didn't work. It was disastrous. But I'll come to that later, shall I?'

There are about twenty-five different varieties of wild blackberry growing in the British Isles. Most people think only one kind is to be found, but you have only to look at the difference in leaf formation, not to mention the size, shape and colour of the berries, to understand how they vary. The frail-looking young woman in a faded tracksuit who was picking blackberries, filling a wicker basket and eating as many as she picked, informed Martin Cook of these facts unasked.

'Interesting,' said Cook. 'What are you going to do with those?'

'Cook them with elderberries and crab-apples. Make an autumn compote.' She gave Burton Lowry an appraising look. Cook was used to that. His DC attracted black and white women alike. 'I don't suppose you've come here for a lesson in Elves' cuisine, have you?'

'I'm looking for Gary Wilson and Quilla Rice.'

'You won't find them here, they've gone. Had a bit of harassment in mind, did you? I'm afraid you'll have to make do with me.'

Cook ignored that. He wouldn't go on ignoring such provocation but he would for a while. 'And what might your name be?'

The young woman shrugged. 'It *might* be any number of things. My mother wanted to call me Tracy and my father liked Rosamund, but in fact what they actually called me is Christine. Christine Colville. What's yours?' When she got no answer she said to Lowry, 'Would you like a blackberry?'

'No, thanks.'

Cook turned away and looked into the depths of the wood. The first tree-houses at Elder Ditches were just visible in the distance. He could see someone sitting in a clearing, apparently holding a musical instrument, but all was silent. 'Is there someone' – he hardly knew how to put it – 'well, in charge here?'

'You want me to take you to our leader?'

'If you've got one, yes.'

'Oh, we have one,' she said. 'The King of the Wood. Haven't you heard of him?'

The name came back to Cook. He remembered the statement to the *Kingsmarkham Courier*. 'He's called Conrad Tarling?'

She nodded. She picked up her basket, turned to them and beckoned. 'Follow me.' As she walked along she plucked bunches of elderberries from the bushes which filled about an acre before the tall trees were reached. Cook and Lowry walked along behind her.

'I'll come back for the crab-apples,' she said. 'I don't suppose you've ever heard of the King *in* the Wood, have you?'

'You just said it was Tarling.'

'Not that one,' she said scornfully. 'In Italy, by the lake of Nemi, in ancient times. This man was called the King in the Wood. He walked round and round this tree, nervous and afraid, armed with a sword, ever-watchful, because he knew men would come and fight him, would try to kill him, so that the killer could be the next King.'

'Oh, yes?' said Cook.

But Lowry said, 'He was a priest and a murderer, and sooner or later he would be murdered and the man who killed him would be priest in his stead. Such was the rule of the sacred grove.'

Christine Colville smiled but Cook said, 'The what?'

It sounded a lot like Sacred Globe to him. She eyed his puzzled face and began to laugh. Cook hadn't the faintest idea what she and Lowry had been talking about, but he was pretty sure she at least was sending him up. When they reached the trees, once they were among them, Christine Colville set down her basket, lifted her head and whistled. It was a whistle like a bird calling – pu-wee, pu-wee.

Faces appeared among the branches.

'Someone needs to talk to the King,' she said.

It was then that Conrad Tarling showed himself, as if called forth by the magic word 'King', the Open Sesame word. He emerged from a tree-house on to the platform on all fours. He was naked to the waist, his shaven head bluish and gleaming.

'Police,' said Cook. 'I'd like to talk to you.'

Tarling retreated behind the flap of tarpaulin which served his crow's nest as a front door. Cook was wondering what to do now when he reappeared, wrapped up this time in his all-enveloping sand-coloured cloak. For a moment Cook thought he would swing down from this considerable height, hand over hand on this branch and that, foot over foot on protuberances on the gnarled trunk. But instead he flicked his fingers at someone unseen and within minutes Christine and a man in shorts and anorak had propped a ladder up against the tree.

Face to face with Cook in the clearing, he was a good six inches taller. His head was rather small, his neck long. The face was an arresting one, hard, clean-cut, as if carved from wood.

Cook asked him about Gary Wilson and Quilla Rice but the King of the Wood wanted identification before saying a word. Having gravely studied Cook's warrant card, he asked in a grand manner what the police wanted them for.

'To ask them a few questions.'

Tarling laughed. He had an audience now, half a dozen Elves squatting on the platforms of their tree-houses, listening, while Christine Colville and her companion in the anorak, sat close by, cross-legged on the grass. Tarling's voice was very deep and soft, yet ringing. They could probably hear what he said in Pomfret, Cook thought bitterly.

'That's what you always say. The words of totalitarianism. A few questions. A spot of interrogation. A smidgen of inquisition. And then the fun and games in the police cell – is that it?'

'Where do you people keep your vehicles?'

Another laugh, this time directed at the gallery. 'Ugly sort of word that, isn't it? "Vehicle". It's what I'd call a police word, like "proceeding" and "inquiry". Those of us who have *vehicles* keep them in a field kindly – very, very kindly, and I mean that – lent to us by Mr Canning, a farmer who is an angel of light compared with others of his kind and, like us, opposed to this damnable bypass.'

'I see. And where might this angel's field be?'

'Between Framhurst and Myfleet. Goland Farm. But Quilla and Gary didn't use it. They haven't a *vehicle*. They must have hitched, they usually do.' Picking up his basket and turning his attention to an elder tree, Tarling said less aggressively, 'They'll return in a week or so. For your information, as you'd doubtless put it your *good* self, they've gone to the SPECIES rally in Wales and they'll soon be back. No one believes this environmental assessment is the end, you know. Things don't happen so easily as that.'

'And you?'

'I beg your pardon?'

'Do you have a' – Cook rejected the offending word – 'a car?'

If Cook was unacquainted with the works of Lewis Carroll, Lowry was not. Wexford too would have recognised the quotation but to Cook it was gibberish. He turned away in disgust. Tarling's words and the tree people's consequent laughter pursued him.

' "I have answered three questions and that is enough,"
Said his father, "Don't give yourself airs.
Do you think I can listen all day to such stuff?
Be off or I'll kick you downstairs." '

Walking back to the car, he said to Lowry, 'I'm getting a bit pissed off with you pulling your university rank on me.'

'What did I do?' said Lowry indignantly.

Barry Vine was in the car with Pemberton. They had been at the Savesbury Deeps camp but appeared to have learnt less than Cook had. Half the tree people had gone, many of them on other pilgrimages to seek out other violations and injustices.

'Your words?' said Cook belligerently.

'Theirs,' said Vine with a shrug. 'I'm off to Framhurst, have a cup of tea in the village.'

A surprised glance was the response to that. Vine explained.

'I'd like to know where they get that muck from they call non-lactic soymilk. I mean, can you buy it in a supermarket or is it only supplied to restaurants as against retail outlets? And when we've refreshed ourselves Jim and I will go and have a word with Farmer Canning.'

Nicky Weaver knew a lot about Brendan Royall's Winnebago by this time. She knew its registration number, that its colour was white, that it was three years old and that he was usually but not invariably alone in it.

The best piece of information she had about it was that it had been seen that morning on the M25, heading for the M2, by a police car on speed control. That rather reduced the impact of the piece of news she had just had phoned in from the Elder Ditches camp by DS Cook, that Royall might be found at a SPECIES rally in Wales. Of course, she had checked out the rally and discovered it was to be in Neath, near Glencastle Forest, and due to start on Tuesday. Please God, they would have found those hostages by Tuesday . . .

If Royall was planning to go there he had been heading in the wrong direction. It wasn't likely he would go near his parents but she couldn't take that for granted. On the other hand, it was practically certain he would pay a visit to the Panicks.

She walked among the desks in the old gym, looking at computer screens, watching for anything new that might have come in. Everyone knew about the SPECIES rally by now. It was an important event in the protestors' calendar. Should the force be there, a presence, among all those activists?

She glanced out of one of the long windows on the car park side. A car was coming in that she didn't recognise, a small white Mercedes, probably come to fetch Dora Wexford. Back in Myringham, at the Regional Crime Squad, she would have known every car that came in and out, and would have questioned any unfamiliar ones. They were nearly all unfamiliar here . . . No harm in noting down the registration number though. Better safe than sorry. She did so as the car turned the corner round the back of the building and disappeared from sight.

'Let's just get this straight,' said Burden. 'Gloves, the one in gloves, you saw less of him than of any of the others. You saw him on the Wednesday morning at breakfast, but not again till you were due to leave. Is that right?'

'Not quite. I saw him on the Wednesday but not again till the Friday, only it was at midday on the Friday.'

'Right. Now food. What did they give you to eat? No, I'm perfectly serious. Food could be a clue as to where you were.'

'Do you mean, what did they give us that Wednesday evening?'

'For a start, yes.'

'I don't think it will be of much help. There were three large pizzas, cooked but cold, some more of the white bread, five slices of processed cheese and five apples. The apples were badly bruised. Oh, and more instant coffee and that non-lactic stuff. If we wanted anything else to drink we just got it ourselves from the water tap. And since we didn't have a cup or a glass or anything we had to put our mouths under the tap.'

Dora drank some of the tea Archbold had brought in to them and took a chocolate biscuit with the appreciation of someone who has recently subsisted on a diet of cold pizza and sliced bread.

'It was Tattoo and The Hermaphrodite that evening. Tattoo and Rubber Face were probably the strongest and the most . . . well, the most ruthless of them, or that's the impression I had, but The Hermaphrodite was certainly the weakest, and I could see the moment they came in what Owen had in mind.

'What Roxane did, it wasn't deliberate, I mean it wasn't part of a plot, it was just spontaneous. She jumped up and said to Tattoo that she wanted to talk to him. "I want to talk to you," she said. And then she said, "And I want you to talk to us." He just stood there, looking at her. Or I suppose he was looking at her – you can't tell when a person's wearing one of those hoods.

' "You've left us all day without food," she said, or something like that. "You've left us all day without anything to eat. It's outrageous what you're doing," she said. "What have we done? We are innocent people. We have done no one any harm. You give us hardly anything to drink," she said, "and this is the first food we've had for ten hours.

759

What is it you're doing?" she said. "What do you want?" He didn't say a word, just stood there, very close to her.

'The Hermaphrodite was holding the tray, a large, heavy tray with all that food on it. I could see Owen keying himself up and Ryan too, poor kid, playing at adventures. The door was shut but it wasn't locked. Roxane – oh, she's a courageous girl – she looked into Tattoo's face, his mask, it was about six inches from her face, and she said, "Answer me. Answer me, you bastard!"

'He hit her. He hit her as hard as he could across the head. That was when his sleeve fell back, he was wearing a shirt with quite loose sleeves, and I saw the tattoo, a butterfly on his left forearm. As Roxane fell over on the bed Ryan made a rush for The Hermaphrodite. Well, The Hermaphrodite dropped that tray and food went everywhere, pizzas upside down on the nearest bed, apples rolling across the floor and the tray making a terrific crash. Ryan had hold of him/her by the shoulders, Tattoo sprang round and pulled out a gun. Owen had got the door open but he never actually got out.

'Everything happened at once, it's quite hard to sort it all out, but the gun went off. I still can't tell you if it was real or not. It made a loud bang and whatever was fired out of it went into the woodwork round the window. Would a replica gun make a noise like that?'

'It might,' said Burden. 'Any sort of gun makes a noise.'

'I don't actually think it was aimed at anyone. Kitty was screaming her head off. She was lying on her bed, drumming her fists into the mattress and screaming. Maybe it was that or maybe it was the gun, but Owen hesitated and you know what they say about the person who hesitates. The Hermaphrodite aimed a kick at Ryan, a really high, hard kick, and it caught him in the stomach and sent him flying, clutching at his body. Roxane was groaning, holding her face. I didn't do anything, I'm afraid, I just sat there. That gun going off had rather mesmerised me.

'Tattoo must have had handcuffs with him because he got them on to Owen. It was quite remarkable the way while this was all going on neither of those two spoke a word. Owen was shouting and cursing, threatening them with all sorts of punishment to come, "They'll shut you up in high security for ever," that kind of thing. Ryan was rolling on the floor whimpering, Roxane was groaning and Kitty was screaming, but those two were utterly silent. I can tell you, it was sinister, it was a lot more effective than anything they could have said.

760

'It dehumanised them, you see. People are people because they speak and these two had become machines. They were science fiction creatures. Anyway, you don't want the philosophy. I'll tell you what happened next. I suppose they always carried handcuffs because they put a pair on Ryan and another pair on Kitty who sobbed while they did it. Tattoo manhandled Roxane into the washroom and locked the door.

'That frightened me because I knew how she felt about enclosed spaces. But I thought that if I told them that, it would make things worse, not better. So I said nothing. Tattoo stayed with us while The Hermaphrodite went away and came back with hoods for the Struthers. The hoods were put on and the Struthers were taken away and that was the last I ever saw of them. It was at about half-past seven on the Wednesday evening.'

Burden interrupted the narrative once more. 'You never saw them again?'

Dora shook her head, realised this movement would be recorded and said. 'No, I never did.' She went on, 'But I've no reason to think any harm came to them. I think they were just taken to somewhere Tattoo thought would be safer. Kitty was sobbing all the time they were being taken out of there.

'Ryan was more or less all right, just very shaken. Later on a terrific bruise came up on his stomach. He got himself up and said something about knowing better than to have tried that on. But I was extremely worried about Roxane. There was an awful silence from behind that door and I thought perhaps she'd fainted. I considered trying to break it down. Have you ever tried to break a door down?'

They all had. All had succeeded but it hadn't been easy. It hadn't been like on television where a shove and a kick will do it.

Wexford said, 'Did you try?'

'Yes, because the silence didn't go on. She started screaming and pounding on the door. It wasn't like Kitty's screaming, this was real phobic terror. I put my shoulder to the door and I kicked it. Maybe I'd have succeeded but after a moment or two Rubber Face and Tattoo came in. They moved me out of the way, Rubber Face just lifted me and dumped me on my bed. Don't look like that, Reg. I wasn't hurt.

'They let Roxane out but not at once. It was nasty what happened. They looked at each other, those two – well, the heads in the masks turned – and I just had this feeling they knew and they, or one of them, was enjoying it. They'd discovered her fear of enclosed spaces and they were *pleased*. They stood there listening to her pounding on the door and her pleading.

'Eventually, they unlocked the door. She staggered out and fell on her bed, sobbing bitterly. It was awful, it really was dreadful. But life in there had to go on. I hugged her and tried to comfort her.

'Then Rubber Face and Tattoo found my handbag and Kitty's – Roxane didn't have one, they don't at that age – and took them with them and went away, I don't know why, having left Ryan handcuffed. The handcuffs didn't come off him till next morning and he was very uncomfortable and in pain.

'We just settled down, the three of us, to make the best of things. I picked up the food that wasn't filthy or otherwise ruined; the pizzas were all right and I washed the apples. I got them to sit down with me and eat as best they could and then we talked. We played a sort of game, each of us to tell a true story about a member of our families. It was dark, you see, they never brought the light bulbs back.

'Well, I started the ball rolling by telling a story and then Roxane told one about her aunt meeting Gershwin when she was a child. It was in New York. And Ryan told one about his father winning some county athletics championship. Still, you won't want to know any of this. We all went to sleep. Even Roxane did, though she was in pain with her face. It was very swollen and black with bruises, and a cut on her temple was bleeding. They were to take her away next day but I didn't know that then.

'I was the only one who hadn't been hurt in some way and that made me feel guilty. Ridiculous really, but I suppose people do feel guilt in my situation . . .'

DC Edward Hennessy went out to the car park just before four. His car happened to be parked alongside Chief Inspector Wexford's. Between the two cars, on the tarmac, stood a dark-brown fibre suitcase, with the initials on its side: D.M.W., and beside it two large, full plastic carriers, one green, one yellow.

Hennessy didn't touch any of it. He went back inside, knocked on the door of Wexford's office and told him. Dora Wexford was still there, taking a break from recording. She jumped up. 'That has to be my case,' she said. 'And it sounds like my parcels.'

She was right. The carriers contained her presents to Sheila:

babyclothes, a shawl, a kimono for a nursing mother, two new novels, a flagon of perfume and one of body lotion. She identified the case as hers and watched while it was opened to reveal her undisturbed, carefully folded clothes. On top of them was a sheet of paper, on which were printed the words of Sacred Globe's next message.

No more delays, please. The media must be told at once. This is the first step in our negotiations. We are Sacred Globe, saving the world.

# 15

The contents of the suitcase were, as far as she could tell, as Dora had packed them. 'This is like what they ask you at airports,' she joked. 'Did you pack your case yourself? Has it been left unattended at any time? It's yes to the first one and heaven only knows to the second.'

'I think I saw the car it came in,' Nicky Weaver told Wexford. 'A white Mercedes. For some reason – God knows what guardian angel inspired me – I took down the number. It's L570 LOO.'

'That'll be the car they brought Dora home in. The L-something-five-seven car.'

'Cheeky bunch, aren't they?' Burden sounded half admiring. 'Not your usual villains.'

'Let's hope they're too clever for their own good.'

'I don't like it,' said Wexford, and when they looked at him inquiringly, 'I don't like their jokes and I don't like it that our decision to lift the embargo coincides with their demand to lift it. It can't be changed now, but it looks as if we're complying with what they ask.'

Dora had been having a cup of tea with Karen Malahyde. She had at first seemed awestricken by the reappearance of her suitcase and parcels, almost as if it evinced supernatural powers on the part of Sacred Globe, and her husband recalled what she had said about science fiction characters who were not quite human. He sat down opposite her and the recorder was started.

'Can we come to Thursday morning, Dora?'

'Well, I'm still on Wednesday night really. Something happened on Wednesday night. Two of them came in while we were asleep, or they thought we were asleep. Roxane and Ryan were, and I pretended I was; I thought it was safer.

'I saw and heard the door open and two of them came in. I think it was Gloves and Tattoo but I can't be sure. They were in their usual hoods. That was when I shut my eyes, so I don't know what they were there for, what they did, but they were wandering about in there for some minutes. Before they left they came and stood over us, checking we were asleep, I suppose. You know how you can always tell something like that, you can sense it.

'On Thursday morning,' Dora began. 'Roxane's face was dreadfully bruised and her left eye was quite closed up. I know it shouldn't, but it somehow made it worse, doing that to such a beautiful girl.

'Rubber Face and The Driver brought our breakfast. It was more white bread, dry bread, and a slice of some sort of tinned meat, the cheapest sort like spam, and three packets of crisps. That must have been to sustain us through the day because again we got nothing else till the evening. Nothing to drink either but water from the tap.

'But they did come back for the tray. Roxane didn't shout at them this time. She just started asking when they were going to let us go, what they wanted, how long this was going to go on. You have to understand that we didn't know they called themselves Sacred Globe. We didn't know they wanted the bypass stopped or their threats or anything. And Roxane desperately wanted to know. Of course neither of them answered. As I've said, they never spoke. They never even seemed to hear, though it's hard to tell a thing like that when someone's face and head are covered up.

'In the middle of the afternoon Roxane began hammering on the door. Ryan had been very subdued after being thrown on the ground the evening before, and his stomach hurt, but once she'd started he helped her. They banged on that door and kicked it and this went on for a good half-hour.

'At last the door was opened and Rubber Face came in with Tattoo. I was very frightened, I don't mind admitting it, because I thought they were going to beat Roxane up and maybe Ryan too. But nothing like that happened. Tattoo simply got hold of Roxane and pinned her arms behind her. She screamed and yelled but he took no notice. He handcuffed her like that with her hands behind her. Rubber Face manhandled Ryan out of the way and when he tried to put up a bit of resistance, grabbed him and locked him in the washroom.

'They had a hood with them and they put it over Roxane's head and took her away. They just took her away, I've no idea where or what happened to her. She spoke to me, she said, "Goodbye, Dora," through the hood, it was sort of muffled but that's what she said. I never saw her again.' Dora paused. She shrugged a little, shaking her head. 'I never saw her again,' she repeated. 'They may have put her with the Struthers, wherever they were, I just don't know. All I can say is that about ten minutes afterwards for the first time I heard footsteps overhead, but that may have had no connection with where they put Roxane.'

'One set of footsteps or more than one?'

'I don't know. More than one set, I think. Ryan was let out of the washroom after an hour. Tattoo and The Driver came in and let him out and after that he and I were alone. We just sat there and played word games. I don't think I've ever in my life so longed for something as I longed for a pad of paper and a pencil – or, come to that, Scrabble or Monopoly. After a time we just talked. He told me things I don't think he'd ever told anyone before.

'His father had been killed in the Falklands war. They'd been married just three months, his father and mother. She was pregnant when the news came and he was born seven months later. The reason she was in hospital was to have a cone biopsy – that's the operation where they take off a bit of the cervix because of pre-cancerous signs. It was the second she'd had. She was going to get married again and she wanted more children – she's only thirty-six now – but it's not likely she'll have any after all that. I'm sorry, I don't suppose you want to hear all this, it's not relevant. It just seemed to me a heavy burden to lay on a boy of fourteen, confiding it all to him.

'Anyway, he confided in *me*, and that's how we passed the evening. They were very late bringing our breakfast on Friday morning. I suppose they'd seen to the others first, I mean to Owen and Kitty and Roxane, wherever they were. It was Tattoo and Rubber Face. They brought us bread rolls, very stale, jam in those individual containers and an apple each.

'Ryan and I had decided we'd ask them what had happened to Roxane, though we didn't think we'd get an answer. We did ask and we didn't get an answer. I think that was the longest day of my life. There was nothing to do. Ryan went completely silent, maybe he thought he'd said too much the evening before, maybe he was embarrassed. Whatever it was, he didn't answer me when I spoke to him. He lay on his back on his bed, staring at the ceiling. For the first time I seriously began thinking we'd never be released, we'd go on like this for weeks and then we'd be killed.

'Gloves appeared at lunch-time. It was the first time we'd seen him since the Wednesday morning. I thought it was Rubber Face at first, but his build was much slighter than Rubber Face's. Tattoo was with him. That was when I saw Gloves's eyes. I said I only saw the eyes of one of them, didn't I? Well, it was Gloves's eyes.

'The holes in his hood must have been bigger than in those worn by the others. Anyway, I could see his eyes quite clearly. They were brown, a clear, deep brown. He came close to me for a moment, peered at me as if he was trying to . . . well, verify something about me, and that's when I saw his eyes. But it's not much help, is it? I suppose half the population have brown eyes.

'It was that evening they let me go. I've told you all about that. Oh, they fed us first if that's of any interest. Tinned spaghetti in tomato sauce, cold of course, bread, more jam. Tattoo and The Hermaphrodite brought it. I was preparing for another night in there when they came in and took me out. Ryan was left there alone. As I've said, I've no idea what happened to the others.'

Wexford got up as Barry Vine put his head round the door and asked if he could have a word. 'It's about food, sir,' he said when they were outside. 'And it's all pretty negative. You remember the non-lactic soymilk at the Framhurst teashop?'

'Of course I do.'

'I don't know why, but I got it into my head that if that place was the only outlet for the stuff in the south of England . . . Anyway, forget it, because you can buy it everywhere. You can buy it in supermarkets. Thanks to Sunday opening, I've done a pretty thorough check on that. You can buy it at the Crescent in Kingsmarkham and every one of their other branches too. Nation-wide.'

'Another lead bites the dust,' said Wexford.

In the Chief Constable's living-room in his house outside Myfleet, Wexford sat eating pistachio nuts and drinking a single malt. Donaldson had driven him there, would drive him back and was at this moment sitting in the car eating a ham sandwich and drinking a can of Lilt. No one had time for proper meals any more.

Wexford was there to talk about the release of the hostage story to the media. In the morning. Tomorrow morning. But they had agreed on how it should be done, how limited it should be and how free, the hour of release and the defensive measures they would take. And now Montague Ryder wanted to talk about Dora. He had listened to the tapes, all of them, and had heard the last one twice.

'She's done very well, Reg, superlatively well. She's an observant woman. But yet . . .'

I do not like 'but yet', reflected Wexford, quoting someone or other. Cleopatra, he thought. He said quickly, 'I know. There's a lot there and at the same time there isn't much.' But could you have done as well? Could I? In a misogynistic way, normally quite foreign to him, he thought how most women he knew would have collapsed under Dora's ordeal, caved in, been stricken dumb. 'They were clever, sir,' he said. 'Clever and cocky. They must have been, to take the risk of letting her go.'

'Yes. Odd that, wasn't it? We still think it was because they found out who she was?'

Wexford nodded, but dubiously. The Macallan bottle was raised along with the Chief Constable's eyebrows and he was tempted, but he said no. He could have gone on drinking all evening, but what was the point? He had to stay sensible tonight and be alert tomorrow.

'You know what I'm thinking, Reg?'

'I think so, sir.'

'Hypnosis. Would she consent?'

It was a method, newly fashionable, of extracting information and observations which lay buried, which would probably remain buried, unless unearthed by means other than the subject's own volition and intent. Wexford hadn't much experience of it. He knew, or had heard, that it often worked. He felt a sudden violent revulsion against putting Dora through it. Why should she have to suffer this . . . this *assault*? This taking away of her free will, this indignity.

'I don't know if she'll consent,' he said. Surprisingly, he had no idea what her reaction would be. Horror or interest, recoil or even attraction? 'I must tell you' – this was very hard to say, to express, to a man of so much higher rank and power, but he wouldn't sleep if he didn't say it – 'I must tell you, sir, that I'm not prepared to persuade her.'

Montague Ryder laughed, but pleasantly. 'Suppose I ask her?' he said. 'Suppose I ask her tonight and then, if she agrees, we'll get hold of the psychologist to hypnotise her tomorrow? Would you mind that?'

'No, I wouldn't mind,' said Wexford.

# 16

Television stole the press's thunder and the Kingsmarkham kidnap story appeared on ITN's news at eight-forty-five and BBC1's at nine-fifteen, prefaced in each case by the words, 'News is just coming in . . .'

By the later time Dora was in bed with a gin and tonic and a hint from her husband that Monday could be the day of her encounter with a hypnotherapist. Wexford regretted now that the hostages' names had been released, or rather that the name of a former hostage had. But even he was unprepared for his doorbell ringing at seven in the morning and for the arrival of three reporters and four cameramen on his doorstep.

The two daily newspapers he took had already come. Both used the story as their front-page lead. Somehow, one of them had got hold of a photograph of Roxane Masood, and this, with pictures of the bypass site, a facsimile of the first Sacred Globe letter and a picture of himself – the hated portrait of him all smiles, holding up a beer tankard, that they kept in their archives – dominated the broadsheet. He was glancing through the text when the doorbell struck his eardrums with a reverberating peal.

Luckily he was dressed. He could imagine another photograph featuring the crimson velvet dressing-gown. Before he opened the door he knew who it was. The chain was on, he had put it on for some reason ever since Dora had come back, and the door opened only six inches. His grandmother, a Pomfret native, used to open her front door a couple of inches to unwelcome callers and snap, 'Not today, thank you.' He had been very small when she died but he remembered, though he restrained himself from repeating her words now. 'Press conference at the police station at 10 a.m.,' he said.

Flash bulbs went off and cameras clicked. 'I'd like an exclusive interview with Dora first,' one of them said impertinently.

And I'd like your head on a plate. 'Good-morning,' he said and shut the door. The phone rang. He snapped into the receiver in his grandmother's words, 'Not today, thank you,' and pulled out the plug.

A photographer had got round the back and was looking through his kitchen window. For the first time he was glad of the 'Roman' blinds Dora had had put up the previous summer. He pulled them down, drew curtains, made the tea, poured a cup for Dora and a mug for himself, and took them upstairs. She was sitting up in bed with the radio on. News of the Kingsmarkham Kidnap – the title had been coined and would be kept – had displaced everything else: Palestine, Bosnia, party political wrangling and the Princess of Wales.

'Is there a ladder in the garage?' he asked her.

'I believe so. Why on earth do you ask?'

'Show no surprise if a head appears at the window any time now. The media are here.'

'Oh, Reg!'

On the previous evening the Chief Constable had been to see her. She was very tired, had been lying on the sofa in her dressing-gown, but even though she had been warned of his coming, hadn't dressed. Wexford was glad she hadn't. He welcomed her independence of spirit and expected a further show of it when the request was made. She would say no. She would say it politely, even apologetically, but she wouldn't agree to some shrink putting her in a trance.

She said yes.

And now she was saying it again, even apparently looking forward to it. 'I must get up. I'm being hypnotised this morning.'

As far as he could remember, there had never been so many press men and women in Kingsmarkham. Not for a serial killer. Not even for the murder of Davina Flory and her family. They had parked their cars everywhere and traffic wardens were out in force, taking numbers, leaving tickets. Wheel-clamping would soon start.

He could picture the invasions of the cottage in Pomfret, Mrs Peabody's little house in Stowerton and the onslaught on Andrew Struther at Savesbury House. He could picture it without going to see. They must defend themselves as best they could, and perhaps it was all to the good, maybe this tremendous publicity would help.

Already, at nine, the phone lines into Kingsmarkham police station were jammed by callers with information. He looked over the shoulder of one of the busy phone operators at the computer screen on which everything that came in was recorded. Roxane Masood hadn't been abducted, she had been seen in Ilfracombe; Ryan Barker was dead and his body would be released for £20,000. The Struthers had been seen in Florence, in Athens, in Manchester, looking out of an upper window of a factory in Leeds, on a boat in Poole harbour. Dora Wexford had never been abducted but had been planted as a spy, a decoy, a detective. Roxane Masood was going to be married in Barbados to the son of a woman who would tell them the whole story for a sum to be negotiated . . .

Wexford sighed. All these people's calls would have to be followed up and all of them would either be mistaken or malicious. Unless, of course, one was authentic, just one provided a lead . . .

He had got Dora out of the house, a big hat and tent-shaped coat concealing most of her, into a car driven by Karen Malahyde. After what she had been through she didn't want anything covering her face and he hadn't argued. The press had run after the car for a bit, taking photographs. When he came back from the old gym, where he left her listening to her own tapes and checking what she had said, he found Brian St George waiting for him.

The editor of the *Kingsmarkham Courier* was deeply aggrieved. In the same grey pinstripe and dirty white sweatshirt, he came up to Wexford, pushing his face close to him. His breath smelt of periodontal gum disease. 'You don't like me, do you?'

'What makes you say that, Mr St George?' Wexford retreated a couple of feet.

'You lifted the embargo on this story on the worst possible bloody day of the week for me. Lift it on a Sunday and I've got five days before the *Courier* comes out. *Five days.* The story'll be dead by then.'

'I'm sure I hope so,' Wexford said.

'You did it out of spite. It might just as well have been last Thursday or have waited till this Wednesday, but no, you have to do it on a Sunday.'

Wexford appeared to reflect. 'Saturday would have been worse.' As the red mounted fiercely up in St George's face, he said imperturbably, 'You'll have to excuse me, I have work to do. You'll no doubt be getting a lot of calls from the public, even though you haven't the advantages of the nationals, and we'd like everything passed directly here, please.'

Craig Tarling, older brother of Conrad Tarling, was currently serving a ten-year prison sentence for his animal rights activities.

'It's not a common name,' Nicky Weaver said. 'I spotted it on the computer and checked him out.'

Damon Slesar raised his eyebrows. They were on their way to Marrowgrave Hall and he was driving. 'A man's not responsible for what his relations do,' he said. 'My father grows fruit and veg on the old bypass and my mum spins yarn out of animal hairs. People send her their pets' fur in bags.'

'There's nothing wrong with that. It's perfectly respectable.' Nicky spoke rather sharply. Her mother worked in a greengrocer's part-time – in the rest of her time she helped look after the Weaver children – and Nicky didn't like his tone. 'And so is fruit-growing. You shouldn't talk like that about your family.'

'OK, OK, sorry I spoke. You know me, my wit runs away with me. What did this brother do?'

'Conspired – master-minded might be the better word – to set off fifty firebombs. His targets were rabbit and chicken farms, butchers' shops, an agricultural college and an agency selling tickets for circuses, among others. I expect he'd have targeted ostrich farms, only this was five years ago and there weren't any then.'

'What went wrong? I mean wrong for him and right for law and order?'

'A shop assistant thought it strange for one man to buy sixty timing devices and told the police.'

On the horizon, standing out against a yellow and black sunset, stood ruined Saltram House where, long ago, Burden had found the body of a missing child in one of the fountain cisterns. Nicky asked Damon if he had ever heard that story, it had been about the time Burden's first wife had died, but he shook his head, his brown eyes contrite.

The car turned into the drive. In the pale sunshine of morning Marrowgrave Hall looked no less forbidding and seemed more than ever closed up, secured against the outside world. Nicky got out of the car and stood for a moment staring at the façade, at the windows and the brickwork in its shades of dried blood and baked clay.

'What is it?' Damon asked.

'Nothing. It just seems such an unlikely place for those Panicks to live in. I'd expect a nice big seaside bungalow at Rustington.'

Dressed up for Sunday, Bob in a dark and shiny suit, Patsy in a flowered silk tent, the Panicks had been at table. Perhaps they always were and when they got up it was only for the clearing away of one meal and to begin the preparation of the next. Patsy carried a large white linen napkin to the door with her and was still wiping her mouth when she opened it. Once more she lumbered ahead of them down the passage towards the kitchen. The smell today was of a breakfast, the kind seaside cafés call a 'full English breakfast', served almost late enough to be brunch, but Panicks no doubt made their own gastronomic rules. At the table, opposite Bob Panick, sat the woman called Freya, Elf, tree-house-building expert and recent resident of the Elder Ditches camp.

She made a strange contrast with her hosts, for she was as thin as they were fat and dressed as unconventionally as they were formal. Face and hands were an unhealthy waxen white but what the rest of her was like it was impossible to tell. She was swathed from head to foot in something like a very old faded sari, frayed and tattered, which, bundled round her though it was, still provided no illusion of adding bulk to her emaciated shape. But she was eating as heartily as the Panicks. In front of her was a plateful of bacon, scrambled eggs, fried bread, fried sausages, fried mushrooms, tomatoes and potato crisps, identical to those set before Bob and Patsy.

She showed no sign of alarm at their entry, unless giving Damon Slesar a long assessing glance was the result of fear. More likely she fancied him, as Nicky said to him afterwards. Patsy said she was sure they wouldn't mind if she went back to her meal and wasn't it funny the police always seemed to call while they were eating?

'Hungry, I dare say,' said Bob with his mouth full. 'Give them something to keep the pangs away. There's a nice bit of ham from last night and if they don't mind carving it themselves, so as not to interfere with your meal *again*, Patsy, that would go down a treat with some of that granary loaf and Branston pickle.'

'Nothing for us, thank you,' said Nicky.

Damon said, in a way she thought uncalled-for, that it was very kind of them, and then he redeemed himself by asking Freya if she was a friend of the Panicks.

Patsy, helping herself to more bacon from the pan, answered for her. 'She is *now*. I hope anyone who comes here and enjoys our hospitality can be termed a friend, don't you, Bob?'

'You're right there, Patsy. Is there another sausage going?'

'Of course there is. And give Freya one. As a matter of fact, Freya is Brendan's friend. A special friend, is that right, Freya?' The woman's tiny eyes twinkled deep in the piled flesh, like lights at the ends of tunnels. 'Brendan brought her here last evening, just had a quick bite and then had to be on his way.'

Nicky remembered Mrs Panick's undertaking to let her know if and when Brendan Royall turned up. She had been surprised by that promise and wasn't surprised it hadn't been honoured. 'On his way where?' she said.

The woman called Freya reacted as if her patience, sorely tried for the past ten minutes, had come to breaking point. She threw down knife and fork, sending a splatter of fat to strike the centre of the napkin that was tucked inside Bob Panick's shirt collar. 'Why can't you leave him alone? What's he done? Nothing. Do you know what a visitor from Outer Space would think if she came to this planet? She'd think you were all psychotic. Not only do you fuck up the whole planet, but you punish people who try to stop it being fucked.'

Bob Panick shook his head almost sorrowfully and helped himself to bread.

His wife said conversationally to no one in particular, 'That's what they mean on the TV when they say the next programme contains strong language. Have you noticed that?' She smiled, eyes twinkling, at Damon Slesar. 'I always take it as a sign to come out here and get us a cup of tea and a packet of bikkies. Brendan,' she said to Nicky, 'has just popped over to the bypass site, dear.'

'Why do you have to tell them that?' shouted Freya. 'What's your motive, that's what I'd like to know? You don't have to talk to them, you know. You've done nothing. Brendan's done nothing. Brendan never talks to them, he doesn't speak, he just stays silent, you want to take a leaf out of his book. Why d'you let them fuck you over? Brendan wouldn't say a word to them, he wouldn't utter.'

'So where is Brendan now?' This was Nicky, being patient.

'Something about going to have a look at a – what was it, Bob?'

Bob Panick considered, rubbed his forehead. 'Folks from Europe, that Common Market, some environment they're making. He's gone in the Winnebago.'

The environmental assessment. Yes, Brendan Royall would want to take a first-hand view of that, would probably photograph the proceedings, having parked at Goland Farm.

The meadows here were steep hillsides on which sheep grazed, the hedges tight and dark-green and the woods clustering, and the sudden sight of a field packed with cars, vans and trailers, few of them in pristine condition and most downright shabby, jarred the imagination. The farmhouse that they expected to be a picturesque half-timbered building looked instead like a converted chapel.

Such conversions had become quite common in the south of England as congregations grew smaller. They provided large, comfortable dwelling houses, if you didn't mind church windows and what Wexford called an 'odour of sanctity'. This one, called Goland Farm, was of red brick with a grey slate roof and a lot of unsuitable window-boxes. Any of its shabby outbuildings might have been the original farmhouse, wedged now between tall, uncompromising silos.

Damon parked by the gate, they walked in among the tree people's cars and there they found Barry Vine contemplating an empty Winnebago.

A fax had arrived from the Neath police, a Chief Inspector Gwenlian Dean. Crowds were gathering for the SPECIES conference, but so far everything was proceeding in orderly fashion. The rally was to be conducted in the open, a good many delegates had arrived in caravans or with tents, but the hierarchy were staying in an hotel where the AGM would take place on the following morning. Gary and Quilla had not yet arrived or had not been located. Gwenlian Dean would be in touch again as soon as she had anything to report.

Wexford went into the old gym to assist the Chief Constable at the press conference. They photographed him as he walked in and he wasn't sorry. Anything to replace that beer tankard picture that constantly reared up to haunt him.

Montague Ryder gave a reasonable, measured and civilised explanation of what had happened and what was being done.

'You must have some idea where they are.' This was a stiletto-eyed young woman with long blonde hair. 'After all this time you must have some clue.'

'We have a good many ideas.' Wexford tried to speak calmly, to follow the Chief Constable's example. 'It must be obvious that we can't disclose any of these ideas at present.'

'Are they in the London area or somewhere in the south of England?'

'I can't answer that.'

And the inevitable question that maddened him, asked this time by a fat reporter, male, in a grey suit and with shoulder-length shaggy grey hair. 'How come it was your wife they let go?'

Ryder answered for him, simply, 'We don't know.'

'Yeah, well, they must have had a reason. Was it they found out she was your wife? D'you reckon they were scared to hold on to her? She wasn't ill, was she? I mean, not a diabetic, not someone takes regular medication?'

'Oh, no,' said Wexford, calm again. 'Nothing like that. Nothing at all.'

Burden had Christine Colville in his office, believing correctly that if she saw the inside of an interview room she would send at once for a lawyer. She was less aggressive and superior with him than she had been with DS Cook and seemed more than willing to give him Conrad Tarling's history.

'You an anthropologist, are you, Miss Colville?'

She gave him a long look, the kind usually called withering. 'I'm an actress. That doesn't mean I have to be ignorant about everything but dramatic art.'

He nodded. 'Resting, I presume?'

'You do presume. I'm not resting, as a matter of fact. Apart from taking part in this protest *with my friends* I'm acting in Jeffrey Godwin's play at the Weir Theatre.'

It came back to him. Wexford had mentioned it. A play about the bypass, the environment, the activists. What was it called? He wasn't going to ask her. Ah, yes, *Extinction*.

'Have a big part, do you?'

'The female lead.'

The only love affair of his life – it had happened between the death of his first wife and his second marriage – had been with an actress. But she had been beautiful, a white-bodied, red-headed woman with a strawberry mouth and grape-green eyes. Not at all like this small, compact creature, short and sturdy with a round brown face and dark, wiry hair, cut to within an inch of her scalp.

'You were telling me about the King of the Wood.'

'From which you distracted me,' she said, quick as a flash. 'Conrad's family live in Wiltshire. Sometimes when he goes to see them he walks. It's eighty miles from here but he walks. People used to do that a hundred years ago, they used to walk huge distances but no one does now. Only Conrad.'

'He's got a car,' said Burden sceptically.

'He hardly ever uses it. Mostly he lends it to others. Conrad's a sort of saint, you know.'

King, god, leader, and now saint. 'Right. Go on.'

'His brother Colum's in a wheelchair. He'll never walk again. He gave his strength and his *mobility* for the cause of animals. And the other brother Craig's in prison for his own part in the struggle.'

'Sure,' said Burden. 'He was going to blow up a couple of hundred innocent people.'

'People are never innocent.' In her words and her look he recognised the authentic voice of fanaticism. 'Only animals are innocent. Guilt is exclusively the attribute of mankind.' She tapped her fist on his desk. 'Conrad has never had a job,' she said, as if speaking of some spectacular achievement and, slightly amending what she had said, 'He has never been gainfully employed. But he survives by his own efforts.'

'Like Gary Wilson and Quilla Rice.'

'No, not like them. He isn't in the least like *them*.' Christine Colville used an expression he had thought long dead and gone. 'They are very small fry. Conrad is above the sort of odd jobs they do. His family are very poor, they are aristocratic but poor. His followers keep him.'

'What, the other tree people? What money do they have?'

'Not much,' she said. 'It mounts up if everyone contributes.'

'I'll bet.' Burden repressed what he had been going to say, that Tarling had a nice little earner going. 'Does he have contacts round here?'

She misunderstood him or affected to do so. 'Everyone in the woods knows the King.'

'Maybe I'll come and see your play,' he said and escorted her out.

A throng of reporters and photographers rushed her. Burden went back into the old gym where Wexford had sent out for lunch from the new Thai takeaway. He drank from the can that had come with the green curry and coconut, and made a face. Pushing it away he said, 'What is this stuff?'

'It would seem to be alcoholic lemonade.'

'God.' Burden read the label. 'Whose idea was that? There's probably some law or rule about not bringing alcohol on to these premises.

'It tastes disgusting anyway. If I drink alcohol I want it to taste like alcohol, I want to feel the kick, not lemonade with a mystery sting in its tail. It'll be alcoholic milk next.'

Wexford glanced out of the window. He wouldn't have put it past some wily cameraman to be lurking out there, hoping for a pot shot of him holding a drinks can, *any* sort of drinks can. But there was no one in the car park. 'Mike,' he said, looking at his watch, 'it's gone two. We haven't heard a word from Sacred Globe since five yesterday. I don't understand it, it doesn't add up. It must appear to them, much as I regret it, as if we're simply yielding to their demands. Firstly by calling a halt to work on the bypass, secondly by releasing the story to the press when they asked us to. The fact that we were going to release it at that particular time anyway is neither here nor there. They don't know that. So, why, if it seems as if everything is going the way they want it, don't they take advantage of their apparently strong position and come right back with their final demand?'

'I don't know. I don't understand it either.'

'I'm going to see how Dora got on under hypnosis.'

# 17

As soon as he saw him Burden recognised Brendan Royall. He didn't know he knew him but when he was brought into the police station, into Interview Room One, Burden remembered him from six or seven years back. It had been one afternoon when he had gone to meet Jenny from Kingsmarkham Comprehensive. Royall was standing on the school steps, on the top just outside the entrance, holding forth to a group of his contemporaries who surrounded him.

He had been only sixteen then, a tallish, weedy boy with a light aureole of Harpo Marx hair. It was the eyes that Burden remembered. They were astonishingly dark, as if the hair must be dyed, and burning bright, the eyes of the fanatic, under thick, sprouting eyebrows like animal fur. And the voice was memorable too, harsh, haranguing, with an ugly flat accent, the vowels hollow, the ends of words gabbled.

The years between had brought about little change in his appearance. The hair was rather darker and longer than Burden recalled but the eyes were still fierce and with that crazy brightness, the eyebrows still like a strip of rabbit skin. How he had been dressed in those days Burden had forgotten but on this Monday afternoon Royall was dressed from head to foot in green-and-brown camouflage. In woodland he might have melted into the background, which perhaps was the idea. As to the voice, Burden couldn't tell if it had changed or not, for Royall declined to open his mouth.

He had brought his lawyer with him. Or this solicitor, not a local man, summoned on the Winnebago's phone, had appeared on the police station steps coincidentally with Royall's own arrival. He had very little to do and could have given his client no better code of conduct than that adopted by Royall without his advice.

The man, who looked as if about to take part in some jungle assault course, sat silent and grave on one side of the table, his solicitor next to him. Even while he was starting the recorder, announcing that the interviewee and his lawyer were present, along with DI Burden and DC Fancourt, Burden knew it was a farce. The solicitor could barely conceal his smiles.

Next door, in Interview Room Two, Nicky Weaver with Ted Hennessy confronted Conrad Tarling, the King of the Wood. His solicitor had taken longer in arriving and Tarling had waited there for nearly an hour before the young woman called India Walton turned up.

Tarling sat in his chair in his robes, the long, full sleeves of his outer garment ostentatiously turned back to show his bare smooth arms, heavily laden with silver and copper bracelets chased in Celtic patterns. He too at first was silent, still as stone, his eyes fixed on the small, high window as if a fascinating scene could be discerned through it instead of the brick wall of the Magistrates' Court.

Wexford was tempted to put his head round the door, but the Codes of Practice for the Police and Criminal Evidence Act prohibit the interruption of interviews in all but exceptional circumstances. A senior officer's curiosity would hardly fall into this category so he had to content himself with a glance through the tiny interior window. The sight he saw reminded him of a story he had heard in his schooldays in the Latin lesson of those old Roman statesmen who went to into the Senate when they heard the Goths were coming and sat marble-like and unmoving on their thrones. Taking them for statues, the Goths prodded and poked them until one rose up and struck back, whereupon all were slain. Wexford, tired and frustrated, would have liked to prod Tarling into life, into some reaction, but knew how untenable such a course must be.

DC Lowry had just told him that the white Mercedes whose number Nicky Weaver had taken had been found abandoned on the Stowerton industrial estate. A stolen car, of course, dumped outside a disused factory building where there were no witnesses, its windscreen smashed and its tyres deflated.

Now Lowry came up to him again and said, 'Can I have a word, sir?'

The man looked like a black Marlon Brando, Wexford thought, but Brando in his *Streetcar Named Desire* days. 'Yes, what is it?'

'Your wife mentions a man who always wore gloves. It occurred to me he might have done that because his hands were like mine.' Lowry held up his long-fingered narrow hands, the colour of a plum on which the bloom still lingers. 'I mean because he was black.'

'Good thinking,' Wexford said and he went back to Dora, who was in the old gym listening to her own voice speaking as if she had never heard it before.

Tarling became as vociferous as Royall was silent. In spite of India Walton's discreet suggestions that he had no need to answer this or that, that he was not obliged to respond to that question and that this one was in the circumstances outrageous, Tarling talked. He held forth. Not that he answered any questions or even appeared to have heard them. He simply talked as if he was making an inflammatory political speech, even as if there was no interrogator present but only a silent, receptive audience.

He talked about his brother Craig, his high principles, his love of animals and his equating of all animals from the humblest to the greatest with mankind. Therefore, if animals could be used in vivisection, human beings could, with equal justification, be blown up. In his eyes, the only difference was that the human beings died a quicker death. He talked of the injustice of Craig Tarling's fate, his courage and undaunted demeanour in prison. When he had finished with his older brother's biography he talked about his younger brother who had been seriously injured under the wheels of a lorry transporting live sheep to Brightlingsea. He paused quite courteously for Nicky to question him and responded by talking about himself, his history, his devotion to the English countryside and what he called the 'restoration of Nature'.

'It's particularly interesting,' he said, 'that all three of us children of bourgeois conservative parents, all the products of distinguished public schools and the two great universities, have each committed his life to a different branch of the protection of created things: my brother Craig to ill-used small mammals, my brother Colum to the beasts of the field and myself to the whole of the natural world. You may well ask yourselves why this has happened . . .'

'I might ask *you* if the name Sacred Globe was your personal invention, Mr Tarling,' Nicky said. 'It's very much in accord with the sort of thing you've been telling us. After all, you call yourself the King of the Sacred Grove.'

'. . . and what was the nature of the inspiration that came to us individually to reject what is known in our society as a "normal" life and take up the despised cause of the vulnerable, the tender, the fragile, without whom, however, life as we know it on this planet must face hideous destruction . . .'

Her face was different. No doubt it would later revert to normal but at the moment her expression was not only bemused, it was if he were seeing her face slightly out of focus, a little blurred, as if she had lost control of it and the features had become untidy. She was like someone asleep whose eyes were nevertheless open, a sleepwalker who isn't walking.

Karen must have left her for a moment, perhaps to get tea. She hadn't seen him. The voice which spoke, her own voice, dwindled and faded away and there was silence. He saw her reach up to switch off the device but she didn't know how to do this. She shrugged, turned, saw him.

'Dora,' he said.

At once she was herself again. She smiled at him radiantly and said, 'It's amazing, Reg. I not only didn't know I knew all that, I didn't know I'd said it. Not till it was played back. And yet my voice sounds just like it always does.'

'I'm glad you weren't upset.'

'Not at all, not a bit. Dr Rowland was very nice. He just asked me to make myself comfortable and relax as much as I could. Then he said all that stuff you read about hypnotists saying, only it was very reassuring and not a bit mumbo-jumbo-ish. I thought it would be like the dentist when they give you that drug that doesn't send you to sleep but puts you into a sort of half-doze and when the tooth's out or the root canal's done or whatever, it seems as if only a moment has passed. But it wasn't. It was like a dream. Yes, like a dream, the kind you don't know you're dreaming. And then the tape was played back to me and I found I'd said all that about the blue thing . . .'

'The what?'

'I remember now, of course I do. But I don't think I would have if I hadn't been hypnotised. I could tell you all of it now or you could listen to the tape. What would you like?'

'Both,' he said, 'but I can't now. I've got to go on television.'

The camera crews were already coming in. A trestle table was set up for them at one end of the room. The Chief Constable sat in the

782

middle with Wexford on his left, Audrey Barker on his right, Andrew Struther next to her and Clare Cox with Hassy Masood on Wexford's left.

The hostage families had been instructed to say nothing in the nature of a plea to Sacred Globe, to say nothing at all if possible, just to be there.

As it turned out, Andrew Struther answered for all of them, and as he was probably the most articulate, this was just as well. In answer to the inevitable question he said, 'We're leaving this to the police to handle, the best and only possible thing to do in the circumstances. This isn't the time or the place for airing the grief and anxiety we all feel. All we can do is wait and leave it to the experts.'

Audrey Barker began to cry. It was good television, but it didn't help the determined and businesslike atmosphere Wexford had hoped to create. Someone asked if it was true Chief Inspector Wexford's wife had originally been among the hostages and if so, why was she released? The scene was cut before anyone answered.

The phones that had quietened during the past few hours began ringing immediately the next news item came on. A man in Liverpool had seen Roxane Masood going into a cinema with a dark man, probably an Indian. A Mr and Mrs Struther had just left a Little Chef restaurant on the A12 near Chelmsford. Were the police aware that a huge conservationists' rally, master-minded by Sacred Globe, was about to take place near Glencastle Forest?

By coincidence, another fax had arrived from Gwenlian Dean in Wales. Gary Wilson and Quilla Rice had arrived at the SPECIES rally and their camping place noted by her officers. Did Wexford wish her to have them questioned? He sent back a message to the effect that he was anxious to know their movements after his encounter with them at Framhurst, when they had left for Glencastle and what connection they had with Conrad Tarling.

Awaiting him was a report on the white Mercedes L570 LOO. It was the property of a William Pugh, of Swansea, and had been stolen three weeks before from outside a house in Ventnor, Isle of Wight, where the Pughs were spending their summer holiday. Forensic work was proceeding on the car's interior.

'I'm going to listen to my wife's hypnosis tape now,' said Wexford, 'and then I'm going home to hear it all over again from her own lips.'

Barry Vine, pale and tired, said, 'I don't think you are, sir. I don't think you will when you hear.'

783

'Hear what?'

'A body's been found. On that bit of waste ground where Contemporary Cars park. It's in a sleeping bag dumped up against the fence ...'

# 18

The barren piece of waste ground where the Railway Arms had once
stood was bounded by chain-link fencing, up against which grew the
kind of trees and bushes always found on sites of this sort, elders and
brambles and the suckers from felled sycamores. Nettles abounded,
at this time of the year waist-high. On the wall of the bus station on
the right-hand side graffiti faced faded lettering on the opposite
building. Long before the aromatherapist and the photo-copiers and
hairdresser came, but not before the shoe repairer, the words Cobbler
and Bootmaker had been printed on the pale brickwork. The graffiti
consisted of the single rubric, Gazza, and the paint used had run
from the brush in long red drips.

Around Contemporary Cars' trailer the turf had become a dusty
hayfield, sprawled with litter. Visitors to the pub and the discount
store discarded their cigarette packets and crisp bags over the fence.
The sleeping bag, camouflage-patterned, was in the farthest corner
among the nettles, half under the brambles. The zip which fastened it
along the whole length of the right-side had been opened about
eighteen inches to disclose what appeared at first to be only a mass of
black silky hair.

'I didn't undo the zip,' Peter Samuels said, anticipating censure
that never came. 'I knew better than that. I could see what it was, I
could see that hair, without touching it.'

'I undid it,' Burden said. 'Her knees have been bent to get the
whole of her inside that bag. When did you find her?'

'Half an hour ago. It was a bit after six. I'd been in there watching
you on the telly and I came out to my car, looked over here and I
saw. I don't know what made me look, I just glanced up and saw it: a
brown-and-green sleeping bag. I reckoned someone had just dumped

it. You'd be surprised the rubbish people unload here. I saw the hair, I thought it was an animal at first . . .'

'All right, Mr Samuels. Thank you. If you'd like to wait in the trailer we'll come and have a word with you in a moment.'

As soon as he had arrived at the site Wexford had felt a sinking of the heart, a dread and apprehension he didn't want justified, that he would have liked to run away from. There was, of course, no running away and no help. A glance at Burden's face had been enough anyway, his pale, cold face and the set mouth. Vine said nothing and Karen said nothing. They turned and watched Peter Samuels walking back across the scrubby grass and then they looked at Wexford. He trod heavily across the nettles to the other side of the sleeping bag, closed his eyes, looked.

The face, of which only the left profile was visible, was badly bruised and with death the bruise colours had become livid, yellowish, green and brown. But the features were unmistakable and he thought of a portrait, a tranquil, gentle, beautiful face and clear, dark eyes. 'It's Roxane Masood,' he said.

Dr Mavrikiev, the pathologist, took no more than fifteen minutes to get there. The photographer arrived at the same time with Archbold, the Scene-of-Crimes officer. Mavrikiev undid the zip to its fullest extent and knelt down in front of the body. It was now possible to see that what Burden had guessed was true and the girl's legs had been bent to an angle of ninety degrees. The body was dressed in black hipster trousers, a red T-shirt and red velvet jacket. A hand, waxen yet delicate as ivory, slid off her thigh as the pathologist gently turned her over.

Wexford had come if not to like, to have a certain respect for Mavrikiev. He was a young man, of Baltic or Ukrainian descent, very fair with pale eyes like crystal quartz, an unpredictable creature, rude or charming according to his mood. Unlike his seniors, particularly Sir Hilary Tremlett, he never indulged his wit at the expense of the corpse, never talked about the 'dead meat' or speculated unkindly as to how the body might have looked in life. But it was impossible to tell what he was thinking, or to read anything in the cold face that might have been carved out of birch wood it was so immobile.

'She's been dead for at least two days,' he said. 'Maybe longer. I will, of course, be able to be more accurate about that later on. But a time-honoured method of assessing the time of death will show you

786

that, for rigor mortis has come on, established itself and worn off again. Note the limpness of that hand. If it's of any help to you at this stage' – he looked up at Wexford – 'I'd very approximately put the time of death as late Saturday afternoon.

'Now when she was brought here I can't tell you but she must have been put in that bag fairly soon after her death because once rigor was established it would have been impossible to bend the legs into that position without breaking the knees. Incidentally, the legs *are* broken but not in aid of getting them into the bag. So you can calculate that the body was placed into the bag on Saturday evening, at any rate before midnight on Saturday.'

'And the cause of death?' said Wexford.

'You're never satisfied, are you? You want everything and you want it at once. I've told you before, I'm not a magician. She's obviously been the victim of a violent attack or attacks. Look at her head and face. As to the *cause* of death, you can see for yourself she hasn't been shot or stabbed and there's been no ligature round her neck.' Sir Hilary would have made jokes about poisoning at this stage but Mavrikiev simply got to his feet without even a shake of the head or rueful smile. 'You can do whatever you have to do and take her away. I'll do the post-mortem tomorrow, nine a.m. sharp.'

Photographs were taken. Archbold went about measuring things and got badly stung by nettles. Wexford, free to touch the inside of the bag now, began to search it, felt the padded cover, slid his hand under the body.

'What are you looking for?' Burden asked.

'A note. A message.' Wexford stood up. 'There's nothing. I don't understand this, Mike. Why? Why do this, any of it, why this girl, why *now*?'

'I don't know.'

Peter Samuels was repeating his story of his discovery of the body when Wexford went into the trailer. 'How d'you know it hadn't been there all day?' he asked.

'What, all day since the morning? No, it couldn't have been, no way.'

'Why not? Did you go over to that corner? Did you look? Did any of you? You were busy, no doubt, with your fares, in and out. Did you even look?'

'If you put it like that, well, no. I don't reckon we did. Well; *I* didn't. I can't speak for the rest of them.'

'So it could have been put there on the previous night? It could have been put there on Sunday night?'

'No. No way. Well, come to think of it, I suppose it could, I mean, I doubt it, I doubt it very much, but it *could*.'

A mounting anger was making Wexford's head swim. Not with Samuels. Samuels was no one, of no account. The rage that filled his head and drummed in his brain was with Sacred Globe. He found himself feeling above all a bitter resentment. This, when everything must seem to them to be going their way, when, however politic and previously planned, events must seem to them to be in compliance with their demands . . .

And now no more demands, no promised 'negotiation', not even an impudent thanks for an apparent meeting of ultimata. A murder instead. But he thought sickeningly how often in the history of abductions that happened, just that. All was going well, all seemed to be progressing both from the point of view of the hostages and the hostage takers – and then a hostage murdered, her body sent home, presented to those who searched for her.

At least they hadn't returned the poor child to her mother. It was a measure of the kind of life he led and the sort of people he encountered, he thought, that his imagination could conceive of such a thing. But it reminded him of what he had to do now. He would do it and he would do it himself.

No message from Sacred Globe had come in on the police phones, though there had been plenty of the other sort, from those deluded or fake witnesses claiming to have seen the hostages in far-flung cities or to live next door to where they were held. The screens he glanced at as he passed carried list upon list of names, addresses, descriptions, offences committed, of everyone closely or remotely connected with nature, wildlife and animal protest. Cross-references, possible connections, records of interviews. He forgot, briefly, his sympathy with so many of these people, their aims, their laudable desires, their ideal, fading world, and lost everything in a red tide of anger. Breathing deeply, calming his racing heart, he found a voice with which to make a phone call. The Posthouse Hotel. Mr Hassan Masood, please.

'Mr Masood is in the dining-room. Would you like me to page him?'

As so often happens when contact is made with a reasonable, polite person from what seems another world, anger was quenched.

Wexford thought of the horror of fetching the man from his dinner, from his wife and sons perhaps . . .

'No, thank you.' He would go himself. He phoned his home, got his daughter Sylvia.

'Dad, what on earth happened to you? Mother's been waiting for you for hours.'

He said he had been delayed, knowing it wasn't Dora but she making the fuss, put the phone down softly on her expostulations. The media, yes. They could wait till tomorrow, even till late tomorrow. He drove out to the Posthouse, walked into the pine-and-glass and tweed-carpeted interior and there the first person he saw was Clare Cox. It hadn't occurred to him she might be there too. It never crossed his mind. She was back in her floor-length dress, a shawl round her shoulders, her greying, tawny hair flopping from its combs. Masood and she had their backs to him. They were side by side at the reception desk, ordering, as he later discovered, a taxi to take her home.

'I had to bring her here,' Masood said when he saw who it was. 'Reporters, photographers, they were all over her house and garden. One of them followed us but I shut her up in my room and the hotel kept them out. This is an excellent hotel, I recommend it.' He beamed at the receptionist and the receptionist simpered back. 'I think maybe it's safe to go home now – what do you think?'

It seemed not to have occurred to him to see Wexford in his angel-of-death role. But Clare Cox, herself rather resembling a Fury or a Fate with her dishevelled hair and trailing clothes, went white in the face and came up to him with outstretched hands. 'What is it? Why are you here?'

Not the mother if he could help it. He made that a rule. 'I'd like you to come back into Kingsmarkham with me, Mr Masood, if you would.' The euphemisms, the circumlocutions! But what else at this moment? 'There's been a . . . development.'

'What kind of a development?' She clutched at his sleeve. 'What's happened?'

'Miss Cox, I think this is probably your taxi that has just arrived outside. If you would like to go home in it I promise you Mr Masood and I will come straight to you if need be.' It sounded as if he was promising hope, relief, yet his voice had been grave. 'I can tell you no more at present, Miss Cox. If you will just do as I ask.'

The taxi wasn't from Contemporary Cars but All the Sixes. He felt an obscure relief. Immediately it was out of sight Masood began asking about this 'development'. They got into Wexford's car and Wexford stalled for a while, but when they were nearly there he told him. A sanitised version. The sleeping bag, the waste ground, the bent legs weren't mentioned. He would see the bruising for himself and nothing could help that.

There had never been any real doubt. Masood looked at the beautiful, discoloured face, made a small sound, nodded, turned away.

Wexford thought that if it had been one of his daughters, so foully dead, beaten in the face before her death, he would have rounded on this policeman, in his grief and misery yelled at him, perhaps seized him by the shoulders, shouted into his face, Why? Why have you allowed this?

Masood stood meek, with head bent. Barry Vine, who was with them, offered him tea. Would he like to sit down?

'No. No, thank you.' He looked up, turning his head in a curious sideways manner as if his neck hurt him. 'I don't understand this.'

'I don't understand it either,' said Wexford.

He remembered then that he had told Burden he thought Sacred Globe were getting cold feet, Sacred Globe were at a loss with no notion how to proceed ... Well, they had proceeded.

'I have sent my wife and sons home to London,' Masood said in a calm, almost conversational tone. 'I am glad now. It was just as well.' He cleared his throat. 'My duty now will be to Roxane's mother. You will come with me?'

'Of course. If you wish it.'

In the car, on the way to Pomfret, Masood said, 'If anyone had told me my daughter would die young I can think of many things I might have said but not what I *feel* now. It is the waste I feel. So much beauty, so talented. Such a waste.'

Remembering what Dora had told him, Wexford wanted to say what is sometimes said to the parents of dead soldiers, that Roxane had surely died bravely. But he lacked the heart for it, he doubted if he would be able to speak the words.

Clare Cox had been drinking since she got home. A reek of whisky came from her. If it had been drunk to save her, to anaesthetise her against what she feared was coming, it was ineffective. Standing close to her, holding her hand, Masood told her, and there was no waiting for the news to sink in, for shock to pass, for a stunning to yield to grief. Her screams began at once, like a chemical reaction, as sharp and insistent as a starved baby crying for the pain of hunger to go away.

'Go home, Reg,' the Chief Constable said on the phone. He was in bed himself. He too had had a long day. 'Go home. There's nothing more you can do. It's ten-past eleven.'

'The press have got it, sir.'

'Have they now. How did that happen?'

'I wish I knew,' Wexford said.

Dora was asleep. He was glad, because it meant he didn't have to explain. The thought of telling her Roxane was dead horrified him almost as much as being with Clare Cox had done. The woman's screams still rang in his ears. Yet Hassy Masood had passed on the news of his daughter's death to the media. In spite of what he had said to the Chief Constable, Wexford was sure of it. Masood had told the news to Roxane's mother – had done his best, no doubt, to calm her – and then told the media his daughter was dead. Well, Masood had other children, a second family, a new life, and to him Roxane had been the grateful recipient of his largess and someone to take occasionally to expensive restaurants. Her death was no more than the waste of her beauty, looks that in her case meant capital. Because Dora was there beside him, he slept like the dead. It took the alarm to wake him and it woke her first.

'I'll go down,' he said quickly, seeing her already up and in her dressing-gown.

He had to get to the papers first. There it was, all over the front pages: HOSTAGE MODEL FOUND DEAD, ROXANE THE FIRST TO DIE, ROXANE MURDERED, A FATHER'S GRIEF . . . So he had been right. He went back upstairs and told Dora.

At first she refused to believe him. It was too much. There was no *reason*. With tears running down her face, she said, 'What did they do to her?'

'Don't know yet. I have to go in a minute. I'm sorry but I must. I have to be at the post-mortem.'

'She was too brave,' Dora said.

'Very likely.'

'She said goodbye to me, she said, "Goodbye, Dora".'

Dora turned her face into the pillow and sobbed bitterly. He kissed her. He didn't want to leave her but he had to.

Tuesday. One week since the hostages were taken. The press reminded him of that as they crowded him on his way into the mortuary.

'Two down, three to go,' one of them said.

'How did you get your wife out, Chief Inspector?' asked a girl from a television news programme.

Mavrikiev was already there. 'Good-morning, good-morning. How are you today? Mr Vine is about somewhere. Shall we get started?'

They all got into green rubber gowns and put on gauze masks. This was Barry Vine's first time and though not particularly squeamish when faced with a dead body, this, Wexford thought, might be different. The sound of the saw got to people, that and the smell, more often than the sight of organs being removed.

Now that the body was exposed, Wexford saw what he hadn't seen the night before. The right side of the head was shallowly stove in, the hair matted with dark clotted blood. It seemed to him, though, that the facial bruising was less marked, less violently coloured, appearing as yellowish-green streaks and blotches on the waxen skin.

Mavrikiev worked swiftly and always in silence. While other pathologists might extract an organ, hold it up and comment on some peculiarity in its structure or progress of its deterioration, he proceeded coolly, speechlessly and deadpan. If Barry Vine had turned pale it wasn't obvious to Wexford. The mask and green cap hid so much, but after a few moments and a muffled 'Excuse me' he left the room with one gloved hand over his mouth.

Breaking his rule, Mavrikiev gave a small, tight laugh and said, 'A case of the eye being stronger than the stomach.'

He worked on, picking something out of the head wound with tweezers. Plastic containers now held the stomach, lungs, part of the brain and whatever it was he had picked from the wound. He finished, stripped off his gloves and came across the room to where Wexford had retreated. 'I'll stick to what I said about the time of death. Saturday afternoon.'

'I suppose I can ask my other question now?'

'What did she die of? That blow to the head. You don't need any

792

medical degrees to see that. Skull's fractured, brain severely damaged. I won't go into a lot of technical stuff, it'll be in the report.'

'You mean someone struck her a violent blow to the head? With what? Can you say?'

Mavrikiev slowly shook his head. He handed Wexford one of the containers. It held a dozen or so small stones, some black with blood. 'If someone struck her he must have hit her with a gravel path. I picked these out of the wound. I don't think she was hit, I think she *fell*. I think she fell from a height on to a gravel path.'

Barry Vine came back into the room, looking sheepish. He kept his eyes averted from the slab on which the body, now neatly covered in plastic sheeting, lay. Wexford ignored him.

'Fell? Or was pushed or thrown?'

'For God's sake, you're at it again. I'm not a magician, how many times do I have to tell you? I don't know. If you expect a great handprint in the middle of her back, that kind of thing doesn't happen.'

'You could tell if she'd struggled,' said Wexford coldly.

'Fingernails full of flesh and blood, eh? There was none of that. If someone did it he'd likely have been left-handed but there was no someone. Her right arm is broken, two of her ribs are broken, her left leg is broken in two places and her right in one. The body's bruised down the right side. I think she fell from a height, perhaps as much as thirty feet, and she fell on to her right side.

'And that's it for the time being, gentlemen. I'll thank you for your attention' – here a supercilious glance at Barry Vine – 'and be off home to my brunch.'

Vine nodded to him.

'Feeling better?' asked Wexford breezily. 'It's just occurred to me that Brendan Royall, when we saw him, was dressed from head to foot in camouflage. Can it be coincidence?'

# 19

Stanley Trotter was still in bed in Stowerton, in the two-roomed flat in Peacock Street, when Burden called on him early on Tuesday morning. One of the Sayem brothers who kept the grocery market downstairs let him in, took him up and pounded on Trotter's door. Perhaps he bore a grudge against the upstairs tenant for something or other, for when Trotter came to the door in pyjama bottoms and dirty vest, Ghulam Sayem smiled smugly to himself. His face had worn much the same expression when Burden announced himself as a police officer.

It was quite a warm day, sultry and windless, but Trotter's windows were tight shut. The room smelt unpleasant. It was exactly what Burden had expected and he analysed the smell as compounded of sweat, urine, Malaysian takeaway and mould, the kind that forms on damp towels that are left about unwashed. Somewhat vain of his appearance and careful of his clothes, he didn't like sitting on the greasy chair with the cigarette burns on its arms, but he hadn't much choice. He dusted it with a tissue he had in his pocket.

Trotter watched him. 'I don't know what you think you've come for,' he said.

'Seen a paper this morning, have you? Seen the telly? Listened to the radio?'

'No, I haven't. Why would I? I was asleep.'

'You're not interested then? You don't want to know what I'm on about?'

Trotter didn't say anything. He rooted about in the pockets of a garment lying across the bed, found cigarettes and lit one. It brought on a liquid, spluttering spasm of coughing.

'You should put yourself down for a heart-lung transplant,

Trotter,' said Burden. 'They tell me the waiting list's as long as your arm.' He coughed himself. It was infectious. 'How long were you going to leave the body there?' he snapped.

'What body?'

'How long were you going to leave the sleeping bag there, Trotter? Or were you going to find it yourself? Was that the idea?'

'I'm not saying anything to you without my lawyer,' said Trotter. He put the cigarette down on a saucer, but without stubbing it out, got into bed and pulled the clothes over his head.

The sleeping bag had gone off to the forensic science lab at Myringham. It was made by a company called Outdoors and according to its label manufactured from a fabric that was part polyester, part cotton and part lycra, lined with nylon and thinly filled with polyester fibre.

Meanwhile, an examination of the stolen car had yielded a mass of cat hairs, pebbles from a south-coast beach and sand, which in the opinion of the earth and soil expert, was from the Isle of Wight. There wasn't a fingerprint on it anywhere, inside or out.

The car had been stolen from Ventnor, Isle of Wight. But the hostages couldn't be there, Wexford thought. Dora would have known if she had crossed water. Her captors would never have taken the risk of using the ferry and that was the only way to reach the island.

William Pugh, of Gwent Road, Swansea was the owner. Wexford put through a phone call to him and asked if he had a cat. Two cats, in fact, for the hairs were from a Siamese and a black. Pugh said he hadn't but he had a Labrador, which had been in kennels while he and his wife were away, as if Wexford were conducting a survey into pet statistics.

'I suppose you went on the beach, Mr Pugh?'

'We did not. I am seventy-six and my wife is seventy-four.'

'So you couldn't have transferred sand from your shoes to the inside of the car?'

'The car was stolen within three hours of our getting there,' said Pugh.

Another fax had come from Gwenlian Dean in Neath. Gary and Quilla had been interviewed by one of her officers. At first they claimed to know nothing of any meeting with Wexford in Framhurst but when their memories were jogged Quilla realised who was meant and they both talked with apparent frankness about that encounter. Chief Inspector Dean wrote that her officer had no reason to doubt the truth of what they said, that if they had even heard Wexford's name when he gave it to them it had scarcely registered and they had soon forgotten it.

They didn't intend to return to Kingsmarkham for the time being but were going on to north Yorkshire where a protest was being mounted over the proposal to build a housing estate. Only one factor in all this had surprised Inspector Dean and this, contrary to what she had been led to suspect, was Gary's and Quilla's ownership of a car. They had arrived by car and were going to Yorkshire by car, a respectable-looking four-year-old Ford Escort. Had Wexford any further interest in them?

The inquest on Roxane Masood was fixed for the following day and still there had been no message from Sacred Globe. It was as if Sacred Globe had died or disappeared, taking its hostages with it. Wexford found himself constantly looking at his watch, counting up the hours since they had last been in touch, forty, forty-one . . . He phoned Gwenlian Dean, thanked her for her trouble and said he would see Gary and Quilla on their return. By then he hoped, he said stoutly, that he wouldn't *need* to see them.

Meanwhile he had Karen Malahyde keep Brendan Royall under surveillance and Damon Slesar tail the King of the Wood.

Tanya Paine told Vine she had never looked in the direction where the sleeping bag was found. She never did, she never had cause to. They were in the trailer and her phones kept ringing. In the lulls between calls she craned and twisted her neck, leant forward, shifted her chair, in an effort to prove to him that no matter what contortions she had put her body through she couldn't have seen that corner where the sleeping bag was, an area now cordoned off with blue-and-white crime tape.

Vine had never before seen fingernails like hers. He couldn't imagine how they were done. Each one had a design on it like a piece of blue, green and violet paisley-patterned satin. Was it printed or had some artist done it with a very fine brush? Or did you buy transfers, stick them on and lacquer over the top? It was as much as he could do to keep his eyes off those fingernails while Tanya stretched and craned. 'I'm not talking about when you were in here, Ms Paine,' he said. 'But when you arrived and when you left,' and remembering her tastes, 'and when you went out for your chocolate bar and your capuccino.'

'I could have seen it then, I suppose, but I didn't.' She gave him a sideways glance, resentful, cagey. 'And I don't eat things like that any more. I'm trying to lose weight. It was an apple and a Diet Coke.'

No distress over the other girl's violent and shocking death was apparent in her manner. She had seen about it on breakfast television and bought a newspaper on her way to work, the kind of newspaper – it lay between her phones – that carries the maximum of black seventy-two-point headline and the minimum of text. This one's front page said only, MY LOVELY GIRL framing a model agency's photograph of Roxane in a bikini.

'You were a friend of Roxane's, you were at school with her.'

'I was at school with a lot of girls.'

'Yes,' said Vine, 'but this is the one who was abducted and is now dead. It's a bit strange, isn't it? Let me put it like this. First of all the people who abducted her, this Sacred Globe, first of all they choose a car-hire firm where *you* work, and when one of the hostages is dead they return the body to where *you* work. The body of your friend. Bit of a coincidence, wouldn't you say?'

One of her phones rang. She answered it, wrote down a time and a place on her pad. It seemed an inefficient and old-fashioned way of doing things. The design on the ballpoint pen matched her fingernails.

'Bit of a coincidence?' Vine said again.

'I don't know what you mean. You keep saying "my friend". She wasn't my friend. I just knew her.'

'She made a point of booking taxis from here because you were here. She liked a chat on the phone to you.'

'Look,' said Tanya, 'I can tell you why she liked talking to me, it was so as I knew she'd got a rich dad and how she was going to be a model – fat chance, I thought – and that she could afford taxis when others have to get the bus. I thought, for two pins I'd say to you, at least my mum and dad was married and are still together.'

So that was a point of advantage in today's youth meritocracy? Wexford would be interested. No one got married any more, but if your parents were married and *still* married, status was conferred on you.

'You didn't like her?'

Tanya seemed slowly to have realised that it might be unwise to tell a policeman that a victim of violence was personally antipathetic to you. 'I'm not saying that. You're putting words into my mouth.'

'Why do you think her body was put here?'

'How should I know?' Now evidently seemed to her the time to tell an essential truth. 'I'm not a murderer.'

'Have you a boyfriend, Miss Paine?'

He had astonished her. 'What do you want to know that for?'

'If you'd rather not answer . . .'

She watched him write something down, said, 'No, I haven't, since you ask. Not right now.' It was an admission she would infinitely have preferred not to make and she fidgeted uncomfortably, twisting her body and showing him that she did indeed need to lose weight. 'Temporarily, right now, I don't, no.'

Her phone rang.

Neither Leslie Cousins nor Robert Barrett could give Lynn Fancourt any idea of when the sleeping bag containing Roxane Masood's body was brought to the parking area. But while Barrett would only repeat monotonously that he hadn't seen any strange cars about, Cousins was able to state firmly that it hadn't been there at midnight on Saturday when he returned from taking a fare from Kingsmarkham station to Forby.

'How can you be so sure?'

'I went down there. To the back fence.'

'Why? Because you saw something?'

Lynn could tell he didn't want to say. His face had reddened. She remembered the occasional behaviour of her father and her brothers, and marvelled at the curious ways of men who often, even when they have bathrooms or public conveniences not far away . . . 'You went down there for a natural purpose, did you, Mr Cousins? To relieve yourself against the hedge?'

'Yeah, well, you know . . .'

'It was easier in the days when police officers were always male, wasn't it? Less embarrassing.' Lynn gave the rather hard, bright smile she had seen on Karen Malahyde's face. 'You went down to the back fence to relieve yourself and at that time, midnight, there was nothing lying among the nettles under those trees – right?'

'Right,' said Cousins with a sigh of relief.

The bus station might have been a mile away instead of next door, for all anyone working there could have seen. The high, blank brick wall blocked off everything. On the other side the shoe repairer had closed up and gone home at five on Saturday afternoon, the hairdresser at five-thirty and the photo-copiers at the same time. Only the aromatherapist lived on the premises.

The windows of her first-floor flat looked towards the Engine Driver at the front – she had had those double-glazed – and at the back over the comparative peace of the waste ground. She invited Lynn into a strongly scented living-room that obviously also did duty for client consultations. The walls were covered with photographs and highly stylised drawings of flowers and grasses. A much larger photograph was of the aromatherapist herself, apparently thrown into a state of ecstasy by the scent emanating from a flagon she held to her nose.

She told Lynn her name was Lucinda Lee, which sounded unlikely, but the truth was that people did have unlikely names.

'Half the time I get no sleep here at all,' she complained. 'What with the pub at the front and those cars going in and out at the back. They're threatening to put my rent up and when they do I'm going.'

Had she seen anything untoward between Saturday midnight and Sunday evening? To Lynn's astonishment she had.

'They don't usually work that late,' said Lucinda Lee. 'Or maybe I should say that early. I'd just got off to sleep, it was all of one in the morning, and this car came in making an unbelievable noise.'

'What sort of noise?'

'I don't really approve of cars. I mean, they're the biggest agent of pollution of all, aren't they? I haven't got one, I wouldn't, and I don't know much about them. I can't actually drive. But this one sounded as if he'd got in here in it but he couldn't get it to start again.'

'You mean the engine stalled?'

'Do I? If you say so. Anyway, I got up and looked out of the window. I was going to shout at him. I mean, midnight's bad enough. They use the end there as a toilet, those fellows, it's disgusting – are they allowed to do that?'

Lynn said gently, 'You were telling me you looked out of the window.'

'Well, I didn't shout. The car was standing there and he was doing something up the end, bending over something – well, it's embarrassing, isn't it? Worse than dogs, at least a dog is natural.'

It was necessary to deflect her from her pet subjects of pollution,

Contemporary Cars and lavatorial lapses. Lynn interrupted her again. 'Could you describe him and the car?'

Soon it became plain that the car used was small and red. At first Lucinda Lee had thought the man was Leslie Cousins, but he was too tall to be Cousins and too thin. She described him as wearing jeans and a zipper jacket.

Later on Sunday morning, mid-morning it had been, when she looked out again she had seen the camouflage sleeping bag but she was so used to seeing rubbish dumped there that she took no further notice.

Brendan Royall had spent the night at Marrowgrave Hall. Karen left her car at its gates and made her way into the grounds, wishing there were more cover than these second-growth trees, scarcely more than saplings, and these ubiquitous nettles. Wexford had once said to her that we were lucky in that the English countryside wasn't dangerous as some places were, the worst to fear being adders and nettles, and whoever saw adders these days? Luckily, she didn't react much to nettle stings.

Rabbits were everywhere, hundreds, in her estimation. They had cropped the turf so that it looked as if someone had shaved it, but still they went on eating what was left. She had been there about fifteen minutes when Royall came out of the front door with a camera. He stood there photographing the rabbits, which must have been too far away to appear as more than dark dots on the film. This done, he began walking forward, and Karen could hear the strange high-pitched whistle he was making. If it was intended to pacify the rabbits, or even attract them to him, it failed and had the opposite effect. Each animal seemed to freeze, before running helter-skelter for the safety of the bushes.

Then Freya came out, draped like a statue on a Roman frieze. She said something to him and handed him something. Royall hung the camera round his neck and got into the Winnebago. This was enough to send Karen racing back to her car. By the time the Winnebago emerged she had moved back on to the edge of the ditch and under the shelter of overhanging branches. Royall turned left towards Forby. It was a cumbersome vehicle to be driving along these narrow lanes. He took them slowly and Karen stayed a long way behind.

There was no way of bypassing Kingsmarkham from this direction

800

and Royall took the Winnebago right through the town, causing a severe hold-up in York Street which was already double-parked. He was heading for the bypass site, Karen thought, or at any rate for its environs. She wondered how Damon Slesar was getting on – Damon who, by coincidence really, had the other surveillance task, that of keeping Conrad Tarling under observation. If anyone got the evening off, if there was any let-up in the hunt for Sacred Globe, she was meeting Damon for a meal in Kingsmarkham at eight. It wouldn't be the first time they had been out together, but it was the first time a meeting between them had happened by design and not by chance or from simple convenience.

Brendan Royall was heading for Myfleet, she supposed, by way of Framhurst. If he was going to one of the camps he would have turned off sooner, certainly by the time they reached Framhurst Cross. The lights were against him, she could see from a long way away, and she slowed almost to a stop. He had moved off up the Myfleet road before she got to the junction and by then the lights had turned red again. Karen thought maybe she wasn't very good at this and she wondered if Damon was making a better job of it.

A lot of tree people were sitting at tables outside the Framhurst teashop. She could even see, from the car, those little pots of non-lactic soymilk. The lights changed and she accelerated after the Winnebago, but it had disappeared from her view round one, or several, of these bends between the twelve-foot-high banks. Of course she had to meet another car, it was just her luck. She had to reverse about fifty yards before she found, not exactly a lay-by but a slight widening of the lane. She pulled into it and saw the Winnebago, the unmistakable large white mobile caravan, far away on the horizon, pursuing its course over the hillside and now disappearing into the valley.

She hadn't much choice but to continue in the same direction, down into the dip, up the hill, bends and windings everywhere, down into the valley, and there ahead of her was a field full of cars. Goland Farm. The car park for the tree people's vans and bangers. The Winnebago in the middle of it was like a swan in a pond of ugly ducklings. She sat in her car waiting and watching it. It couldn't have been there for more than five minutes before she arrived.

There were people outside the house that had once been a chapel. She looked at them through her binoculars. A woman and two men, neither of whom was Brendan Royall. He must be sitting in the cab or in the back, the living area. After all, that's what it was, a place to live in as well as drive, to sleep in, eat in, read in and probably watch television in for all she knew. She moved the car to where she had the Winnebago well in her sights. The binoculars showed her an empty cab.

The Winnebago had curtains, but these were all fastened back. Her excellent glasses had no difficulty in revealing the entire interior to her. Unless Royall was hiding under the bed he wasn't in there; no one was, it was empty. Suddenly she knew exactly what had happened. The something Freya had handed him outside Marrowgrave Hall was a set of car keys. He had come here in the Winnebago and left again in Freya's car.

The message might come by letter, as the first one had. Wexford could think of about a hundred addresses, authorities, companies, firms, public bodies, to whom such a letter might be sent. He could only trust to it that if any of them received a letter they would pass it on. It wouldn't be fax or e-mail, he had been through all that before. A letter or a phone call or nothing.

Nothing until the next body . . .

After all, though they had talked of negotiations, they had no need of them. Their demands were known, their *demand* really. The building of the bypass was not to be postponed or suspended, but cancelled altogether, presumably in perpetuity. It was a ridiculous condition because even if any government were prepared to promise such a thing, the guarantee couldn't be binding on its successors – or could it? Suppose the land was set aside and preserved in its present state, as he had heard certain royal forests were, or Hampstead Heath was? Suppose it was purchased, for instance, by the National Trust?

He found himself ignorant of the law in these respects. But Sacred Globe would have made themselves conversant with it. It was well within the bounds of probability that they would ask for a promise from the National Trust as to the future of the bypass site.

He asked the Chief Constable for permission to address Sacred Globe through the medium of television, appeal to them, ask for the return of the remaining three hostages and require them to state their demands. Permission was refused.

'These people may not fulfil the definition of terrorists as we know it, Reg, but terrorists they are. We can't be seen to negotiate with them. They can address us, but we can't address them.'

'Only they don't address us,' said Wexford.

'How long is it now, Reg?'

'Forty-eight hours, sir.'

'And in that time they've done what you might call their worst.'

'Their worst so far,' said Wexford.

Damon Slesar caught up with him as he was making his way into the old gym. Wexford, turning round, thought he looked tired. Those dark, almost emaciated people showed their tiredness in bruise marks round the eyes and Damon's eyes were sunk in grey hollows. He wondered how his showed – in a general ageing, no doubt.

'Tarling hasn't been anywhere apart from the Elder Ditches Camp,' he said. 'He's been back home since mid-afternoon. He went to take a look at the environmental survey, met Royall there and they went back to the camp together. And that's about it.'

'Perhaps you'd like to tell Karen,' Wexford said not very pleasantly. 'She'll be interested to know where Royall was, seeing that she lost him.'

You could tell so much from a person's eyes, he thought, the subtle changes to the whole face. Criticism of Lynn Fancourt or Barry Vine would scarcely have affected Slesar, but when Karen was its object he became as vulnerable as if it had been directed against himself. Still, all he said was, 'I'll tell her, sir.'

Something in the tone of his voice told Wexford Slesar would make occasion to speak to her, but if Brendan Royall came into the conversation it would be purely incidental.

'OK. After the meeting you can call it a day.'

They assembled in front of him with their news, their successes – not many of these – their ideas – even fewer. He saw the exchanged glance between Karen and Damon and told himself now was no time to take an interest in the involvement of human beings. In passing only would he notice and be pleased that the exacting Karen, feminist, sharp critic, perfectionist, had perhaps at last found someone to suit her.

The day was over. An hour of peace had come and he was going to use it to listen to Dora's hypnosis tape. At last.

# 20

The voice he expected would be a sleepwalker's, bemused, proceeding as from a medium in a trance. He prepared himself to be unnerved by it. Instead, what he heard were Dora's measured tones, steady, sane, almost conversational. She sounded perfectly at ease, occasionally excited by what had been dredged up out of her unconscious and what she immediately seemed to recognise as truth.

'It was the boy,' she said now. 'Ryan. He had such a thing about his father, he was always talking about him. His father died months before he was born. In the Falklands war. Did I tell you that?'

Silence. Dr Rowland didn't speak.

'It's rather strange, isn't it, having so much love and admiration for someone you never knew and couldn't have known?'

This time the hypnotherapist said, 'People idealise a lost or far-distant parent. That, after all, is the parent who doesn't punish, who never says no, who doesn't get exasperated or tired or cross.'

'Yes.' Dora seemed to be considering this. 'His father left him a book of drawings of . . . wildlife, I suppose you'd call it, that he'd made. Well, he didn't exactly leave it to him, he left it behind, and Ryan's mother gave it to him when he was twelve. They were drawings of pond life, frogs and newts and caddises, and all the things he'd seen when he was Ryan's age and which now weren't there any more, had disappeared or were greatly endangered. He treasures that book. It's his most precious possession.'

The hypnotist said, 'Talk about the room.'

'Big, thirty by twenty. Feet, I mean, not metres. I can't do metres. Whitewashed walls. Five beds. Three up one end, those were mine and Ryan's and Roxane's, and two up the window end for the Struthers. Owen Struther moved their beds up there himself. To be

804

away from the rest of us, I suppose. And when Owen and Kitty were gone they didn't take the beds away.

'The floor was concrete, cold underfoot. It was always cold to touch. The door was very heavy, made of oak, I think. When they opened it I could see green and grey outside, and some red brick. The green was grass. The grey was stone.'

The other voice said very gently, 'What could you see out of the window?'

'Green and grey, a stone step, I think. Oh, and there was blue too. Patches of blue.'

'Blue sky?'

There was a silence. Then Dora said, 'It wasn't the sky. It was something else blue. Opposite the window. Sometimes it was high up and sometimes lower down. I don't mean it moved while I watched it. I mean that one day, the Wednesday, I think, it was a small blue patch high up, about eight feet up, and on the Thursday it was a smaller blue patch about three feet up.'

Silence again, a silence so protracted that Wexford knew it was the end. Disappointment had succeeded earlier euphoria. Was that all? Dora had been put through an involuntary – she couldn't have refused and remained a responsible member of society – changing of her consciousness and therefore a loss of her dignity, for that?

He felt like kicking the recorder but he switched it off instead and went home. She was asleep and that didn't surprise him. A message was on the answering machine from Sheila to the effect that she would come back to Kingsmarkham whenever they liked but wouldn't Mother like to come and stay with them?

'Look what happened last time she tried,' Wexford said aloud.

He went to bed and dreamed. It was the first dream he had had since she had come back. He was in a place of vast buildings, warehouses, factories, mills, old railway stations, some of which were recognisable. The Molino Stucky in Venice, the Musée d'Orsay in Paris. He wandered among them, awestricken by their size, by John Martin's *Pandemonium* and Piranesi's *Imaginary Prisons*. It was as if he had strayed miraculously into a book of old illustrations and at the same time, more prosaically, into the Stowerton Industrial Estate. That it was a dream he knew from the first, there was never a moment of illusion. He passed along a street of Blake's dark satanic mills and, turning a corner, came upon Westminster Abbey. Then he knew. He was looking for the place where the hostages were.

Without finding them or their prison he woke up and it was morning, inquest day. His newspaper, on an inside page, carried an article by a well-known feature writer suggesting that any more concessions made to Sacred Globe would constitute a 'Terrormentalists' Charter'.

Dora, making coffee, getting breakfast, said, 'I didn't sleep very well. I kept thinking about them all. That poor Roxane, when she was locked in the washroom. I don't think I'll ever get her cries and her panic out of my head. And the Struthers, they were both so pathetic really. She simply collapsed, she hadn't any inner resources at all. Well, I wasn't very enterprising but at least I didn't cry all the time.'

'Or at all.'

'I was pretty near it sometimes, Reg.'

'I heard your tape,' he said. 'You must be unique.'

'What do you mean?'

'You must be the only person on earth without an unconscious. It's all in your consciousness. You told us everything, didn't you? Kept nothing back. Well, except that blue thing.'

She looked sideways at him, smiling warily.

'What kind of blue was it?'

'Sky-blue,' she said. 'A perfect, true sky-blue. The blue of the sky at noon on a fine summer day.'

'Then it was the sky you saw.'

'No.' She was adamant. She hooked two pieces of toast out of the toaster on the tines of a fork, flipped them on to a plate, reached into the cupboard for the marmalade jar. 'No. It wasn't the sky. You want some coffee? Oh, sit down, Reg. You can take half an hour off for your breakfast.'

'Ten minutes.'

'It wasn't the sky, it was just sky colour. Anyway, was there any cloudless blue sky while I was in there?'

'I don't believe there was.'

'No. This was more like something hung out of a window or painted on, but the difficulty with that is that it moved. It was high up on the Wednesday and low down on the Thursday. And on Friday at lunch-time Gloves boarded up the window a bit more. Did he do that so that I wouldn't be able to see the blue thing?'

'You didn't come up with any reason for why they let you go?'

'If they knew I'd seen things they'd have been more likely to keep

806

me, wouldn't they? Or killed me. Oh, don't look like that. I was telling you about the Struthers. Owen Struther was too young to have been in any war yet he behaved like an old soldier, all that courage-in-the-face-of-the-enemy stuff, the obligation to escape. It was ridiculous.'

'Perhaps he was an old soldier. You can be a soldier without a war to fight.'

'He wasn't. I asked him. He didn't like being asked, he seemed quite affronted. Ryan admired him. I think he'd have followed wherever Owen led. I suppose the poor boy is always looking for a father figure – or is that too psychological?'

'The trouble with psychology,' said Wexford epigrammatically, 'is that it doesn't take human nature into account.'

Mavrikiev gave his evidence as an expert witness to the Coroner's Court, most of it technical and obscure, an analysis of the nature of certain wounds and fractures. When he was asked if in his opinion Roxane Masood had been pushed from or thrown off a height, he replied that he had no opinion, he was unable to say. The inquest was adjourned, as Wexford had known it would be.

Sacred Globe's silence hung over Kingsmarkham like a fog. Or so it seemed to him. Not to the rest of the world, the country, perhaps. The kidnapping, someone had told him, had even got into the American papers. There was a tiny paragraph on the foreign pages of the *New York Times*. To Wexford it was as if the hostages had been removed as far away as that, thousands of miles. The sun was shining, it was a bright day, but all the time he was conscious of this enveloping mist.

'Sixty-eight hours,' he said to Burden. 'That's how long it's been.'

Burden had the morning papers. POLICE IN THE DARK. VANISHED: RYAN, OWEN AND KITTY. MY BEAUTIFUL DAUGHTER, A FATHER'S STORY.

'I'm not in the dark about how she died,' Wexford said. 'I think I know exactly how that happened. Last Thursday, when they took her out of the basement room, they put her somewhere else and it wasn't with Kitty and Owen Struther. The Struthers may not even have been together at that stage. They put Roxane on her own somewhere and it was somewhere high up.'

'On one of the floors above the basement room?'

'Maybe. The trouble is – one of the troubles is – that we don't know what kind of a building we have to deal with here. Or even if it's only one building. It could be a factory complex or a barn or a big house with a basement or a farm with cats. On the coast, somewhere with a beach. Whichever it is, Roxane was taken to an upper floor, perhaps three or four storeys high, and shut up in a room. I think it was a small room, Mike.'

'You can't possibly know that.'

'Yes, I can. She was claustrophobic and they knew that. Sacred Globe knew it. Dora saw them look at each other, the pair who were outside the washroom door while Roxane was inside screaming and beating on it. They knew and they acted on that knowledge. To subdue her. To punish her.

'I was thinking the other day that whatever Sacred Globe might be, they aren't cruel or stupid, but I've had to revise that view. So many people are cruel when they have the opportunity, don't you find?'

Burden shrugged. 'I dare say. I wouldn't be surprised.'

'Give them power and someone or something weaker than themselves. That seems to be enough to make them torment that someone or something. Have psychiatrists ever investigated this? Have they tried to find out why something weak and vulnerable inspires compassion in some people and cruelty in others? I don't know and I don't suppose you do.' Wexford shook his head, in sorrow, in anger. 'They put her in a small room high up. That would have been some time on Thursday. She endured it for nearly two days, at what cost we'll never know.' He was silent for a moment. Then he said suddenly, 'Have you got a phobia?'

'Me?' said Burden. 'I'm not very partial to snakes. I get a bit jumpy in a reptile house.'

'It's not the same thing. If it was a phobia you couldn't go *near* a reptile house. I've a phobia.'

Burden looked interested. 'You have? What is it?'

'That's the last thing I'd tell you. Oh, not you, anyone. My wife knows. The point about being phobic is that you don't tell anyone, you daren't. *Phobos* means fear. Suppose some joker sent you the thing you're phobic about through the post in a parcel? That was why Roxane should never have let Sacred Globe know about her phobia, but she couldn't help herself, poor girl. They couldn't send her the thing she was phobic about, but they could shut her up in a small room.

'On the Saturday afternoon, when she was nearly mad with terror,

808

she tried to escape. Perhaps there was a drainpipe, or some climbing plant to give a foothold, perhaps there was a roof that could be reached, or a ledge. Or she thought could be reached. But it couldn't and she fell. She fell thirty feet to her death, Mike.

'In falling she broke her arm, her ribs, both her legs, and she struck her head a great blow. Perhaps she wouldn't have fallen if she had been – how shall I put it? – in her right mind? But phobics aren't, not when they've been exposed to the thing they're phobic about for two days and a night.'

Reflecting on this for a moment or two, Burden said, 'Sacred Globe couldn't have expected that. It's possible they were appalled by what happened.'

'If they were amateurs who'd bitten off more than they could chew, they'd be appalled all right. The likelihood is that they hoped to get what they want and release all the hostages unharmed. That's no longer possible. There they were with a body on their hands, a body they hadn't killed.'

'You could say they murdered her when they put her in that room,' said Burden.

'You and I could, Mike. It wouldn't stand up in court.'

'Why did they bring her back here?'

Wexford considered. 'Perhaps because they didn't want the body. The body was a further liability to them. What were they to do with it? Burial is the only real possibility if you've a body on your hands. We can forget about weighting it down and dumping it in water unless they're on the coast. And we've no reason to think they are. They'd have to have access to a boat, total privacy, darkness.

'But *they didn't kill her*, Mike, they only put her into a position for her to kill herself by accident. If they compounded it by burying the body and it was found later, as it surely would have been, who would then have been made to believe they weren't directly responsible for her death? This way a pathologist would soon discover her death almost certainly to have been accidental. So they got rid of the body. They took it away on Saturday night, in the small hours of Sunday morning probably, first putting it into a sleeping bag they happened to have.

'I think they took it to Contemporary Cars because they had a grievance against them. Thus they kill two birds with one stone. Maybe they've got it in for Samuels and Trotter and co. because they so quickly contacted us after the hold-up. I'm beginning to think they're a vindictive lot.'

They were interrupted by the arrival of Pemberton, who believed he had found the source of the sleeping bag.

'London?' said Wexford. 'Where in London?'

'Outdoors don't supply many retail outlets,' Pemberton said, 'and they only deal with sports shops, not department stores. Most of their stuff goes to the north of England, but they do supply a shop in north London in NW1, and one in Brixton.'

Brixton . . . why did that ring a bell? It would be on the computers somewhere, whatever it was there would be a record. 'Go on.'

'The north London one's in Marylebone High Street. That's when I had a bit of luck, sir. They'd taken six of those sleeping bags, the camouflage kind, and six in green and purple, but while the coloured ones had all sold, they hadn't been able to shift any of the camouflage.'

'Negative sort of luck, wasn't it?' said Burden.

'I went to Brixton. The shop's called Palm Springs in High Street, Brixton. They told me they only had four of those sleeping bags and two of them were still in stock. The manager himself took one of them, they came in just before he went on a camping trip, that was August twelve months. He remembered it without any trouble, but then I reckon you would. Better than that, though, he remembered selling the other one because it was on the same day.'

'I don't suppose he knows who he sold it to?' said Burden.

'Yeah, well, that's too much to expect, isn't it? It was a woman, he knew that. And he remembered she was going to Zaïre. Well, he said Zimbabwe at first but then he corrected himself.'

'Right,' said Wexford. 'Well done. And now you can get yourself in front of Mary's computer and go through a million kilobytes to find the connection.'

'There's a connection?'

'Oh, yes, I'm sure of it.'

Seventy hours and not a word from Sacred Globe.

Having swapped cars with Damon Slesar, Karen sat outside the gates of Marrowgrave Hall, awaiting developments, awaiting anything at all. It had seemed wise to be in a grey car today and let Damon have the blue one, though she didn't think it had registered with Brendan Royall on the previous day that she was following him.

810

She had started off at Goland Farm, parked among the tree people's cars. The Winnebago was there, but whether or not Brendan Royall was she couldn't tell. His curtains were drawn and all her binoculars could do for her was show her that the cab was empty. Today there was no one about and all the windows in the house were shut as if its occupants had gone out for the day.

She was tired. She and Damon had met for a meal the evening before at a much more up-market place than she had had in mind. La Méditerranée, the Olive and Dove's newly opened restaurant. They had eaten and talked and found they had a tremendous amount to talk about, that they were interested in all the same things, the state of the world, the millennium, what was happening to their own environment, the equality of the sexes, as well as crime and punishment. It had made the conversation at their previous meetings seem like small talk, and after the restaurant indicated that it wanted to close up, they had gone on to a drinking place in the High Street that stayed open till all hours.

By that time they were only drinking Cokes but really she should have been at home in bed. He wanted to come up to her flat with her but she'd said no regretfully and they'd kissed good-night, passionately but like stars in an old Hollywood movie, the kiss leading nowhere except to the mutual promise to see each other again soon. So now she was tired when she shouldn't be and sitting here in a warm car, the sun shining outside in a mild sort of way, she was afraid she might fall asleep.

Fear of that sent her out to walk around a bit. She didn't really look like a tree person but she could just have passed for one in her jeans, black T-shirt and cotton jacket. No one, in any case, would take much notice of her in her flat shoes, neutral clothes and with her long hair scraped back tight and her face as nature made and coloured it.

Somewhere a dog was barking, or several dogs were barking, yapping and howling. The noise was coming from the Winnebago. Well, Royall was said to be an animal lover. No doubt he had dogs of his own, but that they were there meant he would be back, and soon.

Near the house were a lot of concealing trees and high hedges. She had a look at the back of it, with its churchy windows. Would a church or chapel, which was what this had once been, have a crypt? There was no sign of anything like that and the windows weren't

811

hidden or any arches plastered over. She had just returned to her car and was winding down a window to let in some fresh air, when a yellow 2CV came tearing into the field and swept round between the rows like something taking part in the Monaco Grand Prix.

Royall got out of the car, followed by Freya. She opened one of the rear doors and four small beagles bounded out. It took her and Royall some minutes to catch them and thrust them into the Winnebago. Freya was in her usual mummy wrappings and she tripped on the hem of her skirt and fell sprawling. Brendan made an attempt to brush mud off her and then she got back into her car and he got into the cab of the Winnebago.

Karen expected them to return to Marrowgrave Hall and they did. Patsy Panick appeared outside the front door as they drove up and laughed and clapped her hands when all the dogs were released. Karen had heard of someone shaking like a jelly but never before witnessed this phenomenon. Patsy's fat shook as if balloons were inside her clothes.

The beagles ran around in circles, wagging their tails. Karen counted eleven of them. Brendan and Freya managed to catch the dogs, carrying them or otherwise propelling them into the house and Patsy, no doubt exhorting everyone, dogs and all, to have something to eat, shut the door behind them.

The sleep problem reappeared. It was hotter now and Karen did in fact doze off but only for a split second. Barking awakened her. The two people she was keeping under surveillance had re-emerged from the house in the midst of their gambolling pack. While they got them into the Winnebago and Brendan also stowed a suitcase, backpack and large draw-string bag, Karen called in to Kingsmarkham police station.

'They're leaving,' she said. 'I'm going to stay with them, see where they're going, but I think they're going a distance.'

'Chief Inspector wants to talk to you. I'll put him on.'

Wexford said, 'When you're done with that I want you back here. Remember a woman in London who was ill, who'd been in Africa?'

'Yes, of course, sir.'

'She's your pigeon. When you've done with Royall and his girlfriend.'

The Winnebago was packed now with dogs and luggage. Freya, it seemed, wasn't going with him. For a moment Karen thought she was leaving separately but she was only putting her car away in the big empty garage. Patsy and Bob had both come out now, Bob with a slice of something in his hand, a piece of pizza or pie or even a sandwich. All Freya got from Brendan by way of farewell was prolonged eye contact while he held both her hands, but Patsy was hugged and perhaps kissed too, only Karen was too far away to tell. Brendan gave Bob a slap on the back, waved goodbye, apparently to the house, and jumped into the cab. Karen retreated under the trees.

He drove out a lot more cautiously than he had when at the wheel of the 2CV. The beagles were all barking and yelping. Karen followed the Winnebago through Forby and along the Stowerton Road. She had been right, he wasn't going anywhere near Kingsmarkham or the bypass site, but heading for the M23 and then perhaps for its link to the M25. She kept behind him until he came to the approach road to the motorway, watched him enter it and then she turned back for the old bypass and Kingsmarkham.

At the police station the first thing she did was ask if there had been anything from Sacred Globe. Damon, who told her how he had followed Conrad Tarling about all day on foot – it was true the man never used a car – said there had been nothing. It was more than seventy-two hours, or three days which sounded even more, since the message in Dora Wexford's suitcase. Damon had left Conrad Tarling up a chestnut tree, where he had retreated into his tree-house, pulled down the tarpaulin curtain and no doubt curled up inside like a squirrel.

'I'm hoping we can meet this evening.'

Karen, who had turned back to her computer screen, said they could in a way, of course they could.

'What do you mean, in a way?'

'You and I can both go up to London and talk to a woman called Frenchie Collins who may just possibly have bought a camouflage sleeping bag. Will you drive?'

'Sure,' he said. 'I'd love to.'

'The bones those kids found in the heap of earth at Stowerton Dale,' Wexford said, leafing through the forensic reports that had come in, then sitting down and reading. 'Shin of beef and pork knuckle, much as we thought. Now the clothes Dora was wearing, brown linen suit, amber-and-white spotted voile blouse – what the devil is voile, Mike, or should it be "vwahl"? – tan calf pumps – that's shoes – tights in a shade called 'nearly brown', bra and pants in white silk and lycra, white silk slip with coffee lace. Sounds right.

'A small food stain on the blouse has been identified as made by instant coffee and a liquid soya compound. That'll be the non-lactic soymilk. Dora kept herself very clean, I must say, I should have been coated in spaghetti and jam. Now here's something rather more encouraging. A great many interesting substances were taken from her skirt: her own hairs and someone else's, a young person's, long and dark, therefore most likely Roxane Masood's; a cocktail of grains of chalk, breadcrumbs, cobwebs, powdered limestone, sand and cats' hairs. Rather a large quantity of hairs from a Siamese cat and a black cat.'

'There are seven million cats in Great Britain,' said Burden in a neutral tone.

'Are there really? There aren't, however, seven million cases of a black cat and a Siamese found in conjunction.' Wexford referred back to the report. 'Iron filings, which rather points to some kind of factory or workshop. But listen to this. They also found the kind of dust they suggest could be the substance that adheres to the wings of butterflies and moths.'

'*What*?'

'Apparently – there's an explanation here – butterflies' and moths' wings aren't solid colours, painted on, so to speak. They're not like the colours of a bird's feathers or an animal's fur, but the patterns are made up by an arrangement of coloured dust. If this is worn away or rubbed off, the insect can't fly. The suggestion is that what may have happened is that Dora's rather long full skirt brushed against a cobweb in which a butterfly or moth had been caught and had died . . .'

'What is it? What's the matter?'

Wexford had fallen silent. His eyes moved up the page again. He laid the sheets of paper down, looked up. 'Mike, the dust was rose-pink and brown.'

'So? A lot of butterflies are pink and brown.'

'Are they? I can't think of any. Black and red, white, yellow and orange, but pink? The only insect I can think of that is predominantly pale-brown with pink wings, *rose-pink underwings*, is the rare Rosy Underwing. They're found in Europe and in Japan, but in this country only in parts of Hampshire and east Wiltshire.'

'How on earth do you know?'

'I've been interesting myself in this sort of thing lately. Must be this bloody bypass. Anyway, I read up about this rare Map butterfly and in the course of that I came across a lot of other stuff.'

Burden looked at him, half smiling. The Chief Inspector never ceased to give him cause for wonder.

'I don't know why I remember about the Rosy Underwing but I do. Of course we'll check all this out. Maybe on the Internet? But I do remember that part about the few specimens being native to Wiltshire. Who do we know lives in Wiltshire?'

It took Burden only a few seconds to remember. 'Conrad Tarling's family.'

'Exactly. Do we have an address?'

'On the computer.'

Twenty minutes and they had it all in front of them: British and European butterflies and the Conrad Tarling printout with biography and family history. The Tarling parents' address was Queringham House, Queringham, Wilts. Wexford had already been studying the *Great Britain Road Atlas*, calculating distances. He felt a small anticipatory shiver that came with a sense that this could be it, this could be the breakthrough.

'Queringham's right on the Hampshire border, Mike, half-way between Winchester and Salisbury.'

'Not the seaside, though, is it? And it's too far away. We've fixed on a radius of sixty miles, remember.'

'This *is* sixty miles. Sixty-three or four, I'd reckon. Your actress friend was wrong when she said Tarling walked eighty miles, a spot of sycophant's hyperbole, that was. This is a big country house by the sound of it, Mike, no doubt with a lot of outbuildings, right in the middle of Rosy Underwing country – and Rosy Underwing dust came off Dora's skirt.'

'The home of known activists, of one terrorist,' said Burden. 'Of a man who half killed himself in an animal transport protest.'

'We'll put through a polite phone call to the Wiltshire Constabulary and, with their consent, we'll make our way to Queringham Hall. Now. No time like the present.'

# 21

Did they need back-up?

The Wiltshire Constabulary had armed-response vehicles patrolling their roads, as Mid-Sussex had. If Wexford was in need of that sort of assistance . . . ? The whole country was on the alert for the Kingsmarkham Kidnappers.

Wexford said he wasn't in need, thanks. All he was doing was taking a look. He hadn't even a search in mind, unless the Tarling family would agree, for he wasn't going for a warrant at this stage. But there would be four of them, himself and Burden, Vine and Lynn Fancourt. There was even a certain amount of relief in getting away from the police station and from the incident room in the old gym. They would let him know at once if a message came from Sacred Globe, but at least he wouldn't be there waiting.

Seventy-two hours exactly since the last one.

It wasn't a bad run, not as much traffic as he had feared. They crossed into Wiltshire at six-thirty and the River Avon a few minutes later. Queringham was between Mownton and Blick, a gentle pastoral countryside of downs and quiet meadows, surrounded by areas of beauty designated NT for National Trust.

These old landowners, as Wexford remarked, knew how to conceal their properties from the curious eyes of the populace. You could never see them from the road. They built the house – whenever it was, a couple of hundred years ago – and then they planted the trees. So that now, as you approached, what you saw was apparently a forest. Entering the drive, you had the impression that you might not succeed in penetrating, that the track might come to an end up against a wall of foliage.

Suddenly, all trees ceased and open land was displayed with the house behind it. But here were no gardens of rare plants, here was no view. This was literally a clearing, from which everything seemed to have been scraped or seared away but for a few small stunted bushes and two large stone urns in which grew withered cypresses. Wexford had been right about the outbuildings. There appeared to be a stables wing with a small central clocktower, while to the left, behind the house, was a large barn and an even larger, very ugly, cylindrical silo.

The first thing that struck him was that their visit, the surprise visit of four police officers, two of whom were of considerable rank, was hardly a cause of astonishment to Charles and Pamela Tarling. Like the Royalls, they were used to this sort of thing. Whatever they might be, however self-effacing and law-abiding, their children constantly attracted the attention of the police. No doubt officers from other forces, possibly from all over England, had come up this path, rung this doorbell, asked these questions, and many times before.

Not quite these questions, though.

They were invited in, led into a large English country house drawing-room. It was shabby and weary and worn as only such places can be, the great blue-and-yellow carpet threadbare and faded to grey and straw, the upholstery frayed, the long yellow curtains, hundreds of yards of them, transparent with age. A huge chipped bowl of dead flowers stood in the centre of a table, dead flowers, not dried ones, dropping grey pollen on the white-ringed mahogany surface.

The place suited its owners. They too looked as if they had started life in colours, in strength and trimness and with a certain polish, but time and the expense of this house and the trials of those children of theirs and of living with those children, had stained and bleached and worn all that away. They even looked rather alike, thin, tall, round-shouldered people with small heads, wrinkled faces and untidy grey hair.

'We're interested primarily in your son, Mr Conrad Tarling,' Wexford said.

The father nodded wearily. It was as if he had heard it all before. He had perhaps answered all the questions before as well, the ones about where Conrad was now, when he had last seen him, if he frequently returned to Queringham Hall. Then Burden mentioned Craig, one of the other sons, the bomber.

Pamela Tarling reddened. A dark and painful blush suffused that

817

faded, lined face. She put her fingers to her cheeks as if to cool them. Somehow you knew those fingers would be icy cold.

'They *are* our children,' she said gently. It was something she had probably said many times before. 'We have always tried to be loyal to our children. And . . . and they are brave, dedicated people with the right aims and principles, it's just . . . just that they . . .'

'All right, Pam,' said her husband. 'Actually, I endorse that. May I ask you what you want to do now?'

'Have a look outside here, Mr Tarling, if we may. It's up to you to refuse if you wish. I'd like to have a look in some of these outbuildings of yours.'

'Oh, I never refuse,' Charles Tarling said. 'I never say no to the police. There seems no point. They always come back with a warrant.'

He might, of course, have been a very good actor. Wexford simply couldn't tell. He went outside with the others but the Tarlings stayed where they were, sitting opposite each other on a pair of decayed sofas, eyes meeting despairing eyes across a battered late-Victorian table.

To what use had that silo been put? Had the place done duty as a farm? The stable roofs were missing half their tiles and the doors of the loose boxes hung off their hinges. The clock was going but no one had altered the hands when clocks went an hour forward in March and now it would soon be time to put them back again. Wexford looked inside, Burden looked inside. Vine pushed open the door of a place that might have been a dairy or a woodshed or even a grain store. A big blind moth flew blundering out and Wexford got a good look at it. But it wasn't a Rosy Underwing, more like one of the giant hawkmoths.

No one had used the place for fifty years and more. That was apparent. It had a stone floor, shelves covering one wall, a window high up and under it a large stone sink. But no washroom built on, no upper floors overhead. Wexford looked out of the window and instead of giving on to greenness and greyness – and an occasionally occurring blue patch – the outlook was to a brick wall criss-crossed with half-timbering.

'It's a dairy,' he said. 'Where they're kept, the basement room, is a dairy.'

'But not this one,' said Vine.

'No, not this one.'

The sound of wheels, rapidly trundling, made Wexford turn round. The man had come across the cluttered courtyard, propelling his wheelchair as fast as a bicycle. It might have been Conrad Tarling himself, the resemblance was so great. Were they twins? If you could imagine him brought down from his graceful eminence, reduced to what sat in the chair before them, his golden cloak discarded, his strength laid waste, this might have been the King of the Wood.

Like Conrad's, his head was shaved. He could have been as tall as Conrad but his body was reduced and bent, his knees drawn up under the rug that covered them. Large but stubby-fingered hands lay on those knees. The face was Conrad's but even more the Last of the Mohicans, sharp, dark, as if made of bronze, and it was full of pain.

'What are you looking for?' The voice was beautiful, low-pitched, scornful.

Burden's answer made Colum Tarling laugh. 'Just a routine check, Mr Tarling.'

Colum laughed bitterly, without amusement, it wasn't even a genuine laugh, but staged, contrived. To force laughter is much easier than to achieve real tears. 'We get a lot of those,' he said. 'Don't let me stop you. Well, I can't stop you, can I? I can't do anything. Not any more. You can't do much when your spinal cord has been destroyed.'

If such people as he have any compensation, Wexford thought, it must be that of a unique power of embarrassing others. If that was what you liked and wanted.

Colum Tarling evidently liked it, for he said, 'You love all the good things and you work for those good things, to keep them and make them endure, civilisation and living creatures and decent behaviour and mankind, and they punish you for that by cutting up your spine under the wheels of a truck. Have you got an opinion on that?'

Wexford had. He could have talked about it for half an hour without pausing or hesitation. 'You kindly said we should continue, Mr Tarling, so if you'll excuse us, we will.'

Such courtesy he hadn't expected. 'Christ,' he said, 'a gentleman, a real gentleman. In the wrong job, aren't you?'

His father had come out and was standing behind him. Wexford had noticed a spasm of pain pass across Charles Tarling's face when his son spoke so brutally of his destroyed spine. He laid a hand on his son's shoulder and whispered something. More loudly he said, 'Come inside, Colum, come inside now.'

'They're only doing their job,' Colum said. 'Is that what you whispered to me? I didn't quite catch.'

But he turned the wheelchair and moved back to the house, more slowly than he had come out. That father no doubt endured more of the same daily, Wexford reflected, and yet more of the same when the King of the Wood came visiting, walking his sixty miles across country, sleeping under hedges, and even more when he went to see his son in prison. And the mother would hear morning and evening the details of the horror under that lorry's wheels, its precise physiological results, the clinical details, the pain. That would be the conversation in this house, with genteel poverty its backdrop. It didn't bear thinking of. And yet . . .

Tarling, the father, was still there. He said to Wexford, low-voiced, 'His mind is rather badly disturbed. You mustn't think . . .'

'I am not thinking anything in particular, Mr Tarling.'

'I mean, his spine, "destroyed" isn't the word. Not at all. His back was broken but they can mend backs these days, and of course he's lost a lot of height. But it's all, so much of it, in his poor mind . . .'

Wexford nodded. 'I'd like to take a look in those sheds,' he said, 'and then we'll go upstairs if you'll allow us.'

Rebuffed, Tarling said an indifferent, 'Oh, certainly.'

His son Colum seemed to think, or affected to think, they were searching for explosives. He sat in his wheelchair at the foot of the stairs, haranguing everyone, his parents and the four police officers, on vivisection, endangered species, game hunting and, more obscurely, the destruction of the dodo.

Since neither Charles nor Pamela Tarling objected, they investigated the two top floors. Here again, in some curious, almost supernatural way, features of Queringham Hall resembled aspects of the place Wexford had constructed for where the hostages might be held. No, 'resembled' wasn't the word. Mirrored, provided a kind of mirror image? Rather, it was as if Queringham Hall was in one dimension and the hostage house in a parallel universe where things were similar but subtly different because in some past time events and structures had developed in different ways and along different paths.

Just as the basement room presented itself here as a disused dairy, so among the attics they found what might have been Roxane

Masood's prison, small, square, low-ceilinged. But the window was too small for even a very thin woman to squeeze out of and six feet below the flat roof of a bathroom protruded far enough to break a fall.

It was only that English country houses often resembled each other, Wexford thought. It told him one thing, though. A country house was what he was looking for, not a factory or workshop or barn.

If she had shown disapproval of this room and perhaps its occupant on her previous visit, Karen Malahyde was unaware of it. She always tried to maintain a neutral expression and demeanour, no matter how dirty or poor, or come to that, ostentatious and luxurious, a place might be. But she must have given some hint of her true feelings all unawares, must have put something of disapprobation into her tone, or distaste into her cool eye, for Frenchie Collins refused point blank to talk to her.

'I'm not saying a word to a right little tight-arse like you.' She appealed to Damon. 'Look at her face, real sour apple, like she's walking around with a bad smell under her crinkled-up nose.'

'I'm sorry, Ms Collins,' Karen said rather stiffly, 'but I truly don't have any feelings of that sort.'

It was, of course, an outright lie, for she was even more horrified than last time by the squalor of this tiny back room, its view of a grey brick wall and, indeed, by the smell which reminded her of something she hadn't smelt since the chemistry lab at school: the rotten cabbage stink of calcium carbide.

'We simply wanted to ask you a few questions.'

'You simply wanted that before,' said Frenchie Collins. 'And you simply acted like I was something the dog brought in – no, correction, like something the dog did on the floor.'

You could tell she was young, though it was hard to say how, yet she had all the lineaments of age: dry, greying hair, coarse, lined skin, two missing front teeth, wrinkled hands which shook. Her skeletal body was wrapped in a once-white towelling dressing-gown and her feet buried and lost in grey woolly socks.

'Ms Collins . . .'

'I said I wouldn't talk to you. I don't mind talking to him. He seems a nice enough young guy.'

Karen and Damon exchanged a glance.

'All right,' Karen said, 'if that's what you'd like. I won't say a word.'

'I don't want you *here*,' said Frenchie Collins. 'Right? Understood? I'll talk to him on his own, though Christ knows what I can tell him, I don't know anything about those Sacred Globe people. You,' she said to Karen, 'can sit in the car. No doubt there *is* a car?'

Karen went down and did just that. She had a feeling Frenchie Collins knew something that she could get out of her but that Damon couldn't. Of course it was absurd to think like that about a person who refused to talk to her. Because she was a sensible woman and ambitious, with an eye to rising in the police force, she spent the time waiting for Damon in some honest analysis of her own behaviour, examining recent attitudes towards some of the people Wexford called 'our customers'. If you had very high standards of hygiene and method and order it was hard not to apply them to others, but she would try. The great thing was to be aware of your shortcomings, for that was the first step in setting things to rights.

Am I smug, she was asking herself, am I complacent? An honest answer – yes, I am, yes, I am, and intolerant and near to bigotry – was being forced out of her when Damon came back.

It had all been in vain. Frenchie Collins had bought the sleeping bag, as they thought, had taken it to Zaïre but had abandoned it there along with much of her other property. She had been too ill and weak by that time to carry more than the bare essentials.

'So she says,' said Karen.

' "Africa has killed me", she said. Those were her words. And you have to admit she looks in a bad way. I suppose it could be AIDS.'

'No, it couldn't. Hasn't been time. I don't think she'd have thrown that sleeping bag away, abandoned it or whatever she says. People like her never have any money and they don't abandon things like that. She'd have been more likely to have got inside it at the airport and had herself carried on to the plane.'

'The sleeping bag could have been bought in the north of England where Outdoors' other outlets are.'

Karen remembered that she was supposed to be nice and tolerant, not prejudiced and not smug. Especially with this man she wanted to be nice. It was a long time since she'd known any man she wanted to seem as nice to as she did to this one. 'The rest of the evening is ours,' she said and she smiled. 'We could spend it up here, but it would be nicer to go home, wouldn't it?'

822

It was after nine when Wexford got back. No message from Sacred Globe. He knew there wouldn't be, or they would have called him, but he was still disappointed. More than disappointed. A feeling he seldom had these days, one he hadn't experienced much since he was young, flooded over him. It was panic and he clenched his hands, suppressing it, breathing deeply.

He had been in his office ten minutes. He didn't know why he had come up here. There was nothing to do tonight. Go home, tell Dora all those things he was beginning to have doubts about. Oh, no, they won't kill them, of course not. We'll find them. We'll find Sacred Globe. We'll find the man with the tattoo on his left forearm and the one who smells of acetone. What kind of illness could you have that made you smell of nail varnish remover? Something wrong with the kidneys? The pancreas? The body manufacturing too many ketones?

But we'll find them. The man who has to wear gloves because something disfigures his hands. Eczema perhaps or scars. Or because he is black. The woman who wears heavy boots to help her look like a man. The house with a black cat and a Siamese which has a dairy from whose window you can see a shifting patch of blue that's as blue as the sky but isn't the sky.

He went down in the lift, walked across the foyer as Audrey Barker burst through the swing doors.

The duty sergeant called out, 'Excuse me!'

She looked, he realised, as he had never seen her before. She looked happy. More than that – elated, almost manic with happiness. Hair is supposed to stand on end through shock or horror but hers flew out in that wild way from joy. She was smiling, laughing, as if she couldn't stop. 'He phoned me,' she shouted. 'My son phoned me!'

Wexford said, 'Mrs Barker, just a moment . . . What exactly are you saying?'

'I didn't want to phone you, you don't know who you're talking to on the phone, but my son, Ryan, he phoned me half an hour ago. I thought you'd be here, you'd still be here. At a time like this . . . I couldn't keep still, I had to move, run, I came straight here, to tell you myself.'

Wexford nodded. He said very steadily in an effort to calm her, 'Yes, you tell me. Tell me all about it. Let's go upstairs to my office.'

'His voice, I couldn't believe it, I thought I was dreaming, but I knew it was real, and he's all right, he's fine . . .'

'We'll go upstairs, Mrs Barker. The lift's on its way.'

They got in. She jumped into it. She clutched his arm with a shaking hand.

'He's all right. He's quite all right. He likes them and they like him. He's *joined* them, and now they won't hurt him!'

# 22

Audrey Barker sat opposite him on the other side of his desk with a cup of tea in front of her. She was calmer now and some of the wild joy had gone out of her face. The anxious look was returning, the mouth-pursing that prematurely pleated her upper lip. He let her sip the strong, sweet tea, noticing the shaking of the hand that held the cup, the chatter of teeth against the china. Let her take her time. It was, in any case, now far too late to attempt a tracing of the call.

Sweat broke on her upper lip. 'I should have phoned you, shouldn't I?'

'I'm not sure if it would have made any difference, Mrs Barker. Will you tell me what Ryan said?'

'I nearly fainted when I heard his voice. I couldn't believe it. I was stunned. I thought I was dreaming or going mad. He said, "Mum, it's me" and of course I knew it was him, but I still said, "Who is that? Who is it?" and he said, "Mum, it's Ryan, calm down, it's Ryan" and then, "Listen," he said, "this is a message from us," so I said, "Who's us? What do you mean?" And he said, "Sacred Globe. I'm one of them now." I mean, it was something like that he said, I may not have got his exact words.'

'But you're sure he said that. He said, "I'm one of them now"?'

'Yes, I'm sure. "I'm one of them now." I didn't know what he meant and I asked him.' She had been looking down, her hands clasped in her lap, as she made an effort to remember accurately, but now she raised her head and met Wexford's eyes. 'He said he simply meant what he said. He'd joined them. They'd asked him to join them. He was flattered, of course, he was *proud*. He's only a *child*. He can't make those sort of choices. I was feeling happy and I'm not

825

any more. It was stupid of me, wasn't it? I was happy because he's all right, he's alive, but now I realise he's one of *them* I . . .'

'What else did he say?'

'He said – and it didn't sound a bit like him talking – he said, "Our cause is just. I didn't know, but I do now. We want the best for the world. It's 'we', Mum, do you understand?" '

'Did you ask him where he was?'

She put one hand up to her head. 'Oh God, I didn't think of it. He wouldn't have told me, would he? He said something like, I can't remember exactly, "We want the bypass rerouted" or he may have said re-something else, I don't know. But that's what he meant. "I'll come back to you tomorrow," he said, and I didn't know, I *don't* know, what that meant. I mean, could it be he meant he's coming *home*?'

'It sounds more as if another message will come. Mrs Barker, I'd like you to repeat what you've told me and we'll record it on tape. Will you do that?'

At first Wexford had been astonished by Ryan Barker's allying himself with Sacred Globe. But, of course, it wasn't new, it certainly wasn't unknown, this defection of a hostage to his captors and the espousal of their cause. And this cause in particular held a special appeal for young people. It was the young who were fired with outrage at the destruction of the environment – their future environment – and with a burning fervour to reverse 'progress' and restore some unspecified natural paradise.

He said to Audrey Barker when she had finished recording her conversation with Ryan, 'He idealises his father, doesn't he? I wonder if he sees Sacred Globe as something his father would have approved of, or that he thinks he'd have approved of. I understand his father was particularly keen on natural history.'

She looked at him as if he had suddenly, inexplicably, begun speaking to her in a foreign language. A huge weariness had settled on her, causing a sagging of her face and a slumping of her shoulders. He repeated what he had said, embellishing and rephrasing it.

'I know your husband was killed in the Falklands. I know about the album of drawings. My impression is that Ryan has done what some children who have lost a parent do, make paragons of them, idolise them, and model themselves on them. Erroneously, of course,

826

Ryan sees Sacred Globe as an organisation his father would have admired and wanted to support. So he supports it in his stead.'

She shrugged her shoulders, lifting them to an exaggerated extent, as if to make a total denial. Her voice was bitter. 'He wasn't my husband. I've never been married. I told Ryan his father was killed in the Falklands – well, he was killed at the time of the Falklands, that was true.'

Wexford looked at her inquiringly.

'Dennis Barker was killed in a knife fight. In Deptford. They never got anyone for it. Didn't bother, I dare say, they knew the sort he was. I had to tell Ryan something, so I made up all that and my mother stuck by me and told the same tale.'

'And the natural history?' said Wexford. 'The drawings? The album?'

'They were my father's. John Peabody's. Look, I never told him otherwise but kids . . . well, they deceive themselves to sort of make things better.'

And adults too, thought Wexford. 'The point here,' he said, 'is not what is fact but what he has taught himself to think of as fact. In doing this he's putting himself in his father's shoes, he's being his father.'

'His father, my God! A backstreet thug. Well, he's going the right way about it, isn't he, joining up with a bunch of terrorists?'

'I'll have someone drive you home, Mrs Barker. I shall have a trace put on your mother's phone. I shall have all your phone conversations recorded and take the precaution, with your permission, of having one of my officers in the house with you tomorrow for when Ryan calls again.'

If he called. If they didn't send a letter or another body . . . He had to tell Dora.

She surprised him by not being surprised. 'He was waiting for something like that,' she said. 'I had that impression when we talked. I thought he'd found it in a person, in Owen Struther, a father-hero. But Owen let him down, or he must have seen it as letting him down, when he and Kitty were handcuffed and taken away. I see now that Ryan was waiting for something to aim at, a cause, a reason for living. Of course he's only a child . . .'

'That's what his mother said.'

'The poor woman.'

He told her about the real father and the fantasy father, expecting

827

her to be at least a little affronted. None of us likes to be deceived, even if the deceiver is barely aware that he is lying and his listener a dupe. But she only shook her head and held out her hands in that gesture of submitting to the inevitable.

'What will become of him?'

'When we catch them, d'you mean? Nothing, I should think. As everyone keeps saying, he's a child.'

'I wonder what happened,' she said.

'What do you mean, what happened?'

'I told you they never talked to us. There was no communication. How did they come to change that and talk to him after I was gone and he was alone? Did they approach him or he approach them? I'd think the latter, wouldn't you? I mean, he must have been lonely and desperate for a human voice, so he started talking to them, perhaps asking them why they were doing this, what they wanted. And they saw their chance. It was to their advantage, wasn't it, to have a willing guest rather than a hostage? All hostage takers with a real cause must want that.'

'Only up to a point,' said Wexford. 'If all your hostages convert you lose your bargaining power.'

'The Struthers would never convert. Never. That just leaves them now, doesn't it? Owen and Kitty, just the two of them.'

'It's almost as valuable to Sacred Globe to have two hostages as to have five,' said Wexford.

They were both awake early next morning and she began talking to him about the two people of whom, up till now, she had said least. It was as if she had either been thinking about them during the long watches of the night or else her thoughts and analyses had crystallised while she slept. She brought him tea and sat on the bed. It wasn't yet seven.

'Kitty was only in her early fifties but still I'd say she belonged to a dying breed. All their lives they're protected by men, they do nothing for themselves, make no decisions, have no enterprise. Oh, I know I'm just a housewife myself, but not in that helpless way, doing nothing but a little cooking, a little gardening, a little telling the cleaning woman what to do. They always have just one child, these women, it's funny but it usually seems to be a boy, and they send him away to boarding-school as soon as they can.

'That was Kitty Struther. She hardly talked, but somehow I knew all that. Confronted by something different, something threatening, she just went to pieces, she collapsed like a jelly. All she ever said really was, "Owen, you have to do something" and "Owen, *do* something". And his response was to behave like a prisoner of war bent on escaping from Colditz. You could tell what their marriage was, she utterly dependent on him for everything and he sustaining the illusion of being brave and admirable, finding it necessary to impress her all the time.'

'The little woman? That's what empire builders used to say.'

'The big man and the little woman . . . It makes you shudder. Do you remember when Sheila was married to Andrew and his mother used to refer to her as his "little wife"?'

'I'd better get up,' said Wexford, 'or I won't be impressing anyone.'

'They won't kill them, will they, Reg?'

It was the only question he'd anticipated that she had actually asked. 'I hope not,' he said, and then, 'not if I can help it.'

Savesbury House and a trace on Andrew Struther's phone, a trace too on Clare Cox's, though Wexford thought it unlikely Ryan Barker would call her. Her daughter was dead and her involvement, as far as Sacred Globe was concerned, was over. Most probably the call would come to Audrey Barker once more. At least the messages were coming. Anything was preferable to that silence.

Burden, taking Karen Malahyde with him, had gone to Rhombus Road. There, in Mrs Peabody's front room, they would sit it out till the call came. If it came. The computers in the old gym continued to store information, hundreds of thousands of bytes of it, adding now Dora Wexford's comments on the Struthers, Audrey Barker's tape, Karen Malahyde and Damon Slesar's negative results from the interview with Frenchie Collins. Wexford sat in front of Mary Jefferies' screen, reading the document he hoped would at last lead him to Sacred Globe.

A basement room, rectangular, twenty feet by thirty, one heavy door in, one lighter door out to a washroom. One window high up with a sink under it. The window barred with a cross-hatched wooden structure outside it. Something green and a grey stone step visible. The floor of stone flags, the walls whitewashed. A dairy, he knew that now – did that knowledge do him any good?

The non-lactic soymilk, which at first had seemed so promising, was obtainable all over the country. That damned Rosy Underwing

829

had only led them on a wild-goose chase – a wild-moth chase – half across the south of England.

There remained the blue thing that came and went outside the window. Washing hanging out to dry? Did people still hang out washing? A car? It could be a blue car. That would be moved from one place to another and blue was always a popular colour for cars. Yes, but eight feet up in the air? A window which when opened revealed a blue lampshade inside or a blue curtain? He didn't much like any of those ideas. It was the way the blue thing moved that was confusing.

A report had just come in of the theft of twenty beagles from a research laboratory near Tunbridge Wells. The dogs had been taken and the premises set on fire. Kent that was, not his responsibility, not Montague Ryder's responsibility.

Someone, he saw, had already made the connection with Mid-Sussex. Karen Malahyde had all the evidence against Brendan Royall. Did that mean Royall was, after all, unconnected with Sacred Globe? Probably. And Damon Slesar had had no success with Conrad Tarling, who, though occasionally going off for long walks to inspect different areas of the site, was mostly holed up in his tree-house.

Driving to Savesbury, Wexford passed near the camp. A stillness hung over the whole bypass area. At this point, roughly the centre of the proposed construction, no work had yet been done. No trees had yet been cut down. It was still the unspoilt countryside of deep lanes, rich meadows, hilly terrain and, distantly, high downs. The farmer who had removed his sheep from the fields here had brought them back again. Savesbury Hill was still unravaged, a single-standing tor with its crowning ring of trees, its roots in the feeding ground of the Map butterfly. Still. He had no time to waste but for all that he made enough of a detour to see if he could spot evidence of the environmental assessment, but there was no sign of it, unless he was looking in the wrong place.

Last time he had passed this way a fitful sun had been shining. The wind was high enough to blow clouds constantly across the sun's face so that the bright light came and went, and cloud shadows were swept across the green hillsides like flocks of great dark birds. But today it was dull, the thick grey sky threatening rain. The woods must be full of tree people, biding their time, waiting to know what the next move would be, but he could see none of them. Someone

830

had told him that up at the Stowerton end of the bypass site, where the children had found the bones, grass and weeds were already growing on the mounds of upturned earth.

Outside the Framhurst teashop tree people sat at tables, or they might only have been walkers backpacking. No Conrad Tarling, no Gary nor Quilla, no Freya. Perhaps they were all somewhere guarding the Struthers, but he didn't think so. Somehow he knew it wasn't that way at all, it was quite different, he had been looking at this whole thing from the wrong angle. But what was the use of that if you didn't know how and where it was wrong?

Bibi opened the door to him. She had been alerted to his coming, said Andrew was about somewhere and Wexford might find him 'round the back'. He walked through a brick archway on to an area with a floor like a checkerboard of stone squares and turf squares. Tubs of striped petunias and Jamaican daisies stood about, evidence of Kitty Struther's horticultural skills. The dog Manfred was in the act of lifting its leg against a leafy climbing plant which rambled across one of the walls. Wexford turned as Andrew Struther appeared round the side of the Georgian building and followed him back to the house.

The house seemed tidier, better tended, more the way poor Kitty Struther would want to find it when she came home. Sitting in her gracious living-room with its chintz and its rugs in their muted colours, its silver and its Chinese porcelain, Wexford looked once more at the framed photograph of the two remaining hostages, a copy of which Andrew had brought him. You wouldn't guess from this, he thought, that Kitty Struther would bend and break so quickly under pressure and her husband transform himself into a strutting Blimp. In the picture she looked rather more adventurous than he, a well-kept almost athletic skier who had long ago graduated from the nursery slopes. Owen Struther reminded him of photographs from his youth of Sir Edmund Hillary, and Owen appeared as capable of climbing the world's highest mountain.

'You have some news?' Andrew Struther asked.

'Nothing to comfort you much, I'm afraid. I'm here to tell you that your parents are now the only hostages that Sacred Globe hold.'

'What about the boy?'

Wexford told him. Struther clenched his hands and after a moment or two bowed his head and brought his fists up to his forehead. He seemed to make a massive effort at self-control, breathing deeply and

tensing the muscles of his shoulders. He was very different now from
the arrogant and supercilious man who, a week ago, had shown
Burden and Karen the door. Stress had broken him.

'A call may come here. We have a trace on your phone, but I
would like you to co-operate just the same.'

'If by that you mean telling the little bastard what I think of him
I'll co-operate all right.'

'I mean exactly the reverse of that, Mr Struther. I would like you to
keep him talking for as long as you can. Don't antagonise him. Talk
about your parents if you like. It would be natural for you to ask
after their welfare, and the more you ask and talk the more likely he
is to give you some indication of where they are.'

'You think he'll phone *here*?'

'No, I don't think so. I just want to be prepared.'


If royalty had been visiting Mrs Peabody could hardly have cleaned
and garnished her house more thoroughly. She had had notice of the
coming of the two officers since eight o'clock on the previous evening
and that had been enough. The spring-cleaning must have taken
place between then and nine in the morning when Burden and Karen
arrived. Mrs Peabody had probably got up at five. One of the
antimacassars on the back of an armchair was still slightly damp
from the wash, though carefully starched and ironed. Karen touched
it with her fingertip and smiled. Then she told herself that she could
become like that if she didn't watch it. In about thirty-five years' time
she could be a Mrs Peabody, plumping up cushions before guests
came, even making someone, whoever it was – Damon Slesar? – take
off his shoes when he came in the front door.

'Penny for your thoughts, Sergeant Malahyde,' said Burden
because she had gone rather pink.

'I was just thinking I could turn into a finicky old *hausfrau* like
Mrs P. if I wasn't careful.'

'And so could I,' confessed Burden, 'or the male equivalent.'

Audrey Barker was to answer the phone herself. If it rang, when it
rang. She hovered, coming and going, helping her mother with
whatever was left for Mrs Peabody to do, returning with creased-up
face and anxious eyes. Alone for a moment with Karen in the kitchen
she volunteered, unasked, the information that her operation had
been for gallstones. So much for Ryan's more sensational version of
that surgery, repeated by Dora Wexford on tape. Karen marvelled at

832

the mind, not to say the imagination, of a fourteen-year-old boy who could give his mother a cone biopsy.

The first time the phone rang was at twenty-past ten. Mrs Peabody had just brought in cups of milky frothy coffee, the Rhombus Road version of capuccino. A lace-trimmed cloth was on the tray and a paper doily on the biscuit plate, the sugar was the loaf kind and there was an apostle spoon in each saucer. Audrey Barker looked at it with the loathing of a woman who cares very little for the appearance of domestic appurtenances but has all her life suffered under the reproofs of a houseproud mother. The phone ringing made her jump and bring her hands up to her head. Burden nodded to her and she picked up the receiver.

It was immediately clear this wasn't Ryan. Burden – and Wexford – had wondered about the man Ryan had told Dora his mother was engaged to. Was this another figment of his hungry imagination? Apparently not, though, as Audrey Barker explained, putting the phone down after a minute or two. 'My friend' she called him. 'He phones me every day. Well, two or three times a day.'

The time went by. To Burden it passed very slowly. Mrs Peabody took away their coffee cups, picked up two invisible biscuit crumbs from the area of carpet between his feet. For something to do, he asked Audrey Barker about her son, his tastes, his interests, his progress at school, and she told him, manifestly becoming less tense. Ryan shone, apparently, at biology and geography, a prowess which surprised no one. He possessed a considerable library of books on natural history. She had given him a field guide to British birds for Christmas and had already bought a set of wildlife videos for his coming birthday . . .

The phone rang again at midday and because it was precisely twelve noon, which somehow seemed a likely time for Sacred Globe to phone, when Audrey lifted the receiver Karen got up and stood close enough to her to hear her caller's voice. It might have been a likely time but it wasn't the right time. The caller was Hassy Masood.

'He phones every day too,' Audrey said when the short conversation was over. 'It's what he calls being my support group. Very kind, I suppose, though frankly I could do without it. She's not up to talking and I don't wonder. He always explains she's not up to it.'

Next time the phone rang it was a wrong number. Watching

833

Audrey, Karen thought she had never before quite seen the significance of the phrase 'jumping out of one's skin'.

The forensic science laboratory naturally gave Wexford no clue as to the provenance of the sleeping bag. Nicky Weaver had made tracing it her task, now that it was clear they had been wrong in supposing it to be identified with the one bought in Brixton and sold to Frenchie Collins. She had also eliminated the north-London source, and she and Hennessy had widened their search to the Midlands while Damon Slesar kept up his surveillance of Conrad Tarling.

But if there was nothing in the lab report on the sleeping bag's origin, a great deal of evidence had been gathered as to where it had been after it came into the possession of Sacred Globe.

It was made of washable material and had been washed at least once in its lifetime. After the Collins woman brought it back from Africa, thought Wexford, only she hadn't brought it back, it wasn't hers. She had told Slesar it wasn't hers and why should she lie?

Few of the substances on Dora's clothes had been found on the inside or outside of the sleeping bag, except for the cat hair. There was plenty of that. Small stains on the outside of the bag had been made in one case by coffee, black coffee without milk, and in the other by red wine. Three small irregular stones inside the bag were the constituents of gravel, all of them tiny flint fragments, but perhaps the most interesting find was a withered leaf. It had been in the bottom of the bag and in the opinion of the forensic scientist had very likely adhered to one of Roxane's shoes. The leaf was not from a wild plant but from the cultivated climber Ipomoea rubro-caerulea, the Morning Glory.

Wexford read that part of the report again. He had once tried growing Morning Glory in his own garden but the summer had been so bad that the first flowers on the sickly attenuated plant failed to come out till October, only to be immediately nipped by frost. Parts of it – seeds? Root? Leaves? – were alleged to produce hallucinations, Sheila had told him, she knew people who chewed it, but when he looked up Ipomoea in a herbal he had found only that it was a source of the purgative, jalap.

On Roxane's clothes had been found stains made by her own blood, by body lotion – presumably deposited before her abduction – by non-lactic soymilk and by tomato sauce. He turned the pages back to the beginning and looked, unseeing, out of his window.

Ryan Barker phoned his mother at the very moment when Burden was giving up hope, was thinking they were in for another of those long waits. Days of waiting once more perhaps, God forbid.

Mrs Peabody made them the kind of sandwiches that are called 'dainty', little crustless triangles of white bread with wafer-thin ham or cress between the slices. She sat and watched them eat. An hour later she made tea. She brought in a cake, the kind of confection Patsy Panick might have admired, chocolate with chocolate icing and ornamented by chocolate flake bars. To Burden's astonishment the sight and smell of it brought a breath of nausea up into his throat, but thin, tense Karen took a small slice.

Her eye drawn to a speck of something on the mantelpiece that shouldn't have been there, Mrs Peabody came back with a duster and got to work. She rubbed feverishly, polishing ornaments. It reminded Karen of a cat who suddenly senses some trace of scent or dirt on its apparently spotless paw and begins a manic licking.

The phone gave a preparatory click. It hadn't done that before or if it had they hadn't noticed. The bell seemed disproportionately loud, a shrill shattering sound. Audrey gave the number as they had instructed her, in monotonous dalek-speak.

The fiancé once more. Burden wished he had asked Audrey to tell him not to call again that day. He did it now. She nodded but she didn't ask. She put the phone down and it rang at once.

Karen was immediately at Audrey Barker's side as she grabbed the receiver. Again the number was given in that mechanical monotone.

A boy's voice, long-broken but unsteady and perhaps pitched high through nervousness.

'Mum? It's me.'

# 23

'Did you pass on the message, Mum?'

'Of course I did, Ryan. I did what you said.'

Audrey Barker was no actress. Her voice sounded stilted, as if the words had been learned by heart for the dramatic society's play.

'They have to reroute the bypass, you got that?'

'I got it, Ryan, and I passed it on. Like you said, Ryan.'

That stilted voice made him suspicious. 'Is there anyone there with you?'

She almost screamed. 'Of course not, of course not!'

'It has to be announced. Officially. By the government. And if it's not Mrs Struther dies. Have you got that? Before nightfall tomorrow or Mrs Struther's dead.'

'Oh, Ryan . . .'

'I think you've got someone there. I'm going to ring off. I won't call again. Remember our cause is just. It's the only way, Mum, it's the way to save the planet. And when it's a matter of saving the planet one woman's life is of no account. I'm going now. Goodbye.'

That was the conversation Karen Malahyde heard directly. Later on, Wexford was to listen to a tape of it, but before he could do so the call had been traced.

To the Brigadier public house on the old Kingsmarkham bypass.

It had started to rain. The rain, which had been gloomily forecast, which had been expected for days, fell rapidly out of swiftly gathered black clouds, then in torrents, fountaining, crashing rain. It held them up. They might have been there in fifteen minutes, that was the minimum it took, but the rain was the kind that doesn't merely slow traffic, it drives it for safety's sake off the road.

Pemberton, driving Burden and Karen, was forced to pull into a lay-by. It was like being under some great waterfall, he said, maybe Niagara Falls. Barry Vine and Lynn Fancourt, in the next car, caught them up and pulled in behind them. By the time the rain had lessened, had been reduced to a normal heavy storm, twenty minutes had gone by. Half an hour had passed by the time they got to the Brigadier, roaring in over that crunchy gravel approach like cops in an LA car chase.

Twenty-five minutes to six, and William Dickson had opened for the evening trade thirty-five minutes before. He was serving the couple in the saloon bar with a pint of Guinness and a gin and blackcurrant when the five policemen came in – crashed in as hard as the rain – and Vine, with Pemberton behind him, strode across to the door into the public bar.

Burden snapped, 'Who else is in the house?'

'The wife. Me,' said Dickson. 'What is this? What's going on?'

Vine came back. 'There's nobody in the public.'

'Of course there isn't. I said. There's this lady and gentleman and me, and the wife's upstairs. What is all this?'

'We'll take a look,' said Burden.

'Suit yourselves. You might ask. Politeness never did no harm. You're lucky I'm not asking to see your warrant.'

The couple in the bar, the woman at a table, her companion at the counter preparing to pay for his drinks, stared with cautious pleasure. The man kept his eyes on Burden while pushing a five-pound note towards Dickson.

Vine went into the back hallway where the pay-phone was. This was the phone Ulrike Ranke had used back in April when she had made the last call of her life. He looked inside various rooms, an office with another phone, a small sitting-room or snug. There was no one about. Karen followed him. Pemberton and Lynn Fancourt went upstairs.

The rain was coming down heavily again. Sheets of it, falling on the empty car park, almost obscured the outline of the dismal building Dickson called a ballroom. Burden told the man and the woman he was a police officer, showed them his warrant card and asked them how long they had been in the pub.

'Now you wait a minute,' said Dickson.

Burden rounded on him. 'Your wife is being fetched to take over

837

the trade in here. I'd like you to go into that snug place of yours and wait for me. I want to talk to you.'

'What about, for Christ's sake?'

'I regret having to speak to you like this in front of your patrons, Mr Dickson, but you'll go into that room *now*, or else I'll arrest you for obstructing me in the execution of my duty.'

Dickson went. He kicked the doorstop in a petulant way, like a cross child, but he went. Pemberton came back with Dickson's wife, a top-heavy blonde woman of about forty wearing black leggings and high-heeled sandals. Burden nodded to her and asked the couple with the drinks if they would mind his joining them at their table. Rather bemused, the man shook his head. He said his name was Roger Gardiner and his friend's was Sandra Cole.

Barry Vine said, 'I'd like to ask you a few questions' and repeated the one Burden had already asked.

'We came in when it opened,' Gardiner said. 'We were early and we waited outside a bit. In the car.'

'Other people were here then. A boy of about fifteen? And others with him?'

'He was older than that,' Sandra Cole said. 'He was taller than Rodge.'

'We were in here by then,' Gardiner said. 'Been in here a couple of minutes. A man and a woman – well, a girl – they came in, ran into the bar with the boy, and the girl asked the manager, the owner, whatever, if they could use the phone.'

'She said the boy was in something-shock, ana-something shock, and they had to get an ambulance.'

'Anaphylactic shock?'

'That's it. It was urgent, she said, and the owner, he told them where the phone was . . .'

'I told them where the phone was,' Dickson said to Burden. 'Not that pay one, the one in my office. It was urgent, see, she said the kid might die if he didn't get to a hospital. So I reckoned they didn't want to be messing about with a pay-phone . . .'

'Developed a conscience since the Ulrike Ranke business, have you?'

'I don't know what that's supposed to mean. They went off into the office and I never saw them again.'

'Come on, Dickson, you can do better than that. You let them use your phone, you were worried the boy might die, but once you'd seen the back of them the whole thing went out of your head?'

'I did go in there,' said Dickson, 'but they was gone. I asked the wife if she'd heard the ambulance because I hadn't, but she didn't know what I was on about.'

'Show me the phone.'

It was on the desk among the welter of papers and magazines, a brown telephone constructed of a substance that has a glossy surface.

'Has it been touched since?'

Dickson shook his head. A tic had started at the corner of his mouth.

'Don't touch it. And close the place. Most likely you can open again tomorrow.'

'What's all this about? I can't close just like that!'

'You don't have a choice,' said Burden.

He had heard a car arrive. You could hear anything on that gravel. A sparrow walking across it would have been clearly audible. He had heard a car and thought it was customers for the Brigadier but it was Wexford, driven up here by Donaldson. He was in the saloon bar, talking to Linda Dickson, who was now holding a diminutive Yorkshire terrier in her arms, its face pressed up against her brightly painted cheek. Gardiner and his girlfriend were doing their best to describe to Karen Malahyde the appearance of the man and the woman who had accompanied Ryan Barker.

'I never saw them,' Linda Dickson said. She looked around for her husband, but he was locking and bolting the front doors. 'I thought I heard a car, but it must have been that lady and gentleman.'

'Why "must have been"?'

'You can hear everything on that gravel. If this was a free house I'd have that concreted but the brewery won't spend the money.'

'There's no need to go over the gravel if you drive straight into the car park at the back, is there?'

'That's what they must have done.'

'I'm not much of a hand at describing what people look like,' said her husband. 'See too many of them, I reckon. The boy was tall, he was a very tall lad, tall as me . . .'

'We know what the boy looks like, Mr Dickson,' said Wexford, his eye on the tattoo on the man's left forearm. Butterfly? Bird? Abstract design? 'The boy is Ryan Barker, one of the hostages. You keep asking what this is about – well, it's about Sacred Globe. Do

839

you think that will jog your memory when it comes to describing these people?'

Dickson's mouth fell open. 'You have to be kidding.'

'No, I don't have to be. If I was in the mood for it I could think up a better joke that that.'

'Sacred Globe. Bloody hell. You do mean those lunatics that kidnapped those people and killed the girl?'

'Try describing those lunatics, will you?'

His description, when it finally came, tallied with those of Roger Gardiner and Sandra Cole. None of the three was particularly observant, none apparently much interested in his or her fellow human beings. The plausible tale of anaphylactic shock which, it now appeared, had been told solely by the woman, and which might have been expected to attract their interest, had registered only as an account of something alien and unpronounceable. They considered. Roger Gardiner had actually scratched his head. After a massive shrug of his heavy shoulders, William Dickson came up with the best he could do.

The woman was small but wiry and fit-looking. She wore no make-up and her hair was hidden under a baseball cap. She was young but no one could suggest her age more precisely than to describe her as between twenty and thirty. Her companion was a tall, thin man, also wearing a baseball cap and a pair of dark glasses. Their clothes were so unremarkable that no one could specify what they wore. Jeans, perhaps, jackets of dark or neutral colours. No one had noticed eye colour or a single peculiarity. The man had spoken. The woman's voice was . . . just an ordinary voice.

'Like *EastEnders*,' said Roger Gardiner.

Wexford knew what he meant, or thought he did. London working class, only it wasn't politically correct to use expressions like that these days. Cockney – did anyone use the word anymore? Or did he mean like an actor in a television soap? Asked, Gardiner didn't know, couldn't answer, could only repeat what he had said. Like *EastEnders*.

'I'd like to have a look outside,' Wexford said to Dickson.

'Be my guest, guv'nor. I hope I'm a reasonable man, I hope I know how to co-operate. Only there are some not a million miles from where I'm standing who don't know the meaning of the word manners.'

The car park was awash. Puddles were more like shallow lakes and rain dripped off the eaves of the barrack-like building which loomed over the sheets of water. By now the rain had stopped but the dark-grey sky was heavy with more to come. A wind had got up, tearing at the branches of the chestnuts in the meadow beyond the fence.

Wexford hadn't much hope. The truth was that now he had no hope, but he was going to look inside that building just the same. A dance hall – well, if you stuck a few bits of neon on the outside, flung open those double asbestos doors, had some cheerful people selling tickets . . . No, it would always be a dreary dump, a cavernous barn of a place, and the best thing for it would be to pull it down.

Cavernous was right. The whole area must have been sixty feet by forty and the ceiling – or roof of girders and plasterboard – a good thirty feet high. There were metal-framed windows all along both sides, a stage of sorts at one end. Vine opened the door that seemed to lead behind the stage and they trooped through. But nothing was to be seen apart from two lavatories, one with a picture of a peacock with fanned tail on the door, the other of a drab peahen – the most sexist thing she'd seen in years, Karen said angrily – a passage and a large unfurnished room that might once have been used for making tea and even preparing food. The place was dusty and untended, and when Dickson said it hadn't been used for years no one had any difficulty believing him.

Yet why had those two brought Ryan here? What was the point of it? Returning to the main premises of the Brigadier, Wexford wondered if it might be from fear of returning to the phone or call box they had used three times before, while they obviously couldn't use any phone that might be installed where the hostages were. Did they know the pub would be largely unfrequented at that time of day? That Dickson and his wife were scarcely perceptive people?

'You've closed up, Mr Dickson,' he said. 'You'll be at a bit of a loose end this evening, so with your permission I think we'll use it to have a talk about your patrons. Who comes here, who's a regular, that sort of thing.'

Still clutching the Yorkshire terrier, Linda Dickson said shrilly, 'You're taking him to the police station?'

Wexford regarded her calmly. 'Would that present a problem, Mrs Dickson? But no, I'm not. I thought we might talk here. In your office.'

Hennessy was unplugging the phone with gloved hands, dropping the instrument into a plastic bag.

'He can't have my phone!'

'The property of Telecom, as a matter of fact, Mr Dickson. We'll clear it with them. You'll soon have it back.' Wexford sat down without waiting to be asked. He was pretty sure he wouldn't be asked. 'Now, you'd never seen these people before, I take it?'

'Never. Not one of them.'

'Do many of the locals use the Brigadier or do you depend on a passing-through trade, people on their way to the coast?'

Once it was plain to Dickson that Wexford's questions were not to involve him directly, not aimed at jeopardising his livelihood or discourage his clientele, he began to enjoy himself. People usually did, Wexford had found. Everybody likes imparting information, and the ignorant and unobservant correspondingly enjoy it more.

'Well, it's all the lot, isn't it?' said Dickson. 'We get a lot of the young. There's not many senior citizens, on account of you need transport to get out here and that they don't have a lot of. Mr Canning from Framhurst, he's in here a lot.'

'He means Ron Canning from Goland Farm,' said Linda Dickson, putting the Yorkshire terrier on the floor where it stood shivering. 'You know, him as lets those tree people use his field for their cars. If,' she added, 'you can call them cars.'

The dog sniffed Wexford's shoes, gave his left toecap an exploratory lick. He shifted his feet, not easy in so confined a space. 'What's that tattoo on your arm, Mr Dickson? Some sort of insect, is it, or a bird or what?'

'A swallow, it's supposed to be.' To Wexford's surprise, Dickson flushed. 'I'm going to have it removed, the wife's not keen on it. Haven't got round to it yet, that's all.' He picked up the dog, pressed its face against his red cheek and reverted quickly to the original subject. 'Those Weir Theatre people come in. From Pomfret. They call themselves the Friends of the Weir Theatre and the leading light in that's a chap called Jeffrey Godwin. He's like an actor.'

'Been in *Bramwell*,' said Linda. 'No, I tell a lie, it was *Casualty*.'

'I don't mind that, I can tell you,' said Dickson, holding the dog against his shoulder and rubbing its spine as if in an effort to bring up wind. 'I mean, folks like him coming in. Attracts trade, that's what it does. Lot of punters come in just to get a look at him and I always point him out, the least I can do. I always say, that's Jeffrey Godwin, the actor. He's very gracious, I must say.'

Dickson spoke as if he were the proprietor of a restaurant in mid-

842

town Manhattan where Paul Newman was frequently to be seen at a particular table. He smiled reminiscently and settled the dog on his lap, where it immediately fell asleep.

'Look at him,' said Linda fondly. 'You can see he loves his daddy. Can I get you a drink, Mr Wexford? I'm sure I don't know what's happened to my manners. Must be all this upheaval.'

Wexford refused.

'Little something for you, Bill?'

While Dickson was considering this offer, Wexford asked him if he'd noticed any newcomers recently who had become regulars. Did any of the protesters, for instance, use the Brigadier?

Dickson made no secret of his contempt for those involved in any kind of protest against, or even dissent from, totally orthodox convention. Wexford knew at once, from the expression on his face, from the curl of his lip, without his having to say a word, exactly what his attitude would be to those who attempt to save whales, ban fox-hunting, prohibit chemical fertiliser, favour organic foods, are thrifty with water, use lead-free petrol or recycle anything at all.

'Needless to say,' said Dickson, 'I haven't got a lot of time for those gentry. And don't get me wrong, that's not on account of they don't *drink*, not to say *drink*, because they're the sort that imbibe a good deal in the way of your mineral waters and Britvics, and that's where your licensee makes his profit, so no, it's not that. It's not that they've got no money for their Perriers and Cokes and whatever. I'll tell you what it is, it's like the way they're interfering in life, our life, yours and mine, guv'nor. Life what has to go on, if you take my meaning. *What has to go on.* Right?'

He drew breath, reached for the tankard his wife had brought him. 'Thank you, my sweetheart, that's very kind of you. Now who else can I tell you about? Well now, there's this lady Stan drives up here now and again. Don't know her name – d'you know her name, Lin?'

'I don't, Bill. Quite an elderly lady she is, from Kingsmarkham, and she comes up here regular Tuesdays and Thursdays to meet a gentleman. I said to Bill, that's very sweet, I said, that's touching, them being not a day under seventy. But I don't know her name and I don't know his. Stan would know.'

Wexford wondered what possible connection the Dicksons thought a pair of superannuated lovers who chose to meet in the Brigadier of all places – was one of them married? Were both of them? – could have with Sacred Globe. 'Stan?' he said.

843

'Stan Trotter,' said Linda. 'Well, Stanley, to give him his full name. He drives her up here on account of her not driving herself, not having a licence, I dare say. I say "drives her" but it's not been going on for more than – what would you say, Bill? A month?

'The first time, a Tuesday it was, Stan came into the lounge bar with her and that was the first time I'd seen him since April, as a matter of fact, since the night that German girl got herself killed.'

Wexford looked at her and watched the colour flood her face.

# 24

For the second time in six months Stanley Trotter had been arrested, but this time he would appear on the following morning at Kingsmarkham Magistrates' Court, charged with the murder of Ulrike Ranke.

'I owe you an apology, Mike,' Wexford said. 'You were right all along. I dare say I was rude to you – can't remember what I said but I expect it was nasty.'

'I didn't *know*, you know. I was doing your intuitive thing. It was just a very powerful feeling. I didn't know Trotter's second wife was Linda Dickson's sister. I didn't go into his family tree, though maybe I should have.'

'He was only married to her for five minutes,' said Wexford.

'The mystery is the woman feels she owes him some sort of loyalty. She came out with it quite involuntarily. "Well, he's my brother-in-law, isn't he?" was what she said. She seems to subscribe to the curious notion that once a brother-in-law always a brother-in-law, irrespective of intervening divorces and remarriages. These days that must give some people very large extended families.'

'Dickson didn't mention it, though?'

'Dickson didn't know his wife saw Trotter. Or maybe he just didn't want to know. When she was questioned she said she'd gone to bed and to sleep. Only in fact she was looking out of the window. They're not exactly a compassionate couple, are they? Not what you'd call well endowed with empathy? Can she actually have been *concerned* about Ulrike?'

Burden shook his head, but in the way someone does when he doubts rather than denies. 'She's a woman and Ulrike was a young girl. There's always so much we don't know in a case like this, so much we'll never know.'

'Are you saying this was simple anxiety as to Ulrike's ultimate welfare?'

'I don't know. Do you?'

'Maybe I do. Suffice it to say for now that she did look out of the window, she sat in the window waiting and saw Trotter arrive at about eleven. Trotter didn't ring the bell or knock on the door because he didn't need to. Ulrike was waiting out there and he didn't even have to drive across that gravel and thus announce his coming to Dickson who was clearing up in the bar.'

'And when Dickson finally went upstairs Linda didn't say a word about seeing Trotter come for the girl? Didn't say anything then or when the girl went missing, or when her body was found?'

'Look at it this way, Mike. Linda was relieved when Trotter came, a load had been taken from her mind, so she got into bed and fell asleep. Remember she'd had a heavy day. Next morning she'd no reason to feel anxious about Ulrike. Trotter had picked her up and driven her wherever she wanted to go. But when Ulrike was missing, when the papers were full of it, what did she think then?'

'We've never gone any more deeply into why Dickson performed the callous act of sending Ulrike outside to wait for the taxi. He hasn't given a reason, just said they were closed and it wasn't a cold night. But suppose it was Linda who made him send her outside? Linda who even took her to the door, closed it and locked and bolted it? Poor Ulrike isn't alive to tell us.

'My idea is that Linda is a jealous woman, who's been given reason in the past to be jealous. She wasn't leaving Dickson alone with a young woman in the middle of the night, but for herself, she was exhausted, she was dying for her bed . . .'

'Yes, but Reg, Ulrike was a personable young woman of nineteen and Dickson – well, he's not exactly love's young dream, is he?'

'Not to you or me or Ulrike maybe, but perhaps he is to Linda.' Wexford smiled. 'When someone asked James Thurber why the women in his cartoons weren't attractive he said, "They are attractive to my men." Dickson is attractive to Linda and therefore she thinks he must be to everyone else. So she sent Ulrike outside and watched from upstairs to see the taxi come. Because if it hadn't come Ulrike might have come back inside, been *allowed back inside* by Dickson.'

Burden nodded. 'And later?'

'After the body was found, d'you mean? By then she knew Dickson had nothing to do with it. But she had her loyalty to her ex-brother-in-law. To be fair to her, she was probably quite unable to confront the fact that a member of her family, however briefly and tenuously a member, could be a murderer. Few people can do that. He picked Ulrike up, he was driving the taxi, but someone else killed her.'

'I'll never understand human beings.'

'You and me both,' said Wexford. 'Trotter drove Ulrike to Framhurst Copses, raped and strangled her. Perhaps she'd offered him a large sum of money to drive her all the way to Aylesbury and he'd seen what money she'd got. He took it and the pearls. She may have offered him the money and the pearls as the price for her life, so he must have been disappointed when he only got tuppence halfpenny for a necklace he thought worth over a thousand.' He shook his head. 'As for Sacred Globe, they fetched us there for fun. To amuse themselves.'

Ryan Barker's last message, his demand, had not reached the media. A blanket of not so much silence as negativity had fallen over Sacred Globe and the inquiry, drawn down by Wexford, as if he had pulled a cord and released some heavy drapery. The newspapers carried stories of failure, of police ineptitude, of hostages' lives at increased risk, but they held no *news*, no single new development. No word of Ryan Barker's defection had been released to them.

It was as if Sacred Globe and its three captives – its two captives? – were passing into the realm of hostage-taking terrorists associated with a Middle Eastern political scene. The hostages were taken, there was international outcry, demands were made, all negotiation was repudiated, more demands were made with more threats, and then gradually the whole situation grew stale, to be replaced by new excitements. And meanwhile the hostages remained, languished, half forgotten as the days passed, the weeks, the months, the years.

The new excitement in Kingsmarkham was Stanley Trotter's court appearance. A brief one it would be, followed by an immediate remand to a higher court, but the press were on the scene in good time, the same faces, the same cameras, as on the morning the news of Sacred Globe broke.

It had been a big story, Ulrike Ranke's disappearance and the discovery of her body. She was female, young, blonde, good-looking. If that wasn't enough, she had been wandering by night in what was to her a foreign country, carrying drugs, money, jewels, the stuff of sensation.

The aim would be to establish some link between her death and Sacred Globe, or her death and Roxane Masood's. Unfortunately for this pack of people, speculation as to Trotter's links with Sacred Globe would now be *sub judice* and strictly to be kept out of print until a guilty verdict could be returned some months afterwards. Unfortunately, too, the cell in Kingsmarkham police station where Trotter had been held overnight was no more than fifty yards from the entrance to the Magistrates' Court.

A coat was thrown over his head and he was bundled across the paving, while the television cameramen got their shots for early evening news programmes and Newsroom South-East. A small crowd of the public, none of whom had known Ulrike or Trotter or had any personal interest whatever in her murder, waited about in time to boo and yell imprecations, while the hooded figure made his short journey. They too would be on television, which was perhaps what they most wanted.

Nicky Weaver said she couldn't understand it. She never wanted to hear the words 'sleeping' and 'bag' coupled together again as long as she lived. But she knew as surely as it was possible to know anything of this nature that every Outdoors camouflage sleeping bag sold in the British Isles had now been traced. There had been thirty-six, the green-and-purple version being more popular.

'It's a blessing we weren't trying to track down the coloured ones,' she said to Wexford. 'There were ninety-six of them. The thing is, of the camouflage type, Ted or I have seen every one of them. I mean, actually cast our eyes over them. Most hadn't been sold, as I say they aren't popular, people think they look like old army surplus. But we also tracked down a couple to people's homes, one in Leicester and one in a village in Shropshire.'

'So what are you saying?'

'I'm saying it has to be the bag Frenchie Collins bought in Brixton and says she abandoned at the airport in Zaïre.'

'Why would she lie, Nicky?'

'Because she gave or sold that bag to a friend who's involved with

848

Sacred Globe and she knows it. She's probably a sympathiser herself, or maybe more than that.'

Burden would appear in court but not Wexford. He had brought Dora in again and she sat in the old gym. She joked that she never went anywhere but the police station. Did he realise she hadn't been out at all since her release except here and on a single visit to Sylvia?

'Permission to go out tomorrow night, please,' she said.

Like the kind of husband he had never been, would never be, he asked, 'Where do you want to go?'

'Oh, Reg. They're not going to grab me again. Be sensible. I want to go to the Weir Theatre to see Jeffrey Godwin's play. Jenny says she'll go with me.'

'Because I'll say you need a keeper?'

He knew he couldn't shut her up at home, like a woman in purdah, like one of Bluebeard's wives. She had become more precious to him than she had ever been since the first year of their marriage. Now he knew he had undervalued her and wanted years ahead of them in which to show constantly his appreciation.

'I will never stop you doing anything,' he said.

Nicky Weaver came in and he started the recorder.

'It's the distance we're interested in, Dora,' he began. 'It's a matter of how long you were actually in the car. Now, according to what you've already told us, you were in it for only about an hour when you were taken to wherever it was.'

'That's right.'

'But when they brought you home you say you were taken out of the basement room at about ten, yet you didn't get back to Kingsmarkham, to within a quarter of a mile of our house, until half-past midnight. Rather later than that, in fact. Because you came in through our front door just before one.'

'Yes. On the return journey I think I was in the car for nearly three hours. I assume he was just driving round and round. I've got a theory about that.' She looked from one to the other of them almost shyly. 'Sorry, I shouldn't have, should I? But do you want to hear it?'

'Of course we do,' said Nicky.

'Well,' Dora took a deep breath. 'Well, on the way out it didn't matter so much to them, the distance, I mean. They didn't know then that I'd ever come back. Maybe they thought they'd kill me, I don't know. But on the return journey to Kingsmarkham they knew the first thing I'd do was talk to Reg, then to you all. I'd be bound to and it would be fresh in my mind. So they really had to deceive me and they made the journey as long as they reasonably could.'

'Sounds feasible,' Wexford said. 'But were they deceiving you on the outward journey as well? You see, you've said you could have been taken anywhere within a radius of about sixty miles, but could it have been far less than that?'

'I suppose it could.'

'Could it have been within thirty miles? Or twenty? Or ten?'

She put one hand up to her mouth. It was as if the possibility of this frightened her. 'You mean, were they driving round in circles? Sort of on to the old bypass and round the roundabout and back again and out to Myringham and turn back and up the old bypass again?'

He smiled at her. 'Sort of, yes.'

'It never occurred to me,' she said. 'But I don't see why not. I really don't see why not. I wouldn't have known. I couldn't see a thing. We did go round corners and I think we went round roundabouts. Now you mention it, I think we went all the way round one roundabout. It didn't seem important when I was talking to you the first time but now – I think we did go all the way round.'

A satisfied expression on his face, Burden came back from the court after less than an hour. The proceedings had been swift, Stanley Trotter having been committed for trial and remanded in custody. He found Wexford in the old gym, talking to Nicky Weaver.

'What do we do then, bring her in? It's the Met's ground, Brixton, but I doubt if they'll have any objection. I wonder if she'd ever lived round here, if she has any connection with this neighbourhood.'

Burden said, 'Who are you talking about?'

'This woman called Frenchie Collins. I'm wondering if she knows any of these tree people. If, for instance, she's acquainted with the King of the Wood.'

'Why do you ask?'

Wexford said slowly, 'Because we've been talking about the hostages being within a radius of sixty miles, but that was much too wide, that was too generous. They're not in London or Kent or down on the South Coast. They're here, very near here, and the radius is going to be more like five miles.'

'That's just guesswork.'

'Is it, Mike? The non-lactic soymilk isn't proof of anything but it's

850

evidence. It may not have come from the Framhurst teashop but it very likely did. Ryan Barker made his second phone call from the Brigadier, and though that again proves nothing, it does give a strong indication.'

Wexford sat down. He hesitated, then said, 'Who would be most likely to want this bypass stopped? Environmental activists, yes, professional protesters, maybe. Any green group opposed to destroying England, that's for sure. But more than that would be someone, or more than one, who would be personally affected by the building of the bypass.'

'You mean, people whose livelihood might be endangered by it?' Nicky asked.

'That of course. By what I mean is simpler. People whose outlook, view, of the countryside would be spoilt. Those who'd see the bypass when they looked out of their windows or hear it when they walked in their garden. Wouldn't they have a deeper, more emotional interest than a professional protester who doesn't care where whatever is happening is happening, whether it's a power station in Cumbria or a flyover in Dorset?

'Imagine a group of people – *amateurs*, mostly – getting together in ... well, in despair, deciding that desperate situations call for desperate measures, all or some of them householders whose views, whose domestic peace and quiet really, will be wrecked by this bypass. Maybe one of them meets someone in the know, someone who's used to this sort of thing, who's not an amateur, and then they start getting things organised.'

'Meets them how?'

'Well, through KABAL, or going to that actor-manager's theatre, the Weir Theatre – where, incidentally, our wives are going together tomorrow night – or maybe on a demonstration. Even on the big march of July.

'One of the group is already in possession of a large suitable house, probably a beautiful country house. After all, that's the point, isn't it? Once the bypass is built it won't be beautiful any more, or its surroundings won't be. In the outbuildings is an old dairy, not exactly underground but half subterranean, for coolness's sake when it *was* a dairy. They have a washroom built on and a guard to half cover the window. Say there are half a dozen of them, an ample supply of guards. They haven't much else to organise, have they, except to do it?'

Builders are hard to find. The regular, steady, orthodox firms are a different matter. They advertise, they are in the phone book. As for the others, the money-in-the-back-pocket brigade and the moonlighters, the cowboys here today and gone tomorrow, recommendation of their skills, or more likely their low prices, are passed on by word of mouth or begin with an unsolicited knock at the door.

One of these had built the washroom on to the basement room for the specific purpose of answering the needs of a group of hostages; more likely the cowboys, the Bodger and Sons, than a limited company with premises in the High Street. At some point a phone call had been made to them and an estimate asked for. Or not an estimate. Simply a request to do it. Do it as soon as you can and never mind the cost.

In a way, Wexford thought, it was interesting that the washroom had been built on at all. So much was implied by it, so much could be inferred from it.

'They're terrorists, Mike,' he said to Burden. 'However we may shy away from that word, that's what they are. My dictionary defines terrorism as an organised system of violence and intimidation for political ends. But look at what we know of these particular examples of the breed. In most parts of the world terrorists wouldn't worry about their hostages' hygiene arrangements. A bucket in the corner would do for them. But these people went to the trouble of having a washroom with basin and running water and flush lavatory built on to their prison. Not so much civilised as essentially middle-class, wouldn't you say?'

Burden wasn't very interested. He disliked listening to Wexford's disquisitions on social vagary and psychological symptom. What was the point of it except to distract? He had already got Fancourt, Hennessy and Lowry on to Kingsmarkham, Stowerton and Pomfret builders. The ones in the phone book were easy, the others, those who did this work after their legitimate jobs, were the hardest to find. Kids leaving school who have painted their mothers' front rooms think of taking up building work, Wexford had once said, in the same way as anyone who can type thinks he has a book inside him.

'I'll tell you what I'd say. It's that they did it themselves. Sacred Globe. One of them's an amateur plumber, there's a lot of it about. A frequent visitor to the DIY on the old bypass.'

Wexford brightened. 'We should get someone out there as well

852

then. See if they have a regular customer or did have a regular customer, who bought a lavatory pan from them and a basin and the pipework and whatever back in, say, June.'

'Reg,' said Burden.

Wexford looked at him, looked hard and silently.

'That washroom could have been built ten years ago. It could have been built on to that basement . . .'

'Dora said it was new,' Wexford interrupted. 'And it's not a basement, it's a dairy.'

'If you say so. I was going to say as a part of a flat conversion that was never finished. It doesn't have to have been built on in the past few weeks, just as the non-lactic soymilk doesn't have to have come from Framhurst or that damned moth from Wiltshire. Sherlock Holmes worked like that, making huge leap assumptions, but we can't do the same.'

'They're in a house near here,' said Wexford stubbornly. 'A house that overlooks the bypass or is seriously threatened by the bypass.'

'I'll take you to the theatre,' he said. 'I know I'm being absurd but I don't want you going out alone. Not yet. Jenny can make her own way but I'll take you.'

Instead of saying she wouldn't go, Dora said, 'You haven't got time, Reg.'

'Yes, I have.'

By the middle of Saturday afternoon, when most builders in Kingsmarkham and Stowerton had been eliminated from the inquiry, Nicky Weaver came up with a positive lead. A. and J. Murray Sisters, an all-woman firm based in Pomfret and specialising in small building jobs, volunteered the information that they had built a shower room on to a flat conversion at a farm in Pomfret Monachorum. The job had been carried out in the previous June.

Ann Murray, an electrician and the elder of the sisters, told Nicky that they had been glad of the work, had jumped at the chance, in fact. Even though the recession was over, they hadn't found it easy to convince the locals that women made as effective building contractors as men, that they all had City and Guilds qualifications and kept their estimates low. The Holgates, of Paddocks, a one-time farmhouse on the Cambery Ashes Road near Tancred, had approached them, she thought, because Gillian Holgate also had a trade usually confined to men. She was a motor mechanic.

The work required was to convert an old larder in a cottage next door to the main house into a shower room. The cottage, then consisting of one room up and one down with a kitchen, was to be a home for the Holgates' daughter. A. and J. Murray Sisters had started the job on 10 June and completed it on 15 June, the plumbing being carried out by Maureen Sheridan and the electrics and decoration by Ann Murray herself. It was the right time and the right place. Or it seemed to be.

Wexford went up there, taking Nicky and Damon Slesar with him. Outside the gate to Paddocks he got out of the car and looked down across the valley. It was hard to say from this point if the bypass site would be visible or not. The woods of Tancred lay between here and the distant river and they would certainly muffle any traffic sound. Perhaps when the bypass was built it might be possible to see a segment of it, a triangle of double white highway between the dark trees and the green hillside.

Slesar opened the gate and they drove in, up a long, straight driveway, macadam, not gravel. The farmhouse had a red shingled façade and a low roof of red tiles. On the hard, dark-grey surface, in a broad patch of sunlight, lay two cats, one asleep, the other on its back, green eyes wide open, white paws gracefully waving. One of the cats was a Siamese, the other a tabby.

Next door, the building that was evidently the cottage was in the process of external painting. A woman up on a pair of steps was applying cream-coloured emulsion to its plasterwork with a roller.

Wexford and Nicky got out of the car, and the woman, who looked about forty, was tall and thin and wearing paint-stained dungarees, came towards them rather diffidently.

'Mrs Holgate?'

She nodded.

Slesar said, 'We're police officers.'

Very taken aback, she said, 'What is it? What's happened?'

'Nothing at all, Mrs Holgate. Nothing for you to be worried about.'

By now Wexford was almost certain this was true, in spite of the cats. The cottage was too small to contain the basement room. Even from here you could tell that the ground area measured nothing like twenty feet by fourteen. But he had to look. Might they look?

Rallying a little from her initial shock, Gillian Holgate said she would like to know what it was about. Nicky said they had information that a room in the cottage had been converted into a bathroom three months before.

'I had planning permission,' Mrs Holgate said. 'Everything was above board.'

Wexford was rather amused to be taken for an official of the county planning department. But Mrs Holgate seemed satisfied without further explanation and ushered them in through the front door of the building she had been painting. The place was obviously occupied, though its occupant wasn't at present at home. The downstairs room was furnished, was rather comfortably untidy and a generous estimate would set its measurements at ten feet by twelve.

Wexford had been uneasy about this annexe or conversion ever since he had heard it described as a shower room, since Dora had been emphatic the room she had used had contained only a lavatory and basin. Of course it was possible the shower had been removed or walled in before the hostages were brought there – possible but unlikely.

And they saw now that this was another dead end. The room the Murray sisters had converted was large, its walls tiled, its shower cabinet of generous size. Its window was of frosted glass and curtained. From the main room quite a big picture window had a view of Tancred woods.

'It must have something to do with those hostages,' Mrs Holgate said wonderingly. 'The Kingsmarkham Kidnap.'

They neither confirmed nor denied. Wexford nodded enigmatically. He stepped out once more into the afternoon sunshine and a young woman who had come running out of the main house almost cannoned into him.

She said breathlessly, 'Are you Chief Inspector Wexford?'

'I am.'

'There's a phone call for you.'

'For me? Are you sure?'

But he had his own phone. Who would know he was here? No one knew.

He followed her into the main house. The phone receiver lay off the hook on a small hall table. He lifted it, said, 'Wexford.'

'This is Sacred Globe.'

'Ryan Barker,' said Wexford.

'We haven't heard from you. You haven't complied with our request. If there is no announcement on the evening news bulletins of a complete revision on the plan for the Kingsmarkham bypass Mrs Struther dies.'

Someone had written it for him. He was plainly reading it and reading it nervously, his voice growing squeaky.

Under his breath Wexford cursed this group of people who could so exploit a child. He said, 'What do you mean by evening bulletins, Ryan?'

'Wait a minute, please.'

Wexford could hear him conferring with a companion. Then, 'By seven. If it's not, Mrs Struther dies and we will deliver her body to Kingsmarkham tonight.'

'Ryan, wait. Stay where you are. Are you at the Brigadier on the old bypass?'

No reply, only an indrawn breath.

'What you ask,' Wexford said, 'isn't possible. You know that.'

'You have to make it possible,' Ryan Barker's voice said, growing cold now, growing remote. 'You have to tell the press and tell the government. Tell them she's going to die. We're ready to kill her.'

He added stiffly, obviously prompted. 'We are Sacred Globe, saving the world.'

856

# 25

When he had phoned the Chief Constable and told him of Sacred Globe's latest message, he walked out of the Holgates' house, drove out of their drive and stood on the road, looking through binoculars across the valley.

Somewhere, in a house, a big house, one of those out there among the hills and woods . . . There were hundreds such. And if he couldn't find which one in the next four hours a woman would die. The second woman. Only this one would be deliberate murder. But it would happen because government would never, not in any circumstances, these or similar, not under any threat, announce the cancellation of the bypass. Therefore it would happen unless, in the next four hours, he found which house among so many held the two hostages.

'Nothing to the media,' Montague Ryder said when Wexford walked into the suite at the Constabulary headquarters. 'We must keep it dark from them as long as we can.'

'As long as we can' had a sinister ring. It meant, until Kitty Struther's body is found.

'I know they aren't far from here, sir,' Wexford said.

He glanced at the map on the wall. It was a blown-up sheet from the Ordnance Survey, the central part of the Mid-Sussex area. Ryder nodded to him and he drew with his right forefinger an oval shape that encompassed Kingsmarkham, Stowerton, Pomfret and Sewingbury, the villages of Framhurst, Savesbury, Stringfield, Cambery Ashes and Pomfret Monachorum. Places south of the town were excluded. None of them would be menaced by the new bypass. No house in their vicinity would have a view of it.

'And that's your criterion?'

857

'One of them,' Wexford said. 'Maybe the most important one.'

Did she know they intended to kill her? He didn't ask Montague Ryder that because Ryder could only guess as he could. She had been, and no doubt still was, the most fearful of the hostages, the most vulnerable, the least self-contained and with the fewest inner resources. Was she with her husband or had they too been separated?

And now he found himself in the dreadful position at this juncture of having nothing to do. For ten days they had all worked so hard, had worked to the utmost of their capacity, and the result had been only to narrow down the place they were looking for into something like fifty square miles. Nothing remained but to pick out the needle in the haystack or wait for the discovery of another sleeping bag containing another woman's body.

'We'll keep Contemporary Cars' ground under surveillance,' he said to Burden. 'I doubt if they'd come to the same place twice, but I daren't take the risk.'

'The police station's another possibility. So is Ms Cox's and Mrs Peabody's. The Concreation building. The Brigadier.'

'Your house. My house.'

They were there now, sitting in Burden's living-room. Or, rather, Burden was sitting. Wexford was pacing.

'The *Courier* offices,' he said. 'The Stowerton end of the bypass site. The Pomfret end.'

'You said that kid said Kingsmarkham.'

'That's true. He did. We can't police all these places, anyway. We haven't got the back-up.'

'Has anyone thought of using a helicopter? To find where they are, I mean. We know they're in our fifty square miles.'

'What could you see from a helicopter, Mike? A house with outbuildings? There are hundreds. The hostages aren't going to be up on the roof, waving distress flags.'

Burden shrugged. 'Sacred Globe will watch the BBC's early-evening news, which is at five or five-fifteen on a Saturday, and ITN's half an hour later. If there is no announcement, and of course there can't be, they proceed to kill Kitty Struther. Is that what will happen?'

'I don't know about "will", Mike,' Wexford said bitterly. 'It's twenty to six now. It may be happening now and we can't do a thing to stop it.'

*

Upriver from Watersmeet, where the stream that ran under Kings-markham High Street met the larger waterway, the Brede flows among wide meadows and winds between groves of alders and stands of willows. At one point the stones of the river bed are large enough and regular enough to form a dam, over which the determined water gushes and spouts into the deep pool below. This is Stringfield Weir and it is overlooked by Stringfield Mill, built long ago when some of the farming was arable and the means were needed for grinding corn.

The waterwheel was long gone. Sails there had never been. The building of white weatherboard and red brick, a huge, graceful structure, had been converted some ten years before into a theatre and became the regular venue of repertory companies. The lane that led down to it from Pomfret Monachorum was of reasonable width and serviceable surface. Once there, the theatre-goer had everything the civilised in pursuit of culture could wish for: a large car park concealed by tall trees, a restaurant with river frontage, a splendid view across Stringfield Bridge to the woods, meadows and downs beyond and, of course, the auditorium that was big enough to hold four hundred people.

One of its disadvantages was that actors on stage were bedevilled by flying insects, drawn in by the light, moths and lacewings and daddy-long-legs. Legend had it that a bat had tangled itself in an actress's hair while she was playing Juliet. Wexford, who had never been there before, thought there might be mosquitos and he counselled Dora and Jenny to avoid the river terrace and stay inside for their pre-performance glass of wine.

'I'll come back for you,' he said. 'Will ten-forty-five suit?'

'Reg, we can call for a taxi,' Jenny said. 'I should have brought my own car, I don't know why I didn't. It's not as if we intend to go boozing.'

'Well, now you can. A bit. I'll come back for you so you needn't worry.'

*Extinction*, with Christine Colville and Richard Paton, ran for three hours, not including the two intervals. He read that on the programme up on the foyer wall. This play, by Jeffrey Godwin himself, alternated its performances with a modern-dress version of *Twelfth Night* and with Strindberg's *The Ghost Sonata*. An ambitious company, who set their sights high.

A voice behind him said, 'How's Sheila?'

859

He turned and saw standing at his shoulder a tall genial-looking man with brown curly hair and beard.

'You must be Jeffrey Godwin,' he said. 'Wexford – but you know that. Sheila's fine, got a baby daughter.'

'I saw it in the paper,' said Godwin. 'Lovely. I hope to see mother and child in the not too far distant future. Are you coming to tonight's performance?'

Wexford said he wouldn't be and explained that he was particularly busy at the moment. But his wife was here and her friend. He said goodbye to Godwin and made his way back to the car park, skirting the mill's still sunlit gardens, from which came a heavy scent of late-flowering roses.

Back in Kingsmarkham he went to the police station and into the old gym. Damon Slesar was there with Karen Malahyde and three staff working at computers. Wexford said to the two detective sergeants that the witching hour was past, it was gone seven-thirty now. Give Sacred Globe a couple of hours and the time would come for the returning of Kitty Struther's body.

'It may be an empty threat,' Damon said.

Karen looked at him, shaking her head. 'I don't think so. Why would they start being merciful and civilised at this stage? They're more likely to be made cruel by desperation.'

'Merciful' was an interesting word for her to have used, Wexford thought. He asked her what duties had been arranged for her and Slesar that evening.

'I'm doing Contemporary Cars, sir, and Damon'll be at Mrs Peabody's.'

A pity they couldn't be together, he thought. It was obviously what they would have liked. But he hadn't got the personnel, the back-up. They needed everyone, even himself, for surveillance duties. On the watch, there was a good chance of catching Sacred Globe, he thought optimistically. But what a price to pay for catching them! Kitty Struther's death. He imagined Monday morning's papers. Tomorrow's television, come to that. He switched off, because thinking like that was negative and pointless, and saw Slesar's hand just close quickly over Karen's before leaving the old gym.

After Karen too had gone he sat at the window, eyeing the precincts of the police station and its car parks, front and back, the entrances to both of which could be seen from this point. If they caught someone tonight and followed him – or her – back to where they had come from, what would he need in the way of assistance?

He thought of the gun which Rubber Face had had with him in the car when Dora was taken. Rubber Face had again had a gun when bringing food to the hostages in the basement room, and on that occasion he had fired it, probably only to frighten, but could they be sure of that?

Very likely, since Rubber Face had it both times, there was only one gun. Perhaps Rubber Face was the only shot. Possibly the gun was a replica, very possibly, or a child's toy from a toyshop. If Kitty Struther was shot they would know, he thought grimly, that would be a way of knowing for certain.

And when they knew, when they had followed the driver of the car that brought Kitty Struther's body, would he need arms himself?

Armed response vehicles patrolled the roads for sixteen hours each day. In Mid-Sussex there were two such on patrol and carrying arms. Authority to utilise and deploy firearms officers could only be given by an officer of the rank of Superintendent or above except in special circumstances. These would certainly be such circumstances but armed officers could never be interspersed with unarmed in any operation. If the severity of risk was great, all officers involved in the attack would be fully armed and work as a team of four as a minumum, or more likely eight.

Wexford and his own would be a hundred yards away, watching through binoculars. And the price of all this was Kitty Struther's life.

At eight-thirty he left his watch for Lynn Fancourt to take over and drove to Pomfret and Clare Cox's house. Ted Hennessy was outside in his car on the opposite side of the road, but Wexford ignored him, went up to the front door and knocked.

She came to the door after he had knocked again and rung as well. Hassy Masood had gone back to London with his second family – what interest had he in any of this, now his daughter was dead? She was alone. Her bereavement had aged her twenty years and now she had a madwoman-in-the-attic look, her face gaunt and grey, her hair a shaggy fleece with the colour and texture of dried grasses. Deep down in dark sockets her eyes stared wildly at him. Impossible for him to say now that he wanted to talk to her about the remaining two hostages, that he held the strong belief – he hardly knew why –

that a woman's body would be delivered here within the next few hours.

'I came to see how you are.'

She stepped aside to let him enter. 'As you see,' and then she said, 'Not good.'

There are some situations in which there is nothing to say. He sat down and so did she.

'I do nothing all day,' she said. 'I'm alone and I do nothing. The neighbours get my shopping.'

'Your painting?' he hazarded, thinking of what they all said, that work was the remedy for sorrow.

'I can't paint.' She smiled, a ghastly, shadowy smile. 'I shall never paint again.' Tears in her eyes began to flow down her face. 'When I think at all I think of her in that room being afraid. So afraid that she lost her life trying to escape from it.' She put up her hand and wiped the back of it across her eyes. It induced a little shiver the way she read his thoughts. 'That other woman they've got, they'll kill her, won't they? Do you think they'd take me instead? If I offered? If I got it in the papers somehow, that they could have me? I'd like them to kill me.'

Despair he had seen before in all its forms. This was just another example. To suggest counselling to this woman, some kind of bereavement support, would be insulting. All he could do was look at her and say, feeling how wretchedly inadequate it was, 'I am very, very sorry. You have my deepest sympathy.'

As he left, his phone began to bleep. He sat in his car and listened to Burden's account of the car with two men in it who had driven into the car park of the Concreation building. They had got out, opened the boot and lifted out a black plastic bag, sealed at both ends and the length of an average human body.

'I really thought this was it, Reg. The only thing was that one of them could easily lift it on his own. But he held it the way one *would* carry a body – carry a living person, for that matter.'

'What was it?'

'They'd been clearing out a loft,' said Burden. 'It was the usual sort of rubbish from a loft, old newspapers, old clothes, most of it recyclable.'

'Then why didn't they take it to the dump to be recycled?'

'They explained all that. They were scared stiff. Originally they'd been going to stick all the stuff in dustbins – they're brothers-in-law, by the way – but they've got environmentally conscious neighbours that they didn't want seeing paper and cloth disposed of like that. But the dump, with the recycling bins, is three miles away, while Concreation's yard, with a council skip that was brought in empty yesterday, was two minutes from home.'

Wexford sat in his car for a few moments, but it was too near Hennessy's, it would attract attention. He drove back to Kingsmarkham and along the deserted, coldly lit High Street. All those shops, he thought, with bright lights in their windows and not a soul about to look into them. Cars in plenty, though, parked cars whose owners were in the Olive and Dove, the Green Dragon, the York Wine Bar, and who would move on to Kingsmarkham's only night-club, the Scarlet Angel, when it opened at ten.

The sky was dark now, and bright with scattered stars. There was no moon, or none had yet risen. He tried to remember whether there had been a moon on the previous night and if there had been, whether it had been full or a mere curve of light. His phone rang again while he was parked in Queen Street.

Barry Vine. He was at the station. One of the taxis in the Contemporary Cars fleet had just dropped a fare on the station approach. The fare had one large suitcase and a long bundle, so heavy that the driver couldn't lift it out of the boot. A porter was sought but, of course, there had been no porters at Kingsmarkham station for twenty years.

'The chap just disappeared,' Vine said. 'I mean, I thought he had. There was this bundle lying there on the pavement, the cab had gone and this fellow had vanished into the station. I was looking at it when he came back.'

'What was it?' said Wexford for the second time that evening.

'Golf clubs.'

'I trust it's not still there.'

'Someone found him a trolley in what used to be the left luggage department.'

He looked at his watch. It was nine. He would go to Rhombus Road, Stowerton, and then to Savesbury House on his way to the Weir Theatre. Maybe not to go into either place, just to run his eye over them, to check for he hardly knew what. Sacred Globe, after all, had said Kingsmarkham, not Stowerton or Framhurst.

Nicky Weaver must have had the same idea, for she was in her car parked in front of a house a few doors down from Mrs Peabody's.

863

This time Wexford interrupted the surveillance. He went over to her car, tapped on the window and got in beside her. She turned to him her pretty face, the intent eyes, the look of sharp intelligence. He saw all this in the momentary light brought by the door opening. Her geometrically cut black hair, turned under at the tips, reminded him that when he was young such a style was called a pageboy. And he saw her tiredness too, the permanent strained pallor of the woman who has a high-powered job and is a wife and mother too.

'Has anything happened?' he asked her.

'A man called at the house. At about seven. I think he must be Audrey Barker's fiancé. Anyway, he hugged her on the doorstep and he's been inside ever since. Mrs Peabody went out. I thought she was being tactful, leaving them alone together, but she'd only gone to the corner shop for a pint of milk.'

'That Indian place Trotter used to live above?'

'Small world, isn't it?' said Nicky.

'They won't bring Kitty Struther's body here. They'll do something entirely unexpected.'

Driving in the Framhurst direction, he passed the start of the bypass site. If it was never built and those now grass-grown earth hillocks never removed, scholars in future ages would describe them as tumuli or the burial mounds of Saxon heroes. But it would be built. It was a matter not of protest, nor of environmental assessment, but only of time.

Framhurst was as empty as the town but for three boys standing by their motor bikes and smoking outside the bus shelter. Bright strip lighting in the window of the butcher's illuminated nothing but empty white trays and sprigs of plastic parsley. The teashop was locked up and its canopy furled. Night obscured the view of the valley from the ascending lane. It was merely a dark spread, punctured by many lights, a mirroring of the starlit sky. The winding river had vanished but the Weir Theatre shone brightly, a torch on the invisible waterside.

DC Pemberton was in his car outside the gates of Savesbury House.

'It's the only way in, sir. I checked. But the grounds are big and there's only fences or hedges round them. Anyone could get in almost anywhere across the fields.'

'Stay where you are. But they won't come here. It's too far out. It's not Kingsmarkham.'

864

Ten-fifteen. The play wouldn't yet be over, but he would drive down to Stringfield Mill, take it slowly. How pleasant and comfortable it must be not to be endowed with imagination! He didn't want his, he'd had enough of it, anyone could have it. But imagination wasn't something you could get rid of, any more than you could determine not to love. Or not to be afraid.

That was the worst thing, thinking of her fear. All her life she had had someone else to take the strain, to – what were the words of the marriage service? – love her, comfort her, honour and keep her. Literally, it appeared, those things had been done for Kitty Struther. By parents once, by a husband of course, by a son too. She had never lived alone, earned her own living, known want or even straitened circumstances, never probably even travelled alone. But now she was alone. For ten days she had lived on a diet the like of which she had never previously known, had slept – if she had slept – in the kind of bed she had never even seen before, had been cold and hungry, deprived of all the small comforts of life, without a bath or a change of clothes. And now they had taken her husband from her and were going to kill her.

Imagination, the curse of the thinking policeman. He laughed wryly to himself. The lights of the Weir Theatre blazed ahead of him, dazzling out the stars. He put the car into the car park, walked slowly up the lane towards the river. Ten minutes yet before the curtain would fall. Consolations were always to be found in this life and one thing he could be glad about was that he hadn't just sat through three hours of *Extinction*.

A gate in the stone wall led into the mill's gardens. It would provide a short cut and a pleasant one. He unlatched the gate and pushed it open. The lights were all directed away from here and the gardens lay in a cloud of pale shadow, but as he looked southwards he saw the moon rising, a perfect orange-coloured crescent. A waning moon, and now he remembered. It had been full the night Dora came home, eight days before.

Most flowers close up at night. He found himself surrounded by flowers whose blossoms had become buds again, shut at dusk, but still giving off their various perfumes. But the roses, whose scent had come to him when he was here before, remained open, rosy-gold clusters on long stems and flat yellow faces pressed against the mossy grey wall.

Was this a private garden? Godwin's own garden? There was no sign that visitors to the theatre ever came out here. He turned a bend in the path and saw Godwin himself sitting on the topmost of the crescent-shaped steps that splayed out from closed french windows. The wall behind him was hung with roses, white and red, and with other climbers whose flowers had folded themselves away for the night.

'I'm sorry,' he said. 'I'm using your private gardens as a short cut. I didn't realise there were parts of the mill grounds shut off from the public.'

Godwin smiled and made a deprecating gesture with his hand. 'The public won't want it when the bypass comes.'

'It will pass very near here?'

'At the nearest point about a hundred yards from the end of this garden. I was born here – not *here*, I mean, but in Framhurst – and I lived here till I was eighteen. It's twelve years since I came back. There have been more changes in those twelve years than in all the rest – I won't tell you how many. Too many.'

'All changes for the worse?'

'I think so. Destruction and spoliation but additions as well. More petrol stations, more white and yellow paint on the roads, more road signs, more hoardings, more stupid useless information in print everywhere. That Framhurst's been twinned with a town in Germany and another one in France, for instance. That Sewingbury is the floral capital of Sussex. That Savesbury Deeps has been designated a picnic area. And all the new houses. The Dragon pub in Kingsmarkham renamed Tipples and Grove's wine bar turned into a night-club and called the Scarlet Angel . . .'

Wexford nodded. He was going to say something that he didn't believe about progress and inevitability, but he said nothing at all for a moment because he was looking at the climber which ascended the wall to a height of perhaps ten feet between the red rose and the white.

It was a delicate-leaved plant with fine, pointed leaves and curling tendrils. Flowers it had had and by day they must make a considerable show, but now all were closed up, some furled like rolled umbrellas, others withered.

He spoke now. He said to Godwin, 'What is it? This plant, what is it?'

'Now, look.' Godwin got to his feet. His voice, formerly so gentle and meditative, changed in a flash and became immediately surly.

866

'Now, look, if you're going to search for hallucinatory drugs or whatever in garden plants, you've got your work cut out. There are hundreds of them. Ordinary poppies, for instance. But this isn't cannabis, you know. This is Morning Glory, it's quite hard to grow, it doesn't bear much, you wouldn't get enough seeds to fill an egg-cup, you . . .'

'Mr Godwin. Please. I am not in the drugs squad. I am looking for two hostages at present in the hands of those who abducted them ten days ago. This plant' – Wexford thought he could postpone too detailed an explanation – 'this plant, or one like it, may be visible from the place where they are kept.'

'Well, for God's sake, they're not kept here.'

Wexford looked about him, at the gardens, the rising moon, the flower-hung rear wall of the mill. No outbuildings, no sheds or garages in sight. The moonlight, strangely white for a radiance that proceeded from that golden crescent, now lit everything, showed every detail of the garden. 'I know that,' he said. 'Please don't be so defensive, Mr Godwin. I am not accusing you of anything. I only want your help.'

The look he got was warmer. There couldn't be much doubt in the mind of anyone who knew about these things that Godwin was guilty and suspicious because he had himself sampled a good many of these garden drugs, probably grew cannabis somewhere, smoked catalpa beans, chewed magic mushrooms. The list, as he had implied himself, was endless. But now was no time for taking an interest in that.

'Tell me about this plant, will you? It's blue?'

'Look.' Godwin picked a closed flower off a stem. He unwound the spiralled petals and disclosed an interior the brightest and richest of sky-blues. 'Nice colour, wouldn't you say? The wild one that grows here as a weed is white, of course, and its little cousin is the pink convolvulus.'

'Does it come up every year?' Wexford sought for the unfamiliar word. 'Is it a perennial?'

'I grew it from seed.' Godwin's geniality had returned. 'Come into the theatre. I'll buy you a drink while you're waiting for your ladies. Mind you,' he added in a challenging tone, 'I'd kidnap a few people myself if I thought it'd stop that goddamned bypass.'

Wexford followed him up the steps, round the side of the mill, out of the moonlit shadows and into bright artificial light. He held in his hand the flower bud and the leaf Godwin had given him. Where had he seen buds and leaves like that before? Seen them very recently?

'Would it move?'

They were in the empty bar now, Wexford confining himself to sparkling water, Godwin with a pint of lager. He said, 'How do you mean, move?'

'Would the flowers be out in one place one day and another the next?'

'Each one only lasts a day, so broadly speaking, yes. You're quite likely to get all the flowers out in one patch and then another lot out on a higher patch. If I make myself clear. Mind you, they wouldn't come out at all on a really dull day.'

On a dull day, such as they had had recently . . . Where had he seen that plant before?

# 26

His mobile was silent. There were no messages on the phone at home. When he had driven Dora to their home and Jenny to hers, when Dora had gone to bed and at once to sleep, he put through calls to all those people who were on the watch. There was nothing. The town was quiet, less busy at night than usual, less traffic, it seemed. Only two incidents had been reported: an attempted break-in at a shop in Queen Street, a case of driving over the permitted limit.

It was eleven-fifty. Nearly five hours had passed since Sacred Globe's deadline. He realised how he had been measuring this case out in minutes. Time, time, it was all a matter of time. Had they killed her? Would they kill her? Her body could even now be no more than half a mile from where he was, sitting silently in the dark in his own house.

He remembered another midnight, the night Dora had come home. Moonlight falling on his face had awakened him or else it was the sound of her footfalls on the gravel. Gravel had been in the sleeping bag with Roxane Masood's body. Hold on to that. And the dust from the wings of a moth only found in Wiltshire had been on Dora's clothes. Cat hairs and a smell of acetone. A butterfly tattoo. He opened the french windows and went out into the garden. A dreadful idea had come to him.

Last time, when Dora had come home, he had thought it was a messenger from Sacred Globe. He had thought they would target him personally. Suppose, now, they brought Kitty Struther's body here? They could have done so while he and Dora were out.

The sickle moon was overhead now, sailing silver-white in a wrack of cloud, not full enough or bright enough to shed much light. He fetched a torch, searched the garden. His heart knocking, he opened the garage doors, flashed the torch inside. Nothing. Thank God. The garden shed remained. For fifteen seconds he knew what he would find when he unlatched that door, but he held his breath and unlatched it and found what was always in there, a lawn-mower, tools, old plastic bags and other junk.

It proved nothing. Of course it didn't, yet that wasn't the way his mind saw it. He began to see all sorts of unreasonable things and he sat down in his chair in the dark and started to think.

The blue thing. He knew what that was now and and, suddenly, he knew where it was. It came to him clearly, a revelation, a picture in green and grey. Only that wasn't possible, that couldn't be. After a while he fetched the London phone book, the S–Z section. He punched out the number he found but there was no reply. Then he phoned Burden.

It was gone midnight but Burden wasn't asleep. He wasn't even in bed. When he heard Wexford's voice he said, 'Have they found her?'

'No.' Wexford could state it categorically and with perfect confidence. 'And they won't.'

'What do you mean?'

Instead of replying, he said, 'When would you like to go to London? Now or at six in the morning?'

There was a short silence and then Burden said, 'Do I have a choice?'

'Sure you do.'

'I shan't sleep. I'm too strung up. So let's go now.'

Once, driving must always have been like this. Deserted lanes, empty roads, a scent in the air of fields overgrown with camomile, not petrol and diesel. For the first ten minutes even the motorway was empty until a Jaguar passed them, roaring up the fast lane at twenty over the limit. The bright, cold lights drowned the moon in their white haze. In the outskirts of London they saw an owl sitting on a telephone cable and in Norbury a fox crossed the road in front of them.

'It's Sunday now,' Wexford said, 'but I've got on to Vine and told him to dig up someone in the morning and swear out a warrant.'

Burden, who was driving, said, 'Should I take the turn for Balham and go over Battersea Bridge?'

'Turn left or go straight on, doesn't matter so long as we cross the river more or less in the centre.'

Neither of them knew London well. But it was easier at this time of night, at two o'clock as it now was, though the traffic had thickened and begun to hold them up. The journey from the river up through Kensington and Notting Hill seemed interminable. Burden, who had been hoping to go through the park, found it closed and took Kensington Church Street instead. Then came the confusions of the Bayswater Road and Edgware Road.

'Easy to see you never did the knowledge,' Wexford muttered.

'The what?'

'What taxi drivers do before they get to be taxi drivers. Going about on bicycles with maps in their hand, learning one-way streets.'

'I'm a policeman,' said Burden austerely, 'thank you very much.'

But five minutes later he had to ask if it was all right to park on a single yellow line.

'Quite OK after six-thirty,' Wexford said, sounding more confident than he was.

They were in Fitzhardinge Street, off Manchester Square. No one was about and the place was as silent as anywhere ever is in central London. A thin stream of traffic continued to pass down not-far-distant Baker Street, making a ceaseless throb of background noise. They got out of the car, crossed the street and stood in the entrance to the mews.

This was approached by means of an archway in the terrace on the south side of Fitzhardinge Street. The street was well lit so that it was almost as bright as day, but inside the mews, on the other side of the brown sandstone arch, a single lamp burned, casting its yellow radiance over the cobbles. Of the buildings in there, some consisted of one storey above a garage, others were narrow Victorian houses, flat-roofed or with a single gable, designed for the coachmen employed by the dwellers in Manchester Square or Seymour Street. Poor little artisans' houses, all of them, but prettified with roof gardens and window-boxes, porches and new front doors, grown punishingly expensive to buy.

'If you lived up here,' Wexford said softly, 'in London, I mean, you wouldn't have to worry about wetlands and yellow caddises and butterflies' habitats. There aren't any to lose.'

Burden looked at him in amazement. 'I don't worry about those things and I like living in the country.'

'Yes,' Wexford said. 'I know.' And then, not to be patronising and

871

mean-spirited, 'You did well remembering this address. I'm not sure I would have.'

'My mother's maiden name was Fitzharding,' Burden said simply, 'only without the e, of course.'

They walked into the mews through the arch. Outside the house they had come to, number four, stood two green tubs in which grew standard bay trees, their crowns spheres of dark leaves. The front door was at the side, with two sash windows to the right of it and two more above. No lights showed. In the entire mews, apart from the single street lamp, only one window had a light behind it and that was at the farthest end up against the wall of Seymour Street.

Wexford rang the bell of number four. Although the house wasn't divided into flats, there was an entryphone with a brass grille. He didn't expect an answer to his ring and he didn't get one, neither then nor when he rang again. He knocked on the door, pushing at the letter-box lid so that it rattled loudly.

All was in darkness, all was silent and no window was open. But he knew the house wasn't empty. He could feel the presence of occupants, he hardly knew how, perhaps by some strange sense long discounted as feasible to human beings, but which animals understood. An emanation of tension, of strain growing intolerable, communicated itself to him through the pale walls of the house, through the sealed windows. It almost throbbed as if, instead of people, a crouching monster waited inside, breathing rhythmically, flexing its stubby claws.

And the sense of this reached even Burden who said, 'There's someone there all right. They're in there.'

'Upstairs,' said Wexford. 'In the dark, behind those curtains.'

He rang the bell again, putting his ear to the grille. And this time a strange thing happened. A receiver was lifted at the other end, making a sound like a sigh or the opening of a door that lets in a gust of wind. The sighing sound, the wind blowing, should have been followed by a voice but there was no voice. Up there someone crouched with the phone to his ear, not speaking.

Wexford said, 'Detective Chief Inspector Wexford and Detective Inspector Burden, Kingsmarkham CID.' Too late he remembered he should have said Crime Management. 'Open the door and let us in, please.'

The receiver went back before he had spoken that last sentence.

'Do you remember what Dora said?' he asked Burden. 'When she

872

talked of breaking down that washroom door and asked us if we'd ever done something like that? And we all had.'

Grinning, Burden pressed the bell again. Once more the receiver was lifted. He said harshly, 'Open up or we'll break your door down.'

He had already taken the necessary steps backwards and was running up to give the door a mighty kick, when it opened. A man stood there in a dressing-gown of dark-blue foulard over cream-coloured pyjama trousers. He was tall and lean, and the vee of the dressing-gown showed a mat of whitish-blond hair covering his chest. The hair of his head was pepper-and-salt and, if he wasn't quite recognisable from his photograph, his resemblance to his son both in facial features and colouring was unmistakable.

He said nothing. He stood there. On the narrow staircase behind him a woman was slowly descending. Her feet in red slippers came first into view, then her bare legs with the stiff skirts of a red quilted housecoat reaching to the calves, then the rest of her and her white face, set and grim and ready for what must come.

'Owen Kinglake Struther?' said Wexford.

The man nodded.

'You do not have to say anything. But it may harm your defence if you do not mention when questioned something which you may later rely on in court. Anything you do say . . .'

# 27

The morning had started off hazy and cool, an autumn morning of mist penetrated by shafts of pale sunshine. But the mist had lifted now and the sun was no longer pale but bright and strong. Wexford looked up at the brilliance in the blue where the sun was and blessed it for shining when he wanted it to shine. It would show him and all of them what he wanted to see.

Vine had the warrant. They would go in two cars and Wexford would ask for back-up if he needed it. Maybe even if he didn't need it. He should have been tired. In the event, he and Burden had had perhaps two hours' sleep. But he felt elated, adrenalin running, every nerve in his body alert and waiting.

It had worked last night. After entry to the house in Fitzhardinge Mews everything had gone straightforwardly. The Struthers had capitulated in an entirely middle-class, stand up, speak up and play the game way. The curious thing was that neither of them seemed to see that they had done anything particularly wrong.

'My husband planned it all,' Kitty Struther said proudly. 'It was his idea, absolutely his brainchild. The rest of them – well, we had to bring them in. For sheer force of numbers, you understand.'

'Kitty,' Owen Struther said.

'Well, it's all over, isn't it? It doesn't matter what we say now.' She had looked up at Wexford. 'That was your wife, wasn't it? There was the boy and the . . . well, the coloured girl. She jumped out of a window, she wasn't pushed. I wonder what your wife said about us. We put on a jolly good act, you know. Good as professionals. Owen was Colonel Blimp and I was the terrified little woman.'

'Kitty.'

She started laughing. The laughter caught in her throat on a sob

874

and she began to cry, rocking herself back and forth. Wexford thought how Dora had said she cried so much. What had been acting and what real?

'You haven't asked why,' Owen Struther said. 'Personally, I think we were justified. I longed for that house all my life and managed to buy it ten years ago. It was all going to be taken from us, it was going to be ruined by a ghastly road more suited to Los Angeles or Birmingham.' He touched his wife's arm. 'Kitty.'

'I can't help it,' she sobbed. 'It's all so sad.'

'You should be more discreet.'

'What does it matter now? If they build the road what does anything matter? They can execute me if they like.'

'Get dressed now,' said Wexford, 'and we'll be off.'

They were back in Kingsmarkham at twenty-past four. He had snatched his bit of sleep, woken promptly and checked on the warrant with Barry Vine. Now, in the first car, he directed Pemberton where to go.

Pemberton didn't question it. He knew the area and he had his map, and if he was surprised he didn't say so. It would all be over in an hour, Wexford had said, and this afternoon he, James Pemberton, was playing golf with his brother-in-law. The Chief Inspector was in the back with Inspector Burden and DS Malahyde next to him, riding shotgun.

He had used that phrase and Wexford heard it and said, 'I don't believe in Sacred Globe's gun. Not a handgun.'

'Dora said a handgun,' said Burden.

'I know she did and that's why I don't think it was real. Let me put that another way. If she'd said they had a shotgun or even a rifle I'd believe in the possibility of its being real because dozens of people round here have shotgun licences.'

They went the Pomfret way. Marginally quicker, Pemberton said. It would be a lot slower, though, when the bypass was built. Unless they built underpasses or bridges. Burden said his wife had told him of a new proposal she had heard rumoured, that they were going to put a tunnel under the Brede at Watersmeet to save the yellow caddis.

Framhurst was even quieter this morning than it had been last evening, but as they passed over the crossroads church bells started ringing for some early-morning service. For the first time Wexford took note of the car behind him, the car Hennessy was driving. He looked back, craning his neck. Vine was next to him and his heart took a little lurch because of who was in the back with Nicky Weaver.

But he had to be wrong about that. He really knew he was. It was just that he had a horribly suspicious mind, the kind of antennae that locate ugly things, awful things that wouldn't cross other people's minds. But if Brendan Royall hadn't furnished Sacred Globe with Burden's name and telephone number, who had? He had to be wrong. He *was* wrong and since he would never tell anyone, not a soul would know of the doubt in his heart, his nose for the scent of treachery.

Frenchie Collins wouldn't talk to Karen Malahyde, only to her companion. And before he went to the Holgates he had told only those standing close to him that he was going up there in quest of recent building work. Yet Ryan Barker had phoned him while he was there. And as for Tarling's movements . . .

'I think it may all go quietly,' was all he said aloud.

They were climbing Markinch Hill. The bright sun lit up the whole valley, the green and the black-green, the dark massy woods, the sparkling silver river, white houses and red houses, flint and brown, chalk scree on downland slopes. The shadow of a thin strip of cloud floated lightly across it all.

'House up here, is it, sir?' Pemberton asked.

'On our left now,' said Wexford.

Pemberton got out to open the gates.

'Leave them open,' Wexford said. 'Leave the car here. We'll walk up. We'll go quietly.'

The other car had been close behind them. He walked over to it, repeated to Vine what he had just said and said to Nicky and Damon Slesar, 'I'd like you to stay in the car. Wait here till you're called for. I've got more back-up coming.'

The six who weren't staying anywhere began to make their way towards the house. Not on the drive, not to crunch the gravel, but through the shrubberies, between the trees where, through the branches, here on the ridge, the panorama of the valley opened out and spread itself like a great green tapestry unfurled. The sun made dapple patterns on the fine pale soil, the brown leaves of last autumn. On an island in a sea of trees the house stood with its outbuildings, the double house, Jacobean at one end, Georgian at the other. The trees thinned and the house emerged, the lower floors of the

Georgian part hidden by a two-storey building of cut flints with a slate roof.

'Sacred Globe are probably asleep still,' Wexford said. 'Why not? They've nothing to worry about. Or they don't think they have.'

Burden was behind him and Karen now. They came up alongside a wall with a gate in it, opened the gate and passed through, entering an almost enclosed courtyard with a checkerboard floor of stone squares and mown grass squares. Tubs stood about filled with pink-and-white-striped petunias and yellow Jamaican daisies. Ahead of them was an arched opening between the Jacobean part of the house and the encircling wall, an arch he had passed under and seen a dog and a man, greenness and greyness . . .

He pointed in silence at the flint-walled building. Its single window faced the rear of the Georgian part of the house, a wall hung with a creeping plant that covered it to a width of about four feet and a height of eight. As he had expected, the sun which was already high in the sky had brought out its flowers, and on the left-hand side at the top and the right-hand side half-way up, had opened perhaps twenty blue trumpets.

Half close his eyes and he could see a patch of blue and another smaller patch. The isolated blossoms disappeared, returned when he opened his eyes. Blue as the sky at noon on a summer's day.

'I wonder if the door's locked,' he said softly.

A stout, heavy door, oak probably, with locks top and bottom. He tried the handle and the door opened. It was a strange feeling, seeing the place at last. The basement room. The prison. It was very much as Dora had described it, about twenty feet by thirty, with the stone sink under the window, the shelves, the door into the washroom. The five camp beds were still there and the blankets folded quite neatly on top of them.

Two stone steps down to the stone-flagged floor. A chilly place, cool enough once to have kept dairy products sound, with shelves on the wall and a lot of cobwebs hanging. He went to the window, saw a sky-blue patch about six feet up, and saw it, because the rabbit hut structure had been taken down, much more clearly than Dora would have. The wood in the window frame was splintered and there was a hole where that bullet had gone in.

Outside again, he half expected a Siamese cat to come sauntering out from one of the outbuildings or, when he looked up, to see a black cat sunning itself on top of a wall. But, no. He knew almost for certain now that he wouldn't see them, just as he wouldn't find any sand from the Isle of Wight.

He had calculated that there were very likely four people in that house, six if he was lucky. Who would answer the front door?'

Andrew Struther. It was usually Andrew Struther, and so it was this time. Probably they had fixed it that it was always he who came to the door. To be on the safe side. But not quite safe enough. Andrew hadn't long been up, you could see that, had perhaps only this minute got up. He was wearing khaki shorts and a dirty white T-shirt, trainers on his feet, no socks.

'I expect you thought policemen took Sundays off, didn't you, Mr Struther?' said Wexford.

'Should I know what you're talking about?'

'We'll have the explanations inside.'

They pushed past him into the hall. Bibi was there in jeans and the heavy boots Dora had described, holding the dog Manfred by its collar.

Wexford said to her, 'Lock that dog up somewhere. Anywhere. Do it now.'

'What?'

'If it touches one of us it gets destroyed, so for its protection, lock it up.'

'The Hermaphrodite,' said Karen softly.

'Exactly. Where are the rest of you, Andrew?'

Burden remembered the man's insistence on his surname and style, and Struther remembered too. It showed in his face but he made no reference to it, only said again, this time more querulously, 'Should I know what this is about?'

'We have your parents in custody. They were arrested in the early hours of the morning,' Burden said. 'Now, where is Ryan Barker?'

'You're making a mistake.'

The girl came back without the dog, went up close to Andrew Struther, looked into his face. 'Andy?'

'Not now.' Struther said to Wexford, 'He's not here. He's been kidnapped, remember?'

'Search the house.'

'You can't do that!'

'Show him the warrant, Mike,' said Wexford, and to Vine, 'If you go down the back here and turn to the left it should bring you into

878

the tall part of this house. On the top floor you'll find the room where Roxane Masood was kept. The window is in the wall where that blue climber is in flower.' He said to Andrew Struther, 'Where's Tarling?'

Andrew said nothing. He took hold of Bibi and put his hand over her mouth. She quailed a bit, shrinking into herself.

'Let her go!' Wexford said, and to Burden, 'Have they been cautioned?'

'They have. I've phoned for back-up.'

The door opened and Vine came in with a tall gangling boy in jeans and a sweatshirt. His face looked bewildered, his mouth slack. When he saw Andrew and Bibi he made a little sound.

'Sit down,' Wexford said. 'Over there. You too.' He nodded in the direction of Andrew and Bibi, who now stood trembling, rubbing her arm where Andrew had clutched her. 'You sit down over there and wait. Where's Tarling?' he asked again.

'Locked himself in his room next to where the kid was,' said Vine.

Andrew laughed. 'He's got a gun, you know.'

'No, I don't know.' Wexford shook his head at him. 'I find it hard to believe a word you say.'

'Pemberton's gone to fetch Nicky and Slesar,' Burden murmured to Wexford. 'The three of us can get him out and by then the back-up'll be here.'

Andrew half rose out of his chair. He clenched his fists, said, 'What did you say?'

No one answered him. Bibi came up to him, took his arm, said, 'I want my dog. Make them let him out.'

He ignored her, repeated, 'You said Slesar. What else did you say?'

Wexford heard the police vehicles' sirens. They were coming up Markinch Hill. He left the room, crossed the hall, walked out through the front door. Emerging from the shadowy avenue were Pemberton and Slesar, coming on to the wide gravel sweep, Slesar a little way ahead. Tarling he didn't see until it was too late but he heard the cry behind him, up at a window, a howl of rage and despair, 'You betrayed us!'

The bullet must have passed quite close to his own head. It was at the sound that he ducked, involuntarily, the deafening report. Even then he thought, a rifle, not a shotgun. Damon Slesar stood utterly still, his hands slowly rising up, even from this distance the hole the bullet made clearly visible on his white shirt, by his heart.

He said something. Perhaps it was 'no', but Wexford couldn't hear, no one could have heard. Slesar's knees buckled and he fell forward and sideways, blood pouring out of his mouth.

The two cars, the van, came up the drive, and the first one, its siren still wailing, had to swerve to avoid the dead man on the gravel and the two who bent over him. Car doors burst open and the men came out. Wexford turned back to the house as Karen Malahyde came from the front door, calm, cold, staring, but uttering the same small sound of protest as Ryan Barker had made not long before.

She stood and looked at Slesar's body but, unlike the others, she resisted kneeling beside him.

# 28

'Kitty Struther described it as her husband's "clever idea",' Wexford began, 'but it looks as if the original plan came from Tarling. He had been at school with Andrew Struther and though they might appear to have little in common, in fact they both shared with Andrew's father Owen a hatred of authority interfering in their lives, or rather, imposing its will on their lives and thus changing them for the worse.'

He was filling in the details for Montague Ryder, and Burden was there too, in the Chief Constable's suite at Myringham. It was Monday and that morning five people had appeared at Kingsmarkham Magistrates' Court charged with abduction and unlawful imprisonment, and one of them with the murder of Detective Sergeant Damon John Slesar. They had all, in spite of Wexford's guesses and belief, been charged with the murder of Roxane Masood.

'Tarling,' Wexford said, 'was also, of course, very much concerned with protest over green issues and with animal rights. He and Andrew Struther encountered each other by chance in Kingsmarkham, back in the spring when the bypass looked as if it would become reality and the activists first began coming here. I don't know how yet and perhaps it doesn't matter. Suffice it to say that they did – Struther was down here visiting his parents – recognise each other and began discussing the bypass.

'Now the occupants of Savesbury House would be a good deal less affected by the bypass than would almost anyone living in a semi on the outskirts of Stowerton or a cottage in the neighbourhood of Pomfret, but the threat seemed appalling to them. Devastating. That's a word that everyone bandies about these days and I don't like it, but here it's appropriate. The valley which their windows

881

overlooked, which they could see from their garden, would indeed be devastated – that is, laid waste. And they would hear the traffic. Their peace would be broken, their silence that hitherto was only disturbed by birdsong, would be lost to the muted but pretty well incessant roar of the bypass users.'

Burden interrupted him. 'But why should Andrew Struther care enough to involve himself in this? He doesn't live at Savesbury House. He's young and young men aren't usually much concerned about birdsong and peace and quiet. Yet he was prepared to risk his liberty . . .'

'Money, Mike. Money and inheritance. Savesbury House would be his one day. Perhaps he wouldn't want to live in it, he lives in his London mews, but he'd want to sell it. Estate agents in Kingsmark-ham are saying the bypass will reduce the value of all property in its vicinity, some of it by as much as fifty per cent. In this case that means cutting the value of Savesbury House from three quarters of a million to not much more than three hundred thousand, not to mention making it unsaleable.'

The Chief Constable glanced at Burden. 'It's a different league, Mike, but it's there.'

'I suppose it is, sir.'

'There was money available,' Wexford went on. 'For instance, the building and plumbing of the washroom. I'm pretty sure Gary Wilson did that. He's a builder by trade. He told me so, only it didn't register at the time. Oh, he didn't know what he was doing it *for*. But he was glad of the work and the money, and even more happy, if mystified, when he and Quilla were presented with a car to get them to Wales and thence to north Yorkshire, on the understanding he was to stay out of the way for a couple of months.

'It was money accomplished that. Owen and Kitty Struther had money and they were just as keen on the plan as Tarling and their son. And it was Owen Struther's idea to set it up by using Contemporary Cars. He had used them a few times to get himself to Kingsmarkham station and he knew that the last thing they were was contemporary, he knew their slapdash arrangements. But before the plan could be put into operation they had to have a place to put the hostages and, so to speak, a staff to guard them.

'Three of them would, of course, be Tarling, Andrew and Andrew's girlfriend Bettina Martin, known as Bibi. It wasn't enough – well, it was enough for the guard duty, bearing in mind that Owen and Kitty would only need to *appear* to be guarded – but the car abduction plan necessarily must involve more manpower. So Tarling brought in a man we've called The Driver just as we know Tarling as Rubber Face – it was the stocking over his face that turned his features from sharp into rubber – Andrew Struther as Tattoo and Bibi Martin as The Hermaphrodite. And there was one more.'

Wexford hesitated. He got up and walked over to the window where he stood for a moment, looking across another garden, another view. On some mental retina he saw it happening again and heard the shot, he saw the shocked, whitening face and the blood on the shirt where the heart beat beneath. And then beat no longer.

He turned round, said, 'I didn't suspect him until the night before we left for Savesbury House. And then I didn't exactly . . . Frankly, I thought it was me, seeing villains everywhere, believing nothing and no one. I should have stopped him from coming with us. I only knew he *was* coming when I looked round and spotted him in the car behind. And then, believing nothing and no one as I've said, I didn't believe Tarling had a gun. Or if he did that he'd use it in those circumstances.'

'You have no need to blame yourself, Reg,' said Montague Ryder.

Wexford shook his head, a gesture of self-anger, not denial. He glanced at Burden, knowing what he was thinking, some monstrous version of its being all for the best anyway. What kind of a future, a life, would there have been for Damon Slesar?

'He wasn't at school with them, was he?' the Chief Constable asked.

'Not so far as I know, sir. Myringham Comprehensive, I believe. But he was a member of KABAL, which is perfectly respectable, and of SPECIES, which is perhaps not quite that. Strictly speaking, he shouldn't have joined that latter organisation, but then his life for the past six months has been a catalogue of things he shouldn't have done.

'We have to believe that all these people thought their plan would work. They thought that taking hostages would stop the bypass because they thought the government would give in. This wasn't the Middle East, this wasn't Thailand. This was England and English people holding English people, a monstrous act that would have the desired result. They really thought that. Slesar thought that.'

'He had some special reason for being opposed to the bypass?'

'I suppose you could say that,' Wexford said thoughtfully. 'Like

883

Andrew Struther, he was concerned for his parents, though in his case it was their livelihood, not a question of his future inheritance. All he could inherit would be a smallholding out on the old bypass, not far from the Brigadier pub.'

'That place where they sell veg and pick-your-own strawberries?' asked Burden. 'I didn't know that.'

'Most businesses on the old bypass will be threatened by the new one,' said Wexford. 'The old one won't be used much, or that's the theory, there won't be many people stopping off for PYO strawberries. Slesar was against the bypass because it would bankrupt his parents. His father grew fruit. His mother had a subsidiary business spinning thread and weaving garments from animal hair.'

'But how did he get into all this?'

'Through SPECIES, I think. Probably at one of their rallies. Prior to the one that's just ended in Wales they had one in Kent in the spring. Very likely he met Tarling there and the rest followed. They would have worked pretty hard on him, the Struthers particularly, because they really needed someone like him, an insider.'

'Why do you say the Struthers "particularly", Reg?'

Wexford said bitterly, 'Struther's a rich man. Not far off a millionaire.' He shrugged. 'Happily for all of us in this country – there are still some things to be thankful for – there is no one a rich man can bribe to stop something like this bypass. It can't be done. But the Damon Slesars of this world are corruptible. I don't know this yet, but my theory is that Struther bribed Slesar considerably, probably went on raising the price until Slesar yielded. No doubt he got enough to set his parents up elsewhere even if they did lose their livelihood.

'Being their mole inside the force,' Wexford went on, 'Slesar knew Mike Burden's address and phone number for Tarling to phone there with the second message – it was usually the voices of Tarling and Andrew Struther that were heard – and knew I would be at the Holgates' on Saturday afternoon to receive another message there. Of course the sleeping bag which Frenchie Collins bought in Brixton was the one in which Roxane Masood's body was found, as she told Slesar once she was alone with him.'

'She knew?' Burden asked.

'I don't know. Maybe not. Maybe she just took against Karen Malahyde. Anyway, whatever she told Slesar wasn't going to find its way back to me.'

884

'Poor Karen,' said Burden.

'Yes. But I don't think it had gone very deep with her. And knowing what she now knows will have its effect. While she was tailing Brendan Royall he should have been tailing Conrad Tarling. Needless to say, he wasn't. Tarling went back and forth between the camp and Savesbury House as much as he pleased. Doubtless he went down to Wiltshire, also whenever he pleased. At some point, on his clothes, he brought back moth-wing dust from Queringham Hall and by chance transferred it to the room where the hostages were kept.'

Wexford was silent for a moment. They were all thinking, he supposed, the same sort of thing, the horror of a police officer succumbing in this way, and with bribery added to treachery. And then he wondered what thought had passed through Slesar's mind as he saw Tarling at that window with the gun, his fanatical face, the shotgun aimed. He had stared, the blood drawn from his face, his hands rising as if in an ineffectual warding off of death.

'You said something about the place where the hostages were kept,' said the Chief Constable in a welcome changing of the subject.

Wexford nodded. 'A lot of these old houses that have been farms as well as country houses have a dairy. Mostly they're just used to store stuff in, repositories for junk. This one probably was. My wife called it a basement room but it wasn't really, just rather dark and with one small window slightly high up. I expect they renewed the door, had new locks fitted and so on. Of course they didn't dare get a building firm in to convert a cupboard into a washroom, but Tarling knew someone who would do it and say nothing, someone who lived nowhere and would very likely disappear after a few weeks.

'So they took their hostages, and I think we know already exactly how they did that. Of course, in the case of the Struthers, Owen and Kitty just walked across from the main house and put their hoods on outside the dairy door. Then they had their fun, playing the hysteric and the brave soldier. I suppose it helped pass the time for them until Owen staged his mock escape and they were taken away, first back to the comforts of Savesbury House and then off to London to hide themselves in Andrew's house. Incidentally, I wonder what Tarling thought when she carried her act as far as spitting at him. Still, you don't give the boss a smack in the face.

'It must have been a shock for them when they realised they'd got my wife and they would have done much earlier than I thought at first. They didn't have to know the name or be told who I was. Slesar knew on the day he came along with the other two from the Regional Crime Squad. No doubt he was on the blower to Sacred Globe immediately.'

'You've done well, Reg,' the Chief Constable said.

'Not well,' Wexford said. 'I could have saved a man's life and I didn't.'

Dora said she ought to have known. She ought to have guessed about the Struthers. After all, they weren't actors, were they?

'Everyone's an actor these days,' said Wexford. 'They learn it off the TV. Look at all those people who get interviewed after disasters. They've no shyness, they all behave as if they've learnt scripts by heart or got monitors in front of them.'

'Why did they let me go, Reg?'

'At first I thought it was because they'd found out who you were, through Gary and Quilla. But that wasn't so. They knew who you were. They knew because Slesar knew. Incidentally, he wore gloves not because he had something wrong with his hands, but to make you think there was something wrong with them. And not because they thought you might have seen the Morning Glory . . .'

Dora interrupted him. 'I don't understand why they didn't just cut that thing down.'

'Probably because Kitty Struther wouldn't let them. She grew it from seed, remember. No doubt she loved it. On no account are you to cut down my Ipomoea, she'd have said, and you don't argue with the boss. No, they let you go because they'd planted false clues on you.'

'They did what?'

'You were my wife, so when you got home they knew the first thing that would happen would be questioning you in depth and subjecting your clothes to forensic tests. If Roxane, say, or Ryan had been released, who knows what would have happened to their clothes before they reached us? Maybe gone into a washing machine or at any rate been carefully brushed by Mother.' Wexford paused for a moment, thinking of Clare Cox, who would never again tend her child's clothes. He sighed.

'They knew that would never happen here. They knew what would happen and did happen, that I'd drop your clothes into a sterile bag as soon as you took them off. They planted clues on that

886

skirt of yours. Iron filings. Cats' hairs, easy for Slesar to obtain from his mother who spins and weaves with pet animal hair. Just as they made sure you'd carry away a picture in your mind of a tattoo on a man's arm and a smell of a man with some kind of kidney disease, a tattoo easily achieved with a transfer and a smell produced by pocketing a tissue soaked in nail varnish remover.

'A lot of this was Slesar's brainwave. And some of it, I think – I hope I'm not being paranoid – was Slesar getting back at me. He bore a grudge against me, you see, for what he saw as my humiliating him in public.'

'Did you do that?'

'Let's say he saw it that way.'

She shook her head wonderingly, 'Reg, you've accounted for them all but The Driver. You still don't know who The Driver was.'

'I do. He'll be arrested tomorrow. And then those unfortunate Tarlings may be the only parents in Britain with three sons serving life sentences. The Driver was Conrad's brother Colum.'

'Isn't he in a wheelchair?'

'Anyone can sit in a wheelchair, Dora. So much of it, as his father told me, was in "his poor mind". You did say he walked oddly, stiffly, but none of us thought much of that.'

'So it's all over?'

'All over. It was all for nothing. A young woman with all her life before her is dead, a misguided young man is dead, a boy who can't tell truth from fantasy is going to present the shrinks and social workers with a problem for years to come, and six people are going to prison. And the bypass will still be built.'

'Not if we can help it,' said Dora stoutly. 'There's a meeting of KABAL tonight to prepare for next Saturday's demo. If all this has taught us anything it's that the Brede Valley and Savesbury Hill are worth fighting for. There'll be twenty thousand people pouring into Kingsmarkham at the weekend.'

He sighed and nodded. Probably this wasn't the first case of an investigating officer being entirely in agreement with the aims of hostage takers, while hating the way they tried to secure their ransom. Probably not – if it mattered. He smiled at his wife.

'And, Reg, after that I'd like to go up and see Sheila and the baby for a few days.' She looked at him with a half-smile. 'If you'll drive me to the station.'

887